W9-BQT-079

Dear Parents:

Congratulations! Your child is taking the first steps on an exciting journey. The destination? Independent reading!

STEP INTO READING® will help your child get there. The program offers five steps to reading success. Each step includes fun stories and colorful art or photographs. In addition to original fiction and books with favorite characters, there are Step into Reading Non-Fiction Readers, Phonics Readers and Boxed Sets, Sticker Readers, and Comic Readers—a complete literacy program with something to interest every child.

Learning to Read, Step by Step!

Ready to Read   Preschool–Kindergarten
• big type and easy words • rhyme and rhythm • picture clues
For children who know the alphabet and are eager to begin reading.

Reading with Help   Preschool–Grade 1
• basic vocabulary • short sentences • simple stories
For children who recognize familiar words and sound out new words with help.

Reading on Your Own   Grades 1–3
• engaging characters • easy-to-follow plots • popular topics
For children who are ready to read on their own.

Reading Paragraphs   Grades 2–3
• challenging vocabulary • short paragraphs • exciting stories
For newly independent readers who read simple sentences with confidence.

Ready for Chapters   Grades 2–4
• chapters • longer paragraphs • full-color art
For children who want to take the plunge into chapter books but still like colorful pictures.

STEP INTO READING® is designed to give every child a successful reading experience. The grade levels are only guides; children will progress through the steps at their own speed, developing confidence in their reading.

Remember, a lifetime love of reading starts with a single step!

READER
WALLYKAZ

15/299 JAN 2015

Visit us on the Web!
StepIntoReading.com
randomhousekids.com

Educators and librarians, for a variety of teaching tools, visit us at RHTeachersLibrarians.com

ISBN 978-0-385-38767-5 (trade) — ISBN 978-0-385-38768-2 (lib. bdg.)

Printed in the United States of America   10 9 8 7 6 5 4 3 2 1

STEP INTO READING®

STEP 1 READY TO READ

nickelodeon

Wallykazam!™

Bath Party!

by Christy Webster

illustrated by David VanTuyle

Random House 🏠 New York

Gina Giant is having a party!

Dragons love parties.

Dragons also love mud!

Norville is muddy.

Muddy Norville wants
to party!

He needs
to take a bath
before Gina's party.

Wally uses
his magic stick
to make a bathtub.

Dragons do not
like baths.

Wally holds up

his magic stick.

Wally makes the
bathtub bounce!

Bouncing baths
are fun!

Dragons still do not
like baths.

Norville hides.

Gina wants Norville
at her party.

Wally has an idea!

Wally uses

his magic stick.

He makes a band.

Wally makes balloons.

Wally makes bubbles!

It is a bath party!

Dragons love parties.

Dragons even
love parties
in the bath!

Thank you for letting me read The SIECUS Circle *prior to publication.*

I was extremely impressed. The sheer amount of dogged rooting after facts is awe-inspiring. The detail on individuals and organizations piles up irrefutable findings and inspires damning but logical conclusions.

I have never seen a better researched book. As one who fought SIECUS during the Sixties in my capacity as California's state superintendent of schools, I can testify that to my own personal knowledge, The SIECUS Circle *tells the truth.*

Max Rafferty
Dean, School of Education
Troy State University

It is a mistake to regard the assault on life and the family as an isolated phenomenon. Rather, that assault arises from the imperatives of an anti-God religion. This religion is Secular Humanism, which shares a common materialism with Marxism. According to this secular religion, one cannot affirm that man is immortal or that he has any significance greater than a chimpanzee. Secular Humanism is now the official religion of this nation. One of its principal objectives is the re-education of the American people so that they will never know or will forget the nature and the Author of Life. The SIECUS Circle *is a valuable book in its demonstration of the consistent efforts of many activists and their dupes to advance the secular cause. It is a most useful book and it should be widely read.*

Charles E. Rice
Professor of Law
Notre Dame Law School

The
SIECUS
Circle

A Humanist Revolution

By Claire Chambers

WESTERN ★ ◊ ★ ISLANDS

Dedicated to

the preservation of Christianity

and the God-given principles

upon which our Nation was founded

Copyright © 1977 Western Islands
Published by Western Islands, Belmont, Massachusetts 02178
Library of Congress Catalog Card Number: 75-41650
ISBN: 0-88279-119-2

Sex Information and Education Council
137 North Franklin Street, Hempstead, Long Island, New York 11550

The ancient yin-yang symbol was chosen by SIECUS as its official emblem. According to ancient Chinese tradition, yin *represents the passive feminine principle in nature, which is exhibited in darkness, wetness, evil, and death;* yang, *the active masculine principle, is exhibited in light, dryness, good, and life. The union of the two is said to produce all that comes to be.*

The symbol itself dates back at least to the fourth century B.C., and has been identified with the Eastern philosophical religions of Confucianism, Buddhism, and Taoism. In the Western world it has long been adopted into the symbolism of myth, magic, astrology, and witchcraft. In each case it represents a man-centered natural universe made up of male and female principles with no place for God.

The selection of this esoteric symbol by SIECUS to represent its own philosophy immediately suggests a close relationship with the man-centered philosophies that the symbol has historically represented. The SIECUS Circle *is an attempt to explore the history of SIECUS itself and the many facets of its relationship with other members of an atheistic cartel operating in America.*

Contents

Conclusion

Appendixes

A Word from the Publisher

The SIECUS Circle has been several years in the writing. When it was first conceived and titled, the author did not suspect the extent of the interlocking and overlapping of membership among the dozens of humanist organizations in the United States. Only after years of intensive research did the well-concealed humanist underground come clearly into view, with SIECUS as one of its most visible and vocal organizations.

A word of explanation is therefore necessary: This book is not exclusively — nor even primarily — about the Sex Information and Education Council of the United States. It is about the SIECUS *circle*, the network of humanist individuals and organizations that is seeking to transform America into a secular and collectivist state. The influence of this network is enormous; the influence of its humanist philosophy is greater still. A Madalyn Murray O'Hair would have been powerless to remove prayer and Bible reading from the government schools if the Supreme Court of the United States had not drunk deeply at the humanist fountain. A crèche would still be a part of the national and official observance of Christmas if the federal judiciary had not believed the humanist perversion of history which holds that America was founded not as a Christian state but as a secular state.

Organized humanism, as *The SIECUS Circle* thoroughly demonstrates, has launched an attack on America through education and religion. Yet the insidiousness of this attack has not yet been grasped by one patriot in one hundred. Perhaps most parents are aware of the controversy over sex education in the government schools and the role of SIECUS in it. Yet how many are aware of the humanist influence in the United States history courses and textbooks their children are required to study? How many are aware of the humanist influence in the life science courses taught in the schools their children attend? More important, how many are capable of distinguishing between humanism and Christianity so that they may know what is true and what is false, what is right and what is wrong?

It is the sincere hope of the publisher that this book will serve to alert many thousands of readers to the humanist network that threatens America. Only an informed people can hope to retain — and be worthy of — that freedom with which our nation has been blessed.

Western Islands

Foreword

ONCE A CIRCLE IS DRAWN, it is difficult to trace its beginning. The SIECUS circle is similar to others in this respect. Few others than its actual architects can be certain of its origin. We do know that the nucleus, SIECUS (Sex Information and Education Council of the United States), became a physical reality in 1964, shortly after an international symposium for the study of universal sex education was held. Since then, the SIECUS orbit has expanded to envelop publishing houses, film producers, governmental and private agencies, foundations, medical societies, educational institutions, and religious bodies. This massive network of interlocking organizations is the power structure through which SIECUS operates to exert pressure on local schools and an unsuspecting public to adopt its sex education program. SIECUS, then, is the pivotal point, the nucleus. However, light must be shed equally on its vast spheres of influence within this interlocking power structure, if we are to be able to cope with its skillful technique of deception.

The main thrust of this book, therefore, is to trace the SIECUS influence within the circle of organizations that make up this network. This specific endeavor has been undertaken in view of the fact that, once a community becomes aware of the SIECUS philosophy and pressure is exerted on the school, the administration generally moves in one of two directions: It either attempts to rid its sex education/home and family living program of the SIECUS influence, or it unites to convince concerned parents that it has done so, often by turning to another program from a source with another name. Parents, private citizens, school personnel, clergy, and all other groups involved should be made aware that, as the present study will disclose, it is now virtually impossible to divorce sex education from SIECUS. It should be understood, however, that we are speaking in terms of comprehensive sex education, rather than the former sensible approach of a few separated sessions in health and hygiene. More realistically, the only way to expel the SIECUS influence from comprehensive sex education is to remove the subject from the school curriculum entirely and return it to its rightful owners, the parents.

Although this particular study is basically concerned with the public schools, the current upsurge in SIECUS-style sex education was never intended to stop at the academic level. A 1970 SIECUS brochure, for example, asserted that SIECUS "serves as a clearing house for educators, physicians, nurses, youth and social workers, and others . . ." while acting as counsel to "professionals and government officials from other nations who are developing programs in family life and sex education."[1] In 1971, SIECUS took another giant step, launching a promotional campaign to finance conferences for teacher-trainers, educational administrators, the clergy, and even law enforcement officers.[2] This phase should be kept in mind if the SIECUS network is to be seen in its true perspective. The emphasis of this study is primarily on the classroom, but this should not obscure or minimize SIECUS's virtual stranglehold on many other areas of community endeavor.

As a prelude to our exploration of SIECUS-related organizations in PART II, a general background of the philosophy fostered by SIECUS and its associates seems essential. Specific attention is focused on their promotion of Humanism, an atheistic belief diametrically opposed to the basic tenets of our Judeo-Christian heritage, and their intention to force-feed a steady diet of situation ethics to American youth via the classroom. Attention is also given to documenting the substantial Communist influence within the top ranks of this highly sensitive field.

It is expected that this particular exposure will generate criticism from many seemingly "objective" sources, probably including the familiar charges of "character assassination," "witch-hunting," and "McCarthyism." Students of leftist strategy will recognize this maneuver as having been conceived by the Communists for the sole purpose of directing the spotlight away from themselves and their collaborators, as they skillfully aim their oratorical guns at their exposers. The exposers then suddenly find themselves "on trial" to justify the simplest factual statement of plain truth. It is unfortunate that the constant repetition of this exercise in deception, transmitted through carefully selected propaganda circles, has "conditioned" many innocent bystanders to parrot the Party line — thereby greatly increasing the effectiveness of the enemy's vicious campaign to conceal the truth. This semantic manipulation by the Communists has allowed them to enjoy success unsurpassed in the history of psychological warfare.[3]

In addition to sex education, Humanism, and subversion, the book explores various other areas in its study of SIECUS and its associates. Population control, legalized abortion, homosexuality, pornography, sensitivity training, and even drugs, it was discovered, all are part of the general theme. These topics are introduced into the book at certain points to reveal the incredibly broad range of influence wielded by the SIECUS complex.

Several other points seem to require clarification. Since SIECUS's fifty board members usually serve a term of three years, some have come and gone during the writing of this book (although they generally continue to support SIECUS), while others still linger. Throughout the book, these individuals are referred to interchangeably as "SIECUS board members," "SIECUS directors," or "SIECUS officials." Appendix A contains a listing of all known SIECUS board and staff members up to January 1975.

The terms "SIECUS-recommended," "SIECUS-endorsed," and "SIECUS-selected" in connection with authors, books, or films are also used interchangeably. These terms are applied to authors and books found in SIECUS's official listings, *Human Sexuality, Selected Reading in Education for Sexuality*, and the quarterly SIECUS Newsletter; and to films listed in SIECUS Study Guide No. 7 and the 1971 SIECUS booklet, *Film Resources for Sex Education.*

SIECUS, of course, flatly denies that it "recommends" any materials. For example, on Page 4 of SIECUS Study Guide No. 7 is the statement: "Inclusion of a film in this guide does not constitute endorsement by SIECUS." But in scanning the second SIECUS reading list, *Human Sexuality*, we find such descriptive passages as "excellent," "useful and well-illustrated," "valuable," "scholarly," and "one of the best resources available today" — expressions obviously intended to influence the reader's choice.[4]

A final point of explanation concerns the selection of organizations appearing in PART II. This compilation is by no means complete. For example, numerous college curricula have a strong SIECUS influence, yet only a few are included, indicating the trend. It would be an endless task to include them all. Many less significant organizations or agencies were omitted in order to get the book completed and published in time to be effective. It is hoped that even this admittedly incomplete study will give the reader an incentive for further investigation within his particular sphere of interest.

Part I

When we see a lot of framed timbers, different portions of which we know have been gotten out at different times and places and by different workmen — Stephen, Franklin, Roger, and James, for instance — and when we see these timbers joined together, and see that they exactly make the frame of a house or a mill, all the tenons and mortises exactly fitting, and all the lengths and proportions of different pieces exactly adapted to their respective places, and not a piece too many or too few . . . in such a case we find it impossible not to believe that Stephen and Franklin and Roger and James all understood one another from the beginning, and all worked upon a common plan or draft drawn up before the first lick was struck.

— Abraham Lincoln

CHAPTER 1

A Round of Rudiments

Drafting the Blueprint

IN TRACING THE EVENTS that led to the formation of SIECUS and its circle, the most significant point of departure appeared to be the United Nations. Since its inception, the U.N. has advanced a world-wide program of population control, scientific human breeding, and Darwinism. As a prerequisite toward achieving its goal, advocates have long recognized the necessity of erasing traditional concepts of morality in order to condition the populace for acceptance of the control of human destiny by the State. Sex education/home and family living is one of the more recent instruments utilized by UNESCO (United Nations Educational, Scientific, and Cultural Organization) for implementing population control. Under this guise, the U.N. and

3

associates aim to prepare a whole generation of youth to reject "outmoded" morality, as a "new age" of scientific human breeding is ushered in by the U.N. master planners. Certain other by-products of this major thrust are evident, as will be indicated in later chapters; however, it is no longer a matter for dispute that population control is a dominant theme of sex education.

A case in point is UNESCO's quarterly journal, *Impact of Science on Society.*[1] In the fall of 1968, almost an entire issue of this publication was devoted to population control themes, featuring as its lead article, "Technology, Science and Sex Attitudes," by SIECUS board member Jessie Bernard.[2] In her article Professor Bernard laid the foundation for the revolutionary concept of population control by examining the basic, immediate effects of science and technology on such questions as contraception and related medical innovations, while simultaneously propagating the radical views of SIECUS officials Isadore Rubin and Ira Reiss. Swedish author Birgitta Linner followed with an essay extolling the permissive "virtues" of Swedish sex education. Interestingly, she revealed that the Swedish Association for Sex Education (Sweden's counterpart of SIECUS) is a member of the International Planned Parenthood Federation, and that Swedish-style sex education views population control as a major concern. An article by Russia's Edward Kostyashkin lauded the Communist approach to sex education in the U.S.S.R., where intimate relations are "codified and controlled by the State." Two final articles were devoted to the study of "genetics," the implication being that the near future may bring scientific control of human breeding.

This essential point was consistently made throughout the UNESCO quarterly, culminating, in the publication's concluding paragraph, with a quotation from an address delivered by G. M. Carstairs at the 1967 International Conference of the International Planned Parenthood Federation:

> When, because of increasing over-population, the standards of living actually decline at the very time when people's aspirations

have been raised, the stage is set for further outbreaks of collective irrationality and violence.

It is imperative that we recognize the gravity of this threat, because mankind today possesses weapons of such destructive power that the world cannot afford to risk outbreaks of mass violence; and yet the lesson of history points to just such a disaster, *unless population control can be achieved* . . . .[3] [emphasis added]

(The issue of "over-population" requires further exploration and will be dealt with in PART TWO, under the entry for the organization, *Planned Parenthood-World Population.*)

Even as far back as 1945, a UNESCO Preparatory Committee urged that a study of "modern sexuality" be made by UNESCO and its member States. The director of this committee was Humanist Julian Huxley, also first Director General of UNESCO, who in 1948 wrote in *UNESCO: Its Purpose and Its Philosophy*:

> Thus, even though it is quite true that any radical eugenic policy [controlled human breeding] will be for many years politically and psychologically impossible, it will be important for UNESCO to see that the eugenic problem is examined with the greatest care, and that the public mind is informed of the issues at stake so that much that now is unthinkable may at least become thinkable.

Later, in an essay, "Too Many PEOPLE!" he wrote:

> [It is] the duty of the United Nations, supported by the technologically developed nations, to carry out research on human reproduction and its control. . . .
> Already a few countries have an official or unofficial policy of population control . . . but they need world encouragement and their policies should be integrated into a general and official world policy.
> Public opinion is ready for this.[4]

Still active in UNESCO affairs, Humanist Huxley attended UNESCO's 1959 symposium, which marked the 100th anniversary of the publication of Charles Darwin's *On the Origin of Species*. During this time, he used his position at UNESCO to propagandize the subject of "birth control." Other key personnel instrumental in arranging this symposium were Socialist-Hu-

manist Bertrand Russell and Humanists G. Brock Chisholm,
S. I. Hayakawa, and Hermann J. Muller (who once taught "genetics" at Moscow University). Chisholm, former head of the
World Health Organization, had also participated in the 1945
preparatory work, laying, with Huxley, the foundation for sex
education/ sensitivity training by way of three lectures delivered
in Washington, D.C., where he had appeared by special request
of his close friend, the notorious Alger Hiss. There Chisholm
advocated starting sex education in the fourth grade, urging
elimination of the "ways of the elders" by force, if necessary,
and insisting on "eradication of the concept of right and
wrong."[5] *

Another prominent sex education proponent, Elizabeth S.
Force, has referred to UNESCO as an initiator of family life
programs. As director of family life education for the American
Social Health Association, she cooperates extensively with various U.N. agencies. In the February 1964 issue of *Journal of
Marriage and the Family*, Mrs. Force wrote of a UNESCO
conference at which she delivered a paper entitled "The Role of
the School in Family Life Education."[6] Commenting on this
paper, the editor of the journal wrote: "We think the paper
performs an important service for family life teachers in the
United States by linking them and their efforts to a movement
which is world-wide in scope." [emphasis added]

To indicate the real "scope" of the movement, Mrs. Force
went on to cite the United Nations' 1959 proclamation, the
"Declaration of the Rights of the Child." This declaration set
forth ten principles having certain implications for the family
and family education, and called upon governments to recognize
these rights and to bring about their observance by legislative

*Mary Calderone's husband, Frank, served under Chisholm for four years as
Chief Administrator of WHO. More recently, as a member agency of the
American Association for World Health, SIECUS participated in hosting
WHO's 21st World Health Assembly, held in Boston in 1969.

S.I. Hayakawa, now a U.S. Senator, was then president of San Francisco
State College and an advisor of Esalen Institute, a center for sensitivity training.
Hermann J. Muller is perhaps best known for his suggestion that sperm taken
from persons such as Einstein be frozen and used to "improve" the human race.

and other measures. Mrs. Force continued: "In 1960, the sixth White House Conference on Children and Youth, the Golden Anniversary Conference, reiterated specific recommendations for including family-life education in schools and in the broader community" by advocating "that the school curriculum include education for family life, including sex education."[7] (Significantly, four of the nine participants in the Family Life Forum of this conference later became SIECUS board members: Reuben Hill, the Reverend John L. Thomas, David Mace, and the Reverend William Genné.[8])

More recently, in 1967, U Thant* made public a world leaders' "Declaration on Population."[9] This document was signed by the heads of thirty nations, including the then President of the United States, Lyndon Johnson. It carried a proposal that governments throughout the world should recognize the "population problem" as a deterrent to the achievement of long-range goals, affirming that contraception is a "basic human right." This declaration was to serve as the launching pad for a wave of legislative changes that would ultimately grant governments authority to control a citizen's "right" to reproduce.

Incredible as it may seem, this sentiment has been repeatedly expressed by leaders in the sex education movement, and has often gone unnoticed. SIECUS executive director Dr. Mary Calderone, at a 1969 meeting of Planned Parenthood–World Population (PPWP), advocated "marriage control" as well as "birth control." She continued, "There are enormous numbers of people who *should not marry*. . . . and an increasing number of people who *should never have children*."[10] [emphasis added]

Her colleague, PPWP president Alan F. Guttmacher, contended in an article on the subject of birth control that appeared in the *New York Times*: "Each country will have to decide its own form of coercion, determining when and how it should be

*During April 1970 U Thant praised Lenin, founder of the Communist State, as an "outstanding scholar and prominent humanist." Thant's statement was read at a UNESCO symposium on the occasion of the 100th anniversary of Lenin's birth, as UNESCO's tribute to the Communist revolutionary. (Reported in *New York Daily News*, April 7, 1970.)

employed." He added, "The means presently available are compulsory sterilization and compulsory abortion."[11] In earlier describing free conception as "a form of cannibalism," Guttmacher had asserted that an effective program of contraception could offer a "significant contribution" to a new world order.[12] Just how this new world order was to be achieved had already been defined by G. Brock Chisholm, former Director of the World Health Organization: "What people everywhere must do is to practice birth control and miscegenation [racially-mixed marriage] in order to create one race in one world under one government."[13]

Further, trial balloons have consistently been launched by U.S. government officials and their sympathetic contemporaries in the academic field to "desensitize" Americans for acceptance of eventual population control. Robert Finch, then Secretary of Health, Education, and Welfare (HEW), during a speech given before a 1970 ecology conference, was asked what people could do on a voluntary basis to improve the environment. Secretary Finch answered, "I would begin with recommending that they start with two children." He also said the government might offer "disincentives" to discourage parents from starting big families, but did not elaborate.[14]

Of course his comment referred to "voluntary measures." He omitted to mention the fact that an HEW document notes a concerted effort in many states "to make sterilization compulsory for various classes of relief recipients," and forecasts the possible success of "a revitalized eugenics movement" within the United States.[15] Another government spokesman, Stewart Udall, then Secretary of the Interior, stated in 1967 that it was necessary for the federal government to specify "optimum population levels" and to take punitive measures against parents of large families.[16]

On the academic scene, Dr. Melvin M. Ketchel of Tufts University has recommended: "If the birth rate cannot be controlled by voluntary means, then it is, I believe, a necessary and proper function of the government to take steps to reduce it." He further stated that ". . . drugs should be developed which can be administered to a whole population to statistically reduce the number of children born."[17] Addressing the same issue in a lecture before the 77th annual convention of the American Psychological Association, "sex therapist" and long-time Humanist Dr. Robert A. Harper* suggested that the only way to curtail the population explosion would be for nations to take away "the right to reproduce" from their people, "whether or not it was with the individual's approval and consent."[18]

Stanford University's Nobel Prize-winning physicist, Dr. William Shockley, also a Humanist, has offered as his solution to this problem the temporary sterilization of all young women by contraceptive inoculation.[19] Closely following his footsteps, biologist Dr. Paul Ehrlich, also of Stanford, has urged the creation of a federal population commission "with a large budget for propaganda." Ehrlich pleaded his case by saying, "It must be made clear to our population that it is socially irresponsible to have large families." He further stipulated the necessity for "federal laws making instruction in birth-control methods mandatory in all public schools" across the nation. "If all these steps fail to reverse today's population growth, we shall then be faced with some form of compulsory birth regulation," he predicts. "We might institute a system whereby a *temporary sterilant would be added to a staple food or to the water supply*. An antidote would have to be taken to permit reproduction." [emphasis added] Suggesting that the distribution of the antidote be *under government control*, Ehrlich added, "The operation will require many brutal and tough-minded decisions."[20]

By mid-July 1968, U Thant's previously mentioned "Declaration on Population" was being implemented by the United States government in the form of a President's Committee on Population and Family Planning. John D. Rockefeller III and Wilbur J. Cohen, formerly Undersecretary of Health, Educa-

---

*Dr. Harper is listed as a member of the SIECUS "Army of Liberation" in an article titled "Who Killed the Stork?" by SIECUS official Vivian Cadden, which appeared in the January 1968 issue of *McCall's* magazine.

tion, and Welfare,* were appointed to this committee as chairman and co-chairman respectively; SIECUS executive director Mary S. Calderone had a starring role as technical advisor to the committee.[21] Other advisers were UNICEF's most avid supporter, Katherine Oettinger, who later became U.S. Deputy Assistant Secretary of HEW for Family Planning and Population, and Philip Hauser, former consultant to UNESCO. (Hauser, who is also director of the University of Chicago's Population Research and Training Center, was reported by the *Chicago Daily News* of May 7, 1968, to have stated that government must assume many traditional functions of the family, which in turn will be playing an ever less important role in the future.)

Offering it as its solution to the "world's population problems," this committee submitted a list of recommendations, including a resolution that "Federal appropriations for domestic family planning services be steadily increased . . . to a total of $150,000,000 in 1973." Considering Dr. Calderone's strategic position as technical advisor to this committee, its recommendations are significant:

> Support for enlightened population policy and the attainment of its goals requires that information about population matters, *including family planning* and responsible parenthood, be incorporated into the system of education . . . .
> The attention the schools are now giving to population matters, *particularly sex education*, has been largely stimulated by voluntary agencies and private foundations. The effort should now receive increased support from the Federal Government. The Office of Education should be directed to expand both its own effort in this area and its grant support for the preparation of educational materials in *population dynamics and family life education.*[22] [emphasis added]

---

*Wilbur J. Cohen is a contributor to *The Humanist* (see May–June 1969 issue, page 17). He has been a member of the Washington Committee for Aid to China, cited as "Communist-controlled" in the *Guide to Subversive Organizations and Publications* (Page 168); the Washington Committee for Democratic Action, cited as "subversive and Communist" (Pages 119–120); and the Washington Bookshop Association, also cited as "subversive and Communist" (Page 169). See also *Investigation of Un-American Propaganda Activities in the United States*, Special Committee on Un-American Activities, Appendix IX, "Communist Front Organizations," 1944, Page 1685.

Apparently, Dr. Calderone's versatility is unbounded. Her service on the President's Committee gave her the opportunity to represent the combined policies of Planned Parenthood–World Population, the International Fertility Association, the Committee on Human Reproduction of the American Medical Association, the American Society for the Study of Sterility, the Commission on Marriage and Family Life of the National Council of Churches, the World Health Organization, and SIECUS — in all of which she holds membership.

But her versatility is exceeded by her "sense of perception." In SIECUS's *Annual Report 1967–1968*, President Lester Doniger wrote: "Dr. Mary S. Calderone, executive director, had the vision to see the need for an organization such as SIECUS, gave it its structure, standards and goals, saw it through its infancy and early childhood, and in the face of almost insurmountable odds brought it to maturity in the remarkably short period of four years." Considering her sizable influence in the organizations just named, as well as the generous grants made to SIECUS by tax-free foundations and the U.S. Department of Health, Education, and Welfare, one wonders what the "insurmountable odds" were. As for "vision," her close ties with such organizations as Planned Parenthood and the U.N. afforded her a bird's-eye view of coming events.

One of these events took place shortly before the founding of SIECUS, conveniently setting the stage for the new concept in sex education now fostered by SIECUS and associates. This event took the form of a UNESCO-sponsored International Symposium on Health Education, Sex Education and Education for Home and Family Living, held in February 1964.[23] Participants in this symposium included educators from all parts of the free world, as well as the Iron Curtain countries. The findings made by U.N. participants in 1964 were forerunners of the familiar phrases now being parroted by sex education proponents, such as: "Children learn about sex elsewhere . . . rarely in the home"; sex education is needed because "sex is emphasized commercially in the mass media"; "sex education should begin at an early age" and be "integrated into the whole curriculum"; "boys and girls should be taught together"; "anti-dogmatic methods of teaching" must be used; and "moral norms are relative concepts which change with time."

Other familiar-sounding methods of implementation were suggested, such as "discussion techniques, role-playing, psycho- and socio-drama [all sensitivity training methods], youth conferences, parent conferences, well-planned PTA meetings, counseling, films, pamphlets."[24]

Birgitta Linner, author of *Sex and Society in Sweden*, in reporting on the 1964 U.N. conference, verifies that the sex education proposal for universal use as "put forth by two Swedish delegates . . . was accepted by the majority of the delegates."[25] The Swedish program had the following subject outline:

- Differences between the sexes (anatomical, physiological, emotional, psychological, genetic), structure and function of the genitals, menstruation, masturbation
- Boy-girl relationships
- Childbirth, conception
- Sterility, impotence, and frigidity
- Abortion
- Birth control
- Venereal disease
- Sexual deviations[26]

In short, the SIECUS concept of sex education is a carbon copy of the Swedish program, as adopted by UNESCO. It is apparently no coincidence, then, that SIECUS was formed only a few months after UNESCO's 1964 symposium, receiving its charter in May and beginning to function on July 1.

Since then, SIECUS officials have wasted no time in propagating the calculated plan to foster population control by means of public school sex education. As an illustration, SIECUS founder Lester Kirkendall emphasized this aspect in an issue of *The Humanist* magazine that was devoted entirely to the topic of human sexuality. Here he utilized a study by SIECUS-endorsed authors Lee Rainwater and Karol Weinstein, to show that sexual knowledge is *a matter of necessity* in achieving "population control." Kirkendall advises:

> In short, Rainwater and Weinstein demonstrated that effective contraceptive methods, and in the long run population control, were linked closely with physiological knowledge about sex, a capacity for free discussion, and attitudes toward sex roles and sex itself. *Sex education is thus clearly tied in a socially significant way to family planning and population limitation and policy.*[27] [emphasis added]

Framing the Timbers

Since the direction an organization takes depends on who charts the course, it is essential to explore the backgrounds of the six SIECUS founders, the value systems to which they adhere, and their respective fields of endeavor. It was SIECUS past president Lester Doniger who credited Dr. Mary Calderone with structuring SIECUS and setting its standards and goals. It must therefore be assumed that hers was the major voice in the selection of co-founders, and that all met on a common philosophical ground. It is also logical to assume that these six founders, in turn, chose board members of persuasion and ideology generally coinciding with their own.

Commenting on the founding of SIECUS, Mary Calderone stated that it "was the result of the pooled anxieties and concerns of six individuals from the fields of religion, medical public health, sociology, health education, family life education and the law."[28] These six founders, then, held the key to the success or failure of SIECUS. Of necessity, the measure of moral integrity each possessed would be a major determining factor in producing the final result. The backgrounds of the founders are discussed in some detail below.

Mary Calderone

Dr. Mary Calderone represented the "medical public health" segment at the formation of SIECUS. Keeping in mind the "world population control" aspect mentioned earlier, it is significant that Dr. Calderone had served as medical director of Planned Parenthood–World Population for eleven years immediately before the founding of SIECUS.

As the first executive director of SIECUS, Dr. Calderone has been acclaimed as a major guiding force on the national sex education scene. It is in this capacity that she is frequently found propagating her unorthodox views in a fashion bold enough to evoke any reaction from an uneasy blush to angry indignation. For example, in a TV interview by Alexander Cohen (Channel 9, New York City) on January 18, 1968, Dr. Calderone said: "I accept and advocate masturbation as part of the evolutionary sexual development of the individual." A more recent interview by *Playboy* magazine brought forth this comment on whether or not the topic should be incorporated into the school curriculum: "Yes, if it's done calmly and objectively, with the teacher simply pointing out that masturbation is almost universal, doesn't hurt anyone, and it is useful as a release from tension. . . . "[29]

The same TV interview exposed another favorite sport of the lady's — deriding the religious concepts of the Bible as "myths" — as she urged that "the whole relationship of man to woman MUST be changed." The *Washington Star Ledger* quoted her as foreseeing a sex-emancipated future, in which there will be "different kinds of marriage for different purposes at various times in the life of an individual."[30]

More recently, Dr. Calderone reiterated her previous sentiments by supporting the theories put forth in Humanist Rudolf Dreikurs' book, *The Challenge of Marriage*. His proposals include:[31]

- Merging or reversing the sexes or sex roles.
- Liberating children from their families.
- Abolishing the family as we know it.

Other oracles of wisdom pronounced by Dr. Calderone on various occasions include the following:

- *On* Sexology:

  Sexology magazine is no more pornographic than the Bible.[32]

- *On sexual experimentation:*

  The adolescent years are, among other things, for learning how to integrate sex usefully and creatively into daily living, therefore, we must accept that adolescent sexual experimentation is not just inevitable, but actually necessary for normal development.[33]

- *On pre-marital sex:*

  I advocate discussion of it, so that young people know they have choices beginning with masturbation, of course, and petting to climax and mutual orgasm before moving on to intercourse.[34]

- *On extra-marital sex:*

  An extra-marital affair that's really solid might have very good results.[35]

Although she is perhaps best known for flavoring her own maxims with four-letter words, the fact that Dr. Calderone chose to educate her daughter Francesca at the socialist New School for Social Research in New York City is less well-known. Co-founded by Alvin Johnson, editor of *The New Republic* magazine — journalism's voice of Fabian Socialism — Communist Fronters John Dewey[36] and Charles Beard,[37] and others, the radical New School for Social Research has long been a haven for professors of socialist, Humanist, and Communist persuasion, including the notorious Communist fronter and founder of the American Civil Liberties Union, Humanist Roger Baldwin.[38]

The roster of authors whose books have been published by the New School for Social Research for use by students is dominated by Humanists Sidney Hook, Ernest Nagel, Milton Konvitz, Charles Morris, Max Otto, V. M. Ames, H. M. Kallen, and J. H. Randall, Jr., to name a few. Maxwell S. Stewart, identified Communist and editor of the SIECUS-recommended

Public Affairs Pamphlets, has lectured there, as did W. E. B. DuBois, a self-proclaimed Communist. Professors Harry Overstreet,[39] John Dewey, and Corliss Lamont,[40] all Humanists who have been cited for numerous Communist front affiliations, are other exponents of the type of philosophy this school favors in its selection of lecturers.

More recently, lecturers at the New School for Social Research have included such personages as Humanists Erich Fromm, Eugene McCarthy, Thomas Mann, and Margaret Mead. The institution's current president is John R. Everett, a reviewer for *The Humanist* magazine.

Another connecting link between Dr. Calderone and the New School for Social Research is the J. M. Kaplan Fund, Inc. This fund gives financial support to both SIECUS and the New School, and J. M. Kaplan serves the latter as a long-time trustee.

Interestingly, at least one faculty member at the New School for Social Research is affiliated with *Sexology* magazine — also a favorite medium of expression for Dr. Calderone's colleagues at SIECUS. The April 1969 issue of *Sexology* features an article titled "Erotic Messages on Lavatory Walls," by Professor Robert Reisner of the New School, in which he gives his readers a "sneak preview" of the type of lewd scribbling one might encounter in a public rest room. Professor Reisner apparently finds this subject fascinating — so fascinating that he teaches a course on the subject of graffiti at the New School. He also has the unique qualification of having authored such works as *Great Wall Writing*; *Graffiti: Selected Scrawls from Bathroom Walls*, and *Captions Courageous*, which are no doubt destined to make the SIECUS "top ten list" in the future.[41]

The private life of Mary Calderone is also tainted with an "erotic message" that should not be forgotten. Although she often flaunts her concern for young people who are victims of a sex-saturated environment, her husband, Dr. Frank A. Calderone, at the same time is involved with burlesque. One of the Long Island theaters he owns, the Mineola, imported the Minsky Burlesque from Las Vegas in 1967 and 1968, and had slated the show again for 1969. Certain portions of the show, described as "very lewd" and "obscene" by the office of Nassau County District Attorney William Cahn, were not permitted to go on as staged.[42] One of Cahn's aides asserted that, as owner, Calderone was responsible for what was presented in his Mineola theater.

Nevertheless, the same year found his wife and her SIECUS colleagues making such public protestations as the following:

> WHY DOES SIECUS EXIST? To meet an urgent and increasing need that did not exist in earlier days. Parents no longer can control the environment their children grow up in [especially when it is infested with such theaters as the Mineola] as they once could. The fact is that we live today in a society that is saturated with sex and sex symbolism [thanks in part to Mary Calderone's husband Frank]. But the commercial and entertainment use of sex is flagrantly exploitive, focusing attention on women and men as sexual commodities and on sexual activity as an end in itself. . . . SIECUS came into being to help people live their total lives as whole human beings, neither sex machines nor repressed hermits, neither sexual exploiters nor sexually exploited.[43]

As for Dr. Calderone's "religious" persuasion, it is significant that the atheistic American Humanist Association, which is committed to the establishment of an amoral, secular world order, named her "Humanist of the Year" for 1974. This distinction places her in the same category with at least two other SIECUS founders: Lester Kirkendall and Harriet Pilpel, both Humanists as well. However, so far as Dr. Calderone's proclaimed "public image" is concerned, she identifies herself as a Quaker, a fact which is also relevant — since certain aspects of Quakerism can be identified with the Humanist movement.*

Of further significance is the fact that certain leaders of a radical Quaker group, the American Friends Service Committee (AFSC), have publicly thrown their support behind her. At least two members of the AFSC — Stewart Meacham and Communist fronter Stringfellow Barr — have joined with the National

---

*See Chapter 3, *A Round of Religion.*

Committee for Responsible Family Life and Sex Education by signing a full-page newspaper advertisement in support of SIECUS. (Meacham was recently cited by the House Internal Security Committee as one of 65 Communist-oriented men and women who have dominated the campus speakers' circuit in this country.)

Appearing in the October 16, 1969 issue of the *New York Times*, the "support SIECUS" ad stated: "The undersigned National Committee for Responsible Family Life and Sex Education reaffirms that enlightened Americans support the concepts of SIECUS: That sex education and family life training are a community trust and are essential to self-awareness and human development." The March 1970 SIECUS Newsletter subsequently announced the formation of this committee, proudly displaying the names of all signers of the advertisement.* A substantial number of signers of this ad have far left and subversive connections (see Chapter 4).

The leftward-leaning record of the American Friends Service Committee is extensive. The AFSC encourages pacifism, draft card burning, and opposition to military preparedness. Entering the campaign to defeat the loyalty program in California, it also lent its support to the Federation for Repeal of the Levering Act, cited as a Communist front by the California Senate Investigating Committee on Education.[44] Like Stringfellow Barr, AFSC Chairman Henry J. Cadbury and Executive Secretary Clarence Pickett have numerous Communist front citations in their records.

Dr. Calderone's acceptance of support from members of this humanistic Quaker unit, to which she has in turn given financial assistance, coupled with her "Humanist of the Year" award, strongly indicates that her true allegiance lies with the atheistic forces of the far left. Moreover, it brings her into close harmony with the radical convictions of other SIECUS founders.

*See Appendix G for complete list of signers.

William H. Genné

Chosen to represent "the field of religion" in the founding of SIECUS was the Reverend William H. Genné, who has a record in official government files of affiliation with at least three identified Communist front organizations.[45] The Reverend Mr. Genné rejects the Christian doctrine of moral absolutes, following instead the "situation ethics" principle in resolving moral issues. He concluded a speech delivered at ORTHO Pharmaceutical Corporation's sex education symposium by saying: "Just as we strive to free young people from the tyranny of 'Thou Shalt Not,' so we must strive to free them from the tyranny of 'Thou Shalt!' We must make them truly free because no weight of statistics or percentages can dictate which moral choice a person should make."[46] In his lecture, Genné extolled the late heretical Bishop James A. Pike, another well-known promoter of situation ethics, recommending as "excellent" Pike's book on ethics, *Doing the Truth.*

One of Genné's most notable contributions to the field of sexuality is his proposal, "Let's Celebrate the First Menstruation" (like a bar mitzvah), which was presented in an editorial in *Sexology* magazine, a bawdy publication on which he serves as a board consultant.[47]

Any objective appraisal of *Sexology* magazine must conclude that it is obscene and borders on the pornographic. The April 1969 issue, for example, crassly displayed a nude model on its front cover. Featured articles in that issue carried such titles as "Erotic Messages on Lavatory Walls," "Men with Penis Envy," "Women Who Seduce Teenagers," and "Sex in Nudist Camps." The last-named article was accompanied by a photograph of ten naked male and female adults holding hands and frolicking on a beach. The April 1970 issue carried an article by the late Isadore Rubin titled "Helpful and Harmful Sex Devices," which described a vibrator as "helpful" and "useful as a training device in bringing about female orgasm." Nevertheless, reprints from *Sexology* are recommended for teacher and student use by a number of firms publishing sex education materials. SIECUS itself mentions them as resources in many of its Newsletters.

In clamoring for the defense of *Sexology*, SIECUS representatives have cited the outcome of a legal action taken against the magazine in New Jersey, in which it was ruled not obscene (*State of New Jersey v. Irving Fetter*, Indictment No. 319-58, August 5, 1961). However, it should be remembered in connection with this case that in the year 1961, all publications, including *Sexology*, were far more cautious about using openly salacious material than they had become by the more permissive end of the decade.

Besides Genné, four other SIECUS officials serve on *Sexology's* executive staff or board of consultants: Humanist Lester Kirkendall, John Money, Wardell Pomeroy, and Aaron Rutledge. Before his death Isadore Rubin served with them.* Other SIECUS directors — Warren Johnson, E. James Lieberman, David Mace, and Clark Vincent — are contributors to the magazine. Humanists who have contributed articles and who also serve on the *Sexology* board of consultants include LeMon Clark, Robert A. Harper, Ashley Montagu, and Walter Stokes.

Genné, who is the director of the National Council of Churches' Commission on Marriage and Family Life, is typical of the clergy in the top echelons of that radical organization. The type of "Christian" ideals advanced by the National Council of Churches (NCC) is best exemplified by its own publications. A pamphlet published by NCC in 1961, titled *Called to Responsible Freedom: Meaning of Sex in the Christian Life*, advised young people: "For the Christian there are no laws, no rules, no regulations. . . . Life is a series of grays and not pure blacks and whites."[48] The author of this pamphlet was Dr. William Graham Cole, an ordained minister who later became a SIECUS director. The pamphlet further asserted:

---

*On July 31, 1970, Isadore Rubin met with a fatal automobile accident. His demise was reported in the SIECUS Newsletter for October 1970, with a eulogy. However, since his influence is still very much alive and his contributions to SIECUS-generated sex education are innumerable, he is extensively covered in the next few chapters.

> You are now bound by detailed rules of behavior, telling you that it is "all right" to go so far in expressing affection for a member of the opposite sex, and "all wrong" to go further. No one outside yourself can tell you that — not really . . . .
>
> You have to make up your own mind. . . . what your standards of conduct are going to be. . . . There just aren't any rules, you do whatever strikes your fancy.

As for NCC's religious fervor, a survey of the views of its leadership published in *Newsweek* on June 26, 1967, showed that "over one-third could not state they have a firm belief in God . . . over 40% do not believe Jesus Christ was divine . . . only one in six accepts the Bible doctrine of man's sinful nature. Slightly more than 60% of the delegates look forward to a life after death."[49] Little wonder, then, that NCC supported and commended the Supreme Court decision that removed prayer and Bible reading from the public schools.

How has all this been accomplished? An examination of NCC leadership provides the answer. NCC is an outgrowth of the Federal Council of Churches, whose guiding genius was identified Communist Harry F. Ward.[50] Over 1,000 persons at the leadership level in NCC have either Communist-front records or records of service to Communist causes.[51] This may explain why the NCC has consistently gone on record as favoring abolition of all loyalty oaths, all national security laws, and all federal and state investigative agencies aimed at exposing Communist subversion. Further, a 1957 reading list published by NCC recommended works by Herbert Aptheker (leading theoretician for the Communist Party, USA), W. E. B. DuBois, his wife Shirley G. DuBois, and Victor Perlo, all well-known Communists; Gordon Allport, E. Franklin Frazier, and Ruth Benedict, who are Communist fronters; and pro-Marxist Gunnar Myrdal.[52]

There is no doubt that Genné and Dr. Calderone (who also serves on NCC's Commission on Marriage and Family Life) are right at home in this revolutionary camp. It also seems entirely possible that the next edict to be drawn from the well of the National Council of Churches will call for "equal time in the pulpit for Satan."

Clark Vincent

Clark Vincent, who represented the field of sociology at the birth of SIECUS, is director of the Behavioral Science Center at the Bowman Gray School of Medicine, Winston-Salem, N.C. "Behavioral science" is the recently adopted new name for sociology. Its advocates define human behavior as fixed and determined by material circumstances, without any control by "free will." It claims people are pawns of their environment, and therefore should be "understood" and excused for any wrongdoing. The ultimate goal of behavioral science is the establishment of scientific control over individuals and society. A primary vehicle used to achieve this goal is "sensitivity training," a technique largely developed by Humanists and strongly advocated by SIECUS.

Sensitivity training is frequently referred to by other terms, including:

Auto-criticism	Interpersonal competence
Basic encounter groups	Interpersonal relations
Broad sensitivity	Marathon
Class in-group counseling	Nude evaluation
Group confession	Operant conditioning
Group dynamics	Prayer therapy
Group training	Rap sessions
Human potential	Self-evaluation
workshops	Self-honest sessions
Human relations	Synanon games clubs
Human relations lab	T-group training

Former Congressman John G. Schmitz defines sensitivity training as follows: "Sensitivity training is defined as group meetings, large or small, to discuss publicly intimate and personal matters, and opinions, values or beliefs; and/or to act out emotions and feelings toward one another in the group, using the techniques of self-confession and mutual criticism.

"It is also 'coercive persuasion in the form of thought reform or brainwashing.' "[53]

The quoted phrase that equates sensitivity training with brainwashing is taken from page 47 of *Issues in Training*, a manual for group leaders published in 1962 by the National Training Laboratories of the National Education Association[54] (see entry for *National Education Association* in PART TWO). This technique of self-confession and group criticism reduces man to animal level, subjects him to the will of the "group," destroys all forms of personal conviction, and ultimately conditions his mind to accept emotional enslavement. It is a technique based on the Pavlovian theory of conditioned reflexes and is designed to pave the way for a collectivist society. Of course it can succeed only in an atmosphere where fixed moral absolutes have been eliminated. Once a collectivist state is firmly established, sensitivity training is used by those in power for perpetual control and subjugation of their subjects.

As recently as the spring of 1969, a special advisory committee to the State Board of Education in California concluded after a thorough investigation of the subject:

> Sensitivity training is being used by those who are in fact aligned with revolutionary groups acting contrary to public policy; that is, they intend to use the schools to destroy American culture and traditions.

A measure of the effectiveness of group criticism is the frequently observed fact that young people who attend schools where the prevailing climate of values differs from that of the home usually end by rejecting parental values.[55]

It is only logical to assume that teachers would first be subjected to this conditioning process, in order to enable them to conduct their own sensitivity training sessions and transmit new values to their students. In speaking of a new course at New York University, the *Washington Post* of February 21, 1969, reported: "The sensitivity training is a major part of a new course, the Nation's first master's degree program for teachers of elementary school sex education." By now it is apparent that sensitivity training has become prerequisite for teacher training in sex education, nationwide.

Clark Vincent leaves no doubt that he strongly backs a moral code of situation ethics that denies fixed moral absolutes. Speaking at the same ORTHO sex education symposium as Genné, Vincent said: " 'Is premarital coition right or wrong?' 'Is it bad or good?' Such questions, while appearing to be worldly and sophisticated, are actually naive in the extreme. . . . Such questions are akin to asking: 'Is surgery right or wrong?' Such questions can only be answered with reference to specifics. One needs to know for what purpose surgery is being performed, on whom and by whom."[56] (Reviewing the evidence, and applying Dr. Vincent's own words, perhaps one rather "needs to know for what purpose" a fraudulent sex education program is being perpetrated, "on whom and by whom.")

In league with some of his associates at SIECUS, Clark Vincent has linked himself with other medical renegades on the staff of *Sexology* magazine. He was the editor of a textbook for medical students entitled *Human Sexuality in Medical Education and Practice*, to which the editor and the medical editor of *Sexology* each contributed several chapters.[57]

Wallace Fulton

Speaking for health education at the founding of SIECUS was Wallace Fulton, who in 1967 took part in the development of one of the "unhealthiest" education programs yet devised. This was the 3M Company's "School Health Education Study" program, known as SHES, which was constructed under the direction of Elena M. Sliepcevich. Miss Sliepcevich is a life member of the National Education Association and a member of the World Health Organization and the International Union Health Association, all affiliated with the United Nations. Elizabeth Force, mentioned earlier as a sex education proponent and a close associate of SIECUS, also aided in the development of the SHES program as a member of its board of advisors, together with Granville Larimore, a member of the subversive Public Affairs Committee (see section headed *Maxwell S. Stewart*, in Chapter 4).

The SHES program is divided into ten health concepts, with Concept 6 focusing on sex education. It employs the technique of sensitivity training; treats evolution as accepted fact; promotes anti-capitalist sentiments; treats sex in a nihilistic manner, without moral restraints; makes use of transparencies of which at least a dozen range from prurient to pornographic; and constantly pits child against parent. SHES has been used in certain areas of the country as a vehicle to bring sex education into the classroom under the guise of school health.

A strong SIECUS influence can be perceived throughout the SHES program. For example, under the heading "Resource Materials for Teachers and Students" in the basic document, the writings of the following SIECUS personalities are recommended:

Mary S. Calderone	William H. Masters
Catherine S.Chilman	James A. Peterson
Evelyn M. Duvall	Ira L. Reiss
Warren R. Johnson	John Rock
Lester A. Kirkendall	Helen Southard
David R. Mace	Clark Vincent

Also suggested here are the works of such Humanists as Curtis Avery, Erik Erikson, Edgar Z. Friedenberg, Sidonie M. Gruenberg, Alan F. Guttmacher, Margaret Mead, and Dr. Benjamin Spock, as well as various publications (the Study Guides) of SIECUS, the Humanist-founded Child Study Association of America, Planned Parenthood–World Population, the Public Affairs Committee, and Science Research Associates, with which Lester Kirkendall is associated. "Additional References for Teachers and Students" features various reprints from *Sexology* magazine.

Concept 9 of the SHES program, which deals with drugs and drug addiction, features in its references such works as *The Psychedelic Experience* and *Beyond LSD: The Latest in Psychedelic "Trips,"* by Dr. Timothy Leary, fanatical "high priest" of the LSD drug cult. (Leary, it will be recalled, fled from

American justice to Communist-controlled Algeria in late 1970.)
Among other pro-LSD literature found in 3M's *Teacher-Student Resources* guide for Concept 9 is Masters and Houston's
Varieties of Psychedelic Experience. (See section on *Drugs* in
entry for *Guidance Associates of Pleasantville, N.Y.*, in PART II.)

A number of other books listed in 3M's *Teacher-Student
Resources* guide are as objectionable as those above. At least
three of them promote not only legalization of marijuana but its
use and enjoyment as well. These are *The Addict and the Law*,
by Alfred R. Lindesmith; *The Book of Grass*, edited by G.
Andrews and S. Vinkenoog and published by Grove Press; and
Pot: A Handbook of Marihuana, by John Rosevear. Rosevear's
book is also promoted in a brochure advertising hard-core
pornography published by Humanist Lyle Stuart.

Considering that most of the SHES concepts were originally
developed in the NEA's National Training Laboratories Institute for Applied Behavioral Sciences, there can be no doubt that
this health program was structured on the behavioral sciences
and it is clearly designed to change the thinking and behavior
patterns of American youth.[58]

SIECUS founder Wallace Fulton is given credit in the
SHES Program, along with Dr. Mary Calderone and others, as
one of those "who provided reviews of the framework materials
related to the health content areas within their specialized fields
for the final version of this document."[59]

Harriet Pilpel

Harriet Pilpel, who represented the legal profession at the
founding of SIECUS, is a member and past trustee of the New
York Ethical Culture Society, as well as a member of the
advisory committee of the American Ethical Union's Board of
Ethical Lecturers. Both are Humanist organizations. Mrs. Pilpel
is also a vice chairman and member of the national board of
directors of the American Civil Liberties Union, an organization
that claims at least two other SIECUS officials — Ira Reiss and
Ralph Slovenko — as members. A further point of interest is

that ACLU was in part founded, and is supported, by the Ethical Culture Movement, as reported in the March–April 1967 issue of *The Humanist*. Mrs. Pilpel's strong liaison with ACLU, whose cryptic objectives have been exposed by various U.S. government investigative committees over the years, suggests the need for a closer look at this organization. (See Appendix I.)

Founders and leaders of ACLU include such persons as Dr. Harry F. Ward, an identified Communist, who was its first chairman; William Z. Foster, former head of the Communist Party, U.S.A.; and Humanists John Dewey, Clarence Darrow, Norman Thomas, Jane Addams, and Roger Baldwin. (Baldwin, who incidentally has a long record of Communist front citations,[60] has written extensively for Public Affairs Pamphlets, which are promoted by SIECUS.)

After concluding its first decade under the directorship of Roger Baldwin, ACLU came under the scrutiny of the U.S. House of Representatives Special Committee to Investigate Communist Activities in the United States. That Committee's report, dated January 17, 1931, contained the following statement:

> The American Civil Liberties Union is closely affiliated with the Communist movement in the United States, and fully 90 per cent of its efforts are on behalf of communists who have come into conflict with the law. It claims to stand for free speech, free press, and free assembly; but it is quite apparent that the main function of the A.C.L.U. is to attempt to protect the communists in their advocacy of force and violence to overthrow the Government, replacing the American flag by a red flag and erecting a Soviet Government in place of the republican form of government guaranteed to each State by the Federal Constitution.

Again, in 1943 and 1948, the California State Legislative Committee investigating un-American activities concluded:

> The American Civil Liberties Union may be definitely classed as a Communist front or "transmission belt" organization.[61]

In 1969, former police undercover operative David E. Gumaer revealed that a grand total of 206 past leading members of

ACLU had a combined record of 1,754 officially cited Communist front affiliations. As for current officials, Gumaer
added:

> The present ACLU Board [as of 1969] consists of sixty-eight
> members, thirty-one of whom have succeeded in amassing a total
> of *at least* 355 Communist Front affiliations. That total does not
> include the citations of these individuals which appear in reports
> from the Senate Internal Security Subcommittee.[62]

In examining its past performance, we find that ACLU has
served as legal defense for citizens who aid Fidel Castro, for
flag burners, and for the Communist DuBois Clubs; and the
ACLU attorney, Humanist William Kunstler, was cited in 1970
by the House Internal Security Committee as Communist-oriented.[63] ACLU has opposed voluntary prayer and Bible reading
in public schools, has fought laws which protect America from
subversive organizations, has worked to erase the words "under
God" from our Pledge of Allegiance, and is fighting for the
repeal of state narcotics laws. Even this brief summary of an
unsavory record should be sufficient to confirm the harmony
between ACLU's activities and the leftist persuasion of both its
founders and its current leaders.

Leaving no stone unturned in its effort to weaken and
undermine the American way of life, ACLU had managed to
capture control of the 1968 Presidential Commission on Obscenity and Pornography through its chairman, William Lockhart,
and its general counsel, Paul Bender, both of whom were ACLU
members. It was no surprise that, in 1970, the ACLU-dominated
Commission issued a call for a federally financed " 'massive
sex education effort' among adults and youths involving the
family, school, church, and other agencies," as a means of
combating pornography. Ably promoting this neatly packaged
conclusion with personally prepared testimony before the
Commission was none other than SIECUS executive director
Mary Calderone.

Among the other key figures who delivered testimony was
ACLU executive director John de J. Pemberton, a last-minute

substitute for Harriet Pilpel. As reported in ACLU's Press Release No. 29-70, Mrs. Pilpel had been scheduled to deliver the ACLU testimony as chairman of the Union's Communications Media, but had been "detained in New York on legal business." In part, this testimony reaffirmed ACLU's opposition to any laws regulating obscene or pornographic material, adding that the Union knew of "no clear or convincing empirical proof of a causal relationship between allegedly obscene material and antisocial behavior [such as criminal sexual conduct]" — a position that was later incorporated into the Pornography Commission's final conclusions.

In addition to her close affiliation with ACLU and the above episode, SIECUS founder Harriet Pilpel is a senior partner in the New York law firm of Greenbaum, Wolff and Ernst. This was the law firm that assisted in the preparation of the SIECUS Certificate of Incorporation. Morris L. Ernst, a partner in this firm, was one of the founders of ACLU and has been a long-time top official of the organization. He was also a founder, and served on the national executive board, of the National Lawyers Guild, "cited as a Communist front which 'is the foremost legal bulwark of the Communist Party, its front organizations, and controlled unions' and which 'since its inception has never failed to rally to the legal defense of the Communist Party and individual members thereof, including known espionage agents.' "[64]

In addition, Ernst has been affiliated with other organizations cited as Communist fronts in reports of the House Committee on Un-American Activities and elsewhere.[65] One in particular focuses additional attention on a book Ernst sponsored and edited, titled *American Stuff*. Excerpts from *American Stuff* read into the *Congressional Record* in November 1938 were in part so vile that they were unprintable.[66]

It seems to be more than a coincidence that Ernst's law firm, through Harriet Pilpel, was chosen to officiate at SIECUS's incorporation proceedings. Equally significant is the fact that Humanist Harriet Pilpel currently serves as general counsel to SIECUS, the Association for the Study of Abortion, the Association for Voluntary Sterilization, and Planned Parenthood–World Population. Thus another SIECUS official is linked to the master planners of world population control.

Lester Kirkendall

Representing the field of "family life education" at the founding of SIECUS was Dr. Lester Kirkendall, also active with Planned Parenthood. Although *Who's Who* lists him as a Unitarian, Dr. Kirkendall himself publicly describes his religious persuasion as Baptist. This is confusing in view of the fact that, in 1966, he assumed the directorship of the atheistic American Humanist Association, which is dedicated to the eradication of God from the universe. He is presently serving in a dual capacity as a member of the AHA board of directors and member of the editorial board of the association's official voice, *The Humanist* magazine.

Among other past or present staff members who have worked with Dr. Kirkendall on *The Humanist* are UNESCO's Julian Huxley, Lester Mondale (brother of Vice President Walter Mondale, also a Humanist), Stephen Fritchman, and Corliss Lamont. Stephen Fritchman is listed in the files of the California State Senate Investigating Committee on Education as having been affiliated with numerous Communist fronts and causes,[67] although he is called "Reverend." Corliss Lamont was named by Louis Budenz as "a one-time Communist," and has been cited by a California Senate investigating committee in connection with "more than 50 Communist-front organizations."[68] His leftist record is so extensive that he was included in the 1956 Senate Internal Security Subcommittee's list of the eighty-two most active sponsors of Communist front organizations. Lamont currently contributes articles to *The Worker*, a Communist publication.

Other leftists who write for *The Humanist* are Algernon Black (with a record of thirty-two Communist citations);[69] Anatol Rapoport (a self-admitted former Communist Party member, who participated in anti-Vietnam teach-ins);[70] Carey McWilliams (affiliated with eighty-five Communist front organizations);[71] Roger N. Baldwin (a veteran Communist fronter);[72] and Arthur J. Goldberg (former Supreme Court Justice, cited for three Communist front affiliations).[73]

Mr. Goldberg has demonstrated that his sympathies still reside with the far left. On January 21, 1970, he acted as host for the American Civil Liberties Union's 50th Anniversary Party honoring ACLU founder Roger Baldwin.[74] Although Baldwin has been affiliated with at least thirty-five Communist fronts and causes, he is perhaps best known for a statement made before the Fish Committee, to the effect that "the American Civil Liberties Union upholds the right of aliens or nationals to advocate murder, assassination, and overthrow of our Government by force and violence."[75] Goldberg served as chairman of the ACLU dinner; former Chief Justice Earl Warren was billed as honorary chairman.

Abraham H. Maslow, staff member of Esalen Institute (a sensitivity training center, notorious for its nude "marathons"), has served on *The Humanist's* publication committee. Professor Maslow, a past president of the American Psychological Association, was a signer of an "Open Letter" issued by the National Committee To Repeal the McCarran Act, which was officially cited in the U.S. Government's *Guide to Subversive Organizations and Publications* as a Communist front.[76] Also contributing their views to *The Humanist* are such left-wing radicals as Joan Baez, Black Panther official Eldridge Cleaver, and Yippie leaders Abbie Hoffman and Dave Dellinger.

A frequent contributor to *The Humanist* and a member of its editorial board is SIECUS "fellow-swinger" Albert Ellis. In 1969 Dr. Ellis developed for this magazine a series of articles dealing chiefly with the Humanist approach to sexuality, which were edited by Lester Kirkendall. Using typical SIECUS jargon, Ellis theorized: "There probably cannot ever be any absolutely correct or proper rules of morality, since people and conditions change over the years and what is 'right' today may be 'wrong' tomorrow. Sane ethics are relativistic and situational."[77] This is a view which Editor Kirkendall readily accepts.

Dr. Kirkendall's long list of literary achievements clearly demonstrates that he is a consistent supporter of moral relativism and sexual permissiveness. He has gone a step further in showing his willingness to consort with the left by serving as co-editor (with identified Communist Isadore Rubin) of *Sex in the Adolescent Years: New Directions in Guiding and Teaching Youth.* Another Kirkendall affiliation is with Public Affairs Pamphlets, edited by Communist Maxwell Stewart (see Chapter 4). It should also be noted that Socialist-Humanist G. Brock Chisholm wrote the preface of Kirkendall's *Premarital Intercourse and Interpersonal Relationships,* which appears in numerous "Home and Family Living" program bibliographies for high school students throughout the nation. This book became notorious for its case histories of 668 premarital intercourse experiences, as reported "in living color" by 200 college-level males.

Dr. Kirkendall serves on the staff of the salacious periodical *Sexology* as editor of parent guidance. In addition, this magazine's April 1970 issue lists him as a member of its board of consultants, together with SIECUS officials William Genné, John Money, Wardell Pomeroy, Aaron Rutledge, and *Sexology* editor Isadore Rubin, in a virtual crusade to promote lewd living.

The religious dilemma of Lester Kirkendall, mentioned earlier, is complicated by the fact that he is listed as a financial contributor to the cryptic Temple of Understanding. This temple, designed to resemble the sun, with six "rays" — housing respectively the religions of Buddhism, Christianity, Confucianism, Hinduism, Judaism, and Islam — is described in Temple literature with the typical occultist phrase, "six rays of hope." Although supporters of the Temple refer to it as a "spiritual United Nations," it is perhaps more explicitly described by syndicated columnist Edith Kermit Roosevelt, as follows:

> This futurist building in Washington, D.C., will serve as a politically useful symbol in rallying support around the Grand

Design to build a super-secret world government that includes Communist countries.[78]

A Temple brochure states: "Universal understanding must inevitably replace nationalist limitations."[79] Reduced to simplest terms, this means replacing all national loyalty and love of country with allegiance to a one-world order. The Temple of Understanding opens the door to this development by establishing a "world center" to amalgamate all religions into a single body. This absorption process can only result, eventually, in diluting each religion until all identity is lost and nothing essential remains — particularly in the area of traditional religious codes. Perhaps this is why Temple literature promotes an attitude of moral relativism, with emphasis on the theme of "the many facets of truth." Accurately translated, this negates eternal truths in favor of the situation ethics principle of no moral absolutes — again, the same philosophy promoted by Dr. Kirkendall.

Assisting in the operation of the Temple of Understanding is the United Lodge of Theosophists in New York, which uses funds donated by the tax-free Lucis Trust. This trust has been linked with the occult for nearly a century through its forerunner, the Lucifer Press, London publisher of *Lucifer* magazine.* *Lucifer* was at that time the official voice of the Theosophical Society — a group whose "secret doctrine" paid homage to Satan.

It appears that the roots of Theosophy were entwined with Humanism at least as far back as 1891,the year when Humanist-Fabian Socialist Annie Besant inherited the leadership of the Theosophical Society. A prolific writer, Mrs. Besant assumed the editorship of *Lucifer* magazine, whose name she changed to *The Theosophist*. Despite its name-change, however, this magazine perpetuated the traditional link between the occult and Satan worship, as evidenced by information given on its August 1913 cover.

---

*Lucifer Press was subsequently transferred to New York under the name Lucis Trust.

Mrs. Besant was also deeply involved with the Lucis Trust, which is now recognized as a non-governmental cooperating agency by the United Nations and which currently maintains the U.N.'s "meditation room."

The Temple's most visible columns of support come from more than a score of well-known Communists, as well as Theosophists, Humanists, Quakers (particularly the radical American Friends Service Committee), national and international bankers, corporation and news media executives, notable collectivists, and numerous one-world-oriented associations. The following are prominent among the Temple's list of supporters:[80]

- *Jerome Davis* and *Kirtley Mather* — both veteran Communist fronters, who were on the U.S. Senate Internal Security Subcommittee's April 1956 list of eighty-two most active and typical sponsors of Communist front organizations. In addition to Davis and Mather, there are at least a score of other Communist fronters among the sponsors of the Temple.
- *Rabbi Roland B. Gittelsohn* — fellow traveler, SIECUS-endorsed author, and signer of the "Support SIECUS" advertisement that appeared in the *New York Times* of October 16, 1969.
- *Max Lerner* — Humanist, ACLU advisor, syndicated columnist, and supporter of public school sex education.
- *James Linen* — president, Time-Life, Inc. (publisher of the controversial sex education book, *How Babies Are Made*); also a member of the Council on Foreign Relations (CFR), whose admitted goal is to replace our constitutional Republic with a world government.
- *Robert S. McNamara* — an advocate of one-world government and population control, and a "Support SIECUS" ad signer. McNamara is president of the United Nations' World Bank, which finances public school sex education in the developing countries.
- *Margaret Sanger* — Humanist and founder of Planned Parenthood.

- *Norman Thomas* — Humanist Socialist leader, and American Civil Liberties Union founder and director emeritus.
- *Thomas Watson* — member of CFR and president of the IBM affiliate, Science Research Associates, which retains Lester Kirkendall as a consultant and has utilized the services of such other SIECUS personalities as David Mace and Sally R. Williams.*

At least two other SIECUS officials are linked, like Lester Kirkendall, to the Temple of Understanding: Dr. Robert Laidlaw and Dr. Emily Mudd. Dr. Mudd participated in the Temple's second "Spiritual Summit," held in Geneva, Switzerland, in early 1970. The Temple's spring newsletter for that year listed her as a special advisor for this "Summit," opening a special session on the "population problem." As might have been expected, a major conclusion reached by this special session was the agreement that all religions should be concerned both with the fact of overpopulation and with the means of controlling it. (Dr. Mudd's husband, Dr. Stuart Mudd, also participated in the Temple's "Summit" as special advisor.)

In October 1975, the Temple's fifth "Spiritual Summit" featured, with other noted speakers, SIECUS associate and Humanist Dr. Margaret Mead, who led the "Summit's" call for the "spiritual unity of humankind." The conference chairman of the "Summit" was Jean Houston, president of the Foundation for Mind Research and co-author of *The Varieties of Psychedelic Experience.*†

* * *

We have watched as the house of sex education was patiently framed with timbers that were molded "at different times and places, and by different workmen" who apparently "understood one another from the beginning." As the pieces

*Sally R. Williams wrote eight units for SRA under the title, *1968–1969 Family Life and Sex Education Extension Service*, David Mace was one of several consultants in the preparation of SRA's *Worth Waiting For* program, which comprises six records, sixty discussion guides, and one instructor's manual. Lester Kirkendall has written at least five guidance booklets for SRA.
†See entry for *Guidance Associates* in PART TWO.

were joined together, "exactly adapted to their respective places," a pattern has emerged suggesting that the final framers, SIECUS's six founders, "all worked upon a common plan," under the guise of promoting "healthy, responsible sex relations," to formulate a nihilistic sexual philosophy. These founders then chose a sufficient number of like-minded people to help implement one of the most fraudulent programs ever foisted on an unsuspecting public. The SIECUS philosophy and its close alliance with the forces dedicated to total control over human destiny will be thoroughly examined in the next three chapters.

> *It all depends on the situation . . . . In some situations unmarried love could be infinitely more moral than married unlove. Lying could be more Christian than telling the truth. Stealing could be better than respecting private property. No action is good or right in itself. It depends on whether it hurts or helps people, whether or not it serves love's purpose — understanding love to be personal concern — in the situation.*
>
> — "The Law of Love" according to Joseph F. Fletcher, Humanist and father of situation ethics[1]

CHAPTER 2

A Round of Philosophy

"THE LAW OF LOVE" is the basis of the situation ethics philosophy. Situation ethics can be defined as a doctrine that includes no moral absolutes, under which concepts of "right" and "wrong" are governed by the particular situation. Under this code, any acts — adultery, homosexuality, promiscuity — can be redefined as moral, if they "serve love's purpose."

Speaking in terms of *whose* morals will be taught in the classroom, Arthur E. Gravatt, M. D., a leading sex education proponent, said:

> "What shall be taught?" has been sharply redefined by the current theological dialogue concerning ethics. The morality or immorality of any behavior, including sexual behavior, has been put in the context of "situation ethics." In this approach moral behavior may differ from situation to situation. Behavior might be moral for one person and not another or moral at one time and not another. Whether an act is moral or immoral is determined by "the law of love"; that is the extent of which love and concern for others is a factor in the relationship.[2]

This statement, immediately followed by Fletcher's "Law of

37

Love," was made at the ORTHO Pharmaceutical Corporation's 1966 Symposium on Sex Education, which was dominated by various SIECUS officials and their philosophy.[3] Dr. Gravatt was the editor of the symposium proceedings, which were subsequently published.*

Considering that SIECUS states its major purpose is "to promote healthy, responsible sex relations," it is ironic that it has chosen the situation ethics philosophy as the basis for its approach to sex education.[4] Among the vehicles used by SIECUS to accomplish its proclaimed purpose are its Study Guides, which cover various aspects of human sexuality. These were primarily designed to guide professionals in teaching sex education, and they have been widely distributed from coast to coast. These guides not only express the opinions of their respective authors, but are said to represent "the collective voice of SIECUS." As stated in SIECUS's own literature: "All SIECUS Study Guides are subject to review and acceptance by the *entire* SIECUS Board of Directors."[5] [emphasis added]

Of special interest is that the authors SIECUS mentions most frequently as references in its Study Guides are its own board members. Those who appear most frequently are Isadore Rubin, Lester Kirkendall, and Ira Reiss, all Humanists. For "scientific data," SIECUS often refers to the studies of Dr. William H. Masters and Virginia Johnson (both SIECUS board members and Humanists†) and to the Kinsey Reports, which,

---

*Participating in this symposium with Dr. Gravatt (a contributor to the SIECUS handbook for teachers, *The Individual, Sex and Society,* were SIECUS officials Warren Johnson, Clark Vincent, Ethel Nash, and the Rev. William Genné.

Another ORTHO-sponsored symposium held in Toronto, Canada, in September 1967, on the topic "Family Life Education — A Community Responsibility," featured Dr. Mary Calderone as the keynote speaker. The bibliographies of both symposia are replete with works of the usual SIECUS coterie: Dr. Calderone, Harold T. Christensen, Evelyn Duvall, Warren Johnson, Lester Kirkendall, John Money, Emily Mudd, Wardell Pomeroy, Ira Reiss, Isadore Rubin, *et al.*, and they also list SIECUS Newsletters, SIECUS Discussion Guides, and the socialist-oriented Public Affairs Pamphlets and other SIECUS-influenced materials.

†Having been involved in a bizarre event in 1970, the research team of Masters and Johnson merits more than just a passing glance. Keeping in mind that these

according to sociologist Dr. Albert H. Hobbs, "not only failed to meet necessary standards of scientific procedure but were notoriously slanted."[6] In fact, a Special Committee To Investigate Tax-Exempt Foundations, appointed by the 83rd Congress. made an exhaustive investigation and went one step further by concluding that the foundation-supported Kinsey Reports had been deliberately designed as an assault on Judeo-Christian morality.[7]

Of course Kinsey's establishment, the Institute for Sex Research in Bloomington, Indiana, has close ties with SIECUS. Wardell Pomeroy, a SIECUS director, was one of Kinsey's chief investigators, while another SIECUS official, John Gagnon, has been a trustee and senior research sociologist at the Kinsey Institute since 1959. A connecting link between the two groups is found in a common referral system for information requests recently set up by SIECUS and the Institute.*

Another author whose works are frequently used as references in the SIECUS Study Guides is the notorious smut-peddler and Humanist, Albert Ellis. And although Joseph Fletcher's name appears only once among these references, the views of the father of situation ethics can be detected much more frequently.

---

two individuals are acclaimed as respectable, legitimate, scientific interpreters of human behavior, we find that one of their latest "research" projects terminated in a law suit filed by a New Hampshire husband. As reported in the *Paterson* (N.J.) *News* of August 25, 1970, two unnamed male patients, at the instigation and direction of Dr. Masters and Miss Johnson, "engaged in a course of sexual activities culminating in several acts of sexual intercourse" with the plaintiff's wife. It was further revealed that the male patients had paid Masters and Johnson for this "treatment," which included the acts of sexual intercourse with the New Hampshire housewife, who was reimbursed a total of $750 for her services, by the research team — all, of course, in the name of "science." Shortly afterward, Masters divorced his wife and married Miss Johnson. (Masters and Johnson initially became notorious for their provision of mechanical devices for use in sexual experiments on their subjects, both married and unmarried, in the somewhat shady corners of their Reproductive Biology Research Foundation in St. Louis.)

*Not surprisingly, the hedonistic Hugh Hefner Foundation has been a major "sugar daddy" of the Institute for Sex Research. This foundation, set up by Hugh Hefner, publisher of *Playboy*, has also contributed approximately $750,000 to sex researchers Masters and Johnson over a period of ten years.

Due to the tremendous influence the study guides have had in shaping the structure and philosophy of sex education programs in America, parents and professionals should be aware of their content. Critical analysis suggests that SIECUS's real purpose is to erase the traditional moral values of the Judeo-Christian code and replace them with situation ethics and "the new morality." Although these concepts are heavily promoted in the SIECUS Study Guides, they are even more blatantly advocated in other SIECUS literature, such as quarterly newsletters, reprints of writings by professionals, and *The Individual, Sex, and Society: A SIECUS Handbook for Teachers and Counselors.* Together, these publications set forth the SIECUS Program, the existence of which SIECUS denies.[8]

The fallacy that SIECUS has no "program" has filtered down to the local level, and opponents of public school sex education are constantly challenged on this point. Perhaps a statement made by SIECUS executive director Mary Calderone to the *Philadelphia Inquirer* will clear up the matter once and for all. In defining her interpretation of the application of sexuality, she said:

> We should teach our children that this force [sexuality] can and must be integrated into the total personality of the individual, and that people must learn to manage it and use it creatively and constructively in relationships with one another as men and women.
> *The best program I know for doing this is the one I helped formulate* for the Sex Information and Education Council of the United States — SIECUS — the organization for which I work.[9] [emphasis added]

A half-page SIECUS ad appearing in a special issue of *The Humanist* for Spring 1965 announced that it was the intention of SIECUS to go even a step further by becoming involved in teacher preparation:

> Using specialized advisory committees, SIECUS will develop teaching standards and syllabi for professional schools and public schools at all levels, and also plans to conduct its own teaching institutes for the continuing education of physicians, teachers, social workers, etc.

Broadly defined, the SIECUS program, as formulated by Dr. Calderone, recommends integrating coeducational sex education into as much of the curriculum as possible, preferably in all grades, K through 12, with situation ethics as the basis of morality, and sensitivity training as an "educational tool."[10] As previously mentioned, the SIECUS Study Guides are often used in the implementation of this program. Although this chapter does not deal with each study guide in depth, portions of some will demonstrate a consistent trend in the SIECUS philosophy.

SIECUS Study Guides

Study Guides #1, #5, #9, and #10 are chiefly concerned with moral values. It is principally in their pages that Judeo-Christian principles are methodically undermined and situation ethics propagated. The technique most often used is the repeated promotion of freer sexual attitudes, accompanied by an assault on traditional values.

Study Guide #1

Humanist Lester Kirkendall launches the first attack in Study Guide #1, which is titled *Sex Education*. Characterizing former sex education programs as "weak," he complains: "The sex education usually received by children can more accurately be labeled 'reproduction education' or 'moral instruction' than sex education," adding that an "openness of approach" is clearly needed more than "injunctions and moralisms that provide little or no insight." Kirkendall's contempt for traditional morality is evidenced by such statements as:

> Sex education must be thought of as being education — not moral indoctrination. Attempting to indoctrinate young people with a set of rigid rules and ready-made formulas is doomed to failure in a period of transition and conflict.[11]

Obviously, a "transition" to situation ethics and "the new morality" is what SIECUS hopes to prepare educators and parents to accept. Take as an illustration an observation made by Kirkendall later in this guide:

> Today the significance of such sexual expression as youthful erotic play, masturbation, homosexuality between consenting adults, mouth-genital contacts, and other variations from genital heterosexuality is being re-examined in the light of new knowledge.

Considering all of the above, a reason given by Dr. Kirkendall for adult sex education — "To provide the informed public opinion needed *to support desirable changes in attitudes*, education, and laws as they relate to sex" [emphasis added] — becomes more significant.

Study Guides #2 and #3

Study Guides #2 and #3, dealing with homosexuality and masturbation respectively, subtly promote both practices, implying that the major problem is not the practices themselves, but the "punitive" attitudes of both parents and the community. This is accomplished through use of a carefully selected vocabulary — so effective that it has been incorporated almost verbatim into the syllabi of many school systems from coast to coast.

Identified Communist and Humanist Isadore Rubin composed Study Guide #2. The author of Study Guide #3 is Warren Johnson, another SIECUS director, whose humanistic and anti-Christian tendencies need little coaxing to surface and express themselves openly. One occasion when this occurred was at a Symposium on Sex Education of the College Student, held in October 1966. There Johnson contended that the Judeo-Christian tradition was chiefly responsible for undermining male-female relationships, making a healthy sexual adjustment virtually impossible in adulthood, and transmitting a moral code that is no longer appropriate.[12]

Study Guide #5

Guiding the reader toward acceptance of more liberal religious attitudes and sexually permissive standards, Ira Reiss — also a Humanist — states in Study Guide #5, *Premarital Sexual*

Standards: "The choice of a premarital sexual standard is a personal moral choice, and no amount of facts or trends can 'prove' scientifically that one ought to choose a particular standard. . . . Our religious institution also stresses autonomy of choice, as does our political system. There are signs in the political institution supporting the permissive trends with the governmental dissemination of contraceptive information and generally liberal censorship decisions by the Supreme Court. The religious institution also seems to be in part more acceptant of views held by men like Bishop Pike and Harvey Cox." (The late Bishop Pike, a SIECUS-recommended author, was at one time tried for heresy by the bishops of his Protestant Episcopal Church, while Harvey Cox has enjoyed the unique distinction of acting as Chaplain for the Black Panthers.) Reiss continues: "All these institutional structures are responding to our general type of society and displaying increased permissiveness."

Apparently a believer in the power of suggestion, in subsequent passages of his guide Dr. Reiss offers his readers the following: "The Scandinavian countries have developed even further than we a type of affection-centered premarital sexual permissiveness. We seem to be heading toward a Scandinavian type of sexuality. . . . In particular, it seems that permissiveness with affection will have a larger role to play in courtship in America in generations to come."[13]

Study Guide #9

Study Guide #9, *Sex, Science, and Values*, by Harold T. Christensen, openly acknowledges situation ethics as "the common ground" for professionals to stand on in dealing with the subject of morality in the classroom. Christensen begins by saying: "The strict Judeo-Christian codes inherited from the past, in which chastity is prescribed, are being challenged. Rational enquiry is replacing blind faith. . . . A so-called 'new morality' is being ushered in. . . ." Characterizing the traditional Christian position of morality as "a dogmatic one," he continues: "It is a morality of commandment, based upon *the assumption* that transcendental powers and eternal truths exist." [emphasis added] From the full context of these statements, it becomes obvious that Christensen has already prejudiced the issue by his general tone and selection of words. In fact, the major portion of this author's discourse on traditional Christian morality questions its merit and casts suggestive insults at Christians who follow it. Continuing, he discusses the "relativistic position" in which followers "do not see right and wrong as eternal entities; rather they distinguish between what is wise and foolish in actions that vary according to time, place, and circumstances." He then explains: "It [the relativistic position] is essentially the same thing as so-called 'situation ethics,' except that its full development requires more than logic or argument; it requires precise testings of empirical data by means of the scientific method.

"Thus, the newer relativistic position on sexual morality *is a rational one*, backed up by research. . . . this is the approach *that seems to offer the most hope* for consensus under modern conditions."[14] [emphasis added]

Joseph Fletcher's argument for a "law of love," quoted at the head of this chapter, is later used to support the relativistic position on sexual morality in Christensen's effort to guide teachers and students toward "responsible decision-making."[15]

Study Guide #10

Study Guide #10, *The Sex Educator and Moral Values*, by its very title can be considered the most important of all, since it deals specifically with morality, the pivotal point of all sex education. Significantly, it was written by identified Communist Isadore Rubin and released for publication two months after the expiration of his term on the SIECUS board. Rubin bases his concept of morality on four "core values," which he urges sex educators to apply in determining an ethical framework for making sexual decisions. Briefly stated they are: respect for truth, respect for the basic worth of each individual, cooperative effort for the common good, and recognition of the individual's right of self-determination. Rubin's own application of these values clearly demonstrates that he has based them on the situation ethics principle. He says: "Applied to sex conduct, these values suggest the right of the individual to engage in any form of sex behavior (1) within the limits of social obligation and welfare and (2) except where exploitation, violation of another's personality, or cruelty is involved." Rubin advises teachers that their "acceptance of truth as a core value would also imply that the effect of all sex practices would be described [in the classroom] as objectively and scientifically as possible, whether or not the results conformed to the official mores or to a particular social code."[16]

He also tells teachers that premarital sex is a debatable subject, and suggests: "The wisdom of chastity has been seriously questioned on a regular basis in mass-circulation magazines like *Playboy* and *Cosmopolitan*. . . . A sizable number of influential churchmen have declared that — even from a Christian point of view — no absolute rule can be laid down concerning the morality or immorality of all sex before marriage. For the sex educator to rule out premarital intercourse as a debatable subject in the classroom does not rule out the subject as a debatable one."

An even more revealing insight into Rubin's ideological makeup can be found in his article, "Transition in Sex Values — Implications for the Education of Adolescents."[17] This work, in part, was used in the development of Study Guide #10, and has been widely circulated among sex educators throughout the country. In the article, Rubin lists six major competing value systems that exist today, which he categorizes as:

(1) traditional repressive asceticism [traditional Judeo-Christian morality]
(2) enlightened asceticism [no specific code, with an open forum on sexual questions]
(3) humanistic liberalism [situation ethics, no moral absolutes]
(4) humanistic radicalism [virtually complete sexual freedom]
(5) fun morality [hedonism]
(6) sexual anarchy [anything goes][18]

In his description of these values, Rubin places traditional morality at one end of the moral spectrum, making it appear "extreme," counterbalanced by sexual anarchy at the other "extreme." This skillful technique then reclassifies humanistic liberalism, or situation ethics, as the middle-of-the-road position. Most Americans, having been conditioned to avoid "extremes," are thus led toward acceptance of "the new norm."

What type of society can we expect to see, if the foregoing values as fostered by SIECUS continue to flourish in the classroom, as young minds are encouraged to choose their own moral behavior patterns via situation ethics? Rubin has answered this himself in his article, "Transition in Sex Values," by acknowledging: "There is no doubt that there is an extremely difficult problem for social control when the individual is allowed a choice in moral behavior. Landis asserts: 'When acts are no longer forbidden to all, when the individual is authorized to decide whether or not violation will be advantageous, *the moral code vanishes.*' "[19] [emphasis added]

A Pattern of Inconsistencies

The general theory behind the SIECUS approach in supplying alternate codes of conduct is that, in the past, youth has been exposed to only one moral code, which emanated from the Judeo-Christian tradition, and that it has been "undernourished" by not being exposed to varying standards. SIECUS claims to subscribe to a more "modernistic" outlook, which would supply our youth with alternative codes, the final selection being left to the student.

This concept is riddled with false premises and fallacies, as is readily seen in light of the few simple facts that follow.

Man, since the very beginning of time, has been exposed to moral alternatives, arising from his own carnal nature, which challenge his spiritual conscience. The tempting alternatives come naturally, from within; they do not need to be ferreted out by pseudo-psychologists to entice him further.

SIECUS has no intention whatsoever of even giving the individual a choice in the matter; rather, it is the generator of a calculated plan aimed at the phasing out of all existing standards of sexual morality. Otherwise the design of its study guides would not have been so consistently slanted in favor of situation ethics; nor would its authors have gone out of their way to depict traditional morality as corny, humdrum, and obsolete. Further, the founder's selection of board members would have provided for a fair cross section of philosophical thought on morality, which is not the case, despite the claims of SIECUS. The SIECUS-enlisted clergy both on and off the board, who SIECUS maintains are representative of a more traditional viewpoint, would not have revealed themselves repeatedly in their own writing as moral apostates and, in some cases, religious heretics. And finally, the SIECUS selection of movies, slides, books, and periodicals, reviewed and commended in SIECUS newsletters and book lists, would not be so consistently built to accommodate an endless stream of "new morality" propagandists. If a true choice was meant to be offered, why were the writings of moral traditionalists not included among the vast array of reading references compiled by SIECUS?

The 1970 SIECUS book list, titled *Human Sexuality*, deserves special comment to make a further point. This book list might be described as a road map for detouring educators and other professionals to a morally bankrupt dead end. Largely compiled by Isadore Rubin, the diet of pestilent pottage it offers includes, among many others, the following resources, labeled by SIECUS as valuable in the field of human sexuality:

- *Guide to Sexology*, a collection of articles that first appeared in the bawdy magazine *Sexology*.
- *Commonsense Sex*, by Humanist Ronald Mazur. This title is also advertised in the pornographic *Evergreen Review*.
- *Pornography and the Law*, by Drs. Phyllis and Eberhard Kronhausen. This husband and wife team were the collectors of an erotic art display, portions of which were seized by the U.S. Justice Department on the grounds that they

were obscene and ought to be kept out of the country.[20] In recommending *Pornography and the Law* for teenage consumption as part of a basic sexology course, author Arthur Cain, in his *Young People and Sex*, commented: "Once they have perused these examples, there is no point in searching for further material; there is little, if anything, on the market (black market or otherwise) which is more pornographic."[21]

- *Honest Sex*, by Humanists Rustum and Della Roy, who proclaim that "traditional marriage is dead," and recommend, among a variety of choices, that extra-marital sexual experiences should occur only with "very close friends."[22]

- *The Playboy Philosophy*, by Humanist Hugh Hefner — a collection of reprinted installments from *Playboy* magazine, spelling out Hefner's hedonistic philosophy. Humanist Charles S. Blinderman has described *The Playboy Philosophy*, in part, as a work which contends that "institutionalized religion, particularly Christianity, is found to be the culprit responsible for many of the crimes against humanity."[23] (Characteristically, Hefner's "Playboy Advisor" column in the December 1968 issue of the magazine recommended SIECUS sex education materials to parents.)

- *5,000 Adult Sex Words and Phrases*, edited and compiled by John Trimble, published by Brandon House — an extensive collection of some of the filthiest words imaginable, accompanied by vivid, lewd definitions. (Brandon House publishes and distributes hard-core pornographic books, magazines, and films. Brochures advertising incredible filth are usually enclosed in the same envelope with the book. The purchaser, who may be a teenager, then becomes the target of an avalanche of pornography from as far away as Denmark.)

SIECUS itself, in fact, maintains close liaison with the pornography cartel through its connection with Elysium Institute, located in Los Angeles. This hedonistic haven prides itself on the programs of nudism, sensitivity awareness, and group sex activities which it offers to its patrons. SIECUS is listed in the Elysium Institute Directory as pursuing the same objective as, and maintaining an exchange of information with, Elysium, as are also the Sexual Freedom League (of Berkeley); Castalia (Timothy Leary's "League for Spiritual Discovery"); the Institute for the Study of Non-Violence (whose co-director is Humanist Joan Baez); the Institute for Rational Living (headed by Humanist Albert Ellis); the University of Humanism; and the Underground Press (dedicated to the promotion of drug usage, sex, sensitivity training, and obscenity).[24]

The published aims of SIECUS and Elysium, which are amazingly similar in phraseology, have been compared on a point-by-point basis in a special newsletter published by a group of physicians opposed to SIECUS-style sex education.[25] Particularly striking is the fact that Elysium Institute's publishing arm, Elysium, Inc., also prints *Nude Living, ANKH, Jay Bird,* and *Sun West* — magazines that feature totally unretouched male and female nudes in a variety of lewd and suggestive poses. The physicians' newsletter further discloses that, while Elysium, Inc., is entrenched in the field of pornography, it nevertheless wishes to retain some semblance of respectability, and thus assumes the fictitious name of "PANU-CO" when advertising certain obscene publications in its magazines.

*   *   *

In the last analysis, it appears that the strategy of SIECUS calls for a breaking down of moral values by sensitivity training reinforced with steady doses of situation ethics, erotica, and humanistic ideology. Its thrust is apparently aimed at preparing Western civilization for a new life style, which is to include everything from the new morality to total moral degeneracy.

It is obvious, then, that SIECUS's stated purpose of promoting "healthy, responsible sex relations" is merely a front to lure well-meaning citizens into rallying behind a cause which, in reality, has as its goal the eradication of traditional Judeo-Christian principles. This, of course, will lay the groundwork for the ultimate denial of God. Once this is accomplished, sexual nihilism and anarchy will enjoy full reign; for, as Thomas Altizer (contemporary leader of the "Death of God" movement) observes:

> Once God has ceased to exist in human experience as the omnipotent and numinous Lord, there perishes with Him every moral imperative addressed to man from a beyond, and humanity ceases to be imprisoned by an obedience to an external will or authority.[26]

Professing themselves to be wise, they became fools,

And changed the glory of the uncorruptible God into an image made like to corruptible man, and to birds, and four-footed beasts, and creeping things.

Wherefore God also gave them up to uncleanness through the lusts of their own hearts, to dishonour their own bodies between themselves:

Who changed the truth of God into a lie, and worshipped and served the creature more than the Creator, who is blessed for ever.

— Romans I: 22–25

CHAPTER 3

A Round of Religion

SIECUS OFTEN DESCRIBES ITSELF as a "voluntary health organization."[1] Since the term "health," as currently defined, can apply to the condition of body, mind, or spirit, students of the SIECUS philosophy should seek to determine which implication is intended.

Throughout SIECUS's extensive literature, we find the peculiar term "sexual being" used consistently to describe man. For example, the "SIECUS General Information" pamphlet observes "the need to understand oneself as a sexual human being; that all children are born and grow up as sexual beings. . . ." Lester Kirkendall elaborates on this in SIECUS Study Guide #1, saying: "Once and for all, adults must accept as fact that young people of all ages are sexual beings with sexual needs."[2] SIECUS board member Warren Johnson further expands the idea by saying that sex education should help young men and women "understand and accept themselves and each other as

51

sexual creatures, physically *and psychologically*."[3] [emphasis added]

Considering that SIECUS chooses to substitute "sexual" for "spiritual" being, it becomes clear that the intent is purely secular in nature. This is further clarified in SIECUS Study Guide #1, *Sex Education*, which says, once again omitting any reference to the spiritual aspect, "Since sex behavior is a function of the total personality, sex education must be broadly conceived, concerning itself with the biological, psychological, and social factors that affect personality and interpersonal relationships."[4] In fact, the word "spiritual" becomes conspicuous by its absence from the organization's publications.

Yet an examination of the SIECUS Articles of Incorporation, dated April 20, 1964, shows that SIECUS includes as one of its purposes that it is to be "religious" in scope. Specifically, this point is made in Article Third, paragraph (g): "To conduct and carry on the work of the Council not for profit but exclusively for *religious*, charitable, scientific, literary, or educational purposes. . . ." [emphasis added] These five fields of endeavor are mentioned several times in the charter, with the term "religious" consistently first.

The question now arises, what religion? Some may, at first, suppose that the betterment of all religion is intended, since SIECUS retains on its board clergy of the three major faiths. However, as has already been shown, the SIECUS Study Guides, recommended reading lists, and symposium proceedings clearly reveal intolerance for Judeo-Christian philosophy and the standards it traditionally upholds.

It is apparent that we are dealing with an organization that claims to have a "religious" purpose, while it simultaneously maligns and discredits Judeo-Christian values at every opportunity, consistently utilizing a vocabulary of secular terms. The logical inference is that those on the SIECUS board — including its clerical members — who speak out against the religious codes of the Bible, or condone doing so, must by their own definition be of some different "religious" persuasion.

Man Versus God

What, then, is the common denominator that unites these individuals in "religious" endeavor? A gathering of information indicates that the answer is "Humanism."

One definition of Humanism can be found on the inside cover of the March–April 1970 issue of *The Humanist* magazine, published by the American Humanist Association (AHA): "Humanism sees man as a product of this world — of evolution and human history — and acknowledges no supernatural purposes. Humanism accepts ethical responsibility for human life, emphasizing human interdependence." Julian Huxley, longtime spokesman for the Humanist movement, put it this way:

> I use the word "Humanist" to mean someone who believes that man is just as much a natural phenomenon as an animal or plant; that his body, mind and soul were not supernaturally created but are products of evolution, and that he is not under the control or guidance of any supernatural being or beings, but has to rely on himself and his own powers.[5]

According to this rationale, man alone (having divorced himself from God's laws) makes the final decision on all matters, including life and death. Thus he can justify such acts as abortion and euthanasia — both of which are not merely condoned but extensively promoted in Humanist literature.

The major tenets of Humanism, as recorded in the first "Humanist Manifesto"* (published in 1933), may be summed up as follows:

Humanists —
    a. Deny God as Creator and accept the evolutionary theory of man's origin as fact.†

*For full text of *Humanist Manifesto I* and its signers, see Appendix B.
†Although professedly atheists or agnostics, some Humanists on occasion do make reference to God in their writings. Some, when referring to "God," speak in a pantheistic sense. (*Pantheism*: the belief that the total material universe is God; or that God is the life principle in all nature — stones, grass, trees, animals, etc. — rather than a personal, spiritual Being.)
Then there are those who deliberately mislead because of the sensitive positions they may hold. For example, in a book review written for *The*

b. Label traditional religious concepts as inadequate.

c. Believe there is no life after death.

d. Do not tolerate worship or prayer.

e. Formulate values by means of "scientific inquiry."

f. Strive for control of all human institutions, in order to impose their philosophy.

g. Assert that man is essentially a product of his environment. [This concept, otherwise known as economic determinism, is completely alien to the Americanist principle of success through individual initiative.]

h. View the free enterprise system as grossly inadequate and believe a socialized and cooperative economic order must be established for the common good.[6]

Harold R. Rafton, founder and president of the Humanist Fellowship of Boston, when asked, "Do Humanists believe in a supreme being?" answered, "Emphatically, yes. That supreme being is man. Humanists have no knowledge of any being more supreme."[7] This central theme is encountered throughout Humanist literature.

Humanism, then, sees man as God, and as the sole prime mover of his own destiny. Thus, in Humanism there are no moral absolutes, and a situation ethics value system takes their place. AHA president Lloyd Morain confirmed this with the statement: "The humanist revolution of our times consists in the recognition that acts are to be judged by their consequences, not by their rhetoric."[8] Describing a "Decision-Making Kit" used in Humanist schools as an aid in guiding the morals of youth, an "Ethical Education" pamphlet quotes Dr. Milton Senn, who helped to prepare the kit, as stating: "Most denominations believe in teaching absolutes — right and wrong. . . . We're trying to do the opposite."[9]

Humanist (July–August 1960 issue, page 242), Llewellyn Jones had this to say about Humanist Edward Scribner Ames, former pastor of the Disciples of Christ (Campbellite) church: ". . . The fact that Ames could be humanistic and naturalistic in his philosophy or religion — and he was, through and through — and at the same time 'feel' the experience of religion and mediate it to a congregation as pastor, using in this capacity the traditional language of personal religion, even invoking God, was a source of great perplexity to his Humanist friends. . . . Ames as a pastor felt, however, that his first duty was to communicate to his congregation: *this was their language and so he used it.*" [emphasis added]

But perhaps a more significant definition of the Humanist philosophy in its relationship to morality was given by Scott Beach, then editorial associate, in *The Humanist's* September–October 1965 issue: "I think that the most accurate name for the new morality is Humanism."

The foregoing attitudes are undoubtedly in complete harmony with the concepts exemplified by SIECUS.

The "Scientific Approach"

Further evidence that the SIECUS "cult" is Humanistic can be found in the fact that SIECUS literature consistently stresses the "scientific approach" as a fundamental basis for sound moral decision making. As an illustration, on pages 14 through 16 of SIECUS Study Guide #9, *Sex, Science and Values*, the point is made that "scientific research — though not providing final answers and not completely satisfying everyone — is perhaps unique in offering us the possibility of reaching a common ground."

A heavy reliance on this so-called "scientific approach" is apparent in much other SIECUS material. "The SIECUS Purpose," which is repeated in most SIECUS publications, clearly establishes that it is the organization's purpose "to dignify [man's sexuality] by openness of approach, study and scientific research designed to lead towards its understanding." And finally, in the July 1967 issue of *The Journal of Religion and Health*, Mary Calderone posed a number of questions that, she said, "science must dare to answer and religion must dare to free science to answer."

This approach is fully in accord with Humanism's firm commitment to the scientific method in making all judgments, moral or otherwise. For example, Lloyd Morain said on pages 27 and 17 of *Humanism As the Next Step*: "Whereas in most other religions and in some philosophies certain matters have been laid down, accepted on faith and held to be true for all time, this is not true in humanism. We hold in high regard the scientific

method — the constant search for information and the willingness to change opinions as facts warrant." Commenting again
on the scientific method, Morain said: "No other idea has been
of more practical importance to the humanist movement than
this one."

So vital, in fact, is this principle that it is emphasized over
and over again in Humanist literature. And for a very good
reason, since, if a population could be persuaded to accept
science as a major factor in determining values, master planners
then could easily control the moral climate by providing simu-
lated "scientific" data. The noted geneticist and Humanist,
Hermann J. Muller, expressed a related thought in American
Humanist Association leaflet No. 210, titled *Science for Humanity.* Speaking of the necessity for deep changes in attitudes
and practices, he made the point that there must be a fundamental reorientation of young and old alike toward the scientific
viewpoint, "not only for population control in the larger sense,"
but in order that every citizen may be taught to "sympathize
with the purposes of science" and may possess "a proper base
from which to meet the varied problems of the scientific age."
Muller contended that the reorientation toward the scientific
viewpoint would then serve to prepare the populace for eventual
scientific human breeding.

The application of the scientific method by SIECUS as the
final authority in determining "ethical" standards obviously
harmonizes with this major tenet of Humanism.

The Humanist Coterie

It cannot be substantiated at this time that all SIECUS
officials are Humanists, although this is entirely possible. The
research necessary in order to document this particular point
adequately would be a massive undertaking. However, a substantial number of Humanists have been discovered — obviously
enough to have inspired the promotion of a Humanist-oriented
philosophy through the pages of the SIECUS Study Guides,

which, the reader will recall, "are subject to review and acceptance by the entire SIECUS Board of Directors." Consider, for example, that of the existing twelve guides, at least seven were written by three identifiable Humanists (Kirkendall, Reiss, and Rubin), the remainder by various others of like persuasion. Perhaps even more significant is the fact that the very core of the SIECUS philosophy — situation ethics — was originated by inveterate Humanist Joseph Fletcher, a signer of *Humanist Manifesto II.* The following SIECUS officials, past and present, can be identified as Humanists:

> Alan P. Bell
> Mary Calderone
> Deryck Calderwood
> Evalyn S. Gendel
> Virginia Johnson
> Lester Kirkendall
> Daniel H. Labby
> Judd Marmor
> William H. Masters
> John Money
> Jerome Nathanson
> James A. Peterson
> Harriet Pilpel
> Ira L. Reiss
> Isadore Rubin
> Esther Schulz*
> Helen Southard
> Earl Ubell

Names of other SIECUS board members have appeared in the pages of *The Humanist* in such a way as to indicate *at the least* that a basic rapport exists. William G. Cole and Ethel M. Nash, for example, fall into this category.

Other Humanists who are or have been involved with sex education, population control, ecology, sensitivity training, drug

*A SIECUS staff member.

education, and other related fields, as authors, promoters, or supporters are:

Wesley J. Adams	Robert Francoeur
Gina Allen	Jerome D. Frank
Walter C. Alvarez	Lawrence K. Frank
Curtis Avery	Betty Friedan
Luther G. Baker Jr.	Edgar Z. Friedenberg
Marion Bassett	Erich Fromm
Maj-Briht Bergstrom-Walan	Sol Gordon
Eric Berne	Sidonie M. Gruenberg
Algernon Black	Alan F. Guttmacher
Bonnie Bullough	Helen Mayer Hacker
Vern L. Bullough	Marian Hamburg
Elizabeth Canfield	Garrett Hardin
Donald J. Cantor	Frances R. Harper
Anton J. Carlson	Robert A. Harper
Bette Chambers	S. I. Hayakawa
Stuart Chase	Fred Hechinger
Emanuel Chigier	Grace Hechinger
G. Brock Chisholm	Hugh Hefner
LeMon Clark	Inge Hegeler
Helen Colton	Sten Hegeler
Barry Commoner	Hudson Hoagland
Joan M. Constantine	Prynce Hopkins
Larry L. Constantine	Julian Huxley
George W. Corner	Clyde Kluckhohn
Joseph Darden	Hilda S. Krech
Charles Darwin	Lawrence Lader
Alice Taylor Day	Alfred McClung Lee
Manfred DeMartino	Eda LeShan
Rudolf Dreikurs	Lawrence LeShan
Albert Ellis	Birgitta Linner
Erik Erikson	Archibald MacLeish
James Farmer	Abraham H. Maslow
Joseph Fletcher	Rollo May
Anna K. Francoeur	Ronald Mazur

Margaret Mead
Ashley Montagu
Anson Mount
Hermann J. Muller
Gardner Murphy
Gunnar Myrdal
Bonaro Overstreet
Harry Overstreet
Raphael Patai
Linus Pauling
Edward Pohlman
James W. Prescott
Robert H. Rimmer
J. A. T. Robinson
Carl R. Rogers
Alice S. Rossi
Della Roy
Rustum Roy
Edward Sagarin

Frances S. Salisbury
Winifield Salisbury
Leon Salzman
Margaret Sanger
Virginia Satir
Michael Schofield
William C. Schutz
Herbert Seal
Milton Senn
George Simpson
B. F. Skinner
Benjamin Spock
Walter R. Stokes
Lyle Stuart
Thomas H. Szasz
Harold Taylor
Paul Tillich
Robert N. Whitehurst
Charles Winick

H. Curtis Wood Jr.[10]

"Humanist of the Year" awards* have been granted by the American Humanist Association to several of those on the above list, including:

Mary S. Calderone (co-recipient, 1974)
Anton J. Carlson (1953)
G. Brock Chisholm (1959)
Albert Ellis (1971)
Joseph F. Fletcher (co-recipient, 1974)
Betty Friedan (co-recipient, 1975)
Erich Fromm (1966)

---

*To clarify the exact meaning of this award, an editor's note appearing in the March-April 1958 issue of *The Humanist* (page 108) had this to say: "Each year at its annual members' meeting, the American Humanist Association awards the title of 'Humanist of the Year' to one of its members who has achieved distinction in some field of endeavor relevant to the philosophy and purposes of Humanism."

Hudson Hoagland (1965)
Julian Huxley (1962)
Abraham H. Maslow (1967)
Hermann J. Muller (1963)
Linus Pauling (1961)
Carl R. Rogers (1964)
Margaret Sanger (1957)
B. F. Skinner (1972)
Benjamin Spock (1968)
Thomas H. Szasz (1973)

Early Harbingers of Humanism

The roots of Humanism extend into the earliest periods of recorded history. Among those who may be regarded as adherents to the "Humanist tradition" were Xenophanes in Asia Minor, Democritus in ancient Greece, Lucretius in Rome, Spinoza in seventeenth-century Holland, Diderot and Voltaire in France during the French "Enlightenment," and Charles Darwin, Herbert Spencer, and Thomas Huxley in nineteenth-century England. More recently, in twentieth-century England, Bertrand Russell and Julian Huxley contributed considerably to the advance of Humanism, as did their American counterpart, John Dewey.

Although the present movement was not officially organized until 1941 (the year the American Humanist Association was incorporated in Illinois as an educational institution), its roots were firmly fixed in American soil long before 1900, in the form of the Ethical Culture Societies and other smaller constituents of the Humanist complex.

Ethical Culture Societies

The oldest known Society for Ethical Culture was founded in New York City on May 15, 1876, by Dr. Felix Adler, a former rabbi. This was the first of some thirty Societies and Fellowships now existing in the United States. These groups are autonomous, joined together nationally by the American Ethical Union and internationally by the International Humanist and Ethical Union.

Dr. Adler wasted no time in getting started on the long list of educational, economic, and social reforms on his agenda, including the founding of the Free Kindergartens, the Neighborhood Guild, the Good Government Club (now known as the City Club), numerous Settlement Houses, and a quarterly journal. Through these channels and many others to come he would spread his tradition. By 1889 Adler had a national federation of Societies, and 1893 found the Ethical Movement organized internationally.

In 1904 Felix Adler established the Philosophy Club of Faculty at both Columbia University and Union Theological Seminary.[11] Johns Hopkins, Princeton, and Yale University groups were later members. Other groups founded either by or with the help of Ethical Culture were the Child Study Association of America, the Legal Aid Society, the National Association for the Advancement of Colored People, the American Civil Liberties Union, and numerous Planned Parenthood centers.[12]

Particularly strong ties exist between past and present leaders of the Ethical Culture Movement and the New School for Social Research, Columbia University, the National Committee for a SANE Nuclear Policy (SANE), the Fabian Socialist Movement, World Federalists, U.S.A. (formerly the United World Federalists), Americans for Democratic Action (ADA), and various agencies of the United Nations.

So far as Ethical Culture's "religious" philosophy is concerned, there can be no doubt it is Humanist. For verification we need only look to portions of a declaration adopted at the 1966 Assembly of the American Ethical Union, which is considered to be a position paper of the Fraternity of Leaders:

> Ethical Culture is a Humanist movement. Even before the designation Humanist gained currency as one of our common descriptive terms or names, Ethical Culture was a Humanist movement in its essential purposes and values.[13]

American Ethical Union (AEU)

Founded in 1889, the American Ethical Union is a federation of more than thirty Ethical Culture Societies and Fellowships; it is headquartered in New York City. Through this national association the Ethical Societies are able to cooperate in joint endeavors and to coordinate their activities. Together, for instance, they support the United Nations and the work of UNESCO, UNICEF, and the Human Rights and Trusteeship Commissions. The Women's Conference of the American Ethical Union is accredited as a non-governmental organization at the United Nations.

Other AEU activities are centered on ecology, prison reform, amnesty for draft dodgers, repatriation and restoration to citizenship of war resisters abroad, racial busing, and, formerly, American withdrawal of troops from Vietnam.

The field of race relations has also intrigued the leaders of the Ethical Movement. Felix Adler acted as prime mover and one of the chief officials of the first World Congress of Races, held in London in 1911 to bring together leaders and scholars from Africa and Asia.[14] This Congress immediately followed the founding of the National Association for the Advancement of Colored People (NAACP) in 1909–1910, as a result of a call signed by five leaders of Ethical Societies. Then came the founding of the Chicago Urban League in 1917 by the Chicago Ethical Society. Today, in almost every city where there is an Ethical Society, its members work closely with the Urban League.[15] In 1963 the AEU organized its Commission on Race and Equality, setting up a "4-point program in education for integration in Birmingham, Alabama."[16] The American Ethical Union is also affiliated with the National Committee Against Discrimination in Housing (which has provoked widespread racial unrest), and the Civil Liberties Clearing House.

Where youth is concerned, besides helping to found the National Committee on Child Labor and the Play Schools Association, through the years leaders and members of the Ethical Movement have been supporters and officers of such groups as the Public Education Association, the Citizens' Committee for Children, and many Child Guidance Centers. Other activities include the operation of camps for children, work camps, and the Encampment for Citizenship for Youth project. These encampments, incidentally, were conceived and developed by the veteran Communist fronter and Ethical Movement leader, Algernon Black, for the purpose of preparing youth for leadership in the envisioned Humanist society.

Other prominent figures in the American Ethical Union, besides Dr. Black, are Horace L. Freiss, Henry B. Herman, James F. Hornback, David S. Muzzey, and SIECUS director Jerome Nathanson, who was appointed to a fellowship in the New York Society in 1937. Mr. Nathanson was for years chairman of the Fraternity of Leaders, and assumed the directorship of the Institute for Ethical Leadership in 1962. He was a member of the Board of Directors of the International Humanist and Ethical Union from 1952 to 1962. The political interests of Mr. Nathanson include membership in the leftist Americans for Democratic Action (ADA).[17]

As mentioned earlier, SIECUS official Harriet Pilpel is also involved in the Ethical Movement, as a past trustee of the American Ethical Union and current member of the AEU's Board of Ethical Lecturers advisory committee. Furthermore, keeping in mind that Mrs. Pilpel is affiliated with Greenbaum, Wolff and Ernst, the same law firm which officiated at SIECUS's incorporation proceedings, it is interesting to find the November–December 1964 issue of *Ethical Culture Today* reporting: "The office of Greenbaum, Wolff and Ernst provides legal counsel for the American Ethical Union."

Fellow members with Mrs. Pilpel of the advisory committee of AEU's Board of Ethical Lecturers are, among others, SIECUS official Earl Ubell, SIECUS-recommended author Sidonie M. Gruenberg, and Saul K. Padover, professor of political science at the New School for Social Research in New York City.[18] The chairman of the advisory committee is Herbert Rothschild, a member of ACLU, Americans for Democratic

Action, the National Education Association, and the National Committee for an Effective Congress. One of the first participating lecturers of the Board of Ethical Lecturers was Eugene J. McCarthy, a contender for the U.S. Presidential nomination in 1968 and 1976, who publicizes himself as a "Catholic."

Of particular interest is the fact that the AEU filed an *amicus curiae* brief in the U.S. Supreme Court at the time of the 1965 *Seeger* decision (*U.S. v. Daniel A. Seeger*) — a case that challenged the constitutionality of the requirement of belief in a "Supreme Being" as a basis for granting conscientious objector status under the Selective Service Act. Once again, the familiar firm of Greenbaum, Wolff and Ernst appears, this time as counsel on the brief, together with Leo Rosen, an attorney who is connected with the firm in New York City.[19] Rosen, a Humanist, also chairs AEU's Law Committee, as reported in the Summer 1971 issue of *AEU Reports*.

A final note concerns AEU's close liaison with another group, the American Humanist Association — an affiliation accomplished only recently. Werner Klugman, then president of the AEU, announced in the March–April 1969 edition of *The Humanist*: "This issue of *The Humanist* marks the joint sponsorship of the magazine by the American Humanist Association and the American Ethical Union. . . . We welcome the joint publication of *The Humanist* as the voice expressing the point of view of all those who believe in the potential of man, his capacity for change, and his capacity for growth."[20] Among publications printed solely by AEU are *AEU Reports, Ethical Culture Today, Ethical Foundations*, and *Ethical Impact*.

Modern Manifestations of Humanism

American Humanist Association (AHA)

The year 1933 marked the beginning of another chapter in the Humanist saga: the signing of the first *Humanist Manifesto*. Among the thirty-four signatories were John Dewey of Columbia University; Robert Morss Lovett, editor of the leftist

New Republic; John H. Randall, Jr., of the Department of Philosophy of Columbia University; Anton J. Carlson, professor of physiology, University of Chicago; Jacob J. Weinstein, a rabbi and advisor of Jewish students at Columbia University; and Maynard Shipley, who, according to *The Humanist* of February 1975, was "the heart of the defense in the Scopes trial." Shipley was a close colleague of attorney Clarence Darrow.*

In 1941, the American Humanist Association was founded in Illinois as a non-profit, tax-exempt organization, conceived for educational and religious purposes. With the signing of the incorporation papers, this group became the formal representative of Humanists in the United States and Canada. Although AHA "stemmed largely from Unitarianism as a movement of Religious Humanists,"[21] other originators included Universalists, Ethical Society leaders, professors of philosophy and education, scientists, heads of smaller Humanist factions, rationalists, and other freethinkers.

About this same time, the magazine *The Humanist* — which admittedly is ". . . written from a secular and nontheistic point of view" — came into existence as the official voice of Western Humanist opinion under the auspices of AHA. This publication's editorial office is located at the Department of Philosophy, State University of New York at Buffalo, an institution that teems with Humanist professors. The year 1962 found the movement achieving international scope with the birth of the International Humanist and Ethical Union, of which AHA was a founding member.

*An interesting sidelight of the Scopes trial is found in Irving Stone's biography of Clarence Darrow (Doubleday and Co., Garden City, N.Y., 1941). The author points out that the American Civil Liberties Union stage-managed the whole series of events that led to the trial of John Scopes, who taught evolution in violation of Tennessee's Anti-Evolution law. George Rappelyea, a representative of the ACLU, concocted, with Scopes, a plan that included Rappelyea's swearing out of a warrant for the arrest of Scopes in the full knowledge that the ACLU stood ready to defend this as a test case. Accordingly, all four defense attorneys at the trial were members of the Humanist-spawned ACLU, including Darrow himself, who was a Unitarian and an ACLU founder.

Serving on the editorial staff of *The Humanist* in 1974 were the following individuals:[22]

Editorial Board: Bette Chambers, Edward L. Ericson, Roy P. Fairfield, Paul Kurtz (chairman), Gordon C. McCormick, Lloyd L. Morain, Mary Morain, Howard Radest, Arnold Sylvester, Jack Tourin, Maurice B. Visscher, Miriam Allen deFord, Albert Ellis, James Farmer, Herbert Feigel, Jerome Frank, Charles Frankel, R. Buckminster Fuller, Hector Hawton, Julian Huxley, Lester A. Kirkendall, Corliss Lamont, Eda Le Shan, Lester Mondale, B.F. Skinner, Thomas S. Szasz, Harold Taylor, Edwin H. Wilson. *Editor*: Paul Kurtz. *Associate Editors*: Roy P. Fairfield, Khorn Arisian. *Executive Editor*: James Robert Martin. *Assistant Editors*: Rita A. Wilson, Doris Doyle. *Film Reviews*: Harry M. Geduld. *Drama Reviews*: Julius Novick. *Poetry*: M. L. Rosenthal. *Contributing Editors*: Lionel Abel, David T. Bazelon, Paul Blanshard, Edd Doerr, Leslie A. Fiedler, Anthony Flew, Richard Kostelanetz, Robert L. Tyler. *Editorial Associates*: Jean S. Kotkin, David Rosenthal, Marvin Zimmerman, William Geller, Broady Richardson, Marvin Kohl, Cynthia Dwyer, Charles E. Roessler, Anna Marko. *Broadcast Consultant*: James H. Schoonover. *Circulation*: Patricia Pliss, Sally-Ann Garner.

Some other periodicals published by AHA to coordinate its efforts are *Free Mind* (AHA's membership bulletin), and a small newspaper by the name of *Involve*. These are supplemented by a wide variety of smaller leaflets, brochures, and books on specific subjects.

So far as its physical structure is concerned, the AHA is the command vessel for a flotilla of federated associations that are moored in strategic locations in the United States and Canada. Humanist House, the AHA's official headquarters in San Francisco, is a five-story mansion overlooking Golden Gate Bridge and the Pacific Ocean. This building was officially opened on December 10, 1967, Human Rights Day, with the raising of the United Nations flag.[23]

Like its affiliates, AHA directs its energies toward a seemingly endless list of "religious," educational, social, cultural, and scientific interests. In the fall of 1973, AHA leaders and their Humanist associates updated the first *Humanist Manifesto* for the purpose of making clear which interests warrant top priority as Humanists approach the twenty-first century. Like the original Manifesto, *Humanist Manifesto II* criticizes religious dogmatism and denies the existence of a Creator. It asserts that humans alone must solve the problems that threaten their existence on earth, stating: "No deity will save us; we must save ourselves." As its answer to mankind's present plight, the document affirms, among other things, the right to complete sexual freedom, birth control, abortion, divorce, euthanasia, and suicide.

Opting for world government as another solution to our earth's problems, *Humanist Manifesto II* contends:

> We deplore the division of humankind on nationalistic grounds. We have reached a turning point in human history where the best option is to *transcend the limits of national sovereignty* and to move toward the building of a world community in which all sectors of the human family can participate. Thus we look to the development of a system of world law and a world order based upon transnational federal government. [emphasis in original]

The one-world cartel that drew up *Humanist Manifesto II* also proclaimed that "extreme disproportions in wealth, income, and economic growth should be reduced on a worldwide basis." (For the full text of *Humanist Manifesto II* and its signers, see Appendix C.)

Insight into some of AHA's past accomplishments is offered in the following excerpt from the publication titled *American Humanist Association — Philosophy, Purposes, and Program*:

> The AHA is not quite like any other organization. Many innovative ideas on birth control, human rights, science for humanity, education, sexual equality, humanistic psychology, and moral relativity, now commonly accepted and practiced, were first introduced and advocated by humanists.

Other Humanist literature reveals that the AHA Divisions of

Humanist Involvement and Humanist Service are structured with subcommittees working for peace, support for the transnational work of the U.N.; encouragement of world-mindedness; conservation and pollution control; population limitation; abortion law reform; euthanasia; prison reform; separation of church and state; funeral reform; and "humanizing" of public education.

Some of these Humanist goals are worth a searching look, in order to understand what meaning they have for Humanists, and how they are being accomplished.

PEACE — "Peace" is perhaps the most universally accepted of the Humanist goals. In one Humanist pamphlet,[24] the so-called "peace symbol" is shown as one of the six symbols of Humanism.* This symbol, which the Humanists thus claim as their own, can be traced as far back in history as the first century A.D. Then called the Nero Cross, this broken and inverted cross became known as the symbol of the Anti-Christ — for such was the reputation earned for the Emperor Nero by his relentless persecution of both the early Christians and the Jews.[25]

Satanists in the Dark Ages adopted the Nero Cross to mock the religious zeal of Christians. In the early Middle Ages this symbol was recognized as the "crow's foot" or "witch's foot," and, again, as the insignia of Satan.[26] "In the Twentieth Century," according to the scholarly Marquis de Concressault, "this same symbol was painted on the doors of churches closed by the Bolsheviks in Russia. . . ."[27]

It was in the late 1950's that Humanist Bertrand Russell revitalized and popularized the "peace symbol" by using it on an "Easter Peace Walk" in Aldermaston, England, protesting the use of nuclear weapons and urging unilateral disarmament by Britain. Russell, one of the most avid anti-Christians of contemporary times, wrote in *The Will To Doubt*: "I am a dissenter from all known religions and I hope that every kind of religious

*For a description of the six symbols of Humanism, see Appendix D.

belief will die." It is evident that, considering its historical background and present-day sponsors, the "peace symbol" is a made-to-order trademark for Humanism.

As part of its program to promote world "peace," much AHA activity has been centered on the complete withdrawal of American forces from Vietnam; the repeal of the draft; participation in anti-war protests, such as the April 24, 1971 demonstrations in Washington, D.C., and San Francisco (primarily planned by the National Peace Action Coalition and the People's Coalition for Peace and Justice, which were both cited as operating under substantial Communist influence);[28] universal disarmament followed by the formation of a world security force under United Nations control; and the promotion of world government.

The last activity is more specifically defined in an article in the July-August 1966 issue of *The Humanist*:

> Internationally, what do humanists propose? Nationalism, rooted as it is in arbitrary geographical units, must be superseded by a globalism based on the oneness of man. There must be a worldwide organization to which national sovereignty could be relinquished in all international affairs. The UN has the potential to be effective, but it cannot achieve the goal envisioned here until all peoples of the world are represented.[29]

Subsequently, at its 1969 annual meeting, AHA passed a resolution to "mundialize" itself, calling upon all chapters and affiliates to undertake activities to help bring about a world community. It was further resolved that all AHA members and associations should take steps to "mundialize" their cities and other organizations in their communities, and that all AHA members become registered *world citizens*. Following acceptance of this resolution by an overwhelming majority of AHA members, the American Humanist Association acknowledged in the March–April 1970 issue of *The Humanist* that it was "the first national organization to be mundialized (*i.e.*, made part of the world community)." Shortly afterward, certain communities here and there across the nation began to follow suit.

So enthusiastic have Humanists become in their zeal for a one-world order that, in 1971, some of their leaders combined forces with leading advocates of population control and nationalized abortion, World Federalists, and others, in the formation of the American Movement for World Government. This group's full-page advertisement in the *New York Times* of July 27, 1971, called for a "world federal government to be open at all times to all nations without right of secession," with the power to curb overpopulation.

Other essentials supported by this group of twenty-six signatories of the *Times* ad are a "civilian executive branch with the power to enforce world laws directly upon individuals" (which would automatically supersede the U.S. Constitution); and the "control of all weapons of mass destruction by the world government with the disarmament of all nations, under careful inspection, down to the level required for internal policing." (The latter, of course, could conceivably allow for the stationing of Russian or Chinese Communist troops on U.S. soil.) And, as was further stated in the ad, ". . . a federal world government must be established at the earliest possible moment by basic transformation of the UN or other reasonable means."

Participating in this movement as signatories to the advertisement were such Humanists as Hudson Hoagland and Lawrence Lader. Other signers were veteran Communist fronter Louis Untermeyer, who has been cited for more than thirty Communist-front affiliations as recorded in U.S. Government files,[30] and SIECUS sponsor Mark Van Doren, who has six Communist-front associations.[31] Another notable in this group was Dr. Paul R. Ehrlich, author and honorary president of Zero Population Growth, Inc.

No doubt dutiful members of the AHA whole-heartedly supported this call to give vigorous moral and financial support to the world government movement; for, as was brought out in a recent editorial in *The Humanist*, "If there is one principle upon which all humanists are united, it is the continued commitment to a world order based upon world law."[32]

CONSERVATION AND POLLUTION CONTROL (ECOLOGY) — In the

November–December 1970 issue of *The Humanist*, which was almost entirely devoted to ecology, an editorial appeared on the subject that contained the following statement:

> "*The Humanist*" has long been in the forefront of the battle for conservation and preservation of the environment. A scrutiny of our issues as far back as a decade or two ago will show that we were one of the first magazines in America alert to the dangers of an uncontrolled technology.[33]

Further emphasized in this article was the point that the problem is "*global in character*" and so a worldwide strategy is essential to cope with it.

This pet project of the AHA has received tremendous support from rank and file Americans — and understandably. Only a callous brute would turn his back on nature's progeny in fur and feathers, who supposedly teeter on the brink of disaster as an encroaching world of smog and concrete moves in to engulf the wilderness. But behind this propaganda screen, so skillfully designed that its very existence can be scarcely more than guessed at, lies a Pandora's box of troubles requiring closer study.

This subject will be examined in a greater detail in PART II (see entry for *Planned Parenthood–World Population*), but the point should be made here that the "nature-saving" aspect of the ecology movement is simply a façade to convince followers (many of whom may be dedicated, legitimate conservationists) that the movement is drastically needed, that it is bona fide, and that the top leaders are sincere. Once this is established, followers will have been conditioned to accept later phases. These will include further seizure of land by state and federal authorities; more stringent government controls over production, transportation, and industry; nationally legalized abortion and euthanasia; and compulsory population control.

POPULATION LIMITATION — World population control has taken high priority among AHA activities for a number of years. Illustrating this fact, an editorial in the January-February 1970 issue of *The Humanist* named as one Humanist "imperative" for the seventies "the urgent need for worldwide population control." Two major components of AHA's population limitation program are legalized abortion and euthanasia. Abortion law reform was declared by the AHA board of directors to be "the top social action priority for the AHA in 1967."[34] Since then it has continued to command the attention of members throughout the country (see entry for *National Association for Repeal of Abortion Laws* elsewhere in PART II).

Euthanasia became an official Humanist project during the 1966 AHA annual conference at Asilomar, California. The conclusion reached by a special study committee read as follows:

> . . . euthanasia, mercy killing of individuals suffering from incurable and painful illnesses or disabilities, *is an acceptable alternative to the unnecessary prolongation of life*. Every precaution against abuse of this option must be taken, and the consent of the patient should be obtained *if possible. For humanists, it must be remembered that the dead, being nonexistent, cannot regret being dead.*[35] [emphasis added]

In conjunction with this callous attitude, a number of prominent Humanists are in the vanguard of what is termed the "Euthanasia Educational Fund." This group publishes forms for "A Living Will,"[36] intended to provide for the event that an individual is physically or mentally disabled by a terminal illness at some future time. Requiring the individual's signature, this "will" is a clear-cut authorization to his family, physician, clergyman, and lawyer to administer drugs to alleviate suffering of the terminally ill "even if they hasten the moment of death."

Serving on the Euthanasia Educational Fund's board of directors with others is Humanist and SIECUS official Jerome Nathanson. Other Humanist members of the Fund's advisory council, include SIECUS sponsor Walter C. Alvarez; Algernon Black; Joseph Fletcher, father of "situation ethics"; and Dr. Alan F. Guttmacher of Planned Parenthood–World Population.

It should be kept in mind that, once euthanasia is accepted and legalized, a logical further step is the "mercy killing" of *any* person whom the State may regard as expendable —

economically, socially, *or politically.*

Another Humanist-spawned organization promoting euthanasia, the National Commission for Beneficent Euthanasia, was convened at AHA's 1975 annual conference in Webster Groves, Missouri. Co-chairman of this newly formed Humanist front is Professor Marvin Kohl, a signer of *Humanist Manifesto II.*

PRISON REFORM — Another subject dealt with at the 1966 AHA Annual Conference in Asilomar, California, was crime and punishment. The conclusion reached by this particular discussion group was that punishment of criminals should be discontinued in favor of rehabilitation utilizing the techniques of the behavioral sciences.

The AHA is also on record as being opposed to capital punishment, in a prepared statement presented by *The Humanist* on December 17, 1968, to the New York State Legislature's Committee on Codes, which was holding hearings to determine whether or not capital punishment should be reinstated.[37]

As an alternative, Humanist leadership favors the establishment of massive rehabilitation clinics in which criminals will be the subjects of an intensive program of sensitivity training structured on the behavioral sciences. Presumably this is aimed at excluding all "mind pollution" from their brain waves.

In recent years, society has just begun to feel the pressures being exerted in this direction, as the mass media encourage a trend toward rehabilitation and away from punishment, and the public is urged to consider the criminal "a victim of circumstances." An additional point should not be overlooked: the fact that for years small corps of Humanists and ACLU lawyers have been touring state prisons counseling prisoners and agitating for their "human rights."

Among scores of prisons where Humanists have been at work is Soledad, in California. By mid-1970, a Humanist prison group had been established,[38] following the murder of a Soledad guard in January of that same year. Since then, trouble has erupted sporadically at Soledad, the toll of murdered employees having reached three by May 1971. Further, as reported in the "Humanist and Ethical News" section of *The Humanist* for March–April 1972, that year found Arthur M. Jackson, executive director of the Humanist community at San Jose, California, working unofficially as Soledad's prison chaplain.*

But perhaps the most notorious incident of prison unrest in recent years was the outbreak of violence at Attica (N.Y.) State Prison. Shortly after the bloody rioting of 1,000 prisoners in September 1971, which took the lives of thirty-two inmates and eleven hostages, a full-page advertisement in the *New York Times* made an almost hysterical plea to readers for financial support "to avenge Attica."[39] The ad pressed "for major and minor reforms" and prisoner *rehabilitation*, as opposed to punishment. Its sponsors pledged to prevent future Atticas by "attacking every aspect of our prison systems." The ad continued: "At the moment, we're representing prisoners in 63 separate cases, including Attica," adding that the legal group sponsoring this ad had already won victories in Arkansas, Ohio, Maine, and elsewhere. It comes as no surprise to find that the *Times* ad was sponsored by the NAACP Legal Defense and Educational Fund[40] — the same NAACP that was founded in part by Ethical Culture Humanists, acting in concert with Communist W.E.B. DuBois and others of like persuasion.

Combined with other particulars, the Attica story follows a classic pattern. Notably, not only had Attica prisoners been coached from the inside by Humanists, but Humanist lawyers were foremost in their defense, coming from the ranks of the ACLU (led by Humanists William Kunstler and Herman

*The same issue of *The Humanist* contained the following information: ". . . Dr. Ernest Baker, long-time member of the American Humanist Association and a Humanist Counselor, became California's first official humanist prison chaplain at the state correctional facility at Vacaville on December 17, 1971. Dr. Baker meets with about 25 inmates every other Sunday afternoon to discuss humanist issues. . . . Humanist Counselors in California are now planning to attempt to become humanist chaplains in other state correctional institutions."

Schwartz), the Legal Aid Society (founded by Ethical Culture), and the subversive National Lawyers Guild (cited as "a Communist front").

With Humanists and Communist revolutionaries so snugly tied together in the Attica package, violence was only to be expected. And there was more. For behind the grisly spectacle were elements bordering on the macabre. As reported by the Attica chaplain, militant convict Sam Melville (killed while attempting to blow up Attica installations during the recovery of control) had been dressed in a chasuble — an outer garb worn by priests during celebration of the Mass.[41] In addition, Attica's entire chapel had been demolished by the rioters in typical Satanist fashion, with only the marble altar left standing. According to the Reverend James P. Collins, the prison chaplain, the chapel was violated "by Marxist revolutionaries to show their contempt for Christianity."[42]

In attempting to appraise the Attica uprising, it should be remembered that the leading agitators are revolutionaries who despise the system, and their cry for "reform" is only a façade. As with campus uprisings, grievances and issues are used only for agitational purposes. The revolutionaries' sole interest is to present non-negotiable demands that are impossible to fulfill, so that their rejection can be used as an excuse to start a revolution.

HUMANIZING PUBLIC EDUCATION — Besides spearheading the entire sex education movement, Humanists in recent years have nearly achieved control of certain other segments of the public school curricula. Following are just a few examples of what Humanist leadership proposed in the July–August 1966 issue of *The Humanist*:

> Remove the competitive grading practices of our school systems. . . . Work toward teaching cooperative sports with particular attention toward developing appreciation of group participation rather than winning enjoyment at the expense of others through aggressive and competitive sports.

One of the latest innovations in education — the "open classroom" approach, sometimes called "open education" or "informal education" — harmonizes perfectly with this overall scheme, because of the nongraded atmosphere and the emphasis on "group" thinking. This approach, as promoted by the Humanists, is aimed at erasing any trace of the competitive spirit that is so essential to the successful operation of a free enterprise system. A society that has lost this spirit would be ripe for participation in the socialistic system the Humanists are working overtime to create — a system that thrives on "group" thinking. Of course it is no coincidence that leading educators have credited John Dewey (a Humanist and Communist-fronter) with planting the virus of this scholastic malady with his book titled *Schools of Tomorrow*.[43]

Another item often used in school curricula is a social studies course for the fifth grade level, titled *PACOS (People: A Course of Study)*, formerly known as *MACOS* (*Man: A Course of Study*). This course was designed by a team of psychologists under the primary direction of Humanist B. F. Skinner, and has been promoted and marketed by the National Science Foundation (an independent agency in the executive branch of the federal government) to the tune of $7 million. In keeping with Humanist aspirations, the *PACOS* course is intended to mold children along lines that would alienate them from the moral values and beliefs of their parents. *PACOS* materials abound in references to cannibalism, violent murder, elimination of the weak and elderly, killing of female babies, wife-swapping, adultery, communal living, and promiscuity.

A more recent Humanist innovation in the field of education is termed "Parent Effectiveness Training" (PET). PET is a program that claims to offer parents a revolutionary new method of child rearing. It draws heavily on the behavior modification techniques of such Humanists as Carl Rogers and Sidney Jourard, and focuses on "*modifying the parent* rather than the child." PET further emphasizes the situation-ethics concept that there are no "right" solutions to problems, and discourages disciplining of the child.

PET is one component of a four-part program that is admittedly designed to "humanize" families and schools. The remaining three parts are "Teacher Effectiveness Training," "Leader Effectiveness Training," and "Human Effectiveness Training."

AHA members have labored, also, to create and maintain a secular atmosphere in the classroom. In 1958 AHA's Committee on Church and State formulated "A Guide to Action" for the use of association members and friends. This guide states: "We steadfastly oppose the use in any public school of any religious ceremony, pageant, monument, symbol, costume, textbook, or system of instruction which favors or promotes any religion."[44]

Included in the AHA committee's twelve-point action program are such instructions as the following:

> • Study carefully any course offered in public schools in "moral guidance" or "spiritual welfare" to see that it does not contain propaganda for supernaturalism or preference for orthodox institutions; and if it does, challenge its constitutionality. . . .
> • Challenge all religious ceremonies in public schools, including prayers, devotional use of the Bible, and Christmas pageants, wherever the local laws and the climate of local opinion are such that there is a reasonable prospect of successful action.[45]

All of the above activities, and more, are being carried out by Humanists in their respective communities, as they vigorously labor to restructure American education on the cornerstone of secularism and "progressive" Deweyism.

A final case in point is the 1963 Supreme Court decision that outlawed prayers and Bible reading in the public schools. Most Americans viewed the initiator of this court case, Madalyn Murray (now Mrs. O'Hair), as a self-proclaimed atheist who seemingly stood alone. Few realized that she had close liaison with the Humanist Movement, which included editorship of *The Free Humanist* in 1961. This liaison culminated in 1965 with her election to the board of the American Humanist Association. In 1973 she was again elected to the board for a four-year term. Mrs. Murray's associate in the 1963 Schempp-Murray case was

Edward L. Schempp, who was identified as a Humanist in the May–June 1963 issue of *The Humanist*.

Moreover, among organizations actively assisting Madalyn Murray in the legal battle to oust God from the classroom were the American Humanist Association, which filed an *amicus curiae* brief in the Schempp-Murray case, and the American Civil Liberties Union, a favorite haven for Humanists.

MORALITY — Although not mentioned earlier as part of the established AHA program, other interests have captured the attention of the AHA leadership through the years. A case in point is the vulnerable field of morality. Besides having developed and promoted the situation ethics principle and the concept of sensitivity training, Humanists have been active in the promotion of:

1. *Free love* — The 1966 AHA annual conference referred to under *Prison Reform* formulated the assertion that "laws against fornication, or any laws which attempt to prevent young people from coming together in circumstances where sexual activity might take place, *i.e.*, hotels, motels, are non-humanistic approaches which do more harm than good."[46] Similarly, *Humanist Manifesto II* in 1973 affirmed the right of any consenting adult to engage in any form of sexual activity.

2. *Communal living* — In speaking of the single person's "right" to "meaningful relationships," AHA representatives have gone on record with the following statement:

> . . . The social stigma and prejudices maintained against unmarried persons in our society must be erased. Perhaps the traditional biological family unit is not the best institution for fulfilling human needs. . . . Further, families of several adults living together, producing children of various combinations of parents, might have positive advantages.[47]

3. *Sexual equality* — From a perusal of Humanist literature it becomes evident that Humanists basically support the same causes championed by the current Women's Liberation Movement. One reason for this may be that a substantial number of

the founders and activists of the movement are themselves Humanists, Socialists, or Marxists.*

The most prominent Humanists in this category are Betty Friedan, Gloria Steinem, Gina Allen,† Miriam Allen deFord, Florynce Kennedy, Alice Rossi, Margaret Mead, and admitted Lesbians Del Martin and Phyllis Lyon; while Roxanne Dunbar, Jo Freeman, Robin Morgan, and Naomi Weisstein rank among feminists of the New Left. Similarly, the writings of Shirley Chisholm, Bernadette Devlin, and Simone de Beauvoir have expressed a decidedly Socialist theme.

In general, an examination of the continuous flow of literature from the militant feminist movement shows an inclination to dissolve the institution of marriage and the traditional family unit and displays a markedly Socialist orientation. In fact, the movement's intended ideological purpose has been well summed up by women's lib activist June Sochen in her book, *Movers and Shakers*, with the following statement:

> . . . Most women's lib groups accept both the class and sex analysis of the women's dilemma in American society; that is, they share the Marxist-Leninist perspective of the evils of a capitalistic society. . . .

It should then come as no surprise to discover that a central thrust of women's liberation is to promote Humanist values. For example, during a three-day national convention in Los Angeles in early September 1971, a women's liberation group pledged "to bring a universal end to war and to create a society in which feminist, humanist values will prevail. . . ."[48]

---

*Likewise, leaders in the original wave of feminist agitation during the early 1900's included the following: Humanist-Socialists Jane Addams and Margaret Sanger; Socialists Crystal Eastman and Henrietta Rodman; Marxists Elizabeth Gurley Flynn, Kate Richards O'Hare, and Rose Pastor Stokes; Unitarians Susan B. Anthony, Elizabeth Cady Stanton, Lucretia Mott, and Lucy Stone. (See June Sochen, *Movers and Shakers: American Women Thinkers and Activists, 1900–1970*. New York, Quadrangle/The New York Times Book Co., 1973. See also Judith Hole and Ellen Levine, *Rebirth of Feminism*. New York, Quadrangle Books, Inc., 1971.)

†Gina Allen serves on the American Humanist Association's board of directors and is also a member of the NOW Task Force on Sexuality.

Further, in speaking of the existing male involvement with the women's liberation movement, Warren Farrell of the National Organization for Women (NOW) stated in the June 25, 1972 issue of the *New York Sunday News*: "Ultimately, this is a humanist movement . . . ."

Like the Humanists, the women's lib movement does not shun lesbianism. On February 18, 1973, a task force of NOW voted to join forces with lesbians in their fight to legalize their perversion, by passing a resolution that "NOW [National Organization for Women] make civil rights for lesbians and positive attitudes toward lesbians a top priority." And again, in 1975, NOW formally endorsed so-called "lesbian rights" at its annual convention.

4. *Homosexuality* — A report by Humanist Donald J. Cantor on the status of homosexuality in the United States was made to the faithful in the September–December 1967 issue of *The Humanist*. Cantor's essay fully supports the British "Wolfenden Report," which recommended that private, adult, consensual homosexual acts be made lawful.

Significantly, Cantor asserts that ". . . it was the late Dr. Kinsey's study of the sexual habits of the white American male and female which provided the impetus for the homosexual movement."[49]

Cantor concludes his article (which advocates repeal of all U.S. laws governing adult homosexual activity) with the statement: "Equality for the homosexual is an ethical imperative and the American people are beginning to realize this [obviously with the help of the Humanists and their fellow travelers] "[50]

5. *Drugs* — That certain Humanist leaders condone drug use is evident. For instance, prominent British Humanist Aldous Huxley was a known user of drugs. In a series of articles regarding drug dependence, written by a special committee of the American Medical Association, the point was made that "by the early 1960's an increasing number of persons were abusing (self-administering) the drug (LSD), perhaps abetted by the

publications of Aldous Huxley and of Timothy Leary and his associates lauding its 'consciousness expanding qualities.' "[51]

Recently, in May 1971, an AHA member, psychiatrist Thomas S. Szasz, at the annual meeting of the American Psychiatric Association, presented a paper on drugs titled "The Ethics of Addiction."[52] This paper was an argument for making hard drugs, such as heroin, available to adults, and it affirmed that other drugs, such as marijuana, "ought to be simply sold over the counter like aspirin and cigarettes." Szasz further asserted: "The decision as to whether to use or take drugs should be a personal choice and an individual responsibility; the state should not respond in any way, either by calling the drug user 'sick' and forcing treatment on him, or by calling him 'criminal' and imprisoning him."[53]

This mode of thought is clearly set forth by the top echelons of AHA. Writing in the November–December 1966 issue of *The Humanist*, AHA executive director Tolbert H. McCarroll envisioned four "Religions of the Future," one of which, termed "Private Humanism," he saw emerging as possibly "the largest religious body of the future."[54] McCarroll maintained that Private Humanism's members would be users of LSD, mescaline, peyote, and marijuana.

In describing this new "religion," the AHA official quoted excerpts from testimony of Arthur Kleps, chief of the Neo-American Church, as given before the Special Senate Judiciary Subcommittee on Narcotics, May 25, 1966:

> It is our belief that the sacred bio-chemicals such as peyote, mescaline, LSD and cannabis [marijuana] are the true host of God and not drugs at all as that term is commonly understood. We do not feel that the government has the right to interfere in our religious practice, and that the present persecution of our co-religionists is not only constitutionally illegal but a crude and savage repression of our basic and inalienable rights as human beings.
>
> The leader of the psychedelic religious movement in the United States is Dr. Timothy Leary. We regard him with the same special love and respect as was reserved by the early Christians for Jesus. . . . [55]

In his closing remarks, Mr. McCarroll stated:

> It is too early to predict whether Timothy Leary's newly formed League of Spiritual Discovery (L.S.D.) will develop into the private humanism which has been described here. Its primary function might become an attempt to legalize the "sacramental" use of LSD and marijuana. But the rallying call of the L.S.D., "Turn on, tune in, drop out," will probably survive as a religious motto.[56]

Further confirmation that certain Humanist leaders subscribe to Mr. McCarroll's sentiments is the fact that a later issue of *The Humanist* carried an advertisement for the Neo-American Church's drug cult. The ad read:

> THE NEO-AMERICAN CHURCH believes: Everyone has the right to expand his consciousness and stimulate visionary experience by whatever means he considers desirable. The psychedelic substances, such as LSD, are the True Host of the Church, not "drugs." They are Sacramental Foods. Peace and Love.[57]

This ad was preceded, in the same column, by the following statement:

> . . . All advertising must be in keeping with the character of the American Humanist Association and The Humanist. We reserve the right to reject any advertisement we consider unsuitable.[58]

Unitarian-Universalist Association (UUA)

A significant bond between the Unitarians and the Humanists is evident upon further examination of the first *Humanist Manifesto*. Nearly 25 per cent of the original signers were Unitarians. The point is also made by a past director of the AHA, Edwin H. Wilson, that the AHA "stemmed largely from Unitarianism as a movement of Religious Humanists."[59] The Unitarians can still be found at the core of the Humanist movement; in fact, 170 Unitarian-Universalist ministers were signers of *Humanist Manifesto II* in 1973.

Among notable past and present Unitarian-Universalists are found the names of many prominent persons, including Chester Bowles, Albert Camus, Sigmund Freud, Dag Hammarskjöld,

Arthur M. Schlesinger Jr., Bernard Shaw, Adlai Stevenson, and Senators Joseph Clark, Norris Cotton, Paul Douglas, Maurine Neuberger, Robert Packwood, Leverett Saltonstall, and Harrison A. Williams.

In commenting on the growing swell of Humanism within this fellowship, author Howard Radest reported in *The Humanist*:

> In a recent survey of Unitarian-Universalist fellowships, more than half of those responding identified themselves as "humanistic." A small group of Jews organize themselves under the banner of humanistic Judaism. At Exeter, New Hampshire, Unitarian-Universalists, humanistic Jews, the Fellowship of Religious Humanists, the American Humanist Association, and the American Ethical Union have found common ground in an annual dialogue. Internationally, many of us have been joined together for over 18 years in the International Humanist and Ethical Union. We are also working together in the Council of Humanist and Ethical Concern, our Washington, D.C.-based office interested in large public issues.[60]

Humanist official Lloyd Morain elaborates further on the same theme:

> Here in the United States the number of Humanist groups has doubled in each of the past several years. Some of these groups, for example many of the Unitarian Fellowships, are functioning under the auspices of a liberal religious denomination. Each year more and more Protestants, Catholics, and Jews, as well as many without any previous religious affiliation, are coming to follow as their own this way of life.[61]

A policy statement prepared in 1956 (before the merger of Unitarians and Universalists) by a special Committee on Intergroup Relations of the AHA, chaired by Dr. Rudolf Dreikurs, was adopted by the Board of Directors. It stated:

> With respect, particularly, to the Unitarian and Universalist churches, we recognize certain unique responsibilities and an unusual relationship to them based upon their relation in history to the A.H.A. Members of these groups have been active in our Association since its founding, and it is our duty to strengthen and uphold Humanists in those churches in any way possible.[62]

In light of the Unitarian Church's loose acceptance of any or no belief on the part of its members, it would appear that this institution's primary function, so far as Humanist leadership is concerned, is to serve as a gateway between the believing and non-believing worlds; a perfect spawning ground, in other words, from which to draw new converts to Humanism.

A final note on the Unitarian-Universalist facet concerns the UUA's rather broad publications program, which encompasses magazines, pamphlets, books, and newsletters. Operating "under the auspices of the Unitarian-Universalist Association" as its publishing arm is Beacon Press of Boston, Massachusetts, which is represented in Canada by Saunders of Toronto, Ltd., and overseas by Feffer and Simons, Inc.[63]

Fellowship of Religious Humanists (FRH)

According to an FRH brochure, Religious Humanism's foundation stems from "a unitary naturalistic world view."[64] Another definition given cites Religious Humanism as "the position of those who arrive at humanism through a critical study of religious trends and experience." It continues: "Organized humanism before and after the 'Humanist Manifesto' was issued in 1933 began that way. In fact, religious humanists antedated the contemporary 'Death of God' theologians by half a century. And, as pointed out in a Ralph McGill column, they had a more positive message — that of faith in man, all men."[65]

Followers of this particular branch of Humanism claim to supplant a conventional reliance on supernatural revelation with such mystic sensations as "aesthetic insight and illumination"; even more esoterically, Religious Humanism promises "psychic grounding in a universe of all enveloping mystery."[66] Other sensations offered are "self-transcendence combined with illumination" and "peak experiences" that can be understood only by the specially initiated.

In 1963 a group of liberal Humanist clergymen founded the FRH with the aim of drawing into the Humanist movement Protestant ministers who regard Humanism as a religion. Located in Yellow Springs, Ohio, this Humanist faction is affiliated with the American Ethical Union, the American Humanist Association, the Unitarian-Universalist Association, and the International Humanist and Ethical Union.[67] FRH publishes a quarterly journal, *Religious Humanism*, and a membership bulletin, *The Communicator*, in addition to sponsoring conferences with the above groups and another less well-known fraternal organization, the Society for Humanistic Judaism.* A branch of FRH's Humanist Center Library is located at Cocoa Beach, Florida. This library houses the archives of the Humanist movement in America.

FRH stands among those who voice the hope that a "comprehensive world religion will develop through the creative processes of our times."[68]

As of Winter 1969, FRH's officers were: Lester Mondale, president; Joseph H. DeFrees, vice president; Charles B. English, secretary; James M. Hutchinson, treasurer; Edwin H. Wilson, administrative secretary; and Margaret H. Feldman, administrative assistant.

Directors of FRH for the same year included: Elizabeth L. Beardsley, Fred A. Cappucino, Dale DeWitt, J. Harold Hadley, Edward H. Redman, Farley W. Wheelwright.

Named on the masthead of FRH's quarterly journal, *Religious Humanism*, for 1969 were:

Editorial staff: Edwin H. Wilson, editor; Doris E. Young, managing editor: James Hutchinson, book editor; Doris Slaughter, circulation manager. *Associate editors*: Hubert P. Beck, Edward L. Ericson, John A. Farmakis, Robert S. Hoagland, Kwee Swan-Liat, Calvin J. Larson, Thomas J. Maloney, Lester Mondale, John M. Morris. *Editorial advisory board*: George E. Axtelle, Eleanor D. Berman, Brand Blanshard, Randall S. Hilton, Horace M. Kallen, Charles W. Morris, Kenneth L. Patton, Howard A. Radest, Paul Arthur Schilpp, Herbert W. Schneider, Gerald Wendt, H. Van Rensselaer Wilson.[69]

---

*The Society for Humanistic Judaism in Farmington, Michigan and operates under the leadership of Rabbi Sherwin T. Wine, Birmingham Temple.

International Humanist and Ethical Union (IHEU)

In 1952, the International Humanist and Ethical Union held its first Congress in Amsterdam, Holland. Here representatives gathered from Austria, Belgium, Canada, Ceylon, France, Germany, Great Britain, Holland, India, Israel, Italy, Japan, New Zealand, Norway, the United States, and Yugoslavia. Among notables actively involved in this organizational activity were Hermann J. Muller of the United States; H. J. Blackham, Julian Huxley, and Lord Boyd Orr of England; M. N. Roy of India; and J. P. Van Praag of Holland.[70]

The Declaration of the Congress that inaugurated IHEU stated that Humanism, "the outcome of a long tradition that has inspired many of the world's thinkers and creative artists, and given rise to science," was offered as an alternative way out of the "present crisis of civilization."[71]

Among other fundamentals, this Congress advocated "a worldwide application of scientific method to problems of human welfare," during this "age of transition," and affirmed that ethical Humanism is "a way of life for everyone everywhere if the individual is capable of the response required by the changing social order."[72]

IHEU currently promotes Humanist thought and action on a large scale by uniting thirty-five full member organizations and associate groups in twenty-three countries throughout the world. Moreover, like other Humanist groups, it seeks to infiltrate, subvert, and capture control of any other existing organizations that are internationalist in structure, design, or purpose. Perhaps this explains why IHEU has linked itself to the United Nations as a Non-Governmental Organization with consultative status.

As a measure of the Humanists' success in advancing their principles in world affairs, the November–December 1969 issue of *The Humanist* boasted of the roles certain members had played at the U.N.:

> . . . three members of the American Humanist Association [and IHEU as well] were instrumental in the development of three

important agencies of the U.N.: Julian Huxley was director general of UNESCO; Brock Chisholm was director general of the World Health Organization; and Lord Boyd Orr was director general of the Food and Agriculture Organization.[73]

It is no coincidence that Humanists have been planted in a number of strategic positions of influence at the U.N. in recent years to carry out the goals of Huxley, Chisholm, Orr, and others. Although any number of U.N. agencies might be selected at random as illustrations of this, such an undertaking would require a chapter to itself. UNESCO has been singled out as a case in point.

Shortly after UNESCO's founding, Humanist Ashley Montagu headed the committee that drafted UNESCO's 1950 Statement on Race. Further, various UNESCO publications are generously seasoned with Humanist rhetoric. Two prime examples are UNESCO's quarterly journal, *Impact of Science on Society*, founded in 1952 by American Humanist Association official Dr. Gerald Wendt, who was then in charge of world-wide development of science education for UNESCO in Paris; and *International Directory of Philosophy and Philosophers*, coedited by Paul Kurtz, editor of *The Humanist*.

Other UNESCO-Humanist entanglements are evident. Frederick H. Burkhardt, formerly a member of *The Humanist's* editorial advisory board, has served as chairman of the U.S. National Commission for UNESCO. But more significant is the fact that Humanist Gerald Wendt was for many years president of the UNESCO Publications Center in New York City. Although Wendt is now dead, his widow continues to work in the capacity of secretary for the Publications Center.

In addition to the AEU and AHA, some other full members of IHEU include:*

- British Humanist Association, 13 Prince of Wales Terrace, London, W. 8, England.
- Centro-Coscienza, Corso di Porta Nuova 16, Milan, Italy.

*For complete listing of IHEU member and associate member groups, see Appendix E.

- Humanistisch Verbond, P.O. Box 114, Utrecht, Netherlands.[74]

IHEU's publications committee consists of the following: *Editors*: Dr. Paul Kurtz, Tolbert H. McCarroll; *Associate Editors*: Dr. Wilhelm Bonness, Karl Hyde, Franco Ottolenghi, Th. W. Polet, Dr. Matthew Ies Spetter; *Managing Editor:* Stephanie von Buchau.[75]

IHEU's headquarters are located at 152 Oudegracht, Utrecht, Netherlands. Since organizing internationally, the Humanist movement has managed to recruit three million members, of whom perhaps 250,000 are in the United States, according to a report in the *New York Times* for August 26, 1973.

Quaker Friends

Although it must be emphasized that the Quakers (otherwise known as the Religious Society of Friends) are not a formal unit of the Humanist organization, there is some evidence suggesting the existence of significant rapport between them. One piece of such evidence is found in an item in the November–December 1964 issue of the journal, *Ethical Culture Today*:

> . . . Historically, the draftsmen of the First Amendment must have envisioned its protection of non-theistic belief, considering the prominence and standing of the Quaker sect among the religions of the time. *Like Ethical Culture, the Quaker faith does not dictate a belief in a Supreme Being.*[76] [emphasis added]

In fairness it must be recognized that there are undoubtedly many Quakers who believe in God, though others tend toward Naturalism, which rejects a supernatural deity. It is the latter faction of the Quakers which is the subject of this entry.

One member of this Quaker faction is Ernest Morgan, a former member of the AHA's Board of Directors. In speaking of Mr. Morgan, Humanist Alfred E. Kuenzli, writing in an early (1963) issue of *The Humanist,* asserted, ". . . he is a long-standing member of the Society of Friends. He is also a long-standing and very dedicated Humanist."[77] Contending that the Humanists have "many friends among the Friends," Dr. Kuenzli led his readers to the real vortex of political-social reform in twentieth century Quakerism — the radical American Friends Service Committee (AFSC), saying:

> In the summer of 1961, it was my good fortune to serve as a member of the faculty of the annual Midwest Institute at Williams Bay, Wisconsin, sponsored by the American Friends Service Committee. On that occasion I came to know many Quakers personally. Mainly these were members of the younger generation who are active in the fields of race relations and international affairs. Several of these persons were Humanists and practically everybody shared our basic values.
>
> We held regular discussions on the Quaker orientation and it was my conclusion that Humanists and Friends have very little to quarrel about.[78]

A former director of the AHA, Dr. Kuenzli summarized his 1963 *Humanist* article in part as follows:

> Probably the most significant convergence of Humanism and Quakerism in coming years will be the point of action. I am convinced that the work of the American Friends Service Committee is our kind of work. If the organization didn't exist, we should have to create it.[79]

This similarity of purpose can easily be detected by reading the AFSC literature. For example, an integral part of AFSC's community development program is orientation toward family planning and eventual population control. Another AFSC pamphlet said: "The American Friends Service Committee was founded in 1917 to provide young conscientious objectors during the First World War with an alternative to military service . . . ."[80] This same ploy was used by both the AFSC and Humanists during the Vietnam war.

Like the AHA, AFSC has a close affinity with the United Nations. AFSC's International Affairs Division, for example, maintains permanent representatives at the United Nations, receiving advisory and financial help from headquarters in London. An AFSC leaflet titled *Quaker United Nations Program* provides further insight:

Quaker House, the home near the UN where the Quaker Program director and his family live, plays a unique role in this work. As a quiet meeting place for informal and friendly discussion among people who are at the UN or who have close connections with it, Quaker House is much appreciated by those who gather there. . . .

The American Friends Service Committee carries primary responsibility for administering and financing the Quaker UN Program, which relates officially to the UN under the accreditation of the Friends World Committee for Consultation. [emphasis added]

Special attention has been given to "Quaker Friends" because of the fact that SIECUS's executive director, Mary Steichen Calderone, is a Quaker, a regular financial contributor to the American Friends Service Committee, and, as mentioned earlier, a co-recipient of the "Humanist of the Year" award for 1974. It should further be kept in mind that, in their own words, the Quakers place "the authority of conscience, individual experience, and communal consensus above the authority of scriptures, creeds, or traditions"[81] — a position that Mary Calderone obviously shares.

"Humanizing" the Major Faiths

The special discussion of the Quaker-Humanist kinship is in no way intended to ignore or overlook the considerable influx of Humanism into most major faiths over the past decades. Humanist official Lloyd Morain, for example, answered the question, "Do Humanists Expect Other Churches to Close Their Doors?" by saying:

No. They merely believe that the established churches will continue to become more humanistic. They point with pleasure to the growing concern about social conditions [as opposed to pure gospel preaching] within leading churches throughout the world. They note the liberalizing influences at work within Jewish and Protestant groups in America and the changing attitude of many Catholics.[82]

This all aids, of course, in "humanizing" the churches. Morain further notes:

> Some of the larger liberal churches which have humanists among their members receive the literature of the [American Humanist] Association, and keep in close contact with it for help in programming and many other ways. A significant number of ministers and liberal rabbis are members.[83]

So deeply entrenched is this infiltration that, today, in an overwhelming number of churches, the doctrine of Humanism is being covertly preached from the pulpit under the name of Christianity. And there can be no doubt that this heretical influence extends into the highest echelons of church leadership.

One indication is the "Catholic-Humanist Dialogue" held in Brussels, Belgium, on October 2–4, 1970. This meeting was the second such "Dialogue" during a five-year span, and it ended the nearly 2000-year-old conflict between the Catholic Church and atheism. Co-sponsored by the International Humanist and Ethical Union and the Vatican Secretariat for Unbelievers, the "Dialogue" concluded that differences in the beliefs held by the two parties "need not interfere with a humanistic approach to pressing world problems."

Of further interest here is the statement made by Paul Kurtz, a "Dialogue" participant and editor of *The Humanist*, in commenting on the timeliness of the Brussels meeting in the magazine's May–June 1971 issue:

> There are remarkable humanist trends now building up within the Church, especially since the Second Vatican Council. Many Catholic reformers are calling for fundamental Church reform and for a new humanist politics, morality, and religion. *A crucial movement within the contemporary Church is thus the humanist movement.* [emphasis added]

Professor Kurtz is co-editor, with Monsignor Albert Dondeyne of Belgium (another "Dialogue" participant), of the recent book, *A Catholic-Humanist Dialogue*, published by Prometheus Books of Buffalo, an Ethical Humanist Press.

Monsignor Dondeyne's convenient patronage of the "Dialogue" as a participant becomes transparent in light of the fact that he is a member of the board of consultants of the magazine *Humanitas*, whose editor is humanistic psychologist

Adrian Van Kaam, and whose pages boast a long list of prominent Humanists as consultants and contributors. These include Erik Erikson, Herbert Marcuse, Rollo May, Margaret Mead, and Carl Rogers. *Humanitas* is published by the Institute of Man at Duquesne University, a Catholic institution.

Is Humanism a Religion?

Although some Humanists consider Humanism a philosophy, a substantial number of its leaders look upon it as a religion. Lloyd Morain, current president of the American Humanist Association, has stated:

> Down through the ages men have been seeking a universal religion or way of life. . . . Humanism . . . *shows promise of becoming a great world faith.*
>
> Humanists are content with fixing their attention on this life and on this earth. *Theirs is a religion without a God*, divine revelation, or sacred scriptures.[84] [emphasis added]

Another Humanist, Edwin H. Wilson, a prominent leader in the Fellowship of Religious Humanists, has asserted:

> Many well-known thinkers have given voice to the hope of Religious Humanism that a comprehensive world religion will develop through the creative processes of our times. Roy Wood Sellars in 1927 held humanism to be the next step in religion. John Dewey, in his book *A Common Faith*, believed that we have all the materials available for such a faith. Sir Julian Huxley predicts that the next great religion of the world will be some form of humanism.[85]

It is apparent that the Ethical Culture Movement also falls into this category. The November–December 1964 issue of *Ethical Culture Today* accentuates the religious aspect of this organization's structure, stating:

> Ethical Culture is listed as a religion in the Census of Religious Bodies published by the Federal Government, and in various religious publications and general reference works. Federal tax exemption rulings have been issued to the American Ethical Union and to the various Ethical Societies.[86]

Looking once more at the original *Humanist Manifesto*,

which was adopted in 1933 and reaffirmed in 1966, we find this:

> While the age does owe a vast debt to the traditional religions, it is none the less obvious that any religion that can hope to be a synthesizing and dynamic force for today must be shaped for the needs of this age. *To establish such a religion* is a major necessity of the present. [emphasis added]

How Is Humanism Viewed by the Court?

In dealing with this question, another prominent Humanist, Edward L. Ericson, has revealed:

> In the landmark *Seeger* decision (*United States v. Seeger*, 1965) the Supreme Court held that a humanistic and ethical belief that is sincerely professed as a religion shall be entitled to recognition as religious under the Selective-Service law. If one professes such a faith or belief, he is entitled to have his belief respected under the law as "parallel" to the belief in God of the traditional believer. . . .
> The case of the *Washington Ethical Society v. District of Columbia*, to determine whether a group committed to a non-theological ethical purpose could qualify under the law as a religion, decided favorably in 1957; the case of the Fellowship of Humanity of Oakland, California, to determine under California state law the same issue, also decided favorably at about the same time; the Torcaso case of 1961, in which Humanism and Ethical Culture were footnoted by the Court as examples of nontheistic religions existing in the United States; a series of church-state cases in which the American Ethical Union and the American Humanist Association entered briefs *amicus curiae* in defense of religious minorities and secularists; and testimony over a period of years on related church-state issues before committees of the House and Senate, all helped to provide the precedents and constitutional history for the Seeger decision and subsequent actions.[87]

Further light was shed on the Torcaso case by Humanist Corliss Lamont in his book, *The Philosophy of Humanism*:

> In 1961 the U.S. Supreme Court took official cognizance of religious Humanism in the case of Roy R. Torcaso, a Humanist who was refused his commission as a Notary Public under a Maryland law requiring all public officers in the State to profess

belief in God. In delivering the unanimous opinion of the Court that this statute was unconstitutional under the First Amendment, Justice Hugo L. Black observed: "Among religions in this country which do not teach what would generally be considered a belief in the existence of God are Buddhism, Taoism, Ethical Culture, Secular Humanism and others."[88]

In the current semantic sense, the word "religion" appears to have many facets of meaning. For instance, one standard dictionary has defined it as "any system of belief, practices, ethical values, etc., resembling, suggestive of, or likened to such a system (humanism as a religion)."[89] Combining this definition with the views of the U.S. Supreme Court and certain leaders of the Humanist movement, it may be possible to regard Humanism as a "religion" in the broadest sense.

This brings up a current contention of Humanists and their sympathizers that persons actively engaged in exposing Humanism are attacking a religion. This amounts to little more than a semantic exercise probably concocted to turn the spotlight from the accused to the accusers and distract attention from the fact that it is the Humanists who attacked religion in the first place. It would be more accurate to assert that, if the exposers of Humanism are attacking anything, they are attacking a militant *anti*-religion that is Satanic in origin, purpose, and effect.

The question is sometimes raised of whether Humanism in its broadest sense is not simply equivalent to "humanitarianism." The two terms should be *contrasted* rather than equated or even compared. "Humanitarianism" is merely an interest in human affairs, with no particular philosophical foundation. A Humanist author, John H. Dietrich, elaborates this thought in an American Humanist Association pamphlet entitled simply *Humanism*:

> . . . so a distinction should be made between Humanism and humanitarianism. The latter is a more or less sympathetic interest in humanity, while the former carries with it a definite faith in man as the director of his own destiny, founded upon the latest scientific conception of the universe and man's place in it.

Humanism Versus Christianity

The Humanist attitude toward God, man, and morality is not as "fresh and modern" as Humanists would have us believe. Since earliest times, man has rationalized the substitution of his own reasoning powers for the majestic wisdom of divine judgment. The passage from Romans quoted at the beginning of this chapter is pointedly illustrative of this.

Man's apostasy from God was first recorded as far back as the Book of Genesis. Adam's fall occurred after he professed himself to be wiser than God — and so it was with Cain when he slew Abel. That murder illustrated the destructive potential of *human* brotherhood, when one brother takes it upon himself to decide what is "right" and what is "wrong." The degeneration of Sodom and Gomorrah further exemplifies the depravity of man, once he has separated himself from God. The Book of Proverbs reminds us, "There is a way which seemeth right unto a man, but the end thereof are the ways of death."[90]

Love of man, in the Christian sense, cannot be fully realized until man first loves God, becomes His spiritual child, and follows His commandments. The counterfeit *human* brotherhood then gives way to God's plan for authentic *spiritual* brotherhood, in which man's conduct is guided by the divine wisdom of God through faith, prayer, and the Holy Scriptures. Only those who acknowledge the Fatherhood of God can truly see others as spiritual brothers in God's holy family.

In contrast, those who look upon mankind as something that has evolved from the mud by its own efforts have professed themselves to be wiser than God and, in so doing, have "become fools." Darwin, for instance, said: "Man is developed from an ovule about 1/125th of an inch in diameter which differs in no respect from the ovules of other animals."[91] In commenting on this, the noted Christian minister, Dr. Donald G. Barnhouse, added: "This is a statement as foolish as to say that the California redwood tree develops from a tiny seed that differs in no respect from the seed that produces the ragweed. Darwin knew nothing about genes and chromosomes. The result is that today there is no authentic scientist in the world, Christian or non-Christian, who believes in Darwin's guesses. The horrible thing is that they still hold to the results of the theory without believing in his method."[92]

But Darwin's theory accomplished much more; for, as was stated plainly in an article in *The Humanist* some years back:

> . . . Darwin's discovery of the principle of evolution sounded the death knell of religious and moral values. It removed the ground from under the feet of traditional religion.[93]

Even more tragic is the fact that Darwin's successors — more specifically SIECUS and its associates with their pseudo-scientific mentality — apparently think the public is now gullible enough to swallow the idea that a Humanist-oriented philosophy is original and is urgently needed in this scientific age. In reality, the pages of history reek with the stale odor of Humanism, and we are now witnessing another desperate move for a repeat performance. Those individuals who fall into Humanism's murky waters are destined to an existence of confusion and spiritual destruction. Moreover, it takes no great intellect to see that, as our twentieth century world becomes more humanistic, mankind more rapidly succumbs to moral anarchy and cold-blooded barbarism.

It must be recognized that Humanism and Christianity cannot co-exist, simply because they are diametrically opposed to one another. Whereas the most fervent of Christians is content to win his converts with God's truth as recorded in the Holy Scriptures for man to accept or reject, the militant Humanist uses *any* means — including deception — to justify his ends, and will not rest until God is evicted from the universe and the last fire of faith is quenched in the heart of the last Christian.

Furthermore, Humanism has only recently taken the form of a concerted, worldwide movement — and it is convinced that it is winning. Hector Hawton, editor of the British magazine, *Humanist*, exulted in an American Humanist Association publication:

But the fact is that the generation which now refuses to conform will be in control tomorrow, and it would be remarkable if they all take their places tamely in the rat race and the power game from which they have opted out. They are groping for an alternative to the values of a materialist society that measures success by bank balance. Whether they are conscious of it or not, many of the values that inspire them are primarily humanist values. . . . Frightened conservatives are fighting in the last ditch to preserve the old order and the authority that is enshrined in outmoded ideologies, religious and secular. But the winds of change are blowing in our favor, for humanism is a disturber of the status quo. Far from leading down the road to ruin, as its enemies warn, humanism is man's coming of age.[94]

In view of the information brought forth in this chapter — particularly the court cases which uphold Humanism as a "religion"; the affirmations of the SIECUS Charter relative to the collective "religious" intent of its six founders; and the presence of a Humanist-oriented philosophy within SIECUS-generated sex education — it would appear that the SIECUS program is in conflict with the principle of separation of church and state, which prohibits public schools from engaging in any form of religious indoctrination. The existence of a double standard further complicates matters. For if it is forbidden to honor God with Bible-reading and voluntary prayer in the public schools, it should also be forbidden to denounce God, teach the evolutionary theory of man's origin as fact, and promote amoral, atheistic concepts emanating from a Humanistic "religion."

In any event, if the fraudulent ideology of Humanism continues to permeate the atmosphere of our nation's schools as well as other public institutions and churches, we may come to see one Humanist's forecast approach reality:

By the year 2,000, institutionalized religion, already on the wane as a significant factor in everyday life, will have faded to a point where it is only of slight importance in the community. Theology may still exist as a scholastic exercise, but in reality the God of Authoritative Answers will not only be dead but buried.[95]

Here is a terrifying aspect of Communism — its effort to indoctrinate the rising generation, to mold these minds in the atheistic tenets of Marxism-Leninism, to make them mere soulless cogs of a brutal machine, where man is degraded and debased.

— J. Edgar Hoover, former director, Federal Bureau of Investigation[1]

CHAPTER 4

A Round of Subversion

AFTER CLOSE SCRUTINY of the atheistic philosophy and Socialist-oriented objectives of Humanism, along with concepts proclaimed in both Humanist Manifestos, only one logical conclusion can be drawn: that it is the intent of the Humanist hierarchy to meld all people of the world into an apostate religion under the control of a one-world Socialist government — a goal also envisioned by the Communists in their determined drive for the obliteration of Western Christian civilization. Perhaps that is why so many leading Humanists are also found in the ranks of the Communist "fifth column."

The partners in this unholy alliance, all of whom seek the same ultimate goal, must first secularize all institutions and corrupt America's youth if they are to triumph. The schools were long ago chosen as the site for the major battle. Sex education is just one of the many deadly weapons in the armory of the Communist-Humanist complex.

The charge that sex education is tied in with the Communist conspiracy has often been ridiculed by advocates of this program. SIECUS President Harold Lief testified at a New Jersey Joint Legislative public hearing on sex education: "The notion that SIECUS is somehow connected with some kind of Communist conspiracy is again totally absurd."[2]

The September 1969 issue of the *New Jersey Education Association Review* (an adjunct of the NEA) echoed this sentiment: "National organizations, such as the John Birch Society, try to attach sex education to the 'Communist conspiracy' to ruin American youth. Such 'conspiracy' claims have no basis."

Our national news media, for the most part, have parroted this line. The late columnist and editor of the *Atlanta Constitution*, Ralph McGill, characterized Robert Welch, founder and president of The John Birch Society, as a "stand-up comic like Will Rogers" because he suggested that sex education in the nation's public schools is the result of a Communist plot to destroy the morals of youth. McGill continued, "That's real funny. It's a pity Mr. Welch doesn't chew gum and twirl a lariat when he delivers such rib-tickling lines."[3]

Statements dealing with this particular aspect are rather consistently handled in similar fashion. By ignoring the specifics — names, dates, and subversive affiliations of persons involved in the upper echelons of sex education — the media avoid bringing the real facts of the issue before the public. Instead, charges of subversion are either dismissed as "totally unfounded," with no reason given, or the smear tactics of ridicule and scorn are employed. And so the public is lulled back to sleep with the tranquilizer of evasive jargon.

It is the purpose of this chapter to cover the subversive element in sex education to the degree necessary to counteract the gross distortions perpetrated by those who wish to suppress the truth. But here several points of clarification are needed.

First, the list of Communist fronters and leftists mentioned in this chapter is by no means inclusive. It is merely a sampling, intended to show that a significant segment of the forces at work in this highly sensitive field is subversive. And in the interest of conserving space, the Communist front citations given under each individual's name may in some cases represent only a portion of the total citations listed for him in official government sources. Documentation for the full complement of citations can be found in the respective footnotes.

Another point to be noted is that some of the most success-ful attacks on personal liberties have been launched by subver-sive fronts with deceptively innocent-sounding names. As was brought out in the U.S. Government's *Guide to Subversive Organizations and Publications*, "the first requisite for front organizations is an idealistic sounding title."[4] As an illustration, what could sound more innocuous than the National Federation for Constitutional Liberties? Yet the description of this orga-nization given by the House Committee on Un-American Acti-vities was as follows:

> There can be no reasonable doubt about the fact that the National Federation for Constitutional Liberties — regardless of its high-sounding name — is one of the viciously subversive organizations of the Communist Party.[5]

Perhaps it is not merely coincidental that a substantial number of individuals with subversive backgrounds covered in this chapter were at one time or another connected with this Communist front.

Finally, it seems desirable to provide an official definition of a Communist front:

> A front is an organization which the communists openly or secretly control. The communists realize that they are not welcome in American society. Party influence, therefore, is transmitted, time after time, by a belt of concealed members, sympathizers, and dupes. Fronts become transmission belts between the Party and the noncommunist world.[6]

Another source provides the following description:

> Communist-front organizations are characterized by their common origin, the rigid conformity of these organizations to the Communist pattern, their interlocking personnel, and the methods generally used to deceive the American public. Being part of a conspiratorial movement, their essence is deception.[7]

The "Fundamental Lesson"

The quotation appearing at the beginning of this chapter

contains a chilling description of atheistic Communism for what it really is: an effort at mass enslavement of mankind. Another definition states: "Communism is more than an economic, political, social, or philosophical doctrine. It is a way of life; a false, materialistic 'religion.' It would strip man of his belief in God, his heritage of freedom, his trust in love, justice, and mercy. Under Communism, all would become, as so many already have, twentieth-century slaves."[8]

Of course, the Communist masters were quick to recognize that, before man can be enslaved, his state of mind must be reduced from spirituality to carnality. He must learn to think of himself as basically an animal with no spiritual purpose. Once man is freed from his obligations to God, the way is cleared for his ultimate obedience to the Communist State as his master. In effect, then, he is "conditioned" so that he can be ordered and enslaved. This conditioning process has its roots in the so-called scientific socialism of Karl Marx, whose theories were intended to bring about the destruction of religion in order to create the Communist man.

Obviously, if the citizens of a target country can be conditioned *before* that nation is conquered, so much the better. And what could be more desirable than to achieve this through an agency such as the schools, which are in a position to mold the thought and behavior patterns of a whole generation? As far back as 1954, FBI Director Hoover, one of the foremost authorities on the Communist menace, pointed out: "Being good tacticians, the Communists realize that one concealed Party member in education may be worth a dozen in less strategic fields, and some of their more successful propagandists in this area have influenced, and are influencing, the ideas of thousands of impressionable young people."[9]

As early as 1940, an investigative committee of the New York State Legislature reported that the New York City Teachers Union was completely under Communist control, and that more than a thousand Communists were teaching in the New York City school system.[10] The committee's final report concluded: "The communists and those under their influence in the Teachers Union comprised nearly one-fourth of all personnel in city colleges."[11] A similar (and increasing) percentage of Communist infiltrators throughout other key areas of the United States over the years represents a sizable network of influence on our youth.

With the recognition of this, as well as the fact that the evolutionary theory of man's origin is part and parcel of SIECUS-generated sex education, observations made by Bishop Cuthbert O'Gara become much more significant. In describing the Communist takeover of Yuanling, a Chinese province, he wrote:

> . . . When the Communist troops overran my diocese they were followed in very short order by the propaganda corps — the civilian branch of the Red forces. . . . The entire population, city and countryside, was immediately organized into distinctive categories — grade school and high school pupils and teachers (Catholic, Protestant and pagan), merchants, artisans, members of the professions, yes, and even the lowly coolies. Everyone, for a week or more, was forced to attend the seminar specified for his or her proper category and there willy-nilly in servile submission listen to the official Communist line.
>
> Now what, I ask, was the first lesson given to the indoctrinees? One might have supposed that this would have been some pearl of wisdom let drop by Marx, Lenin or Stalin. Such however was not the case. The very first, the *fundamental*, lesson given was man's descent from the ape — Darwinism! . . .
>
> Are you surprised that the Chinese Communists chose Darwinism as the corner-stone upon which to build their new political structure? At first this maneuver amazed me. I had taken for granted that they would begin by expounding the economic principles of Marx. Later on when in a Red jail the reason for this unanticipated tactic became very obvious to me. . . . Religion must be destroyed.
>
> Darwinism negates God, the human soul, the after-life. Into this vacuum Communism enters as the be-all and end-all of the intellectual slavery it has created.[12]

Besides being a Humanist in the formal sense of the word, Darwin laid the cornerstone for the Humanist ideology. As Humanist Julian Huxley pointed out, Humanism's "keynote, the central concept to which all its details are related, is evolution."[13]

A Parallelism of Purpose

The SIECUS perspective, with its strident overtones of Humanistic Darwinism, is firmly based on a "scientific" approach to man. Whether or not it was intended, this perspective is in harmony with the "scientific" dicta of Communism:

> There is no God. When communists deny God, they simultaneously deny every virtue and every value which originates with God. *There are no moral absolutes, no right and wrong. The Ten Commandments and the Sermon On The Mount are invalid.*[14] [emphasis added]

In keeping with this thought, J. Edgar Hoover noted: "In making Marxism–Leninism the 'perfect science,' the communists characterize religion as a superstitious relic."[15]

The similarity between the SIECUS perspective and "scientific" Communism frequently reveals itself in the statements and writings of certain SIECUS spokesmen. References that categorize the traditional religions as outmoded, puritanical vestiges of the past are often made. The specific terminology used, as well as the frequency with which it occurs, makes it appear that this parallelism of purpose is more than just a coincidence. As one illustration, compare the following quotations, one from a SIECUS director and the other from a former Communist Party official:

> The simple fact is that through most of our history in Western Christendom we have based our standards of sexual behavior on premises that are now totally insupportable — on the folklore of the ancient Hebrews and on the musings of medieval monks, concepts that are simply obsolete. — *David R. Mace, past president of SIECUS.*[16]

> Religion has now been made obsolete by science. . . . It has now become virtually impossible for a thoroughly modern person, even if he wants to do so, actually to believe the old legends, primitive philosophies, and imaginary history upon which all religions are founded. — *William Z. Foster, former chairman of the Communist Party, U.S.A.*[17]

In connection with the so-called scientific approach to man, a specific observation is essential. Although those who employ the scientific method consistently strive to give the impression that it is more "factual" and "authentic" than Biblical history, it is frequently presented without any documentation at all. And evolutionary propaganda is often expressed in evasive terms, *double entendres*, and equivocations. Whatever "facts" are presented are usually wrapped in a neat package of slanted statistics — all in the name of "science."

Besides being a self-proclaimed "scientist," Karl Marx was a Humanist, viewing man as his own creator. Marx's own definition of Humanism reads: "Humanism is the denial of God, and the total affirmation of man. . . . Humanism is really nothing else but Marxism."[18] The inclusion of this statement is not meant to imply that all Humanists are Marxists, but rather, that all Marxists are essentially Humanists. That certain aspects of Humanism are closely related to Marxist principles is confirmed by the titles of lectures given during an international symposium on "Socialist Humanism," which was subsequently edited for publication by Erich Fromm, a Socialist-Humanist and SIECUS-endorsed author:

> "The Sources of Socialist Humanism" — Ivan Svitak
> "Socialism Is Humanism" — Leopold Senghor
> "Marx's Humanism Today" — Raya Dunayevskaya
> "Socialist Humanism and Science" — Umberto Cerroni
> "Marxian Humanism and the Crisis in Socialist Ethics"
>   — Eugene Kamenka[19]

Further evidence that Communism and Humanism have common goals is provided by the summary of the *Humanist Manifesto* given in Chapter 3 (for full text see Appendix B). Interestingly, all the *Manifesto's* major points coincide with the beliefs and goals of Communism. In the Foreword to *Witness,* Whittaker Chambers called Communism "man's second oldest faith. Its promise was whispered in the first days of the Creation . . . : 'Ye shall be as gods . . . .' The Communist vision is the vision of Man without God." This is Humanism *par excellance.*

It is obvious, then, that Communists work in concert with Humanists to promote Humanistic concepts within their particular sphere of influence. It is also apparent that Humanists who do not subscribe to the full Marxist doctrine nevertheless aid Communism by their promotion of atheism, evolution, and situation ethics. In view of this, and of the fact that the SIECUS pattern of comprehensive sex education is shaped to conform to Humanistic concepts, it can be seen why the late Congressman James B. Utt felt it necessary to warn his constituents: "One of the basic activities of the Communists is their promotion of complete sex education in almost all school grades."[20]

Of course the Communists would not bother to support something that does not aid in the advancement of Communism. How, then, does SIECUS-generated public school sex education help the Communist cause? The following are some of the ways:

1. The very concept of teaching sexual morality on a mass scale is collectivistic. The Americanist tradition reserves this fundamental right for parents within the privacy of the home.

2. Sensitivity training is employed; this, in essence, is a form of "brainwashing."

3. Darwinism is the prevailing theme. Most sex education materials consistently speak of man as an animal, omitting any reference to him as a spiritual being.

4. The program blatantly teaches students to formulate their values on the basis of Humanism's "situation ethics," rather than on the laws of God.

5. Some of the materials pit the child against his parents, in an effort to break down parental authority and redirect the child's obedience to the authority of the State.

6. A negative outlook toward traditional family life is promoted. The abolition of the family as we know it is another Communist objective.

7. Other home and family living materials pit race against race, another tactic used in Communism's "divide and conquer" strategy.

8. Often injected into the curriculum is pornography, which ultimately debases man.

9. Individualism is discouraged by an emphasis on "group conformity," a concept that "ripens" human beings for eventual subjugation.

10. Birth control is treated in such a way as to prepare youth for world population control — another collectivist concept.

11. Materials designed to stimulate sociological discussion usually deride the free enterprise system and promote instead the socialistic concepts of a Marxist State.

SIECUS's Core of Subversives

In answer to charges of Communist influence within the field of sex education, SIECUS and associates have become experts at skirting the issue. In an article by Humanist Dr. Luther Baker of Washington State College, titled "The Rising Furor Over Sex Education," which SIECUS distributes and frequently quotes, we find the statement: "IT IS NOT TRUE that sex education is un-American. This charge is so ridiculous as hardly to merit reply."[21]

We would reply to Dr. Baker that many individuals with backgrounds of subversive activities have been involved in the sensitive field of sex education in recent years. Only a small number of persons in this category can be covered here; but even these few will demonstrate the considerable strength of this group.

Individuals

ISADORE RUBIN — In commenting on the accusation that SIECUS director Isadore Rubin (now deceased) was an identified Communist, Dr. Baker had this to say: "The truth is that Dr. Rubin was never officially charged with being a member of the Communist Party. In 1948 he was called for questioning by the House Committee on Labor in connection with a statement which had been taken out of context and used to challenge his patriotism."[22]

In another publication, Paul Putnam of the National Education Association fell into step with Baker, stating:

The truth: Dr. Rubin has never been charged with subversion by any agency of the U.S. Government; he denied membership in the Communist Party, under oath, before the House Labor and Education Committee in 1948, and was not subsequently indicted for perjury.[23]

The facts about Isadore Rubin's record were quite different. Both Baker and Putnam chose to omit two events in Rubin's life subsequent to the 1948 hearing: (1) In 1952 he invoked the First and Fifth Amendments to evade questions on this same charge;[24] and (2) in 1955 he was identified as a member of the Communist Party in sworn testimony by a special undercover agent of the New York Police Department, Mildred Blauvelt, who had attended Communist cell meetings with Rubin.* In addition, while serving in the U.S. Army during World War II, Rubin had been a direct contributor to the Communist Party's fund drive. A later incident found him serving as editor of the *New York Teachers News*, published by the Communist-controlled Teachers Union of New York.

Rubin was the only SIECUS director to have been officially identified as a Communist. But despite this identification, he exerted tremendous influence, as chairman of the SIECUS Publications Committee and as editor of the SIECUS Newsletter. He is also given special recognition by SIECUS for his extensive help in compiling the 1970 SIECUS book list for professionals. Further, of the twelve original SIECUS Study Guides, Rubin wrote five and his writings are cited as authoritative references in two others. Rubin's contribution thus represents close to 50 per cent of the Study Guide materials, which were designed to help in the structuring of sex education courses throughout the country, from grade school level through college. This is a perfect illustration of a point that has been emphasized by former FBI Director Hoover:

Never must the strength of the Communist Party be measured

---

*In an effort to establish the truth about Rubin once and for all, the testimony delivered on May 3, 1955, by undercover agent Blauvelt is reprinted in Appendix F for the benefit of those who are unable to obtain a complete copy.

by numbers alone. Experience has shown that by strategic place-
ment of members, Communists are able to exercise influence far
beyond their own membership.[25]

It is astonishing that Rubin's Study Guide #10, which is
intended to pilot teachers over the particularly rough course and
sensitive area of moral values, should have been published by
SIECUS eight months after his subversive background was
revealed — or is it? For although Rubin left SIECUS suddenly
in 1969, at the height of the controversy, there was a proud
announcement of his return to the SIECUS board in the March
1970 SIECUS Newsletter, and a glowing eulogy in the October
1970 Newsletter, following his death.

REVEREND WILLIAM GENNÉ — As was mentioned in Chapter 1,
which dealt with the six SIECUS founders, the Reverend
William Genné has been officially cited in connection with the
following Communist fronts:[26]

- Committee for Peaceful Alternatives to the Atlantic Pact
  — cited as "a Communist front organization."
- National Committee To Repeal the McCarran Act — cited
  as a Communist "front established to defend the cases of
  Communist lawbreakers."
- World Peace Appeal (also known as Stockholm Peace
  Appeal) — cited as "part of the [Communist] Party's
  peace program in the late 1940's and early 1950's. . . ."

EMILY AND STEWART MUDD — Dr. Emily Mudd has
seen long service on the SIECUS board of directors, having been
allied with the organization since its inception in 1964. Emily
Mudd is also a member of the Public Affairs Committee,
which publishes the Socialist-oriented Public Affairs
Pamphlets (covered separately later in this chapter). As far
back as 1949, a California Senate Fact-Finding Committee on
Un-American Activities listed her among the sponsors of the
Cultural and Scientific Conference for World Peace,[27] cited by
the House Committee on Un-American Activities as "a Commu-

nist front set up to 'mobilize American intellectuals in the field of arts, sciences and letters' as a propaganda forum for Soviet foreign policy and 'Soviet culture.' " This conference served to prepare the way for the Communist-oriented World Peace Congress held in Paris the same year.[28] Co-sponsors with Emily Mudd were numerous Humanist Communist-fronters, among them Algernon Black, A.J. Carlson, Sidonie M. Gruenberg, Corliss Lamont, Carey McWilliams, Judd Marmor, Gardner Murphy, and Linus Pauling.

Further, Emily Mudd and her husband, Dr. Stuart Mudd, are shown in official U.S. Government investigative committee files as sponsors of the fourth anniversary dinner of American Youth for Democracy,[29] cited as "subversive and Communist" by Attorney General Tom Clark.[30] This front was described by the House Committee on Un-American Activities as "a determined effort to disaffect our youth and to turn them against religion, the American home, against the college authorities, and against the American Government itself."[31]

Stuart Mudd has been affiliated with at least two other Communist fronts: with the publication of Soviet Russia Today,[32] and, as signer of an "Open Letter,"[33] with the National Committee To Repeal the McCarran Act. Appearing once again on the latter committee's roster were many inveterate Humanist/Communist-fronters, among them Algernon Black, Anton J. Carlson, Dorothy Canfield Fisher, William H. Kilpatrick, Carey McWilliams, Dr. Alexander Meiklejohn, and Lewis Mumford.

Sharing his wife's interest in population control (see Chapter 1), Stuart Mudd co-edited The Population Crisis: Implications and Plans for Action.[34] This book's thirty-one articles are a compilation of the opinions of such Humanists as G. Brock Chisholm, Alan F. Guttmacher, Julian Huxley, and H. J. Muller. In a review in the January–February 1966 issue of The Humanist it was described as "the indispensable book for anyone interested or working in the field of population control."[35]

EVELYN MILLIS DUVALL — In 1940 author Evelyn Duvall, later a SIECUS director, lent her sponsorship to the Chicago affiliate of the League of Women Shoppers.[36] Although this Communist front bears a particularly innocuous-sounding name, it was nevertheless described by the U.S. House Committee on Un-American Activities as "an organization which this committee found to be a Communist-controlled front by indisputable documentary evidence obtained from the files of the Communist Party in Philadelphia."[37] Further characterizing this organization, the House Committee said: "In its eagerness to aid strikes it is worthy of note that the League of Women Shoppers concentrated its support upon unions which were Communist-controlled and which received the aid of the *Daily Worker*, official organ of the Communist Party. . . ."[38] It is also interesting that Mrs. Duvall was listed as sponsor of this Chicago-based front together with Mrs. Carl Sandburg — the wife of the poet, who was Mary Calderone's uncle, and a veteran Communist-fronter in his own right.

Nor did the passing of time diminish Evelyn Duvall's enthusiasm for Communist causes. In 1952, the Communist *Daily Worker* reported that eighty-nine "prominent Chicagoans" had sent an open letter to President Truman requesting executive clemency for atomic spies Ethel and Julius Rosenberg.[39] Among the signers of the letter listed by the *Daily Worker* were Evelyn Millis Duvall, Humanist Eustace Hayden of the Chicago Ethical Society, and Humanists Anton J. Carlson, Curtis W. Reese, and Anatol Rapoport. The Chicago group was cited as a "local auxiliary" of the National Committee To Secure Justice in the Rosenberg Case,[40] the latter having been designated as "a Communist front organized at least as early as November, 1951."[41]

The present finds Evelyn Duvall still mingling with the Left, as a contributing author to the Socialist-oriented Public Affairs Pamphlets.

MAXWELL S. STEWART — Maxwell Stewart is currently editor of Public Affairs Pamphlets, whose soft-covered booklets are used as required reading or authoritative references in numerous home and family living programs. Stewart's subversive background is given thorough coverage in Felix Wittmer's informative exposé of American education, titled *Conquest of the American Mind*. The passage reads as follows:

> Maxwell Slutz Stewart has been the editor of Public Affairs Pamphlets since their inauguration in 1936. Despite occasional protests he has held this position ever since, during a period in which more than eighteen million copies of two hundred different pamphlets have been distributed in schools, colleges and among organized societies. It would be ridiculous to argue whether or not Maxwell Stewart ever was a Communist. No one that we can recall, who has not been an ardent champion of the Marxian world revolution, ever was permitted to be an associate editor of the *Moscow Daily News*. But Stewart, in addition, has served on the editorial boards of such Communist publications as *China Today* and *Soviet Russia Today*. Throughout the decades, he has supported dozens of Communist fronts.
>
> Louis Francis Budenz told the McCarran Committee under oath that Stewart was a Communist, and that Earl Browder called him "one of the reliables of the Party."[42]

For those who are interested in delving further, Stewart's long list of Communist-front affiliations has been documented in the files of various government investigative committees.[43] He denied under oath, however, that he was a Communist.

Altogether, there are approximately 200 Public Affairs Pamphlets, about 137 of which fall into the category of sex education/home and family living. Since these pamphlets are frequently featured in both teacher and student sex education bibliographies from coast to coast (45 of them are part of the San Mateo County [California] program, for example), they merit more than just a passing glance.

As a starter, it should be noted that the headquarters of the Public Affairs Committee, publishers of the pamphlets, is located at the same address as the Communist-run International Publishers (381 Park Avenue, South, New York, N.Y.). Among early leaders of the Public Affairs Committee were such notables as Robert P. Lane (original head of the American

Student Union, cited as "a Communist front"); Frederick Vanderbilt Field (identified many times under oath as a Communist); and Evans Clark (secretary to Ludwig C. A. K. Martens, one of the first Communists to be forcibly deported from this country).[44]

Predictably, the current Public Affairs Committee is full of leftists of varying degree, including Communist fronters Algernon Black, Hubert T. Delaney,[45] and Vera Micheles Dean;[46] Telford Taylor, a consistent defender of leftist and Communist clients such as Junius Scales, North Carolina Communist Party chairman; Michael Harrington, chairman of the American Socialist Party; and Harry Laidler, founder of the Intercollegiate Socialist Society. Although Stewart himself has written over thirty of the 200 pamphlets published by the Public Affairs Committee, numerous other leftist authors are responsible for others, including Roger Baldwin, Benjamin Gruenberg, and Swedish pro-Marxist Gunnar Myrdal.

Small wonder, then, that Public Affairs Pamphlets, ever since their inception, have been injecting doses of Red poison into the bloodstream of American education. In official testimony delivered before the House Committee on American Activities on July 21, 1947, Walter F. Steele* stated that the Public Affairs Committee "issues higher quality pamphlets on subjects related to those adopted for propagation by the Communist Party."[47]

These pamphlets are classic examples of the cryptic technique of deception that has been so skillfully utilized by the collectivists who wish to reconstruct American society. These change agents are quick to realize that the age-old failure, socialism, never advances through open advocacy. Instead, they have successfully adopted the Fabian method — cloaking col-

---

*In commenting on Mr. Steele's testimony as chairman of the National Security Committee of the American Coalition of Patriotic, Civic, and Fraternal Societies, a California Senate Fact-Finding Committee on Un-American Activities noted: "Mr. Steele has done an outstanding work in compiling data on subversive activities in the United States." (*Fifth Report, Un-American Activities in California, 1949*, Regular California Legislature, Sacramento, page 539.)

lectivism under any other name than its own, while at the same time pressing toward its realization. Essentially, the pamphlets convey by skillful innuendos a steady stream of subtle attacks on the American way of life, while at the same time placing emphasis on the merits of the socialistic system.

Further illustrating this point, Felix Wittmer made this observation:

> There is something diabolically cunning in the general framework of these pamphlets. Only a Marxian mastermind could fool Americans so completely. . . .
>
> As a matter of camouflage, the veteran sponsor of the Communist causes and editor of P.A.P. [Maxwell Stewart] has published numerous pamphlets of a medical, hygienic or otherwise socially useful nature. Attractively made up, such booklets are the delight of those citizens who want good information in capsules. "Vitamins for Health," "Epilepsy," "Good News About Diabetes," "Polio Can Be Conquered," "Alcoholism Is a Sickness," and "Loan Sharks and Their Victims" are almost infallible bait for the innocent; for, after gaining confidence in P.A.P. through these neat and competent pamphlets, hundreds of thousands proceed to reading the others, which suggest the advisability of public (socialistic) planning and disregard the wisdom of limited government.[48]

Among books frequently found in sex education bibliographies is *Facts of Love and Marriage for Young People*, edited by Aron Krich. This book, which is promoted by the Humanist-founded Child Study Association of America, is a compendium based largely on earlier Public Affairs Pamphlets.

Like so many other organizations in the Socialist-Humanist orbit, the Public Affairs Committee in recent years has gotten its teeth into the movement to legalize abortion. Public Affairs Pamphlet No. 429, *When Should Abortion Be Legal?* makes a subtle plea for the revision of our abortion laws. It was authored by Humanist Harriet Pilpel of both SIECUS and Planned Parenthood–World Population and Kenneth P. Norwich, a member of the Humanist-laden Association for the Study of Abortion, Inc.

SIECUS officials William Genné and Emily Mudd and SIECUS sponsor Dr. Leona Baumgartner are members of the Public Affairs Committee. A number of SIECUS directors, though not members of the Committee, contribute their talents as writers of Public Affairs Pamphlets; these include Evelyn Millis Duvall, Lester Kirkendall, David Mace, James A. Peterson, and Harriet Pilpel.

Among Humanists who are members of the Public Affairs Committee are Algernon Black, Sidonie M. Gruenberg, Alfred McClung Lee, and Mark Starr. A considerable number of other Humanists have contributed writings to Public Affairs Pamphlets, among them Fred M. Hechinger (a member of the *New York Times'* editorial board), Alan F. Guttmacher, Hilda Krech, Eda LeShan, Gunnar Myrdal, Saul K. Padover, and Sidonie M. Gruenberg.

SIDONIE M. AND BENJAMIN GRUENBERG — Mrs. Gruenberg's activities do not stop with the Public Affairs Committee. She is also deeply entrenched in the Humanist movement, as a member of the advisory committee of Ethical Culture's Board of Ethical Lecturers. Moreover, the files of the House Committee on Internal Security list her as having been affiliated with the following subversive activities:[49]

- National Council of American Soviet Friendship — cited as "subversive and Communist."*
- Congress of American Women — cited as "subversive and Communist and supported at all times by the international Communist movement."
- Cultural and Scientific Conference for World Peace — cited as "a Communist front."
- Peoples Radio Foundation — cited as "a subversive and Communist organization."

*Originally listed as a sponsor and member of this Communist front as early as 1944, Mrs. Gruenberg became a member of its board in 1946. Describing this front as "a direct agent of the Soviet Union, engaged in traitorous activities under the orders of Stalin's consular service in the United States," a California Senate fact-finding committee further disclosed: "The National Council of American-Soviet Friendship has followed the Communist line of the Seventh Period of strategy in the United States since 1945 with undeviating subservience." (*Fifth Report, Un-American Activities in California, 1949,* Regular California Legislature, Sacramento, page 540.)

- Progressive Citizens of America — cited as a "political Communist front."

In addition, Mrs. Gruenberg's book, *More Favorite Stories, Old and New*, was originally promoted in *The Worker*, an official organ of the Communist Party.[50]

As the director of the Humanist-founded Child Study Association of America for twenty-five years, Mrs. Gruenberg's influence on American education has been very great. The CSAA retains her as a special consultant, and she is said to be "one of the most outstanding and beloved leaders in the field of child development and parent education." In fact, there is hardly a home and family living program in existence which does not include her works. Perhaps best known is her SIECUS-recommended book, *The Wonderful Story of How You Were Born*, which subtly promotes the concept of evolution as it force-feeds the intimate details of sex to young children in adult terminology.

Another member of the Gruenberg family is actively involved in the sex education field. Mrs. Gruenberg's husband, Benjamin, also writes for Public Affairs Pamphlets, and is touted by them as "one of America's leading authorities on sex education."[51] Professor Gruenberg is credited with having assisted his wife in the development of *The Wonderful Story of How You Were Born*. He has been affiliated with the following subversive activities:

- American Committee for Protection of Foreign Born — cited as a "Communist front organization," "subversive and Communist," and "under the 'complete domination' of the Communist Party."
- National Federation for Constitutional Liberties — cited as "subversive and Communist."

Other leftist activities of Professor Gruenberg include past membership in the Communist-infiltrated Teachers Union in New York City, and defense of the commissioning of Communists in our armed forces. Moreover, he formerly taught at the

Socialist-spawned New School for Social Research, which was discussed earlier.

A daughter of the Gruenbergs, Humanist Hilda S. Krech, follows in her parents' footsteps as a contributing author of Public Affairs Pamphlets.

DOROTHY BARUCH — Dr. Dorothy Baruch is another SIECUS-recommended author who contributes articles to Public Affairs Pamphlets. Her book, *New Ways in Sex Education*, is frequently found in sex education bibliographies throughout the country.

The California Senate Fact-finding Subcommittee on Un-American Activities lists Dr. Baruch as a sponsor of the following Communist fronts:

- Los Angeles Emergency Committee To Aid the Strikers — cited as "a Communist front."
- American Youth for Democracy — cited as "subversive and Communist," and further described, as previously noted, as "a determined effort to disaffect our youth and to turn them against religion, the American home, against the college authorities, and against the American Government itself."[52]

RUTH BENEDICT AND GENE WELTFISH — Another subversive whose writings have tainted home and family living bibliographies is the late Ruth Benedict, who was also a contributing author of Public Affairs Pamphlets. One pamphlet, *Races of Mankind*, of which she and Gene Weltfish were co-authors, was banned by the United States Army with the explanation that its evident aim was to create racial antagonism.[53] It was this same pamphlet that provided the basis for the film, *Brotherhood of Man*, which appears in McGraw-Hill's film catalog with other films used in current home and family living courses.

Professor Benedict is listed in the files of the House Committee on Un-American Activities as "among the well-known supporters of Communist-front organizations"; the same source also cites her in connection with at least ten Communist fronts and causes.[54]

Dr. Gene Weltfish has surpassed her former colleagues by almost three to one, having chalked up a total of twenty-nine affiliations with Communist fronts or causes.[55] In addition, Dr. Weltfish has been cited five separate times for defending Communists and the Communist Party. As an example, one citation was for supporting the right of Communist Party leader Robert Thompson "to teach and advocate the violent overthrow of the U.S.Government."[56]

With such notorious backgrounds, it is little wonder that the chosen theme of these two authors was in perfect harmony with a prime objective of the Communists; that is, to create racial antagonism.

ALGERNON BLACK — Algernon Black, a Humanist/Communist-fronter of long standing, participated with SIECUS officials Mary Calderone and Helen Southard in a 1966 panel discussion on sex education sponsored by the Child Study Association of America. The entire proceedings of this conference have been published by CSAA as a book with the title, *Sex Education and the New Morality — A Search for a Meaningful Social Ethic*. As might be expected, the book is saturated with Humanist, situation ethics concepts. It appears in sex education bibliographies from coast to coast.

In introducing Dr. Black to this conference as "a religious leader of prominence and now a senior leader of the New York Society of Ethical Culture, . . ." Moderator Mildred Rabinow omitted mention of a significant portion of his background. Official investigative committees of the U.S. Government have cited Black as having been affiliated with at least thirty-one Communist fronts and causes. A few of them are American Friends of Spanish Democracy; American Student Union; League of American Writers; Associated Film Audiences; National Federation for Constitutional Liberties; and Film Audiences for Democracy.[57]

Like many other Communist fronters, Dr. Black is a contributing author for *The Humanist*. His association with Ethical Culture dates back to the thirties; by 1934 he had assumed a leadership position in the American Ethical Union.

Politically, Black is an active Socialist, a bitter critic of anti-Communists, a sympathizer with Red China, and a board menber of the radical ACLU.

JOSEPH F. FLETCHER — Held in high esteem as a SIECUS-recommended author, the Rev. Joseph F. Fletcher (S.T.D.) has dropped many pearls of wisdom in his six books, which include *Situation Ethics–The New Morality*, and *Moral Responsibility–Situation Ethics at Work*. In the latter, as a brief illustration, Fletcher soberly offered his readers: "The personal commitment, not the county clerk, sanctifies sex. A man or wife who hates the partner is living in sin. A couple who cannot marry legally or permanently but live together faithfully and honorably and responsibly, are living in virtue — in Christian love."[58]

As mentioned earlier, Humanist Fletcher is credited with having developed the concept of situation ethics, which has been adopted by sex education experts as the criterion for all moral decision-making.

Ordained to the Episcopal ministry in 1929, Fletcher later became a faculty member of the Episcopal Theological Seminary in Cambridge, Massachusetts. There he worked incessantly on Communist Party projects, as revealed in the sworn testimony of Herbert Philbrick, undercover agent for the FBI. In describing how he and his fellow Communists used church facilities for their own purposes, Philbrick stated: "This happened over such a long period of time that it was simply incredible and impossible that the minister in charge did not know or could not have known what was going on."[59] When later asked to name the ministers involved, Philbrick testified: "Donald Lothrop is one. The Reverend Joseph Fletcher, F-l-e-t-c-h-e-r, of the theological seminary, Episcopal Theological Seminary, in Cambridge, Mass., is another. Joe Fletcher worked with us on Communist Party projects and on an enormous number of tasks."[60]

In addition, Fletcher has chalked up an impressive score of at least seventeen affiliations with Communist fronts and causes, including the Win-the-Peace Conference (or Congress); the Committee of Welcome for the "Red" Dean of Canterbury; the National Federation for Constitutional Liberties; the People's Institute of Applied Religion, Inc.; the School for Democracy; the National Council of the Arts, Sciences, and Professions; the National Free Browder Congress; and the National Council of American-Soviet Friendship.[61]

ERICH FROMM — There is scarcely a home and family living bibliography in existence that does not include books by Erich Fromm. The philosophy in Fromm's books is heavily intermingled with Marxian socialism. It is apparent in his most popular work, *The Art of Loving*, that Fromm's heroes are Karl Marx, Herbert Marcuse (a Marxist and Humanist), Friedrich Nietzche (an atheist), and others of similar persuasion. Despite its title, much of this book is devoted to subtly questioning the existence of God as a Supreme Being, and the merits of the capitalistic system. In the book's summation, Fromm lashed out strongly against capitalism, stating: "The principle underlying capitalistic society and the principle of love are incompatible."[62] He arrived at the conclusion that "radical changes in our social structure are necessary," and offered as a substitute for capitalism the socialistic principle whereby workers share the work, rather than the profits.[63]

Fromm's extra-curricular activities include membership on the National Advisory Council of the ACLU, and also membership in the National Committee for a Sane Nuclear Policy, a leftwing, pacifist group, and in the Socialist Party. The establishment of socialism is of course viewed by its advocates as a transitional stage between capitalism and Communism. This particular point was illustrated by John Strachey, a top official in the Labor-Socialist Party of Great Britain in 1950. Having been for many years an openly avowed Communist, Strachey wrote in his book, *The Theory and Practice of Socialism*:

> It is impossible to establish Communism as the immediate successor to Capitalism. Accordingly, it is proposed to establish Socialism as something which we can put in the place of our present decaying Capitalism. *Hence Communists work for the establishment of Socialism as the necessary transition stage on the road to Communism.* [emphasis added]

In 1966 Fromm served on the National Conference for New Politics, a "classical united front third party movement largely controlled by the Communist Party."[64] Also in 1966, he sponsored the National Voters' Pledge Campaign, which was headed by Socialist-Humanist Norman Thomas, veteran Communist-fronter William Sloane Coffin, and Sanford Gottlieb, the political director of the National Committee for a Sane Nuclear Policy. Fromm has also been affiliated with the National Committee To Abolish the House Un-American Activities Committee, which was cited as "a 'new organization' set up in the summer of 1960 'to lead and direct the Communist Party's Operation Abolition campaign.' "[65]

The previously mentioned collection of thirty-six essays, edited by Fromm under the title *Socialist Humanism*, is so akin to Marxist ideology that the book was boldly advertised in the May 1970 edition of *News and Letters*, a periodical describing itself as "an organization of Marxist Humanists."

HARRY AND BONARO OVERSTREET — Two persons who have won favor in the top echelons of sex education are the late Harry Overstreet and his wife, Bonaro, both Humanists. Hailed as "experts on extremism," their writings have provided the basis for articles prepared by SIECUS, the PTA, and other groups within the sex education establishment in an effort to "aid" the community in dealing with opponents of sex education who, purportedly, are "extremists." For example, SIECUS's publication titled *Extremist Tactics* proudly recommends the Overstreets' book, *The Strange Tactics of Extremism*, as an additional source of information. Coincidentally, a similar article published by the national PTA, titled "Extremist Groups," was prepared by the PTA's editorial staff, of which Bonaro Overstreet is a member. Professor Overstreet and his wife served as consultants to the PTA over a period of many years. Their book, *Mind Alive*, and Mrs. Overstreet's *Understanding Fear* appear in various home and family living bibliographies throughout the country.

However, Professor Overstreet's activities were much more diversified than the above would indicate. He had been a member of the American Humanist Association as far back as 1944. Furthermore, listed in information from the files of the House Committee on Internal Security, there are nine Communist front affiliations for Harry Overstreet:

- American Committee for Democracy and
  Intellectual Freedom
- American Committee for Protection of Foreign Born
- American Committee To Save Refugees
- American Friends of Spanish Democracy
- Descendants of the American Revolution
- Friends of the Abraham Lincoln Brigade
- National Federation for Constitutional Liberties
- Schappes Defense Committee
- Spanish Refugee Relief Campaign[66]

It would be unfair to omit to mention Overstreet's 1953 statement, in correspondence with the House Committee on Un-American Activities in regard to his subversive affiliations: " . . . I did not know at the time of my affiliation that I was serving Communist ends by lending my name or by becoming a member."[67] However, it should be noted that four of these organizations (the second, third, and the last two on the above list) had been cited as subversive *before* Overstreet gave them his support.

Furthermore, at the time of his 1953 statement, Overstreet's socialist record was already more than thirty years old. He had at one time held membership in the John Reed Club, a notorious arm of the Communist Party.[68] In any event, as recently as 1964, the year he and his wife collaborated in writing *The Strange Tactics of Extremism*, a major thrust of the attack by the authors was against *anti*-Communists.

An earlier work of the Overstreets, written in 1958, should not be ignored. *What We Must Know About Communism* was best described by author Edward Janisch, as "a stupendous attempt that was designed to soften us at the very hour of our crisis . . . because the book attempts to make palatable certain notions which would, if accepted by large numbers of Americans, render us helpless in the face of the onslaught of World communism."[69] Janisch continued: "Here is a book on Communism in which not one of J. Edgar Hoover's somber warnings is mentioned . . . a book in which espionage, a major activity and purpose of the Party, gets less than a page of asides. In short, it is a book as conspicuous by what it omits as by what it includes." Janisch summarizes: "The question to be asked is: *Why has Overstreet completely omitted military strategems and force, the bolshevik standard tactics, as well as subversion and espionage, from his study?*" [70] Included, by contrast, were pleas for more "tenderness" and less hostility (toward an enemy that had already butchered and enslaved millions); the halting of nuclear testing (at a time when it was obvious the Russians were accelerating their test program); and continual bargaining, negotiations, and summit conferences — all consistent with the Communist objective of rendering America powerless while the Reds continue to engulf what remains of the free world.

Considering the book's contents, it is easy to see why Communist-fronter Gordon Allport gave *What We Must Know About Communism* the following endorsement:

> So readable and informative and so vitally important that one can scarcely lay it down.

This glowing commendation by so notorious a Communist sympathizer as Gordon Allport leaves no doubt that what we *really* must know about Communism is unlikely to be found in the Overstreets' book.

GORDON ALLPORT — In addition to writing reviews, the late Gordon Allport, another Humanist, had achieved an entrance of his own into the field of sex education. His *Pattern and Growth in Personality*, for example, is listed in a sex education bibliography published by the U.S. Catholic Conference's Family Life Division. Moreover, Allport's *The Nature of Prejudice* appears on a book list issued by the National Education Association, titled *The Negro American in Paperback*, along with works by Communists Herbert Aptheker, W. E. B. DuBois, Langston Hughes, Maxwell S. Stewart, and Victor Perlo.[71] Other leftists on the list include Communist fronters E. Franklin Frazier and Carey McWilliams.[72] Purportedly designed to improve race relations, this NEA book list was compiled for use in the teaching of American Negro history.*

Professor Allport was described in Wittmer's *Conquest of the American Mind* as ranking "among the nation's most persistent Communist fronters," having publicly supported a dozen or more Communist fronts and causes.[73] Some of the fronts named are the American Committee for Protection of Foreign Born; the American League for Peace and Democracy; the Coordinating Committee To Lift the Embargo; the National Emergency Conference; and the National Federation for Constitutional Liberties.[74]

RABBI ROLAND B. GITTELSOHN — Rabbi Gittelsohn's *Consecrated Unto Me* appears on SIECUS-recommended reading

*This was not the first time the National Education Association had promoted pro-Communist literature. In 1940, for example, they had urged the use of the "Building America" series of social studies texts in American schools. After it had been widely adopted, a Senate Investigating Committee on Education of the California Legislature condemned this series for subtly playing up Marxism and denigrating American traditions. The Senate report ". . . found among other things that 113 Communist-front organizations had to do with some of the material in the books and that 50 Communist-front authors were connected with it." (*Report, Special Committee to Investigate Tax-Exempt Foundations*, 83rd Congress, pages 154–155.)

lists, and in numerous sex education bibliographies as well. He is shown as a sponsor of the Mid-Century Conference for Peace in its Call and Program dated May 29–30, 1950. This conference was cited as a "Communist front" by the Internal Security Subcommittee of the U.S. Senate Judiciary Committee.[75]

Gittelsohn was also a sponsor of the American League for Peace and Democracy, cited as "the largest of the Communist 'front' movements in the United States . . . " by a Special Committee on Un-American Activities of the House of Representatives.[76]

His third affiliation was as a signer of an "Open Letter" to Congress opposing the Internal Security Act of 1950 (press release dated January 19, 1951). This letter was issued under the auspices of the National Committee To Repeal the McCarran Act, also cited as a Communist front by the Internal Security Subcommittee of the U.S. Senate Judiciary Committee.[77]

LEWIS M. TERMAN — SIECUS Study Guide #4 and various sex education curricula list this author's *Psychological Factors in Marital Happiness* in their selected bibliographies.

The late Professor Terman had affiliated himself with at least four Communist fronts and causes: the Federation for Repeal of the Levering Act; the National Federation for Constitutional Liberties; the Schneiderman-Darcy Defense Committee; and Consumers Union.[78]

In addition, the Communist *People's World* included him among those who were actively engaged in fighting the loyalty oath in California during the early 1950's.[79]

E. FRANKLIN FRAZIER — Frazier's book *The Negro Family in the United States* appeared in the 1970 SIECUS book list for professionals, which was titled *Human Sexuality*. Described by SIECUS as "a classic study of the Negro family in America," this book is one of a number written by Frazier on the subject of race relations. Skillfully cloaked in a cryptic style similar to that of the Public Affairs Pamphlets, Frazier's book subtly injects frequent doses of racial antagonism between blacks and the white "master race" (to use Frazier's own terminology), and between blacks and Negroes of mixed blood.

Moreover, he displays a persistent distaste for the light-skinned, "middle-class" Negro throughout, while revealing, and encouraging in his readers, a preference for "the black proletariat" — a Marxian term denoting the working class.

Another of Frazier's books, titled *The Negro in the United States*, so promoted the Marxist cause that it was advertised in the Communist Workers Book Shop catalogs for 1949 and 1950, after also receiving favorable reviews in the Communist publications *Daily Worker* and *People's World*.[80] This book, as well as others by Frazier, appears on the recommended reading list of the National Council of Churches, and the National Education Association's book list for American Negro History.

The files of the Committee on Un-American Activities of the U.S. House of Representatives contain eighteen citations of Frazier's connection with Communist fronts and subversive causes in America, including the Washington Committee for Democratic Action; Council on African Affairs, Inc.; Committee for a Democratic Far Eastern Policy; Civil Rights Congress; Southern Conference for Human Welfare; Southern Negro Youth Congress; Citizens' Committee To Free Earl Browder; National Council of the Arts, Sciences, and Professions; and National Federation for Constitutional Liberties.[81]

ANTON J. CARLSON — The late Anton J. Carlson was among those who signed the *Humanist Manifesto*, which signalled the beginning of the American Humanist Association. He had the distinction of having received the first "Humanist of the Year" award ever presented (1953), and he received the American Medical Association's Service Gold Medal in the same year.

Born in Sweden in 1875, Dr. Carlson went on to become president of the American Association for the Advancement of Science and consultant to the U.S. Food and Drug Administration. His book, *The Machinery of the Body*, is among the considerable number of works by Humanist authors that have been strategically placed in current sex education curricula.

In typical Humanist fashion, Carlson lent his support to at least thirteen officially cited Communist fronts and causes. Besides having been listed as national president of the American Association of Scientific Workers (cited as a "Communist front organization"),[82] Carlson was also affiliated with the National Council of the Arts, Sciences and Professions; World Peace Conference; American Committee for Protection of Foreign Born; Consumers Union; American Friends of Spanish Democracy; National Federation for Constitutional Liberties; American Peace Mobilization; National Emergency Conference; and Abraham Lincoln School.[83]

Publishers

In addition to some of the authors described in this chapter, the 1970 SIECUS reading list titled *Human Sexuality* contains a curious blend of pro-left publishers whose presence merits special notice. Only a few can be listed in the space available, and no implication that this number is all-inclusive is intended.

VANGUARD PRESS — This publishing house was cited by the House Committee on Un-American Activities as a "Communist enterprise" established by the Garland Fund (officially known as the American Fund for Public Service, and cited as a "Communist front").[84]

Among those who have served as directors and officers of the Garland Fund or its subsidiaries are veteran Communist fronter Roger Baldwin and Morris Ernst of the SIECUS-connected law firm of Greenbaum, Wolff and Ernst.[85]

LYLE STUART, INC. — Humanist Lyle Stuart has maintained a close liaison with leftist forces that dates back many years. In 1963, for example, the operation of Fidel Castro's Fair Play for Cuba Committee in the United States was investigated by the U.S. Senate's Internal Security Subcommittee.[86] The inquiry revealed that this pro-Castro committee's first treasurer was Lyle Stuart, publisher of a monthly magazine and of books with various pro-Castro, anti-religious, and unconventional sexual themes. Stuart's cozy associations with Communism include his seating on the reviewing stand with the Castro brothers at a May Day celebration in Havana shortly after the Communist take-over.

Stuart's firm issues such books as *Secret Techniques of Erotic Delight*, which it describes as "everyman's guide to success in seduction and sexual intimacy"; *The Cruel and the Meek*, "an examination of sexual cruelty, whipping, bondage, high heels 'disciplining,' etc."; and *Sarv-A-Nez*, a series of erotic art essays examining the ancient Persians' sexual interest in animals as well as their needs in women.[87]

The Independent, a Lyle Stuart monthly (once called *Exposé*), is publicized in *The Humanist*, along with other period-icals of similar anti-religious persuasion.

UNIVERSITY BOOKS, INC. — According to the *New York Times Book Review* of November 9, 1969 (page 45), this publishing firm is a division of Lyle Stuart, Inc.

GROVE PRESS — SIECUS also lists Barney Rosset's Grove Press in its roster of publishers pandering to prurient interests.

Rosset was featured in the January 25, 1969 issue of the *Saturday Evening Post* in an article titled "How to Publish 'Dirty' Books for Fun and Profit." When not focusing on pornography, Rosset spends his time propagating the Commu-nist ideology with such books as Ernesto "Ché" Guevara's *Rem-iniscences*; Communist Herbert Aptheker's *Nat Turner's Slave Rebellion*; Communist Kim Philby's *My Silent War*; and *Red Star Over China*, by Edgar Snow (identified as a Communist by Louis Budenz and distinguished for at least five cited affilia-tions with Communist fronts and causes).[88]

Grove Press is the distributor for Marxist Abbie Hoffman's handbook for thieves, *Steal This Book*, which contains instructions on how to loot, pilfer, and shoplift, and at the same time preaches revolution. So blatantly criminal are the contents of Hoffman's book that thirty outraged publishers rejected it before Hoffman decided to publish it himself, and many large wholesalers and the majority of bookstores have refused to handle it.

BEACON PRESS — As mentioned earlier, Beacon Press is operated under the auspices of the Unitarian-Universalist Association, which is formally affiliated with the Humanist movement. Publishing primarily in the field of the humanities, the social sciences, and liberal religion, it can be verified that a preponderance of Beacon Press books are not only written by Humanists, but also convey the tenets of atheistic Socialism. An examination of Beacon's Fall 1969 catalog discloses the works of a swarm of Communist-front authors as well, some of them featured in this chapter: Gordon Allport, John Dewey, Joseph F. Fletcher, E. Franklin Frazier, Corliss Lamont, and Mark Van Doren, to name only a few.

In 1971, the Unitarian-Universalist Association and its publishing arm, Beacon, together launched a sex education curriculum series titled *About Your Sexuality*, aimed at the junior high school level (ages 12 to 14). According to Beacon's own description, the program "is structured so that students — not teachers — decide the topics they want to explore, and in what order. . . . No effort is made to impose values on students."

The principal author of this curriculum series is Humanist Deryck Calderwood of SIECUS. In addition to recordings of young people describing their first heterosexual intercourse, the course includes a filmstrip showing three separate acts of coitus by three different couples.[89] Other topics covered in *About Your Sexuality* are contraceptive practices, masturbation, slang terms, homosexuality, and other sexual deviations. In short, the UUA-Beacon curriculum is the most explicit and controversial set of materials ever assembled for use in a classroom — and probably the most pornographic.

Not surprisingly, the American Humanist Association has

taken the lead in endorsing this program, its members having approved a resolution commending the UUA for its series at the AHA 1972 annual membership meeting.[90]

Beacon further links itself to pornography by ads appearing in the lewd magazine, *Evergreen Review*.[91] Subjects of books promoted in these ads other than pornography include draft-dodging and revolution. One finds, for instance, such titles as *An Essay on Liberation*, by Herbert Marcuse — a Marxist and Humanist, and chief mentor of Communist Angela Davis.

CITADEL PRESS — Co-proprietor of Citadel Press is Philip S. Foner, identified as a Communist Party member in testimony before the Subversive Activities Control Board in 1955.[92] In addition to writing for the Communist journal *Political Affairs*, Foner has taught at all major Communist schools across America, and was a founding sponsor with Herbert Aptheker (chief theoretician for the Communist Party) of the American Institute for Marxist Studies.[93]

Numerous Citadel Press books bear the names of various authors who have been identified as Communists, including Morris U. Schappes,[94] John Howard Lawson,[95] Maxim Gorki,[96] and Herbert Aptheker.

In recent years, Communist Party bookstores across the nation have begun to carry Citadel books dealing with demonology and the occult. In fact, of the thirty most malignant books sold in these stores that focus on the theme of Satanism, more than half are published by Citadel.

A "Support SIECUS" Front

Numerous other identified Communist fronters, radicals, and leftists have pushed into the forefront of support for SIECUS, as members of the previously mentioned National Committee for Responsible Family Life and Sex Education.*

*For a complete listing of committee members, see Appendix G.

This committee of nearly 200 members sponsored an ad in the October 16, 1969 issue of the *New York Times*, reaffirming that "enlightened Americans support the concepts of SIECUS." Labeling opponents of public school sex education as "extremists," the ad made an urgent — almost desperate — plea to communities to adopt the SIECUS brand of sex education.

Of the committee's membership, a large percentage have been associated with organizations cited by the United States Government as Communist, Communist front, or subversive. In order to present specific cases, for whatever help it may give in bringing this information to light, a list of twenty signers of the ad has been compiled. The list is not by any means complete, for to include all subversive individuals with appropriate documentation would be a monumental task. This committee's membership also includes a significant number of Humanists whose activities often aid, either directly or indirectly, the advancement of Communism.

The following list states the name of the individual, the number of citations he or she has received for participation in Communist fronts, causes, activities, committees, organizations, and campaigns, and the pertinent documentation:

- *Margaret Culkin Banning* — five citations (House Committee on Un-American Activities, Appendix IX, *Communist Front Organizations,** pages 668, 775, 941, 977, 1702).
- *Stringfellow Barr* — seven citations (California Legislature, 1953 Regular Session, Eleventh Report, Senate Investigating Committee on Education, pages 15, 23, 24–25, 34, 41, 110; *see also* HCUA, Appendix IX, page 1235; *see also* Francis X. Gannon, *Biographical Dictionary of the Left*, Volume I, page 227).
- *Ralph Bunche* (deceased 1971) — three citations (HCUA, Appendix IX, pages 1293, 1456, 1697). One of these citations was based on the fact that Dr. Bunche served on the editorial board of the openly Communist publication,

*Referred to hereinafter as "HCUA, Appendix IX."

Science and Society, for more than four years. Bunche seems to have had some ties with Communism even closer than those cited. Two former high-ranking Communists, both Negroes, swore under oath at a U.S. Civil Service loyalty board hearing in 1954 that they had known Bunche in the Communist Party (Francis X. Gannon, *Biographical Dictionary of the Left*, Volume I, page 261).

- *Dr. Allan M. Butler* — seven citations (Fifth Report, Un-American Activities in California, 1949,   pages 480, 489, 499, 507, 509, 513, 531).

- *Bennett Cerf* (deceased 1971) — nine citations (HCUA, Appendix IX, pages 673, 696, 943, 957, 965, 1171, 1179, 1449, 1648, 1772).

- *Stuart Chase* — six citations (California Legislature, 1951 Regular Session, Eighth Report, Senate Investigating Committee on Education, page 53). Stuart Chase, a Humanist, is a member of the National Advisory Council of the American Civil Liberties Union.

- *Norman Corwin* — fifteen citations (Final Report, Un-American Activities in California, to the 1949 Regular California Legislature, Supplementing Committee's Fifth Report, page 2981).

- *George S. Counts* — twenty-six citations (Verne P. Kaub, *Communist Socialist Propaganda in American Schools*, revised edition, 1967, pages 142–143; *see also* Francis X. Gannon, *Biographical Dictionary of the Left*, Vol. II, pages 288–293).

- *Rev. William H. Genné* — three citations (for documentation, see reference 45, Chapter 1).

- *Rabbi Roland B. Gittelsohn* — three citations (for citations, see discussion of Rabbi Gittelsohn earlier in this chapter.

- *Arthur J. Goldberg* — three citations (for documentation, see reference 73, Chapter 1).

- *Chaim Gross* — six citations (Review of the Scientific and Cultural Conference for World Peace, House Committee on Un-American Activities, April 19, 1949, pages 23, 50; *see also* HCUA, Appendix IX, pages 433, 485, 577, 1075, 1119, 1338).

- *Hugh B. Hester* — two citations (Francis X. Gannon, *Biographical Dictionary of the Left*, Vol. I, pages 366–367; see also *Guide to Subversive Organizations and Publications*, pages 117, 69–70). In addition to the organizations mentioned in these citations, Hester has been associated with the Fair Play for Cuba Committee (Communist-subsidized); such Communist publications as *The Worker, National Guardian, New World Review,* and *Political Affairs*; the left-wing American Friends Service Committee; and others. Hester was also co-author, with the veteran Communist-fronter Jerome Davis, of *On The Brink.* (Davis was referred to as a "Soviet Government propagandist" by former Communist Benjamin Gitlow, in testimony appearing on page 258 of the California Legislature, 1958 Budget Session, Sixteenth Report, Senate Investigating Committee on Education. Further, in 1956, the Senate Internal Security Subcommittee included Davis' name in its list of the eighty-two most active and typical sponsors of Communist front organizations.)

- *Rockwell Kent* (deceased 1971) — eighty-five citations (Fifth Report, Un-American Activities in California, to the 1949 Regular California Legislature, Sacramento, page 498). According to a story in the *Newark Sunday News* of March 14, 1971, Rockwell Kent visited Moscow in 1967, to accept the Lenin Peace Prize for that year, and later donated $10,000 of the prize money to the Communist North Vietnamese.

- *Archibald MacLeish* — twelve citations (California Legislature, 1953 Regular Session, Eleventh Report, Senate Investigating Committee on Education, page 22; *see also* HCUA, Appendix IX, pages 535, 668, 732, 753, 785, 957, 969, 1340, 1391, 1765, 1772).

- *Lewis Mumford* — eighteen citations (California Legislature, 1951 Regular Session, Eighth Report, Senate Investigating Committee on Education, pages 61–62; and California Legislature, 1953 Regular Session, Eleventh Report, Senate Investigating Committee on Education, page 58; *see also* HCUA, Appendix IX, pages 319f, 322, 332, 770, 1179, 1472, 1474).

- *Reinhold Niebuhr* — twelve citations (California Legislature, 1953 Regular Session, Eleventh Report, Senate Investigating Committee on Education, pages 19, 32; and Eleventh Report, Un-American Activities in California, 1961, to the 1961 Regular California Legislature, Sacramento, pages 127–130; *see also* HCUA, Appendix IX, pages 371, 389, 632, 658, 669, 768, 1304, 1455, 1772, 1774).

- *Mildred Scott Olmstead* — three citations (California Legislature, 1953 Regular Session, Eleventh Report, Senate Investigating Committee on Education, page 58; and Fourth Report, Un-American Activities in California, 1948, Communist Front Organizations, page 320; *see also* HCUA, Appendix IX, page 398).

- *Harold C. Urey* — thirteen citations (HCUA, Appendix IX, pages 328–331, 349, 358f, 670, 754, 776, 981, 1203, 1207, 1210, 1357, 1648, 1702f; *see also* Francis X. Gannon, *Biographical Dictionary of the Left*, Vol. I, pages 570–571).

- *Mark Van Doren* — six citations (Fourth Report, Un-American Activities in California, 1948, Communist Front Organizations, pages 241, 263, 331, 338; *see also* HCUA, Appendix IX, pages 473, 1562).

In recent years, SIECUS gained sixteen official sponsors,* whose names appear on SIECUS stationery beneath those of the Board of Directors. Three of these sponsors — Rabbi Roland B. Gittelsohn, Chaim Gross, and Mark Van Doren — were included in the foregoing listing of signers of the ad in support of SIECUS.

Another SIECUS sponsor, Leona Baumgartner (also a mem-

*For a complete list of SIECUS sponsors, see Appendix H.

ber of Maxwell Stewart's Public Affairs Committee, publisher of Public Affairs Pamphlets), was a featured speaker at a 1944 conference held by the notorious Communist front, the National Council of American-Soviet Friendship.[97] There she was joined by Humanist Sidonie M. Gruenberg, whose Communist front affiliations were mentioned earlier in the chapter. Humanist Margaret Mead and Chaim Gross were other friends of SIECUS associated with Dr. Baumgartner as sponsors of the National Wartime Conference of the Professions, the Sciences, the Arts, the White-Collar Fields, which was "stacked with well-known Communists and fellow travelers," including SIECUS supporter Rockwell Kent.[98] In fact, it is obvious that a substantial number of persons whose names appear in this chapter have at one time or another been associated in organizations cited as subversive.

The welcoming of these four more leftists into the fold as official SIECUS sponsors makes it evident that SIECUS remains unaffected by charges that the sex education it advocates is Red-tinged, and is advancing boldly, confident that the news media will continue to surround this issue with a curtain of silence.

The Last Go-Round

More than forty persons involved in subversive activities, all of whom are connected in some way with sex education and/or sensitivity training, have been covered in this section. Although these forty are a minority of the total sex education corps, many of them are in the top echelons of the movement's leadership, promoting each other and the works of authors whose philosophies coincide with their own. This represents a substantial influence on the program, since the amount of pressure that can be exerted from their vantage point is sufficient to achieve any goals deemed desirable.

One example of how such pressure is exerted by a few strategically placed persons is sensitivity training, which is being used in both sex education and drug education programs. This technique was pioneered by Dr. J. L. Moreno, heralded as the founder of sociometry[99] — a science that utilizes such sensitivity training methods as psychodrama, sociodrama, role-playing, and the like. In his book, *Who Shall Survive?* Dr. Moreno acknowledges that the way was prepared for this new field by the thinking of such pioneers as George H. Mead (a luminary of the Humanist movement) and especially professor John Dewey[100] (the earlier-mentioned Humanist and notorious Communist fronter).[101] Moreno notes further that another pioneer in sociometry was Gardner Murphy (also a dedicated Humanist and Communist-fronter). He indicates Murphy's stature with the statement: "Without Murphy the acceptance of sociometry by social scientists in the colleges and universities might have been delayed by a decade."[102] (Murphy was described by a California Senate Fact-Finding Committee as having been affiliated with at least eleven Communist front organizations.[103])

In contemporary times, persons active in the pro-left, Humanist camp are found in the forefront of current sensitivity training activities. Among these are Abraham H. Maslow, Communist fronter and "Humanist of the Year" for 1967, and Humanist William C. Schutz, author of *Joy: Expanding Human Awareness*, both of whom are affiliated with Esalen Institute, a sensitivity training center at Big Sur, California. The director of this institute is Humanist Virginia Satir, whose book, *Conjoint Family Therapy*, has been incorporated into many family life programs, including that of San Mateo, California. Another Humanist prominent in sensitivity training is Dr. Carl Rogers, a Resident Fellow in the Western Behavioral Sciences Institute at La Jolla, California. Dr. Rogers is referred to in *Psychology Today* literature as "the father of Group Encounters," and is further credited in sex education bibliographies with being the author of the book, *On Becoming a Person.*

A final illustration of how subversive influences have been working in the schools occurred as far back as 1947, in the town of Chico, California. Despite the long time lapse, it is well worth study as a case in point because of its close similarity to the SIECUS story. After examining sex education materials in "Basic Twelve" (a family relations course at Chico High School), a California State Legislature Joint Fact-Finding Committee on Un-American Activities found that the material "was totally unfit for high school students."[104]

Under the subtitle, "Communist Party Line in Sex," this committee's report began: "It is the considered opinion of the committee that the books in question strike at the sanctity of marriage, at the family, and religion."[105] Among authors whose books were placed in the "Communist Party Line" category were Norman E. Himes and Henry Bowman. Both authors' works are now recommended by SIECUS and are found in current sex education bibliographies. Books that came under heaviest attack by the committee were *Marriage for Moderns*, by Bowman; *Your Marriage*, by Himes; *Coming of Age*, by Esther Lloyd Jones and Ruth Fedder; and *Marriage and Family Relationships*, by Robert Geib Foster.

The book list on which these authors' works appeared came from the California State Department of Education. The man named as responsible for "heading up the work" was Dr. Ralph Eckert, a writer for the subversive Public Affairs Committee and a currently SIECUS-recommended author. Dr. Eckert's name can still be found gracing sex education bibliographies across the country. Following its extensive investigation, the California fact-finding committee concluded:

> The books under examination are pornographic in content, immoral in many respects and totally unfit for high school students. . . .
> The books, either wittingly or unwittingly, follow or parallel the Communist Party line destruction of the moral fibre of American youth. Disrespect for parents, religion, and the law of the land is subtly injected throughout the hedonistic context. . . .

And finally:

> The Chico incident is not an isolated one. The Committee is in possession of sufficient facts to indicate an over-all pattern. The

> presence of [Humanist and Communist-fronter] Carey McWilliams in Chico at or about the time of the inception of "Basic Twelve," is a fact that the Committee is not overlooking.[106]

The 1947 Chico incident, then, is a classic prototype of the current national sex education hoax. The names, concepts, and rhetoric remain the same; only the date and place have changed. The original transcript of the investigative proceedings strikes a familiar note, all the way from the contrived method of introducing sex education into the school system to the hand-wringing pleas of innocence on the part of school officials chagrined by exposure. But the most significant cause for concern is the shocking increase in the number of subversives in American education, for whom sex education has proved to be a fertile field.

Yet opponents of public school sex education have been constantly rebuked and ridiculed by school administrations and the press for even suggesting that home and family living courses may be Red-tainted. The cry of "Extremist!" all too often dogs the footsteps of those who are courageous enough to bring these unwelcome facts to light. Concerned citizens should not submit to this tactic, which is designed to bully them into retreat. In the words of the late FBI Director J. Edgar Hoover: "Communism can exist only where it is protected and hidden. The spotlight of public exposure is the most effective means we have to use in destroying the communist conspiracy."[107]

The highly sensitive area of sex education has opened new channels through which the conspirators can operate to paralyze the spirit and will of American youth in preparation for a final takeover. This fact was perhaps best stated by Congressman John Rarick of Louisiana, speaking in the House of Representatives on June 25, 1968, on the topic of SIECUS-generated sex education:

> Through the promotion of pornography, drug use and the "New Morality," the will to resist the International Communist Conspiracy is being awakened . . . "situation ethics" and the idea

that there is no longer any "right or wrong" way to act, along with the downgrading of the influence of the family and religion play right into the hands of the Communists.[108]

Despite the abundant evidence at hand, many persons will no doubt continue to view the subversive element in SIECUS-generated sex education as non-existent, and in so doing will aid the Communists in the sinister scheme to debase a whole generation of American youth.

In any event, the conspiracy against Christianity and civilization is now totally organized. And it goes deeper than just Communism. Communism is only one of several interdependent movements working in concert with the master planners of world revolution. Socialism is another. Like its counterparts, socialism has its own role to play. Famed historian Nesta Webster examined this role in her scholarly study, *Secret Societies and Subversive Movements*, saying:

> Socialism, with its hatred of all superiority, of noble virtues — loyalty and patriotism — with its passion for dragging down instead of building up, serves the purpose of the deeper conspiracy.[109]

Other movements in the conspiracy include Humanism, which breeds atheism and labors to produce the desired stage of moral anarchy; the Council on Foreign Relations, whose central purpose is to merge the United States into a one-world government;[110] many tax-exempt foundations, whose grants support the revolution;[111] and theosophy and many other obscure factions of the occult, whose secret, anti-Christian doctrines make them appropriate satellites of the world movement toward a new secular world order. Although it may not be realized by all of the rank and file members of these movements, the top directorate of this sinister conspiracy that coordinates them is working for the annihilation of all traditional religion, all established governments, and all human institutions. Remarkable insight into this aspect of the conspiracy was shown nearly half a century ago by Mrs. Webster, when she wrote:

> For the final goal of world-revolution is not Socialism or even Communism, it is not a change in the existing economic system, it is not the destruction of civilization in a material sense; the revolution desired by the leaders is a moral and spiritual revolution, an anarchy of ideas by which all standards set up throughout nineteen centuries shall be reversed, all honoured traditions trampled under foot, and above all, the Christian ideal finally obliterated.[112]

The revolution foreshadowed by Mrs. Webster is already well under way. Only the dedicated and concerted action of all citizens will enable America to survive its onslaught. For if a whole generation of American youth can be turned away from God to self-worship and reduced from spirituality to carnality; if it can be persuaded to turn its back on eternal truths and to become preoccupied with the search for "pleasure" through drugs and animalistic sex; and if its will to resist can be finally broken, it is doubtful that our nation will long endure. When the season arrives for that generation to assume the guardianship role in our society, and nothing of value is left to preserve, we will already have reached a point where we can be ordered and enslaved.

Part II

The Circle of Organizations

THE PRECEDING FOUR CHAPTERS that make up PART I have been an in-depth study of SIECUS and the atheistic Humanist movement that founded and continues to steer that organization. The primary thrust of PART II is to trace the SIECUS influence within a network of interrelated, interlocking groups that are pertinent to our study.

This detailed study of the circle of organizations affiliated or otherwise associated with SIECUS was initially sparked by a SIECUS form letter dated September 1969, which suggested contacting eight other organizations as sources of additional aids to be used in formulating sex education programs. The eight were:

> American Association for Health, Physical Education
>   and Recreation
> American Medical Association
> American Social Health Association
> Child Study Association of America
> Family Service Association of America
> Henk Newenhouse, Inc.
> National Council on Family Relations
> Planned Parenthood Federation of America

Literature sent on request by these organizations in turn recommended SIECUS, SIECUS materials,* materials individ-

---

*"SIECUS materials" have been defined by the California State Board of Education in a resolution on sex education dated April 10, 1969, as "materials either published or promoted by the Sex Information and Education Council of the United States." (See SIECUS Newsletter for April 1969, page 6.)

As mentioned in the Foreword to PART I, SIECUS-selected authors are authors listed in the official SIECUS publications, *Selected Reading in Education for Sexuality*, *Human Sexuality*, and the quarterly SIECUS Newsletter. Many of these SIECUS-selected authors have been covered in PART II, as representative of one facet of the SIECUS influence, for a specific purpose. In examining a number of their books, it became obvious that many subscribe to the SIECUS-Humanist gospel. For example, a great many promulgate the situation ethics philosophy, omitting any reference to spiritual values; many explicitly or by inference equate man with the animals. Others frequently pit child against

ually created by SIECUS officials, and other items written by SIECUS-selected authors. Also recommended were visual aids and films. In some cases, it was discovered that SIECUS board members — though not identified as such — had actually assisted in the production of these, while many other films were the same as those promoted in SIECUS Study Guide #7, *Film Resources for Sex Education.*

Moreover, it was discovered that, of the eight organizations listed above, six had SIECUS directors as members, or even on their staffs. A seventh, the American Association for Health, Physical Education and Recreation, is under the direct jurisdiction of the National Education Association, which is linked to SIECUS by the membership of SIECUS officials Sally R. Williams, Elizabeth Koontz, Virgil Rogers, and Bennetta B. Washington. The remaining organization, Henk Newenhouse, Inc., was named in the 1969 SIECUS form letter as the central source for sex education materials at a time when SIECUS and Henk Newenhouse were sharing an address and stationery in Northfield, Illinois.

The replies to subsequent requests for sex education program guidelines from numerous other sources, such as those developed by the New Jersey State Department of Education, indicated similar associations with SIECUS. And so, as each segment of this consistent pattern revealed itself, the outline of a circle began to take form: the starting point, SIECUS, spinning its rings of influence around a multitude of organizations, each ring ending where it began.

Nor did the story end with sex education. A tragic sequel began to unfold as other spheres of influence exerted by the Humanistic complex of SIECUS and associates emerged. A case in point is drugs. Particularly noticeable was the fact that some of the same persons and organizations involved in the sex

---

parent, encourage a negative outlook toward traditional family life, promote population control, and utilize illustrations and phraseology that border on the pornographic. Even books that are seemingly innocuous lead the reader back to works of SIECUS officials and their Humanistic collaborators through their bibliographies.

The works of a few of these authors may not fall into any of these categories. To read all the SIECUS-selected books would be a monumental undertaking. It should be noted, however, that the books that were carefully studied were sufficient in number to demonstrate an overall conformity with the usual SIECUS philosophy. A number of them will be found reviewed in the discussions of the organizations covered in PART II.

education drama suddenly reappeared as "experts" when the drug issue exploded. Furthermore, substantial research into this field uncovered certain serious misrepresentations that seemed intrinsic in a number of drug education programs. The following are just a few of them:

- That the use of drugs is like any other "habit" — such as taking aspirin, smoking, and drinking tea, coffee, or cola beverages.
- That marijuana is not physically harmful — that it is, in fact, less harmful than alcohol.
- That marijuana use is not a direct cause of mental or emotional illness.
- That use of marijuana does not of itself lead to the use of other drugs.
- That law enforcement is the real danger to marijuana users, not the drug itself.
- That the legalization of marijuana could serve as society's answer to the problems caused by its use. (This point is often put across by subtle implication rather than by an outright appeal for legalization.)

In view of the above, sections on drug education programs have been inserted under appropriate organizations in PART II.

An expansion of some topics originally presented in PART I has also been injected into portions of PART II. These topics include Humanism, sensitivity training, pornography, and population control — the latter issue having been the spearhead of the drive to repeal all state abortion laws in preparation for federal regulation of population growth. (See entries in Part II for *National Association for Repeal of Abortion Laws* and *Planned Parenthood–World Population*.)

Finally, several other points should be made. First, not all members of organizations covered in PART II should be stigmatized, nor should some of the organizations as such. In most cases, it has required only a few persons in strategic positions to carry out the nefarious schemes of the Humanist-Socialist conspiracy. Second, since it took several years to gather all the data reported in PART II, the facts presented will not necessarily be completely up-to-date at the time of publication. Some of the individuals named both here and in PART I may be deceased, or may, before the publication date, have assumed new positions within their respective organizations, or been replaced by other individuals of like persuasion. Also, some organizations will have changed their addresses or altered their titles. Third, in compiling various lists of names of SIECUS directors and others in PART II, it was not always feasible to divide the lists and categorize certain individuals as Humanists. Should the reader require this information, he may refer to the list of Humanists in sex education and related fields given in Chapter 3. Finally, in reading PART II, it would be well to keep in mind that SIECUS is a Humanist front and a major force in the atheistic juggernaut that is working to transform America into an immoral, Godless nation.

American Academy of Pediatrics (AAP)
1801 Hinman Avenue, Evanston, Illinois

THE HEAVY INFLUENCE exerted by the Humanist complex of SIECUS and associates on the American Academy of Pediatrics is best exemplified in an AAP pamphlet, *Selected References on Sex Education*. Just as a starter, the following paragraph is found on the inside front cover:

> This pamphlet, prepared by Dr. Lester A. Kirkendall, Professor, and Mr. Deryck Calderwood, both of the Department of Family Life and Home Administration, Oregon State University, Corvallis, in cooperation with J. Roswell Gallagher, M.D., was reviewed and approved by members of the Section Committee and other authorities in the field.

Lester Kirkendall and Deryck Calderwood, both Humanists, are not identified anywhere in the pamphlet as the SIECUS personnel that they are; nevertheless SIECUS has left its traces on every page. For example, the works of SIECUS officials Evelyn Duvall, William Genné, Lester Kirkendall, Ira Reiss, and Helen Southard are listed.

SIECUS-recommended authors whose books appear in this sex education bibliography are Albert Abarbanel, Kenneth C. Barnes, Dorothy Baruch, Lester F. Beck, M. A. Cassidy, Maxine Davis, Karl de Schweinitz, Helen Driver, Albert Ellis, Marie Ets, Sylvia F. Fava, Lawrence K. Frank, Sidonie M. Gruenberg, Alan F. Guttmacher, Jerome Himelhock, Phyllis and Eberhard Kronhausen, Milton I. Levine, Marion Lerrigo, Morris Ploscowe, and Jean H. Seligmann.

A review of Karl de Schweinitz's *Growing Up*, which is one of the works listed for the lower primary grades, seems appropriate at this point. This 73-page story of reproduction is replete with evolutionary concepts and shows an irrepressible urge to tell too much too soon. Consider, for example, the following passage:

> The sperm of men, like those of the four-legged animals, live in two testes in the scrotum, the little bag under the penis.
> The father places the sperm in the body of the mother in much the same way that the four-footed animals do, but more lovingly, and the mother and father can lie together facing each other. The penis, which is usually soft, becomes erect and then can fit into the vagina of the mother which has its own special opening underneath the opening for the urine or waste water.
> When the sperm leave the father they are in something like the milt in which the sperm of fish live. It is called semen.[1]

Humanist George Corner's twin books, *Attaining Manhood* and

Attaining Womanhood, head the reading list for young teenagers in this AAP pamphlet. Although Dr. Corner does not appear in the roster of SIECUS-recommended authors above, he could surely qualify. Numerous graphic illustrations of male and female genitalia appear in his books, including a huge "bird's-eye view" of the vulva, from clitoris to vagina, all "properly" labeled with clinical terms. Later, in a discussion of masturbation (which he classifies as "not harmful"), Dr. Corner reassures his young readers with the statement: "Serious worry over the possible sinfulness of it, or violent efforts to repress it on the part of people in whom the desire is almost irresistible, do much more harm than the act itself."[2]

This author's humanistic tendencies are often revealed in casual remarks like the following: "Ever since in the slow climb of evolution mankind became too wise to live by animal instinct alone. . . ."[3] Moreover, throughout his pages, Dr. Corner consistently credits "Nature" for the marvelous workings of the reproductive system; God as its Creator is never mentioned.

To summarize: 75 percent of the sex education materials listed in the AAP pamphlet can be traced to SIECUS. A final indication of the close affinity between AAP and SIECUS is the fact that SIECUS has regularly participated in AAP annual meetings.

American Association for Health, Physical Education and Recreation (AAHPER)

A Department of the National Education Association
1201 Sixteenth Street, N.W., Washington, D.C.

As SUGGESTED BY SIECUS in its September 1969 form letter, the American Association for Health, Physical Education and Recreation was contacted for supplemental sex education/home and family living information. This request brought the following materials:

- "The Development of Healthy Sexuality," an article by Humanist Mary S. Calderone, executive director of SIECUS, in which she chants the usual SIECUS roundelay, frequently citing her SIECUS associates as experts. In AAHPER's own words, this article is "based on her address presented at the AAHPER Convention in Chicago, March 1966."

- A brochure titled *AAHPER 1968-69 Publications*, listing five booklets by Humanist Helen Southard, a SIECUS official, in collaboration with SIECUS-selected author Marion Lerrigo. These booklets make up what AAHPER terms its "Sex Education Series."

- "Sex Education — Where, When, and How Should It be Taught?" by Helen Manley. This pamphlet supports the SIECUS concept of an integrated, comprehensive K-12 family life program. In fact, Miss Manley's views are so closely in tune with those of SIECUS as to have won her a place as a contributing author in the SIECUS sex education handbook for teachers, *The Individual, Sex, and Society*. Miss Manley is an honor-fellow of AAHPER, having also received the organization's highest recognition, the Luther Gulick award. She served as AAHPER president in 1946-47, but is perhaps best known for her *Curriculum Guide in Sex Education.*

    Published the same year SIECUS was founded, this curriculum guide is rife with SIECUS-Humanist influence. It employs the techniques of sensitivity training; flagrantly invades the privacy of the student and the home; pits child against parent; teaches situation ethics; encourages loose attitudes toward masturbation and homosexuality; covers such topics as sexual intercourse, premarital sex, and birth control as early as Grade 4; and

149

utilizes vulgar gutter language in its junior high school curriculum. Its bibliography suggests that students read SIECUS Study Guides on Sex Education, Homosexuality, and Masturbation, and other SIECUS selections. All in all, close to 60 per cent of the materials and visual aids in the Manley curriculum can be linked to SIECUS.

- A pamphlet titled *What Parents Should Know About Sex Education in the Schools*, published by the National Education Association. which suggests that persons interested in generating sex education programs contact SIECUS for assistance.
- A copy of *NEA News* for May 27, 1969, written in defense of SIECUS. This ten-page newsletter makes a violent attack on the opponents of public school sex education, portraying them as villains of the piece and SIECUS as hero.
- A cover letter suggesting three other sources of sex education information, with SIECUS heading the list.

Several other links between AAHPER and SIECUS merit comment. In June 1968, the two collaborated in formulating *A Resource Guide in Sex Education for the Mentally Retarded*, which should leave no doubt as to where AAHPER stands regarding SIECUS. As might be expected, this guide and its accompanying bibliography and audiovisual section are marked by the stealthy footprints of the SIECUS coterie. April 1971 once again found the two organizations cheek-to-cheek, with SIECUS' educational exhibit on display at AAHPER's 86th Anniversary Convention in Detroit. Delivering the keynote address to some 10,000 educators at this function, according to SIECUS' April 1970 Newsletter, was Humanist Margaret Mead, an inveterate SIECUS fellow traveler.

In view of the act that AAHPER is a department of the National Education Association, it is not surprising to learn that at least four SIECUS officials — Sally R. Williams (president, NEA Department of School Nurses), Elizabeth Koontz (NEA past president), Virgil Rogers (director, NEA Educational Implications Automation Project, since 1963), and Bennetta B. Washington — are also members of NEA.

American Association of Marriage Counselors, Inc. (AAMC)*

3603 Lemmon Avenue, Dallas, Texas

THE AMERICAN ASSOCIATION OF MARRIAGE COUNSELORS, founded in 1942, is an organization "dedicated to professional marriage counseling and to the field of marriage and family relations."[1] Its membership roster includes more than 600 persons, including psychologists, social workers, ministers, physicians, sociologists, attorneys, and educators.

The president of this organization during 1971 was Dr. Thomas C. McGinnis, then also vice president of the SIECUS front organization, the American Association of Sex Educators and Counselors. He is director of the program in sex education at New York University's Graduate School of Education, and is publicized as "a pioneer in techniques of group, family, and marathon therapy."[2] In explaining the significance of sensitivity training in Dr. McGinnis' course at the University, the *Washington Post* of February 21, 1969, reported:

> The sensitivity training is a major part of a new course, the Nation's first master's degree program for teachers of elementary school sex education.

The foreword of Dr. McGinnis' book, *Your First Year of Marriage*, was written by SIECUS official David Mace, then executive director of the American Association of Sex Educators and Counselors.

Another past president of AAMC is SIECUS board member Wardell Pomeroy, who is also on the board of consultants of *Sexology* magazine. Other SIECUS officials who have previously served as president of AAMC include Warren Johnson, Sophia Kleegman, Robert Laidlaw, Emily Mudd, Ethel Nash, James A. Peterson, and Aaron Rutledge.

One AAMC supervisor is Dr. Helene Papanek, a Humanist and an active member of the New York Society for Ethical Culture. She is also a consultant to the Veterans Administration, director of the Alfred

*Since this entry was written, AAMC has changed its name to American Association of Marriage and Family Counselors, and is now located at 225 Yale Avenue, Claremont, California. However, despite the change in name and address, the organization maintains its liaison with SIECUS. It elected Dr. Laura J. Singer of SIECUS as its president for 1972.

Adler Institute, and supervising psychiatrist for group psychotherapy at the Postgraduate Center for Mental Health and the Alfred Adler Mental Hygiene Clinic. Some advisory committee members are the Reverend William Genné, Lester Kirkendall, Sophia Kleegman, Harold Lief, and David Mace — all of SIECUS. Another SIECUS director, Elizabeth Koontz (an activist in the "women's liberation" movement), is an honorary member of AAMC. Other SIECUS board members who are also members of AAMC, some having served in executive capacities, are Mary Calderone, Harold T. Christensen, Evelyn Duvall, Harriet Pilpel, Isadore Rubin, Rabbi Jeshaia Schnitzer, Ralph Slovenko, and Clark Vincent.

According to a promotional brochure, the American Association of Marriage Counselors works closely with other professional groups to "establish and revise state laws pertaining to marriage, divorce, licensing of marriage counselors and related subjects. AAMC has held cooperative conferences with the American Association of Obstetricians and Gynecologists, the National Council on Family Relations, the American Bar Association, the American Psychological Association and many other organizations."[3]

The promotional brochure continues: "AAMC officers and members provide factual material on marriage and family problems to newspapers, television, radio and magazines. Members speak to many lay groups and write extensively for periodicals and professional journals."[4] Apparently, AAMC's sphere of influence knows no bounds in the field.

Considering all the ties noted between AAMC and SIECUS, what AAMC executive director Edward J. Rydman has to say in answer to inquiries for help in setting up sex education programs seems ludicrous: "For information on sex/family life education programs write to SIECUS, 1790 Broadway, New York 10019."

American Association of Sex Educators and Counselors (AASEC)

815 Fifteenth Street, N.W., Washington, D.C.

THE STATED PURPOSE of the American Association of Sex Educators and Counselors is "To assist those responsible for counseling on sex-related matters and those responsible for sex education programs in the schools and elsewhere through training, education and research."[1] This organization was founded in 1967, when SIECUS was in its infancy, and since its inception has had a sizeable number of SIECUS officials and associates at its controls. For this reason, AASEC is considered by some to be a SIECUS "front."

With AASEC assuming the role of associate director in the sex education drama, a familiar cast of stars emerges to thicken the plot. Playing dual roles, for example, are the following individuals:

SIECUS official	Office or capacity at AASEC
Warren Johnson	Past president
Lester Kirkendall	Advisory Committee member; former vice-president
Sophia Kleegman	Advisory Committee member
Elizabeth Koontz	Honorary member
Harold Lief	Advisory Committee member
David Mace	Advisory Committee member
James A. Peterson	Advisory Committee member
Isadore Rubin	Advisory Committee member (deceased 1970)
Philip M. Sarrel	Advisory Committee member
Gilbert Shimmel	Advisory Committee member

Like its parent organization, SIECUS, the AASEC has a close relationship with the bawdy magazine, *Sexology*. At least nine members of AASEC's Advisory Committee — Rev. William Genné, Warren Johnson, David Mace, and Humanists LeMon Clark, Sol Gordon, Robert Harper,* Lester Kirkendall, Isadore Rubin, and Walter Stokes — have either served on *Sexology's* staff or contributed articles to it.

*Besides being a contributor to *Sexology*, Dr. Harper is a former president of the American Association of Marriage Counselors and is co-author with fellow Humanist Dr. Albert Ellis of *Creative Marriage*.

153

At least three members of the AASEC Advisory Committee — Rabbi Balfour Brickner, Rev. William Genné, and Isadore Rubin — have also been involved with Communist causes.

Other notables serving AASEC in some capacity include: *Dorothy Harrison* (AASEC president, 1970–72), who is also director of a Head Start project that is concerned with creating a national health curriculum including Family Life and Sex Education; Communist fellow traveler *Wilbur J. Cohen* (AASEC honorary member), formerly Under Secretary of Health, Education, and Welfare; *Dr. Carl Schulz* (AASEC honorary member), also Director, Office of Population Affairs, U.S. Department of Health, Education, and Welfare; *Gertrude Hunter* (AASEC Treasurer, 1970–72), U.S. Office of Economic Opportunity; *Nancy Blackmun* (AASEC Northeastern regional chairman) of Cambridge, Massachusetts, daughter of Associate Justice Harry Blackmun of the Supreme Court; SIECUS ad signer *John Chandler Jr.* (AASEC Board of Directors, 1970–72), also vice president of the National Association of Independent Schools; *Mrs. Elizabeth Nichols* (AASEC Board of Directors) of Planned Parenthood–World Population; and *Dr. Charity Runden* (AASEC Advisory Committee member), a staunch SIECUS supporter, Unitarian, and executive director of the Educational Foundation for Human Sexuality at Montclair (N.J.) State College, whose sex education materials are inundated with SIECUS-Humanist philosophy.

In keeping with its heavy SIECUS accent, AASEC has generously seasoned its programs and conferences with SIECUS-Humanist concepts and personalities. In fact, AASEC's Second Annual Conference, held at the Sheraton-Park Hotel in Washington, D.C., in April 1969, must have brought sheer ecstasy to SIECUS and company.

Delivering the keynote address at the conference was Humanist Lester Kirkendall, and his SIECUS colleagues took turns on the podium as featured speakers.[2] Another presiding officer for the conference was Dr. Eleanor Hamilton, also a member of AASEC's Advisory Committee and author of *Sex Before Marriage*. In her book, Dr. Hamilton advises readers sixteen years old and under to employ mutual masturbation as a substitute for too early intercourse. Providing her young readers with detailed instructions for manipulation, she recommends, as a precaution against possible frustration, that "if two teenagers do decide to pet, they would be wise to see to it that each comes to orgasm." As for the boy of fifteen or older who is not satisfied with such trifles as mutual masturbation and wishes to experience intercourse, Dr. Hamilton suggests that "he can have it with a prostitute," or "he can *force* his girl to have intercourse with him"; but, she adds, he will be "less than satisfied with the result." Rather, he might "find a sympathetic and experienced older woman with whom he can establish a tender and loving relationship." Although not a SIECUS board member, Eleanor Hamilton can often be found at SIECUS "happenings."

Also cooperating in the 1969 conference as a panel discussion participant was another AASEC Advisory Committee member, Monsignor James T. McHugh, director of the Family Life Division of the U.S. Catholic Conference. The association of a Catholic priest with AASEC is a paradox in itself, considering the fact that AASEC membership is generously laced with Planned Parenthood activists. Furthermore, the "Get Acquainted Reception" for that conference was sponsored by Ortho Research Foundation and EmKo Company, both suppliers of contraceptive devices.[3]

In 1970 the Third Annual Conference of AASEC had — according to an announcement in the March 1970 SIECUS Newsletter — many SIECUS board members, including Gerald Sanctuary, then executive director of SIECUS, as speakers and discussion leaders.

In 1971, a noteworthy function sponsored by AASEC was the Fourth National Sex Institute, which was conducted at the Sheraton-Jefferson Hotel in St. Louis, Missouri, April 15–18. Virginia Johnson of the Masters and Johnson sex research team, SIECUS director and Humanist, chaired a panel at this event. Special features of this meeting included sensitivity training sessions for all those wishing to participate; a session in which male and female homosexuals conveyed to the audience their views of each other and their goals; and the use by guest speakers of such common sewer language as "screwing," "organ grinding," and "a kiss on the lips, a brush on the breasts, and a pipe in the pelvis."

The most offensive program event was introduced by Dr. W. Cody Wilson, former executive director of the President's Committee on Obscenity and Pornography — the same which concluded that there was a "need" to legalize pornography in the United States. Following a few comments to set the pace, Dr. Wilson presented a German-made color film without name or credits. It featured a performance in which a man and woman entered a room, embraced and undressed one another, caressed each other's genitals, and performed oral stimulation on each other. The man masturbated, and the couple performed sexual intercourse, which was photographed from several angles. After the film ended, AASEC executive director Patricia Schiller commented gleefully, "The chandelier is tingling and so is our audience."

The Sixth National Sex Institute, held March 29–April 1, 1973, was adorned with such SIECUS personalities as Dr. Mary Calderone (who received an AASEC award), Lester Kirkendall, Warren R. Johnson, John Money, Derek Burleson, David Mace, James McCary, and Rev. William Genné, as well as pornography peddler Dr. Albert Ellis, who participated as a leader of the Institute's Human Growth Sessions.[4]

Among the participants in the conference preliminary to the above Institute were representatives of such organizations as the American Association of Marriage and Family Counselors; the American College of Obstretricians and Gynecologists; the American Home Economics Association; the Citizens Committee on Population and the American Future; the National Association of Social Workers; the National Council of Churches; the National Council On Family Relations; the National Institute of Mental Health; the U.S. Department of Health, Education, and Welfare; and the Unitarian-Universalist Church.[5]

In addition to its cooperation with SIECUS, AASEC initiates cooperative action with Planned Parenthood-World Population, the National Education Association, and the American Association of Marriage and Family Counselors.

American College of Obstetricians and Gynecologists (ACOG)

79 West Monroe Street, Chicago, Illinois

AT THE ELEVENTH ANNUAL MEETING of the American College of Obstetricians and Gynecologists, held in New York City on May 22, 1963, Humanist Alan F. Guttmacher of Planned Parenthood addressed ACOG's Committee on Maternal Health, suggesting that ACOG "assume its proper role and offer leadership in dealing with the socio-medical problems related to their specialty: contraception, therapeutic abortion, sterilization, illegitimacy, perinatal mortality, teenage marriage and divorce, venereal disease, and family life (sex) education."[1] At this same time Dr. Mary Calderone was in her eleventh year as medical director of Planned Parenthood, in close association with Dr. Guttmacher.

In May 1964 — the same month and year the SIECUS Charter was granted — the executive board of ACOG established a standing Committee on Education and Family Life, which later developed a booklet entitled *Family Life Education — A Professional Responsibility*. Its fourth edition (1968) acknowledges the encouragement and support of seven members of this standing committee, and further states:

> . . . We are also indebted to Mr. Deryck Calderwood, Consultant for Educational Services, SIECUS (Sex Information and Educational Council of the U.S.), and Mr. William Carlyon, Consultant for Health and Fitness, American Medical Association, who reviewed the contents and provided us with their professional appraisal of the material.[2]

The printing of the 39-page booklet, which was intended to aid physicians in developing programs in family life education, was financed by a grant from Ortho Pharmaceutical Corporation.

Although the ACOG booklet boasts "a wide selection of the best audio-visual and printed materials presently available," it soon becomes obvious that ACOG's featured bill of fare is à la SIECUS. The following authors listed in the booklet as being endorsed by ACOG are SIECUS board or staff members:

Jessie Bernard	Catherine S. Chilman
Mary Calderone	Cornelia V. Christenson
Deryck Calderwood	Evelyn Duvall

Reverend William Genné	Emily Mudd
John H. Gagnon	Ethel Nash
S. Leon Israel	James A. Peterson
Warren R. Johnson	Wardell Pomeroy
Lester Kirkendall	Ira L. Reiss
Harold Lief	Isadore Rubin
David Mace	Helen Southard
Frederick Margolis	Clark Vincent
James L. McCary	

A number of the above are also Humanists.

Furthermore, the works of at least fifty-nine SIECUS-selected authors can be found in ACOG's catalog — in this case, too many to list. As for films, 60 per cent of those offered are either SIECUS-endorsed or produced with the assistance or consultation of an individual SIECUS official. There are at least sixty references to SIECUS in this brochure.

ACOG, incidentally, rates the controversial slide series, *How Babies Are Made*, as "excellent" for preschool and "outstanding" for elementary grades.* These slides have become so controversial that even SIECUS is denying its major role in their development. It should be noted, however, that the entire book of the same name is an exact reproduction of the film strip. And the first page of the book states: "The contents of this book were prepared in consultation with the Sex Information and Education Council of the United States (SIECUS) and the Child Study Association of America, to whom grateful acknowledgment is made."

In addition, ACOG soberly suggests for senior high school students

---

How Babies Are Made is a set of colored slides depicting, in paper sculptures, various animals in the act of sexual intercourse. Designed for tots from three to eight years of age, the slides come equipped with a narrative for use by the teacher. One scene shows a male dog sitting up with genitalia exposed, including an erect penis. The narration reads: "In dogs, as in cats, horses and many other animals, the father's sperm come from parts of his body called testicles. The sperm go out of his body through a special tube between his legs called a penis. Close behind the dog's penis are two little bags that hold the testicles."

In the following scene the male dog is shown mounting the female, as the narrator explains: "When a father dog wants to place his sperm in a mother dog, he climbs on her back. This is called mating. He places his penis inside an opening in her body called the vagina and then lets his sperm go into her."

Another scene involves the same performance with a rooster and a hen. Later, the slides take a similar approach in their account of human mating, showing a striking view of father's and mother's sex organs, and culminating in a bedroom scene of father and mother under the covers.

the notorious *Guide to Sexology* — a compilation of articles that have appeared in *Sexology* magazine, with a heavy accent on the sexually bizarre — as well as SIECUS Reprint No. 04, a *Sexology* article dated January 1967, written by SIECUS board member Warren Johnson.

ACOG's organization itself has experienced the "SIECUS touch." At least two SIECUS officials, Sophia Kleegman and Humanist William Masters, are members of ACOG, as well as diplomates of the American Board of Obstetrics and Gynecology. The latter organization sets the standards for this particular field of medicine. And finally, sitting in the editor's seat of ACOG's official voice, the *Journal of the American College of Obstetricians and Gynecologists*, from 1965 until his death in 1971, was SIECUS board member Dr. S. Leon Israel.

American Medical Association (AMA)

535 North Dearborn Street, Chicago, Illinois

WHEN THE AMERICAN MEDICAL ASSOCIATION was contacted for assistance in setting up sex education programs, as suggested by SIECUS in its September 1969 form letter, a reprint of a speech by Dr. Mary Calderone of SIECUS, and a pamphlet, *AMA Health Education Materials Catalog*, were received. Page 13 of the catalog lists seven booklets which make up AMA's "Sex Education Series." Of the seven, five are written by Humanist Helen Southard (SIECUS board member) with Marion Lerrigo (SIECUS-selected author). The five booklet titles are: *A Story About You, Finding Yourself, Approaching Adulthood, Facts Aren't Enough,* and *Parents' Responsibility.*

The series is approved and published by the Joint Committee on Health Problems in Education of the American Medical Association and the National Education Association, and is somewhat less offensive than most of its kind. However, certain points cannot be overlooked. First, of all the physicians available in the United States, the authors chose as their medical consultant Humanist Milton J. E. Senn, M.D., who by his own admission does not believe in teaching moral absolutes. Second, many of the graphics of the sex organs seem unnecessary, and much of the information presented is too descriptive for the age level at which it is directed. Space permits detailed review of only one of five Southard-Lerrigo booklets, *Finding Yourself.*

Finding Yourself was designed and written for ages 12 to 13. This booklet offers such details as the following:

> . . . The outside opening of the vagina is between the legs, where it is protected by folds of skin and flesh known as the *vulva.* Where the inner folds of the vulva meet in front there is a small, sensitive tip called the *clitoris.* The opening of the vagina may be partially closed by a rather thick membrane, which is called the *hymen.*[1]

Presumably, following such passages, a teacher might turn to an enlarged diagram of the female genitalia, making this the topic of classroom discussion, with both sexes present. (One wonders how even *adults* might react in a similar setting.)

The following chapter carries on, discussing the male genitalia:

> The penis hangs in front of the testes. It is shaped something like a

thumb, but is usually larger, although it varies in size. A tube, known as the *urethra*, runs through the length of the penis.

Shortly afterward, we find:

Although usually limp and soft, the penis, under sexual excitement of mind or body, fills with blood so that it becomes firm, and an erection occurs. In a boy whose sex organs have matured, semen may then spurt out of the erect penis as a result of the contraction of certain tissues. This is called an ejaculation. The penis then becomes limp again. Erection and ejaculation are accompanied by sensations in the sex organs that are intensely pleasurable.

Other topics dealt with include:

- *Masturbation* — Like most of its kind, this booklet implies that the only harmful effects of masturbation are the "guilty feelings" that may result; no attempt is made to discuss the moral ramifications.
- *Sexual intercourse* — Students are given a detailed account of the sex act.

The bibliographies in the books of this series carry the SIECUS message via the works of such authors as Dorothy Baruch, Karl de Schweinitz, Marie Hall Ets, Sidonie M. Gruenberg, Eric W. Johnson, Milton Levine, and Jean Seligmann — all SIECUS-endorsed authors — as well as SIECUS official Evelyn Duvall. In addition, the series suggests the reading of pamphlets by:

> Child Study Association of America
> Public Affairs Pamphlets
> Science Research Associates, Inc.

In February 1966, the *Journal of the American Medical Association* (*JAMA*), the official voice of AMA, carried an article by Dr. Thomas E. Shaffer titled "The Role of the School and the Community in Sex Education and Related Problems." In it Dr. Shaffer expressed enthusiasm for public school sex education beginning at preschool level. After outlining this need, he exulted in the fact that schools could now exert their influence on even the tiniest tots in the matter of sexuality:

Newly developing programs like "Operation Head Start" provide a special opportunity for getting closer to mothers and young children . . . . What a novel chance this is for schools and other institutions and agencies to get in "early licks" never before so attainable!

In later speaking of SIECUS in his conclusion, Dr. Shaffer said: "I recommend this council for information and stimulation in the coming years."

There can be no doubt that AMA took his advice. The late 1960's found this association hobnobbing with SIECUS in public; SIECUS was featured as a participant in AMA's 1968 and 1969 conventions.

Then, AMA tackled a *Handbook on Human Sexuality*, designed as an aid for physicians and medical students. The handbook idea was proposed by the AMA's Committee on Human Reproduction, of which Dr. Calderone was a member. AMA trustees assigned the supervision of its preparation to SIECUS official Dr. John C. Ballin,[2] who was secretary of the AMA committee. To make matters cozier, two of the six-member editorial committee formed in 1969 for the purpose of developing the handbook were from the SIECUS staff: Doctors Harold Lief* and Philip M. Sarrel.[3] The 200-page handbook the committee produced encompassed "every aspect of human sexuality." It was designed for use in the nation's medical schools, and thus will, no doubt, permeate the medical profession with the SIECUS message until the desired saturation point is reached among physicians and ultimately among their patients.

In keeping with the anomalous tendencies of SIECUS, the AHA's Council on Mental Health issued a statement supporting the drive of the Gay Liberation movement to legitimize homosexuality, according to the *New York Times* of June 6, 1974. The governing board of AMA has also endorsed the concept of "decriminalizing" marijuana. This action links AMA with a list of other organizations that have arrived at the same position, including the American Bar Association, the American Public Health Association, the National Commission on Marijuana and Drug Abuse, the National Council of Churches, and the National Education Association.

But perhaps the most significant turn of events occurred in June 1973, when the AMA House of Delegates affirmed the right of physicians to perform abortions:

*Harold Lief, M.D., served as president of SIECUS during this period. He is also director of the University of Pennsylvania's Center for the Study of Sex Education in Medicine. Training courses at the center include (1) a postgraduate program in marriage counseling and family life, and (2) proposed programs concerning continuing education, and work on a master's degree in family planning and sex education.

In Dr. Lief's opinion, as stated in *American Medical News* (April 26, 1971), the important thing about the center is that it serves as a communications network reaching the deans of all U.S. medical schools. In the decade ahead, Dr. Lief predicts, all medical schools will teach courses in human sexuality, and training in family planning will be integrated with instruction in sex and marriage counseling.

Dr. Lief's predecessor at the center was SIECUS' Dr. Emily Mudd. She has since moved on to serve as co-director of training at the Humanist-run Masters and Johnson clinic.

The Principles of Medical Ethics of the AMA do not prohibit a physician from performing an abortion that is performed in accordance with good medical practice and under circumstances that do not violate the laws of the community in which he practices.

It is not surprising to learn that for years Humanist Mary Calderone, an AMA member, had been working behind the scenes, using her strategic position as medical director of Planned Parenthood to inject pro-abortion propaganda into AMA's bloodstream. The *New York Times* of February 7, 1977, credited Dr. Calderone with having carried on for years a personal crusade to induce AMA trustees to reverse the organization's anti-abortion stand. Finally, between the pro-abortion pressure exerted by Dr. Calderone and her Humanist colleagues within AMA and the anti-life decisions of the Supreme Court in 1973, the prestigious physician group caved in and sanctioned a procedure it had long condemned as highly improper and unethical.

For the record, at least eleven SIECUS directors are members of the AMA. They are John C. Ballin, George Packer Berry, Mary S. Calderone, Evalyn Gendel, Sophia Kleegman, Robert Laidlaw, Harold Lief, Emily Mudd, William Peltz, John Rock, and Philip M. Sarrel.

American School Health Association (ASHA)

515 East Main Street, Kent, Ohio

Sex Education

THE AMERICAN SCHOOL HEALTH ASSOCIATION publishes one of the most widely used sex education guidelines, offered to the nation's schools as a suggested program for Kindergarten through Grade 12. Titled "Growth Patterns and Sex Education," this guideline was presented in the May 1967 issue of *The Journal of School Health,* a monthly periodical published by the ASHA.[1] The guide (as is brought out in its Foreword) had its inception in the sex education program of the Worthington (Ohio) Public Schools. However, the concepts in the guide coincide conspicuously with concepts found in the *Handbook on Sex Instruction in Swedish Schools*, published by the National Board of Education of Sweden.[2]

The decision to establish sex education guidelines was reached at ASHA's annual meeting on November 10, 1963, just a few months before SIECUS was founded. Already in the early stages of development by 1964, the guide was further refined and clarified in 1965–66. Members of the ASHA's 1966 Committee on Health Guidance in Sex Education, which was responsible for the final draft, were SIECUS director and Humanist Evalyn Gendel, and Sally R. Williams, who would be a SIECUS official by the time the guide was in print. Sally Williams is perhaps best known for having initiated the sex education program for Anaheim Union High School in California, considered to be a "SIECUS showcase." Another committee member who made a significant contribution to the guide was Humanist Joseph S. Darden, then assistant professor of Health Education at Newark State College, now known as Kean College, in Union, New Jersey.

Close scrutiny of AHSA's guidelines reveals a heavy SIECUS influence: an obvious absence of moral absolutes, repeated encouragement of role-playing (a feature of sensitivity training), and the usual probing into every possible aspect of the private life of the student and his family. In the chapter for Grade 8, the subject of masturbation is dealt with in such a way as to encourage its practice. Page 78, for example, gives this definition:

> Masturbation is the process of self-stimulation of the genital organs to

the point of orgasm. Many authorities agree that, under some circumstances, it may serve as a constructive temporary outlet for physical tensions related to the sex drive.

Listed under resources for students and teachers are the works of SIECUS board members Evelyn Duvall, Warren Johnson, and Humanists Lester Kirkendall, the late Isadore Rubin, and Helen Southard. Also listed are writings of the following SIECUS-selected authors:

Dorothy Baruch	Rabbi Roland Gittelsohn
Henry A. Bowman	Sidonie M. Gruenberg
Michael Cassidy	Marion Lerrigo
Lawrence Crawley, *et al.*	Bishop James Pike
Maxine Davis	Mary McGee Williams
Ralph Eckert	

Taking the lead in ASHA's film resource listings are the same films SIECUS promotes, especially the slide series *How Babies Are Made,* recommended for Kindergarten through Grade 1.

A few other individuals associated in some way with the American School Health Association should not be overlooked. Listed among associate editors of the monthly *Journal of School Health* are SIECUS official Evalyn Gendel and Elena Sliepcevich, who played a major role in the development of 3M Company's School Health Education Study (SHES) — a decisive SIECUS "creation." Also affiliated with ASHA as an honor-fellow is Helen Manley, a contributing author to SIECUS's handbook for teachers and counselors, *The Individual, Sex, and Society.*[3]

Drug Education

Channeling its activities into new fields, ASHA (like many organizations discussed in PART II) has recently embarked on a program of drug education, creating an implication that cannot be avoided: namely, that the same Humanist-oriented groups promoting the SIECUS ideology of situation ethics in sex education have drafted many of the courses in drug education. Consequently, the situation ethics phraseology has already infested this new field.

According to catalog accounts, these drug programs "avoid preaching," "omit scare tactics," are non-moralizing, confront the student with "many points of view," and encourage him to make his own decisions "based on the information presented." ASHA's new teaching guide, *Teaching About Drugs*, designed for Kindergarten through Grade 12, takes the same course. This guide was prepared by ASHA and the Pharmaceutical Manufacturers Association jointly. A few passages as quoted in a newspaper account are illustrative. Just how dangerous teenagers will consider mind-crippling drugs to be after they are presented with the following "facts" is anyone's guess:

> In the 1800s, the United States had a sizable population of middle-aged ladies who were opium addicts. They sipped patent medicines — such as Mrs. Winslow's Soothing Syrup and Pierce's Golden Medical Discovery — that were generously laced with opium and morphine. . . .
>
> Marijuana, too, was used in patent medicines in the 19th Century, promoted as a cure for "all cases of consumption, bronchitis, asthma, catarrh, nervous debility and all nervous complaints." . . .
>
> Marijuana was not declared illegal until 1937, after an energetic campaign by Bible Belt congressmen armed with lurid tales of sinful acts committed by marijuana-drugged men and women. . . .[4]

And from the same news report:

> . . . Scientists have discovered a direct link between excessive drug use and body damage in only four cases: barbiturates, alcohol, cigarettes and glue. With other drugs, the effect on the body has not yet been determined.

The foregoing is, at best, a gross misrepresentation of facts in view of the abundant scientific information that is available. Consider, for example, the following medical data, which are supported by an ever-increasing number of authoritative sources:

1. Doctors Harold Kolansky and William T. Moore, both Philadelphia psychiatrists, made a five-year study of marijuana smokers. According to their report published in the April 19, 1971 *Journal of the American Medical Association*, marijuana is anything but safe. They found in their patients "serious psychological effects, sometimes *complicated by neurologic signs and symptoms.*"[5] (emphasis added) Some patients who smoked marijuana four or five times weekly for many months showed indications of neurologic impairment, such as slurred speech, staggering gait, hand tremors, thought disorders, and disturbed depth perception. These symptoms clearly indicate physical damage to the brain and are not connected with the psychological effects of marijuana.

2. Writing in *Current Medical Digest*, James C. Munch stated: "The serious results following exposure to Marijuana, especially when smoked . . . appear to be due to progressive, irreversible damage to various parts of the brain."[6] Dr. Harry Wilmer supported this opinion regarding marijuana in the *Journal of the American Medical Association*: "There are often signs of organic brain damage and it appears to us that some residual impairment, some permanent defect, will be the lot of many of our patients."[7]

These findings are further corroborated by a research paper published in the December 4, 1971 issue of *The Lancet*, a British medical journal. According to this report, ten youthful patients with three-to-eleven-year histories of marijuana use showed serious brain atrophy comparable to the atrophy that normally takes place between the ages of 70 and 90. The researchers concluded, in part: "We feel that our results suggest that regular use of cannabis produces cerebral atrophy in young adults," adding: "It must be stressed that cerebral atrophy indicates irreversible brain damage."

3. Dr. Irwin L. Lubow, a leading New York dermatologist, has stated:

Regardless of what you may have heard, drugs, including marijuana, do have specific pharmacological effects on the internal systems of the body as well as on the skin and hair . . . in our own practice we have seen more than 100 cases of excessive hair loss among both boys and girls. Acne also is caused by drug use, particularly among girls. Why? Our research suggests that drugs affect the function of the sebaceous glands and the physiology of the hair structure.[8]

4. One highly respected authority in the field of drug research, Professor Gabriel Nahas of Columbia University, states in his book, *Marijuana: Deceptive Weed*, that marijuana definitely damages the genes. Substantiating this conclusion is Dr. Morton Stenchever, professor of obstetrics at the University of Utah Medical School, who has found that both marijuana and hashish cause measurable chromosome damage.[9] Moreover, current scientific studies show that in countries where hashish and marijuana are used extensively, an unusually high percentage of malformed children are born.

5. A *New York Times* article reporting on the effect of drug use on the vital organs stated, "Hepatitis, or inflammation of the liver, and infections of the heart are said to be common, serious medical complications of drug abuse that can require long, expensive hospitalization."[10] Dr. David C. Dale, chief medical resident physician at the University of Washington Hospital in Seattle, said that a recent 23-year-old patient had apparently suffered a severe heart attack due to an overdose of amphetamines, which she had injected into her veins. The article continued, "The woman is fortunate because she survived her medical complication of drug abuse. However, many addicts die from medical complications of their habit before they even reach a hospital for treatment."

Taking the above reports into consideration, one can only wonder why ASHA's assessment of drug-related body damage is so misleading.

American Social Health Association (ASHA)
1740 Broadway, New York, New York

Sex Education

SIECUS, in its September 1969 form letter, listed the American Social Health Association as a source of additional sex education information. Pulling strings at the ASHA end of the line is SIECUS board member Helen Southard, who is also a member of ASHA, as was Isadore Rubin until his death. Still another connecting link with SIECUS is Dr. Leona Baumgartner, an official SIECUS sponsor, who is a member of ASHA's board of directors.

On request, ASHA sends out a wealth of material on family life/sex education. Its listing of *Selected and Annotated Readings for Family Life Educators* was prepared by Elizabeth S. Force, ASHA's director of family life education. Mrs. Force is also a consultant on family life for the American Social Hygiene Association, as well as for the American Institute of Family Relations, which is linked to SIECUS by Lester Kirkendall and Evelyn Duvall.* But she is perhaps best known for having assisted in the development of 3M Company's notorious SHES (School Health Education Study) Program, which has been described as "designed to create an allegiance to a humanistic, godless world government."[1] Mrs. Force worked diligently with such notables as Dr. Mary Calderone and Wallace Fulton of SIECUS on the SHES program.

The pamphlet on sex education developed for ASHA by Mrs. Force offers the usual SIECUS bill of fare, recommending works by SIECUS officials Jessie Bernard and Harold Christensen, and SIECUS-selected authors Robert R. Bell, Hyman Rodman, Eleanor Maccoby, and Humanist Margaret Mead. Another prominent Humanist, Erik H. Erikson, helped round out this comparatively small reading list of eighteen books. Other books on this list — seemingly unrelated to SIECUS and company — are undoubtedly in keeping with the goals and objectives of SIECUS. A case in point is Carl F. Hereford's *Changing Parental Attitudes Through Group Discussion*, published one year before SIECUS was founded. Mrs. Force's annotation on this book bears the quotation:

*Lester Kirkendall has served on the board of trustees of the American Institute of Family Relations; Evelyn Duvall is their regional consultant.

A report on a scientific procedure designed to test the hypothesis *that parents will change their attitudes if they meet informally with groups of other parents to discuss their problems*, and *that the children of these parents will also show change . . . .* The results set forth leave no doubt about the value of the group-discussion method as described here. [emphasis added]

This should dissolve any remaining doubt as to what the sensitivity training advocates are really up to in their unwavering enthusiasm for group discussion techniques.

Another formal publication of ASHA is titled *About Family Life Education*. In it, SIECUS is named as a "national resource," along with numerous SIECUS-dominated organizations. Also listed as action groups urging the need for this program are UNICEF, UNESCO, and WHO — all United Nations agencies. At least 90 percent of all the avenues for exploration in sex education suggested by this ASHA pamphlet can be linked to SIECUS in some way.

As for its relations with government, ASHA notes:

Regular liaison is maintained with Federal departments such as the U.S. Public Health Service, the National Institutes of Health, the Army, Navy and Air Force, the Federal Bureau of Narcotics, U.S. Defense Supply Agency, the Children's Bureau, the Office of Education, and the National Research Council.

ASHA is largely financed through government grants and United Community Fund campaigns.

Drug Education

In recent years, the American Social Health Association has added drug abuse as a major program area, with the claim of being the "major national voluntary resource for professional consultation" in this field.[2] The same brochure states that ASHA "constantly assists communities to diagnose their problems and produces publications for teachers, guidance counselors and youth workers."

Schools and other agencies selecting drug education materials should do so with knowledge of the following fact: ASHA employs as director of its Narcotics Addiction Program Humanist, Dr. Charles Winick.* The significance of this can only be measured after further study of the Humanist stance on the subject of drugs. One Humanist-related group, the Unitarian-Universalist Association, officially passed a resolution in 1970 calling for legalization of marijuana. As reported in

---

*Dr. Winick is professor of sociology at the City University of New York. He has served as consultant to federal and state legislative and investigating committees concerned with narcotics.

the July 6th issue of the *Paterson* (N.J.) *Evening News*, ". . . the resolution said present laws in both the United States and Canada are 'based largely on public hysteria and myth' and that laws are 'making criminals of and causing undue and unjust punishment to many persons.' " In calling for marijuana's legalization, the report suggested it be subject to the same restrictions as alcohol.

Numerous issues of *The Humanist* indicate a decisive tolerance for marijuana, most articles opposing any legal sanctions against its use. Typically, in 1967 a Humanist-sponsored legal defense fund was established for Professor Leslie A. Fiedler of the State University of New York at Buffalo, a fellow Humanist and marijuana advocate. (Professor Fiedler was convicted in 1970, and sentenced to six months' imprisonment, for "maintaining a premise where marijuana was being used."[3]) While the Fiedler Defense Fund was being organized, an editorial in *The Humanist* expressed the following opinion:

> There is considerable scientific testimony that marijuana is not physiologically addictive, and its use may be less harmful than alcohol or tobacco. Whether it is debilitating in the long run, or whether its use leads to a quest for more intense kicks, is for many still an open question. If it does not have these consequences, then perhaps the same Puritan conscience which outlawed Demon Rum is now committing a grave miscarriage of justice by entrapping and imprisoning occasional users of marijuana and subjecting them to public calumny and vilification.[4]

With the advent of compulsory drug education in the public schools, the Humanist complex has found new channels through which to spread its propaganda. ASHA's drug program is one example. It is apparent from ASHA's literature that, like his fellow Humanists, Dr. Winick adheres to the following opinions:

1. Where drug education is concerned, information should be conveyed "in a nonjudgmental, nonmoralistic manner."[5]

2. Instead of denouncing drug use, drug discussion groups should present "a variety of viewpoints," accompanied by the "pro and con for each point of view."[6] This, of course, is a description of the Humanist "open forum" approach.

3. ". . . the addict should be regarded as a sick person, with a chronic disease* which requires almost emergency action,"[7] rather than

---

*The statement that drug addiction is a "disease" implies that the user originally had little or no control over his destiny, and that he "contracted" his so-called illness in the same way one might succumb to a virus. The fact is that the drug user became addicted by using drugs with the free consent of his own will. Further, no amount of antibiotic or any other known drug, such as methadone, can bring about his total recovery. The suggestion offered by Dr. Winick that drug addiction be removed from the criminal category and declared a "public health matter" can only enhance the social acceptance of drug usage — or,

as a criminal who regularly plunders the private property of innocent citizens to support his habit.

4. Among other "total treatment" institutions, Synanon must be considered a "significant development in terms of treatment"[8] of the addict. (The founder of Synanon, Charles E. Dederich, and Synanon's director, Dan L. Garrett Jr., are both Humanists. So avid are the Humanists for the Synanon method that it was a featured topic at the 1966 American Humanist Association's Annual Conference, the theme of which was "The Humanist Alternative." The program for April 29, 1966, lists "Synanon group techniques and approaches" as the topic for a session led by Dederich and Garrett.[9])

Dr. Winick's talents were further utilized by ASHA as author of the discussion guide for *The Underground Bird*. This play was commissioned and published by ASHA as part of its drug program and is, at best, part of a softening-up campaign to bring about eventual social acceptance of drugs. Written and produced by a division of the Family Service Association of America (whose general director is SIECUS official Clark Blackburn), the play is more closely examined under the "Drugs" heading in the entry for that association, later in PART II.

Among notables serving on ASHA's Drug Dependence and Abuse Advisory Committee is Dr. Granville Larimore, First Deputy Commissioner, New York State Department of Health in Albany. Dr. Larimore is also a member of the notorious Public Affairs [Pamphlets] Committee.

---

worse, induce the legalization of drugs. History has shown that the only effective measure against *all* crime is application of a stringent penalty by law enforcement agencies. The current national scoreboard supports this concept. This nation has experienced the recent sudden escalation of drug addiction only since penalties for drug possession were softened.

Association Press (AP)

291 Broadway, New York, N.Y.

ASSOCIATION PRESS is the publication department of the National Council of the Young Men's Christian Association of the U.S.A. From 1964 until the early 1970's, the director of AP was Dr. Stanley Stuber, who has lectured before the Unitarian-Universalist Association. Over the years Dr. Stuber has done extensive public relations work for the National Council of Churches and has held executive positions with both the Missouri Council of Churches and the Greater Kansas City Council of Churches. He is a member of the United Nations Association of the U.S.A., and has been affiliated with at least six organizations cited by agencies of the federal government as either "Communist" or "Communist fronts."[1]

Books by SIECUS official Evelyn Millis Duvall, who at one time was a member of the board of the Young Women's Christian Association, predominate in the family life education material published by the Association Press. Of the two publications offered, one is entirely devoted to the promotion of her eight-book series on the subject, written for the consumption of pre-teen through adult levels.[2] Two of these (*Being Married* and *When You Marry*) had Reuben Hill of SIECUS as co-author.

Mrs. Duvall's book, *Love and the Facts of Life*, is perhaps the best known of the eight; there is scarcely a home and family living program in existence which does not include the title in its bibliography. This book was prepared by Mrs. Duvall for teenagers, in answer to such questions as: What is normal? What is healthy? What is right? Although some of the advice offered is sound, it is frequently counterbalanced by such relativistic comments as the following:

On masturbation:
> People used to feel that the handling of one's genitals was a very serious affair. . . . Some persons still think that masturbation is a sin, to be avoided at all costs. . . .
>
> In recent years, intelligent, scientifically minded persons [no doubt Mrs. Duvall was thinking of Humanists Masters and Johnson] who have studied these things tell us quite a different story about masturbation. . . .
>
> Today we know that the tendency to relieve sexual tension by rubbing the genital area to the point of release is a very common practice. Statistical studies and clinical findings indicate that between 80 and 90 per cent of

teen-age boys report that they masturbate, and that somewhat fewer teen-age girls also report the practice. With a habit as common as this seems to be, what the harm is, if any, is a very real question.

Psychologists agree that the greatest danger involved in masturbation is that of feeling guilty or ashamed . . .

This sense of wrongdoing is encouraged by certain religious groups that believe such sex play is sinful. If this is the point of view of a person's religion, he must come to terms with his religious beliefs, himself, and his sex life if there is to be any real integration and wholesomeness in his adjustment.[3]

In addition, Evelyn Duvall exposes her teenage audience to several paragraphs in which a detailed account of the act of intercourse is portrayed in a very graphic and offensive manner.[4] One wonders why young students are bombarded with such vivid and sexually stimulating descriptions in school at a time when most parents are urging them to keep their emotions in check until marriage.

The other AP publication is a catalog titled *Professional and Class Resources*, which incorporates a section on family life education. Here also Mrs. Duvall's writings are featured, along with the SIECUS-inspired masterpiece, *Sex in the Adolescent Years: New Directions in Guiding and Teaching Youth*, edited by SIECUS officials Lester A. Kirkendall and the late Isadore Rubin, both Humanists. The latter volume includes writings of such SIECUS personalities as Deryck Calderwood, Aaron Rutledge, Clark Vincent, and Wardell Pomeroy; and *Sexology* magazine's Walter R. Stokes and Robert A. Harper, both Humanists. Of the seven family life education books offered in this AP catalog, five were written by SIECUS directors and the sixth by Sylvanus Duvall, husband of Evelyn Millis Duvall.

The strong Humanist flavor of the AP catalog is further evidenced in the portion devoted to counseling. This section lists a book, *Becoming the Complete Adult*, edited by Simon Doniger. Among the book's contributing authors are three prominent Humanists: Drs. Karl Menninger, Harold Taylor, and Harry Overstreet, whose views "give young adults expert help on growing into adulthood." Topics discussed in the book are physical development, psychology, spiritual values, education, sex, vocational choice, and politics. In the same section, directed to teachers and counselors, the "Rogers Personality Adjustment Inventory," compiled by Humanist Carl A. Rogers, is also listed.

E. C. Brown Trust Foundation (ECB)

3170 S.W. Eighty-Seventh Avenue, Portland, Oregon

THE E. C. BROWN TRUST FOUNDATION describes itself as "a charitable educational foundation" that directs its primary efforts to the area of social health education. By the preference of ECB's founder, the administrator of the foundation has always been the president of the University of Oregon, an institution to which the foundation is closely related. Administrator during the 1960's was Arthur S. Flemming, former Secretary of HEW, a long-time official of the National Council of Churches and active member of the Planned Parenthood cartel. Flemming holds the dual position of Planned Parenthood council member and member of the Population Crisis Committee. Both of these organizations are Humanist-dominated and are working for eventual world population control (see entry for *Planned Parenthood–World Population*). It is also noteworthy that Flemming is a recipient of the Alexander Meiklejohn Award for Academic Freedom, which is named in honor of a prominent Humanist of an earlier day.

ECB's director for twenty-two years prior to his death in 1971 was Humanist Curtis E. Avery, formerly professor of education at the University of Oregon. Avery was a close associate of Humanist Lester Kirkendall of SIECUS, who, in turn, was a recipient of an E. C. Brown research grant. These two individuals shared an interest in the notorious *Sexology* magazine, to which Professor Avery contributed articles.[1]

But their relationship does not end here. Avery and Kirkendall blended their philosophical sentiments in an article that appeared in the Fall 1965 issue of *The Humanist*, titled "Humanistic Convictions and Practices in Life."[2] After denouncing the ethics of dogma and Commandments as satisfactory only to "unthinking persons," Avery and Kirkendall described it as a "tragedy" that many young people in their search for values "are given only the cold and sterile solace of 'thou shalt' and 'thou shalt not.' " Further recognizing that there are many others who are groping and in need of a standard, the two announced:

> . . . we have felt it necessary to work out a more sharply defined concept . . . and one which is geared to basic human needs. We have called this the "interpersonal relationships concept."
>
> The concept may be expressed in this way: Whenever thought and choice regarding behavior and conduct are possible, those acts are morally

good which create trust, and confidence, and a capacity among people to work together co-operatively. Such acts build integrity in relationships, and an enhanced sense of self-respect in the individual. Those acts are morally bad which build barriers and separate people through creating suspicion, mistrust and misunderstanding. Such acts destroy integrity in relationships and decrease the individual's sense of self-respect. *This means that acts in themselves are neither moral nor immoral — good or bad.*[3] [emphasis added]

The above seems to identify both Avery and Kirkendall as co-developers of the so-called "Code of Morality" which graces many a home and family living curriculum under the name, *Basis for Moral Judgments.* So far as is known, its first public appearance was at a teachers' training session in Southern California,[4] where it was presented as part of a position paper titled *A Morality for Twentieth Century Living,* by Dr. Kirkendall. The code follows:

BASIS FOR MORAL JUDGMENTS

Right
1. increased capacity to trust people
2. greater integrity in relationships
3. dissolution of barriers separating people
4. cooperative attitudes
5. feelings of faith and confidence in people
6. enhanced self-respect
7. fulfillment of individual potentialities and a zest for living

Wrong
1. increased distrust of people
2. deceit and duplicity in relationships
3. barriers between persons and groups
4. resistant, uncooperative attitudes
5. exploitive behavior toward others
6. diminished self-respect
7. thwarted and dwarfed individual capacities and disillusionment[5]

This Humanist code has been adopted almost verbatim in school curricula from California to New York, in both public and Catholic schools.* Under the code, which uses situation ethics rather than God's divine wisdom as the basis for determining correct human behavior, any act — premarital sex, adultery, homosexuality, or other perversions — could be requalified as *right* if its participants convinced themselves through human rationalization that they do not violate the criteria expounded by Humanists Avery and Kirkendall: increased trust, cooperative attitudes, confidence in people, etc.

*Kirkendall's code, as well as a number of prurient excerpts from his book, *Premarital Intercourse and Interpersonal Relationships,* are incorporated in the Catholic high school sex education program written by James J. DiGiacomo, S.J., titled *Sexuality: Conscience and Concern* (Holt, Rinehart and Winston, Inc., 1969).

E. C. Brown Trust Foundation has sponsored the making of a five-film audiovisual series for use in sex education programs. The five films, which are all heartily endorsed by SIECUS,[6] are titled *Early Marriage, Fertilization and Birth, Human and Animal Beginnings, Human Growth,* and *Human Heredity.* Author and technical advisor for *Early Marriage* and *Human Growth* is SIECUS-recommended author Lester F. Beck. In reading the following quotation from a review by Dr. Karl H. Brenner Jr. of the companion book for the film *Human Growth,* keep in mind that the film is intended for showing to fifth and sixth graders.

> As the author, Lester F. Beck, Associate Professor of Psychology at the University of Oregon, states, "The main object of the book is to give young people a clear understanding of birth and growth without at the same time involving them with questions of right and wrong." He then proceeds on page 71 to describe the sex act from erection to penetration to climax in vivid detail explaining vaginal lubrication and re-emphasizing penetration by repeating its description twice.[7]

Humanist Lester Kirkendall is listed in the book as having, along with several others, contributed his "professional counsel and advice" to the making of ECB's *Early Marriage.*[8] *Fertilization and Birth* was developed for "all elementary grade levels." Like many of its contemporaries, this film offers youngsters such tidbits as: "The egg is fertilized when the penis of the father goes into the vagina of the mother and deposits the sperm."[9] The *Human Heredity* film guide acknowledges that certain concepts brought forth in this film were developed in part, by Margaret Mead (a SIECUS associate and Humanist).[10]

Another E. C. Brown-sponsored film, titled *Families,* was created for children in the early primary grades, and has as its central theme "the interdependence of all human beings everywhere."[11] "Interdependence" is a collectivist term for the amalgamation of all mankind, in which individual responsibility is to be replaced by dependence on a world government for the fulfillment of basic human needs. This superstructure would regulate all aspects of family life.

Since a major segment of the world's population still frowns on such a scheme, the master planners apparently consider it necessary to "condition" the coming generation for "interdependence" in case the present populace continues to reject it. An essential ingredient of this grand design is, obviously, the reshaping of youth's thought patterns about the family. If the young adult is to accept the ethos of "interdependence," he will have to be reoriented to "group thinking"; that is, to thinking in terms of being part of a larger family outside his own circle. Then, by learning to tolerate "what is best for the group" — which is one aspect of sensitivity training — the individual will voluntarily discard portions of control over his own destiny, one by one, until he suddenly wakens to find himself absorbed within the socialistic world system of "Big Brother," euphemistically termed "the family of man."

Descriptive literature on *Families* sets the stage on this point, stating: "Subtly, it leads to the acceptance of the concept that [Humanist] Margaret Mead has called, 'the family of man.' "[12] Concentrating heavily on this thought, a review by Perennial Education, Inc., continues: "One focal point of class discussion will inevitably have to do with the idea of individual families all belonging to the 'family of man.' "[13] It further implies that a child's total concept of the "family" as he now knows it will be restructured after seeing this film.

This type of indoctrination toward a new world order is being used for the purpose of not only separating the child from his family, but extinguishing all loyalty to his country as well. *Families* and other films like it are undoubtedly laying a foundation for the World Federal Government envisioned by Socialists, World Federalists, Humanists, and their Communist-oriented bedfellows.

Like many home and family living education materials, *Families* has found its way into sociology courses as well — an area of the curriculum that for years has been a spawning ground for one-world-ism. In higher education particularly, professors of the Humanist-Socialist persuasion are no longer in the minority; in fact, it is becoming increasingly difficult to find textbooks in use that encourage allegiance to America.

Little wonder, then, that we are beginning to see colleges here and there in the country, like William Paterson (Teachers) College in New Jersey, adopting World Citizenship resolutions that, first, declare the college "a world campus dedicated to international cooperation and just world law." Secondly, William Paterson's resolution (which, incidentally, was initiated by the Student Government Association) suggests that, during United Nations Week and on other appropriate occasions, the campus display the United Nations flag in all places where the college usually displays the American flag. Thirdly, it proposes a "twinning" program of international cooperation with like-minded colleges in other countries, wherever feasible.

With such films as E. C. Brown's *Families* now indoctrinating students in the early primary grades, it is possible that in the near future, teacher-sponsored World Citizenship resolutions will emanate from the elementary school level — instigated, of course, by enthusiastic graduates of William Paterson and other one-world-oriented teachers' colleges.

E. C. Brown formerly published *Family Life Coordinator*, a quarterly journal which, in recent years, has been taken over by the National Council on Family Relations (of which Humanist Lester Kirkendall is a member and former director). Current ECB publications on family life education are, for the most part, written by either Humanist Curtis Avery (a SIECUS-recommended author) or Lester Kirkendall.[14] Of other printed materials available in ECB's catalog on this subject, 60 per cent are published by Science Research Associates (an IBM affiliate that retains Lester Kirkendall as consultant), and many of them are written by Dr. Kirkendall. Other materials prominently promoted by ECB are the Public Affairs Pamphlets. All in all, 50 percent of the publications offered in ECB's various catalogs (including film brochures) are written by either SIECUS officials or SIECUS-recommended authors.

And finally, the distributor of ECB films is Perennial Education, Inc., formerly Henk Newenhouse, Inc., another organization that has its own entry later in PART II.

Child Study Association of America (CSAA)
50 Madison Avenue, New York, New York

Sex Education

THE CHILD STUDY ASSOCIATION OF AMERICA started as a group of mothers within the New York Ethical Culture Society, a Humanist organization.[1] Sidonie M. Gruenberg, a Humanist, Communist-fronter, and SIECUS-recommended author, was for over twenty-five years the director of CSAA, to which she is now a special consultant. (Mrs. Gruenberg is also editor of *The Encyclopedia of Child Care and Guidance*, author of numerous other works, and co-author with her daughter, Hilda Krech, of the book, *The Many Lives of Modern Woman*.) SIECUS officials Helen Southard and Evelyn Duvall are both members of CSAA; Mrs. Duvall serves on its advisory board.

That CSAA and SIECUS share the same Humanistic philosophy cannot be disputed. Together, they compiled the previously mentioned book and filmstrip, both titled *How Babies Are Made*, which stress animalistic concepts concerning procreation and are devoid of spirituality. Further, in 1966, CSAA enlisted the services of SIECUS-Humanist bedfellows Mary Calderone, Lester Kirkendall, and Helen Southard as major participants in their 42nd Annual Conference, whose overall theme was "Sex Education and the New Morality."[2] Two other prominent members of this discussion panel were the New York Ethical Culture head, Algernon Black, and Dore Schary, chairman of the National Commission of the Anti-Defamation League of B'nai B'rith.

As suggested in the September 1969 SIECUS form letter, CSAA was contacted with a request for aid in setting up sex education programs. Two brochures were received in response to this request, both prepared by CSAA. The first, *Source Materials in Family Living and Sex Education*, features primarily the works of such SIECUS-selected authors as Aline B. Auerbach and Helene S. Arnstein.* One book by Mrs. Auerbach, titled *Parents Learn Through Discussion*, is described by SIECUS as designed to help orient leaders of parent discussion groups, for the purpose of changing attitudes.[3] However, as brought

*Aline Auerbach is a CSAA staff member; Helene Arnstein is vice president of CSAA.

179

out by SIECUS, these techniques may also be applied toward influencing "teachers, young people, guidance counselors, etc."

The second brochure, *Recommended Reading on Sex Education*, was obviously prepared under SIECUS tutelage. Over 85 percent of the listings are written by either SIECUS directors (Lester Kirkendall and Helen Southard) or SIECUS-recommended authors, such as Ralph G. Eckert, Sidonie M. Gruenberg, Alan F. Guttmacher, Eric W. Johnson, and the late Bishop James A. Pike.

At the conclusion of this CSAA brochure appears the following familiar suggestion:

> Those interested in obtaining information about audio-video aids and other materials on sex education may write to: SIECUS, 1790 Broadway, New York, New York 10019.

Drug Education

In 1971, the staff of the Child Study Association of America prepared and published the book, *You, Your Child and Drugs*, with support from the Helena Rubinstein Foundation, Inc. This 72-page parents' guide is clearly in harmony with the permissive attitude toward drugs, particularly marijuana, which is often found in current drug literature. In fact, CSAA's guide seems to have been written chiefly as a defense of today's dissident youth, their life style, and their use of marijuana. The section headed "Marijuana: Fact and Fiction" states: "For a number of adults, the attack on marijuana is really an attack on youth itself — on a new life style that is perplexing and disturbing."[4] It also suggests that adults "must move beyond this polarized thinking" regarding marijuana.

Parents are further advised that they "should anticipate that well-balanced, reasonably mature youngsters may try marijuana." After all, the book argues, "Most marijuana smokers use it occasionally and continue to function in school and at work . . . . They use marijuana as a means of relaxing, *to be used with discrimination, comparable to their parents' drinking a martini before dinner.*"(emphasis added)

The reader has now been prepared for the book's major message: that the punitive measures and "severe" criminal penalties imposed by the Marijuana Tax Act of 1937 were disproportionate to the known dangers of the drug. The implication is that law enforcement is not the answer — seemingly an instant replay of similar attitudes expressed in such books as *Drugs and Youth*, by the Coles, Brenner and Meagher team, and numerous other books that have infested the drug education circuit.

Finally, the question is posed, *"Should the laws against marijuana be repealed?"* After establishing that "enormous controversy" exists — most of which, of course, has been incited largely by the Humanist complex — the pros and cons of this question are presented in such a way as to favor the pro position:

> . . . Those who favor repeal argue that the present laws are excessively severe and unenforceable and — *like the prohibition of alcohol in the past* — encourage crime and disrespect for the law. *Many responsible citizens favor legalization*, with the same kinds of controls that operate in the distribution and sale of alcohol. Opponents are reluctant to add one more legal intoxicant to those already used and abused in our society. *They want to wait for further evidence.* [emphasis added]

It is little wonder then, that Humanist Margaret Mead (an open advocate of marijuana legalization) gave this plug, which appears on the back of the book's jacket: "Sane, responsible, thought provoking, badly needed. A serious attempt to tell parents how young people feel and what they can do about it together."

Churchill Films
662 North Robertson Boulevard, Los Angeles, California

AT THE TIME OF INQUIRY Churchill Films produced only a few films intended for the sex education/home and family living category.[1] The two most often promoted are the companion films, *Boy to Man* and *Girl to Woman*, suggested for use in the years of early adolescence. The two films use basically the same sequence to give a detailed account of the male and female sex organs in the process of reproduction. The most controversial segments are discussions of male ejaculation and masturbation, and an occasional display of nude sketches, guaranteed to bring a blush to the cheek of any pre-adolescent in the classroom.

For example, in *Boy to Man*, a picture of an erect penis appears on the screen, as the formation, storage, and ejaculation of the sperm are verbally described. As ejaculation occurs, a series of animated arrows quickly pass through the urethra. This leads into a discussion of fertilization. In commenting on the emission of sperm on occasions other than those intended for reproductive purposes, the narrator observes suggestively:

> Some may be ejaculated at night during a wet dream. This is called a nocturnal emission. *Or during masturbation a boy may handle his penis to cause an ejaculation.* [emphasis added]

Another comment on this topic is presented, once again in an affirmative manner:

> Neither masturbation nor nocturnal emissions are harmful, but rather, are natural outlets and are normal until you are a grown man and can deposit your sperm into the vagina of the woman.

These films, further, graphically depict the male and female genitalia, breast development, and the growth of pubic hair to the extent of being nearly pornographic. Both films are SIECUS-recommended, with Humanist Lester Kirkendall's booklet, *Understanding Sex*, suggested for teacher preparation in the *Boy to Man* bibliography.

A third film warrants some discussion, since it is also a favorite with SIECUS. *A Quarter Million Teenagers*, a film primarily designed to combat venereal disease, is frequently encountered in home and family living programs. In keeping with an attitude that runs rampant throughout SIECUS publications, the film's Study Guide notes:

"A Quarter Million Teenagers" approaches the subject purely from the standpoint of health and disease, *avoiding any discussion of the moral issues involved.*[2] [emphasis added]

Listed as "References and Sources of Information" in this guide are Public Affairs Pamphlet No. 292 and a Task Force Report on the Eradication of Syphilis, prepared by SIECUS sponsor Leona Baumgartner, for the U.S. Public Health Service, along with several other articles.

The midwest representative for Churchill Films, incidentally, is Perennial Education, Inc. (formerly Henk Newenhouse, Inc.,) another enthusiastic SIECUS fellow traveler.

Family Life Publications, Inc. (FLP)
219 Henderson Street, Saluda, North Carolina

Sex Education

FAMILY LIFE PUBLICATIONS is a private corporation, and should not be confused with the Family Life Division of the U.S. Catholic Conference. Serving on the advisory committee of FLP are five SIECUS directors: Evelyn Duvall, Lester Kirkendall, Harold Lief, David Mace, and Emily Mudd. Another member of FLP's advisory committee is Humanist Walter Stokes of the staff of *Sexology*.

FLP furnishes counselors and teachers with various inventory forms, designed by sociologists, which probe, pry, and penetrate into every aspect of the student's private life and his family's as well. Among these are "A Religious Beliefs Inventory," "A Religious Attitudes Inventory," and "A Parent-Adolescent Communication Inventory, Form A." The latter attempts to assess the type of relationship existing between the student and his parents. But perhaps best known is FLP's "Sex Knowledge Inventory, Form X," revised in 1967. Following is one illustration of the type of question posed to high school students on this form:

68. What does size of male or female sex organs indicate?
   A. Size indicates whether the man or woman will be a good sex partner.
   B. Large sex organs mean greater sex desire and capacity.
   C. Size indicates how much the man or woman has masturbated.
   D. Large sex organs mean much experience in sex relations.
   E. Size of sex organs indicates none of the above.

After a question which centers on effective methods of birth control, the following question appears in such a way as to plant the idea of "population control" in the mind of the young student:

49. If the population of the United States is to remain at its present level, no couple may have more than:
   A. One child
   B. Two children
   C. Three children
   D. Four children

Other questions center on the reasons for sex play prior to intercourse, various methods of clitoral stimulation, and best positions for sexual intercourse.

Also available from FLP is "Sex Knowledge Inventory, Form Y." Form Y "tests for knowledge and teaches the beneficial facts of sex. Also measures and offers opportunity to teach scientific vocabulary pertaining to human reproduction and sexual activities."[1] Neither the X nor the Y form is new to school sexologists. Developed by FLP official Gelolo McHugh, these forms were formerly used in 1961, when the "life adjustment" program created a storm of protest all over the United States.

FLP's publications brochure promotes such guides for counselors as the SIECUS handbook, *The Individual, Sex and Society,* and Helen Manley's *A Curriculum Guide in Sex Education.* Professional journals published by the American Institute of Family Relations and the National Council on Family Relations, two SIECUS partisans, are also given special attention in the FLP catalog, as are books from the "Concordia Sex Educaton Series" of the Luthern Church — Missouri Synod, including, *Life Can Be Sexual,* by Elmer Witt. (See entry for *Lutheran Church — Missouri Synod,* elsewhere in PART II.)

Other books listed in this FLP brochure, too numerous to name here, are written by SIECUS board and staff members, a number of whom are also Humanists:

Jessie Bernard	John Money
Carlfred Broderick	Emily Mudd
Evelyn Duvall	James A. Peterson
Virginia Johnson	Isadore Rubin
Reuben Hill	Aaron Rutledge
Lester Kirkendall	Esther Schulz
David Mace	Helen Southard
William Masters	Sally R. Williams

Some of the SIECUS-endorsed authors whose works are listed in the brochure are:

Helene S. Arnstein	Sidonie M. Gruenberg
Dorothy Baruch	Eleanor Hamilton
Lester F. Beck	Richard F. Hettlinger
Hugo Beigel	Eric W. Johnson
Lawrence Crawley, *et al.*	Richard H. Klemer
Karl de Schweinitz	Dona Z. Meilach
Celia Deschin	Howard E. Mitchell
Geraldine Lux Flanagan	Bishop James A. Pike
Edgar Z. Friedenberg	Rustum and Della Roy
Haim Ginott	Jeanne Sakol
Bert Y. Glassberg	Sara B. Taubin

Drug Education

Family Life Publications also publishes "A Drug Knowledge Inventory." Judging by the catalog description, it appears that FLP is suggesting that drug usage by high school and college students may have merit under some circumstances:

> For class and individual use to help high school and college students learn what they must know to make intelligent behavior choices regarding use of chemical sedatives, hallucinogens, and stimulants as ways to satisfy emotional and social needs.[2]

An examination of the inventory itself shows it was in part developed in 1969 by Gelolo McHugh. This inventory consists of forty-four multiple-choice questions relating to drugs. Although it was prepared primarily for junior and senior high school students and college undergraduates, FLP considers its Drug Knowledge Inventory useful for parents, churches, and civic organizations as well.

Prior to the use of this inventory, the teacher or group leader is advised to study the recommended literature listed at the end of the teacher's discussion guide, which includes a number of books that are favorites of the pro-marijuana cartel. Among these is *The Varieties of Psychedelic Experience*, by Masters and Houston (see "Drug Education" section in entry for *Guidance Associates*, elsewhere in PART II).

As is common practice in many contemporary drug programs, the FLP Discussion Guide tells the leader not to reinforce his teaching with admonitions and scare propaganda, but rather to present the facts in an unbiased manner. The guide says this method will open up opportunities "for an exchange of ideas, feelings and attitudes." Its advice clearly echoes a favorite Humanist cliché often voiced by sex educators — "creating an open forum." In the case of drug education as well, this so-called free exchange of ideas tends to tear down traditional attitudes while it gives the leader the advantage of controlling group behavior.

As for the plea to omit "scare propaganda" from the drug program — another favored cliché — one senses the existence of a double standard. For example, the films that deal with the effects of tobacco smoking, such as are prepared by some of the organizations in PART II, employ every scare tactic imaginable, from grim pictures of cancer-riddled lungs to "irrefutable" statistics that portray the "wide-spread tragedy" caused by smoking. Why the soft pedal when it comes to drugs?

Another enigma calling for further comment is the advice to teachers "to present the facts in an unbiased manner." This injunction harmonizes with the current trend in the schools to present issues without taking a moral position. In his new academic role as "moderator," the teacher must now refrain from making moral judgments. This limits the topic of discussion to the medical and social consequences of drug use.

Certain issues require more than a consideration of these consequences. The only adequate way to treat such topics is by indicating moral approval or disapproval. What would we say, for example to a treatment of the subject of slavery that dealt merely with the medical and social factors, with no mention of the moral wickedness of the practice? Contrary to the prevailing opinion, the young, impressionable mind seeks — even craves — moral guidance. It is sheer folly for the teacher to maintain an unbiased attitude when it comes to drugs — potentially a deadly menace to the user, his loved ones, and society.

Questions 29 through 35 in FLP's Drug Knowledge Inventory deal with marijuana. The answers and comments provided in the teachers' Discussion Guide reiterate a theme that runs through much of today's "educational" material on marijuana; specifically, they make the following suppositions:

1. That marijuana has not been proven to be physically harmful.
2. That marijuana is not the direct cause of mental or emotional illness.
3. That marijuana's effects can be rated as similar to the effects of alcohol.
4. That marijuana, though classed as a narcotic, is not an addictive drug.
5. That marijuana does not by itself lead to the use of "hard" drugs such as LSD and heroin.[3]

The first supposition is covered in the "Drug Education" section of the entry for the *American School Health Association*. The second supposition has been refuted by the authoritative psychiatric studies of Drs. Harold Kolansky and William T. Moore in their report in the *Journal of the American Medical Association* (JAMA) titled "Effects of Marihuana on Adolescents and Young Adults," a portion of which concluded:

> . . . In one subgroup, a clear-cut diagnosis of psychosis was established, and in these patients, there was neither evidence of psychosis or ego disturbance nor family history of psychosis prior to the patients' use of marijuana. Several in this group were suicidal.

As for the third, fourth, and fifth suppositions, Dr. Henry Brill, chairman of the AMA's Committee on Drug Dependence and Alcoholism, gives the following analysis of these often-repeated, almost identical allegations:[4]

Concerning the third supposition — "The pharmacologic differences between these two [alcohol and marijuana] are most important in making the comparison. Increasing the dose of alcohol produces ataxia and stupor, while raising the dose of marijuana produces delusions and hallucinations with acute psychotic bursts."

Concerning the fourth supposition — "This statement is true but contains the hidden conclusion that since the drug causes no symptoms on withdrawal, it is not harmful. The cocainist also has no physical symptoms on withdrawal. By this standard, cocaine also should not be harmful or a narcotic, yet it is notoriously harmful through its capacity to produce psychic dependence and destroy social capacity."

Concerning the fifth supposition — "Clinically it is known that taking drugs for pleasure is often a general tendency and not confined to one substance. Most persons with experience in this field believe that there is more than a chance correlation between the abuse of any drug and abuse of others. The sequence in colleges is thought to be from marijuana to LSD, and in certain slums from marijuana to heroin."

The constant propaganda barrage that belittles marijuana's corrosive effects is currently being directed at teacher, student, and parent alike. If enough of the population is lulled into a sense of security by the presumption that marijuana is relatively harmless, could public opinion then be conditioned for the acceptance of its legalization? Could this in fact be a major purpose of the Humanist influence behind drug education? If so, and if successful, it would then be only a matter of time until the Humanist design for the legalization of all drugs became a reality.

Family Service Association of America (FSAA)
44 East 23rd Street, New York, New York

Sex Education

THE FAMILY SERVICE ASSOCIATION OF AMERICA has 342 member agencies throughout the nation. These agencies provide counseling services to those having family, marriage, or personal problems.

As suggested by SIECUS in its September 1969 form letter, the Family Service Association of America was contacted for additional sex education information. Four lists of suggested reading, loaded with names of SIECUS officials and SIECUS-recommended authors, were received in response.[1] Among those on one or more of these lists were the following individuals, many of whom are Humanists:

SIECUS *Officials*

Clark W. Blackburn	Lester Kirkendall
Rev. Thomas E. Brown	David Mace
Mary S. Calderone	Jane Mayer
Harold T. Christensen	James A. Peterson
William G. Cole	Harriet Pilpel
Evelyn Millis Duvall	Isadore Rubin
Rev. William Genné	Helen Southard
Warren R. Johnson	

SIECUS-Recommended *Authors*

Helene S. Arnstein	Sidonie M. Gruenberg
Curtis E. Avery	Richard and Margaret Klemer
Evelyn N. Bachelor *et al.*	Eda J. LeShan
Dorothy W. Baruch	Norman M. Lobsenz
Lawrence Q. Crawley	Milton I. Levine
Maxine Davis	Elizabeth Ogg
Ralph Eckert	Hyman Rodman
Haim Ginott	Jeanne Sakol
Sol Gordon	Jean Seligmann

An estimated 50 percent of all materials recommended in FSAA's reading lists on sex education can be linked to SIECUS in some way. This becomes germane in connection with the fact that SIECUS officials Reuben Hill and Clark W. Blackburn are FSAA members, Blackburn having been FSAA's general director since 1952.

Drug Education

As its contribution to the drug problem, the Plays for Living Division of the Family Service Association of America wrote and produced *The Underground Bird*. Commissioned and published by the American Social Health Association, this satire was written by Rose Leiman Schiller and has an accompanying discussion guide specially written by Humanist Charles Winick. (Dr. Winick, it may be recalled, is the director of ASHA's Narcotic Addiction Program.)

The purposes of this drama as outlined by Dr. Winick in his discussion guide[2] show clearly that it is structured to comply with the Humanist-inspired concept of the "open forum." This little scheme — at least from the psychological standpoint — has the effect of reclassifying once "forbidden fruit" as "food for thought." Dr. Winick's purposes are stated as being:

   a. To present *a variety of points of view* about drug addiction, dependence, and abuse.
   b. *To suggest the arguments pro and con* for each point of view.
   c. To give young people an opportunity for reflection, expression, and clarification of their own thinking and goals with respect to the use of drugs. [emphasis added]

Dr. Winick continues: "The play deliberately avoids a preachy tone." Later, in offering advice to the group chairman, he says: "The discussion leader has the job of tapping a variety of points of view and *helping the audience to see the relative merit of the various possibilities* without necessarily expressing his own approach." (emphasis added)

The central thrust of the play is to cultivate the view that everyone is "addicted" to *something*. This includes not only narcotics but coffee, cigarettes, and cola beverages. In the play, for example, one character is portrayed as hopelessly "addicted" to the study of maps. After running the gamut of possible "addictions," from drugs to maps, the play advances to the conclusion that, where addictions are concerned, "One is just as bad as the other."[3]

A typical audience reaction to the play's substance is summed up by Dr. Winick on page 7 of his discussion guide: "One common reaction to the play will be that, 'since everybody is on something,' how can we honestly say that drug use is bad but that sex or cards or smoking or coffee or alcohol are better?"[4] This mental reflex, it should be remembered, is subject to the guidance of the discussion leader, whose job is *to help the viewers to explore the merits of the various choices available.* The discussion leader will, in all likelihood, come from the ranks of professionals trained for this purpose at drug education seminars. (An examination of the character of drug seminars is made in the "Drug Education" section of the entry for *New Jersey State Department of Education*, elsewhere in PART II, in an attempt to ferret out whose views are being taught.)

Foundations and Miscellaneous Grants

THE SIECUS ANNUAL REPORT for 1967–68 states: "Since 1964 SIECUS has been supported by contributions, memorial gifts, bequests and legacies from individuals, corporations, and family funds. Major grant support has been received from foundations such as The Commonwealth Fund, The Ford Foundation, Kimberly-Clark Foundation, Inc., and Public Welfare Foundation, Inc."

The Commonwealth Fund

SIECUS official Dr. George Packer Berry is honorary director of the Commonwealth Fund, whose 1974 vice president was Humanist Carleton B. Chapman. SIECUS director Dr. Harold Lief was a fellow of the Commonwealth Fund for the years 1963–1964. This Fund also established the University of Pennsylvania's Center for the Study of Sex Education in Medicine, headed by Dr. Lief, to which 88 medical schools appointed representatives in 1969.[1]

Besides granting monies to SIECUS, the Commonwealth Fund gave $145,700 to Planned Parenthood to start a New York clinic that provides contraceptive assistance to girls under eighteen.[2]

The Ford Foundation

Dr. George Packer Berry of SIECUS is also a member of the Advisory Committee of the Ford Foundation, while SIECUS director Reuben Hill was program consultant on population to the Foundation from 1964 to 1966.

Besides being a major supporter of SIECUS, the Ford Foundation has consistently financed leftwing institutions and causes in recent decades. Such activities are closely related to the stated purpose of the Foundation as disclosed by a top official of Ford before the Reece Committee. At the time that committee was charged with investigating the tax-free foundations, its chief investigator, Norman Dodd, personally interviewed H. Rowan Gaither Jr., then president of the Ford Foundation. Gaither freely admitted to Dodd that the directive by which the Foundation would be guided was "to so alter American Society that it could be comfortably merged with that of the Soviet Union."[3]

The Ford Foundation has also been linked to the Humanist movement, having retained the prominent Humanist Robert M. Hutchins* as associate director from 1951 to 1954. During that time Hutchins, together with others, was granted $15,000,000 by Ford to set up the Foundation's leftist Fund for the Republic. Moreover, during Hutchins' tenure as associate director of the Foundation, Ford gave $1,134,000 to the Humanist-oriented American Friends Service Committee; then, in 1967, Ford gave $300,000 to the Humanist-founded NAACP (National Association for the Advancement of Colored People); $430,000 to the Urban League, which cooperates with Ethical Culture; and $47,000 to the A. Philip Randolph Institute, which is named for the 1970 winner of the "Humanist of the Year" award. More recently, Ford gave grants to the University of California at Santa Barbara and the University of Massachusetts for "exploring more humanistic modes of education."

For the record, SIECUS has also received grants from:

> Chase Family Foundation
> Foundation for Education and Social Development
> Hamm Foundation, Inc.
> Katherine Cornell Foundation
> Kempner Foundation
> Playboy Foundation
> U.S. Department of Health, Education and Welfare

Individuals who have contributed funds to SIECUS include:

> Humanist Hugh Hefner of *Playboy* magazine
> Mr. and Mrs. Steven C. Rockefeller
> Mrs. Van Meter Ames, wife of Humanist Van Meter Ames
> William Benton, former Assistant Secretary of State,
>   former U.S. Senator, present chairman of the board of
>   *Encyclopaedia Britannica* (on which Robert M. Hutchins
>   also serves)
> Mr. and Mrs. John Cowles of Cowles Publications
> Mr. Grant Keehn, president of Equitable Life Assurance
>   Society
> Mr. Corliss Lamont, Humanist and Communist fronter
> Mr. Vance Packard, author (*The Sexual Wilderness*)
> Mrs. James P. Warburg, wife of co-founder of United World
>   Federalists James Warburg (who is also a prominent
>   member of the Council on Foreign Relations)

*Hutchins founded the Aspen Institute for Humanistic Studies, which promotes one-world government and receives grants from the Ford Foundation.

Group for the Advancement of Psychiatry (GAP)
419 Park Avenue South, New York, N.Y.

THE GROUP FOR THE ADVANCEMENT OF PSYCHIATRY is an organization of approximately 200 psychiatrists who "direct their efforts toward the study of various aspects of psychiatry and toward the application of this knowledge to the fields of mental health and human relations."[1] Established in 1946, GAP now has over twenty committees, which work in concert to further GAP's overall aims, which the group states are:

- To collect and appraise significant data in the field of psychiatry, mental health, and human relations;
- To re-evaluate old concepts and to develop and test new ones;
- To apply the knowledge thus obtained for the promotion of mental health and good human relations.[2]

As stated in GAP's 1968–69 Publications brochure, each committee report is circulated to all members of GAP prior to publication, so it reflects the collective judgment of the entire membership.

It is also stated in GAP literature that:

> Collaboration with specialists in other disciplines has been and is one of GAP's working principles. Since the formation of GAP in 1946 its members have worked closely with such other specialists as anthropologists, biologists, economists, statisticians, educators, lawyers, nurses, psychologists, sociologists, social workers, and experts in mass communication, philosophy, and semantics.[3]

Considering the purpose stated above, as well as the fact that so large a body of psychiatrists automatically enjoys a certain prestige, GAP undoubtedly is in a position to exert almost unlimited influence on the public, both in and out of the profession. Therefore it should not be surprising to discover at least five SIECUS officials in the GAP ranks: Drs. Harold Lief, William L. Peltz, Roy W. Menninger, Judd Marmor, and Robert L. Arnstein.[4]

Even less surprising is the fact that the SIECUS book list, *Human Sexuality*, and various SIECUS Study Guides and Newsletters, all promote GAP publications; and, in turn, GAP recommends SIECUS when sex education information is requested.[5] Nor is GAP without its share of well-known Humanists, including Drs. Jerome D. Frank, Judd Marmor, Karl Menninger, and Benjamin Spock.

GAP publishes several symposium proceedings and reports each year. One such publication is Report Number 60, titled *Sex and the College Student*. This report lists Dr. Robert L. Arnstein (of SIECUS) among its contributors. Released in 1965, shortly after the formation of SIECUS, *Sex and the College Student* provided much of the initial thrust for the permissive life style that is prevalent on today's college campuses, by encouraging administrators to condone unrestricted sexual activity in college dormitories. A major portion of this GAP report presents a set of formulated guidelines to college officials that is anything but conventional.

GAP's own review of this booklet, for example, states:

> The authors suggest that responsible heterosexual experimentation *can help some students to develop sexual maturity*, while for others such liaisons lead to conflict and anxiety.
>
> Once an unmarried student becomes pregnant, emotional difficulties cannot be avoided, the study states. Students involved in such pregnancies should have the help of the college in assuming responsibility for the pregnancy and in planning realistically for its outcome. The authors suggest that *students deserve access to information about contraception* through the college health service or a course in sex education.[6] [emphasis added]

As might have been expected, *Sex and the College Student* received a very favorable review in the November-December 1966 issue of *The Humanist*, which revealed that the GAP report further recommended that "students be involved in an advisory capacity in drawing up institutional policies."

In October 1969 GAP once again took the lead in a major social issue, publishing an analysis titled *The Right to Abortion: A Psychiatric View*. This was formulated by the GAP Committee on Psychiatry and the Law over a three-year period, with the assistance of two consultants: Dr. Alice S. Rossi (a Humanist) of the Department of Social Relations at The Johns Hopkins University, and Ralph Slovenko (a SIECUS official) of Wayne State University Law School, under the chairmanship of GAP psychiatrist Dr. Zigmond M. Lebensohn.[7]

This publication is generously reinforced with the supportive philosophy and opinions of other Humanists, such as Garrett Hardin and Erik Erikson, as well as at least one other SIECUS director, Sophia Kleegman. Its central thrust is toward striking down all traditional objections to legalized abortion, rationalizing that these objections "no longer can be sustained by a justifiable state interest."[8] After using the threat of over-population as a scare tactic, the report suggests that legalized abortion might constitute "a secondary means of 'contraception' and planned motherhood in an overpopulated society. . . . If anything," it adds later, "it may be in the interest of the state to permit abortion freely as a secondary measure to limit population where contraception fails."[9]

Next, the GAP psychiatrists tackled the issue of abortion as murder, holding that ". . . this is insoluble, a matter of religious philosophy and religious principle and not a matter of fact."[10] Several other aspects having been considered, the report assumed a position in its summary closely paralleling a position statement of the American Civil Liberties Union[11] (of which GAP consultant Ralph Slovenko is a member). The following conclusion was reached by GAP:

> It is on the basis of the foregoing discussion that we recommend that abortion, when performed by a licensed physician, be entirely removed from the domain of criminal law. We believe that a woman should have the right to abort or not, just as she has the right to marry or not.[12]

Not supported or even recognized in this GAP publication is the unborn child's right to life (a subject considered later in PART II in the entry for the *National Association for Repeal of Abortion Laws*).

The influence of GAP is spread widely by its various committee reports, as well as by means of symposiums, always moderated by GAP members, with panels composed of other GAP members. Some GAP-sponsored symposiums whose proceedings have been published by GAP have such peculiar titles as: "Considerations Regarding the Loyalty Oath as a Manifestation of Current Social Tension and Anxiety"; "Factors Used to Increase the Susceptibility of Individuals to Forceful Indoctrination: Observations and Experiments"; "Methods of Forceful Indoctrination: Observations and Interviews"; and "Pavlovian Conditioning and American Psychiatry."[13]

Research for some of GAP's symposiums has been supported by the National Institute of Mental Health; the National Institutes of Health; the Public Health Service; and the U.S. Department of Health, Education, and Welfare.

SIECUS at one time shared GAP's office space at 419 Park Avenue South in New York. Other groups sharing the offices with GAP are:

> International Conference on Social Work
> Mental Health Materials Center, Inc., and its Information
>   Resources Center for Mental Health and Family
>   Life Education
> National Conference on Social Welfare
> Society for Public Health Educators
> World Federation of Public Health

These offices occupy an entire open floor, without doors or partitions. Literature racks are shared by all the organizations.

Some foundations and organizations which over the years have supported GAP by financial grants include:

Ciba Pharmaceutical Products, Inc.
Hoffman-La Roche, Inc.
The Mona Bronfman Sheckman Foundation
Smith, Kline and French Foundation
The Commonwealth Fund
The J.M. Kaplan Fund[14]

The last two have also given financial assistance to SIECUS.

Guidance Associates of Pleasantville, N.Y. (GA)

A subsidiary of Harcourt, Brace, Jovanovich, Inc.
41 Washington Avenue, Pleasantville, New York

Sex Education

IN 1969, GUIDANCE ASSOCIATES, then a subsidiary of Harcourt, Brace and World, Inc., published an entire curriculum under the title *Family Life and Sex Education*. Divided into two segments, this program is designed, according to the catalog for the curriculum,[1] to give young people "sex education with greater scope and depth to prepare them to cope with their physical, mental, and emotional development, their interpersonal relationships and the social issues they will face." In keeping with this multilateral theme, Guidance Associates' audiovisuals cover a variety of subjects ranging from student rights to birth control, and come with detailed teachers' manuals designed to "encourage an open exchange of ideas and attitudes."

As disclosed in the Guidance Associates catalog, Part I of the program, titled "Human Sexuality: A Modern Approach," was produced "in consultation with a Special Committee of SIECUS." The films listed in Part I are:

- *Sex Education U.S.A.*, by James Lincoln Collier (narrated by Chet Huntley)
- *Growing Into Manhood: A Middle School Approach*, author not named
- *Growing Into Womanhood: A Middle School Approach*, author not named
- *Becoming a Woman: Maturation and Growth*, by Eric W. Johnson
- *Becoming a Man: Maturation and Growth*, by Eric W. Johnson
- *Understanding Human Reproduction*, by James Lincoln Collier
- *Understanding Human Reproduction: A Middle School Approach*, author not named
- *Human Reproduction 100*, author not named

Catalog descriptions of these films and filmstrips confirm that the SIECUS philosophy pervades them.

Part II of the program, titled "Family Life and Sex Education," was produced by the editorial staff of Guidance Associates, aided by "outstanding authorities and pioneering groups in the field." In listing these consultants, the Guidance Associates catalog begins by naming Mary S. Calderone, M.D., executive director of SIECUS. However, the remaining names are given as if they had no connection with SIECUS, since the information in brackets does not appear in the catalog, thus:

> Deryck Calderwood, Family Life and Sex Education consultant [SIECUS staff member]; Evelyn M. Duvall, Ph.D. [SIECUS official]; Richard Hettlinger, Ph.D., Professor of Religion, Kenyon College [whose writings SIECUS promotes and whose book, *Living With Sex: The Student's Dilemma*, is endorsed by Mary Calderone]; Eric W. Johnson, Vice Principal, Germantown Friends School [a Quaker, and an associate of Dr. Calderone, whose writings are recommended by SIECUS]; Lester A. Kirkendall, Ph.D., Professor of Family Life, Oregon State University [founder and board member of SIECUS].

Films listed in PART II of the program are:

- *The Alienated Generation*, author not named
- *Everything But . . .* , by Richard Hettlinger
- *You and the Law,* author not named
- *The Exploited Generation*, author not named
- *Venereal Disease: A Present Danger*, by Eric W. Johnson
- *Learning About Sex*, by Deryck Calderwood
- *Sexual Values In Society*, by Richard Hettlinger
- *Masculinity and Femininity*, by Richard Hettlinger
- *Dare To Be Different*, author not named
- *Developing Your Personality*, by Evelyn M. Duvall
- *Love, Marriage and the Family*, by Lester A. Kirkendall
- *Family Planning Today,* author not named
- *The Population Explosion*, author not named
- *The Accomplished Generation*, author not named
- *And They Lived Happily Ever After? Understanding Teenage Marriage*, author not named
- *The Tuned-Out Generation*, author not named (but film expresses appreciation to Dr. Mary S. Calderone)
- *I Never Looked At It That Way Before*, author not named
- *Sex: A Moral Dilemma For Teenagers*, author not named (but film catalog states it was produced with the consultation of Dr. Calderone)
- *Values for Teenagers: The Choice Is Yours*, author not named
- *Think of Others First*, author not named
- *Tobacco and Alcohol: The $50,000 Habit*, author not named

Judging from catalog accounts, it is evident that one thing many of the above films have in common is their disparagement of parents and parental values. So much is this the case, it causes one to wonder if their final result could be a widening of "the generation gap." One example is *Sex: A Moral Dilemma For Teenagers*, featuring Dr. Calderone, which was removed from a New Jersey high school by the local Board of Education on the grounds that it tended to pit the child against his parents.

Other films are unique in their own fashion. The GA catalog review of Richard Hettlinger's *Masculinity and Femininity*, for example, points out that problems are caused when basic American attitudes toward masculinity and femininity are "exaggerated or over-simplified." In the catalog this is followed by the comment: "Program suggests a *more flexible approach to sexual roles.*" (emphasis added) Another Richard Hettlinger film, *Everything But . . .* , is described in the Guidance Associates catalog as one in which teenagers speak out candidly on the difficulties "of making responsible decisions when sexually stimulated, of judging the effect intimacy will have on a relationship," and further "debate the value of virginity before marriage."

Recognizing that no sex education program would be complete without postulating the need for world-wide population control, Guidance Associates has included several films on this topic. One in particular, *The Population Explosion*, features an exclusive interview with Dr. Alan F. Guttmacher, a Humanist and then president of Planned Parenthood–World Population. The review in the Guidance Associates catalog continues: "Programs initiated by the United Nations and the U.S. Government to help alleviate the problem resulting from over-population are considered."

Of the eight books and booklets promoted by Guidance Associates in this catalog, four should be noted:

- *Human Growth*, by SIECUS-endorsed author Lester F. Beck
- *Love Against Hate*, by Humanist psychiatrist Karl A. Menninger
- *Family Life and Sex Education: Curriculum and Instruction*, by SIECUS official Sally R. Williams and Humanist Esther Schulz
- *Sex Education U.S.A.: A Community Approach*, by James Lincoln Collier and the editorial staff of Guidance Associates, in consultation with a special committee of SIECUS

The last-named booklet, published in 1968 and written by James Lincoln Collier, is a companion item to the Guidance Associates film, *Sex Education U.S.A.* — also written by Mr. Collier. This is often the first film viewed by a community, prior to the "creation" of a sex education program. As is disclosed by the catalog, Mr. Collier prepared this film "in consultation with a Special Committee of SIECUS."

The same year Mr. Collier's booklet, *Sex Education U.S.A.,* was published — in June to be exact — an article bearing his name appeared in *Reader's Digest.* Carefully timed to quench the fires of skepticism about sex education that were beginning to sweep the country, Collier's article no doubt won the confidence of readers perhaps numbering in the millions. Its spurious contents warrant a replay of the author's opening remarks:

A concerned parent queries a well-known expert
Sex Education: Blunt Answers for Tough Questions
An interview with Lester A. Kirkendall
by James Lincoln Collier

Sometime in the next two or three years the small suburban town where I live is virtually certain to put a sex-education program into its schools — whether I like it or not. But before my two boys go into any such classes I want answers to some tough questions — questions I'd probably be embarrassed to stand up and ask at a parent-teacher meeting. And since thousands of other communities across the country are also considering sex education for their schools, it seems likely that millions of parents like myself are troubled by similar questions.

To look for some answers I flew out to Oregon State University to talk with Dr. Lester A. Kirkendall, an extraordinarily perceptive man of 64 who has devoted much of his professional life to working with sex-education programs . . . .

Without question, he is one of the most respected authorities in the whole field of sex education and family life. Here are his answers to the questions I posed.[2]

After reading this, it would seem appropriate to "pose" a question or two to Mr. Collier, such as "How is it possible to write a purportedly authoritative booklet on sex education for Guidance Associates in collaboration with SIECUS and be an uninformed 'concerned parent' — all in the same year?"

Consider an even more puzzling feature of the Collier saga. In May 1971, an article titled "The Procreation Myth" found its way into *Playboy* magazine. The author of the article was one James Collier — the same James Collier who had depicted himself in *Reader's Digest* as too shy to ask questions about sex in public. The *Playboy* article, which carries the theme that "men should copulate at will, with no thought of reproduction,"[3] indicates that the author feels more at home when propagating the hedonistic Humanism of his SIECUS colleagues. Heavily loaded with evolutionary theory and preoccupied with the subject of incessant copulation, his article takes every opportunity to deride the philosophical foundation of Judeo-Christianity where sex is concerned; and concludes that a *new sex code* based solely on sensual gratification must be developed for the next millennium.

Drug Education

By 1970–71, Guidance Associates had developed a full-fledged drug education program. The series offers a wide range of drug-related topics by way of color filmstrips reinforced with discussion guides, reference booklets for parents and community leaders, and advice on how to form "community action groups." But perhaps the most eye-catching segment of information given on this series in GA's catalog is the portion that lists the consultants to the program.

Consultants

Among the "noted authorities" who have acted as consultants to GA's drug education program are:

Dr. David Smith of the Haight-Ashbury Free Medical Clinic in San Francisco, a medical rebel who is, in his own words, dedicated to serving a "deviant population on terms it would accept."[4] Dr. Smith maintains close contact with the hippie movement and, as reported in a Rutgers University publication, *Trans-Action*, is sympathetic to its dreams of new social forms. The first of a growing chain, the Haight-Ashbury clinic operates outside accepted medical channels and caters to drug users who do not trust "straight" private physicians. More detailed coverage is given to Dr. Smith in the "Drug Education" section of the entry for *New Jersey State Department of Education*; this includes exposure of his membership in an organization that is working to legalize marijuana.

Dr. Donald Louria, who plays the role of a "moderate" in the currently rising debate concerning marijuana's legal status. In this role Dr. Louria's stance on drugs approaches the bizarre. For at the same time he affirms that marijuana should not be fully legalized, he is also urging parents, teachers, students, and governmental committees to exempt marijuana users from all but the lightest criminal penalties.[5] This, however, does not apply to the pusher, who, Dr. Louria contends, should be severely punished. This poses another problem. The pusher, as any schoolboy knows, is frequently the user. In fact, a large number of marijuana users regularly push their friends to "try it." In view of this, the pusher and the user cannot always be realistically separated. Lessening the penalty for one may automatically lessen the penalty for the other.

The scheme to greatly reduce penalties for use and possession of marijuana, led by such "national drug experts" as Dr. Louria, is but part of the softening-up process leading to eventual legalization — a step that has been advocated in the highest quarters; for example, by President Nixon's National Commission on Marijuana and Drug Abuse in 1972.[6] Dr. Louria's position on drugs will be further considered later.

Robert E. L. Masters and Jean Houston, directors of the Foundation for Mind Research in New York. The members of this research team are also co-authors of *The Varieties of Psychedelic Experience*, purportedly "the first comprehensive guide to the effects of LSD on human personality."[7] This book's 420 psychedelic travelogs are based on 206 personally conducted LSD or peyote sessions, supplemented by 214 interviews with persons who had experienced their hallucinogenic voyages elsewhere.

The book's opening remarks make it clear that this research team takes the "pro" position on psychedelic drug usage by both psychiatric patients and normal individuals. But no doubt is left that the accent is on the normal individual. Consider, for example, the following:

> . . . we hope to make entirely credible our belief that *the psychedelic drugs afford the best access yet to the contents and processes of the human mind.*
>
> Much already has been written about the psychedelic drugs as they have been used in the treatment of severely disturbed individuals. The present volume, however, is principally concerned with the psychedelic drug-state *as it is experienced by the comparatively normal individual — the "average person" rather than the psychotherapist's patient. It is, then, the remarkable range and richness of the inner life of normal individuals, as revealed in purposeful, controlled drug sessions, that will be described.* And the effort will be made to detail means by which the average person may pass through new dimensions of awareness and self-knowledge to a "transforming experience" resulting in actualization of latent capacities, philosophical reorientation, emotional and sensory athomeness in the world, *and still other changes beneficial to the person.*[8] [emphasis added]

In a meager attempt to counterbalance their stated opinion that for the normal individual the psychedelic experience "holds out the promise of rewards of incalculable value,"[9] the authors admit that there are *some* dangers. This is immediately followed by the contention that certain "alleged dangers have been exaggerated or otherwise misrepresented . . . ."*[10] Shortly thereafter, the authors observe:

> . . . Here, we will remark that we emphatically do not agree with those who would make these drugs available to everyone, or almost everyone, to

---

*The total irresponsibility of this statement is evidenced by the following facts: (1) Dr. Marvin Block, vice president of the U.S. National Council on Alcoholism, has revealed that 250 persons confined in Bellevue Hospital in New York were *totally insane solely through use of LSD*. These patients, he stated, would never recover. (2) According to the Los Angeles Police Department, "Epileptic seizures, suicidal tendencies, successful suicides, and even homicides have been the product of this substance." (3) At U.C.L.A.'s Neuropsychiatric Institute, LSD psychotics seeking treatment have become so numerous that they are no longer admitted. Instead, they are sent directly to Camarillo, a state mental hospital.

use under any conditions at all. The psychedelic experience is one that has to be *responsibly directed* if it is to be of maximum benefit to the drug subject. [emphasis added.]

It is obvious, then, that Masters and Houston consider the potential hazard to be minimal — in fact, almost non-existent — so long as the user is "responsibly directed." In order to satisfy this prerequisite, a trained "psychedelic guide" is recommended. This guide, according to Masters and Houston, should himself have experienced the effects of LSD on several occasions; he need not necessarily be a member of the medical profession.

Considering the fact that *The Varieties of Psychedelic Experience* was used as a support in the making of Guidance Associates' filmstrip, *Marijuana: What Can You Believe?*[11] it would seem important to examine the book's statements about this drug as well. In keeping with the current permissive trend, we find:

> . . . Although physiologically nonaddictive, *and possibly less harmful than alcoholic beverages*, marijuana use can hardly be justified on the basis that it makes a major and positive contribution to society. Certainly, as compared to LSD, peyote, and other powerful psychedelic drugs, its value as a consciousness-expanding agent, vehicle of self-transcendence, or source of visions, is not very great. *On the other hand, it is sheer nonsense to lump marijuana together in punitive legislation with heroin, morphine, or even cocaine.*[12] [emphasis added]

For those individuals who seek it, the Masters and Houston book suggests the possibility of a drug-induced "religious" or "mystical" experience similar to the much-publicized "spiritual discovery" of Timothy Leary. They declare:

> In our own experience, the evidence would seem to support the contentions of those who assert that an authentic religious experience may occur within the context of the psychedelic drug-state. However, we are certainly less exuberant than some other researchers when it comes to the question of the frequency of such experiences.[13]

In later probing this aspect in more specific terms, Masters and Houston claim that some subjects who have "exceptional self-understanding" have been able to reach what is termed a "deep integral level" where an ecstatic sense of what is termed "illumination" takes place. According to the authors, this is similar to the non-drug "peak experience" described by A.H. Maslow.[14] (Humanist Maslow's "peak experience" is often favorably referred to in Humanist literature.)

Judging by this and all other passages quoted from the book, it is no wonder *The Humanist* effervesced with enthusiasm in its review of *Varieties of Psychedelic Experience:*

. . . Masters and Houston calmly, coolly, unambiguously line up with those who find the dharmic [a Buddhist term meaning religious] drugs quite safe *in the hands of trained administrators*. And they end with a sentence Timothy Leary might have written, and which no reader can think of seriously without being excited to the core of his being: "For we doubt that extensive work in this area can fail to result in eventually pushing human consciousness beyond its present limitations and on toward capacities not yet realized and perhaps undreamed of."[15]

With tutors as persuasive as Smith, Louria, Masters, and Houston behind the scenes, guiding the attitudes of students, teachers, parents, and the community at large, it seems necessary to take a close look at some of Guidance Associates' drug education filmstrips.

Filmstrips

GA produces at least seven filmstrips on the subject of drugs:

- *The Effective Teacher: Drug Education* [four parts — (1) The Drug Problem in Perspective; (2) Drugs in the Classroom; (3) Curriculum Approaches to Drug Education; (4) Classroom Dynamics in Drug Education]
- *The Drug Information Series* [four parts — (1) Narcotics; (2) Sedatives; (3) Stimulants; (4) Psychedelics]
- *The Drug Threat: Your Community's Response*
- *LSD: The Acid World*
- *Marijuana: What Can You Believe?*
- *Tobacco and Alcohol: The $50,000 Habit*
- *The Alienated Generation*[16]

Space permits detailed review of only two of these filmstrips:

THE ALIENATED GENERATION (in three parts) — The visual portion of this filmstrip guides the audience through San Francisco's Haight-Ashbury district, the hippie capital of America. Musical impressions interspersed throughout consist of a number of popular "acid rock" recordings.* Such aspects of hippie life as painting psychedelic pictures, rolling marijuana cigarettes, smoking pot, engaging in street demonstrations, and protesting "police brutality" are portrayed as unique, appealing, and intriguing.

Since the main theme of *The Alienated Generation* is the so-called "generation gap," one might expect that the filmstrip's purpose would be to create a better understanding between the generations. This, however, is not the case; for it is evident that the balance is heavily

*"Acid rock" in drug language means "music to drop acid [LSD] by."

tipped in favor of radical youth. As the narrator consistently examines "the alienated generation" in sympathetic tones, hippies are given a generous amount of time to discuss their nihilistic views of life and love and to voice their disgust with parents, school, and the world in general. In contrast, adults are rarely seen or heard from, except for a caustic remark or two aimed at the younger generation. One scowling senior citizen, for example, is more than once heard describing America's rebellious youth as "human garbage."

During Part 2 of the filmstrip, following a round of complaints by teenagers against their parents, Dr. David Smith (the consultant to *Guidance Associates* who was mentioned earlier) is introduced as an adult who is "working hard to understand the mental turmoil of these young people." Not only are his comments 100 percent sympathetic to the hippie culture, but he offers nothing constructive to bridge the generation gap. In fact, Dr. Smith's entire manner of approach implies that the hippie life style and the drug culture offer a justifiable, legitimate alternative to the "straight" world.

Of course, an occasional negative view of the hippie "culture" is aired, but the general tone and substance of this are not sufficient to counterbalance the heavy damage already inflicted by the multitude of comments favorable to this life style. In fact, of the seventy-five units of dialogue in this filmstrip, only fifteen could be considered as negative to the hippie movement, and even this estimate is probably somewhat generous. In short, *The Alienated Generation* can only serve to widen the generation gap.

Page 10 of the discussion guide for this filmstrip contains a short bibliography of recommended reading matter, including *Today's Teen-Agers*, by SIECUS director Evelyn Millis Duvall, and *Identity: Youth and Crisis*, written by Humanist Erik Erikson.

MARIJUANA: WHAT CAN YOU BELIEVE? (in two parts) — Dr. David Smith was script consultant for both parts of this sound filmstrip and narrator for Part I.[17] Early in the accompanying discussion guide the point is made that:

> . . . The counselor should keep in mind during this discussion that the aim of the filmstrip is not to take an authoritative stance with regard to marijuana, but to raise doubts in the minds of the viewers.[18]

Once *Marijuana* has been viewed, this somewhat nebulous intent becomes much clearer. Specifically speaking, the overall message *does not* "raise doubts" about smoking marijuana; but rather, it *does* "raise doubts" as to whether (a) marijuana smoking is dangerous, and (b) its current *illegal status* is justified.

Among major points developed in this filmstrip are the following: (1) A significant portion of the population is moving from an alcohol to a marijuana orientation. (2) Smoking marijuana is similar to drinking alcohol. (3) Marijuana is harmful only under certain conditions; for example, when smoked too often, when the user takes the wrong dosage, or when it is taken to solve personality problems. (4) Marijuana smoking leads to harder drugs only because, along with heroin and harder drugs, it possesses an *illegal status* which places it in the same criminal drug subculture. Dr. Smith argues that this association could be broken by moving marijuana out of the subculture — in other words, legalizing it. Although at one point Dr. Smith says that he does not advocate legalizing marijuana, he nevertheless has this to say in the next breath:

> What I feel is that we should take all drugs and place them in a continuum, and regulate the drugs in direct proportion to the abuse potential of the drug . . . . I feel that because marijuana is a psycho-active agent, and particularly with the more potent preparations, *I would regulate that about like alcohol.* [emphasis added]

The above illustrations are only a few of many seeds of destruction that have been planted in the Guidance Associates program, though it purports to have been designed for the purpose of combating drug usage. As with *The Alienated Generation*, this filmstrip makes a feeble attempt to redeem itself here and there by interviewing several youths who offer their own reasons why people should avoid pot. Again, however, these few sporadic contributions seem grossly inadequate when measured against Dr. Smith's convincing case for marijuana, and the prestige afforded by his profession.

Henk Newenhouse, Inc.
1825 Willow Road, Northfield, Illinois

HENK NEWENHOUSE, INC., is listed in the previously mentioned SIECUS form letter for September 1969 as a central source for sex education materials. Upon receipt of this distributing house's 1969 catalog entitled *Sex Education and Family Living Materials*, it was discovered that close to 80 percent of the listings were either SIECUS-endorsed or SIECUS-produced materials. They included the *SIECUS Study Guides* Nos. 1 through 6.

Henk Newenhouse might more accurately be described as a quick-change artist than as a distributor. During 1969, this company shared offices with the SIECUS Publications Office at the above address. In fact, the two were so close that they also shared stationery. Then in March 1970, during the height of the sex education controversy, SIECUS announced it had severed ties with Henk Newenhouse.[1] Since then, Henk Newenhouse has changed its name to Perennial Education, Inc., though it maintains its offices at the same address. Although Perennial Education, Inc., no longer distributes books, it continues to carry basically the same SIECUS-recommended audiovisual aids as its forerunner, Henk Newenhouse.

Lutheran Church — Missouri Synod
3558 South Jefferson Avenue, St. Louis, Missouri

THE PUBLISHING ARM of the Lutheran Church-Missouri Synod is Concordia Publishing House, located at the same address. Here is printed the church's "Concordia Sex Education Series," which is designed "to help all ages grow toward responsible Christian sexuality."[1] Separate guides for parents and church leaders, and correlated sound filmstrips, were designed to accompany the six basic books making up this series, which are discussed below. Although some of these acknowledge God and are kept within the marriage context, they are nevertheless far too explicit in detail for the various age groups designated. Others are entirely inappropriate for the specific reasons given in the discussions that follow.

I WONDER I WONDER, by Dr. Marguerite Kurth Frey (ages 5 to 8, no bibliography) — This book acknowledges God, and the topic of sex is handled within a marital framework. However, it attempts to tell too much too soon. For example, it describes Daddy as carrying his sperm "in the bag or sack that hangs between a man's legs."

Further, its account of childbirth is crude, and could easily confuse a child in this age group. It seems unnecessary to tell young children that babies come out "between the opening where the waste water comes out and the opening for waste solids." Child psychologist Dr. Rhoda Lorand and other experts have stated that forcing such mental images on children so young can cause acute anxiety and apprehension.[2]

WONDERFULLY MADE, by Ruth Hummel (ages 9 to 11, no bibliography) — Here again is a book which demonstrates a traditional Christian viewpoint, but is nevertheless too explicit in teaching sex to mixed classes. Its discussions of seminal emissions, sexual intercourse, the penis and vagina, coupled with drawings of the male and female sex organs, are out of place in a truly Christian-centered program.

Further, the author's treatment of masturbation is extremely lenient. On unnumbered page 32, there is a discussion of boys and girls fondling their sex organs at certain times, though the word "masturbation" is not used. The following comment is made:

> Some boys and girls may worry about doing such things. They may think
> that it is wrong. It isn't. Almost everyone does it when he is young. It isn't
> wrong. It's just babyish.

In California, where sex education was first introduced, students
have admitted that being told masturbation was not wrong caused them
to masturbate freely "to relieve tensions."

TAKE THE HIGH ROAD, by A.J. Bueltmann (ages 12 to 14) — Although
this book has many Christian principles as a basis, gives some good
advice, and is generally written in a commendable way, it nevertheless
raises topics that are not appropriate for classroom discussion, such as
premarital sex, masturbation, nocturnal emissions, and homosexuality.
Portions of its contents might be considered suitable by some for
reading at home.

But the reader should be prepared for a spot course in the
physiology of sex. For example, no detail is left unexplored in describing the male and female sex organs and their respective functions, with
accompanying drawings. Among numerous lengthy paragraphs describing everything from the length, width, and thickness of the average
testicle to the various causes of penile erection, the following general
discussion of the penis is found on pages 44-45:

> The penis is the other external sex organ. It hangs in front of the
> testicles. It is cylindrical in shape and consists largely of spongy tissue. The
> penis varies in size from person to person. It varies in length, in diameter, in
> general contour, and even in the exact place of the opening at the
> end . . . .
> The penis is usually limp and soft. Under certain conditions blood
> rushes into the spongy tissue that makes up the bulk of the penis. The penis
> then becomes hard and firmly erect at an angle from the body . . . .

Further, the author is exceedingly bland in his discussion of homosexuality, carefully avoiding any use of the word "sin" and any
reference to Biblical accounts of God's punishment of Sodom and
Gomorrah. Parents should also be aware that this book invades many
delicate areas that should remain the responsibility of parents.

It should not be surprising to discover that the book's bibliography
leads the adolescent back to SIECUS. Of ten books listed, three are by
SIECUS directors: *Love and the Facts of Life* and *The Art of Dating* by
Evelyn Duvall, and *Finding Yourself* by Helen Southard. Another is
Love and Sex in Plain Language, by Eric W. Johnson. This author is a
close associate of Humanist Mary Calderone and is vice principal of
Germantown Friends School in Philadelphia, a school for Quakers.
Appearing on page one of the book is a review by Dr. Calderone,
generously praising it. Dr. Calderone is also listed under "Acknowledg-

ments," along with her SIECUS colleagues, S. Leon Israel, Emily Mudd, and William L. Peltz. The assistance of Humanist Alan F. Guttmacher, then president of Planned Parenthood-World Population, in auditing the book's contents, is acknowledged too.

Love and Sex in Plain Language is full of sketches of nude men, women, and children. One illustration compares an uncircumcised penis with a circumcised one; another compares a flaccid and an erect penis. The text accompanying these sketches is even more suggestive, as the author describes fully the course of penile erection, including comments on the angle and length of the erect penis. Equally vivid are the descriptions of intercourse and orgasm. The author's section on masturbation clearly gives this practice the green light. One paragraph reads:

> Since masturbation is harmless, even when practiced frequently, you may wonder why I have written about it in this chapter on problems. One reason is that many people *believe* that masturbation is harmful and are deeply worried about boys and girls who masturbate. This is especially true when people belong to a religious group that considers masturbation a sin. If a young person who masturbates is in contact with others who believe it is evil, he will probably feel guilty and ashamed. Yet he may be unable to stop because masturbation gives him such strong pleasure.[3]

Another chapter is entirely devoted to family planning and population control, and includes nine methods of birth control, complete with instructions for use. *Love and Sex in Plain Language*, along with all the other books mentioned in the bibliography of *Take the High Road*, appears under the caption, "Some Helpful Books," and is apparently intended as additional reading for either teacher or student. The preface of Johnson's book recommends it "for boys and girls of any age." It is endorsed by the Gesell Institute of Child Development.[4]

LIFE CAN BE SEXUAL by Elmer Witt (ages 15 and up) — *Life Can Be Sexual* is an incredible experience. Certain passages of the book could even be interpreted as downright blasphemy. Its title does full justice to the contents. Chapter 1, for example, introduces the subject promptly:

> SEX is being 36-24-36.
> SEXUALITY is knowing the meaning and power of being 36-24-36.
> CHRISTIANITY clues us as to where sexuality — with all its meaning and power — comes from and why.
> And it clues us to do something about it!
> That's the message of this book in a nutshell.[5]

The book's main thrust attempts to blend Freudian concepts with Scripture. This is accomplished in a variety of ways. On page 89, for example, *I Corinthians* is restyled in the following manner:

Though I have all the physical assets of a Playboy bunny but have no love,

I become no more than flowering grass or a sexual symbol. . . .

Another example of Witt's Freudian technique gives a sexual connotation to a traditional Sunday morning worship service in order to make it more exciting. Witt's interpretation of the service is presented in the following manner:

The Service	*On the Sexual Way*
	* * * * *
The Creed	We affirm the presence of the Father, who conceived sexuality, the Son, who redeemed it, and the Spirit, who chooses to make our sexual being his home (temple of the Holy Spirit).
	* * * * *
The Lord's Prayer	Literally loaded; for example: God's will to be done through our sexuality, the daily bread which supports our sexual body, deliverance from the temptations and evil which plague our sexual being.
	* * * * *
The Lord's Supper	The dramatic sharing of Christ's own body and blood along with bread and wine for sexual Christian beings to eat and drink, celebrating His death and resurrection, entering into deep and daily fellowship with Him and all Christians, receiving power for practical, sexual living.
	* * * * *
The Benediction	. . . the Lord bless and keep you in that exciting, tricky, servant-like, fun-filled sexual life back in the world for which He made you, to which He called you, and into which He goes with you.[6]

Then such questions as "Have you ever thought of public worship as sexual?" are introduced; hardly the sort of inquiry one would expect from a former parish pastor.

Although Witt's book is replete with "God-language," it nevertheless refers to man as a "sexual being" — a SIECUS-concocted term — rather than as a spiritual being. Nor is there any clear-cut condemnation of masturbation, such as might be expected. Witt's primary objection to the act of masturbation is that it produces a "sense of guilt," while his discussion of homosexuality is full of sympathetic undertones that tend to minimize God's unequivocal condemnation of this sexual deviation. To be specific, though he acknowledges that God's design in nature is clearly for heterosexuality and against homosexuality, Witt summarizes his thoughts on the subject in such conjectures as: "God in Christ loves, forgives, and accepts *all* people, also those with homosexual tendencies," without noting the need for repentance. In fact, during the entire discussion, Witt never uses the word "sin," nor does he make clear that the only way to merit God's forgiveness for past sins is through sincere repentance and a determined resolve to resist future temptation.

Recommended reading in Witt's bibliography includes works by SIECUS directors Evelyn Duvall and William G. Cole, as well as such SIECUS-recommended authors as Betty Friedan, Margaret Mead, and *Playboy's* Hugh Hefner — Humanists all. Other works listed are John A. T. Robinson's *Christian Morals Today*, which makes a strong case for situation ethics; and Donald Kuhn's *The Church and the Homosexual*, published by the Glide Urban Center in San Francisco. (The Glide Center is in the vanguard of the movement to legitimize homosexuality in the United States. See entry for *National Sex and Drug Forum*.)

The ultimate incongruity of *Life Can Be Sexual* lies in the fact that its author, Elmer Witt, is the executive director of youth work for the Lutheran Church — Missouri Synod.

PARENTS GUIDE TO CHRISTIAN CONVERSATION ABOUT SEX, by Erwin J. Kolb (for parents) — Akin to other books in the Concordia series that are couched in traditional Christian language, this book is anything but traditional in its treatment of such key topics as masturbation, abortion, and homosexuality. For instance, the section on masturbation conveys the idea that masturbation is just a phase of growing up, and (on page 71) even rather encourages the practice with the statement that "some medical authorities now regard masturbation as a step in preparation for adult sexual feelings" (this is a quotation from SIECUS-recommended author Marion Lerrigo's *Your Child From 9 to 12*, which is also quoted verbatim in Concordia's *Christian View of Sex Education*). Although the discussion later offers advice to parents on how to help their children overcome the habit, masturbation is never categorized as "wrong," but only as "immature."

In his coverage of abortion (page 89), author Kolb avoids condemning this practice by simply defining what an abortion is without using such offensive words as "killing" or "murder," and blandly adding the comment: "There is no easy answer to every situation, but many Christians believe that an abortion not judged necessary to save the life of the expectant mother is the taking of a life. Today the church is facing the question of *whether an abortion should be permitted in other situations.*" (emphasis added) No attempt is made to meet the subject head-on in terms of a clear-cut "right" or "wrong"; instead, the reader is left with the feeling that he may make his own decision.

Kolb is indifferent in his approach to homosexuality. Although he acknowledges (on page 103) that "The Christian understands that this way of sexual satisfaction [note that the word "perversion" is not used] is contrary to the normal, God-given use for sex," the reader is nevertheless lured into accepting the SIECUS concept that homosexuality may at times be considered "a temporary step in the process by which emotions mature . . . ." Never mentioned in this section are the severe condemnations of this perversion in both Old and New Testaments; nor is any mention made of the massive damage it can do to the soul. In fact, the only real danger Kolb mentions is that a homosexual "sometimes" becomes a "poor marriage risk."

Concordia's review of this guide claims that it offers parents a "Christian understanding of sex."[7] However, footnote references clearly indicate that the author based some of his material on the opinions of such Humanists as Wardell Pomeroy (of *Sexology* fame), Deryck Calderwood, and Helen Southard, all SIECUS directors.

The author's annotated book list includes works by SIECUS officials Evelyn Duvall, Reuben Hill, Lester Kirkendall, and Helen Southard. Other books are by various SIECUS-selected authors. Public Affairs Pamphlets are also listed, as well as materials from two other organizations discussed in PART II: the Humanist-founded Child Study Association of America and the Mental Health Materials Center.

CHRISTIAN VIEW OF SEX EDUCATION, by Martin Wessler (for teachers and church leaders) — Like other books in the Concordia series, this one is presented within a Christian context; it contains many acceptable portions and much wholesome advice. Among its weaknesses is its equivocal treatment of masturbation, which gives the impression that this practice is not necessarily wrong and may even be desirable as a preparation for marriage. Here again is found (page 10) the familiar thought that, "To the best of the pastor's knowledge, no serious physical consequences result from masturbation. But the consequent sense of shame and guilt can be damaging." This is followed by such statements as the following, which again quotes Marion Lerrigo:

> There is no easy answer for what parents should do if they discover a child masturbating at this age [adolescence], because many boys and some girls masturbate as a part of their experimentation and growth in searching for an expression of their sex urge. *However, "some medical authorities now regard masturbation as a step in preparation for adult sexual feelings."* (emphasis added)

Another significant flaw in this book is its "Resource List for the Christian Sex Educator."[8] Among the materials named as additional aids in the development of a Christian sex education program are many that have been discussed elsewhere, most of them SIECUS-recommended. These books, and their authors, are:

- Lester F. Beck, *Human Growth**
- Child Study Association of America, *What To Tell Your Children About Sex*†
- Karl de Schweinitz, *Growing Up**
- Evelyn M. Duvall and Reuben Hill (both SIECUS directors), *Being Married,*† as well as other books by Mrs. Duvall, including *Love and the Facts of Life**
- Ralph G. Eckert, *Sex Attitudes in the Home*†
- Geraldine Lux Flanagan, *The First Nine Months of Life*†
- Sidonie M. Gruenberg (Humanist), *The Wonderful Story of How You Were Born**
- Alan F. Guttmacher (Humanist), *The Complete Book of Birth Control*†
- Richard F. Hettlinger, *Living With Sex: The Student's Dilemma**
- James L. Hymes Jr., *How To Tell Your Child About Sex*† (Public Affairs Pamphlet)
- Lester Kirkendall (SIECUS founder and Humanist), *Understanding Sex** and *Sex Education as Human Relations: A Guidebook on Content and Methods for School Authorities and Teachers*†
- Helen Manley, *A Curriculum Guide in Sex Education*†
- James A. Pike, *Teenagers and Sex*†
- Isadore Rubin (SIECUS director, Humanist, and identified Communist), *Sexual Life After Sixty*†
- Helen F. Southard (SIECUS director and Humanist), *Sex Morality-Teaching Record Kit*†

Some visual aids offered are *How Babies Are Made, Human Growth* (E.C. Brown Trust Foundation), and *Human Reproduction* (McGraw-Hill, revised edition produced with the assistance of Humanist Mary Calderone).[9] Counseling aids suggested are, among others, the previously mentioned "Sex Knowledge Inventories," Forms X and Y, developed by Family Life Publications, Inc. Promoted under the heading "Organizations Offering Assistance" to church sex education committees are SIECUS and SIECCAN (Sex Information and Education Council of Canada, the Canadian counterpart of SIECUS), as well as a number of organizations interlocked with SIECUS.

*   *   *

In conclusion, it should be emphasized that, despite the noble aspiration expressed in the Concordia series — that of "helping all

*For students.
†For adults.

ages to grow toward responsible Christian sexuality" — and despite numerous pages offering commendable thoughts and advice, the books have serious flaws, as noted, which render the program inappropriate for mixed classroom use. It would seem that a truly Christian program should concern itself primarily with the spiritual, moral, and scriptural aspects of sex, in keeping with Christ's teachings, rather than continually focusing attention on drawings and descriptions of sexual organs and their functions in minute detail. In view of this defect, the Concordia series hardly seems appropriate even for use in the home, between parent and child.

But regardless of where the books are used, there is considerable risk involved. In essence, the Concordia program utilizes a number of the basic patterns developed by SIECUS and associates, tones them down and then carefully weaves a Christian dialogue around them.* Once stripped of its Christian framework, the Concordia program's defects become more conspicuous, and the single most consistent feature of contemporary sex education is revealed: the hidden message that masturbation *is not wrong*, that its only harmful effect is the "sense of guilt" that accompanies its practice; and that the repugnance formerly felt toward the homosexual should be abandoned in favor of sympathy and at least partial acceptance.

It would therefore appear that a Christian teacher, counselor, or parent assumes a critical risk by exposing young children to a number of concepts that are not consistent with the Scriptures, and to detailed descriptions and sketches of sex organs, when there is even the slightest possibility that doing so may cause impure or sensual thoughts and fantasies to creep into young minds and strip away the purity they may still possess. For as Matthew 18:6 reminds us:

> But whoso shall offend one of these little ones which believe in me, it were better for him that a millstone were hanged about his neck, and that he were drowned in the depth of the sea.

To which II John 1:9–11 adds:

> Whosoever transgresseth, and abideth not in the doctrine of Christ, hath not God. . . .
> If there come any unto you, and bring not this doctrine, receive him not into your house, neither bid him God speed:
> For he that biddeth him God speed is partaker of his evil deeds.

*It is not meant to imply that Concordia's authors did this deliberately. In all fairness, the benefit of the doubt should be given, since there is no evidence of direct linkage between these authors and the Humanist-spawned SIECUS. It is probable that, in the course of their research, the Concordia authors relied primarily on SIECUS materials, for there is little else available in the field.

Although Concordia published this sex education series for the Lutheran Church — Missouri Synod in 1967, it is still being widely used by this and other religious denominations, including a number of fundamentalist churches.

Marriage

St. Meinrad Archabbey, St. Meinrad, Indiana

THIS CATHOLIC MAGAZINE offers adult home and family living education to married couples. Owned, edited, and published by St. Meinrad Archabbey, the magazine prides itself on the "distinguished" professionals who offer "service and wisdom" to its readers. Among the members of *Marriage's* editorial advisory board are Dr. David R. Mace and the Rev. William Genné, both SIECUS directors.[1]

Dr. Mace, a Quaker, is professor of family sociology at the Bowman Gray School of Medicine's Behavioral Sciences Center, Wake Forest University, Winston-Salem, N.C. He is also affiliated with several SIECUS-interlocking organizations mentioned earlier, and contributes articles to *McCall's* and *Reader's Digest.*

A frequent contributor of articles to *Marriage* is SIECUS associate and Humanist Ashley Montagu. Like Genné, Dr. Montagu serves on the board of consultants of *Sexology.* Dr. Montagu's views on morality are anything but traditional. For example, speaking of premarital sex in the December 1966 issue of *Sexology,* he said:

> It would, I am convinced, greatly contribute to the mental health and stability of our society were adolescents permitted the self-development and self-discipline of premarital sex. *Not* the encouragement of licentiousness or promiscuity, but the encouragement in the growth and development of a mature and healthy personality. A growth and development in which the experience of sex as the beautiful and greatly humanizing event it can be plays its necessary and proper role . . . .

Father James T. McHugh, director of the Catholic Family Life Bureau (see entry for *United States Catholic Conference*), is another author contributing to *Marriage.* A zealous spreader of the SIECUS "gospel," Father McHugh has been associated with Mace, Genné, and other SIECUS directors as advisory committee members of the American Association of Sex Educators and Counselors, a SIECUS front.

Another Catholic priest who contributes to *Marriage* is SIECUS official Father Walter Imbiorski.* Father Imbiorski can best be described as a Humanist-oriented sexologist in priest's clothing. Thus, his lectures present a curious blend of SIECUS philosophy with a smatter-

---

*Since this entry was written, Father Imbiorski has left the priesthood to marry and is no longer considered to be a Catholic priest in good standing.

ing of traditional religious points of view, and his writings present a kaleidoscopic sort of pseudo-religion that can only serve to confuse and bewilder Catholic readers. One wonders what purpose Father Imbiorski has in quoting such passages as the following in a religious publication, either with or without the comment that immediately follows:

> There once was a lady named Wild
> Who kept herself pure, undefiled
>   By thinking of Jesus,
>   Venereal diseases,
> And the fear of begetting a child.

Facetious as it may sound, this is the situation today. Old threats are gone, and people must make personal moral decisions.[2]

This vulgar and sacrilegious limerick originally appeared in Humanist Joseph Fletcher's book, *Moral Responsibility — Situation Ethics at Work*, to put a similar point across.[3] Moreover, Father Imbiorski's writings and speeches are interspersed with frequent use of Humanist phraseology and are frequently embellished with casual references to dedicated Humanists who are not identified as such.

An occasional contributor to *Marriage* is Humanist Robert Francoeur, a former Catholic priest whose book, *Perspectives in Evolution*, promotes the concept of scientific human breeding. In the March 1970 issue of *Marriage* there is an article by Francoeur titled "Learning How to Play God with Man's Future," an analysis of works by other authors. The books reviewed are all given vigorous approbation, which again is incongruous, considering their subjects. Most books reviewed by Francoeur are Humanist-oriented,* and take the so-called "ethical" approach to the problems of man in a supposedly secular world.

Rosenfeld's *Second Genesis* and Taylor's *Biological Time Bomb* are described by Francoeur as "marvelous, all-enveloping surveys of the biological revolution, from birth in an artificial womb, programmed minds, brain transplants and pregnancy permits to the creation of life, human-computer hybrids, body banks and postponing death."[4]

Of course there are some traditionally oriented articles in *Marriage*; otherwise, its readership might dwindle. But it only takes a small dose of poison to kill — in this case, to kill faith. That this magazine

---

*Francoeur's extensive travels into Humanist territory involve participation in *The Humanist's* "Ethical Forum" for November–December 1973, together with a number of well-known Humanists. This Forum had previously been an official quarterly publication of the American Ethical Union and presented opinions of a purely non-theistic, ethical point of view. When a joint sponsor of *The Humanist* with the American Humanist Association in 1969, the "Ethical Forum" was incorporated into *The Humanist* as a regular feature.

delivers plenty of small doses is evidenced by a letter to the editor that appeared in the March 1970 issue. The letter, from a Cuban reader, is self-explanatory, as its writer begins by listing his objections to an earlier article in *Marriage* magazine on "Family and Revolution in Cuba." His main dissent centers on two false points which the article tried to implant in the mind of its readers:

> . . . the first one is that the policy of the Cuban government regarding abortion and birth control is identical to the Vatican's policy, and secondly, that a person with a family in Cuba can be a perfect practicing Catholic and a perfect "*Fidelista*" at the same time.
>
> Frankly, I had the impression that *Marriage* was a magazine edited with the purpose of bringing good, Christian advice to the American families. I was able to detect the poison in this article because I am familiar with the subject, *but I ask myself how much poison I have swallowed already* from articles on subjects unfamiliar to me.[5] [emphasis added]

It is to be hoped that by now other readers are asking the same question.

McGraw-Hill, Inc.
330 West 42nd Street, New York, New York

THE ONLY KNOWN, OVERT CONNECTION between McGraw-Hill and SIECUS is the fact that Dr. Mary Calderone was the consultant in the remaking of McGraw-Hill's film, *Human Reproduction*. Dr. Calderone's fellow Humanist, Margaret Sanger, founder of Planned Parenthood, is given credit for assistance in producing this film. Perhaps this explains why *Human Reproduction's* story of sex is imparted in a purely animalistic framework that is spiritually void. The film displays in crude but graphic drawings closeups of the female genitalia, nude pregnant women, and the male scrotum and penis, showing penis in full erection, and also in the process of ejaculation.

Despite the fact that McGraw-Hill cannot be otherwise identified with SIECUS, there can be no doubt that the organization has fallen prey to the influence of the same Humanist complex that guides SIECUS. Besides distributing a wide assortment of educational materials that advance Humanist concepts, McGraw-Hill promotes and distributes a number of sex education films that rank high on the SIECUS billboard. Several of these are described briefly below.

THE GAME — Depicts a teenage boy's seduction of a young virgin, and the mixed emotions of the two following intercourse. As his friends find vicarious pleasure in discussing some of the details of his affair as they imagine it, one hears reference made to the girl's "cherry," as well as such remarks as, "Did you bounce her high?" Among other treats in store for young teenage viewers of this film are repeated scenes of dancing, bikini-clad girls with the camera focused on their breasts and abdominal areas, and a suggestive soul-kissing scene. The film concludes with a street scene, in which Peter, the seducer, is debating whether or not to see Vicki again. As he begins to search his conscience, his eye catches the action of a workman's drill in the process of vigorously penetrating the earth. At this point, Peter hurriedly enters a phone booth and begins to dial Vicki's number. Like so many sex education materials, *The Game* opens the door for discussion, and avoids taking sides as to the rights or wrongs of the situation.

PHOEBE — The story of a premarital affair, showing the emotional conflicts of a young teenager on discovering she is pregnant. The film offers no solution, nor does it take a moral stand. The closing scene finds this situation still unresolved, its overall hidden message pointing to birth control. In fact, if a teacher were so inclined, this might well lead her to recommend contraceptives as the best solution.

THE MERRY-GO-ROUND — Features the views of Dr. Albert Ellis — a Humanist, hedonist, and bellwether of the sex revolution. (See entry on *National Sex and Drug Forum.*) McGraw-Hill's catalog describes him as one of several "well-known authorities on sex"[1] appearing in the film. Another is columnist Ann Landers, a SIECUS sponsor.

FOUR FAMILIES — A film narrated by Humanist Margaret Mead, the highly publicized anthropologist-author.[2]

All four of the above films are produced by the National Film Board of Canada (NFBC), for which McGraw-Hill acts as the chief distributor in the United States. NFBC is registered with the Foreign Agents Registration Section, U.S. Department of Justice, as "an agent of the Canadian Government,"[3] which is currently headed by a socialist, Prime Minister Pierre Elliott Trudeau.

Among other noteworthy films distributed by McGraw-Hill (but having no connection with NFBC) are the following, all listed in the annotated catalog, *Sociology*:[4]

BROTHERHOOD OF MAN — The Public Affairs Pamphlet *Races of Mankind*, written by Communist fellow travelers Ruth Benedict and Gene Weltfish, provided the basis for this film. As was brought out earlier, *Races of Mankind* has been described by the United States Army as designed to create racial antagonism.

MARRIAGE TODAY and THIS CHARMING COUPLE — These two films were correlated with the textbook, *Marriage for Moderns*, by SIECUS-recommended author Henry A. Bowman. The book was cited by a subcommittee of the California State Legislature as among those which "strike at the sanctity of marriage, at the family, and religion." McGraw-Hill suggests that these films be shown in Sociology and Home Economics courses.

THE FUTURISTS — Twelve scientists, economists, educators, and writers tell "what they think the world of tomorrow will be like." Produced by CBS News, this film is loaded with the views of such Humanists as R. Buckminster Fuller, Herman Kahn, Lord Peter Ritchie-Calder, Isaac Asimov, and Harrison Brown.

How Do Things Look? — A panel of "five eminent thinkers in the fields of education, international relations, religion and philosophical thought, the arts, and bio-medicine" offer a prognosis of events and attitudes in the twenty-first century. At least two panel members are Humanists: Lord Peter Ritchie-Calder and Robert M. Hutchins. Besides writing a column for the *Los Angeles Times*, Hutchins serves on the national advisory council of the American Civil Liberties Union. He is an avid promoter of world government, being a founder and president of the Committee To Frame a World Constitution. Like SIECUS officials Harriet Pilpel and Earl Ubell, Hutchins is a member of the American Ethical Union's Board of Ethical Lecturers advisory committee.[5]

How Do Things Look? and *The Futurists* are both products of CBS. They were first seen on CBS's "21st Century" series.

Time Piece — The potential psychological damage *Time Piece* could inflict upon young people may be easily ascertained by any honest viewer.

The opening scene commences in a hospital room, where a stethoscope is being applied to the chest of a bearded patient. The sound of his heartbeat is caught and magnified by the sound track. This is synchronized with frequent, sudden psychedelic shifts of scenery throughout the film to produce a dramatic effect.

The patient's life is then shown in a series of flashbacks: working in a factory, and being unmercifully pressured by buzzers, alarms, gongs, and whistles until he runs away, but is unable to escape his misery. As he finally anticipates a modicum of pleasure at mealtime, he is served his own head on a platter, feebly crying for "help."

Following a number of equally distressing scenes, the patient's head is seen in a toilet bowl. As the lid slowly closes, the head once again feebly cries for "help." The camera quickly returns to the hospital room, where a sheet is being pulled over the patient's head. The heartbeat stops. As the film closes, the doctor, who turns out to be the same man as the deceased, faces the audience with a gloating smile.

The general impression created in *Time Piece* is that life is a hopeless rat race, without purpose or meaning — the only escape being death. In short, the film's nihilistic distortion of life is a shocking discredit to our educational system.

This scathing satire was produced in 1965 by Muppets, Inc., in cooperation with Contemporary Films. Its author and star, Jim Henson, is also creator of the Muppets, seen on *Sesame Street*, a television program for preschoolers.

As for McGraw-Hill's organizational structure, this company's president and chief executive officer, Shelton Fisher, is on the board of directors of the United Nations Association of the United States of America, an organization whose long-time goal has been world government. A close colleague of Mr. Fisher is Edward E. Booher, chairman of McGraw-Hill's subsidiary, the McGraw-Hill Book Company. Interestingly, Mr. Booher also served as chairman of the Board of Higher Education for the state of New Jersey when that state's sex education controversy was at its height in 1969.

Medical Aspects of Human Sexuality

Published by Clinical Communications, Inc.
18 East 48th Street, New York, New York

MEDICAL ASPECTS OF HUMAN SEXUALITY is a monthly journal for physicians. Its stated purpose is to "provide authoritative information on sexual problems that affect many patients," to be supplemented by "pertinent current data from sociology, psychology, and other behavioral sciences."[1]

Also a part of this journal's statement of purpose is the declaration that, "As a scientific journal, *Medical Aspects of Human Sexuality* is not designed to promulgate any particular point of view. Our distinguished Consulting Editors represent a wide variety of opinions . . . ." However, this magazine's list of consulting editors contains such familiar names as Harold I. Lief, William H. Masters, Roy W. Menninger, and John Rock — all SIECUS board members.[2] Prior to his death in 1971, Father George Hagmaier of SIECUS was also one of the consulting editors. Others include Edward T. Auer (a member of the Group for the Advancement of Psychiatry), Seward Hiltner (a SIECUS-recommended author and consultant on religion and psychiatry to The Menninger Foundation), and Richard F. Hettlinger (another SIECUS-selected author).

A number of SIECUS officials appear in various issues of this journal as contributing authors; a few of them, also familiar, are Alan Bell, Jessie Bernard, Carlfred Broderick, Harold Christensen, Evelyn Duvall, S. Leon Israel, Warren Johnson, Harold Lief, David Mace, John Money, William Peltz, Wardell Pomeroy, Rabbi Jeshaia Schnitzer, Ralph Slovenko, Father John L. Thomas, and Clark Vincent.

Judging from all of the above and other related symptoms, the SIECUS canker has apparently reached another major target — this time the field of medicine, and particularly the family physician's office.

Mental Health Materials Center, Inc. (MHMC)
419 Park Avenue South, New York, New York

THE MENTAL HEALTH MATERIALS CENTER is a private agency which provides a wide variety of reading matter for distribution in mental health clinics, family service agencies, health and welfare agencies, child guidance clinics, maternal and child health services, general practitioners, pediatricians, parent-teacher organizations, and nursery schools. Topics covered by these publications include sex education, drugs, alcoholism, mental retardation, child training, and suicide.

A close affinity between MHMC and SIECUS cannot be denied. In the spring of 1967, MHMC was retained by SIECUS to conduct a survey of its Newsletter readership.[1] From January 1968 until the spring of 1969, MHMC served as the SIECUS publications office and the two organizations shared the same address. During the time SIECUS was located at this address at 419 Park Avenue South, SIECUS distributed MHMC publications. (This communal office is currently shared by the Group for the Advancement of Psychiatry, the World Federation of Public Health, and other Humanist-oriented groups.)

One division of MHMC, the Information Resources Center for Mental Health and Family Life Education (IRC), publishes the *IRC Selective Guide*. IRC's promotional leaflet for this guide begins with a comment by Humanist Eda LeShan, Family Life Consultant for the National Educational Television network (NET), who lauds the guide as "remarkable and unique . . . sound and extremely helpful." A member of the New York Society for Ethical Culture,[2] Mrs. LeShan is also a SIECUS-recommended author, a writer of Public Affairs Pamphlets, and wife of Humanist Lawrence LeShan, who writes extensively on the subject of mysticism. The November–December 1971 issue of *The Humanist* further identifies Mrs. LeShan as being featured in the NET TV series, *How Do Your Children Grow?*[3]

The *IRC Selective Guide* promotes the usual SIECUS publications, including most of the Study Guides, as well as sex education materials by such SIECUS affiliates as the E. C. Brown Trust Foundation, the Child Study Association of America, the Public Affairs Committee, and Science Research Associates. Among other favorites found in this guide is the booklet, *The Right to Abortion: A Psychiatric View*, which was formulated by a committee of the Group for the Advancement of Psychiatry under the guidance of SIECUS director Ralph Slovenko and

Humanist Alice S. Rossi. (See entry for the *Group for the Advancement of Psychiatry* elsewhere in PART II for a review.) IRC's evaluation of this pro-abortion report as given in Bulletin #142 reads: "A concise, fresh, and authoritative statement on a controversial issue, consistently emphasizing its mental health aspects."

Another IRC selection is worthy of mention. Bulletin #306 accents *Fresh, Variable Winds*, by Nora Stirling, the second in a trilogy of plays called *Temperate Zone: Three Plays for Parents About the Climate of the Home.* According to IRC's review, this play "presents a convincing little episode in a family upset by crisis," while focusing attention on interpersonal relationships between a ten-year-old son and his father, who find it difficult to communicate with one another.

Interestingly, Miss Stirling chose Humanist Lawrence K. Frank (now deceased) to write the discussion guide accompanying this play. Dr. Frank states in his guide that during this period of a boy's adolescence, "he will be repeatedly in conflict with his own ideals of right and wrong," and sympathetically observes that the boy "may have to deny these, forget them, even openly violate them to retain his place in the group." Rather than giving parents and teachers encouragement and support to establish and maintain a code of high moral standards, the guide advises them to remain essentially neutral and to encourage the adolescent to establish his own values.

Dr. Frank wrote discussion guides for other plays by Nora Stirling, including *The Ins and Outs*, which relies heavily on sensitivity training techniques. Until his death, Dr. Frank was a leader in the New York Ethical Culture Society.[4]

MHMC is perhaps best known for publishing the 160-page report, *Teach Us What We Want To Know*, which is based on a survey of 5,000 school children ranging from Kindergarten through Grade 12, conducted by the Connecticut Department of Education. It is claimed that the results of the survey indicated the need for an integrated K-12 sex education program, and a curriculum "that places a strong emphasis on mental, social, and emotional health as well as on the physical aspects."[5] MHMC further describes this report as "one that may well bring about the complete restructuring of the health curriculum in schools . . ."* [6]

---

*The concept of fusing sex education with the health curriculum was introduced at the January 1968 meeting of the permanent Joint Committee of the National School Boards Association and the American Association of School Administrators. Here a recommendation was made to incorporate sex and family life education into a comprehensive K–12 Health Education Program.

In keeping with this scheme, Lester Kirkendall's state of residence, Oregon,

This project's special advisor was Elsa Schneider of the U.S. Office of Education, which funded the survey. She was also one of twelve participants in a sex education workshop, held in October 1966, which provided the essence of the New Jersey State Board of Education Policy Statement on Sex Education,[7] portions of which were nearly direct quotations from the SIECUS Study Guide #1, *Sex Education.*[8]

As might have been anticipated, *Teach Us What We Want To Know* was given a favorable review in the October 1969 *SIECUS Newsletter* and was heartily endorsed by Dr. Mary Calderone in the January 1970 issue of *Eternity* magazine.

---

has adopted a Comprehensive Health Plan containing a sex education unit camouflaged under the title, "Interpersonal Relationships." The health plan itself mentions that SIECUS and the American Association of Sex Educators and Counselors will formulate the portion on sex education. Interestingly, by 1971 some combination of health/physical education was required in 32 states.

National Association of Independent Schools (NAIS)
4 Liberty Square, Boston, Massachusetts

IN JULY 1966, the National Association of Independent Schools undertook a program designed to encourage and assist its 800 member schools with the planning and development of programs of instruction in sex education. The decision to launch this new venture had apparently been made at an NAIS Institute on Sex Education seminar, held at Princeton in April 1966. NAIS literature describes this seminar as a discussion by 50 school administrators and teachers of the need for and the nature of sex education; it was led by Humanist confreres Dr. Mary S. Calderone and Dr. Alan F. Guttmacher, together with Mrs. Millicent McIntosh and the Rev. Richard Unsworth.[1]

A book published in October 1967, titled *Sex Education and the Schools*[2] and presenting the full proceedings of the above Institute on Sex Education, was soon to become a major feature among NAIS materials offered to both public and independent schools on the subject. Since this book subsequently found its way into numerous home and family living bibliographies throughout the country, it may be worthwhile to take a look at its contents. Here are a few excerpts from the proceedings:

Dr. Calderone's Question Period
Question: You use nothing but clinical terms. When you are dealing with children, they use the old four-letter, Anglo-Saxon terms. Do you think it's necessary in dealing with them at their level to keep it clinical?
Dr. Calderone: I think it's necessary to do that which is comfortable for them and comfortable for you. I did use the word "f . . ." once on a public platform of a high school and the skies did not fall in. I did it deliberately when a question gave me a golden opportunity: "Why do some boys like to talk dirty in front of girls?" So I immediately twisted the thing around and said: "It depends on what you mean by talking dirty, and what the fellow means. I have actually heard the word 'f . . .' used in a good and clean way. I have heard the word 'intercourse' used in a dirty way. So, it depends on the *motivation* — what you mean. . . ." Now, I didn't answer the original question, "Why do some boys like to talk dirty in front of girls?" That wasn't important to answer. But I did what I did deliberately to see what would happen, to see if anybody would be shook up. Nobody was.[3]

Several pages later, a staunch SIECUS supporter, the Rev. Mr. Unsworth, comments:

I think this is important, and maybe has something to do with the question stated earlier about the language that's used, and the idea of communicating not just facts but the *aura* of facts. I'd like to see more discussion about language in context. I could name, let's say, four or five terms for coitus used in different literary contexts which would range from the sacred to the diabolic in their aura. The word "f . . ." was used in *Lady Chatterley's Lover* with an almost sacred aura . . . .[4]

Spring 1967 again found NAIS nesting with SIECUS at the NAIS Annual Conference in New York. As might have been expected, the NAIS playbill for this affair featured speeches by Dr. Calderone[5] and others, followed by a lively question-and-answer period. The full proceedings of the conference were recorded on video-tape and were later televised by WNDT, Channel 13, New York. NAIS offers a 90-minute, 16-mm sound film of the entire program. A booklet titled *Planning a Program of Sex Education*, containing the presentations made by the speakers, is also available from NAIS.

NAIS's consultant on sex education programs is its vice-president John Chandler Jr., who also serves on the board of directors of the American Association of Sex Educators and Counselors, a SIECUS front. Mr. Chandler's aim is described in the January 1968 issue of *McCall's* as being "not to blitz the schools with packaged programs *but to expose entire faculties to new attitudes* and new knowledge about sex."[6] (emphasis added) A portion of the SIECUS influence behind this association is brought to the surface as the article continues:

> The NAIS has sponsored some unusually excellent seminars for teachers, directed by Dr. Warren Johnson [a SIECUS director] at the University of Maryland, where invited experts from many disciplines — medicine, psychiatry, psychology, sociology, anthropology, public health — offer teachers a prism of views.

With the foregoing facts as background for the NAIS scenario, it comes as no surprise to find among other sex education properties offered by NAIS the following:

- *Anaheim Program of Sex Education* — largely developed and coordinated by SIECUS official Sally R. Williams
- Guidance Associates of Pleasantville, N.Y., filmstrips — prepared with SIECUS consultation
- *Family Planning, Population Problems and the Secondary School Curriculum* — made available by Planned Parenthood–World Population, a Humanist front that is an avid SIECUS bedfellow
- *How Babies Are Made* — filmstrip made with consultation from SIECUS and the Humanist-founded Child Study Association of America

- *Planning a Program of Sex Education* — a publication by Dr. Mary S. Calderone
- *Sex and Sex Education* — a basic reading list of seven books and several other items for adults. Among the books included are:
  - *Towards a Quaker View of Sex* — published by the Friends Home Service Committee in London. This book maintains, among other things, that "it is the nature and quality of a relationship which matters. Homosexual affection can be as selfless as heterosexual affection and therefore we cannot see that it is in some way morally worse."
  - *Living With Sex: The Student's Dilemma* — by Richard F. Hettlinger (see entry for *United States Catholic Conference*, elsewhere in PART II)
  - *Today's Teen-Agers* — by SIECUS director Evelyn Duvall
  - *Human Sex and Sex Education* — by SIECUS official Warren Johnson
  - The *SIECUS* Newsletter and *SIECUS Study Guides on Sex Education*, *Homosexuality*, and *Masturbation*
  - *Young People and Sex* — by Arthur H. Cain. Although Cain is not a SIECUS director, the contents of this book would make him a likely candidate. Various passages are so lewd, perverted, and vulgar that they cannot be quoted.

One passage gives detailed descriptions of three positions for oral-genital stimulation; another passage condones sodomy under certain conditions.

In a later section, Cain suggests that seven books which he classifies as "pornographic" be introduced into the curriculum at the high school level. He concludes this passage by saying: "Once they [the students] have perused these examples, there is no point in searching for further material: there is little, if anything, on the market (black market or otherwise) which is more pornographic."

This book has been found listed in sex education bibliographies *for students* throughout the country.

National Association for Repeal of Abortion Laws (NARAL)
250 West 57th Street, New York, New York

It will be recalled that, in Chapter 1, Humanist and SIECUS founder Lester Kirkendall was quoted as saying he viewed sex education as a prerequisite for public acceptance of population control. Writing in the Spring 1965 issue of *The Humanist*, Dr. Kirkendall further expounded the need for radical social change and the building of a new sex ethic through re-education, not only of youth, but of the adult community as well.

The SIECUS director further implied that the change in public opinion to be effected through sex education would provide a climate favorable to eventual modification of laws governing sex crimes, pornography, and abortion. Thus, a safe assumption is that SIECUS was instituted by the Humanist complex for the express purpose of bringing about a climate favorable to these Humanist goals and others intrinsic to the population control scheme. The tracing of a SIECUS-Humanist link to the abortion issue is the subject of this particular inquiry. For if the abortion question is ever to be fully understood in its present context, it is vital that we search behind the wave of challenges to state abortion statutes, and accurately identify the forces responsible for the repeal of the statutes.

The sexual revolution of the 1960's left in its wake a number of unfulfilled campaign promises. Abortion law reform was one. State laws on abortion were still standing firm in the mid-Sixties; forty-five states prohibited all abortions except where necessary to save the life of the mother.[1] Penalties for illegal abortions were severe. In New York, for example, abortion was a felony, carrying a sentence of up to seven years.

Then, suddenly, new vistas burst forth. Acting as the avant-garde in what was to become a dedicated and zealous crusade against life, the American Humanist Association (AHA) passed a resolution in favor of elective abortion at its 1966 Annual Conference in Asilomar, California.[2] Shortly afterward, the AHA board of directors passed a motion to make abortion law reform the top social action priority for the AHA in 1967.[3] That same year, Colorado became the first state in the nation to let down legal barriers against abortion.

Existing abortion repeal committees that had emerged here and there were beginning to score some successes, but coordination was needed. One San Francisco group calling itself "The Society for Humane Abortion" asserted: "Our purpose is to organize those who believe as we do into a solid, informed membership, capable of making its voice heard at the propitious time."[4]

Apparently viewing 1969 as the "propitious time," Lawrence Lader and other abortionist leaders convened a First National Conference on Abortion Laws (FNCAL) at the Drake Hotel in Chicago in February of that year. This group formed the nucleus of what was to become the National Association for Repeal of Abortion Laws (NARAL). Attending the FNCAL assembly were many organizations and individuals whose common goal was the total abolition of all existing abortion laws in the United States. Although the task ahead was Herculean, the movement was to gain strength from the new federation.

First National Conference on Abortion Laws (FNCAL)

Examination of the roster of individuals and organizations who participated in the First National Conference on Abortion Laws shows that the entire conference was Humanist-conceived and Humanist-directed. In fact, as will be subsequently shown, the entire abortion repeal movement has been a Humanist enterprise from start to finish. However, like so many other closely guarded secrets of the Humanist movement, this irrefutable fact is rarely revealed to the general public. The following documented description of FNCAL is given to demonstrate the depth of Humanist involvement in the anti-life crusade.

Coordinating Committee Chairmen

All three Coordinating Committee chairmen working for FNCAL were Humanists. Acting as East Coast Coordinating Committee chairman was SIECUS-recommended author Lawrence Lader, well-known to his fellow Humanists as the biographer of Margaret Sanger (founder of Planned Parenthood and 1957 "Humanist of the Year"). Lader's Humanist ties are so strong that he was a signer of *Humanist Manifesto II*; he was also a founder of the New York-based Association for the Study of Abortion* and author of *Abortion*, the paperback edition of which is published by the Unitarian-Universalist Association's Beacon Press.

*The October 1968 SIECUS Newsletter announced SIECUS' participation in the International Conference of the Association for the Study of Abortion at Hot Springs, Virginia, in that year. Humanist Harriet Pilpel of SIECUS is general counsel to and a member of that association.

Functioning as West Coast Coordinating Committee chairman was Humanist Garrett Hardin, sponsor of *The Humanist* magazine's Publication Development Committee[5] and of the Society for Humane Abortion,[6] another Humanist front.

Humanist Lonny Myers was the Midwest Coordinating Committee chairman for this conference. She also has the distinction of having been a panel leader at the same Humanist Day of the World conference[7] where hedonist Dr. Albert Ellis received the 1971 "Humanist of the Year" award. In addition, Dr. Myers was a signer of the October 16, 1969 *New York Times* advertisement in support of SIECUS.

Participating Groups

The following groups participating in the FNCAL conference are known to be either Humanist or affiliated with the Humanist movement:

> American Civil Liberties Union
> American Ethical Union
> American Humanist Association
> California Committee to Legalize Abortion
> Illinois Citizens for the Medical Control of Abortion
> National Emergency Civil Liberties Committee*
> National Organization for Women
> Society for Humane Abortion†
> Unitarian-Universalist Association
> Wisconsin Committee to Legalize Abortion
> Women's City Club of New York
> Women's Liberation

Individual Sponsors

SIECUS officials Sophia J. Kleegman and Wardell Pomeroy are shown on FNCAL's official letterhead as Individual Sponsors of this conference, as are SIECUS sponsor Stewart R. Mott and SIECUS ad signers Marya Mannes and Vance Packard.

Known Humanists who appear on the same letterhead as Individual Sponsors of FNCAL's conference are:

*As recently as 1970, the National Emergency Civil Liberties Committee was cited by the U.S. House of Representatives Committee on Internal Security (HCIS) as "communist controlled."[8]
†Planned Parenthood leader Dr. Alan F. Guttmacher was, before his death, a sponsor of the Society for Humane Abortion, along with other prominent Humanists.

- Dr. Walter C. Alvarez — SIECUS sponsor
- Algernon Black — veteran Communist fronter and SIECUS associate.
- Dr. Prynce C. Hopkins — signer of the "Support SIECUS" ad
- Walter Lawton — leader, Chicago Ethical Society
- Ashley Montagu — SIECUS-recommended author; author of introduction to the book, *Abortion in the United States*, edited by Dr. Mary S. Calderone.
- Aryeh Neier — executive director of the American Civil Liberties Union.
- Dr. Alice S. Rossi — consultant for the report of the Group for the Advancement of Psychiatry on *The Right to Abortion: A Psychiatric View*.
- Herman Schwartz — A lawyer, Mr. Schwartz represents both the American Humanist Association and the American Civil Liberties Union. (During the 1971 Attica prison uprising, Schwartz was a chief aide to Communist sympathizer and Humanist lawyer William Kunstler, also of the ACLU. Both Schwartz and Kunstler acted on behalf of the Marxist militants who sparked the Attica uprising.)

FNCAL's conference proceedings did not run as smoothly as anticipated, due to a clash of views. One faction was content to settle for minor repeals that would accommodate certain restrictive limitations on abortion; another faction, representing the majority, would not settle for less than a total elimination of all restrictions on abortion. It is the latter faction that established the National Association for Repeal of Abortion Laws.

With a Humanist coalition still in control, a concerted anti-life crusade was under way by the late 1960's, giving the needed national thrust to the abortion repeal movement. NARAL was now a reality.

National Association for Repeal of Abortion Laws (NARAL)

When it opened offices at 250 West 57th Street* in New York in March 1969, NARAL became the hub of the abortion repeal movement in America. Almost overnight NARAL's organizational network began chipping away at legislative and public opinion, putting into operation a carefully planned formula for success. One NARAL bulletin expressed

*This address is shared by such anti-life groups as the Euthanasia Society of America, the Society for the Right to Die, Inc., and the Euthanasia Educational Council, as well as with the Abortion Rights Association of New York, which SIECUS promotes in its literature.

the formula this way: "Repeal=Public Support×Organization+Legislative Pressure."[9]

As a result of some earlier victories scored by forerunners of this movement, and through the unswerving dedication of NARAL leadership, abortion reform had left its mark in seventeen states and the District of Columbia by the summer of 1971.[10] Four states — Alaska, Hawaii, New York, and Washington* — now permitted legal abortion for any reason, the decision to abort being left to the woman and her doctor. Similar laws awaited decision in other state legislative chambers as NARAL regrouped its forces for another attack.

Structurally speaking, by early 1972 NARAL listed members from forty-nine states and five foreign countries, in addition to the sixty-one organization members in its standing army. A beginning had been made.

NARAL Leadership

Like FNCAL, NARAL's top echelon is riddled with personalities from the Humanist-SIECUS camp. Verification of this can be found in an article titled *The Abortion Revolution*, by Humanist Lawrence Lader, which appeared in the May–June 1973 issue of *The Humanist* magazine. In this issue Lader joined other Humanists, including Planned Parenthood's Dr. Alan F. Guttmacher, in an editorial spree celebrating the legalization of abortion by the Supreme Court.

According to Lader, the campaign to repeal abortion laws in every state "quickly became the foundation of a 75-organization coalition called the National Association for Repeal of Abortion Laws . . . ." Lader continued, "We started with only a handful of militants in New York and California, *a few organizations like the American Humanist Association, American Ethical Union, Unitarian-Universalists, and New York Civil Liberties Union.*" (emphasis added)

It is further revealed in Lader's article that the NARAL-led abortion campaign undoubtedly had a sizable influence on the 1973 Supreme Court decision. The Court's opinion included seven citations

---

*In the state of Washington, an abortion repeal bill was passed by public referendum in 1970. The forces of atheistic Humanism were hard at work there, expending their total energy in behalf of "Referendum 20." Describing her part in the campaign for passage, Bette Chambers of Spokane, who headed the American Humanist Association's Abortion-Law Reform Committee, expressed jubilation over the hard-won victory in the "Letters to the Editor" column of *The Humanist* for March–April 1971: "The state of Washington has finally passed an abortion law repeal bill. I logged, in all, 29 public addresses, four 'formal' debates, and several rather hair-raising encounters, on behalf of abortion law reform . . . . On Saturday, October 31, right on through sunset, November 2, I walked 45 miles distributing 1500 pro-abortion reform leaflets in seven city precincts . . . . WE WON!!! I've never had such a thrill . . . to really win one!"

from the studies of NARAL's legal counsel, Professor Cyril C. Means, Jr., and seven others from Lader's own book, *Abortion*.

The following roster of individuals from the Humanist-SIECUS camp who hold leadership positions with NARAL is given here simply for the record:

EXECUTIVE COMMITTEE OFFICERS

- *Maurine Neuberger, Honorary Vice President* — A former U.S. Senator, Mrs. Neuberger is a Unitarian-Universalist. Unitarian-Universalist Association leadership, it will be recalled, is in firm alliance with the Humanist movement.
- *Lawrence Lader, Executive Committee Chairman* — An active Humanist, Mr. Lader was also East Coast Chairman of FNCAL.
- *Betty Friedan, Vice President East* — Mrs. Friedan, a signer of *Humanist Manifesto II*, is founding president of the radical, Humanist-oriented women's liberation group, the National Organization for Women (NOW), and co-founder of the recently formed "Womansurge."
- *Lana Clarke Phelan, Vice President West* — A Humanist, Lana Phelan is also co-author of *The Abortion Handbook*, a publication distributed by the American Humanist Association. She is a member of the National Organization for Women and the Society for Humane Abortion.
- *Stewart R. Mott, Vice President, Advisory Council* — Besides having been a sponsor of FNCAL, Mr. Mott appears on the SIECUS letterhead as an official SIECUS sponsor. In addition, he is a member of the executive committee of the Humanist-founded Planned Parenthood–World Population.
- *Helen Southard, Secretary* — Mrs. Southard is a Humanist, a SIECUS official,* and director of the Bureau of Research and Program Resources, National Board of the YWCA.

EXECUTIVE COMMITTEE MEMBERS

- *Patricia T. Maginnis* — A Humanist and women's liberation militant, Miss Maginnis worked with the Trotskyite Socialist Workers Party in San Francisco for the repeal of abortion laws. She is president of the Society for Humane Abortion and co-author with Lana Clarke Phelan of *The Abortion Handbook*.
- *Robert W. McCoy* — A long-time member of *The Humanist's* Publication Committee and former president of the American Humanist Association, Mr. McCoy is also affiliated with the Minnesota Council for the Legal Termination of Pregnancy.

*Another NARAL-SIECUS link is Dr. E. James Lieberman, who serves on NARAL's medical committee.

BOARD OF DIRECTORS
- *Leona Baumgartner* — A SIECUS sponsor.
- *Joseph Fletcher* — A Humanist, veteran Communist-fronter and SIECUS-recommended author.
- *Helen E. Meiklejohn* — A Humanist and member of Planned Parenthood, Mrs. Meiklejohn also serves on the National Advisory Council of the American Civil Liberties Union and is a sponsor of the Society for Humane Abortion. Mrs. Meiklejohn's late husband, Alexander (also a Humanist), was for many years national vice-chairman of the ACLU and, according to the March–April 1965 issue of *The Humanist*, often cooperated with the earlier-mentioned Communist-controlled Emergency Civil Liberties Committee.
- *Lloyd Morain* — Former president of the American Humanist Association.
- *Dr. Lonny Myers* — A Humanist and former Midwest Coordinating Committee Chairman of FNCAL.
- *Dr. Alice S. Rossi* — A Humanist, lobbyist for NOW, and SIECUS-recommended author.
- *Ivan Shapiro* — Member, New York Civil Liberties Union.

NARAL Organizational Members

A listing of its organizational members published by NARAL includes a number of groups that are either Humanist or Humanist-controlled:

- American Humanist Association
- Chicago Area Council of Liberal Churches (Unitarian-Universalist)
- Illinois Citizens for Medical Control of Abortion
- Minnesota Council for the Legal Termination of Pregnancy
- New York Civil Liberties Union
- National Women's Conference of the American Ethical Union
- Society for Humane Abortion, San Francisco
- Unitarian-Universalist Women's Federation
- Wisconsin Committee To Legalize Abortion[11]

NARAL Supporters

Another NARAL publication, titled *Speaking Up on Abortion — Statements by Organizations*, contains strong endorsements of total repeal by other organizations, among them the following Humanist-founded groups:

- American Civil Liberties Union
- American Ethical Union
- American Humanist Association
- National Council of Women of the United States
- Planned Parenthood-World Population
- Unitarian-Universalist Association[12]

Statements of other organizations supporting the repeal of abortion laws also appear in supplementary NARAL literature. The organizations include many of the above, as well as the following:

- *Americans for Democratic Action* — A left-wing political group which is a haven for Humanists.
- *American Friends Service Committee* — The Humanist-oriented Quaker unit.
- *American Psychological Association* — This group has established a division of Humanistic Psychology, which should come as no surprise in view of the fact that Humanists Abraham Maslow and Carl Rogers are both past presidents of APA.[13] The APA, of course, is not without its share of SIECUS board members, including Catherine S. Chilman, Cornelia Christenson, William Peltz, Wardell Pomeroy, and Helen Southard.
- *Association for Voluntary Sterilization* — This Humanist front is dedicated to "the encouragement of a stable population," and after perusal of its literature it must be regarded as simply another segment of the world movement for total population control. AVS's honorary president until his death was Brock Chisholm, "Humanist of the Year" for 1959. The medical consultant to AVS is Dr. H. Curtis Wood, a Humanist and SIECUS-recommended author. Serving on its board of directors are SIECUS officials John L. S. Holloman Jr., Robert W. Laidlaw, and John Rock, as well as Humanists Lawrence Lader, Lonny Myers, and Mary Morain (who was elected to the post of third vice president of AVS in 1971). Various AVS committees have numbered among their members SIECUS directors William Genné and Emily H. Mudd, and such assorted Humanists as Algernon Black, Alan F. Guttmacher, and Harriet Pilpel (also with SIECUS). Of further interest is the fact that AVS has selected Humanist and Communist-fronter Joseph Fletcher to chair its Clergymen's Committee[14] and that AVS field director Cortland Hastings has long served in a leadership capacity with the World Federalists, U.S.A.

    Another noteworthy item concerns AVS's affiliation with

Zero Population Growth and the American Civil Liberties Union: The three groups have jointly initiated a project called "Operation Lawsuit," which was designed to provide legal assistance to individuals who have sought sterilization for other than health reasons and been refused by their local hospitals.

- *Group for the Advancement of Psychiatry* — Publishers of the pamphlet *The Right to Abortion* (see entry for this organization elsewhere in PART II).
- *National Council on Family Relations* — A SIECUS satellite (see entry elsewhere in PART II).
- *National Medical Association* — SIECUS director John L. S. Holloman Jr. is a former president of this association.
- *National Organization for Women* (NOW) — Founded by Humanist Betty Friedan, who is also on NARAL's board of directors.
- *United Methodist Church* — The UMC has SIECUS official Reverend Leon Smith as director of its Ministries in Marriage, Board of Education.
- *Young Women's Christian Association of the U.S.A.* (YWCA) — (See entry elsewhere in PART II; also dicussion later in this entry.)
- *Zero Population Growth, Inc.* — An organization with some 20,000 members, ZPG has as its goal "to stop population growth as soon as possible, first in the United States and then in the rest of the world."[15] Its organizational arm, the ZPG Fund, develops educational materials for schools and the general public.

Another pursuit of ZPG is political lobbying and providing support for political candidates who hold similar views on population, as well as taking part in public demonstrations. In 1972, for example, ZPG participated in an Emergency Demonstration To Defend the Right to Abortion in New York, which was aimed at the New York State Legislature, then considering a bill to reverse that state's newly introduced pro-abortion law. The anti-abortion bill subsequently passed the legislature, but was vetoed by then Governor Nelson Rockefeller. Among those joining ZPG as sponsors of this demonstration were such groups and individuals as:

U.S. Representative Shirley Chisholm
Humanist Betty Friedan of Women's Lib
Rebecca Goldblum of the New York Society for Ethical Culture
Humanist Alan F. Guttmacher of Planned Parenthood
Linda Jenness of the Socialist Workers Party
Humanist Lawrence Lader of NARAL

New York Chapter of the National Association of Social
  Workers
SIECUS official Helen Southard
Gloria Steinem of Women's Lib, a staunch supporter of
  Humanism
United Church of Christ
Westchester Ethical Humanist Society
Women's Caucus, Union Theological Seminary[16]

ZPG leader Dr. Paul R. Ehrlich also serves on the board of directors of the Association for Voluntary Sterilization, which was discussed earlier. Among other prominent ZPG officials is Dr. Edgar R. Chasteen, also president of Compulsory Birth Control for All Americans, Inc. In his 1970 biennial report to the American Civil Liberties Union, Dr. Chasteen stated: ". . . parents no longer effectively own their children; thus, it is not the right of parents to have as many children as they want, but a privilege for them to have even a limited number of children."[17] Representatives of ZPG have attended conferences held at Humanist House in San Francisco.

NARAL Individual Supporters

Among many prominent persons who actively support NARAL are John Lindsay, former Mayor of New York; Congressman Paul N. McCloskey* of California; Congresswoman Shirley Chisholm, black militant and women's lib activist, who is honorary president of NARAL; and LaDonna Harris, a member of the National Advisory Council of the American Civil Liberties Union. Mrs. Harris is the wife of former Oklahoma Senator Fred Harris, who co-authored the Harris-Pryor Bill, proposing that the U.S. negotiate an international treaty to prevent member nations from engaging in seal-trapping.

This introduces a paradox that crops up constantly in the anti-life movement. For at the same time Mrs. Harris was working with NARAL to legalize the extermination of defenseless human babies, her husband was waging a vigorous fight in the Senate to "protect the lives of baby seals and other wildlife."

Chief backers of the Harris-Pryor Bill, who call themselves "Friends of Animals, Inc.," ran a full-page advertisement in *The Humanist* declaring: ". . . We're tired of violence, and we think

*McCloskey, an early candidate for the 1972 Democrat Presidential nomination, received sizable financial support for his campaign from Cleveland industrialist Cyrus Eaton. Eaton, who received the Lenin Peace Prize for his contributions to the Soviet cause, and his wife, were described in the September–October 1971 issue of *The Humanist* as "Humanists Ahead of Their Time."

attacking helpless animals with modern weapons and barbaric clubs is not only short on fair play, but self-destructive in the new ecological terms."[18] Reiterated throughout this ad was concern for animal suffering at the time of death. (An advisor to "Friends of Animals, Inc." is former American Humanist Association treasurer Alex Hershaft,[19] also president of the Environmental Technology Seminar in Bethpage, New York.)

At best, it seems slightly absurd that the very persons who are ostensibly fighting to save the lives of baby seals, whales, and walruses should simultaneously be engaged in a movement to legalize the killing of unwanted human babies — and all in the name of "ecology."

As evidenced by all the foregoing, there can be no doubt that NARAL is operating under rigid control by the same Humanist complex that guides SIECUS.* Even the smaller local groups that have formed for the express purpose of blocking any proposed anti-abortion legislation in Congress are Humanist-directed. One such group is the New Jersey Coalition for Abortion Rights, whose executive director is the Reverend Raymond J. Pontier, minister of the Unitarian-Universalist Fellowship of Wayne, New Jersey. In March 1975, Pontier and a small delegation from his Coalition group traveled to Washington, D.C., to lobby against passage of any Constitutional amendment that would ban abortion. Meeting with the U. S. House Judiciary Committee, Pontier's Coalition (which claims to be composed of a "cross section" of religious groups of all faiths, but which is dominated by Humanists) took the position that abortion is a matter for individual choice, thus upholding the 1973 Supreme Court decision. Since Pontier contends that no single religious viewpoint should be imposed on all citizens, the question may properly be raised: Why then should the religion of Humanism be permitted to impose its pro-abortion dogma on the rest of society?

Methods of Abortion

Having substantially covered the question of *who* is behind the anti-life crusade, it would seem essential to understand *how* abortions are performed before getting at the roots of the issue itself. Dr. Richard Jaynes, an obstetrician, has described the procedure as follows:

---

*The extent of Humanist control of the anti-life movement is by no means limited by the borders of the United States. As an illustration, we read in the September–October issue of *The Humanist* that Dr. Henry Morgenthaler, past president of the Canadian Humanist Association, has been a leading figure in Canadian abortion law reform for years.

There are two methods commonly used to destroy an unborn child — a suction apparatus procedure used up to about four weeks after conception, and curettage.

The suction apparatus involves the creation of a powerful vacuum in a tube. The tube is inserted in the woman's uterus and what's inside is drawn through it into a bottle. The vacuum is so powerful that the process is almost instantaneous. You hardly see the fetus as it zips through the tube . . . .

After about 10 to 12 weeks, however, the developing child has grown too large and solid to pass through the suction apparatus. After that point curettage is generally used.

A roughly spoon-shaped instrument called the curette, about ten inches long and with sharp edges, is inserted into the uterus. The child inside is cut into pieces and pulled or scooped out limb by limb.

In order for the members to be removed, of course, the doctor must stretch the uterine opening. It isn't dilating of its own accord as it would in a normal birth. It can't be stretched too far, however, and in order to pass larger parts like the head, they must be crushed. Some doctors use a ring forceps.

Curettage is rarely used after 14 weeks of pregnancy. At that stage of development a hysterotomy is used as a kind of abdominal surgery similar to Caesarean section.[20]

The particulars of a hysterotomy have been related by Dr. H.P. Dunn, a Fellow of both the Royal College of Surgeons and the Royal College of Gynaecologists and Obstetricians in England:

The woman has a general anaesthetic, an abdominal incision, the womb is incised from top to bottom and the baby lifted out. It makes some weak movement of its arms and legs, and tries to breathe. Sometimes it manages a pathetic cry like a kitten; then after a few minutes it dies an asphyxial death and lies coldly in a stainless steel bowl.[21]

A fourth type of abortion is the salt brine technique, used after the baby is about twelve weeks old. A hypodermic needle is inserted through the mother's abdomen into the amniotic sac containing the child. The fluid in the sac is withdrawn and a strong salt solution is injected. As the child is literally pickled in the mother's womb, it thrashes about violently until it finally succumbs to death. Usually within forty-eight hours, it is expelled from the womb and delivered as a stillbirth.

Some of these babies, who have not been destroyed in the womb by the salt brine method, are left to die after birth in the cold sterility of the delivery room; some struggle for life for two or three hours, while others have been known to live as long as two days.[22]

Fortunately, this brutal carnage is becoming increasingly repugnant to some members of the medical profession, whose consciences can no longer rest. In California, a group calling itself Nurses for Life has filed an *amicus curiae* brief against abortion, stating: "We believe that if other members of our sex could witness an abortion, if they could see the results of the abortion, if they could see the drowning of the child in amniotic fluid, the experimentation on the living child, the disposal of the dismembered child, the emotional trauma of many women after the abortion, they would, hopefully, not choose to exercise what they term their 'civil right' to an abortion."[23]

Of course, not all members of the medical and legal professions are in agreement as to whether or not *abortion* is *murder*. But one thing is certain. Whether it is termed *abortion* or *murder*, whether legalized or not, the aborted babies all have two things in common after the deed is done — they were once living and they are now dead.

Is the Unborn Child a Distinct and Separate Being?

The claim that the unborn child is merely a "glob of tissue" has often been used as a trump card in the abortion advocate's game. As far back as summer of 1967, an American Civil Liberties Union lawyer, Humanist Herman Schwartz, presented this thesis in an article on the subject in *The Humanist* — apparently for the purpose of establishing the official party line. (This is the same Herman Schwartz who vigorously defended the "human rights" of murderers, rapists, and hardened criminals at Attica State Prison.) Schwartz callously offered in his *Humanist* article such rationalizations as the following:

> . . . abortion proponents seek only to permit those who feel it necessary to destroy unborn organisms, often no more than a few inches of proto- plasm with no discernible personality at all, in order to reduce human suffering.[24]

Like so many of his colleagues, Professor Schwartz gives his readers no clue to how he reached this conclusion — no substantiation, no facts. If his statement is true and the abortionists fully accept it, it is all the stranger that they themselves remain deadlocked on the point that is the crux of the matter: *At what exact moment does a baby become human, if not at the moment of conception?* It would seem that the burden of proof is on those who make such dogmatic statements as Professor Schwartz's.

Fortunately for the unborn child — which incidentally is at a grave disadvantage, since it cannot yet defend itself — there are many qualified professionals who are willing to stand up and be counted in its behalf; and their testimonial briefcases are usually well-fortified with facts. One vocal physician is Dr. Eugene Diamond, who has attested:

> To consider the fetus not to be a separate person but merely a part of the mother has not been tenable since the Sixteenth Century, when Arantius showed the maternal and fetal circulations were separate — neither continuous nor contiguous.[25]

In his book, *The Vanishing Right to Life,* Dr. Charles E. Rice, professor of law at the University of Notre Dame, has this to say: "The unborn child is in fact a human being from the moment of conception. When the child in the womb weighs only one-thirtieth of an ounce, he has every internal organ he will ever have as an adult . . . ."[26]

Dr. Paul E. Rockwell, director of anesthesiology at a leading New York hospital, further backed this essential point with his personal witness:

> Eleven years ago, while giving an anesthetic for a ruptured ectopic pregnancy (at two months' gestation) I was handed what I believe was the smallest living being ever seen.
>
> The embryo sac was intact and transparent. Within the sac was a tiny (approximately 1 cm.) human male swimming extremely vigorously in the amniotic fluid, while attached to the wall by the umbilical cord. This tiny human was perfectly developed, with long tapering fingers, feet, and toes. It was almost transparent, as regards the skin, and the delicate arteries and veins were prominent to the ends of the fingers.

It should be noted here that the being Dr. Rockwell is describing as one centimeter, or less than one-half inch, in length, is far smaller than the "few inches of protoplasm" mentioned by Professor Schwartz. The doctor continued:

> The baby was extremely alive and swam about the sac approximately one time per second, with a natural swimmer's stroke. This tiny human did not look at all like the photos and drawings and models of 'embryos' which I have seen, nor did it look like a few embryos I have been able to observe since then, obviously because this one was alive![27]

How's *that* for a "glob of tissue?"

As for his secondary comment, that the tiny human did not resemble certain photos and drawings he had seen of "embryos," Dr. Rockwell has perhaps inadvertently opened up another can of worms in the area of evolution. For, when joined with certain other data, some deeper implications of the doctor's comment appear. Consider, for example, columnist David A. Noebel's relevant critique of the embryo sketches of Ernst Haeckel, one of the first German biologists in the Nineteenth Century to accept and strenuously promote the Darwinian doctrine of evolution:

> To begin with, Haeckel falsified his drawings of embryos to bring them into accord with his theory. Dr. Bolton Davidheiser points out in *Evolution and Christian Faith* that Haeckel even went so far as to *alter pictures of embryos drawn by other people.* Davidheiser concludes, "It seems nearly unbelievable, but it is a fact that in spite of the scandal which arose over Haeckel's drawings of embryos nearly a century ago, *many modern college textbooks republish his drawings to illustrate the embryonic evidence in favor of evolution.*[28] [emphasis added]

This factor at least raises the possibility that the "little curled-up fish" concept of the human embryo may be simply another hoax being perpetrated upon some of the medical profession and the lay public by certain evolutionists.

In any event, it is encouraging that there are still many physicians who know misrepresentation when they see it. In fact, so enraged have some become at those who doubt the humanity of the unborn child that in 1971 a group of 220 physicians rushed to its defense in public protest. Many of them were Fellows of the American College of Obstetrics and Gynecology, and nearly half were established at the professional level in medical schools across the country, including Harvard, Tufts, and Boston Universities. These doctors filed an *amicus curiae* motion and brief with the U.S. Supreme Court, contending that the unborn offspring of human parents is an autonomous human being.

The physicians' group cited as substantiation a host of recent findings discovered in the new medical specialty, *fetology*, which uses such innovative techniques as x-ray fluoroscopy, ultrasound, and miniature fiberoptic cameras and endoscopes that are inserted through the cervix. Among many pro-life points made in the brief is that modern obstetrics has discarded as unscientific the concept that the child in the womb is only tissue of the mother, as well as the idea that the pregnant woman can be treated as a single patient.[29]

In building their case that the unborn child is autonomous, the physicians unveiled a specific time-period development continuum:

■ "From conception, when the sperm and egg unite, the child is a complex, dynamic, rapidly growing organism."

■ "At about 18 days, the development of the nervous system is under way, and by the 20th day the foundation of the child's brain, spinal cord, and entire nervous system is established."

■ "By the beginning of the second month, the unborn child looks distinctly human, yet the mother is not aware that she is pregnant." (As for the question, "When does the embryo become human?" the brief quoted authorities, stating: ". . . the answer is that it always had human potential, and no other, from the instant the sperm and egg came together, because of its chromosomes.")

■ "Even at five and a half weeks, the fetal heartbeat is essentially similar to that of an adult; the energy output is about 20 percent that of the adult but the fetal heart is functionally complete and normal by seven weeks. At this point, the child may be likened to a one-inch miniature doll with a large head, but gracefully formed arms and legs and an unmistakably human face."

■ "By the end of seven weeks . . . there is a well-proportioned small-scale baby. It bears the familiar external features and all the internal organs of the adult, even though it weighs one-thirtieth of an ounce. The body is covered with skin, the arms have hands and fingers, the legs have knees, ankles and toes . . . . The new body not only exists, it also functions."

■ "After the eighth week, no further original organs will form — everything that is already present will be found in the full-term baby."

■ ". . . in the sixth month, the child may even have a slim chance of surviving in an incubator (the youngest children known to survive were between 20 to 25 weeks old)."[30]

Since a high percentage of abortions occur around the eighth week of pregnancy, it is worthwhile to take a closer look at the human embryo in this stage of development. Dr. Richard Jaynes describes it:

> By eight weeks it has all its organs, legs, arms, feet, hands, ears and looks like a human being. It often sucks its thumb at this stage. There is a definite heartbeat. It waves its arms and legs and, if removed from the uterus, often struggles to take a breath into its lungs. It answers all the ordinary criteria for life.[31]

Unquestionably there is substantial current medical and scientific evidence to fully support the autonomous humanity of the unborn child, and to indicate that he is just as human before birth as after. It seems strange that persons who claim "science" as the sole basis for their belief are so quick to ignore its findings when the latter are not in accord with their particular purpose.

The Unborn Child's Right to Life

Although there are nearly a dozen false premises on which the abortionists habitually hinge their case for legalization, the one that is perhaps most frequently used will be dealt with for purposes of this study; that is, the proposition that legalized abortion will obviate bringing "unwanted" children into society. In this area, one is likely to hear such familiar utterances as "Families of the retarded or crippled should be spared their burden," or "Our country has simply *too many people*." Dr. Paul Andreini, who is affiliated with the Mayo Clinic, comments as follows:

> Promoting or accepting the right of people to abortion on demand, is accepting a utilitarian view of human life — if the fetus is not useful or convenient, like a chair or automobile, then we may dispose of it.
> Once we accept this utilitarian outlook, once we admit that man has no inviolable right to life — but only a right depending on usefulness — then none of us can be safe from annihilation.[32]

The utilitarian view of life was also quite common in ancient civilizations, where a man's right to live depended solely upon his usefulness to society. It has more recently been introduced into contemporary life by the Socialist countries. But whereas these nations have either permitted or banned abortion depending upon the current needs of the State, the United States has always upheld man's inalienable right to the life bestowed on him by Almighty God. In fact, this attitude is the exact antithesis of the utilitarian perspective. It is what makes this nation unique among other cultures over a span of nearly 6,000 years of history. It is a principle to be reckoned with by every American who cherishes his freedom, for the very crux on which our liberty hinges is that *every* life is of equal value.

The right to life is one of the first guarantees of the Constitution. Affirmed in the Preamble was the stated purpose of securing "the blessings of liberty to ourselves and our posterity." To this the Fifth and Fourteenth Amendments add the reinforcement that no person shall be "deprived of life, liberty, or property, without due process of law." To those who also recognize the fact that each life is a precious gift from God, another essential truth should immediately be evident: that our blessing of liberty carries with it certain responsibilities which cannot be ignored. The liberty of an individual, therefore, must *of necessity* be limited. A man is free to act so long as he does not infringe upon the life or liberty of another. He may also take a risk or place his own life in jeopardy, so long as he does not endanger the life of another thereby. In other words, the State has no jurisdiction over *personal* morals, so long as only one person is involved; but beyond that, it must intervene. Michigan's Lieutenant Governor James H. Brickley (who has reversed his former pro-abortion stance) emphasizes this logic with these specifics:

> The state should not legislate in the field of "private morals," a violation of which would not affect the rights of others. For instance, it is not a crime simply to tell a lie. It may be personally immoral, but it does not affect another person. It is a crime, however, to tell a lie — perjury for instance — that damages another person.[33]

Substantial insight on this point is offered by columnist Mary Kay Williams, as she examines its significance to the abortion issue:

> Abortion not only damages another's life, it destroys it. Abortion forfeits the very basic right to life from which all other rights proceed. Without question, it is a moral issue — both deeply personal and highly public. Highly public because there are two parties involved, the mother and the fetus.
>
> To deny the fetus this status is to deny all of what modern medical science has been saying about the child's development in the womb —

evidence which should make the fetus more protectable than ever before. Drawn from the disciplines of biology, genetics, fetology, and perinatology, this evidence affirms that:

1. The fetus is different from the parent organism.

2. Fetal life is independent.

3. The fetus is largely in charge of the pregnancy, and the mother is a passive carrier.

4. The fetus is treated as a separate patient by obstetricians.

That there is more than one patient expands the question of abortions from the area of private morals into the area of public morals.[34]

This fact, then, is what thrusts the abortion issue into the public domain. Because of it, abortion cannot be considered a "private" matter between a woman and her physician. As to whether or not the mother has absolute command over her body and, therefore, the right to take her own unborn child's life, Editor James H. Townsend of *The Educator* has this to say:

The woman's body is her own, by gift of God, until she engages in activity that invites a guest to share it with her for a period of time, roughly nine months. Having entered into that solemn obligation, she is bound by the law of God and nature not to disturb the tenant. She had a property right in her body and she, for a consideration, voluntarily relinquished a part of that right to another. Her body no longer is completely her own. That is what pregnancy means.[35]

What we are talking about, then, is simply this: Prior to a pregnancy, a woman *does* have rights — including the right to prevent pregnancy by any means acceptable to her conscience. That is a private, moral decision. But once a woman becomes pregnant, the rights of *two* human beings are involved. The term "private morality" is no longer applicable or valid. We are now in the realm of "public morality," and the state has the obligation to protect the right to life of both persons involved. Rights can never be unqualified. They are always subject to the consideration, "Do my rights infringe upon the rights of others?" In the case of the pregnant woman, obviously, the answer is *yes*. And no amount of rationalization can erase the fact that the woman who chooses to abort in furtherance of *her own* rights is placing her possible embarrassment, emotional strain, or financial burden above *the right to life of her unborn child.*

To accept the utilitarian view of life is to regress thousands of years in the calendar of history. Once this Rubicon is crossed, the way will have been opened for the future extermination of any segment of mankind. If mothers can solve *their* socio-economic problems by legalized abortion, what then is to prevent the State from solving *its* socio-economic problems by compulsory abortion, euthanasia, and other forms of legalized murder? So insane has this business become that already bills have been introduced into at least twenty legislatures to legalize euthanasia. Even Dr. Malcolm Todd, 1974 president of the once solidly pro-life American Medical Association, has publicly taken a stand in favor of legalizing murder of the aged and infirm.

What class of humanity will be the next target of the life-destroyers? Will it be the mentally retarded, the mentally ill, or certain racial minorities? Or is it possible that, once in full power, the Humanist Socialist complex may declare that their ideological adversaries — perhaps including believing Christians — no longer serve the purposes of the new world secular society and should be eliminated? And is it just remotely possible that this has been their goal from the start?

In Higher Places

Many persons prefer to remain in a state of lethargy, trusting that the nation's leaders will protect them from such atrocities. But it should be emphasized that some of the very highest positions in the United States Government — as well as in the national organizations that exert pressure on it — have been infiltrated, influenced, and in some cases are now controlled by the Humanist-Socialist nexus.

Concurrent with this alarming trend, the political pendulum is now swinging in a direction paralleling the major pursuits of the Humanist hierarchy. First, President Nixon's Commission on Population Growth and America's Future, which was heavily stacked with Humanistic anti-life forces (see entry for *Planned Parenthood–World Population* later in PART II), devoted its entire life to creating an atmosphere favorable to public acceptance of a national zero population growth rate and the eventual Supreme Court decision for abortion on demand. Further, certain U.S. Government agencies have vigorously supported the movement for total repeal of abortion laws, led by NARAL. Among these are the Fiftieth Anniversary Conference of the Women's Bureau of the U.S. Department of Labor,* the President's Task Force on the Mentally Handicapped, and the White House Conference on Children and Youth.†[36]

Assisting the Humanist movement on the House side of Capitol Hill is Representative Don Edwards (D.-Calif.). Edwards holds the strategic position of chairman of the House Judiciary Committee's Subcommit-

---

*The Fiftieth Anniversary Conference was headed by former SIECUS official Elizabeth Koontz, who also delivered the keynote address.
†A number of persons named in the list of participants in the White House Conference on Children and Youth, and in its bibliographical references, are either SIECUS officials, SIECUS associates, or Humanists.

tee on Constitutional Amendments. Any amendment that would have the effect of overturning the Supreme Court's 1973 ruling on abortion must be referred to the Subcommittee before hearings can be scheduled. In October 1973, Edwards participated in the American Humanist Association's regional conference in Los Gatos, California, opening a Saturday session with a lecture on "Humanism on Capitol Hill."

Consider further the U.S. House of Representatives. The January-February 1969 issue of *The Humanist* comments on the results of a special study conducted by the National Committee for an Effective Congress (chaired by Humanist Sidney H. Scheuer, a top official in the International Humanist and Ethical Union). According to this magazine, "The report finds that there were about 55 humanists in the last [1968] House of Representatives."[*37]

Moreover, some of our Senators supporting the anti-life movement are not immune to the Humanist virus. One such is Senator Robert W. Packwood (R.-Ore.), a Unitarian, who in 1970 introduced into the U.S. Senate a National Abortion Act, intended to legalize abortion in every state. This act predicated the unborn child's right to life upon the whim of a woman and her physician, permitting abortion to be performed up to approximately the halfway point in pregnancy (four and a half months).

That Senator Packwood is a sometime traveler into Humanist territory should not come as a shock. In an article appearing in the July–August 1970 issue of *The Humanist*, titled "Population and Survival," Packwood sent out a call to all Humanists for unwavering support of his National Abortion Act, coupled with an urgent plea for its passage, apparently in order to save the world from contamination by humanity.

Another backer of abortion-on-demand is Senator George McGovern (D.-S. Dak.), who has stated: "It is my view that abortion should concern a woman and her physician and no one else."[38] To say that McGovern is at home in the Humanist camp is an understatement. The Senator not only contributes articles to *The Humanist*, but has participated in the magazine's "Ethical Forum" as well. He was also a featured speaker at the Humanist-led first Action Conference on National Priorities, held in Washington, D.C., in February 1969, which was sponsored and organized by the Council for Humanist and Ethical Concern (CHEC).[39] CHEC was represented at the First National Conference on Abortion Laws in February 1969,[40] at which NARAL was born.

Senators Packwood and McGovern and Representative Edwards are only three of a substantial number of agents of the Humanist-Socialist cartel in Congress who are laboring to legislate the United States onto a course that leads to Humanist goals.

Outside our government, other influential groups, in step with NARAL, have strained every nerve to bring about the repeal of abortion laws. They include:

> American Association of University Women
> American Baptist Convention
> American College of Obstetricians and Gynecologists
> American Home Economics Association
> American Jewish Congress
> American Psychiatric Association
> American Public Health Association
> B'nai B'rith Women
> Episcopal Churchwomen of the U.S.A.
> National Association of Social Workers
> National Council on Family Relations
> Sierra Club
> United Church of Christ
> United Presbyterian Church in the U.S.A.[41]

Nor should we be surprised to discover behind the scenes the tax-exempt Ford and Rockefeller Foundations, acting as major financiers of the abortion movement; or to learn that the Playboy Foundation is at the financial hub of the abortion wheel. Playboy Foundation began assisting the abortion movement in 1966, with a grant to the Association for the Study of Abortion; subsequently it made grants to the Women's National Abortion Coalition, NARAL, and the Clergy Consultation Service on Problem Pregnancies (an adjunct of Planned Parenthood and an organization member of NARAL).

Even the respected American Bar Association has called for virtually unrestricted abortions in all fifty states. Prior to the 1973 Supreme Court decision, the ABA pressed for an abortion law that would allow any woman to have an abortion performed by any licensed physician, or to perform an abortion on herself under medical supervision, any time during the first twenty weeks of pregnancy. This action by so prestigious an organization has undoubtedly influenced not only the lay public, but members of the legal profession as well.

Familiar "Friends of the Court"

The 1973 Supreme Court decision, which, in effect, legalized abortion, was a predictable outcome of the unrelenting, organized onslaught of the anti-life forces against the right to life. The legislative history of this attack involved numerous challenges to state abortion statutes throughout the country. The two state cases on which the high court's final decision rested were those of Texas and Georgia. In the Texas case, the Federal District Court had held the Texas abortion laws unconstitutional "because they deprive single women and married couples of their right, secured by the Ninth Amendment, to choose whether to have children."[42] In the case of Georgia, the state court had concluded that procedures for obtaining an abortion may be controlled but that the reasons for which an abortion may be obtained may not be regulated, "because such action unduly restricts a decision sheltered by the constitutional right to privacy."[43] It was at these points that Texas and Georgia, respectively, appealed to the Supreme Court.

The two cases were argued in the high court's chambers on December 13, 1971, with both pro- and anti-life forces present. Each side was allotted thirty minutes in which to present its views on so critical a question — one that would mean life or death to millions of unborn babies. But certain other aspects of the two cases should be noted as final proof that the entire abortion repeal drama was staged by Humanist directors.

Texas (Roe v. Wade, *No. 70-18, 1971 Term*) — Acting as vanguard for the anti-life forces in this Supreme Court appeal were such Humanist groups as the American Ethical Union, the American Humanist Association, and the Unitarian-Universalist Association, filing a joint *amicus curiae* brief. Another signatory of this brief was the Humanist-oriented American Friends Service Committee, together with a number of other fellow travelers. Joining with them were the United Church of Christ's Board of Homeland Ministries, and the United Methodist Church's Board of Christian Social Concerns — both organization members of NARAL.[44]

Georgia (Doe v. Bolton, *No. 70-40, 1971 Term*) — The situation was similar in the Georgia case, with the American Ethical Union again delivering an anti-life brief, in league with such Humanist front groups as the American Civil Liberties Union and Planned Parenthood. Representing Planned Parenthood as counsel was Humanist and SIECUS founder Harriet Pilpel, who, it may be recalled, also holds the position

---

*Curiously, Planned Parenthood has condoned what by its own definition is murder, in aligning itself with the anti-life forces. A pamphlet issued by this organization in 1963 states that an abortion "kills the life of a baby after it has begun." (Valerie Vance Dillon, *In Defense of Life,* published by the New Jersey Right to Life Committee, Trenton, N.J., 1970, Appendix, page 156.)

of national vice chairman of the ACLU. Other ACLU attorneys involved were Reber F. Boult, Jr. and Charles Morgan, Jr., both of Atlanta.

Following its deliberations on both cases, which lasted until after the 1972 Presidential election, the Supreme Court on January 22, 1973, ruled unconstitutional the Texas law which had allowed abortion only to save the life of the mother. In a parallel decision, the Court ruled unconstitutional certain sections of Georgia's law, as unduly restrictive to the woman or her physician. It further decreed that unborn children are nonpersons, not covered by the Constitution, and therefore expendable by abortion. No restrictions were placed on abortion until the fourth month of pregnancy, whereafter the state might regulate abortions in ways reasonably related to maternal health.

The majority opinion, written by Justice Harry A. Blackmun, explicitly denied any intention by the Court to resolve "the difficult question of when life begins." Settling that long controversial issue, Blackmun stated, is not the Court's business. Nevertheless, the majority decision was based on the position that an unborn baby does not become a human person with a right to life until it is "viable" — that is, capable of surviving outside the womb. However, the court said that even during the last three months of pregnancy, states might lift restrictions on abortion when it is considered necessary to the life or health of the mother. "Health" here includes both physical *and mental* health, in accordance with an earlier Supreme Court decision delivered in 1971 (*U.S.* v. *Vuitch*). Ironically, this was the same Court that not too long previously had declared capital punishment of convicted murderers to be cruel and inhuman, and had overthrown the death penalty.

Here too it is no coincidence that Humanist forces can be detected at work. As a pointed illustration, we find the late Supreme Court Justice William O. Douglas, a Unitarian, casting a "yea" vote. Douglas's ties to Humanism include a brief stint as a book reviewer for the American Humanist Association's official organ, *The Humanist* magazine, and his contribution to a collection of essays on *Contents of Humanistic Education and Western Civilization* — a book devoted to "the enduring challenge and possibility of humanism in education," written in honor of Humanist Robert M. Hutchins. Douglas was joined at the high court by such Humanist luminaries as Beulah Bullard, a 1970 candidate for the AHA's board of directors, who helds the sensitive post of Supreme Court reference librarian.

District of Columbia (United States *v.* Vuitch*) — In another

*Dr. Milan Vuitch is a member of the NARAL board of directors.

abortion case resolved by the Supreme Court, the Humanists were also predominant. As noted in the American Humanist Association Membership Bulletin of March 1971, for example, we find the AHA's Joint Washington Office for Social Concern* among those filing *amicus curiae* briefs in behalf of the anti-life forces.[45]

In this case, the 1971 Supreme Court ruling upheld the constitutionality of the District of Columbia statute by reversing the decision of Federal District Court Judge Gerhard Gesell that the law was void because of its vagueness.

New Jersey (Princeton YWCA *v.* Kugler, *Docket No. 264-70*) — Upon examination of other lower court cases, Humanist footprints are again to be seen. New Jersey is just one example. On February 29, 1972, two members of a three-judge federal panel overturned the state abortion law on grounds of invasion of privacy and vagueness. Legal action challenging the state statute had been filed in March 1970 by the American Civil Liberties Union in behalf of the Princeton YWCA, its officers, and nine physicians. Head counsel for the "Y" was ACLU attorney Richard I. Samuel, aided by Roy Lucas of the James Madison Constitutional Law Institute† of New York, which works closely with the A.C.L.U.

Another plaintiff in the YWCA case was the New Jersey Chapter of the Women's International League for Peace and Freedom, a group claiming 10,000 members in the U.S., whose national sponsorship is studded with an impressive number of Humanists, including Jerome Frank, Ashley Montagu, Benjamin Spock, and Harold Taylor, and Communist-fronters such as Jerome Davis, Mildred Scott Olmsted, and Hugh Hester. The objectives of the League have been described by the California Senate Fact-Finding Subcommittee on Un-American Activities as being "in conformity with the international Communist Party line."[46]

Among the plaintiffs claiming that the existing New Jersey abortion law was an unconstitutional violation of a woman's right to privacy was the International Planned Parenthood Federation, represented by Humanist Harriet Pilpel, acting as attorney for the law firm of Greenbaum, Wolff and Ernst. Mrs. Pilpel is considered to be the ACLU's top-ranking expert on abortion law reform.*

*This Humanist front is identified in Humanist literature as representative of the social and legislative aspirations of Humanists, Ethical Culturists, and Unitarian-Universalists.
†The James Madison Constitutional Law Institute has changed its name to the Population Law Center; it is still located in New York City. Mr. Lucas has represented other anti-life groups involving themselves in abortion litigation throughout the country, including the Georgia case, *Doe v. Bolton.*

* * *

In summarizing the total substance of the NARAL case, we must recognize the existence of a common pattern. As SIECUS is the Humanists' guiding force in sex education, so is NARAL their guiding force in the anti-life movement. While acting as a national clearing house and coordinator of strategy and activities, the NARAL team stands ready to zero in on any specified area of the country. For, despite the 1973 Supreme Court decision that ruled in favor of abortion-on-demand, NARAL finds its task is far from finished. Shortly after the high court's decision, pro-life forces regrouped for the purpose of seeking a constitutional amendment that would outlaw abortion. Subsequently, in the fall of 1973, NARAL suddenly changed its name to National Abortion Rights Action League; and 1974 found the new NARAL engaged in a state-by-state reorganization in order to counteract the threat of any forthcoming anti-abortion legislation. Of course the new NARAL is controlled by a Humanist coterie similar to the one that presided over the original NARAL.

Many who have watched these momentous events in our judicial and legislative chambers have seen the abortion question as a legitimate struggle for women's rights, through what the viewers imagine to be democratic processes at work in a society moving faster than its laws. Few recognize it for what it really is: *a treacherous assault on the right to life by a vicious, dedicated, atheistic minority.*

It is clearly evident that the Humanist-Socialist coterie leading this procession is not in the least concerned about protecting *anyone's* rights. Were such the case, their cause would of necessity take into consideration the rights of *all* concerned. As already evidenced, NARAL's views are negative when it comes to the rights of the unborn child. It is further apparent that this organization's voice is equally negative with regard to the rights of doctors and nurses. At a 1971 meeting in Boulder, Colorado, for example, NARAL is reported to have favored legislation that would deny to medical personnel and institutions the right to

---

*The power embodied in the ACLU, enabling it to wield immense pressure upon the U.S. judicial system, is staggering. As one illustration, consider the fact that this revolutionary legal lobby commands a corps of about 275,000 members organized into fifty state affiliates. ACLU offices exist in most medium and large-sized cities, and have access to a standing volunteer army of thousands of attorneys across the nation. Other ACLU members are in such fields as journalism, magazine and book publishing, and other areas of the news media. Nor are judges themselves immune from ACLU membership. The precise number of judges in both state and federal chambers who wear the invisible mantle of the ACLU over their supposedly "impartial" judicial robes is known only to the insiders of the system. See Appendix K for listing of ACLU officials in 1977.

refuse to perform an abortion.[47] Even the rights of women — presumably the focal point of this campaign — are on a collision course with the master planners of population control. For, should the latter's scheme be successful, there looms in the very near future the total abolition of a woman's freedom to procreate as she pleases. Her new world will be one of compulsory abortion and forced sterilization.

In the final analysis, each person's attitude toward abortion will be governed by his concept of God. The believer will view each new life as God's creation — and therefore His possession to give or to take away. On the other hand, the atheist or agnostic, who does not see morality through God's perspective, will base his decisions, including legislative ones, on a situation-ethics, man-centered view of life, derived from whatever philosophy may have caught his fancy, whether he calls it rationalism, pragmatism, materialism, hedonism — or Humanism.

The crucial question before us now is whether the judicial and legislative branches of our government will fulfill the responsibility, entrusted to them by the Fifth and Fourteenth Amendments to our Constitution, to protect the God-given right to life, or whether the insidious encroachment of Humanism has already secured its place in the highest offices of the land.

National Council of the Churches of Christ in the U.S.A. (NCC)

475 Riverside Drive, New York, New York

THE PAST FEW DECADES have given evidence of a creeping moral decay within the churches of America. Concurrently with the permissive trend in our educational institutions and society in general, the principle of situation ethics has been embraced by a number of clergymen, and in fact many are preaching it from the pulpit. One aspect of this Humanistic trend can be traced to one of the most influential religious bodies in our nation — the National Council of Churches. Founded in 1950 for the stated purpose of bringing its member churches together for "fellowship, study and cooperative action," the NCC is composed of member denominations of the Protestant and Orthodox faiths. Some of these denominations are:

> African Methodist Episcopal Church
> American Baptist Convention
> Episcopal Church
> Greek Archdiocese of North and South America
> Lutheran Church in America
> National Baptist Convention of America
> National Baptist Convention, U.S.A., Inc.
> Russian Orthodox Greek Catholic Church
> United Church of Christ
> United Methodist Church
> United Presbyterian Church in the U.S.A.

In addition to the above and others, it is stated on page 29 of the NCC's 1966 Triennial Report: "More than 20 denominations which are not members of the National Council are active participants in some of its units and programs. The time has come when a number of these Churches should be encouraged to consider seriously full membership in the Council."

Since then, the NCC has begun a complete reorganization. In an attempt to broaden its ecumenical structure, efforts have been made to bring other denominations, such as the Southern Baptists, the Northern Baptists, the Wesleyans, the National Association of Evangelicals, and the Roman Catholic Church into some sort of common endeavor with the NCC.

That the NCC wields tremendous political influence and power is no longer a topic for debate. One need only consider the sizable accomplishments of its lobbyists at work in our nation's capital. With a total of thirty-three member denominations under its authoritative wing, NCC's hierarchy claims to represent over forty million persons when it solicits its favorite brand of socialistic legislation. In fact, Dr. Eugene Carson Blake, the chief administrative officer of the United Presbyterian Church in the U.S.A., has openly speculated that, "With prudent management, the Churches ought to be able to control the whole economy within the predictable future."[1] The pro-Communist bias of some within NCC's hierarchy* having already been covered in Chapter I, this particular point will not be reiterated. It has been recalled primarily as a launching pad for this discussion of the NCC.

As far back as 1961, the SIECUS caldron was already simmering in the workshops of the NCC. During that year, Dr. Mary Calderone lectured on the role of the churches in sex education before the First North American Conference on Church and Family, convened by the NCC of the U.S. and Canada, which was attended by 500 delegates from thirty-eight Protestant denominations. According to SIECUS, of the seventeen professionals from many disciplines who served as resource persons for the five-day conference, four became co-founders of SIECUS, and five others became SIECUS board members.[2]

In 1968, at the start of the national sex education controversy, an *Interfaith Statement on Sex Education* was approved for release by the NCC in cooperation with the Committee on Family of the Synagogue Council of America and the United States Catholic Conference's Family Life Bureau. This pamphlet has since become a so-called religious backing and frequently used support for sex education, often being displayed at PTA meetings and committee meetings for the study of home and family living programs. By claiming to represent "the common affirmations of the major faith groups of our country," the pamphlet has no doubt swayed the opinions of hundreds of thousands throughout the country.

Looking a bit closer, one finds that the *Interfaith Statement* was drafted by a thirty-member Interfaith Commission on Marriage and Family Life that had been earlier created by the three sponsoring religious groups. The Commission's officers were:

---

*It is not intended to imply that all top officials of the NCC are Communist or pro-Communist. There are obviously many dedicated individuals who are earnestly working for the cause of the churches. However, it should be remembered that, as noted in Chapter I, pro-Communists have gradually edged their way into positions of control until they can now steer NCC onto a course that closely parallels the Communists' own course.

- *Chairman*: Rabbi Mordecai Brill. Rabbi Brill participated in a panel discussion on the *Interfaith Statement* at a workshop session of the Second Annual Conference of the American Association of Sex Educators and Counselors, a major SIECUS front.
- *Vice-Chairman*: William Maughn. Mr. Maughn was chiefly aided in this endeavor by Father James T. McHugh, the director of the U.S. Catholic Conference's Family Life Bureau. An avid SIECUS supporter and AASEC advisory committee member, Father McHugh participated in the AASEC workshop session with Rabbi Brill.
- *Secretary*: Rev. William Genné. One of the original SIECUS founders, the Rev. Mr. Genné is also an advisory committee member of the original AASEC and, as mentioned earlier, he has a number of Communist front citations. Besides serving as director of NCC's Commission on Marriage and Family, Genné was the third participant (with Rabbi Brill and Father McHugh) in the AASEC three-member panel discussion on the *Interfaith Statement*.

   Among others working with Genné as representatives of the NCC in the drafting of the *Interfaith Statement* were Humanist Helen Southard of SIECUS and the Rev. Jesse Lyons of the Riverside Church in New York City, both of whom were later to become top officials of the National Association for the Repeal of Abortion Laws.

The SIECUS influence within the National Council of Churches does not end here. Other individuals who are either past or current members of NCC's Commission on Marriage and Family include SIECUS board members Evelyn Duvall and Clark Vincent, as well as Humanist Mary Calderone, SIECUS executive director. Of further interest is the fact that NCC's president from 1969 to 1973, Cynthia Clark Wedel, is also associate director of the Center for a Voluntary Society of the National Education Association's National Training Laboratories in Washington, D.C., a pioneer in sensitivity training.

A fourteen-page booklet published by the NCC in 1968, titled *Sex Education in Major Protestant Denominations*, covered an in-depth study of the sex education materials most frequently used by these denominations in their church schools and youth organizations. Churches whose materials were examined in this study were: the Episcopal Church; the Lutheran Church in America; the Lutheran Church — Missouri Synod; the Methodist Church; the Presbyterian Church, U.S.; the Southern Baptist Convention; the United Church of

Christ in the U.S.A.; and the United Presbyterian Church in the U.S.A.[3] Since these churches have a combined church school enrollment of over 21,000,000, the study is considered representative of the extent and quality of sex education in the mainstream of American Protestantism.[4]

Among programs given special commendation in the NCC booklet was the Concordia Sex Education Series of the Lutheran Church — Missouri Synod (see entry elsewhere in PART II), which the booklet lauded as "the most complete direct approach to sex education. . . ." It is suggested as one of three programs to be considered as "tentative models for comprehensive programs." In attempting to come to grips with the true meaning of sexuality in Christian terms, the NCC study borrowed a definition from the blasphemous Concordia text, *Life Can Be Sexual*, by Elmer Witt, one point of which is: "As Christians we affirm the joy of God's forgiveness for our misuse of sexuality." The NCC accorded to Witt credit for having designed "perhaps the best delineation of sexuality in Christian application . . . ."[5]

Also commended by the NCC analysis was the book *Sex and Selfhood*, then slated for use as the primary text in a sex education unit (titled "Sex in a Christian's Life") of the United Presbyterian Church, U.S.A. The author of this text is SIECUS director William G. Cole, an enthusiastic proponent of situation ethics.

Even the program of the Southern Baptist Convention — the largest Protestant denomination — has been captivated by the SIECUS beat. In the latter part of 1968, young people of the Baptist faith between the ages of 18 and 24 began studying a unit titled *A Christian View of Sex* that included lengthy excerpts from the writings of SIECUS official Evelyn Duvall and her husband Sylvanus, as well as from SIECUS-recommended authors Seward Hiltner and Humanist Hugh Hefner of *Playboy* magazine.

Other SIECUS scents can be detected on the Baptist trail. The September 1967 issue of *Home Missions*, a Baptist publication, was devoted primarily to the theme, "The Sexual Revolution," and the lead article was written by SIECUS board member David R. Mace.

The over-all impression given by the fourteen-page NCC booklet is that the NCC sanctions a somewhat modified SIECUS approach. While not openly advocating all aspects of "the new morality," for example, the study nevertheless refers to SIECUS authors here and there and subtly acknowledges a need for reform in sex laws. (This feature is in harmony with the views of Church Women United, a Programmed Division of the NCC that is listed in literature of the National Association for Repeal of Abortion Laws as supporting a position similar to that of NARAL on the abortion issue. Further, although SIECUS as an organization is not mentioned in the NCC booklet, writings of some SIECUS board members are approved as appropriate courses of study.

As a member of the World Council of Churches, the NCC has aligned itself with one-world collectivists. An Associated Press story in the *Philadelphia Evening Bulletin* of July 28, 1971, from Geneva, Switzerland, reports, for instance:

> The General Secretary of the World Council of Churches views the Socialist experiment in Chile as a sign of encouragement and stimulus to many other countries who share similar difficulties and similar hopes, the Council said yesterday. A World Council of Churches' statement said that Dr. Eugene Carson Blake, an American, expressed his views in a meeting with President Salvatore Allende during a visit to Chile last week to symbolize the interest of the churches in the Chilean experiment. *Allende, a Marxist, has pledged to transform Chile into a socialist state.* [emphasis added]

This account did not explain, however, how it was possible for an ecclesiastical head to endorse an atheistic regime that had labored strenuously to extinguish all existing religions, especially Christianity. Equally incredible is the fact that the World Council of Churches, which depends solely upon donations from its Protestant members, sent contributions to the North Vietnamese and the Vietcong, and is still contributing to terrorist organizations in Africa.

One solution to the enigma is suggested by the fact that, since 1961, both the Russian Orthodox Church and other Eastern European satellite churches have themselves been members of the World Council of Churches, and have helped to turn the world religious body into another instrument of Soviet propaganda. It should be remembered that these churches do not operate independently, as do churches in the free world, but are mere divisions of the Communist government. For, as the U.S. Senate Judiciary Committee pointed out in its exhaustive study, *The Church and State Under Communism*, the Church is necessary to sell Soviet foreign policy and propaganda.

As for sex education, the World Council of Churches is in complete accord with other organizations in The Circle. Gerald Sanctuary, the executive director of SIECUS, was present at WCC's Symposium on Family Life and Sex Education, held in Geneva during the Fall of 1970, and acted as rapporteur to the meeting.[6] The symposium concluded that it was important to extend sex education as widely as possible throughout the world.

National Council on Family Relations (NCFR)
1219 University Avenue, Southeast, Minneapolis, Minnesota

THE NATIONAL COUNCIL ON FAMILY RELATIONS was one of eight organizations listed in a September 1969 SIECUS form letter, which suggested that these organizations be contacted for assistance in developing sex education programs.

In answer to a request for such assistance, the NCFR sent a listing of home and family living materials, with a form letter inviting membership in the NCFR. Not surprisingly, the closing lines of the NCFR form letter echoed the familiar injunction: "We suggest that you contact SIECUS concerning their Newsletter, which will provide you with additional information."

A brief glimpse into the background of the NCFR is offered on the inside cover of a quarterly published by the Council:

> The National Council on Family Relations was organized in 1938 to bring together in one organization the leaders in research, teaching, and professional service in the field of marriage and the family. Its purpose is to advance the cultural values now principally secured through family relations for personality development and the strength of the nation. It seeks to unite in one common objective, persons working in all the different fields of family research, teaching, and welfare [*i.e.,* education, counseling, ministry, government, medicine, law, and others].[1]

Further insight into NCFR activities is given by this statement in a promotional leaflet:

> The NCFR encourages: Lively local, state, and regional councils, conferences, and workshops. Curriculum development in the schools and universities and in the graduate training programs of professional persons.[2]

The above activities assume greater significance when viewed with awareness that numerous members of the SIECUS hierarchy have held leadership positions in the NCFR over a long span of years. For instance, Humanist Lester Kirkendall served as NCFR director as far back as 1952–1956; David Mace was president during 1961–1962; and Emily Mudd assumed the NCFR directorship in 1963, just one year prior to the founding of SIECUS.

The 1972 roster of NCFR officers and directors showed six SIECUS officials serving on the NCFR executive committee:

Carlfred B. Broderick   Richard K. Kerckhoff
George C. Chamis   E. James Lieberman
Evelyn M. Duvall   Robert E. Staples[3]

The NCFR board of directors for the same year included four SIECUS board members:

Clark W. Blackburn   Joseph Himes
Marjory Brooks   E. James Lieberman

And the following are other directors and former directors of SIECUS who served NCFR in an official capacity prior to 1972:

Jessie Bernard   Ira Reiss
Catherine S. Chilman   John Rock
Harold T. Christensen   Isadore Rubin
Wallace C. Fulton   Aaron Rutledge
Rev. William Genné   Helen F. Southard
Ethel M. Nash   Clark Vincent

Considering that NCFR leadership has been consistently dominated by SIECUS personnel and their associates, it is not surprising to discover that the NCFR often favors them in its awards program. The recipient of its Burgess Award for 1971 was SIECUS official Harold T. Christensen. And in 1971, the NCFR presented to Dr. Richard K. Kerckhoff of SIECUS its Ernest G. Osborne Teaching Award, "in recognition of demonstrated excellence in the teaching of family relationships."[4]

The late Isadore Rubin, a Humanist and identified Communist, was held in high esteem by the NCFR, having been a featured speaker at its 1964 annual meeting, held in Miami, Florida. It was on this occasion that Rubin delivered his paper on "Transition in Sex Values — Implications for the Education of Adolescents," advocating a value system (discussed in Chapter 2) that establishes situation ethics as the standard for teachers to use in guiding their students in moral decision-making.

Among many others from SIECUS headquarters who have participated in NCFR activities over the years is former SIECUS executive director Gerald Sanctuary, who presented a paper on "Sexuality and Violence" at the plenary session of the NCFR's 1970 annual conference.[5]

The NCFR publishes a catalog titled *Family Life: Literature and Films*, compiled by the Minnesota Council on Family Relations (MCFR) — a local affiliate. This annotated bibliography is intended for the use of persons, particularly those in the teaching profession, who need information on marriage and family living. First assembled in 1951, this catalog was updated in 1964, the year SIECUS was founded. In 1967, this catalog's "Human Sexuality and Sex Education" section was extensively revised by educators at the University of Minnesota, Planned Parenthood of Minneapolis, the NCFR, and others.[6]

Several items of special interest regarding recommendations made in this catalog should be noted:

Maxwell Stewart — Recommended works by Stewart, an inveterate Communist fronter, include a Public Affairs Pamphlet titled *The Poor Among Us — Challenge and Opportunity*. In discussing the extent of poverty in the U.S. today, this pamphlet lauds the Socialistic programs of the Johnson Administration, which purportedly were designed to deal with this problem. Another Public Affairs Pamphlet authored by Stewart, *A New Look at Our Crowded World*, is promoted in a special section of the catalog devoted to population control. Numerous other Public Affairs Pamphlets are listed in this guide.

E. Franklin Frazier — Frazier's SIECUS-recommended book, *The Negro Family in the United States*, is described in the NCFR catalog as "The most comprehensive account available of American Negro family patterns." Frazier's affiliations with numerous Communist fronts and causes were covered in Chapter 4. Among other identified Communist fronters whose works are given recognition in the NCFR catalog are Humanist Joseph Fletcher (*Moral Responsibility: Situation Ethics at Work* and *Situation Ethics: The New Morality*) and Robert J. Havighurst[7] (*Developmental Tasks and Education,* and *Older People*).

The Humanist magazine — This periodical is listed in the catalog under a heading that reads: "The following journals occasionally have articles of direct interest and relevance to the family life educator." Also promoted in this directory are Isadore Rubin's article, "The Humanist Bookshelf on Sex" (featured in the Spring 1965 edition of *The Humanist*). Under the heading, "Agencies Offering Various Materials," the American Humanist Association is named.

Sexology — Listed in the *Family Life Education* section of this catalog, *Sexology* magazine is described by the NCFR as "Intended to 'present the best current thinking in the areas of sex research and education in popular and readable form.' "

SIECUS Newsletter — Described in the NCFR catalog as "A must for family life and sex education program."

American Friends Service Committee — Listed in the Audio Visual Sources section of this guide, together with numerous SIECUS-influenced-film agencies and publishing firms mentioned elsewhere in PART II.

SIECUS Board Members — Listed in the Author Index of the NCFR's catalog are the following SIECUS officials, a number of whom are Humanists.

Jessie Bernard	Lester A. Kirkendall
Clark W. Blackburn	David R. Mace
Carlfred B. Broderick	William H. Masters
Mary S. Calderone	John Money
Deryck Calderwood	Emily H. Mudd
Catherine S. Chilman	Ethel M. Nash
Harold T. Christensen	James A. Peterson
William Graham Cole	Harriet Pilpel
Evelyn Duvall	Ira L. Reiss
William Genné	John Rock
Reuben L. Hill	Isadore Rubin
Warren Johnson	Aaron L. Rutledge
Richard K. Kerckhoff	Helen F. Southard

Clark E. Vincent

In addition, the works of more than eighty SIECUS-recommended authors are listed in the catalog.

Humanists — The writings of a number of Humanists who are not members of the SIECUS Board of Directors are also promoted in this guide. They include:

Eric Berne	Alfred McClung Lee
Algernon Black	Eda LeShan
Albert Ellis	Lawrence LeShan
Erik H. Erikson	Margaret Mead
Edgar Z. Friedenberg	Ashley Montagu
Erich Fromm	Alice Rossi
Alan F. Guttmacher	Benjamin Spock
Grace Hechinger	Charles Winick

Other sex education materials that may be obtained from the National Council on Family Relations* include:

*All sex education materials covered in this entry are listed in the NCFR promotional leaflet titled *Available from the NCFR Office.*

Tapes — NCFR's distributor for the following tapes is Perennial Education, Inc., formerly known as Henk Newenhouse.

- *Premarital Sex Behavior* — A dialogue between SIECUS director David Mace (a Quaker) and Humanist Walter Stokes of *Sexology* magazine, taped in 1965, in which each man discusses his own philosophy of sex.
- *The Use of Sex in Human Life* — The dialogue on sexual philosophies presented by David Mace and Humanist Albert Ellis at NCFR's 1965 annual meeting.
- *Sex Ethics, Sex Acts, and Human Need* — Another Mace-Stokes dialogue, presented at NCFR's annual meeting in 1959.
- *Equalitarianism and Male Dominance: A Catholic-Protestant Dialogue on Changing Religious Concepts* — A discussion by David Mace and the late Father George Hagmaier, both of SIECUS, as presented at the 1968 NCFR annual meeting.

Quarterlies — Two quarterlies published by NCFR have been widely distributed for use in college libraries and elsewhere throughout the country. They are:

- *Journal of Marriage and the Family* — This periodical is described by its editors as "a medium for the presentation of original theory, research interpretation, and critical discussion of materials related to marriage and the family."[8] Editor of the *Journal* for 1972 was SIECUS director Carlfred B. Broderick. Among the associate editors were SIECUS official Robert Staples and SIECUS-recommended authors Robert R. Bell, Lee Rainwater, and J. Richard Udry.

    Past issues of the *Journal* reveal a strong SIECUS influence — not surprisingly, since in 1965, this quarterly's associate editors included SIECUS board members Jessie Bernard, Catherine S. Chilman, Reuben Hill, Richard Kerckhoff, Ira L. Reiss, and Clark Vincent; Harold T. Christensen and David Mace were members of the editorial board. In 1968, a similar situation existed. The masthead of the May 1968 issue, for example, billed Catherine S. Chilman of SIECUS as "Special Issue Co-Editor" and a number of familiar SIECUS colleagues as associate editors: Jessie Bernard, Reuben Hill, Richard Kerckhoff, David Mace, Ira L. Reiss, and Clark Vincent. This issue featured an article by Humanist Garrett Hardin on abortion, and carried an advertisement for *Sexology* magazine which included the following testimonial from SIECUS director Warren Johnson, Professor of Health Education at the University of Maryland: "I make a practice of recommending *Sexology* to all my classes."[9]

- *The Family Coordinator* — This quarterly, formerly known as *The Family Life Coordinator*, was established in 1952 by the E.C. Brown Trust Foundation. In 1967, the NCFR assumed sponsorship, and changed the title to *The Family Coordinator*. This periodical is intended to be used as a companion to the *Journal of Marriage and the Family*.

    SIECUS officials who have served on the editorial staff of *The Family Coordinator* include Jessie Bernard, associate editor, 1968; Joseph S. Himes, associate editor, 1972; Richard Kerckhoff, associate editor, 1972; Sally R. Williams, board of editors, 1968 and 1971.

    Some SIECUS associates who have been members of the editorial staff of *The Family Coordinator* are Humanist Curtis Avery, board of editors, 1968; Elizabeth S. Force, associate editor, 1972; and Arthur E. Gravatt, board of editors, 1968.

It should be noted that NCFR's influence on family life educators and other professionals extends far beyond the boundaries of the United States. Assisting NCFR in this endeavor is SIECUS director Evelyn Duvall, as chairman of NCFR's Committee on International Liaison.[10] As part of this program, NCFR supports the International Scientific Commission on the Family through its membership in the International Union of Family Organizations.[11] At the same time, family life leaders throughout the world are encouraged to become overseas members of NCFR, which gives this SIECUS-Humanist front one more vantage point from which to direct its assault on the remainder of Western civilization.

National Education Association (NEA)

1201 Sixteenth street, N.W., Washington, D.C.

THE NATIONAL EDUCATION ASSOCIATION was founded in 1857 by forty-three educators from ten states. It has now become the largest professional organization in the world, numbering nearly one million members in over sixty state groups.

So far as its administration is concerned, NEA has become one of the largest non-governmental bureaucratic complexes in the world. Its numerous commissions and committees are concerned with everything from professional rights to international relations. Outside of its own professional body, NEA maintains joint commissions with the American Legion, the American Library Association, the American Medical Association, the American Teachers Association, the American Textbook Publishers Institute, the Magazine Publishers Association, the National Congress of Parents and Teachers, and the National School Boards Association.

Recognizing this organization's potential for exerting tremendous pressure and influence on American education, the Humanist-Socialist complex wasted no time in seizing control of NEA; this it accomplished as far back as the early 1900's. Early NEA leaders who strove for a one-world Humanistic order included such Humanist-Communist fronters as John Dewey and William Heard Kilpatrick. Harold Rugg and Marxist professor George S. Counts (who now serves on the National Advisory Council of the American Civil Liberties Union) were among the NEA teacher-leaders whose writings helped steer the leftward course of this organization in the early 1930's.

These and other Humanist-Socialist-oriented educators spearheaded a master plan to socialize America under the leadership of John Dewey, then honorary president of NEA. By maneuvering converts into top administrative positions, the master planners gained control of NEA. Humanist Dewey considered NEA to be a potential channel for the dissemination of his educational philosophy, which was based on a wholly materialistic view of life. Through its official organs and recommended texts, NEA soon was affecting the methods and thinking of thousands of professional educators.

That NEA continues to promote the Humanist ideology on the current scene is evident in a number of ways. For example —

- A former division of NEA is still associated with the parent

269

organization and is housed in the same building in Washington, D.C., as the National Training Laboratories. Humanist Abraham Maslow's psychology formed the basic foundation for these laboratories, which since 1950 have been a major innovator in the area of sensitivity training and the behavioral sciences. Today, NEA and NTL together coordinate the work of hundreds of trainers in university training centers throughout the country.

• Humanist W. N. Alexander is past president of NEA's Association for Supervision and Curriculum Development and a former member of the National Committee for the NEA Project on Instruction.[1]

• Long-time Humanist Albert Shanker is an active NEA member and is executive vice-president of New York State United Teachers, an NEA affiliate. He is also president of the American Federation of Teachers, an affiliate of AFL-CIO, and a director of the socialist League for Industrial Democracy.

• In 1967, the NEA's Association of Supervision and Curriculum Development published *Humanizing Education: The Person in the Process*. A portion of this publication, written by Humanist Carl R. Rogers, was titled "The Interpersonal Relationship in the Facilitation of Learning." Editor Mildred S. Fenner, writing in the *NEA Journal* in 1968, described this author's work as "more nearly relevant than anything else we read. . . ."[2]

• Another book published by NEA's Association for Supervision and Curriculum Development (1970) is titled *To Nurture Humaneness*. Under the subtitle "Technology and the Decline of Organized Religion," this book conveys such messages as: "If schools are to move toward humanism, then humanism must become important to all of us, students, teachers, administrators, and the general public."

• A featured lecture given at the Atlantic City convention of the New Jersey Education Association (a division of NEA) held in October 1971 was titled "Developing Humanism in Elementary Schools."[3]

• The humanistic Horace Mann League maintains a memorial room that is connected with the library of the NEA. The League was founded to perpetuate the writings and philosophy of Horace Mann, a Unitarian and initiator of universal, non-sectarian public education.

Like other organizations in PART II, NEA has tried to rid itself of any SIECUS taint by means of such statements as the following, which was part of a 1969 press release: "Despite the extremists' insistence on a tie-up between NEA and SIECUS, NEA has never commended nor condemned the SIECUS movement."[4] Yet, several years earlier, an NEA pamphlet had painted a totally different picture. *What Parents Should Know About Sex Education in the*

Schools offered three specific sources of information for structuring sex education programs:

1. SIECUS was recommended as "a clearinghouse for research and education in sex, as a source of information about sex education in the schools, and as a public forum where consideration of various aspects of man's sexuality can be carried out in dignified and objective fashion."

2. For information on current and projected programs, NEA recommended its subsidiary, the American Association for Health, Physical Education and Recreation. The AAHPER, it will be recalled, not only gives SIECUS top billing in its literature, but also collaborated with SIECUS in formulating *A Resource Guide in Sex Education for the Mentally Retarded.*

3. The Sex Education Series published by the AMA-NEA Joint Committee on Health Problems in Education is listed as "One of the best sources of additional information." All the booklets in this series were co-authored by SIECUS director and Humanist Helen Southard and SIECUS-recommended author Marion Lerrigo, with Humanist Dr. Milton Senn as medical consultant.

As a postscript to NEA's denial of any bond with SIECUS, certain other telltale signs should also be recorded here:

- The following proclamation was made in the March 1970 SIECUS Newsletter:

    "We are very pleased to announce that the National Education Association . . . is producing a community action guide for broad distribution.

    "In order not to duplicate our efforts, SIECUS has decided not to produce its planned Community Action Kit . . . . The NEA has offered to send copies of their guide, free of charge, to people who have indicated interest in the SIECUS Kit. Write to . . . SIECUS if you would like your name to be forwarded to the NEA for receipt of their guide."[5]

- SIECUS Executive Director Dr. Mary Calderone is a frequent contributor to NEA's *Journal.*

- At the same time she held the position of NEA president in 1968, Elizabeth Koontz was serving as a SIECUS board member.

- SIECUS official Sally R. Williams (originator of the notorious Anaheim home and family living program) is president of NEA's Department of School Nurses.

- Marjory Brooks, a SIECUS director, is a member of NEA's national executive board.

- Virgil M. Rogers of SIECUS is also director of NEA's Educa-

tional Implications Automation Project, as well as a former
member of NEA's board of directors.

In 1971, NEA representatives made a first formal visit to Russia,
where they met with members of the NEA's Soviet counterpart, the
Education and Scientific Workers of the Soviet Union, to co-sign a
pledge for "further democratization of education." The NEA team's
trip was in keeping with earlier pronouncements from this organization
to the effect that American education must be more "global" in
concept, and also with NEA's endorsement of most educational concepts and policies emanating from UNESCO, the educational arm of
the United Nations.

Of course it is no accident that NEA is a consistent supporter of a
one-world government under U.N. control. Consider the NEA handbook, *Education for International Understanding in American Schools*.
Designed as a guide for teachers in indoctrinating their pupils in
world-mindedness, this NEA publication maintains, among other
things: "More recently, the idea has become established that the
preservation of international peace and order may require that force be
used to compel a nation to conduct its affairs within the framework of
an established world system. The most modern expression of this
doctrine and collective security is in the United Nations Charter."[6] An
evaluation of the NEA handbook by a 1954 Special House Committee
to Investigate Tax-Exempt Foundations reports in part: "The volume
implies that the creation of the United Nations is only the first step in
the establishment of a world order."[7]

The same report by the 1954 Special House Committee to Investigate Tax-Exempt Foundations uncovered the fact that the NEA was a
component part of a network in the social sciences.[8] Other component
parts included the Rockefeller, Carnegie, and Ford Foundations, the
Commonwealth Fund, the Progressive Education Association, the John
Dewey Society, the pro-Communist Institute of Pacific Relations, and
the socialist League for Industrial Democracy. The social sciences
network was committed to the implementation of the 1934 Report of
the Commission on Social Studies of the American Historical Association, another component part. According to that Report, social sciences
were to be the core of school curricula to foster indoctrination for
collectivism.[9]

Today, NEA has not abandoned its determination to build a
collectivist state, nor has it disavowed leaders of the past for the course
they have followed. For decades, NEA has acted as a propaganda
mouthpiece for the United Nations and one-world collectivists, and in
view of the fact that NEA's executive secretary, Sam Lambert, is also

a member of the board of directors of the United Nations Association of the United States of America,[10] there is every reason to suppose that it will continue to do so.

Other current successors to NEA's top posts continue to further the collectivist cause by lobbying for total federal aid to education, knowing that what government supports it can control. In fact, as revealed by former U. S. Commissioner of Education Dr. Sterling M. McMurrin, at the time of his resignation in 1962, NEA is "moving toward national control of education."[11] Among the significant achievements of NEA to this end were several court rulings in California, Texas, Minnesota, and New Jersey that local financing of schools by property taxes is illegal. These decisions have the effect of handing over control of local schools to the state, and ultimately to the federal government. With local financing and control gone, NEA could direct all educational processes by serving as the mouthpiece for the federal government, with whom it has shared a long and productive relationship. (For one result of such court decisions, see Appendix L.)

Even more alarming is the fact that, on January 10, 1972, a Federal District Judge in Virginia ordered consolidation of three separate school districts in the City of Richmond and the Counties of Henrico and Chesterfield. As reported in one newspaper account:

> With one stroke the Judge ordered creation of a new 101,000 student system, simply disposing of the three existing systems.
> Each government must give its land, buildings, desks, etc. to the new court-created school board. . . .
> THIS IS THE FIRST DECISION THAT DESTROYS GOVERNMENTAL BOUNDARIES ENDANGERING NOT ONLY SCHOOLS, BUT LOCAL GOVERNMENT ITSELF.[12]

In the state of Hawaii, NEA's objective has already been achieved. Hawaii now has only one school district, one superintendent, and one school board. Hawaii is also the first state to have adopted the revolutionary "master plan" for education, titled "Forecast for the '70's," which appeared in the NEA journal, *Today's Education*, in January 1969. Several major points in this forecast were:

1. Educators will assume responsibility for children when they reach the age of two. Enforced or mandatory foster homes are to be available for children whose homes are felt to have a malignant influence.*

*In 1975, corresponding national legislation in the form of the Child and Family Services Act was proposed by Senator Walter Mondale (D.-Minn.), a Humanist. If passed, this legislation would, according to Representative E. G. Schuster (R.-Pa.) permit the government "to legally intervene in the American family," in that it "repeatedly opens the door to increased governmental interference with

2. Children will be given drugs on an experimental basis, to "improve in the learner such qualities as personality, concentration, and memory."[13]

3. There will be widespread busing of children to achieve various goals.

4. Teachers will become "learning clinicians." This title is intended to convey the idea that schools are becoming clinics whose purpose is "to provide individualized psychosocial 'treatment' for the student. . . ."[14]

In answer to those educators who insist the "Forecast for the '70's" is only the opinion of the two proesssors who compiled it, the following excerpt from the report itself should serve as a sufficient reply:

> For the past three years, we have studied approximately 400 published and unpublished articles and books in which such conjectures and projections occur.
>
> These current writings clearly indicate that education and schools, as they exist today, will change drastically during the 1970's and will be modified almost beyond recognition by the end of the century.[15]

Shortly after the forecast was made, financed partially with federal funds, Hawaii's single Board of Education adopted a Master Plan for Public Education in Hawaii, which neatly duplicated the mind-control methods envisioned by NEA. Hawaii rephrased it this way:

> . . . it is possible that drugs can be used to improve the intellectual capabilities and capacities of an individual. In comparison to some of the drug problems encountered today that do not provide constructive results, this approach may have profound and beneficial results.[16]

It was less than a year after Hawaii's pronouncement that a Congressional investigation ensued over the nationwide use of behavior-modification drugs on grammar school children.[17] As a matter of course, SIECUS director and NEA official Sally R. Williams was present at these proceedings to testify in favor of the behaviorists' latest innovation of administering stimulant drugs to small children. In speaking for NEA, which represents over one million teachers in the United States, Mrs. Williams claimed:

> Amphetamines and similar drugs, as well as other drugs affecting the brain, are useful tools which are the most valuable yet found medically to aid in stabilizing the brains of children with learning disorders and

the parental role." The Mondale Bill has received strong support from Humanists in authoritative positions, among them Albert Shanker, president of the American Federation of Teachers.

hyperactivity. *These drugs are unusually safe — much more so than aspirin or penicillin, and when used properly, do not lead to habituation, addiction, or abuse, but rather, help control the underlying psychological and physiological problems which lead to such abuse.*[18] [emphasis added]

At the very time of these Congressional hearings, federal Food and Drug Administration officials were warning physicians in Omaha, Nebraska, against the use of two drugs, Tofranil and Aventyl, that had been commonly prescribed there for the "behavior modification" of school children. As news of this reached the committee holding the hearings, Representative Cornelius Gallagher, chairman of the inquiry, addressed the following remarks to Dr. John E. Peters of Little Rock (who had said he used Tofranil for children with learning disabilities): "You are using drugs that FDA says are dangerous and you didn't even know the drugs were dangerous. . . ."

Concern over school-administered drugs mounted at the hearings as other factors were brought to light, including the discovery that parents from various parts of the country were being pressured by school authorities to place their children on amphetamines. Among other revelations to be found in this hearing's Appendix is the startling fact that, at the time, between five and ten percent of the first- to sixth-graders in the Omaha public school system were on amphetamines, and that, nationally, at least 150,000 to 300,000 grammar-school-age children were getting legal amphetamines from their doctors to curb "hyperkinesis."* (The National Institute of Mental Health estimates that there are up to four million "hyperactive" children in the United States who could "benefit" from stimulant drugs, including Dexedrine and Ritalin.[19])

These and other shocking statistics have been achieved largely through the efforts of NEA, its National Training Laboratories, and other related Humanist-influenced arms of the American education movement. And, considering that this is only the beginning of a much wider range of Orwellian concepts anticipated by NEA in its "Forecast for the '70's" it would appear that the situation demands the closest scrutiny by every responsible educator and concerned parent. For, as NEA itself concedes in another portion of its forecast:

*A *Washington Post* story dated July 22, 1970, titled "Student Pep Talk," by Nicholas von Hoffman, which was reprinted in this Hearing's Appendix, further notes: ". . . often the official line is that the child suffers from 'marginal brain damage'; that is, conjectured damage which shows on no tests and for which there are no clear symptoms." In many states, children are identified for special educational purposes as: minimal brain dysfunction; minimal brain damaged; perceptually handicapped; dyslexia handicapped; learning disabilities; neurologically handicapped; maturational lag; developmental lag; or simply educationally handicapped.

As educators turn a speculative eye on the next decade, they must seek to answer a question that most of them have hesitated to face. For what kind of world should we strive to prepare children and youth who will spend most of their lives in the next century? We say this question is crucial because educational policy decisions in the 1970's will not only anticipate tomorrow, they probably will help to *create* it.[20]

National Institute of Mental Health (NIMH)
5454 Wisconsin Avenue, Chevy Chase, Maryland

ANOTHER AREA NEEDING CLOSER EXAMINATION in our quest to grasp the full scope of the sex education controversy is the mental health movement, since it is closely related to home and family living courses as well as to the general health curricula in the schools. Unfortunately, critics of public school sex education too often find their attention sharply focused on the offensive erotic stimuli being thrust upon young students, without looking further. Consequently, the staggering amount of mental health propaganda — with all its psychological brain-picking — is frequently missed.

Background of the Mental Health Movement

Before covering the National Institute of Mental Health, it is necessary to understand the origins of the American mental health movement — a movement that dates back to the year 1908. Clifford Whittingham Beers, who had himself been mentally ill and from time to time had been committed to a number of mental institutions, in 1908 took the lead in organizing the first Mental Hygiene Society in the country (in Connecticut). A year later, the National Committee for Mental Hygiene, headquartered in New York City, was formed.

These groups sought to enlist public interest to reform existing mental institutions. Working with Beers were such men as Humanist William James (a leader in the early Ethical Culture Movement and chief mentor of Humanist John Dewey) and Anson Phelps Stokes (a Communist fellow traveler who in October 1969 was to become a SIECUS ad signer). From that time onward, the movement spread through North America and to other countries as well. In 1919, Beers formed the International Committee for Mental Hygiene, which held its First International Congress in Washington, D.C., in 1930.

The development of state groups and eventually hundreds of local groups, all operating more or less independently, continued until 1950. In that year, the National Committee for Mental Hygiene merged with two other national organizations — the National Mental Health Foundation, founded by a group of conscientious objectors in 1947, and the Psychiatric Foundation — to form the National *Association* for Mental

Health.* Another notable activist working in the movement, who was himself a member of the National Committee for Mental Hygiene and the National Association for Mental Health, was Humanist Lawrence K. Frank of the New York Ethical Culture Society.

About the middle 1940's, the mental health movement was suddenly discovered by the mass media of communication. The result was a flood of propaganda unparalleled in the history of this field. An account of this is contained in the *Encyclopedia of Mental Health*:

> . . . A series of press exposés swept the country, one of the earliest and most effective being Albert Deutsch's series, "The Shame of the States," beginning in 1945, and for several years used as a model by many newspapers planning reportorial surveys. Some of these exposés were directly instrumental in bringing about reorganization of state hospital systems, increased state budgets, and the creation of new and improved facilities for the mentally ill.[1]

Although Albert Deutsch's personal background was apparently unknown to many of those he influenced, a 1953 Senate Investigating Committee on Education summed it up as follows:

> . . . The Committee on Un-American Activities, House of Representatives, 1949, pages 9–58, lists Deutsch as being affiliated with the following Communist fronts:
>
>> American Youth for Democracy;
>> Equality;
>> Joint Anti-Fascist Refugee Committee;
>> League of American Writers;
>> Progressive Citizens of America . . . .
>
> Albert Deutsch was affiliated with *Masses* and *Mainstream*. *Masses* has been cited as the journalistic voice of the Communist Party; *Mainstream* has been cited as a Marxist quarterly launched by the Communist Party in January, 1947, for the avowed purpose of stimulating "Marxist thinking in literature and the creative arts." It later merged with *New Masses*, the weekly journalistic voice of the Communist Party.[2]

Deutsch also wrote *The Mentally Ill in America* under a grant from the American Foundation for Mental Hygiene; and in 1948 he edited *Sex Habits of American Men*, a symposium of "expert" evaluations of the first Kinsey Report. For several years before his death in 1961,

---

*Today the National Association for Mental Health (not to be confused with NIMH) has state divisions in nearly every state and local chapters in some 1,000 communities. It has more than one million enrolled members and volunteers. A current Humanist influence within the National Association for Mental Health is demonstrated by the presence of such members as SIECUS official Earl Ubell, who is also active with Ethical Culture, and Harry E. Maynard, a member and former secretary of NAMH, who has served on *The Humanist's* editorial advisory board.

Deutsch worked under grants from the National Association for Mental Health and the National Institute of Mental Health[3] — the latter being a U.S. Government agency.

The forties saw new responsibilities assumed by the federal government for the first time, conveniently coinciding with Deutsch's plan to create the proper public climate for ultimate centralization of the mental health field. This, of course, was to be accomplished by provoking a need for more stringent federal controls. In 1946, this having been achieved, the passage of the National Mental Health Act made possible the establishment of the National Institute of Mental Health, which emerged in 1949 as one of the seven Institutes of Health of the U.S. Public Health Service.

Another activity, and one of international significance, was taking place in this same era, following the founding of the United Nations in 1945. As explained by the *Encyclopedia of Mental Health*:

> . . . World War II disturbed most of the countries of the world, and at the end of the war, when it was decided to try once more to bring together all the people who were interested in this particular mental health approach, the United Nations and its specialized agencies had just come into being. The United Nations Educational, Scientific, and Cultural Organization (U.N.E.S.C.O.) and the World Health Organization wished to create an international nongovernmental organization that was more broadly based, representing people from all the human sciences. *The result was that at the Third International Congress on Mental Health in London in 1948, the World Federation for Mental Health was inaugurated.*[4] [emphasis added]

It is clearly no coincidence that the chairman of the International Preparatory Commission for the Third International Congress in 1948 was Humanist Lawrence K. Frank of the New York Ethical Culture Society. Frank also became a member of the Inter-Professional Commission of the World Federation for Mental Health.

Interestingly, at the final session of the Third International Congress on Mental Health, the discussions of those assembled were summed up as follows by Professor J. C. Flugel:

> . . . under present-day conditions full mental health is only possible with reference to "one world." . . . Principles of mental health cannot be successfully furthered in any society unless there is progressive acceptance of the concept of world citizenship. *World citizenship can be widely extended among all people through the applications of mental health.*[5] [emphasis added]

In view of the ideologies of the forerunners of the mental health movement, it is hardly surprising to discover the theme of "one world-ism" pulsing through its veins. In fact, the master planners consider the mental health movement an essential tool for the preparation of the world's people for mass enslavement through thought control.

World Federation for Mental Health

One direct result of the 1948 International Congress on Mental Health, as stated above, was the formation of the World Federation for Mental Health, which was soon to become an international giant in the field. Among top leaders pulling the strings behind this organization were Communist fronter Albert Deutsch, one-worlder John R. Rees (acting as first president and executive director), and Humanists Lawrence Frank and G. Brock Chisholm.*

As part of his own personal commitment to a socialized new world order, Chisholm held traditional concepts of right and wrong to be the real menace to the world. Recognizing the need for a new breed of psychiatrists, to be hand-picked and specially trained for participation in the collectivists' grand design, Humanist Chisholm feverishly urged support for his proposed course of action on more than one occasion. For example, in a lecture delivered to prominent psychiatrists and top government officials in Washington, D.C., in October 1945, Chisholm expressed the following opinion:

> What basic psychological distortion can be found in every civilization of which we know anything? The only psychological force capable of producing these perversions is morality — the concept of right and wrong. The reinterpretation and eventual eradication of the concept of right and wrong are the belated objectives of nearly all psychotherapy.
> If the race is to be freed from its crippling burden of good and evil it must be psychiatrists who take the original responsibility.[6]

So far as its basic structure and activities are concerned, further insight into the World Federation for Mental Health is offered by the *Encyclopedia of Mental Health*:

> The federation, which includes more than 140 professional or mental health societies from forty-four countries, has been as active as its financial situation will allow. It has conducted international study groups and expert committees, international teaching seminars, annual meetings and congresses, and it has had close contact with those working in this field in approximately ninety-four countries. The World Federation for Mental Health has about thirty-six member associations in the United States, many of them national, state, or local mental health bodies. The larger associations in the human sciences are also members. It still is the only widely based voluntary organization in the international mental health field, and, as one of its many activities, serves as a clearinghouse of information.[7]

Besides coordinating mental health programs on a worldwide

---

*A Canadian, G. Brock Chisholm served as president of the World Federation for Mental Health in 1957-58, and was also president of the Canadian National Committee for Mental Hygiene, an outgrowth of Clifford Beers' group in New York City.

basis, this non-governmental organization has consultative status in its cooperative relationship with the United Nations and its specialized agencies, such as UNESCO, WHO, UNICEF, ILO (International Labor Organization), and the Economic and Social Council. As a consultative organization, it has representatives at official meetings of the U.N. and its agencies, where the ideas and recommendations of the World Federation for Mental Health are put forth.

Current members of the World Federation for Mental Health include such personalities as Humanist Margaret Mead (a former president of the organization) and SIECUS director Dr. Harold Lief.

World Health Organization

There can be no doubt that the World Health Organization of the United Nations has had an interlocking Socialist-Humanist directorate since its inception, and that it still does. Instrumental in the founding of WHO in July 1946, for example, was Brock Chisholm, working in concert with other Humanists. Chisholm was executive secretary of WHO's Interim Commission in Geneva from 1946–48, and its director general from 1948–53. He was also honorary president of the World Federalists of Canada, and a member of the World Association of World Federalists. Also on hand at the founding of WHO was Chisholm's close associate, Soviet spy Alger Hiss.[8]

Like the World Federation for Mental Health, WHO from the very outset labored to stimulate the concept of "world mental health." Hiss conjured up a revolutionary definition of "health," which reads: ". . . Health is a state of complete physical, *mental, and social well-being*, and not merely the absence of disease or infirmity."[9] [emphasis added]

The Hiss concept was adopted by WHO for its Constitution and is still widely quoted today. Innocuous though it sounds, this definition clearly revised the traditional "physical" concept of health, giving it a further "psychological" meaning. This concept of health is closely tied in with the master plan to invade all existing areas of the psyche by every means possible, for the purpose of *controlling human behavior.* Envisioning "health" in this perspective has opened up an infinite number of new avenues through which the behavioral scientists can direct their Orwellian techniques to reach an unsuspecting populace.

This new turn in the health field helped prepare the way for the flood of mental health propaganda and brain-picking devices currently invading our public school curricula by way of home and family living programs, as well as health courses, which in most cases are now mandatory.

It should be noted, further, that this redefinition of health has played a significant part in court decisions overturning state anti-abortion and sterilization statutes. Whereas these acts were once legal only if the patient's *physical* health was in jeopardy, they can now be reclassified on the basis of *mental* health considerations.

Following the adoption of the Hiss concept of health, WHO began to weave a network of control around both governmental and independent health agencies all over the world. Its Mental Health Section was organized one year after the founding of the Humanist-conceived World Federation for Mental Health, with which WHO works closely. Besides acting as a collector and disseminator of information, WHO's Mental Health Section has convened a large number of international "expert" committees. These committees, in turn, have produced reports that have been read and acted upon by governments and professionals all over the world. The Mental Health Section has also supplied numerous consultants and granted many fellowships for training.

SIECUS itself is directly associated with WHO. Evidence of this is the following announcement contained in the SIECUS Annual Report for 1967–68:

> As one of the member agencies of the American Association for World Health [an outgrowth of the U.S. Committee for WHO], we shall be privileged to help host WHO's 21st World Health Assembly in Boston in 1969.[10]

Further, Dr. Mary Calderone has served on the Board of Directors of the American Association for World Health, and is a member of the U.S. Committee for WHO as well. Her husband, Frank Calderone, not only assisted in the organization of WHO's services and staff in 1948, but was also WHO's chief administrator.

National Institute of Mental Health (NIMH)

Only with the foregoing background in mind can the role of the National Institute of Mental Health be seen in its proper perspective. As mentioned earlier, this Institute was established in 1949 under the authority of the National Mental Health Act passed by Congress in 1946, the same year the World Health Organization was founded. In view of the interlocking Humanist-Socialist directorate that surrounds the mental health movement, it is easy to guess NIMH's true objective: to change values through application of the behavioral sciences.

So far as sex education is concerned, such governmental agencies as the U.S. Office of Education assumed leadership in the field. That agency retained Humanist Lester Kirkendall as its sex education specialist during 1944–45. By the fifties, NIMH arrived on the scene to promote the infusion of mental health principles into the teaching of sex education. And since that time, a number of SIECUS board members have been or are still connected with NIMH, including:

- Dr. E. James Lieberman, chief of the Center for Child and Family Mental Health, NIMH
- Dr. Clark Vincent, an NIMH fellow, who was also NIMH Scientist Administrator, 1960–64, and consultant to NIMH's Training and Manpower Branch, 1964–65
- Dr. Ira Reiss, a Humanist and recipient of NIMH research grants from 1960–64
- Dr. William A. Darity, an NIMH research project grant recipient for the preparation of a paper presented at the Workshop on Research Approaches to Sex Education, Contraception, Family Planning and Morality, sponsored by NIMH, September 14–15, 1970
- Dr. Alan P. Bell, a Humanist and senior psychologist at the Kinsey Institute for Sex Research in Bloomington, Indiana, who acted as principal investigator of an NIMH field research team on homosexuality in 1969 [11]
- Dr. John Money, an NIMH research grant recipient and a member of NIMH's 1967 Task Force on Homosexuality
- Dr. Judd Marmor, a Humanist, member of NIMH's 1967 Task Force on Homosexuality and also of its Social Problems Research Review Committee. Significantly, Dr. Marmor has been a long-time leader in the American Psychiatric Association, which recently voted to drop homosexuality from its list of mental disorders. This reversed a position held by the APA for nearly a hundred years, by which homosexuality was characterized as a sexual deviation. Marmor is a former vice president of APA and was elected president for the year 1974.

Task Force On Homosexuality

This NIMH-funded project is particularly significant, since it was created at a time when the Humanist complex, including SIECUS, was mustering its forces for an all-out attack on existing sex laws in an effort to "legalize" homosexuality. In September 1967, a Task Force on Homosexuality was appointed by Dr. Stanley F. Yolles,* then director of NIMH, whose selection of members was anything but neutral. Following is a partial list of individuals who served on this fifteen-member panel in addition to Drs. John Money and Judd Marmor, who were mentioned above:

*Dr. Yolles is also a contributing member of the Humanist-oriented Group for the Advancement of Psychiatry.

- Dr. Jerome Frank, a Humanist
- Dr. Paul Gebhard, head of the Kinsey Institute, a SIECUS-recommended author and a contributor to *Sexology* magazine
- Dr. Evelyn Hooker, whose studies on homosexuality made at the University of California were recommended in the Spring 1965 issue of *The Humanist*, in an article titled "The Humanist Bookshelf on Sex," by Humanist Isadore Rubin of SIECUS.[12] Another study of Dr. Hooker's, described in *The Problem of Homosexuality in Modern Society*, was also mentioned in Rubin's article.
- Dr. Edwin M. Schur, a SIECUS-recommended author, whose anthology on *The Family and the Sexual Revolution* was highly praised in the Rubin "Humanist Bookshelf" article. (Dr. Schur serves on the Advisory Board of the radical National Organization for the Reform of Marijuana Laws, a group working for the legalization of marijuana.)
- Judge Morris Ploscowe, another SIECUS-selected author, whose views were presented in a panel discussion on homosexuality in the April 1971 issue of *Playboy* magazine. In general, Ploscowe maintains that the law should assume a neutral stance where homosexual activity between consenting adults is concerned. Ploscowe further stated: "Homosexuality must be socially accepted as a fact of life; a laissez-faire attitude toward the homosexual must develop." Rubin's "Humanist Bookshelf" article recommends Ploscowe's *Sex and the Law* as "The best single book on the need for change in our laws."

According to a SIECUS Newsletter devoted to the subject, the mandate of the NIMH Task Force on Homosexuality was "to review carefully the current state of knowledge regarding homosexuality in its mental health aspects and to make recommendations for Institute programming in this area."[13] In its final report, October 10, 1969, the Task Force recommended the coordination of NIMH activities in the broad area of sexual behavior through the establishment of a Center for the Study of Sexual Behavior, to be funded with tax dollars.

So far as legal recommendations are concerned, the same SIECUS Newsletter revealed that a majority of the Task Force accepted and concurred with the British Wolfenden Commission, the Ninth International Congress on Criminal Law, and the American Law Institute's Model Penal Code, which have all recommended that statutes covering sexual acts be recast such a way as to remove legal penalties against acts in private between consenting adults. Said the Task Force experts: "Although many people continue to regard homosexual activities with repugnance, there is evidence that public attitudes are changing. Discreet homosexuality, together with many other aspects of human sexual behavior, is being recognized more and more as the private business of the individual rather than a subject for public regulation through statute."

Interestingly, another article in the SIECUS Newsletter, titled *Homosexuality and Objectivity*, endeavors to convince its readers that homosexuality should not be frowned upon. Its author, Humanist and SIECUS official Judd Marmor (a Task Force member), quotes Sigmund Freud* in one portion to substantiate the contention that "Homosexuality is assuredly no advantage, but it is nothing to be ashamed of, no vice, no degradation, it cannot be classified as an illness; we consider it to be a variation of the sexual functions produced by a certain arrest of sexual development."

Another recommendation of the Task Force on Homosexuality focused on research: "We recommend that basic and applied research activities in the area of homosexuality be given high priority. . . ."[14] Less than two months later, it was announced that "the most comprehensive study ever done on Homosexuals in the United States" was being conducted by the Kinsey Institute for Sex Research, funded by a $375,000 grant from the National Institute of Mental Health.[15] "It is our hope," said Tom Maurer, director of field research for the NIMH-funded project, "*that the study will produce data to change attitudes, laws, and ideas about homosexuals.*" (emphasis added) Maurer did not comment on whether or not this was the desire of the American taxpayers who paid for the study. Another consideration not revealed was the fact that Maurer is a former president of the San Francisco male homosexual group known as the Society for Individual Rights, and teaches a course on homosexuality at the notorious National Sex and Drug Forum,[16] also located in San Francisco (see entry for *National Sex and Drug Forum,* elsewhere in PART II). Working with Maurer and other members of the NIMH-funded field research team was Humanist Alan P. Bell of SIECUS, who acted as principal investigator for the study.

Encyclopedia of Mental Health

As a second illustration of the Humanist-SIECUS influence behind the National Institute of Mental Health, the previously men-

---

*Significantly, Sigmund Freud is identified as a Humanist in Corliss Lamont's book, *The Philosophy of Humanism*; this should come as no surprise when it is remembered that Freud developed his total sexual mythology on a radical atheistic basis.

tioned *Encyclopedia of Mental Health* has been selected because of its apparently wide distribution and the stimulation it has given to the mental health profession. Although no acknowledgment of a financial grant to the Encyclopedia by NIMH is apparent, there are other indications of a direct linkage through personnel involved in its development.

First, the Encyclopedia was published in 1963 with the full cooperation of Dr. Robert Felix, then director of NIMH, and his staff. Second, two of the eleven-member board of consultants who worked on the preparation of this six-volume set were officially connected with NIMH: Dr. Seymour S. Kety, chief of the Laboratory of Clinical Science, and Dr. David Shakow, chief of the Laboratory of Psychology. Third, at least nine persons shown on the Encyclopedia's list of contributing authors were NIMH staff members.

But perhaps even more significant is the fact that a key personality in this project, and its prime mover, was the previously mentioned Communist-fronter, Albert Deutsch. In the Encyclopedia's own words:

> Albert Deutsch was appointed Editor in Chief on August 25, 1960, and before his sudden death on June 18, 1961, *he had prepared the basic outline for the work and selected most of the contributors . . . .*
> *We are proud that we have followed the basic ideas and plans of Mr. Deutsch in the original Prospectus . . . .*[17] [emphasis added]

Other key figures on the Encyclopedia's eleven-member Board of Consultants were Dr. Emily H. Mudd, who was soon to become a SIECUS official; Humanist Margaret Mead, associate curator of ethnology, American Museum of Natural History, and close SIECUS associate; Humanist Dr. Karl A. Menninger, chief of staff of the Menninger Foundation; and collectivist Dr. John R. Rees, former executive director, World Federation for Mental Health, London.

Listed as contributing authors of this publication, which is among the most comprehensive works in the field, are such Humanists as Frank Barron, Eric L. Berne, Jerome D. Frank, Gerard V. Haigh, Judd Marmor, and Ashley Montagu. Dr. John Money, who soon after became a SIECUS director, is also listed.

NIMH Grants

Over the years, NIMH has become increasingly active in awarding research grants for work performed in the behavioral sciences. An inquiry by Representative Cornelius Gallagher (D.-N.J.) into the extent of the U.S. Government's involvement in this highly controversial field has disclosed shocking figures. The General Accounting Office reported, for example, that literally tens of thousands of behavioral research projects were being financed by government agencies. A preliminary check uncovered 70,000 grants and contracts at the Department of Health, Education, and Welfare (of which NIMH is a division) and 10,000 within the Manpower Administration of the Labor Department.[18]

It is equally disturbing to learn to whom these grants have been made. It merely scratches the surface to mention such recipients as the National Education Association's infamous National Training Laboratories; Communist-fronter Albert Deutsch; Humanist Ira Reiss of SIECUS; and Humanist B. F. Skinner. The latter, and the circumstances surrounding his grant, have in recent years become a center of controversy in government circles.

It was the discovery that the National Institute of Mental Health had granted $283,000 to this 67-year-old Harvard scholar that triggered Representative Gallagher's interest in research grants. Having incorporated the results of his research into the book, *Beyond Freedom and Dignity*,* Dr. Skinner proposed that government institute a "technology of behavior," making full use of scientific methods to alter the environment, and even man himself. Congressman Gallagher has described Dr. Skinner's proposal as a scheme "to alter modern life by conditioning the behavior of each citizen . . . he proposes to choose what is decent behavior and then reinforce it by rewards. And should that not be successful he would then punish negative behavior."[19]

As part of his plan, Skinner advocated the use of "operant conditioning" (a Pavlovian conditioning technique) to remake man through the use of computerized information systems. He rejected the view that men are endowed with "certain inalienable rights," asserting that man's freedom and dignity *must* be sacrificed in order to shape the "new man" in the collectivist image. In fact, Humanist Skinner attacked the very precepts on which our society is based, saying that "life, liberty, and the pursuit of happiness" were once valid goals but have no place in Twentieth Century America or in the creation of the new culture he envisons.[20] Of course it is no coincidence that, under the Skinner system, there would be communal ownership of all property under a world state.

One news account quotes Representative Gallagher as contending that *Beyond Freedom and Dignity* constitutes a threat against the American governmental system.[21] Closely paralleling this view, syndicated columnist Paul Scott commented:

Gallagher doesn't oppose Skinner's right to advocate that America be

*Preparation of this book was supported by NIMH Grant K6-MH-21, 775-01.

run by a dictatorial process of thought control. He thinks Skinner's proposals, if made as a member of his profession or a private citizen, are the good Professor's own business. But Congressman Gallagher does question whether the *government* should subsidize such schemes, since "they threaten the future of our system of government by denigrating the American traditions of individualism, human dignity, and self-reliance."[22]

Reporter Scott summarized the over-all scope of this issue by saying:

> To Representative Gallagher and a number of his colleagues in the House, all this adds up to the use of taxpayers' funds by the National Institutes of Health to promote Dr. Skinner's plan for having the government control our way of life. Gallagher also believes the grant indicates an emerging pattern of government-sponsored behavioral research the aim of which is to alter radically the values and the traditions of the nation, and with them our freedom. He contends that the logical conclusion of proposals like Skinner's must be a dictatorship under the control of those who believe in enforced population control and those who would pop pills into all of us to control our actions.

It cannot be denied that Dr. Skinner wields considerable influence among psychologists and psychiatrists, both in and out of government. In a recent Johns Hopkins University poll, psychology faculties and graduate students around the nation named Skinner as the most respected social scientist alive, despite his thought-control proposals. Similarly, a Southern Methodist University poll concluded that Skinner was one of the ten great minds in the history of psychology, and the only one now living.[23] Seldom if ever revealed is the fact that Dr. Skinner is formally affiliated with the Humanist movement as a member of *The Humanist's* editorial board, where his fellow editors consider him "the leading behaviorist in the world."[24] Skinner's prestige in the Humanist camp soared still higher when he was presented with the "Humanist of the Year" award for 1972.

In attempting to appraise the full significance and far-reaching consequences of the Skinner grant and others like it for our nation, it would be well to reflect upon the closing paragraph of an article titled "Steps Towards Mind Control," by Congressman John Schmitz:

> It is impossible to exaggerate the danger of direct mind control in a world where there are so many people eager to use it to subject the wills of other men to their own. The effect on our nation of a widespread program of enforced mind control could be as irreversibly monstrous as its effect on an individual. It could extinguish not only liberty, but the very desire for liberty. Such an evil is too horrible to think about; yet we *must* think about it, because it is no longer only a terrible shadow on the future, but a menace that confronts us here and now.[25]

NIMH and Drugs

The National Institute of Mental Health has long been involved in a broad and comprehensive program of support for narcotic addiction research, training, and treatment. This program operates through NIMH's Center for Studies of Narcotic and Drug Abuse, its Clinical Research Centers at Fort Worth, Texas, and Lexington, Kentucky, and its Addiction Research Center at Lexington. In 1961, for example, the NIMH supported fifty research projects which had narcotics or drug abuse as their principal focus.[26]

In 1967, the Task Force Report of the President's Crime Commission strongly urged a revitalization of effort, with the formation of a single government agency to prepare and distribute a broad range of drug materials. The Commission promptly suggested NIMH as an appropriate unit to be charged with the major federal responsibility for drug abuse education.

During 1968–69, NIMH made direct contact with the public educational system by initiating a Drug Abuse Education project involving the development of teacher training workshops and resource materials. Under contract with the American Association for Health, Physical Education, and Recreation and the National Science Teachers Association (both divisions of the National Education Association), a two-week pilot workshop on drug abuse education was held in California.

Since then, pilot inservice training workshops have been held in many states. An NIMH publication continues: ". . . two-day preconvention seminars in drug abuse education were held in conjunction with the annual meetings of AAHPER and NSTA. The seminars included programs for teacher inservice training, presentations by authorities on the pharmacological, legal and psychosocial aspects of drugs, and evaluation of teaching aids, both audiovisual and printed."[27]

Of course, numerous materials have been prepared by NIMH for use in school systems and community programs. A series of television and radio spot announcements have been distributed nationally to spur public awareness of the problem; NIMH-sponsored films have been produced; posters have decorated the inner cities; and pamphlets on opiates, LSD, marijuana, amphetamines, and barbiturates distributed by NIMH now number in the millions. The National Clearing House for Mental Health Information of NIMH also makes available to professionals, from its library, the largest in the field, bibliographies and abstracts on drugs.

Although it is impracticable to review fully the vast number of NIMH publications centering on the drug problem, a particular trend should be noted. This trend was accurately described in testimony presented before the Special Studies Subcommittee of the House of Representatives Committee on Government Operations:

> The crisis of drug abuse is used to introduce drug education programs which are identical to the sex education programs in that they insist on exposing children from the earliest possible ages to all aspects of the problem area, including detailed information on illegal and dangerous activities; they refuse to emphasize legal or moral objections (see the NIMH-approved "model" program for the Nation in drug education); they include the use of powerful psychological tools to change personality and attitudes; and they are all created, funded and promoted by agencies of the Federal Government.[28]

A specific trend in the NIMH drug program is the familiar stratagem of exposing the hazards of such hard drugs as heroin, *while minimizing the dangers of marijuana.* For example, NIMH's nationally distributed pamphlet, *Marihuana — Some Questions and Answers*, hammers home the theme that present research evidence is insufficient to answer most of the charges of harmful effects leveled at marijuana. And a subtle reference to its possible eventual legalization is made in the following passage: "All researchers agree that more knowledge of the long-term physical, personal, and social consequences of marihuana use is needed before national decisions about its legal status can be made."[29]

Of particular interest is the NIMH-sponsored booklet titled *Drug Abuse Films*, which reviews almost 100 drug audio-visuals for the benefit of educators and professionals. The reviewing was done by the National Coordinating Council on Drug Education, a nonprofit organization formed in 1968, which is devoted to the coordination and evaluation of drug programs under contract with NIMH.

Serving as vice president of the National Coordinating Council is Dr. Daniel X. Freedman, a member of the Group for the Advancement of Psychiatry, who was assisted in rating the drug films by a number of evaluation panelists. Included among the panelists are actor Peter Fonda, who uses and promotes the use of drugs; William F. Buckley Jr., editor of *National Review*, who supports the legalization of marijuana; Stuart D. Loomis, chief psychologist at the Haight-Ashbury Free Medical Clinic in San Francisco; Judy Seckler, director of the Free Clinic in Washington, D.C. (for a discussion of the Free Clinics, see "Drug Education" section of entry for *New Jersey State Department of Education*, elsewhere in PART II); and others, including drug users, drug addicts, ex-addicts, and inmates of penal institutions.

The films reviewed and evaluated in the National Coordinating Council's booklet, *Drug Abuse Films*, are given either an asterisk (*), designating a *favorable* recommendation, or a dagger (†), signifying a rating of *objectionable*. However, a close examination of these evaluations discloses that in most cases films labeled objectionable by the evaluating panel take a clear anti-drug stance. On the other hand, audio-visuals which have been given the National Coordinating Council's stamp of approval generally take a very soft line on drug usage and, particularly in the case of marijuana, come close to promoting it. Of particular interest are the favorable ratings given many of the drug films produced by Guidance Associates of Pleasantville, N.Y. (see entry elsewhere in PART II), including *Marijuana: What Can You Believe?* — a film structured on comments of Dr. David Smith, a member of the National Organization for the Reform of Marijuana Laws.

Joining the NIMH as members of the National Coordinating Council on Drug Education are such organizations as the American Bar Association, whose two drug committees have called for the legalization of marijuana;[30] the American Public Health Association, which has passed a resolution calling for an end to criminal penalties for marijuana users;[31] the Humanist-founded Child Study Association of America; the NAACP, which was founded in part by Humanists; the National Association for Mental Health, and the Communist-influenced National Council of Churches.

With the passage of several legislative bills in 1970, NIMH's involvement with the drug problem expanded. One bill, which became Public Law 91-527 on December 3, 1970, enlarged the power of the Secretary of Health, Education, and Welfare, of which Department NIMH is a subsidiary, and provided for the development and evaluation of drug programs for use in educational institutions and community projects. It further provided funds for curriculum development in drug education and for the training of persons involved in this field, such as teachers, law enforcement officials, and other public service personnel.

Another bill, which became Public Law 91-513, the Comprehensive Drug Abuse Prevention and Control Act of 1970, was signed by President Nixon on October 27, 1970. It was intended to serve as a model for similar laws in the states. This statute replaced all previous narcotic and dangerous drug control laws other than those concerned with import and export; reclassified possessing or giving away marijuana as a misdemeanor instead of a felony, abolishing mandatory minimum penalties for such offenses; permitted possible expungement of the police record after satisfactory probation in the case of a first offender; and granted greater authority over drug control to the Secretary of HEW.

In essence, the foregoing drug legislation transferred authority over drugs from the Attorney General in the Justice Department, a *law enforcement* agency, to the Secretary of Health, Education, and Welfare, the official *health* agency of the United States Government. This was significant in the light of current efforts to remove drug abuse from the criminal category.

Key Personalities

Inasmuch as one of the significant effects of the above legislation was a shift of power to HEW and its subsidiary, NIMH, it seems desirable to take a closer look behind the scenes at the views on drugs held by some of the key figures in these agencies:

- *Roger O. Egeberg, M.D.*, then Assistant Secretary of HEW. During a hearing held by the House Crime Committee in October 1969, Dr. Egeberg urged softer penalties for the sale and use of marijuana.
- *Stanley F. Yolles, M.D.*, then Director of NIMH. Backing up the testimony of his superior, Dr. Egeberg, at the same Crime Committee hearing, Dr. Yolles was reported to have answered "Yes" to the question, "Would you even favor dropping mandatory jail terms for sellers of heroin who sell to teen-agers?" Yolles further stated: "I am convinced that the social and psychological damage caused by incarceration is in many cases far greater to the individual and to society than was the offense itself."[32]
- *Neil L. Chayet*, a member of the seven-member advisory committee to NIMH's 1968–69 Drug Abuse Education Project, which conducted the previously mentioned NIMH-NEA-sponsored teachers' drug seminar in California, and developed the 1969 NIMH *Resource Book for Drug Abuse Education*. As a contributor to this resource book, Mr. Chayet deplores what he terms the "punitive measures" taken by law enforcement agencies in attempting to deal with the drug problem, and their "gangster-style" raids. So favorably inclined toward marijuana is Mr. Chayet that he later became an advisory board member of the National Organization for the Reform of Marijuana Laws.
- *Sidney N. Cohen, M.D.*, former Director of the Division of Narcotic Addiction and Drug Abuse of the NIMH. Dr. Cohen has stated: "The old myths that marijuana drives you crazy, that it leads you to a life of crime or hard-core heroin addiction, these all seem to be becoming irrelevant in the light of scientific scrutiny of the subject."[33]
- *James L. Goddard, M.D.,* former Commissioner, U.S. Food and Drug Administration, HEW. In 1967, Dr. Goddard said there was

no factual basis to support the belief that marijuana was more dangerous than alcohol, and that he knew of no medical justification for prohibiting its use.[34] In the same year, while still Commissioner, Goddard was further quoted as stating that it would disturb him less if his teenage daughter smoked one marijuana cigarette than if she drank an alcoholic beverage.[35]

- *Julius Axelrod,* NIMH. Axelrod highly recommended Solomon H. Snyder's book, *Uses of Marijuana,* in a *New York Times* ad, September 26, 1971. Dr. James L. Goddard and Humanist Ashley Montagu joined Axelrod in commending the book. According to the ad, Snyder's book "separates myth from medical fact to determine whether [marijuana] is a 'dangerous drug' or whether it may have legitimate medical, *as well as social,* uses."[36] (emphasis added) Not surprisingly, *Uses of Marijuana* is rated "excellent" in literature of the National Organization for the Reform of Marijuana Laws.[37]

- *Kenneth Keniston,* another member of NIMH's Drug Abuse Education Project advisory committee. Keniston is a consultant to Guidance Associates, Inc., and author of the book, *Youth and Dissent,* described by *Publisher's Weekly* as sympathetic toward radical youth.

- *Bertram S. Brown, M.D.,* Director of NIMH (1972). Dr. Brown is considered to be the government's top psychiatrist. In early 1972 he urged an easing of marijuana laws, stating: ". . . I have personally felt for a long time that the penalties (for use and possession) are much too severe and much out of keeping with knowledge about [marijuana's] harmfulness. . . . I have been strongly in favor of decriminalization, but not for total removal of penalties."[38] When asked for his definition of "decriminalization," Brown told reporters it involved "penalties that do not jail people for use." (The use of the term "decriminalization" appears to be no more than a play on words — another way of implying "legalization" without saying it.)

Another outgrowth of the Comprehensive Drug Abuse Prevention and Control Act of 1970, mentioned earlier, was the establishment of a commission to conduct a study of marijuana and to make recommendations regarding its control. This body became known as the National Commission on Marihuana and Drug Abuse. A unanimous recommendation made by this Commission was "that marijuana be legalized for private, personal use," and "that laws be changed to permit casual distribution of small amounts of the drug when little or no money changes hands."[39]

Serving on the thirteen-member National Commission on Marihuana and Drug Abuse were Raymond P. Shafer, former Governor of Pennsylvania, as Commission chairman; Dr. Dana L. Farnsworth, a psychiatrist and member of the Group for the Advancement of Psychiatry; Congressman Tim Lee Carter (R.-Ky.); Senator Jacob Javits; and Mrs. Joan Cooney, president of the Children's Television Workshop and producer of *Sesame Street.*

Other personalities wielding a strong influence on this marijuana study commission as contributors and contractors to its general study of the drug problem were Neil Chayet and Erich Goode, both members of the National Organization for the Reform of Marijuana Laws.

A press release put out by the National Commission on Marihuana and Drug Abuse clearly shows that it was under the influence of another thirteen-member group that conducted a behind-the-scenes, three-day seminar at Endicott House in Dedham, Massachusetts, during the height of the Commission's research. Commission members Shafer and Farnsworth watched the proceedings from a quiet corner, while a tape recorder gathered every sound. The press release says:

> . . . The men and women doing the talking those three days at Endicott House were what might be termed the "42nd Project." What they concluded there was solely for the benefit and guidance of Shafer, Farnsworth, and the other 11 members of the National Commission. Ultimately it might benefit and guide the Congress, the President, and all the people.[40]

Not revealed by the press release was the fact that the thirteen-member body which conducted the seminar for the benefit of the Commission was itself dominated by such Humanists as Jacques Barzun of Columbia University, its chairman; psychoanalyst Rollo A. May; and Kenneth Boulding, professor of economics at the University of Colorado. The same press release disclosed that NIMH had worked closely with the National Commission on Marihuana and Drug Abuse in guiding the decision that called for the legalization of marijuana.

The permissive attitude toward marijuana in the overall NIMH drug program and many others that are flooding our school systems is part of a pattern to condition both youth and adults for the acceptance of drug use. This is apparently only one segment of a broader, syndicated plan that will include the eventual national acceptance of behavior-modification drugs for small children, and later for the entire population, as one means of *controlling human behavior.*

National Sex and Drug Forum (NSDF)
330 Ellis Street, San Francisco, California

SINCE ITS FOUNDING IN 1968, the National Sex and Drug Forum has rapidly become involved in as many aspects of sex and drug education as possible. It has diligently conducted courses in Human Sexuality (heterosexuality, homosexuality, abortion and birth control, prostitution, pornography, development of sexual attitudes and behavior, sex laws, morality) and in Drug Use and Abuse for groups and institutions throughout the country, though its efforts are directed primarily to doctors, clergymen, social workers, and educators. One stated purpose of the organization is "to overcome ignorance, fear, and extremism."

Certain key personnel who run the show at NSDF appear to have an affinity for the bizarre and the sensual. Co-director of NSDF is Ted McIlvenna, who leads the Forum's course on homosexuality. Besides having organized the fight for homosexual law reform in Great Britain, McIlvenna is also a founder in this country of the Council on Religion and the Homosexual, a group which is enthusiastically working to legitimize this perversion. Aiding McIlvenna in the NSDF course on homosexuality are the Reverend Tom B. Maurer, a former president of the San Francisco male homosexual organization, the Society for Individual Rights, and the Forum's assistant director, Phyllis Lyon, a Humanist and former president of the international Lesbian organization, the Daughters of Bilitis. Says Miss Lyon:

> The Revolutions sweeping America — homosexual, black, women, sexual, youth — all seek freedom for the individual. One of the freedoms so desperately needed is freedom from myth and misinformation. The National Sex and Drug Forum is contributing to this freedom in the areas of human sexuality and of mind-altering drug use and abuse.[1]

Co-director of the Forum with McIlvenna is Dr. Joel Fort, whose views on drugs are reflected in the following statement:

> Essentially, Dr. Fort holds that there are no such things as "hard-core" and "soft-core" drugs. For example, more people die annually from aspirin overdose or from long-range effects of nicotine than from LSD; addiction to alcohol is more widespread and socially damaging than heroin addiction.[2]

Dr. Fort is considered by the Forum to be one of the nation's foremost authorities on mind-altering drugs, and he often tours the country in an unremitting effort to spread the Forum fever. In fact, he has been featured in high-level sessions of teachers' drug seminars — a curious spot for one who holds membership in the National Organization for the Reform of Marijuana Laws (see "Drug Education" section in entry for *New Jersey State Department of Education*, elsewhere in PART II).

So far as sexuality is concerned, NSDF's Multi-Media Research Center has issued a catalog of raw pornographic films that masquerade as "sex education." Subjects graphically portrayed in these films are male and female homosexuality, masturbation, heterosexuality, massage for sexual fulfillment, and group sex, demonstrated by nude closeups. One of the wilder heterosexual films, on erotic fantasy, the catalog declares is being used with persons of high school age.

The above films are apparently only a few of a catena of raw movies used by NSDF. In June 1970, a shipment of films slated for an NSDF seminar for clergy in Chicago was confiscated by the Federal Bureau of Investigation after the FBI was informed by United Air Lines that the carrier was holding a shipment of pornographic films.[3]

Teaching techniques used by the Forum are anything but traditional. A special Awareness Room, for instance, is frequently utilized in the NSDF's 14-hour weekend courses for purposes of "information intake." Among the furnishings of this room are huge psychedelic pillows, wall-to-wall carpeting, a control booth equipped for the most sophisticated audiovisual projection techniques, and, according to *Commonweal* magazine, "the sexiest damn water bed this side of Pecos." The Awareness Room was further utilized in an eighteen-month study conducted by the Forum for the President's Commission on Obscenity and Pornography in its quest for "objective" data.*

Other teaching aids include a broad range of publications, written or compiled by the Forum staff, consisting of such items as charts sketching out the main findings of Humanists Masters and Johnson in *Human Sexual Response; The "Yes" Book of Sex* series, designed by the Forum to provide professional counselors with sex information "which emphasizes proficiency rather than constraint"; and papers on sexuality in children and on youth and drugs.

One assumption that underlies the Forum's basic approach to teaching is that learners are entitled to a "meaningful exposure" to a

---

*Following the Commission's recommendation that pornography laws be lifted, a coalition of twenty-five national organizations issued a statement endorsing the Commission's report. According to the April 1971 SIECUS Newsletter, some of the participating organizations were: the American Civil Liberties Committee, the American Library Association, the American Public Health Association, the National Council of Churches, the National Education Association, the National Board of the YWCA, and SIECUS.

wide range of human sexual behavior that extends outside their own area of experience (including, of course, sexual deviation).[4]

Curiously, the Forum's approach and course materials have been adopted by medical schools at the Universities of Minnesota, California, and Hawaii.

In view of all foregoing facts, it should not be surprising to discover such personalities as John Gagnon of SIECUS, and the "Humanist of the Year" for 1971, Dr. Albert Ellis, serving on NSDF's Board of Advisors. The latter deserves a closer look.

Dr. Albert Ellis

Although not a SIECUS director, Dr. Ellis frequents the SIECUS circuit and, in turn, has earned the enthusiastic approval of SIECUS as a "legitimate authority" in the field of sexology.

His books, *Sex Without Guilt, Constitutional Factors in Homosexuality*, and *The Encyclopedia of Sexual Behavior*, are cited as references and recommended for study in some of the SIECUS Study Guides. Other works by Ellis are given recognition in SIECUS newsletters. Identified Communist Isadore Rubin described him as "one of America's leading sexologists." Fellow-Humanist Lester Kirkendall of SIECUS accompanied Ellis on a college campus tour in 1968 and joined him in advising students to add sex to their extra-curricular activities.

In a lecture series at the University of Bridgeport in October 1969, Ellis advocated the practice of masturbation, pre-marital intercourse, and group sex, and he advised students to "get away from home as soon as possible" and to stop listening to people who are "attached to puritanical standards."

Of course Ellis's views on religion are compatible with his perverted concept of sex. Stated in his treatise, *The Case Against Religion*, for example, is the conclusion that:

> Religion is . . . directly opposed to the goals of mental health. . . . It encourages a fanatic, obsessive-compulsive kind of commitment that is, in its own right, a form of mental illness. . . . This close connection between mental illness and religion is inevitable and invariant. . . . In the final analysis, then, religion is neurosis.[5]

Albert Ellis is connected with the following organizations:

- American Humanist Association
- Institute for Rational Living (founder and director)
- Institute for Advanced Study in Rational Psychotherapy
- American Psychological Association (in which he shares membership with a number of SIECUS officials)

- Society for the Scientific Study of Sex (in collaboration with at least ten SIECUS board members)
- *International Journal of Sexology*

But perhaps Dr. Ellis's most significant contribution to the field of "sexology" is his less well-known affiliation with the notorious newspaper, *Screw,* one of New York's hard-core pornographic weeklies.* So salacious is this newspaper that its premises were raided by New York police and its staff arrested in the late 1960's. Dr. Ellis was listed on the inside cover of the April 25, 1969 edition of *Screw* with the title, "Shrink in Residence."[6]

Page 8 of that issue was entirely devoted to an effusion of pornographic prose entitled "Sex Addict," which was boldly headed with a photograph of a nude man and woman. The article contained an advertisement promoting Ellis's Institute for Rational Living in New York City. The advertising segment reads:

> The aesthetic of New Pornography is not to take the poem seriously as you don't take the prettiest girl seriously. My aim is firm poetry cognition, as firmness with girls. You know the sexy feeling like you feel before you are going to f *** somebody new. I give you that.
>
> LEARN THE SECRET OF THE SEX ADDICT. ATTEND SESSIONS AND WORKSHOPS AT THE INSTITUTE FOR RATIONAL LIVING [address and telephone number given]. A girl can feel the Ellisonian Ideology down to her toes; since one's beliefs indirectly affect motor pathways.

This article was so thoroughly corrupt and obscene that no other portion of it could possibly be quoted without offending the reader; in fact, the foregoing passage was the least offensive in the entire article.

Albert Ellis's Institute for Advanced Study in Rational Psychotherapy is connected with the Institute for Rational Living run by the same personnel. Serving on the boards of professional advisors for both institutes are two SIECUS directors, James L. McCary and Wardell Pomeroy — the latter of whom was fêted by a homosexual group, the Mattachine Society of New York, at a fund-raising cocktail party.[7] Some other members of both boards are Humanists Aaron T. Beck, Robert A. Harper, and Heinz L. Ansbacher (a founding sponsor of the American Association for Humanistic Psychology); and John C. Lilly, a former resident at the Humanist-run Esalen Institute who has also worked for the National Institute of Mental Health, and who, in

---

*Humanist Aryeh Neier, executive director of the American Civil Liberties Union in New York, announced the ACLU's support for *Screw* in a letter to the editor that appeared in the December 1971 issue of *Playboy.* In it Neier wrote: ". . . I recall a couple of years ago when New York newsdealers selling *Screw* were being harassed, the New York Civil Liberties Union took action on behalf of *Screw* to end that harassment."

an article appearing in the December 1971 issue of *Psychology Today,* condoned the use of LSD.

Humanist Ellis does not merely "dabble" in pornography, but considers it a profession, as evidenced by the following extracts. One is from an advertising brochure for hardcore pornography, published by Lyle Stuart, Inc.:

> THE CRUEL AND THE MEEK, by Walter Braun,
> with a special introduction by Dr. Albert Ellis.

Here, just made available in America, is a no-holds-barred examination of sexual cruelty, whipping, bondage, high heels "disciplining," etc.[8]

And another, published by Regent House:

> Now available for the first time anywhere!
> THE PHOTOGRAPHIC MANUAL OF SEXUAL INTERCOURSE
> by L.R. O'Connor — Introduction by Albert Ellis, Ph.D. . . . .

Now for the first time, the mystery of sex is unlocked through the aid of over 150 actual photographs of a live man and a live woman together engaged in sexual intercourse positions![9]

The shocking "credentials" of Humanist Ellis should surely cause the most complacent parent to question his close liaison with SIECUS, an organization that claims its purpose is "to promote healthy, responsible sex relations." Even more disturbing is the knowledge that Dr. Ellis's warped dialectic, as expressed in *The American Sexual Tragedy, If This Be Sexual Heresy,* and *Sex Without Guilt,* have found their way into the sex education bibliographies of public school curricula throughout the country.

Glide Memorial United Methodist Church

Another area deserving close scrutiny because of its close liaison with the National Sex and Drug Forum is the Glide Memorial United Methodist Church, under which the NSDF operates as a public service. Established in 1930, Glide is recognized as an "agency of the United Methodist Church,"[10] having had tax-exempt status since 1937.

So far as is known, the Glide church in its earlier years operated in a conventional religious framework. In 1948, however, Bishop Donald Tippett assumed leadership of this church, and is considered to have "engineered Glide on its present track."[11] Just where the Glide church was headed was perhaps known then only by Tippett, whose ideological background is anything but traditional.

Bishop Tippett is on record as having been affiliated with the following subversive activities:

- American Youth for Democracy, cited as "subversive and Communist,"[12] determined to turn American youth against religion.[13]
- Methodist Federation for Social Action, cited as a "Communist front."[14]
- *Protestant Digest*, cited as "a magazine which has faithfully propagated the Communist Party line under the guise of being a religious journal."[15]
- Sponsor of a testimonial dinner for the "Hollywood Ten" (ten Hollywood Communists who refused to testify before the House Committee on Un-American Activities). The dinner was given by the Freedom from Fear Committee, which was cited as "one of the Communist Party's latest fronts."[16]

Besides being active with the National Council of Churches through the years, Tippett held the influential position of president of the Methodist Council of Bishops during 1967–68, and in October 1969 he became a SIECUS ad signer.

In late 1963 the Rev. A. Cecil Williams, joined the Glide'staff; he is now the church's Minister of Involvement and Celebration Like Tippett, Williams has close ties with the conspiratorial Left, having been cited in 1971 by the U.S. House of Representatives Committee on Internal Security as a member of the Communist World Peace Council.[17] He was further accorded the title of "spiritual advisor" to Communist Angela Davis in a March 1971 Glide newsletter.[18]

A typical Glide "celebration" (a term the church uses instead of "service"), as conducted by Williams, includes sensual, captivating chants by him — often ending with an "oooooeee" — with music by the Meridian West Jazz Group and revolutionary readings from a book titled *Quotations from Chairman Jesus.* * This book is a clear attempt to

---

*The foreword to *Quotations from Chairman Jesus* was written by Communist sympathizer Father Daniel Berrigan. Berrigan, while on trial in April 1972 in Harrisburg, Pennsylvania, for destroying draft records, actively participated in a so-called Holy Week program staged in the Pennsylvania state capital.

According to the American Council of Christian Churches in Harrisburg and Valley Forge, events taking place there included a Holy Week parade, led by a thirty-foot devil and his demons. Joining them were U.S. Representative Bella Abzug (D.-N.Y.), American Civil Liberties Union attorney William Kunstler, and others. Two banners glaringly advertised the presence of the Communist Party. Also in attendance were representatives of the Augsburg Lutheran Church and the YWCA–YMCA; a delegation from the United Church of Christ; and some Episcopal Bishops. Lending its support in the form of donated facilities was the Quaker-run Friends Meeting House. During the height of the activities, a collection was taken for the Angela Davis Defense Fund.

As a delegation in the center of the crowd waved the Viet Cong, Red Chinese, and United Nations flags, Father Berrigan placed a telephone call to the Communist Vietnamese delegation in Paris, expressing the Harrisburg rally's support for the Communist emissaries.

portray certain Christian scripture as Communistic. Its title, of course, is a take-off on the official "Bible" of the Chinese Communists, *Quotations from Chairman Mao.*

One particular Sunday "celebration" conducted in 1969 by Cecil Williams is of special interest here. A news account of it relates:

> On Sunday, October twenty-sixth, Comrade Angela [Davis] appeared before an "overflow" crowd at the notorious Glide Memorial Methodist Church in San Francisco. The "Reverend" Cecil Williams (minister at Glide) introduced Angela, remarking that someone had telephoned to criticize her appearance at the Church, calling her an atheist. The "Reverend" Williams then declared: "Now listen to this — the man called Jesus of Nazareth was a communist!" With that, Angela came on to the raucous beat of the Meridian West Jazz Folk Group.[19]

The title "Reverend," as applied to Williams by his church, is somewhat of a misnomer, in view of the fact that he condones homosexuality, free love, and completely unrestrained living; renounces heaven as having no meaning for him; boasts that he killed the church; permits disrobing, sexual acts, and pornographic films in his church; and in general turns Christian values upside down.[20] He nevertheless was recently a featured speaker at the United Methodist Conference held in Atlanta's Civic Center in April 1972.

Another notable personality at Glide is its Minister to the Elderly, the Rev. Edward L. Peet, also executive director of the Glide Involvement Center. Peet's less known credentials include several citations for support of subversive causes. Specifically, Peet was (1) a sponsor of the 20th Anniversary National Conference of the American Committee for Protection of Foreign Born, cited as "subversive and Communist";[21] (2) a signer of an "open letter" to Senators and Congressmen urging repeal of the McCarran Internal Security Act, issued by the National Committee to Repeal the McCarran Act, a cited Communist front;[22] and (3) a signer of the Statement in Defense of Communist Party, U.S.A.[23]

The secretary of Glide Church is Humanist Phyllis Lyon, mentioned earlier as a former president of the Lesbian organization, the Daughters of Bilitis, of which she had been a founder.

In philosophy, Glide is clearly Humanistic and Marxist-oriented. Its leaders place a heavy accent on sensuality, communal living, and community involvement — the last a term that has succeeded in rallying Glide membership behind a flood of leftwing activities.

Those drawn into the Glide ranks include homosexuals, leftwing activists, drug addicts, and especially young drop-outs. Regularly featured by Glide for its flock are such activities as homosexual weddings, paganistic "religious" celebrations, and a constant stream of Communist and other subversive speakers. For example, the church has offered its lectern to the convicted atom bomb spy, Morton Sobell, who spoke at a Glide fund-raising affair for the Communist Party newspaper, *People's World*,[24] and Humanist William Kunstler, legal counsel to many Communist revolutionaries, including Angela Davis.

The Glide Church has given its support to:

- The Soledad brothers
- The Black Panther Breakfast Program, in which inner-city children have been given literature depicting policemen as "pigs" and instructed to assassinate them with knives and other lethal weapons
- The Women's Liberation Movement
- The Committee United for Political Prisoners, a group whose activities parallel the Humanist prison reform movement
- The Council on Religion and the Homosexual, mentioned earlier
- The ecology movement
- The American Friends Service Committee (Quaker).

Apparently Glide is also in league with the Planned Parenthood cartel, having established a Family Planning Clinic on its premises. Operated in cooperation with the San Francisco Department of Public Health, the clinic offers free birth control counseling, contraceptives, VD and pregnancy tests, and abortion counseling to persons of all ages, including "emancipated" minors.[25]

In its role as sponsor of the swinging National Sex and Drug Forum, Glide Church lends its sanctuary at times to NSDF for film showings and other public activities.

New Jersey State Department of Education

225 West State Street, Trenton, New Jersey

Sex Education

In 1967, the New Jersey State Department of Education (Division of Curriculum and Instruction, Office of Health, Safety, and Physical Education) jumped onto the sex education bandwagon, publishing a booklet titled *Guidelines for Developing School Programs in Sex Education.* This booklet was made available to all schools in the state. Shortly afterward, and usually with the help of local Humanists, the *Guidelines* became a prime resource for generating sex education programs. In fact, it has been one of the most widely distributed booklets ever published by this department — and certainly the most controversial.

During the height of the controversy in New Jersey (1969–1970), as tension soared between schools and concerned-parents groups, the State Department of Education continued its drive to force sex education into the schools with statements specifically formulated to pacify the public. One such letter written to anxious parents in Cranford is pertinent to this entry. Typical of evasive rebuttals emanating from the highest education office of the state, it pretends to deal with the question of SIECUS-style sex education. Although the letter is too lengthy to quote in its entirety, the last paragraph is self-explanatory and seems sufficient to make the point:

> As to your objections to SIECUS, the New Jersey Department of Education has no connection with that group, and *SIECUS material is not recommended for classroom use in the State Department guidelines on sex education.*[1] [emphasis added.]

At best, this is adept misrepresentation, in view of the following facts:

1. The Philosophy of Program and Policy Statement on Sex Education in the New Jersey *Guidelines* both contain passages which are so near to being exact duplications of the phraseology used by Lester Kirkendall in the SIECUS Study Guide, *Sex Education*, that it is obvious the study guide was the prototype.

2. Page 10 of the New Jersey *Guidelines* suggests that schools obtain the services of SIECUS as "consultant for "additional insights."

3. Participants in a Sex Education Workshop whose contributions formulated the essence of the State Board of Education's 1967 Policy Statement on Sex Education included SIECUS director Evalyn Gendel (who joined SIECUS in June 1966), and Humanist Joseph S. Darden, a persistent SIECUS promoter, as well as a friend and colleague of an identified Communist, the late Isadore Rubin of SIECUS.

4. Pages 4 and 5 of the *Guidelines* contain "Supportive Statements" on the need for sex education by the Rev. John L. Thomas, a SIECUS board member, and SIECUS executive director Dr. Mary Calderone. The bulk of the remaining "Supportive Statements" in this section emanate from either SIECUS associates or SIECUS-influenced organizations covered elsewhere in PART II.

5. The *Guidelines* suggest for showing to students numerous SIECUS-recommended films, as well as other audiovisuals produced with the direct aid of SIECUS personnel, such as *How Babies Are Made, Human Reproduction, Sex: A Moral Dilemma for Teenagers,* and *The Tuned-Out Generation.*

Typical SIECUS-selected reading matter for students includes Lester Beck's *Human Growth*, Evelyn Duvall's *Love and the Facts of Life*, and Eric Johnson's *Love and Sex in Plain Language.*

6. Among several curriculum outlines recommended on page 22 of the *Guidelines* for perusal by local curriculum committees seeking "specific resource materials" is the Anaheim Union High School District's *Family Life and Sex Education Course Outline*, which was designed by a professional committee chaired by SIECUS director Sally R. Williams, then a school nurse in the Anaheim district. The Anaheim program at the time enjoyed national prominence as "a SIECUS showcase."

7. Teachers are encouraged to draw from the writings of SIECUS directors Evelyn Duvall, William Genné, Lester Kirkendall, Helen Southard, and Clark Vincent as source material; among other teacher resources suggested are the works of numerous SIECUS-selected authors.

Geraldine Lux Flanagan's SIECUS-recommended book, *The First Nine Months of Life*, is one of many suggested in these *Guidelines* that are consistent with their Humanistic trend. Although the book's accurate description of what takes place in the womb during pregnancy is undoubtedly of some value, its contents are contaminated by evolutionary concepts.

For example, one finds statements such as the following:

> The amniotic waters have an evolutionary significance. Through them the higher forms of life make the transition from a marine existence to dry land.[2]

* * *

In these two months [fifth and sixth] a fine woolly fuzz called *lanugo* [the Latin for *wool*] appears — especially on the arms, legs, and back. Most of this falls out before birth. It may be an evolutionary reminder of man's fur-bearing ancestors.[3]

In view of all foregoing data given on the New Jersey *Guidelines*, it would appear that the State Department of Education is being less than candid in attempting to disclaim any connection between SIECUS and the state's suggested program.

Humanizing the Curriculum

There are strong indications that the essence of Humanism has not only penetrated New Jersey's sex education guidelines, but has invaded the highest levels of the State Department of Education itself, and has already begun to affect other areas of the curriculum.

For example, an article appearing in the May 1971 issue of the newsletter, *New Jersey Education*, was captioned, "Commissioner Sees Education Focusing on Humanism, Greater State Financial Support for Schools in 70's." In it, Dr. Carl L. Marburger, then State Commissioner of Education, declared the need for education to place emphasis on "human values" rather than traditional objectives. "This trend toward humanism is not new to the education scene," the commissioner said. Looking at the coming decade, Dr. Marburger forecast the following as among several other "discernible trends":

There will be a tendency for schools to become more humanistic, more open in terms of student and community involvement and less rigidly structured than in the past.[4]

The overall scope of Marburger's scheme would encompass "greater state participation in local affairs," with increased emphasis upon the use of educational television; open, non-graded classes; individual instruction*; and behavioral objectives.[5]

Answering Dr. Marburger's challenge, Waldwick High School soon

*Individual instruction is basically a Humanist-oriented, permissive concept under which the individual student, rather than the teacher, decides upon his own particular learning interest for the day. After making this choice, which is approved by the teacher, the student visits the school's Multi-Media Center (formerly the library), also sometimes referred to as an Instructional Materials Center or Education Media Center. There he is advised what tapes, recordings, filmstrips, books, or magazines are available for his use. As with educational television, the learning process is centrally controlled. Individual instruction can be used in either an open classroom or a traditional setting.

became one of many to "humanize" its curriculum. Less than one year after his article appeared, a special course was instituted at Waldwick called "American Humanities." One newspaper account of this action, headed "Waldwick High Seeks to Humanize Curriculum," cites a few of the authors whose works are listed in the course's bibliography. Of the five contemporary authors mentioned, at least two are known Humanists: William James and Jean-Paul Sartre, the French Marxist; two others are Communist-fronter Reinhold Niebuhr and existentialist philosopher Martin Buber, who is highly regarded in Humanist circles.

Later, other schools throughout the state began to implement Marburger's plan by instituting many of his reforms, including humanistic education and the open, non-graded classroom approach.

As for New Jersey colleges,* recent years have shown a heavy influx of Humanists and their front men into positions of authority in these institutions. Substantiation of this fact can be found in the following illustrations, which have been chosen at random to demonstrate the point: At Trenton State College, *Humanist Manifesto II* signer Gordon Clanton is assistant professor of sociology; Rutgers University retains another signer, Irving Louis Horwitz, as professor of sociology and political science; and at Ramapo College, long-time Humanist leader Howard Radest is strategically positioned as associate professor of philosophy.

Primary targets, as seen by Humanists, are the colleges that train teachers, which include all the above. Most of these can, in fact, be currently designated as Humanist Socialist strongholds. One need only examine a typical college syllabus and its accompanying bibliography in such fields as anthropology, ecology, the humanities, psychology, sociology, and particularly sex education, to discover this.

Newark State College's† sex education bibliography,[6] for example, was compiled by Humanist Joseph S. Darden, who is professor of health education at this college. Dr. Darden's selection of references is almost identical with the selection made by the SIECUS-Humanist complex.

William Paterson College's suggested text for use in teacher train-

---

*New Jersey colleges have begun to introduce "humanistic education" into their curricula. As just one example; William Paterson College opened its whole campus for a three-day symposium on "Humanistic Studies," for the purpose of acquainting its teachers and all participants with such Humanist-oriented innovative programs in education as *values clarification*, transcendental meditation, psychodrama, sociodrama, group interaction, non-traditional learning, and *peace studies*. This function was co-sponsored by the college and the American Federation of Teachers, of which Humanist Albert Shanker is president.
†Now known as Kean College.

ing is the SIECUS-produced handbook, *The Individual, Sex and Society.*[7] This SIECUS creation is loaded with references to the writings of such Humanists as Albert Ellis, Erik Erikson, Alan F. Guttmacher, Garrett Hardin, Virginia Johnson, Lester Kirkendall, Judd Marmor, Abraham Maslow, William Masters, Margaret Mead, Karl Menninger, Edward Pohlman, Alice Rossi, Isadore Rubin, Edward Sagarin, Helen Southard, and Walter Stokes.

Montclair State College's Educational Foundation for Human Sexuality is caught in the same Humanist web. The Foundation is headed by Dr. Charity Runden, a Unitarian, who has contributed at least one of her poetic efforts to *The Humanist* magazine.[8] Dr. Runden's choice of "experts" in the field of sexuality includes Humanists Albert Ellis, Erik Erikson, Erich Fromm, Hugh Hefner, Virginia Johnson, William Masters, Margaret Mead, and Carl Rogers. Suggesting their writings in an article titled *Sex and the Teacher*, which appeared in the October 1968 issue of the *New Jersey Education Association Review*, the Foundation's executive director designated the above as authors whom teachers will "need to read" in order "to develop new self-images, new philosophies of human sexuality, new self-confidence."[9]

So infused with the SIECUS mentality is Dr. Runden's Foundation that in June 1970 it sponsored a conference on human sexuality at Montclair State College, which featured Humanist colleagues Ira Reiss of SIECUS and Alan F. Guttmacher, president of Planned Parenthood–World Population, who spoke on the need for abortion law repeal. At this function awards were presented by the Foundation to Dr. Guttmacher, as well as to Dr. Reiss and his SIECUS colleagues, Wardell Pomeroy and Frederick J. Margolis.[10]

Charity Runden's affinity for SIECUS runs even deeper. Following her attendance at the Second Annual SIECUS conference — one of many SIECUS functions she has visited — Dr. Runden enthused:

> This year's SIECUS Conference I found fresh and interesting in ways that I would have thought cliché and uninspired. Sometimes I grin through gritted teeth realizing that we go ahead more freely with what we really want to do because we know extremists will criticize whatever we do.[11]

Another Humanist connected with Montclair State College is Ethical Culturist Dr. John Seymour, who is chairman and associate professor in the psychology department at this institution.Seymour's Humanistic influence extends into Montclair's Psycho-Educational Center, which retains him as an advisory board member. The Center's director, Elayne Nord, is president of the Lakeland Ethical Humanist Society, where Seymour has lectured. Moreover, at the time when New

Jersey's Department of Education was straining every nerve to launch its program into the schools, Dr. Seymour made speeches urging parents to accept public school sex education.

The above are only a few of countless illustrations that could be offered to show the substantial influence and even dominance wielded by the Humanist-Socialist complex in the education area. So influential are the members of this complex, in fact, that a 1968 study (published in *Psychology Today*) reported that when "activist" students on campuses throughout the nation were asked to identify which of twenty-two "isms" they identified with most closely, 30 per cent listed Humanism as their first choice, 22 per cent as their second, and 12 per cent as their third, for *a total of 64 per cent placing it among their first three choices.* Even among "non-activist" students, a total of 43 per cent placed Humanism among their first three choices.[12]

Drug Education

In response to the much-publicized drug crisis, an act providing for drug education programs for teachers and pupils was passed in 1970 by the New Jersey State Legislature (Assembly Bill No. 1056). This act provided that each school district having secondary school grades (7 through 12) was to incorporate into its health education curriculum a recommended drug education unit.[13] The program was to consist of three phases.

Phase I called for approximately 250 teachers, representing the 200 secondary school districts and 50 regional districts, to be given a three-week training program. During this time, a curriculum was to be developed for training teachers at the local level and for later presentation to the students.

Phase II was to consist of a teacher training program at the local level. This training was to be conducted by the teachers who had attended the Phase I seminar.

Phase III would encompass the actual presentation of the suggested drug education unit to students in the classroom.

Subsequently, teacher drug seminars were conducted at the New Jersey College of Medicine and Dentistry (NJCMD) and Rutgers University to train teachers as future workshop leaders throughout the state. Approximately 100 teacher representatives from local districts attended the NJCMD Drug Abuse Institute for Educators, held between June 22 and July 10, 1970. The Institute's stated aim was "to prepare representatives of the New Jersey educational system to gain insights into and to explore meaningful alternatives to drug-oriented activity."[14]

However, some of those brought in to train New Jersey teachers were persons who have long given indications of bizarre attitudes with regard to drugs. Others were actively promoting the legalization of marijuana. In fact, the theme of this drug conference could very well have been "How to Promote Drug Use While Ostensibly Combating It."

Therefore, many of the participants who steered this Institute's activities and led segments of the discussions require closer scrutiny, particularly so since the NJCMD's Division of Drug Abuse expressed the hope that the seminar would be "a prototype course in 'educating the educators'. . . ."[15]

Earl Ubell

One of the drug "experts" who addressed the New Jersey teachers at the NJCMD's seminar on the subject of *The Mass Media: Effect, Role and Responsibility* was WCBS-TV editor Earl Ubell, a SIECUS director and a Humanist.

Considered to be knowledgeable in the field of narcotics, Mr. Ubell is also the author of the WCBS-produced program series, *The Television Report, Drugs: A to Z*, a transcript of which has been published in pamphlet form.

When read in its entirety, this series covertly glamorizes drug usage; minimizes the dangers of marijuana as it ever so subtly pleads for its legalization; and places emphasis on alcohol and nicotine as hazardous drugs.

Following are several statements made by Humanist Ubell in this series that are typical of his soft stance on drugs:

> . . . There are some experts who believe that marijuana is no more dangerous than coffee or tea, but some say that long-term, continued marijuana smoking does produce personality changes . . . . However, in any comparison of alcohol and marijuana, *alcohol proves to be the more dangerous drug.*[16] [emphasis added]

Interestingly, Mr. Ubell later pursued that thought by saying, ". . . those who want to legalize marijuana say that the drug is safe, safer than alcohol . . ." — a point he had already made.

Mr. Ubell continued:

> . . . There is also agreement among experts that pot rarely generates mental disturbances, and if it does, the disturbance lasts only a short time. At least in the short run, pot . . . does not physically harm the user.

And finally:

> The tide for marijuana legalization is rising. There are many who believe that marijuana will soon join alcohol, coffee and cigarettes as legal mood-changing agents for those who want and need it.

In essence, the heavily biased, scanty statistics in Earl Ubell's compilation leave the reader with the decided impression that the real culprits are alcohol and nicotine, and that a second look at marijuana, heroin, and certain other drugs in a legalized and controlled atmosphere might be in order.

This review of Mr. Ubell's work is not meant to imply that alcohol and nicotine are not hazardous, particularly when used to excess, but rather to suggest the folly of *comparing* rather than *contrasting* them with marijuana. A *comparison* of alcohol and marijuana is essentially unsound for a number of reasons: (a) The active ingredients of the two drugs are totally different substances, having opposite physical and mental effects. Marijuana is an hallucinogen and a stimulant; alcohol is non-hallucinogenic and a depressant. (b) Unlike alcohol, marijuana is nearly always used to the point of total disorientation, and in fact such an effect is the object which the user desires to attain. (c) The effects of smoking a single marijuana cigarette (or "joint") last for twenty-four hours, whereas the effects of one or two drinks of alcohol generally wear off in an hour or two. (d) Moreover, studies made by Kolansky and Moore of patients smoking an average of four or five "joints" per week indicated a consistent pattern of such undesirable effects as very poor social judgment, including sexual promiscuity and subsequent high incidence of venereal disease; poor concentration; confusion; anxiety; depression; apathy; often a slowed and slurred speech; and a paranoid suspiciousness of others.[17] On the other hand, social drinkers consuming an average of four or five drinks per week show none of the above adverse effects as a result and continue to lead normal and productive lives. Comparing marijuana with alcohol can produce no sensible guide to action, and will, in fact, only confuse and distort the issue.

In order to analyze realistically Ubell's true intentions where drugs are concerned, it is only necessary to follow them as far back as the 1968–69 Annual Report of SIECUS — his holding company. There a significant factor is recorded — specifically, that SIECUS is apparently ready to accept certain types of drug usage as a legitimate activity of the future:

> What do we see in the future for SIECUS? In any projection it is necessary to consider that human sexual behavior will certainly be affected before the end of the twentieth century by such profound technical innovations as: major reduction in congenital and hereditary defects; new techniques for adult education; *new, more varied and reliable drugs for control of fatigue, relaxation, alertness, mood, personality, perceptions, fantasies, and other psychobiological states.* . . .[18] [emphasis added]

Considering this SIECUS sentiment and the total essence of Mr.

Ubell's television drug series, it may be assumed that this SIECUS director exerted every effort to inflict his own bias on New Jersey teachers during his presentation at the NJCMD's Drug Abuse Institute for Educators — especially in view of the fact that transcripts of his lecture and those of other participants in this seminar could not be obtained by the tax-paying public.

Joel Fort, M.D., Ph.D.

Another member of the "guest faculty" of the Drug Abuse Institute for Educators was Dr. Joel Fort of the School of Social Welfare, University of California at Berkeley, who addressed the educators on the subject of "Our 'Alienated' Society." Although not a SIECUS official, Dr. Fort is very much at home in the SIECUS camp. His swinging National Sex and Drug Forum in San Francisco, discussed earlier, is served by a board of advisors that includes SIECUS official John Gagnon and SIECUS associate (and Humanist) Albert Ellis.

There is other evidence that Joel Fort associates freely with the SIECUS clan. For example, at the California Teachers Association state conference on education research held November 14–15, 1968, in San Francisco, the featured speakers on topics ranging from drugs to sex included Dr. Fort, as well as such personalities as SIECUS director Lester Kirkendall and SIECUS associates Ralph Eckert and Eleanor B. Luckey.

Dr. Fort is a former consultant on drug abuse for the World Health Organization, which, according to the *New York Times* of June 10, 1973, declared, "Drug-taking in itself should not be considered a crime," and called for efforts to be undertaken to "decriminalize drug-taking . . . in those jurisdictions where such action is a crime." Dr. Fort has also served in the capacity of United Nations Social Affairs Officer. He is author of *The Pleasure Seekers: The Drug Crisis, Youth and Society,* and *Alcohol: Our Biggest Drug Industry and Drug Problem*.

Like Earl Ubell, Joel Fort considers marijuana less harmful than alcohol. For example, in an article appearing in the October 1969 issue of *Playboy* magazine, titled "Pot: A Rational Approach," Dr. Fort offered such comments as the following:

> In short, we seem to have a drug here [marijuana] that makes many users very euphoric and happy — high — without doing any of the damage done by alcohol, narcotics, barbiturates, amphetamines, or even tobacco.
> But we didn't have to wait until 1968 to learn that pot is relatively harmless. Some research has been done in the past . . . .[19]

In the same article, Dr. Fort further proclaimed:

> Not only is marijuana comparatively harmless on the face of all the

evidence, but there are even reasons to believe it may be beneficial in some cases . . . . My own investigations in areas of the world where this folk medicine still flourishes and my study of 20th Century scientific literature lead me to believe that marijuana would be useful for treating depression, loss of appetite, high blood pressure, anxiety, and migraine.[20]

In addition, Dr. Fort has called for removing all drug matters from the hands of the police and placing them under the jurisdiction of the medical profession.[21] So radical is his approach to drugs that in 1967 he was dismissed as director of San Francisco's Center for Special Problems by the chief administrative officer of the city. This dismissal, according to an account in the *Congressional Record* of June 25, 1969, resulted in part from the fact that "Dr. Fort symbolizes the public health and sociologic approach to homosexuals and drug users which radically contrasts with the punitive law enforcement approach."[22]

Another key fact about Dr. Fort is that he serves as an advisory board member of the radical National Organization for the Reform of Marijuana Laws (NORML). This organization's beliefs are boldly expressed in NORML literature by such statements as the following, headed "What the Law Should Be":

> We agree with the many experts, including the San Francisco Committee on Crime, who believe a compelling case exists for the removal of all criminal penalties from the use or possession of marijuana, and for making it available through sellers licensed by the state. . . .
>
> The sale and distribution of marijuana should be subject to government regulation just as alcohol is today.[23]

In short, NORML is seeking total legalization of both sale and use of marijuana.*

Since several members of the "Guest Faculty" at the Drug Abuse Institute for Educators other than Joel Fort are also associated with NORML, it is essential to further scan this organization and its activities. NORML was founded in January 1971; it is financed by Humanist Hugh Hefner's Playboy Foundation.[24] The organization's New York office shares its address (156 Fifth Avenue) and phone number with the American Civil Liberties Union. Guy Archer, head of NORML's New York office, is also an ACLU lawyer. One NORML

*In 1972 the American Health Association (of which at least five SIECUS directors, including Dr. Mary Calderone, are members) joined with NORML and the Institute for the Study of Health and Society to file with the Bureau of Narcotics and Dangerous Drugs a petition asking that marijuana be taken off the list of drugs whose possession and use are regulated under the federal Controlled Substances Act. The objective of the petition was the elimination or considerable reduction of federal penalties for use and possession of marijuana.

publication, titled *The Leaflet*, clearly describes what the two organizations are up to, under the heading, "A.C.L.U. Works for Legalization." It says:

> The American Civil Liberties Union has announced a nationwide legislative campaign aimed at the repeal of all criminal laws pertaining to marijuana. In urging their state affiliates to make this a top priority, the ACLU has offered their own resources combined with those of NORML.[25]

In addition to Fort and others covered in this entry, some members of NORML's Advisory Board who are worthy of mention are:

- Dr. Lester Grinspoon, a member of the Group for the Advancement of Psychiatry's Committee on Social Issues and author of *Marihuana Reconsidered.* In his book he parrots the familiar line so often used by the pro-marijuana coterie: ". . . no amount of research is likely to prove that cannabis [marijuana] is as dangerous as alcohol and tobacco."[26] Accordingly, Dr. Grinspoon denounces "the present punitive, repressive approach to the use of marijuana," while proclaiming that "in the next decade we must move to make the social use of marijuana legal."[27]
- Humanist Aryeh Neier, executive director of the American Civil Liberties Union.
- Humanist Benjamin Spock, M.D.

A consideration of the connections and expressed opinions of Joel Fort should cause taxpayers to question the judgment of those responsible for engaging a man of his caliber to educate the educators about drugs, using public funds.

David E. Smith, M.D.

Guiding teachers at the Drug Abuse Institute for Educators in the area of "the psychedelic scene" was Dr. David E. Smith, director of San Francisco's Drug and Narcotics Abuse Center, founder and director of the Haight-Ashbury Free Medical Clinic, and associate professor of pharmacology at the University of California Medical Center.

"Free clinics," as they are termed, are institutions founded for the purpose of providing medical treatment to the "deviant" members of society: hippies, drug addicts, prostitutes, etc. They operate outside of accepted legal and medical channels and, as such, become sanctuaries for criminals and anarchists during times of civil disorder, and havens from police apprehension.

Furthermore, free clinics are active in distribution of "the pill" to teenagers, treatment of venereal disease, and abortion counseling. They also maintain close liaison with Planned Parenthood. In 1968, a National Free Clinics Council was created to coordinate the dozens of free facilities in Berkeley, Boston, and other major cities across America which modeled their efforts after those of the Haight-Ashbury Free Medical Clinic programs.*

In an exclusive interview with the underground newspaper, *Berkeley Barb*, Dr. David Smith revealed that his free clinic in Haight-Ashbury treated such bizarre personalities as the Charles Manson "family" (convicted slayers of actress Sharon Tate), a group that practiced Satanism and all-out sexual communism. Said Dr. Smith: "I think Communes can be a very positive and meaningful way of life but only if the participants in the movement think for themselves."[28]

Dr. Smith is also an advocate of psychodrama and sensitivity training. The Narcotics and Drug Abuse Center in San Francisco General Hospital, which he directs, uses these techniques during brain-picking sessions with LSD patients. Similarly, the Haight-Ashbury free clinic uses methods developed by Synanon and Esalen Institute.

Not surprisingly, David Smith's views on drugs† coincide with those of Joel Fort and others in the pro-marijuana combine. For example, Dr. Smith assisted in the preparation of a report submitted to the California Legislature which stated that marijuana is less harmful than alcohol.[29] He is so committed to this theory that he now lends his assistance to NORML as a member of its advisory board.

Dr. Smith has two other significant drug-related affiliations: he is the director of the California State Drug Information Project, and also a member of the National Action Committee and Leadership Training Institute, sponsored by the U.S. Office of Education.[30]

Donald B. Louria, M.D.

The "institute advisor" of the Drug Abuse Institute for Educators was Dr. Donald B. Louria, who is professor and chairman of the Department of Preventive Medicine and Community Health, New

*The Long Beach Free Clinic in California is of special interest to this inquiry, having been established by the Peace and Freedom Party — the political arm of· the Communists in California.

The Peace and Freedom Party has become merged with the Human Rights Party and the New Party to form the People's Party. The latter's platform calls for legalization of heroin and marijuana, a guaranteed annual income, support for the women's and gay liberation movement, turning the free-enterprise system into the collective property of the people — *i.e.*, Socialism. The Presidential nominee of the People's Party in 1972 was Humanist Benjamin Spock, M.D., who also serves on NORML's advisory board.

†For a more thorough coverage of Dr. Smith's views on drugs, see entry for *Guidance Associates of Pleasantville N.Y.*, elsewhere in PART II.

Jersey College of Medicine and Dentistry, and president of the New York State Council on Drug Addiction.

An examination of Dr. Louria's opinions on marijuana, as expressed in his book, *The Drug Scene*, indicates that he is more than moderately tolerant of the drug. Although he makes a number of attempts — some perhaps sincere, some half-hearted — to expose certain dangers, they are usually followed by arguments on behalf of marijuana.

As an illustration, the first page of Donald Louria's chapter on marijuana poses the question: "Is marihuana an innocuous drug, a giver of delight, or is it intrinsically evil, leading to debauchery, degradation and criminality?"[31]

After discussing numerous pros and cons, Dr. Louria offers some definitive answers, such as the following:

> . . . It seems to me that our laws in regard to marihuana represent an appalling anachronism. The drug, after all, has limited dangers, does not necessarily lead to other drugs, and does not ordinarily provoke violence; its use must be regarded as a peccadillo, not a major crime. Yet we continue to insist on treating it as if it were a heinous offense.[32]

Dr. Louria contends in *The Drug Scene* that he is not completely in favor of legalizing the drug, stating "legalization would be unwise for our society *at this time.* . . ."[33] (emphasis added) But no doubt is left in the reader's mind that Louria has a decided preference for marijuana over alcohol, which is clearly implied by such passages as this:

> . . . . If the question before us were a national referendum to decide whether we would use for one of our legitimate escape mechanisms either alcohol or marihuana, I might personally vote for marihuana. . . .[34]

So emphatic is Dr. Louria's condemnation of alcohol that on July 10, 1970, on CBS radio, he proposed that it be declared illegal by the U.S. Government.

To summarize, what Dr. Louria is really saying is that as between marijuana and alcohol, marijuana is the wiser choice; that certain marijuana laws should be relaxed now; and that eventually total legalization of marijuana may be acceptable, under controlled conditions, and especially if alcohol is declared illegal.

There are, however, some legitimate drug experts who disagree with Dr. Louria. One outspoken critic is Dr. Robert Baird, head of HAVEN (Help Addicts Voluntarily End Narcotics) Clinic in Harlem. When Dr. Louria's name was mentioned during a special drug program televised on New York's TV Channel 7 on September 20, 1970, Dr. Baird became so angered by Louria's soft stance on marijuana that he twice called for Louria's resignation from the New York State Council on Drug Addiction — once, because of Dr. Louria's call for less severe penalties for possession of marijuana, and the second time, because of Louria's belief that smoking marijuana is no more dangerous than drinking, a point on which Dr. Baird sharply disagrees with him.

Among Dr. Louria's presentations at the Drug Abuse Institute for Educators was a discussion on "Developing a Drug Abuse Curriculum and Training Programs."

Neil L. Chayet

Neil Chayet also addressed teachers at the Drug Abuse Institute for Educators, on "Early Case Finding in Schools." Chayet is an attorney and lecturer at Boston University School of Law and Tufts University School of Medicine. Although the program listing for the institute identified him simply as the counsel for a group called the Committee for Effective Drug Abuse Legislation, it is also worth noting that, besides having given legal aid to the American Civil Liberties Union, with which he has worked on certain cases from time to time, Neil Chayet is also a member of NORML's Advisory Board.

John Finlator

Among other members of the "guest faculty" of the Drug Abuse Institute for Educators was John Finlator, former Deputy Director, Bureau of Narcotics and Dangerous Drugs, U.S. Department of Justice, whose scheduled address was titled "Drug Abuse: Legal Aspects." At this time he held a top post in the Nixon Administration. Not surprisingly, Mr. Finlator later mustered all the prestige his former government position could afford when he publicly announced his pro-marijuana stance and membership in NORML only weeks after his retirement as the country's No. 2 drug law enforcer. In his news release, Finlator reiterated the familiar theme that "both alcohol and tobacco had proved to be more harmful than marijuana."[35]

With Joel Fort, David Smith, and Neil Chayet, Finlator currently serves on NORML's advisory board. This makes a total of at least four members of the "Guest Faculty" of the Drug Abuse Institute for Educators who rallied publicly to the support of legalization of marijuana only months after addressing the New Jersey teachers.

A Familiar Pattern

It is the consensus of many of the "experts" discussed in this entry that marijuana is similar to alcohol, but less dangerous; that marijuana can be considered a mild euphoric drug, with no really harmful effects; that marijuana is not addictive and does not lead to use of heroin; and that the drug crisis could be solved by removing drug matters from the realm of law enforcement and placing them in the hands of the medical profession. This reasoning is the substance of the following three-point process of softening the attitude of the public toward marijuana:

- Equating marijuana with alcohol generates *tolerance.*
- Depreciating the harmful effects of marijuana enhances *acceptance.*
- Removing drugs from the criminal category and labeling their use a "health" matter lays the foundation for *legalization.*

To suppose that New Jersey teachers would leave the Drug Abuse Institute for Educators adequately prepared to deal with the drug problem in their respective communities was anything but realistic. First, a faculty of "experts" such as those discussed could hardly be expected to contribute unbiased information leading to any effective solution. Second, the influence wielded by these "experts" far outweighed their small number. Their status as tutors to teachers not only afforded them the chance to train a top echelon of educators, who were to become in turn a pipeline for transmitting biased drug data to lower ranks in the profession, but also enabled them to assist their trainees in the preparation of a curriculum for use at the local level. After they had been subjected to the barrage of propaganda leveled at them by such personalities as Earl Ubell, Joel Fort, and their like, there is every reason to believe that a considerable number of teachers attending the New Jersey seminar in fact became, as was intended, so many more links in a chain of compromising drug dialogue adeptly slanted toward eventual legalization.

As an indication that this is the specific intention of the pro-marijuana combine, which is directing a substantial number of drug education programs throughout the country, another fact should be considered. A Gallup Poll conducted in March 1972 revealed that eight out of ten Americans were opposed to legalization of the use of marijuana. The report of the poll concluded that this opposition was probably due to "attitudes on the part of the public that marijuana is physically and psychologically harmful, is addictive, and leads to the use of other drugs."[36]

It is surely no coincidence, then, that these are the very points being repeatedly attacked and disputed in films, literature, seminars, newspapers, and on radio and television, as the pro-marijuana cartel subtly whittles away at the percentage of public opinion that continues to oppose legalization. And in fact that 1972 Gallup Poll figure, which showed 81 percent of Americans opposed to legalizing marijuana, was already down from 84 per cent in a survey made only three years earlier, in 1969. Apparently the strategy of this cartel has begun to take effect, and some public officials are now predicting that the drug will be legalized nationally in the near future.*

*   *   *

Since this is the last entry in PART II containing discussion of drug education programs, it seems appropriate to briefly summarize their general structure and substance in order to show a familiar pattern emerging once again:

1. Control is at the national and state levels, with government agencies often financing Humanist-oriented drug programs subtly designed to *augment* rather than *diminish* drug usage.

2. Drug programs are largely based on the Humanist-conceived "open forum" approach, which represents an attempt to discard existing values of absolute right and wrong. This ploy opens other avenues of discussion by which the *benefits* of drug use — as well as the disadvantages, which are often minimized — are brought under consideration. This begins a desensitization process which seeks to soften any hard-line attitude toward drug usage and to neutralize traditional thinking on the subject.

3. Sensitivity training, sometimes masquerading under other names, is applied to both teachers and students whenever possible.

4. A "generation gap" between students and their parents is constantly promoted.

5. Many of those in top positions of influence covertly press for legalization of marijuana and other drugs, while ostensibly waging "war on narcotics."

6. Programs are meticulously planned to erase the "punitive" attitude of the community toward drug addicts, while at the same time

---

*One such official is Dr. Sylvia Herz, chairman of the New Jersey Public Health Association's drug abuse committee, who predicted in 1972 that marijuana "will be legalized within the next five years." As moderator and coordinator of a drug symposium that was held for representatives of the New Jersey State Departments of Health, Education, Law and Public Safety, and Labor and Industry in February 1972, Dr. Herz took a public stand in favor of legalization, stating: "I support the legalization of marijuana for mere possession and use." (*Newark Star Ledger*, February 13, 1976.) Earlier, Dr. Herz was coordinator of the pilot project on Drug Abuse Prevention for the Essex County School Districts and was instrumental in the development of drug abuse guidelines that were mailed to school systems throughout Essex County.

local law enforcement agencies are coerced into adopting a hands-off policy where drug criminals are concerned.

With drug seminars and programs throughout the country following this general pattern, there can be no doubt that, as with sex education, the so-called "experts" are now leading America onto another disastrous collision course — this time with drugs.

Planned Parenthood–World Population (PPWP)

810 Seventh Avenue, New York, New York

PLANNED PARENTHOOD is the last of eight organizations mentioned in the foreword of PART II as having been listed on the September 1969 SIECUS form letter as sources for additional information on sex education.

Planned Parenthood's close identification with the sex education movement is particularly significant, and in fact is intrinsic to the central theme portrayed in Chapter 1: that SIECUS-style sex education is in part a vehicle being used by the Humanist-Socialist complex to foster public acceptance of population control. It is surely no coincidence that, in 1964, Dr. Calderone terminated her eleven years as medical director of the Humanist-founded Planned Parenthood — an organization that names "sex education as a major goal"[1] — to become almost overnight the high priestess of sex education as executive director of SIECUS. Or that several years later, in 1968, she was projected into the strategic position of technical advisor to President Johnson's Committee on Population and Family Planning — a group that urged incorporation of "population matters" and "family planning" into the system of public education. This scheme is much too cozy to be anything but another tile in the SIECUS mosaic.

Then, too, considering that SIECUS in its form letter promoted Planned Parenthood, note should be taken that a number of SIECUS personalities are or have been involved in some way with the Planned Parenthood organization. Among them are:

- Humanist Mary S. Calderone — a member of PP's National Medical Committee.
- Dr. William Darity — PP Executive Committee member.
- Humanist Evalyn Gendel — PP speaker.
- Dr. Sadja Goldsmith — medical director, Teenage Services, PP of San Francisco.
- Humanist Lester Kirkendall (SIECUS founder) — Oregon State PP board member.
- Dr. Sophia Kleegman (now deceased) — medical director of New York State PP, 1936–58; member of PP medical advisory committee; consultant, PP Eastern League.
- Humanist William Masters — member of PP.
- Humanist Harriet Pilpel (SIECUS founder) — PP legal counsel.

- W. Ray Montgomery — a member of PP in Dallas, Texas.
- Dr. John Rock — on PP's medical council; former PP vice president. (Working in 1954 with the late Dr. Gregory Pincus, who had a research grant from PP, Dr. Rock conducted the initial research which led to development of the birth control pill in 1963.)
- Victoria Sanborn — a volunteer at the PP Center of New York City.

Turning to sex education literature emanating from Planned Parenthood offices, one notes a heavy accent on the works of such SIECUS directors as Jessie Bernard, Carlfred Broderick, Mary S. Calderone, Evelyn Duvall, Sadja Goldsmith, Reuben Hill, E. James Lieberman, and John Rock.

Other books, pamphlets, and articles promoted by Planned Parenthood represent SIECUS-recommended authors too numerous to list; still other PP publications rely heavily on the attitudes and advice of known Humanists, including Alice T. Day, Garrett Hardin, Lester Kirkendall, Margaret Mead, Karl Menninger, Harriet Pilpel, the late Isadore Rubin, and Helen Southard.

Moreover, every one of the films recommended in Planned Parenthood's *Guide to Films* under the heading "Sex Education" is also recommended by SIECUS.

SIECUS, Planned Parenthood, and Overpopulation

Before further examining this particular entry, it seems essential to get at the heart of the overpopulation myth that is being propagated by Planned Parenthood, its sister organization SIECUS, and other satellites in the movement, to discover whether or not the issue of overpopulation is a valid one.

One favorite argument of the population propagandists is that "we are running out of land." Actually, in comparison with other countries, the United States is rather sparsely populated. For example, it has a population of 56 persons per square mile, compared with England's 588, Japan's 708, and Holland's 982.

Moreover, the U. S. Census Bureau has indicated that two-thirds of all Americans live on less than 2 per cent of the land.[2] Our problem, then, is not *space* but, rather, *distribution of population.* Scare propaganda disseminated by the population planners through the news media invariably focuses on New York City — the most densely populated city in the nation — and does not reflect an accurate, overall view of America, where what one sees from the air is mostly vast expanses of land, dotted here and there with human habitations. For example,

Alaska, to achieve the same population density as Manhattan, would have to have about 40 *billion* residents.

Even New Jersey, which claims a record 953 persons per square mile, has massive land areas that have not been settled. A report published in 1966 by the New Jersey State Department of Community Affairs indicated that, of the state's total land area of 7,510 square miles, 71 per cent, or 5,331 square miles, was open land.[3] A 1973 estimate by the same office showed that approximately *two-thirds* of New Jersey's land was still unsettled — a significant fact, considering that New Jersey is the nation's most densely populated state.

As for the population growth rate in this country, the 1970 *World Almanac* states that since 1957 it has steadily declined. The downward trend continued to the end of 1972, when, as federal government statistics showed, *for the first time in our history, fertility in the United States dropped below the level needed to achieve zero population growth.*[4]

Indeed, the overall picture in America is so changed that the U.S. Census Bureau has reduced its population forecast and is now projecting a population of approximately one hundred million *fewer* people in the year 2,000 A.D. than it was predicting three years ago.

It is true that in some other parts of the world the overall population is increasing, but what is so often evaded by the "doomsday" propagandists is a comparison of the *growth rate* of a country with its *existing population density*. For the most part, the areas of the world that are experiencing the greatest increase in birth rates, such as Latin America and Africa, are among the least populated. By any sensible standard, these countries are *underpopulated* today. A larger population could only enhance their progress and development.

A number of densely populated countries, such as Norway, Sweden, France, Poland, and England, are experiencing birth rates so low as to threaten the maintenance of their present population levels. In fact, only seven countries in Europe are producing enough children to replace the present adult population.[5]

A second scare tactic being employed by the "doomsday" forecasters is the prediction that "we are running out of food." The fact is that any serious food shortages that may be experienced in the United States can only be attributed to the federal government's socialistic interference in the economic sector. Prior to this interference, the free market economy of the U.S. had always produced a surplus of food. This situation has gradually been reversed through federal subsidies to farmers for *not* growing food, vast credit shipments of American grain to Russia and Red China, and government price controls coupled with the lifting of import bans on beef, dairy products, and other commodities, which have sharply reduced food production in this country.

One of the world's foremost authorities on food resources, Dr. Colin Clark of Oxford University in England, comments in his book, *Starvation or Plenty*, that potential food resources of the world are sufficient to meet the needs of all many times over. Dr. Clark notes that, given the general use of agricultural methods already practiced by the average farmer in Holland and other densely populated Western countries, and without allowing for any further improvements in agricultural methods or technology, for any provision of food from the sea, or for any extension of present systems of irrigation, *the potential agricultural area of the world could provide for the consumption requirements, at contemporary maximum dietary standards, of 35.1 billion people, or over ten times the present world population.*[6]

The trumped-up specter of mass starvation and "standing room only" due to overpopulation has evidently been promoted for a purpose — to give the master planners the excuse to extend their power over mankind. The specific role played by the Planned Parenthood crowd in perpetrating the myth of overpopulation has a long history of its own — a history that sorely needs to be recorded if current events upon the world stage are to be seen in proper perspective.

Planned Parenthood (PP)

Planned Parenthood was spawned in the early 1900's, during the Margaret Sanger era. Although there had been earlier advocates of family limitation, including Mrs. Annie Besant[7] of the Theosophical Society (identified in the pages of *The Humanist* as one of "the most brilliant humanist organizers and propagandists"[8]), it was Margaret Sanger who would later become known as "the Mother of Birth Control." Also labeled a "feminist rebel" by her successor as president of the Planned Parenthood Federation of America, Dr. Alan F. Guttmacher, Mrs. Sanger began her long crusade with only a few devoted followers who were the extremists of their day. In an article appearing in *The Humanist*, author Miriam Allen DeFord describes it this way:

> . . . It was the radicals — political, economic, and religious — among whom Margaret Sanger found her first supporters: and she herself was one of them. Her father, Matthew Higgins, was a Socialist and the "village Atheist" of Corning, New York. . . . [9]

Explaining the religious persuasion of Margaret Sanger herself, the article continues:

The word "Humanism" in its present religio-scientific meaning was not then current. But call it Freethought or Rationalism or Secularism, it was and it remained Margaret Sanger's creed. The first paper she founded and edited was called *The Woman Rebel*, and its masthead bore the motto: "No gods, no masters."

Margaret Sanger

Some less well-known facets of Margaret Sanger's career are perhaps equally significant, including her sponsorship of the occult Temple of Understanding, and her membership on the advisory council of the Euthanasia Society of America, Inc., which was founded in 1938.

Among the early highlights of Margaret Sanger's epochal career was a series of articles she wrote in 1912 for *The Call*, the leading New York Socialist paper at that time.[10] Another leftist affiliation of Mrs. Sanger's was membership in the American Round Table on India, which is cited in the House Committee on Un-American Activities' *Appendix IX* as a "Communist front."[11] The secretary of this front was Robert Norton, cited as a "well-known member of the Communist Party."[12]

A fellow member of Mrs. Sanger's in the American Round Table on India was Albert D. Lasker, who served on its executive committee. During a portion of his life, Lasker was also a member of the board of the American Civil Liberties Union. Later, Lasker's wife, Mary, became an honorary sponsor of Planned Parenthood; she is currently president of the Lasker Foundation, which has its offices in the United Nations Plaza. This foundation gives the annual Lasker Award for special contributions to the field of medical and scientific research and, not surprisingly, has made awards to such individuals as Communist-fronter Albert Deutsch (1949) and Humanists G. Brock Chisholm (1945), Alan F. Guttmacher (1947), Margaret Sanger (1950), and Earl Ubell (1958).

As is often the case in the life of a rebel, Margaret Sanger came into conflict with the law on more than one occasion. A primary instance was her arraignment on August 25, 1914, for having published in *The Woman Rebel* certain articles that had been declared "unmailable" by the Post Office Department.[13] While awaiting trial, Mrs. Sanger fled to England via Canada, leaving her family behind. Once out at sea, she wired her New York associates to release 100,000 copies of *Family Limitation*, a pamphlet she had prepared describing actual contraceptive techniques — information which, at that time, it was illegal to print. Although she did later return to face trial in America, the *American People's Encyclopedia* says that Mrs. Sanger was "relieved of charges by President Wilson (Feb., 1916) when liberal friends interceded."[14]

While abroad in 1914–15, Mrs. Sanger added spice to her life history by a liaison with the notorious Havelock Ellis, who, with Ethical Culture leader Percival Chubb, had been a principal organizer of the socialistic Fabian Society of Great Britain.[15] Ellis was a sexual pervert and drug user, who, with a circle of fellow leftists, pioneered in the experimental use of hallucinogens in private orgies. Having become conditioned to the use of urine and urination in a form of sexual perversion,[16] Ellis was clearly a pathological case. He urged his wife into Lesbianism and drug addiction, and obtained erotic excitement by forcing her to describe her Lesbian experiences to him. The book, *Sage of Sex*, by Calder-Marshall, further reveals that Ellis finally drove his wife into a state of mental collapse, which became complete when he wrote to her about his intimate relationship with Margaret Sanger.[17]

Like Mrs. Sanger, Havelock Ellis was to have a profound effect on the public's attitude regarding sex. He set the stage for sex education with a massive erotic work, *Studies in the Psychology of Sex* (seven volumes, 1897–1928), which was banned from time to time on charges of obscenity.[18] This and other similar works were later used by the Fabians as a wedge for introducing sex education into the schools, starting first in the colleges and working down to the high school level. Today, Havelock Ellis's perversions are standard reference material for sex educators, and he is hailed as the "Father of Social Psychology." Further, an article on sex education in the January 1968 issue of *McCall's* magazine features Ellis in its list of "Sung and Unsung Heroes" in the sex education "Army of Liberation."[19] A supporting cast of "Revolutionary Heroes" on an adjacent page includes Margaret Sanger, and the body of the article is studded with SIECUS-Humanist personalities.

The English Fabian Society, which Ellis helped to found in 1883, is a collectivist group that seeks to establish a one-world socialist government on a piecemeal basis, rather than by violent revolution. A small package of socialism at a time is pushed through the target country's legislative chambers by Fabian lawmakers and lobbyists until total socialism is finally achieved. Such legislation is seldom labeled "socialism," but parades under the banner of "welfare," "humanitarianism," and the like. The public, of course, is not intended to see the full picture of what has happened until it is too late.

So far as the United States is concerned, the Fabian tide reached America's shores in the mid-1880's and has steadily moved forward ever since. Some early leaders of the Fabian Society in America were such Humanists as Roger Baldwin, Clarence Darrow, John Dewey, Julian and Aldous Huxley, Robert Morss Lovett, Harry Overstreet, Mark Starr*, and Norman Thomas.

One year following her return from England, where she had studied literature on contraception and family planning in the libraries of London, Mrs. Sanger founded the first birth control clinic in the United States. It opened on October 16, 1916, in the Brownsville section of Brooklyn. Birth Control Leagues soon sprouted in several cities throughout the country, and in 1917 they were united under the name National Birth Control League, with Margaret Sanger as president. The organization soon changed its name to American Birth Control League, and Mrs. Sanger again emerged as president.

A direct outgrowth of the ABCL was the Planned Parenthood Federation of America — a name admittedly given in order to erase the stigma of the term "birth control" — which was founded in 1941. In 1963 the Planned Parenthood Federation of America merged with the World Population Emergency Campaign, an international group with similar interests. At this time, the long titles of the two were comfortably melded into Planned Parenthood–World Population, although the two names, Planned Parenthood–World Population and Planned Parenthood Federation of America, are still being used interchangeably in the organization's literature.

Until her death in 1966, Margaret Sanger was honorary chairman of Planned Parenthood. Among other significant honors won by Mrs. Sanger in her lifetime was the "Humanist of the Year" Award for 1957.[20]

Recent Leadership

Planned Parenthood's president from 1962 until his death in 1974 was Dr. Alan F. Guttmacher, a signer of the *Humanist Manifesto II*, who inherited Margaret Sanger's role as prime mover in the birth control movement. Besides being a prolific writer, Dr. Guttmacher lectured extensively on such topics as population control, abortion, and sex education. During 1964 — the year SIECUS was founded — he was engaged in research for the National Institutes of Health,[21] a division of the Department of Health, Education, and Welfare.

Alan Guttmacher's medical affiliations included membership in the New York Academy of Medicine, the New York Obstetrics Society, and

*Humanist Mark Starr, a former executive of the International Ladies Garment Workers Union, has traveled extensively about the world on assignment from the U.N. International Labor Organization, assisting various countries with their labor education programs. He is also chairman of the New York City information center of the Esperanto League, a group promoting a one-world language.

the American Eugenics Society. He was associate editor of the journal *Fertility and Sterility*; a member of the Board of Directors of the Margaret Sanger Research Bureau, an adjunct of Planned Parenthood; and a diplomate of both the American Society for the Study of Sterility and the American Board of Obstetrics and Gynecology. Dr. Guttmacher also served as chairman of the International Planned Parenthood Federation's Medical Committee. Two of Dr. Guttmacher's numerous international activities to promote Planned Parenthood were attendance at the 1965 United Nations Population Conference held in Belgrade, Yugoslavia, and participation in the Havana congress of February 1966, in Communist Cuba. In Havana, Dr. Guttmacher addressed a four-hour session on family planning before an audience of physicians, nurses, and health workers.[22]

Other key figures who either have served or are currently serving Planned Parenthood include:

- *Mrs. Philip Bastedo* — a member of the board of directors of the Association for Voluntary Sterilization. Philip Bastedo is a resident member of the Council on Foreign Relations (CFR), a group that covertly wields substantial control over the actions and policies of the U.S. Government in pursuit of the goal of one-world government.
- *Eugene R. Black* — PP vice chairman; a non-resident member of the Council on Foreign Relations; a financial consultant to the Secretary General of the United Nations; a member of the advisory board to the United Nations' Special Fund; former president of the World Bank; and a trustee and chairman of the finance committee of the Ford Foundation.
- *Lammot duPont Copeland* — PP honorary vice chairman; heir to the DuPont chemical fortune; also a signer of the October 1969 *New York Times* ad in support of SIECUS. (The DuPont Corporation is a prominent supporter of the population control movement.)
- *John Cowles Sr.* — PP council member; a financial contributor to SIECUS, member of the Council on Foreign Relations, and partner in Cowles publications.
- *William H. Draper Jr.* — PP honorary vice chairman; sponsor of the First National Conference on Abortion Laws; and CFR member.
- *Marriner S. Eccles* — PP council member; SIECUS ad signer; former governor of Federal Reserve Board and official of numerous international banking concerns, including the Export-Import Bank.

- *John Kenneth Galbraith* — PP council member; a non-resident member of the Council on Foreign Relations; a Fabian Socialist who has been affiliated with the socialist League for Industrial Democracy.

- *Ernest Gruening* — PP honorary vice chairman; another signer of the October 1969 *New York Times* "support SIECUS" ad; a former U. S. Senator (Alaska); a frequent speaker at leftwing protest demonstrations against the Vietnam war. His most widely-publicized appearance in the latter capacity was on December 10, 1965, at the Bill of Rights dinner sponsored by the Emergency Civil Liberties Committee (cited by the House Committee on Un-American Activities as "a front for the Communist Party"[23]). Gruening has also served in an official capacity with the Garland Fund, which was cited by a California Senate Fact-Finding Committee on Un-American Activities as a "source of revenue for Communist causes."[24]

- *Stewart T. Mott* — PP executive committee member; a SIECUS sponsor; a member of the executive committee of the National Association for the Repeal of Abortion Laws; a fund-raiser for the National Organization for Reform of Marijuana Laws.

- *Whitney North Seymour* — PP council member; a member of the Council on Foreign Relations; a past director and long-time member of the American Civil Liberties Union.

Major Supporters

In view of the Humanist persuasion of Margaret Sanger and Alan Guttmacher, it might be anticipated that Planned Parenthood offices and activities would be largely Humanist-controlled, and this is the case. One Ethical Culture pamphlet, for example, discloses that the Ethical Culture Movement helped to found Planned Parenthood centers.[25] Another Ethical Culture publication more specifically states that its New York Society's Women's Conference was "a major participant in the development of the Planned Parenthood Clinic in Manhattan's Upper West Side,"[26] which was founded in 1959.

Moreover, an article in the January–February 1963 issue of *The Humanist*, titled "Intergroup Relations of the American Humanist Association," points out the relationship between AHA and Planned Parenthood, indicating plainly that the causes of Humanism and of Planned Parenthood are closely allied, in the following passage:

> Our Humanist convictions should lead us into active participation in specialized organizations devoted to kindred causes. Without neglecting their primary loyalties, Humanists and Humanist groups should relate to and strengthen such organizations as, for example, the American Civil Liberties

Union, the National Association for the Advancement of Colored People, *the Planned Parenthood Federation*, and Protestants and Other Americans United for Separation of Church and State. [emphasis added]

Similarly, individuals from the Unitarian, Ethical Culture, and American Humanist Association camps work diligently to promote the cause of Planned Parenthood at the local level. Besides the Humanist SIECUS board members mentioned earlier, a spot-check around the country uncovers the following Humanists involved with Planned Parenthood:

- Humanist *Gerald A. Ehrenreich*, a member of PP; also staff psychologist at the Menninger Clinic in Topeka, Kansas.
- Humanist *Norman Fleishman*, executive vice president of PP in Los Angeles.
- Humanist *Carl G. Heller*, a member of the Oral Contraceptives Committee of the International Planned Parenthood Federation.
- Humanists *Tolbert McCarroll* and wife, *Claire*, founders of the PP Association of Oregon.
- Humanist *Helen Meiklejohn*, a prominent member of PP in California; also closely tied to the American Civil Liberties Union and the National Association for Repeal of Abortion Laws.
- Humanist *Ashley Montagu*, a member of PP's Social Science Research Committee.
- Humanist *Lloyd Morain*, former PP board member; member of the American Civil Liberties Union of Northern California; member of the board of directors of the National Association for the Repeal of Abortion Laws.
- Humanist *Mary Morain*, member of the International PP Federation's Western Regional Council, and former vice president of the PP League of Massachusetts.
- Humanist *Janet Oliphant*, former member of the board of PP; she has also served as a legislative consultant for the National Association of Social Workers, and as a member of the boards of both the Mental Health Association and the Unitarian Fellowship for Social Justice.
- Humanist *Howard B. Radest*, a member of the Bergen County (New Jersey) PP Association.
- Humanist *Matthew Ies Spetter*, who has served on the executive committee of the Hudson Valley (New York) PP Center.
- Humanist *H. Curtis Wood Jr.*, medical field consultant to and former president of Philadelphia PP Association; also medical field consultant to Association for Voluntary Sterilization.

The above are only a few examples of what was found to be a national trend in the Planned Parenthood organization. Although it should be recognized that many sincere and dedicated volunteers at Planned Parenthood simply believe in the concept of birth control and are working to promote it, those who have held positions of authority in the organization, from its inception until the present, have for the most part belonged to the Humanist faction.

Purpose and Program

According to the *Encyclopedia of Organizations*, the stated purpose of Planned Parenthood is: "To provide leadership in making effective means of voluntary fertility control, including contraception, abortion and sterilization, available and fully accessible to all; in achieving a U.S. population of stable size in an optimum environment; in stimulating relevant biomedical, socio-economic and demographic research; in developing appropriate information, education and training programs. To support the efforts of others to achieve similar goals in the United States and throughout the World."[27]

As was shown in Chapter I, Planned Parenthood's leadership and its supporters stand ready to scrap the word *voluntary* where fertility control is concerned, and to substitute *compulsory*, if the "overpopulation" panic button can stir up enough political and popular support; and it seems probable that this was their intention from the beginning. On this question, for example, it will be recalled that former Planned Parenthood chief Alan Guttmacher was not inclined to be tolerant. He stated in 1969: "Each country will have to decide its own form of coercion, determining when and how it should be employed," adding, "The means presently available are compulsory sterilization and compulsory abortion."[28]

Planned Parenthood's own literature makes it evident that the overall plan is to extend the organization's program and services into every country throughout the world, and, when acceptance is achieved, to have the operation subsidized and controlled by the respective governments as an initial step toward eventual worldwide population control. Dr. Guttmacher spoke candidly on this aspect in an article appearing in the March 1965 issue of *Cosmopolitan* magazine:

> We're operating a demonstration program. On a world scale, or even in the United States, the problem is so vast we can't begin to make progress through individual philanthropic efforts. *Governments will have to take over.*[29] [emphasis added]

Recent years have seen this plan reach fruition in many countries. At least forty governments throughout the world now support national family planning programs.

Financial support for Planned Parenthood itself has been largely provided by such tax-exempt institutions as the Ford Foundation, which also supports SIECUS; the Commonwealth Fund, another SIECUS supporter; and the Victor-Bostrom Fund, a major sugar daddy in the population control movement.

Various federal agencies are in league with the above foundations. In 1970, grants made by the U. S. Government to Planned Parenthood soared to $1,023,000. In fact, the relationship between PP and our government is so close that, of 139 local agency projects initiated by Planned Parenthood's Center for Family Planning Program Development between 1967–1970, ninety-three were funded by federal grants.[30]

Although the program of Planned Parenthood is far too broad to cover in detail, certain facets require mention. One in particular is noted in the organization's 1970 Annual Report, which states that many PP clinics now serve the unwed and counsel adolescents on birth control methods. These "Teen Clinics," as they are called, also give teenagers contraceptives, sexual examinations, and advice.[31] (Until a very few years ago, Planned Parenthood clinics served only married women, and minors received contraceptives only with parental consent.) As of 1970, PP operated twenty-two Teen Clinics.

The director of Planned Parenthood's San Francisco Teenage Services is SIECUS director Dr. Sadja Goldsmith, who was a speaker at the opening session of the Western Region Planned Parenthood Association's annual meeting in 1971. Among pronouncements made there by Dr. Goldsmith in speaking of her teenage clients was, "I hate the word 'virgin,' with all its 1870 connotations. I'd prefer to call these girls 'planners.' "[32] Dr. Goldsmith highlighted her discussion of the Teen Clinics' current activities with the following statement:

> . . . we're also encouraging young men to come into our centers and take real male responsibility. They should know all about this, *including seeing their girl, if they choose, have a pelvic.* (emphasis added)

Other clinics operated by Planned Parenthood have now extended their services to accommodate the recent relaxing of abortion laws. In 1970, even before the Supreme Court ruling, this organization's clinic in Syracuse, New York, was performing abortions for its patrons, and over one hundred other clinics offered abortion counseling and referral; another fifty-two offered telephone referral services.

As already shown earlier (see entry for *National Association for Repeal of Abortion Laws*), certain Planned Parenthood leaders and personnel are closely identified with the abortion repeal movement itself; and a *New York Sunday News* article pointed out the fact that most women seeking abortions have received prior counseling from organizations such as Planned Parenthood.[33]

Besides abortion and contraception, the term *planned parenthood*, to its proponents, also covers sterilization. Consequently, Dr. Guttmacher was conveniently cast in another role, as a member of the Medical and Public Health Committee of the Association for Voluntary Sterilization — a group that once shared offices with Planned Parenthood at the latter's former address: 515 Madison Avenue, New York City. Like Planned Parenthood, the Association for Voluntary Sterilization is a Humanist front that is working its own angle in the quest for total population control. During the time the two organizations shared the same address (1965), Planned Parenthood did not offer sterilization among its services; it referred inquiries to AVS, which then furnished assistance to the applicant.

Planned Parenthood maintains 695 centers in major cities throughout the United States. Its organizational influence is extended across America by means of its professional journal, *Family Planning Perspectives*, a quarterly which has a circulation of more than 30,000, mostly health professionals. Another related publication is *Advances in Planned Parenthood*, a compilation of papers presented at conventions of the American Association of Planned Parenthood Physicians — a 650-member group of physicians from Planned Parenthood affiliates, health departments, hospitals, and other agencies. The 1970 issue of *Advances in Planned Parenthood* reached 5,000 doctors.

Planned Parenthood has been accorded consultative status at the United Nations, and is a member of the American Public Health Association, National Conference on Social Welfare, National Health Council, American Public Welfare Association, and Community Chest (now United Way of America).

International Planned Parenthood Federation (IPPF)

In 1952, the International Planned Parenthood Federation was organized through the efforts of Margaret Sanger, Lady Rama Rau of India, and Mrs. Elise Ottesen-Jensen of Sweden. The decision to form the Federation had been made at a family planning conference held earlier in Bombay, India. Among other pioneers attending this conference were Dr. C.P. Blacker and Dr. Helena Wright* of the United Kingdom, and Dr. C. Van Emde Boas of Holland. Throughout these

---

*Dr. Helena Wright is the author of *Sex and Society*, a book which was reviewed very favorably by the late Humanist and identified Communist, Isadore Rubin of SIECUS, in the December 1968 issue of *Sexology* magazine. According to Rubin, Dr. Wright's book suggests a new code of morality "based on a belief that sex in a period of contraception should not be confined to marriage."

events Humanist Margaret Sanger continued to maintain a position of leadership, finally emerging as president emeritus of IPPF.

Since its founding in 1952 with eight member associations (those of the German Federal Republic, Hong Kong, India, The Netherlands, Singapore, Sweden, the United Kingdom, and the United States) IPPF has grown until it had seventy-nine in 1971. Interestingly, IPPF's Swedish affiliate, the National Association for Sex Education, was largely responsible for the growth and acceptance of family planning and sex education in Sweden, as was its counterpart, SIECUS, in the United States.

Like Planned Parenthood–World Population (a founding and charter member of IPPF), IPPF encourages, according to a 1971 publication, "the formation of national associations to pioneer family planning services in each country of the world and to bring about a favorable climate of public opinion in which governments can be persuaded to accept responsibility."[34] The same IPPF pamphlet reveals that, as governments respond to these initiatives through their funding of family planning programs, IPPF-affiliated associations provide a nucleus of staff around which an expanded government program can be built. This staff provides training for future personnel, including the government staff, and IPPF association activities are integrated with the government program. In this way, maximum control by IPPF is assured. IPPF has also pressed forward in its effort to join forces with all agencies reaching the community level, such as women's organizations, trade unions, youth groups, and professional organizations of nurses, midwives, teachers, and social workers.

IPPF is financed by voluntary contributions from foundations and private citizens, and only recently by grants from governments. From a budget of $30,000 in 1961, a quantum leap was taken in 1965 with the first government grant to the Federation, made by Sweden. Soon after, the United Nations Fund for Population Activities became a financial contributor to IPPF, and the year 1972 found some $80,000,000 flowing through the Federation's massive system. Today, a federal agency, the Agency for International Development (AID), is the single largest contributor to IPPF's budget for work in the developing countries.[35]

Two committees closely identified with IPPF for purposes of raising financial support are particularly noteworthy, in view of their far-reaching effects on later events in this entry. Descriptions of these two committees, the Victor-Bostrom Fund Committee and the Population Crisis Committee, follow.

The Victor-Bostrom Fund Committee

The Victor-Bostrom Fund Committee is a fund-raising arm of the

International Planned Parenthood Federation. The basis for this committee dates back to 1965. During that year, the Victor Fund was established, with an initial bequest of over $150,000 from Alexander Victor of Victrola fame, to raise at least $13 million for the worldwide budgets of the IPPS during 1966, 1967, and 1968. During the last year, Harold Bostrom, vice president of Universal Oil Products Company of Milwaukee, became a substantial contributor to the Fund, and it was renamed the Victor-Bostrom Fund.

The Fund provided over $1.5 million to IPPF for the years 1969 through 1971. Fund-raising activities expanded in 1972, when members of the Victor-Bostrom Fund Committee raised close to $10 million for use in birth control projects throughout the world.

Chairman of the Victor-Bostrom Fund Committee is William H. Draper Jr., an investment banker, who was a sponsor of the First National Conference on Abortion Laws, out of which came the National Association for Repeal of Abortion Laws. Draper is also the U.S. Representative on the Population Commission of the United Nations; a member of IPPF's Governing Body; an honorary vice chairman of Planned Parenthood–World Population; and a member of the Council on Foreign Relations, the informal supra-State Department of the United States.

Serving with Harold Bostrom as a vice chairman of the Victor-Bostrom Fund Committee is Stewart R. Mott, a SIECUS sponsor and member of the executive committee of both Planned Parenthood–World Population and the National Association for the Repeal of Abortion Laws.

Another member of the Victor-Bostrom Fund Committee is Communist fellow traveler Cass Canfield. Canfield has been affiliated with a wide assortment of Leftwing groups, including the American Committee for Yugoslav Relief,[36] cited by Attorney General Tom Clark as "subversive and Communist."[37] For more than twenty years, Canfield has been a resident member of the Council on Foreign Relations, and he has been affiliated with the American Association for the United Nations and with World Federalists, U. S. A. His devotion to the goal of one-world government is further evidenced by the fact that on July 27, 1971, he joined with other fellow travelers and a number of Humanists in signing a full-page ad in the *New York Times* urging the formation of a world federal government. Canfield is also chairman emeritus of IPPF's governing body, and was chairman of Planned Parenthood–World Population's executive committee in 1965. He is perhaps more widely known as a senior editor of the publishing firm of Harper and Row.

Victor-Bostrom Fund Reports are issued quarterly, each issue focusing on a specific aspect of the world-population panorama. This propaganda mouthpiece is distributed for the IPPF by another related committee of considerable import — the Population Crisis Committee.

The Population Crisis Committee (PCC)

The Population Crisis Committee was founded in 1965 — the same year that the Victor Fund was instituted — and is largely financed by the Rockefeller Foundation. Like the Victor-Bostrom Fund Committee, PCC is mainly concerned with raising money for the IPPF. PCC has also contributed money to Planned Parenthood–World Population and the United Nations for certain birth control projects. By working with the UN, PCC members have helped international birth control programs grow until they took in more than $45 million for the UN Fund for Population Activities in 1970.

The *Encyclopedia of Associations* describes the PCC's central purpose as being: "To bring forcefully to the attention of all Americans and the various agencies of government the population crisis which exists now in many parts of the world and in some parts of the U. S."[38] PCC reaches federal officials by engaging in direct lobbying in Washington — a not-too-difficult task, since PCC membership comprises a substantial number of former and present government leaders. In order to bring its urgent message to the public, the committee utilizes newsletters, pamphlets, the lecture platform, and the news media.

One project sponsored by PCC in association with Planned Parenthood–World Population took the form of a special supplement to the *New York Sunday Times* of April 30, 1972, titled *Population — The U.S. Problem, The World Crisis.* The supplement featured a summary report from the U.S. Commission on Population Growth and the American Future (to be discussed later), as well as articles by prominent one-worlders who have long been in the forefront of the effort to establish worldwide population control, such as John D. Rockefeller III; World Bank President Robert S. McNamara;* IPPF Secretary-General Julia Henderson; and the previously mentioned William H. Draper Jr.

Drawing upon all the expertise it could muster, the *Times* supplement identified the existence of too many people as a major menace to the world, making an almost hysterical plea to governments to adopt a comprehensive long-term population policy to be coordinated under the auspices of the United Nations.

In addition to the 1.6 million copies regularly distributed by the *Times*, PCC undertook as a project the nationwide distribution of the

*Significantly, McNamara has reportedly threatened to withhold World Bank loans from countries without birth control programs.

supplement. As one result, the high school magazine, *Senior Scholastic*, mailed copies with a teacher's guide to some 30,000 teachers, for use with about two million students.[39] Unfortunately, too few knew that the *Times* supplement was sponsored by many of the same people engaged in promoting SIECUS-style sex education, nationalized abortion, Humanism, and one-world government. A PCC membership list, for example, includes SIECUS directors Catherine S. Chilman, E. James Lieberman, Luigi Mastroianni Jr., John Rock, Virgil Rogers, and Gilbert Shimmel. Many Planned Parenthood–World Population and IPPF officials and members also appear, among them, to name a few, Joseph D. Beasley, Eugene R. Black, Lammot duPont Copeland, Ernest Gruening, Mrs. Albert D. Lasker, George N. Lindsay, and Stewart R. Mott.[40]

In addition to American Humanist Association President Lloyd Morain (who was one of PCC's early board members), other Humanists have served or still are serving the PCC, including Morain's wife Mary, Norman Cousins, Alan F. Guttmacher, Hudson Hoagland, Joseph Wood Krutch, Ashley Montagu, Edward Pohlman, Sidney H. Scheuer, and William B. Shockley; and still other Humanists who are Communist fronters as well — among them, Stuart Chase, Morris L. Ernst, Archibald MacLeish, and Carey McWilliams.

Other leftists of varying hues who are members of PCC include: Henry B. Cabot (a CFR member and signer of the world government ad in the *New York Times* of July 27, 1971); John Cowles (non-resident member of the CFR, who has been a trustee of the Ford Foundation); George S. Franklin Jr. (executive director of the CFR); John Kenneth Galbraith (a CFR member and Fabian Socialist); Paul G. Hoffman (a Unitarian, CFR member, trustee of the Ford Foundation, manager of the U.N. Fund for Population Activities, member of Americans United for World Government, and financial supporter of the Temple of Understanding); Whitney North Seymour (CFR member and former director of the national board of the American Civil Liberties Union); and Harold C. Urey (SIECUS ad signer and Communist fronter).

In addition to those named above, PCC's membership roster lists a number of one-world internationalists, international financiers and bankers, corporation executives, news media representatives, leaders in the film industry, and more than eighty past and present U.S. Senators, Representatives, and top officials of the United States government. Among the last group are:

- *William P. Rogers*, former Secretary of State
- *Charles E. Bohlen*, former Assistant Secretary of State and member of the CFR

- *Bertram S. Brown, M.D.*, deputy director, National Institute of Mental Health
- *William H. Draper Jr.*, U.S. Representative on the Population Commission of the United Nations, and CFR member
- *Louis M. Hellman, M.D.*, director, Office of Population Affairs, Department of Health, Education, and Welfare
- *Russell E. Train*, administrator, Environmental Protection Agency, CFR member, and former head of Laurance Rockefeller's radical environmental group, the Conservation Foundation.

So prestigious has the PCC become that its officers have been invited to testify before ten different Congressional Committees and before the Rockefeller-chaired President's Commission on Population Growth and the American Future.

The PCC has a number of things in common with the Victor-Bostrom Fund Committee. The two committees were established in the same year; they share the same address and telephone number in Washington, D.C.; both raise funds for Planned Parenthood–World Population and the IPPF; and they have interlocking directorates and memberships not only with one another but also with SIECUS, Planned Parenthood, the Population Council, the Population Reference Bureau, Zero Population Growth, and other organizations engaged in foisting the overpopulation hoax on the American people.

Planned Parenthood and the United Nations

Bearing in mind that the one-world Humanist-Socialist complex was instrumental in the development of some of the earliest-established agencies and programs of the United Nations, and that Humanist-Socialist strategy continues to be in accord with U.N. goals, it is not surprising that the U.N. is currently playing a leadership role in worldwide population control.

The U.N.'s formal acceptance of this role can be traced back at least two decades. In 1954 a U.N. Population Commission recommended that every country should "have a population policy."[41] The year 1962 found the Economic Committee of the U.N.'s General Assembly debating the population question, urging U.N. activity in this field.

But the "historic breakthrough" came in 1966, when the full General Assembly adopted a broad resolution authorizing the U.N. to give assistance when requested in the field of population. Soon afterward, on "Human Rights Day," December 11, 1967, U.N. Secretary-General U Thant, President of the United States Lyndon B. Johnson, and twenty-nine other heads of State issued a *Declaration on*

Population. This Declaration proclaimed "fertility control" to be a new, so-called basic human right. During the same period, various specialized agencies of the U.N. acted in concert with this edict, developing their own corresponding mandates.

The establishment in 1967 of a U.N. Fund for Population Activities by Secretary-General U Thant, a Marxist, and the subsequent organization and management of the Fund under the administration of Paul Hoffman,[42] a Unitarian and CFR member, was another major advance for the population planners.

While these developments were taking place, IPPF and PPWP leaders were tirelessly pulling strings at every opportunity to hasten the advent of a global, U.N.-based population program. One such leader, William Draper of both IPPF and PPWP, was maneuvered into the strategic position of U. S. Representative to the U.N. Population Commission.

At its meeting in Geneva on November 12, 1971, this Commission adopted a resolution urging, among other things, that all member states:

- ". . . cooperate in achieving a substantial reduction of the rate of population growth" in the countries where it was needed.
- ". . . ensure that information and education about family planning, as well as the means to effectively practice family planning, are made available to all individuals by the end of the Second United Nations Development Decade [1980]."[43]

This Commission further designated 1974 as World Population Year, inviting all Member States to participate in this event, and requested the U.N. Secretary-General, among other things, to:

- ". . . seek the widest possible cooperation of non-governmental organizations, research institutions and mass communication media in furthering the objectives of the World Population Year."
- ". . . study the possibilities of developing a global population strategy, including population movements, for promoting and co-coordinating population policies in Member States with the objective of achieving a balance between population and other natural resources. . . ."[44]

With the adoption of this resolution, the population planners of the international Planned Parenthood cartel were well on their way toward achieving a global population policy under U.N. control.

IPPF's strategy of combining unceasing effort with patient gradualism has won rich rewards. On the basis of resolutions such as the above adopted over the last several years, all major U.N. agencies now have authority to undertake action programs in population and family planning.[45] Further, as was brought out in a Victor-Bostrom Fund Report, an actual *principle of partnership* between the IPPF and the U.N. system was well established by 1971.[46] IPPF had been accorded consultative status with all the major U.N. organizations concerned with advancing world population control.

As U.N. technical consultant, IPPF collaborates closely with the U.N.'s Economic and Social Council, the International Labor Organization (ILO), the World Health Organization (WHO), the United Nations Children's Fund (UNICEF), the United Nations Education, Scientific and Cultural Organization (UNESCO), and the Food and Agriculture Organization (FAO) in matters related to population growth.[47] IPPF staff and associates also participate in World Bank study missions and join other U.N. agencies in sponsoring conferences, seminars, and training sessions in which IPPF wields considerable influence.

One significant undertaking of IPPF with its U.N. partner in the movement for world population control was its participation in the U.N.'s 1972 Conference on the Human Environment, which met in Stockholm, June 5–16. Just prior to the convening of the conference, U.N. Secretary-General Kurt Waldheim expressed the opinion that the conference's leaders "must surely link the increasing pollution of the planet with the increasing population of the planet."[48] Both IPPF and the U.N. have seized every opportunity to fuse ecology with the so-called "overpopulation crisis" as another means to inject their population control propaganda into the public arena. Accordingly, the Stockholm conference urged, among other things:

- "That special attention be given to population concerns as they relate to the environment during the 1974 observance of World Population Year."
- "That U.N. agencies provide increased assistance in birth control to countries which request it."[49]

A study of the conference's proceedings, activities, and recommendations further substantiates a contention made in Chapter 3: that the so-called "nature-saving" aspect of the Ecology Movement as promoted by the Humanist cartel* is merely a façade designed to conceal the eventual implementation of sweeping socialistic controls over man's environment. For example, contained in the Stockholm

---

*One prominent public figure belonging to the cartel is worth noting here: Ralph Nader, whose Humanist affiliation is confirmed by the November–December 1976 issue of *The Humanist*.

Conference's wide range of recommendations and resolutions was a call for:

- The development of mass media "information programs" to propagandize the public on environmental issues and the need for environmental control and management.
- The establishment of an international environmental education program encompassing all levels of education. This program would fall under the jurisdiction of UNESCO and other U.N. agencies, and would also provide for the training and retraining of professional workers and teachers.
- The creation under the U.N. of a global system of not less than one hundred stations to monitor the state of the environment.
- The establishment of international standards of environmental control by the global authority governing the above system, with a design for U.N. agencies ultimately to oversee such public enterprises as housing, health, sanitation, nuclear testing, education, transportation, migration, population distribution, and industry (*i.e.,* automotive, fishing, mining, synthetics, etc.).[50]

A final result of the Stockholm conference was the establishment of a United Nations Environment Program (UNEP). This new division's executive director is Maurice Strong — one of the twenty-one trustees of the Rockefeller Foundation — who previously served as Secretary-General of the Stockholm Conference. UNEP is intended to become the future overseer of a global environmental monitoring system.

In connection with the events of the 1972 U.N. Conference on the Human Environment, note should be taken of a substantial Humanist element that was at work both in its proceedings and in behind-the-scenes activity. The following are just a few significant indications:

1. The concept of a global authority to deal with environmental matters has been consistently promoted by the American Humanist Association and the Humanist-oriented World Federalists. Of particular interest here is an ad sponsored by the World Association of World Federalists, which appeared in a 1971 issue of *The Humanist*. It read:

> World Federalists believe that the environmental crisis facing planet earth is a global problem and therefore calls for a "global" solution — a worldwide United Nations Environmental Agency with the power to make its decisions stick. WAWF has submitted a proposal for just such an agency to be considered at the 1972 U.N. Environmental Conference to be held in Stockholm.[51]

2. A substantial number of Humanist-controlled non-governmental organizations were represented at the Stockholm Conference; to

name just a few, the International Humanist and Ethical Union, the IPPF, and the World Association of World Federalists. Consequently, recommendations presented to the Conference by way of a Non-Governmental Organizations' Declaration had a decidedly Humanist tinge, urging, for example, that "a new dimension of planetary loyalty" be adopted — a loyalty transcending present national and political boundaries in favor of a so-called world view; that an immediate redistribution of the world's wealth and resources in favor of the developing countries be effected; and that the "essentially inter-disciplinary, humanistic, and ethical aspects of environmental education . . . be stressed at every level of education and mass communication. . . ."[52]

3. The general tenor of messages delivered by a number of the featured speakers at the Conference displayed contempt for the modern-day technology that has thrived under the free-enterprise system, scorning capitalism as anathema. One particularly outstanding example was Barry Commoner, a Humanist who played a leadership role at Stockholm as the registered delegate of the International Humanist and Ethical Union.

In general, Commoner's contention was that progress has been ecologically unsound and that certain modern advances must be abolished. According to Commoner, the target for attack so far as ecology is concerned is modern technology, which he claimed is largely responsible for pollution. But in sharp contrast with Commoner's views, reliable statistics published by several U.S. government agencies indicate that, despite the technological advances of heavy industry, power plants, and the automotive industry, U.S. industry in general is polluting the air today less than it did forty years ago.*

If modern technology did not exist, Commoner and millions of other Americans might not have lived beyond the age of twenty. Without modern technology, we, like our ancestors, would still be subject to epidemics of typhoid, cholera, malaria, polio, smallpox, and dozens of other communicable diseases. And without modern technol-

---

*An examination of particulate figures measured over the years by the U.S. Public Health Service and HEW in a substantial number of the largest U.S. cities, including New York, proves the point with the following figures on micrograms of particulate per cubic meter of air:

1930	519
1957	120
1968	96
1969	92

According to the National Science Foundation, a comparison between present-day air samples from around the world with comparable samples taken in 1910 showed that the amount of oxygen in the air today is the same as it was three-quarters of a century ago: 20.95 per cent.

ogy, the threat of famine would loom constantly on the horizon of all nations, as it does still in too many countries where technology is undeveloped.

Attacks on the American free enterprise system appear frequently in Commoner's writings. In fact, so compatible are his views with the overall Humanist design that it seems his plan to reduce America's high standard of living is being promoted so that the Socialist-envisioned merger with the poorer countries can be more comfortably achieved.

There can be no doubt, then, that the United Nations intends to take the lead in shaping the earth's environment to meet its own socialistic designs. Once this purpose is understood, it is easier to understand why, in much of the current educational ecology literature and visual aids, capitalism is scorned as the basic culprit, and the need for a world system to regulate the so-called "crisis" is propagandized. Nor are the mass media negligent in this respect. For example, in December 1972, a *New York Times* magazine section devoted a number of pages, in a feature article on ecology, to convincing its readers that free enterprise and good ecology cannot co-exist. The *Times* article repeatedly disparaged the American competitive economic system, and explained its conclusion that a new world economic order should be established by stating:

> Such an economic system would have to be highly regulated, and because both modern economies and environmental problems cross international boundaries, a worldwide, environmentally responsible economic system would have to be managed by an international team of planners, most reasonably organized by the United Nations.[53]

Perhaps not coincidentally, the *Times* article was in keeping with the general socialistic tenor of the 1972 U.N. Conference on the Human Environment — a conference which, in the words of its secretary-general, Maurice Strong, was "only a stepping stone in the development of a system to manage the global environment."[54]

Planned Parenthood Moves Ahead in Legislation

According to the previously mentioned Population Crisis Committee, the recent entrance of the U.S. government into the area of fertility control had its origins in the early 1940's, during the Roosevelt era. Mrs. Eleanor Roosevelt believed that "family planning services should be supported with federal funds as part of maternal and child health programs if states chose to do so."[55] This socialistic view was only the tip of the iceberg of Mrs. Roosevelt's radical ideology. She was a long-time friend, supporter, and promoter of known Communists and Fabian Socialists.[56] So crimson, in fact, was the former First Lady's complexion during the thirty-three years from 1927 to 1960 that official documents emanating from the Senate Internal Security Subcommittee, the House Committee on Un-American Activities, and other U.S. government agencies show a total of eighty-eight Communist-front affiliations in connection with her name — a fact that was closely guarded by the White House and the news media.[57]

Other Leftist citations of Mrs. Roosevelt include membership, sponsorship, or close association with the American Association for the United Nations, the American Civil Liberties Union, the American Friends Service Committee, the National Association for the Advancement of Colored People (NAACP), and the New School for Social Research. A less well-known activity of Eleanor Roosevelt was her enthusiastic participation in the affairs and activities of Ethical Culture. So cozy was this association that Mrs. Roosevelt was honorary chairman and sponsor of Ethical Culture's Encampment for Citizenship,[58] established in 1946 under the direction and leadership of Humanists Algernon Black and Henry B. Herman. Her seemingly endless affiliations extended further, into the occult; she was a financial supporter of the Temple of Understanding.

However, despite the urgings of Mrs. Roosevelt, state and federal funds for birth control programs were meager until the 1960's. Then with the development of the birth control pill by Dr. John Rock of Planned Parenthood and others in 1963, the U.S. fertility control bandwagon was ready to shift into high gear.

By 1965, U.S. legislative measures surrounding fertility control began to coincide closely with the population planning events at the United Nations that were covered earlier. That year, President Johnson called a White House Conference on International Cooperation, which included a Panel on Population. Among those submitting proposals to the screening committee of the Conference was the American Humanist Association,[59] which by this time had made significant strides in U.S. government circles. This event was, in fact, a milestone for AHA, as it was the first White House Conference to which the organization had been invited as an official participant.

According to Mary Morain (a Humanist and Planned Parenthood member), who took part in the Conference's Panel on Population, another panel participant, John D. Rockefeller III, keyed his opening speech to the following central theme:

> Population stabilization at this point in history is a necessary means to the enhancement and enrichment of human life, a means of release of human energies; the big problem is to convince leaders that their peoples are ready to accept it as such.[60]

Rockefeller concluded with the thought that ". . . we are probably the last generation for which family planning can be a voluntary choice."

In the same report, which was published in *The Humanist*, Mrs. Morain noted comments made by two other panel participants: Senators Joseph Clark (president of World Federalists, U.S.A.) and Maureen Neuberger (a Unitarian-Universalist and Fabian Socialist). The two Senators urged those attending the panel discussion "to rouse more interest in the rank and file of American citizens so that Congress would not be allowed to continue its indifference."

This advice having apparently been heeded, Congress in 1967 allocated over $50 million for population and/or family planning. This action was in line with the recommendations of an HEW task force headed by Oscar Harkavy, a graduate of the Humanist-run New York City Ethical Culture Schools and Program Officer of the Ford Foundation. The task force called for "reprogramming of funds," a "reassignment of existing personnel," and "a clear signal from the [HEW] Secretary" for a population policy.[61]

By 1968, a President's Committee on Population and Family Planning was in existence under the Johnson administration. Its co-chairmen were Communist fellow-traveler Wilbur J. Cohen, then Secretary of HEW, and John D. Rockefeller III, a major financer of the population control movement. Here again is found the familiar interlock of SIECUS associates, Humanists, CFR members, one-worlders, and population control advocates, all working frantically to make their master plan official U.S. government policy. Included among them were:

- *Dr. Leona Baumgartner** — a SIECUS sponsor, a member of both the Population Crisis Committee and the board of directors of the National Association for the Repeal of Abortion Laws, the recipient of an Albert Lasker Award, and former administrator of the U.S. Agency for International Development
- *Dr. Harrison Brown†* — a Humanist, recipient of an Albert Lasker Award, and member of World Federalists, U.S.A.
- *Dr. Mary Calderone†* — a Humanist, former medical director of Planned Parenthood, executive director of SIECUS, and a hearty advocate of one-world government
- *Dr. Oscar Harkavy** — a Humanist, Ford Foundation Program Officer in Charge of the Population Office, and a consultant to both HEW and the U.S. Agency for International Development
- *Dr. Philip Hauser†* — member of Population Crisis Committee

*Committee member.
†Technical adviser to Committee.

- *Dr. Sheldon J. Segal** — director of the Biomedical Division of the Rockefeller-headed Population Council
- *Paul H. Todd Jr.** — chief executive officer of Planned Parenthood at the time of his appointment to the President's Commission.

Judging by the above list, which includes only a few of many persons who could be named as examples, it is apparent that the 1968 President's Committee on Population and Family Planning was composed of individuals who were anything but neutral. Little wonder, then, that its recommendations coincided so closely with the goals of the master population planners. Among them was a call for committee support of government entry into population matters, research, and family planning programs, and the proposal that birth control information and sex education be incorporated into the public school curriculum. And, not surprisingly, the Cohen-Rockefeller Committee reiterated the recommendations of the 1967 Harkavy Report, which had called for giving top priority, sufficient personnel, and adequate funds to population programs.

Using the Cohen-Rockefeller Committee's recommendations as both springboard and buffer, U.S. legislative leaders in the population control movement took a giant step toward what was to become a major legislative breakthrough in their crusade. In 1969, Senator Joseph Tydings (a Population Crisis Committee member), and Congressmen James Scheuer (a SIECUS ad signer), Tim Lee Carter, and George Bush (a CFR member and zero population growth advocate) introduced the Tydings Bill into both houses of the Congress. Once again, the report written by Humanist Oscar Harkavy entered the picture, this time as the basis for the Tydings Bill.[62]

Lead-off witness in favor of the bill was SIECUS director and Planned Parenthood official Dr. John Rock, who highlighted the need for drastic federal effort in researching more effective methods of birth control.[63] And, as might have been expected, a number of familiar organizations rushed to forward as lobbyists to endorse the Tydings Bill's proposals. These included:[64]

> American Ethical Union
> American Humanist Association
> American Medical Association
> American Public Health Association
> Friends of the Earth
> National Education Association

*Committee member.

Planned Parenthood–World Population
Population Crisis Committee
Sierra Club
Unitarian Universalist Association
United Church of Christ, Council for Christian Social Action
United Methodist Church, Board of Christian Social Concerns
Young Women's Christian Association
Zero Population Growth.

In its final form, the Tydings Bill passed the Senate unanimously, the House by an overwhelming majority, and was signed into law by then President Nixon on December 24, 1970, as the Family Planning Services and Population Research Act of 1970. The new law, the first in U.S. history to deal with these matters, authorized $382 million for family planning services, population research, manpower training, and population education and information through 1973.

A "Landmark Luncheon" held on Capitol Hill celebrated passage of the Family Planning Services and Population Research Act of 1970. The luncheon was co-sponsored by the CFR-dominated Population Crisis Committee and Senator Alan Cranston of the World Federalists.[65] Among the Senators honored at the luncheon for their strong support of the act were Humanist Walter Mondale,* Unitarian Robert Packwood, Edward Brooke, and Edmund Muskie, all contributors to the American Humanist Association's official organ. *The Humanist*. With the exception of Packwood, all are members of the CFR.

Further, in a subsequent report on the new law written for the Population Crisis Committee, Senator Tydings noted that this legislation was the result of years of pioneering and public education by such leaders as Senator Ernest Gruening (a Planned Parenthood official,

---

*Vice President Walter Mondale was a major participant in the 5th Congress of the International Humanist and Ethical Union held at the Massachusetts Institute of Technology in August 1970. In his opening remarks, Mondale made the following comment: "Although I have never formally joined a humanist society, I think I am a member by inheritance. My preacher father was a humanist — in Minnesota they call them Farmer Laborites and I grew up on a very rich diet of humanism from him. All of our family has been deeply influenced by this tradition including my brother Lester, a Unitarian Minister, Ethical Culture Leader, and Chairman of the Fellowship of Religious Humanists." (It should be remembered that Mondale was extremely influential in the selection of President Carter's new Cabinet, and as Vice President he presides over the U.S. Senate.)

Other prominent Humanist participants in the 5th Congress included Rita Hauser, then U.S. Ambassador to the United Nations; Professor Noam Chomsky of MIT; Lord Ritchie-Calder of Great Britain; Barry Commoner; and Jo Grimmond, former chairman of Great Britain's Liberal Party and Rector of Edinburgh University in Scotland.

Population Crisis Committee member, and Communist fellow traveler) and Senator Joseph Clark[66] (a World Federalist).

Commission on Population Growth and the American Future

Concurrently with these legislative events, the executive branch of the United States government was exerting its own influence in the promotion of population control. On July 18, 1969, in an unprecedented Message to Congress on Population, President Nixon called on Congress and the American people to recognize the so-called population crisis in both the United States and the world, climaxing his remarks by saying: ". . . I today propose the creation by Congress of a Commission on Population Growth and the American Future."[67] In the next breath, the President reiterated the belief of his administration "that the United Nations, its specialized agencies and other international bodies should take the leadership in responding to world population growth," adding: "The United States will cooperate fully with their programs."

Besides the Commission, the President recommended a number of other measures, including expanded research in contraceptive development and the behavioral sciences, as well as a reorganization of family planning service activities within the Department of Health, Education, and Welfare. Shortly afterward, HEW's National Center for Family Planning Services was inaugurated.

Acting favorably on President Nixon's message, the Congress passed Public Law 91-213 on March 16, 1970, establishing a Presidential Commission on Population Growth and the American Future, with a mandate to conduct an extensive inquiry concerning both the present and future population growth rate in America and "to formulate policy for the future" designed to deal with "the pervasive impact of population growth on every facet of American life."[68]

Under the new law, the President was empowered to appoint the members of the Commission and to designate its chairman and vice chairman; and, like the 1968 President's Committee on Population and Family Planning under the Johnson administration, Nixon's twenty-four member Commission was stacked with individuals dedicated to the population control movement, and/or associated with the one-world, Humanist-Socialist cartel.

Following is an examination of a number of members, staff, and consultants of the Commission on Population Growth and the American Future.

Commission Chairman and Vice Chairman

Commission Chairman was John D. Rockefeller III, a CFR member and honorary chairman of the CFR-dominated Rockefeller Foundation. Over the years, the Foundation has granted large sums of money to propagate the Humanist philosophy of Professor John Dewey and such Humanist-oriented institutions and groups as the National Council of Churches, the Union Theological Seminary of New York, the London School of Economics (British educational headquarters of the Fabian Socialists), and its American counterpart, the New School for Social Research. Nor is it pure coincidence that the Rockefeller brothers have invested scores of millions to promote one-world government, and donated the land for the United Nations complex in New York City.

The Rockefeller Foundation publication, *RF Illustrated*, sums up the Foundation's intentions this way:

> The RF will continue to work in the less-developed world as well as to intensify its efforts in the United States, but *will seek an even greater integration of humanistic and scientific disciplines to achieve its goals.*[69] [emphasis added.]

RF Illustrated also discloses that various committees of the Rockefeller Foundation have been assisted by "Humanists such as Hannah Arendt, Paul Freund, and Hans Morgenthau. . . ." Another Humanist, Michael Novak, acts as Director of Humanities for the Rockefeller Foundation, which in November 1973 made a $19,000 grant to the American Humanist Association's television series titled *The Humanist Alternative.*[70]

The Rockefeller Foundation's president, Dr. John Knowles, has Humanistic leanings of his own, which are depicted in the same issue of *RF Illustrated*. The article describes Knowles' inclinations by saying, ". . . he believes that the post-industrial world cannot survive without standards and values based on humanistic ideals."

John D. Rockefeller III himself has taken a clear-cut stand for Humanism in his Cass Canfield-published book, *The Second American Revolution*. Throughout the book, Rockefeller calls for a "humanistic revolution," and lauds the views of prominent Humanist activists. More specifically, the multimillionaire made a naked plea for "a society in which humanistic values predominate," "a humanistic capitalism," and "a politics of humanism." Moreover, he contends that the humanistic second American revolution is already under way in our society, and predicts its victory in the near future.

The Rockefeller Brothers Fund, another tax-exempt Rockefeller enterprise that supports a number of left-wing causes, has poured $500,000 into the establishment of Worldwatch Institute, which was organized by Humanist Lester R. Brown, a signer of *Humanist Manifesto II*. Worldwatch believes that American farmland must be regarded as "a world trust," and wants to socialize American food production in an attempt to feed all the rest of the world. Brown is also Senior Fellow of the Overseas Development Council, which would have all U.S. aid channeled through the United Nations. Forty-four of the seventy-three directors of the Overseas Development Council, including Humanist Brown, are CFR members.

John D. Rockefeller III was the recipient of an Albert Lasker Award for planned parenthood in 1961, and is chairman of the board of the New York-based Population Council. The council, founded in 1952, is heavily financed by the Rockefeller Foundation, its 1971 grant having totaled $500,000. Other financial supporters of the Population Council are the Ford Foundation and the United Nations, whose agencies often use the council's statistics to substantiate the need for population planning. Since 1963, the Rockefeller Foundation has provided more than $45 million for various population control projects throughout the world.[71]

Vice chairman of the Commission on Population and the American Future was Grace Olivarez, a member of the National Advisory Council of the American Civil Liberties Union (see Appendix J).

Commission Members, Staff, and Consultants

The following is a partial list of *Commission members*:

JOSEPH D. BEASLEY, M.D. — chairman of Planned Parenthood and member of the Population Crisis Committee.

DAVID E. BELL — a CFR member, a recipient of a Rockefeller Public Service Award in 1953, and executive vice president of the Ford Foundation. (Like the Rockefeller Foundation, the Ford Foundation devotes a total of 10 per cent of its income to the so-called population crisis.)

DR. BERNARD BERELSON — president of the Population Council; fellow of the Humanist-oriented Rockefeller Foundation; a former director of the Ford Foundation's Behavioral Sciences Division (1951–1957); and technical advisor to the 1968 President's Committee on Population and Family Planning. Berelson has been affiliated with the National Council of American-Soviet Friendship,[72] cited by former Attorney General Tom Clark as "subversive and Communist," and with the Chicago Ad Hoc Committee of Welcome for the Dean of Canterbury (paying homage to England's most notorious Red clergyman).

SENATOR ALAN CRANSTON — honorary president of World Federalists since 1952, population control advocate, and Communist fellow traveler. Cranston's ties with the Left can be traced back as far as 1941, when he received an appointment to the U.S. government's Red-infiltrated Office of War Information. An investigation made by the

Federal Bureau of Investigation revealed, among other things, that Cranston moved "in Communist circles," and that his "friends seemed to be fellow travelers . . . with Communist sympathies."[73]

SENATOR ROBERT PACKWOOD — a Unitarian, SIECUS-recommended author, and prime mover in the drive to legalize abortion on a national scale. Significantly, both Packwood (a Republican) and Cranston (a Democrat) — the only Senators appointed to President Nixon's Commission on Population Growth and the American Future — were given their assignments after each had introduced population control legislation. The appointments were presumably made for the purpose of creating an illusion that the Commission was politically bipartisan.

HOWARD D. SAMUEL — a Humanist who has served on the Board of Governors of the Ethical Culture Schools in New York City; also a member of the Socialist-oriented Public Affairs Committee (Public Affairs Pamphlets), and a member of the board of directors of the socialistic League for Industrial Democracy (LID).[74] It should be noted that not only did founders and early leaders of the LID subscribe to Socialism, but many of them, such as Stuart Chase, Norman Thomas, and Professors John Dewey, Robert Morss Lovett, and Alexander Meiklejohn, were Humanists and Communist fronters as well.[75]

Founded as the Intercollegiate Socialist Society, LID was renamed in 1921 at the instance of Jane Addams, a leading Socialist of her day, who was also prominent in the Ethical Culture Movement.[76] Miss Addams helped to found the ACLU, and was the founder in 1915 of the Women's International League for Peace and Freedom, a group whose goals, according to a 1961 California Senate Fact-Finding Subcommittee,[77] are world government and total disarmament. Today, LID continues to be under the strong influence of Humanist-collectivists, including George E. Axtelle, Brand Blanshard, LeRoy Bowman, Sidney Hook, Ernest Nagel, Aryeh Neier, and Harold Taylor.[78] LID is officially accredited to and represented on the United States Mission to the United Nations.

JAMES H. SCHEUER — a SIECUS ad signer and co-sponsor of the Tydings Bill.

JOSEPH D. TYDINGS — former U.S. Senator from Maryland and sponsor of the Tydings Bill. Tydings is also co-chairman with Dr. Milton S. Eisenhower (a Planned Parenthood council member) of the Coalition for a National Population Policy, a group that lobbies for immediate enactment of legislation by Congress to declare zero population growth a national policy, and that would fix a voluntary goal of not more than two children per family. The coalition's fifteen-member board is composed of representatives of such organizations as Planned

Parenthood, Zero Population Growth, and the Sierra Club. Another goal of the coalition is a reform of the federal tax structure to penalize families with more than two children.

During the time Tydings served on the President's Commission (he resigned January 3, 1971), he was elected to the board of the Population Crisis Committee.

GEORGE WOODS — former president of the U.N.'s World Bank; trustee of the Rockefeller Foundaton; member of the Population Crisis Committee; and member of the board of directors of the United Nations Association of the U.S.A.

Members of the *Commission staff* include the following:

CHARLES F. WESTOFF — executive director. Westoff is a member of the National Advisory Council of Planned Parenthood and author of books recommended by Planned Parenthood. He is further involved with the fertility control movement through the Office of Population Research at Princeton, of which he has been associate director since 1962, and the Population Association of America (PAA), which he has served both as vice president and as a member of the board of directors. Westoff's colleagues at PAA include Humanist Oscar Harkavy and SIECUS director Harold Christensen.

FREDERICK S. JAFFE — special consultant. A vice president of Planned Parenthood; also a technical advisor to the 1968 President's Committee on Population and Family Planning.

IRENE B. TAEUBER — special consultant. A member of the U.S. Agency for International Development (AID); member and former president of the Population Association of America; senior research demographer for the Office of Population Research at Princeton University; and technical advisor to the 1968 President's Committee on Population and Family Planning. Mrs. Taeuber also assisted William Draper of the Population Crisis Committee in producing a Victor-Bostrom Fund Report that glorified Red China's Mao Tse-tung and his stringent population control policies.[79]

DANIEL CALLAHAN — special consultant. Author of *Abortion: Law, Choice and Morality*, a book financed by grants from the Ford Foundation and the Rockefeller-controlled Population Council.[80] Views expressed in Callahan's book parallel closely the position taken by the National Association for the Repeal of Abortion Laws. The ultimate basis on which Callahan justifies abortion on request under certain conditions is the humanistic assumption that "Man is responsible for everything to do with man, including control over life and death."[81] Dr. Callahan is also identified with the Temple of Understanding (see Appendix I), having participated in the latter's second worldwide

Spiritual Summit Conference, held in Geneva, Switzerland, March 31 through April 4, 1970. It was there that Callahan addressed a special session on the so-called Population Problem, joining Dr. Emily Mudd of SIECUS in delivering papers on the worldwide crisis.

Callahan is a staff member of the Population Council and is co-founder and director of the Institute of Society, Ethics, and the Life Sciences (ISELS), located at Hastings-on-Hudson, New York. ISELS was established in 1969 and was initiated with the financial support of John D. Rockefeller III, by grants from the Rockefeller Foundation and the Rockefeller Brothers Fund.[82] Current projects and programs of ISELS are supported by the Rockefeller, Commonwealth, and Ford Foundations — the latter two also having helped to support SIECUS. ISELS' purpose is to "examine the ethical, legal, and social implications of advances in the life sciences."[83]

Perusal of ISELS literature shows known Humanists at the helm, such as Karl Menninger and Walter Mondale, who are both on ISELS' eight-member advisory council.[84] And not surprisingly, the omnipresent SIECUS is also represented at Callahan's Institute; SIECUS official Robert M. Veatch is ISELS' associate for medical ethics.[85]

Daniel Callahan's close affinity with Humanism is further evidenced by his participation in *The Humanist's* "Ethical Forum" in late 1972,[86] as well as by the fact that both his writings and those of his Institute are frequently flavored with the views of such prominent Humanists as Kenneth E. Boulding, Joseph Fletcher, Charles Frankel, Garrett Hardin, Oscar Harkavy, Walter Mondale, Arthur E. Morgan,* and Edward Pohlman.

Four problem areas, appropriately described as "scientific in origin but Humanistic in implication," have been singled out for special attention by the Institute. They are death and dying (euthanasia), behavior control (including electrical stimulation of the brain), population policy, and genetics engineering (cloning, selective breeding).

A peculiar paradox connected with Callahan's Institute is in need of exposure. ISELS' public image, as conveyed by means of college lecture tours and the news media, has been carefully polished to create the impression that the organization intends to be America's "watch-dog" and protector of the public from the grisly horrors of unre-

*Morgan was the first chairman of the board of the Tennessee Valley Authority and, as president of the Unitarian-founded Antioch College in the 1920's, established that college's well-known cooperative work-study program. He is the father of Ernest Morgan, a former member of the American Humanist Association's board of directors.

strained experimentation on human life that may soon result from recent advances in the life sciences. But in reality, ISELS press propaganda is clearly agitating for eventual changes in public policy and a new social consensus based on Humanistic and Ethical standards.

Consultants to the Commission Staff include the following:

PRESTON CLOUD — a Humanist; recipient of a Rockefeller Public Service Award; member of both the Population Crisis Committee and the Society for the Study of Evolution.

BARRY COMMONER — covered earlier in this entry. A member of the St. Louis Ethical Society, Commoner was the recipient in 1970 of the first International Ethical Humanist Award, given "for his distinguished contribution to the cause of ecology."[87] Commoner has been hailed by *Time* magazine as "the U.S.'s most articulate ecologist."[88] So prestigious is his image that he has delivered ecological testimony before the U.S. House of Representatives' Interior Committee.

PAUL R. EHRLICH — a Population Crisis Committee member, SIECUS-recommended author, and official of the Association for Voluntary Sterilization. Ehrlich also heads Zero Population Growth. (See entry for *National Association for Repeal of Abortion Laws,* elsewhere in PART II.) He is in the vanguard of those who believe governments have been derelict in this matter, and that they should impose drastic controls, including tax penalties for parents having more than two children, and if all else fails, should undertake direct intervention to regulate family size.[89] Ehrlich's book, *The Population Bomb*, was financed by the Ford Foundation.

SOL GORDON — a Humanist; member of the advisory committee of the SIECUS satellite American Association of Sex Educators and Counselors; an author whose works are recommended by SIECUS and Planned Parenthood; a writer for both *Sexology* and *The Humanist*.

An essay written by him for *The Humanist* of January–February 1975, titled "Creative Infidelity: On Being Happy in an Unhappy World," boldly stated:

> The author wishes to use the occasion of this publication to come out of is closet and declare that he is polymorphous perverse. He dedicates this piece to all the women in his life, to all the men in his life, and especially to the wife in his life.

Gordon has also written a series of vulgar sex comic books for young readers. These are known as Zing Sex Comix, and are published by Ed-U Press, which Gordon heads. These sex pamphlets are distributed through Planned Parenthood outlets and promote the erotic pleasures that Gordon suggests youngsters can enjoy through homosexuality, masturbation, bisexuality, oral and anal sex, and pornography. Ed-U Press is the publishing arm of the Institute for Family Research and Education, College of Human Development at Syracuse University, where Gordon is a professor and head of the Family Planning and Population Information Center.

Perhaps the most distressing element of the Gordon story is the fact that HEW's National Institute of Mental Health approved a $250,000 grant to Gordon in 1974, for the purpose of preparing community leaders to instruct parents in how to teach sex to their children according to the titillating gospel of Sol Gordon.

HARRIET PILPEL — a SIECUS director and Humanist; legal counsel for Planned Parenthood; a vice chairman of the American Civil Liberties Union; and a member of both the Association for Voluntary Sterilization and the Association for the Study of Abortion.

CHRISTOPHER TIETZE, M.D. — a consultant to Planned Parenthood; associate director of the Rockefeller-headed Population Council; and a member of the Association for Voluntary Sterilization.

Commission Recommendations

After two years of concentrated effort, the Commission on Population Growth and the American Future transmitted its final report to President Nixon on March 27, 1972. In addition to the overall conclusion that the United States should "welcome and plan for a stabilized population,"[90] the Commission made more than sixty recommendations for action at the federal, state, and local levels, all of which relate in some way to the population issue. Among them were the following:

Internal population distribution

- That an Office of Population Growth and Distribution be established within the Executive Office of the President.
- That "the federal government develop a set of national population distribution guidelines to serve as a framework for regional, state, and local plans and development," and that all levels of that government take appropriate steps to guide and control population movement and distribution.
- That "governments exercise greater control over land-use planning and development."
- That "state development agencies" such as the New York State Urban Development Corporation be established and given "broad

powers to acquire land, to override local ordinances, and actually to carry out development plans."

- That current patterns of racial and economic segregation be eliminated by federal promotion of integrated housing in metropolitan areas and more suburban housing for low- and moderate-income families, such as the "planned unit development," etc.
- That local governments be *reorganized* and *restructured*, with gradual transfer of local municipalities' property taxes to a regional body such as "metropolitan government," which in turn would redistribute revenues "according to need." (This of course would reduce and/or ultimately destroy local control of schools, police, and government in general.)

Population propaganda

- That a Population Education Act be legislated to assist school systems in setting up population education programs to be integrated into the school curriculum, using federal funds.

Fertility control

- That abortion, sterilization, and contraceptive services and information be made available to all Americans, whether married or single, and that "abortion be specifically included in comprehensive health insurance benefits, both public [governmental] and private." Further, that federal, state, and local governments make funds available to support abortion services.
- That minors be given access to abortion, sterilization, and contraceptive services and information without the consent of parents or guardians.

Sex education

- That sex education be available to all through community organizations, the media, and especially the schools. Also, that funds be given to the National Institute of Mental Health "to support the development of a variety of model programs in human sexuality."

Women's rights

- That "the Congress and the states approve the proposed Equal Rights Amendment for ratification as the twenty-seventh Amendment to the U.S. Constitution. (Coincidentally or not, the chairman of the House Subcommittee that held hearings on the ERA was Don Edwards, [D.-Calif.], a Humanist.)*

A New Citizens' Population Committee

No sooner had the Rockefeller-chaired Commission on Population Growth and the American Future officially submitted its report than a substantial number of critics arose in dissent. Sensitive to the rising tide of opposition to its recommendations, John D. Rockefeller III and some of his coterie rushed to defend the report by forming the Citizens' Committee on Population and the American Future (CCPAF) for the primary purpose of softening the public's attitude toward the Commission's highly controversial findings. Nearly half of the forty-two CCPAF members were either former members of or consultants to the President's Commission on Population Growth and the American Future, and/or representatives of such familiar groups as the American Civil Liberties Union, the National Association for Reform of Abortion Laws, the Planned Parenthood–World Population, the Population Crisis Committee, the Public Affairs Committee, and SIECUS.[91]

CCPAF was largely funded by the Rockefeller Foundation, and John D. Rockefeller III served as its honorary chairman. Two of the three co-chairman assisting him were Eleanor Holmes Norton,† a New York attorney who works with the New York Civil Liberties Union, and Hugh Downs, former host of NBC's *Today* show, who acted as front man for CCPAF.

* * *

As specifically demonstrated in this entry and elsewhere, the major thrust of the population and environmental control movements has been spearheaded and engineered from its inception by the Humanist-Socialist one-world cartel through such instruments as the United Nations, Planned Parenthood, SIECUS, NARAL, and other related groups. The movements being promoted by these organizations — abortion, euthanasia, contraception, sterilization, women's lib, and "gay" lib — are all outward manifestations of the overall master plan to drastically reduce the world's population.

As we have seen, each of these movements has a specific purpose.

---

*For detailed coverage of the ERA, including the Humanist–Socialist thrust behind it, see the article, "Behind The War On Women," available as a reprint from *The Review Of The News,* 395 Concord Avenue, Belmont, Mass. 02178.)
†Eleanor Holmes Norton's other activities include membership in the NAACP's Legal Defense Fund (on which she serves as campaign committee member). Here she is joined by a number of Communist fronters, far leftists, and Humanists, such as Joan Baez, Roger Baldwin, Helen L. Buttenwieser, Hugh Hefner, Archibald MacLeish, and A. Philip Randolph — who was named "Humanist of the Year" for 1970.

The population control component embodies all the means necessary for achieving authority over mankind's thought patterns, moral standards, family life, reproductive choices, place of residence, and even his appointed time of death. The environmental control aspect provides the means to increase the financial holdings of the coterie of powerful collectivists whose central aim is the destruction of free enterprise in favor of the gigantic monopolies that are intrinsic to their intended socialistic form of government. Together, the population and environmental control movements provide the building blocks with which the envisioned atheistic one-world order is to be constructed should the master planners succeed in bringing their plan to fruition.

United States Catholic Conference (USCC)
Family Life Division
1312 Massachusetts Avenue, N.W., Washington, D.C.

LIKE OTHER SIECUS-influenced organizations that are discussed in PART II, the U.S. Catholic Conference has made statements that are frequently used by proponents of sex education as indicating ecclesiastic approval of sex education in the schools. One promotional sheet distributed to support the myth that sex education is urgently needed originated with SIECUS, and it seems worthwhile to quote it here, in part, since most of the groups listed are by now familiar to the reader. This sheet, furnished by SIECUS upon request, reads as follows:

> SEX EDUCATION IN THE SCHOOLS IS APPROVED
> BY THE FOLLOWING NATIONAL ORGANIZATIONS:
>
> American Academy of Pediatrics
> American Association for Health, Physical Education and
>   Recreation (AAHPER)
> American College of Obstetricians and Gynecologists
>   (Committee on Maternal Health)
> American Medical Association (AMA)
> American School Health Association
> American Public Health Association (Governing Council)
> National Congress of Parents and Teachers (PTA)
> National Council of Churches
> National Education Association (NEA) and American Medical
>   Association (AMA) (Joint Committee on Health Problems in
>   Education)
> National School Boards Association and American Association of
>   School Administrators (Joint Committee)
> National Student Assembly, YMCA and YWCA
> Sixth White Conference on Children & Youth
> Synagogue Council of America
> United Nations Education, Scientific and Cultural Organization
>   (UNESCO)
> United States Catholic Conference
> United States Department of Health, Education & Welfare
>   (U.S. Commissioner of Education)

As can be seen clearly by now, SIECUS personnel and their Humanist associates have inserted themselves into key positions of control in many different groups, including most if not all of those listed above. The result has been to produce an apparently spontaneous call for sex education by seemingly unrelated agencies and associations with authoritative voices.

Like other organizations and agencies in PART II, USCC is linked directly to SIECUS. The link, in this case, is Walter J. Imbiorski, a SIECUS director who, as a Catholic priest, also served on the advisory board of USCC's Family Life Division. This division's major contribution to sex education, a program titled *Becoming a Person* (BAP) was produced under the editorship of then Father Imbiorski, who later renounced his vows to marry one of his BAP co-authors, Miss Frances Marzec. The BAP program will be covered later in this entry, following some pertinent background material about USCC itself and other related groups.

USCC is the operational secretariat and service agency of the National Conference of Catholic Bishops and is related to it by membership and directive control. Its function is to carry out the civic-religious work of the Roman Catholic Church in this country by providing the organizational structure and resources to coordinate the public, educational, and social concerns of the Catholic Church.

Family Life Division (FLD)

One branch of USCC is the Family Life Division, whose director is Monsignor James T. McHugh. Monsignor McHugh is the editor of two booklets published by the division in 1969: *Sex Education — A Guide for Teachers,* and *Sex Education — A Guide for Parents and Educators*, both to be discussed later. Catholic parents may well be disturbed to discover that, though Monsignor McHugh has never been a SIECUS director like Walter Imbiorski, he was nevertheless a member of the advisory board of the SIECUS-controlled American Association of Sex Educators and Counselors (AASEC) for years,* in company with numerous persons who are SIECUS officials and/or Humanists, Communist fronters, and smut peddlers (see *AASEC* entry elsewhere in PART II). In fact, so much in accord with SIECUS and associates is Monsignor McHugh that he collaborated with SIECUS founder and Humanist Lester Kirkendall in drafting AASEC's policy statement in 1969.[1]

Another distressing point in connection with Monsignor McHugh's sensitive position in the Family Life Division is his consistent affiliation with persons and organizations deeply involved in the population control movement — a cause that should be repugnant to any faithful

*Monsignor McHugh claims that he helped to found AASEC in 1967. He served as a member of its advisory committee from that time until at least July 1973.

prelate of the Roman Catholic Church. As was pointed out earlier, AASEC is chiefly governed by SIECUS officials, many of them actively engaged in the pro-abortion movement and the work of Planned Parenthood–World Population. (See entries for *National Association for Repeal of Abortion Laws* and *Planned Parenthood–World Population* elsewhere in PART II.)

Moreover, the July 1973 SIECUS Newsletter confirms the pro-abortion stance of the SIECUS organization itself. Surely as a long-time SIECUS associate, Monsignor McHugh cannot deny having had knowledge of this. On page 2 of that Newsletter, SIECUS director E. James Lieberman, who is also a member of NARAL's medical committee, says:

> . . . in the short term, then, abortion has had an impact in the obstetrical and pediatric areas which, in public health terms, compares with the discovery of a new vaccine or a cancer cure. . . .
>
> . . . Abortion must become and remain a part of comprehensive family planning services in any case, since, as Dr. Christopher Tietze has pointed out, the safest effective birth control is provided by a combination of conscientious diaphragm use with early abortion as a backup method.

Moreover, pro-abortion material frequently is favorably reviewed in SIECUS Newsletters, and such films as the following are recommended in SIECUS' *Film Resources for Sex Education*:

TOMORROW'S CHILDREN (1972)

> This film carries the message that we are destroying our world through over-population and environmental pollution. It proceeds to advocate birth control and abortion reform, and shows all the methods of birth control and describes their effectiveness.[2]

Of course the AASEC leadership has its own axe to grind in the population control movement — a fact that Monsignor McHugh must surely have discovered. Consider, as an illustration, the activities of the following AASEC officials and members:

- *Rabbi Balfour Brickner* — a member of the board of directors of the National Abortion Rights Action League and member of the Clergymen's Committee of the Association for Voluntary Sterilization.
- *Wilbur J. Cohen* — a featured speaker at one of the National Family Planning Conferences of Planned Parenthood–World Population.[3] It was here that Mr. Cohen promoted the work of the U.S. Department of Health, Education, and Welfare in providing birth control devices as an integral part of its health services program.

- *Warren Gadpaille* — a member of the pro-abortion Group for the Advancement of Psychiatry.
- *Reverend William Genné* — a SIECUS official who, like Rabbi Brickner, is a member of the Clergymen's Committee of the Association for Voluntary Sterilization.
- *Humanist Robert A. Harper* — an enthusiastic proponent of *compulsory* population control.
- *Humanist Lester Kirkendall* — a pro-abortionist, a SIECUS founder and director, and a member of Planned Parenthood of Oregon.
- *Humanist Lonny Myers* — a member of the board of directors of the National Association for Repeal of Abortion Laws.
- *Mrs. Elizabeth Nichols* — executive director of Planned Parenthood of Montgomery County, Maryland.
- *Humanist Harriet Pilpel* — legal counsel for the pro-abortion movement for years.
- *Dr. Philip M. Sarrel* — a SIECUS board member who assists in directing the Sex Counseling Service at Yale University. According to the *SIECUS Report* of January 1973, this service offers abortion counseling and contraceptive prescription and counseling to both married and unmarried students.
- *Gilbert M. Shimmel* — a SIECUS director who is identified in the February 1972 SIECUS Newsletter as faculty advisor to the student group at Hunter College which does counseling on family planning and abortion referral. He is also a member of the Population Crisis Committee.

There are other indications of AASEC's kinship with the population control movement in its organization's own literature. One is the fact that AASEC's 1969 Annual Conference, in which Monsignor McHugh participated, was sponsored by two contraceptive manufacturers: Ortho Research Foundation and Emko Company.[4] More recently, the Hillcrest Abortion Clinic and Counselling Service was listed on AASEC's official program as a contributor to AASEC's sixth National Sex Institute, held in Washington, D.C., in March 1973. At this time Monsignor McHugh was still on AASEC's advisory board. It might be supposed that AASEC's own admission that it initiates cooperative action with Planned Parenthood–World Population — a major catalyst in abortion law repeal — would be embarrassing to Monsignor McHugh. But despite these facts, Monsignor McHugh to date has never publicly repudiated or completely severed his ties with AASEC, though this organizaton is clearly aiming at a contraceptive society where sexual intercourse will be an ordinary pleasure of maturity, needing no sanction by the church.

Although Monsignor McHugh has more than once expressed his own opposition to abortion, his liaison with the persons mentioned above, who promote both abortion and population control, poses a serious question. Is it possible that the Monsignor was unable to discover the pro-abortionist views and activities of his AASEC colleagues in the course of an association lasting for more than five years?* As director of USCC's Family Life Division, Monsignor McHugh exercises a vast measure of influence and authority over his domain of approximately 130 U.S. Catholic dioceses — a position requiring keen insight, great sensitivity, and scrupulous perception. A man in such a position, it would seem, should long ago have divorced himself from such murky associations, for as St. Paul observed in I Corinthians 10:21, "Ye cannot be partakers of the Lord's Table, and of the table of devils."

Little wonder that numerous liaisons between diocesan officials and the population control movement are to be found even at the local level of the USCC's Family Life Division. A significant number of Catholic family life educators, responsible for the formulation and implementation of local sex education programs, are themselves members of AASEC. Moreover, the Newark (Catholic) Family Life Apostolate was a co-sponsor of a sex education workshop conducted at Montclair State College in New Jersey on June 17, 1970. There Planned Parenthood president Dr. Alan F. Guttmacher not only discussed the

---

*Monsignor McHugh is also a member of the board of advisors of the Kennedy Institute for the Study of Human Reproduction and Bioethics at Georgetown University, Washington, D.C. The purpose of this institute is strikingly similar to that of Daniel Callahan's Institute of Society, Ethics and the Life Sciences, which was discussed in the entry on *Planned Parenthood — World Population*. Both have the goal of molding professional and public opinion on such Humanist-generated issues as abortion, euthanasia, fetal experimentation, and genetic control.

Like Callahan's group, the Kennedy Institute has received generous grants from the Ford Foundation and the Humanist-oriented National Endowment for the Humanities, and both enjoy a close liaison with the U.S. Government's National Institutes of Health (which are providing grants for experimentation on live human fetuses).

The Kennedy Institute is linked to SIECUS through Father Robert C. Baumiller, a staff member and geneticist of the Institute's Laboratories for Reproductive Biology. Father Baumiller's unorthodox leanings surfaced publicly in 1972, when he assumed the role of faculty advisor to six medical students at Georgetown University who collaborated in the writing of a 46-page sex manual titled *Human Sexual Response-Ability*. The manual endorsed homosexuality and contraception for unmarried students, and advocated a morality directly contrary to the teachings of the Catholic Church.

Other noteworthy individuals at the Kennedy Institute include Sydney Cornelia Callahan (the wife of Daniel Callahan), who serves on the Institute's board of advisors, and Father Charles Curran (a research scholar of the Institute, who believes that both abortion and homosexuality can be justified under certain circumstances).

need for abortion law repeal, but was specifically honored at the meeting, along with SIECUS directors Frederick Margolis, Wardell Pomeroy, and Ira Reiss.

National Catholic Educational Association (NCEA)

Another agency relevant to our study of the USCC's Family Life Division is the National Catholic Educational Association, which works hand-in-hand with Monsignor McHugh's Family Life Division in the formulation of sex education programs for Catholic schools. In April 1969, NCEA cooperated with the FLD in publishing the latter's booklet, *Guidelines for the Formation of a Program of Sex Education.* Confirming the close relationship between the two groups, one of the earliest FLD sex education bulletins stated:

> The Family Life Bureau, USCC, *with the cooperation of NCEA,* the National Center of the CCD, and the Department of Education, USCC, has undertaken the task of formulating a total program of education in human sexuality that will utilize the resources of home, school and parish.[5] [emphasis added]

NCEA is located in Washington, D.C. It is the oldest and largest professional organization of Catholic educators in the nation, its membership being open to both individuals and educational institutions. It conducts research, works with voluntary groups and government agencies on educational problems, conducts workshops, and offers consultant services. The main objective of NCEA as stated in the 1973 Catholic Almanac is "to promote and encourage the principles and ideals of Christian education and formation by suitable service and other activities."[6] Unfortunately, NCEA has strayed far from its original purpose. For example, it has allowed SIECUS within its periphery on more than one occasion. SIECUS official John Stanavage was a featured speaker at NCEA's 1970 annual convention in Atlantic City, where a combined book exhibit and bibliography for Catholic educators boldly presented the SIECUS-compiled book, *Sexuality and Man* (a collection of the first twelve SIECUS Study Guides, written by such SIECUS directors as Humanists Lester Kirkendall, Isadore Rubin, and Ira Reiss. A year later, SIECUS was invited to exhibit its materials at NCEA's April 1971 annual conference.

More than a passing look at the program of the 1970 Atlantic City meeting is required to discover the ideology behind an association that helped to formulate FLD's sex education curricula. Topping the list as "name performers" at this convention were:

- *Norman Cousins* — a Humanist, population control advocate and member of the Population Crisis Committee, who has also held high-ranking roles with the World Federalists, U.S.A., the World Association of World Federalists, the Council on Foreign Relations, and the pro-abortion American Civil Liberties Union. This speaker's far-Leftist leanings are further exemplified by the fact that he is a sponsor of the Humanist-Socialist Norman Thomas Endowment* at the New School for Social Research in New York City, together with a number of Humanists and Communist-fronters.[7] Cousins was the featured speaker at the NCEA convention's Second General Session.[8]

- *Senator Edmund Muskie* — another population control advocate who was a leading supporter of the Family Planning Services and Population Research Act of 1970, Muskie has flirted with Humanist forces on a number of occasions. He participated in *The Humanist* magazine's "Ethical Forum" and "Reader's Forum," and wrote a solicited article for the magazine on how "to humanize elections in the future."[9]

  Further, following a sweeping victory for Governor George Wallace in the Florida primary, Senator Muskie was quoted in the *New York Times* of March 19, 1972, as having stated that a succession of Wallace victories would be "a threat to the underlying values of humanism and decency and progress. . . ." Muskie was selected as featured speaker at the closing general session of NCEA's convention.

Another major speaker at the convention was Humanist James Farmer, a founder of the Congress of Racial Equality (CORE) and former Assistant Secretary for Administration of the U.S. Department of Health, Education and Welfare. Mr. Farmer's radical record dates back at least as far as 1950, when he began a four-year term as field secretary for the socialistic League for Industrial Democracy.[10] He later served as vice president of the League and as a member of its board of directors. In 1962, he received the League's John Dewey Award, a tribute reserved for prominent leftists of Humanist persuasion. In 1973, he signed *Humanist Manifesto II*. Farmer is also a member of the American Civil Liberties Union, the legal arm of the Humanist-Socialist movement.

*Other prominent members of the Norman Thomas Endowment at the New School for Social Research have included: Supreme Court Justice William O. Douglas, John Kenneth Galbraith, Arthur J. Goldberg, Michael Harrington, Senator Mark O. Hatfield, the Rev. Theodore M. Hesburgh (who is also on the National Advisory Council of ACLU), Julian Huxley, Senator Jacob K. Javits, Senator Mike Mansfield, Eugene McCarthy, Gunnar Myrdal, and A. Philip Randolph.

Some topics for discussion by other participants at NCEA's 1970 convention were: "Helping the Catholic Educator Assume a Global Role," "A More Global Role for Parents," "Non-Graded Programs," and "Man and His Environment." Victor Ferkiss, a teacher of government at Georgetown University, speaking on the last subject, told the 20,000 assembled Catholic educators that mankind faces extinction unless drastic steps are taken. The solution Ferkiss proposed was threefold: (1) adoption of a *zero population growth* policy throughout the world; (2) exertion of certain "pressures" upon parents through the tax structure to "persuade" them to observe the arbitrary limit of two children per family; and (3) the initiation of what he termed "coercive sanctions" in the event taxation pressure is not enough. "Coercive sanctions," in contemporary terms, could of course include forcible sterilization and compulsory abortion. But the obvious question here is why Mr. Ferkiss was invited to address NCEA, thus creating the impression among educators that he spoke for Catholic education in general.

The authors of a number of books promoted at NCEA's Atlantic City Convention could not possibly be considered as representative of an authentic Catholic viewpoint. Among them were:

- *Eldridge Cleaver* — a literary contributor to *The Humanist* and notorious Black Panther revolutionary, whose book *Soul on Ice* brags about rapes he has perpetrated and disparages the Holy Trinity. (Recently, he claims to have been converted.)
- *Norman Cousins* — mentioned earlier.
- *Jessica Mitford* — identified Communist Party member who was a county financial director for the Communist Party, U.S.A., in 1946.[11]
- *Bonaro Overstreet* — Humanist.
- *Harry Overstreet* — Humanist and Communist fronter.
- *Bertrand Russell* — Humanist and Fabian Socialist.
- *Jean-Paul Sartre* — Humanist, existentialist, French Marxist.
- *Pierre Teilhard de Chardin* — the existentialist priest, now deceased, who according to his biographer experienced a complete conversion to belief in evolution between the years 1909 and 1912. It was during that period, in Hastings, England, that Teilhard became involved in the celebrated affair of the Piltdown Man, long believed to represent an important step in the development of man from the ape, but later proven to be a hoax. In 1926, Teilhard's superiors in the Jesuit Order instructed him to cease teaching, and in 1944 he was refused permission by the Pope to publish his most significant work, *Le Phénomène Humain* (*The Phenomenon of Man*). After his death in 1955, a decree of the

Holy Office ordered the withdrawal of his works from Catholic libraries, seminaries, religious institutions, and bookshops. Shortly afterward, *The Phenomenon of Man* was sponsored for publication by a committee of scientists who were sympathetic to Teilhard's views. More recently, in 1962, the Holy Office issued a solemn *Monitum*, or warning, against Teilhard's works, under the authority of Pope John XXIII, on the ground that they contained serious errors, offensive to Catholic doctrine. Nevertheless, Teilhard's works continue to be widely read in Catholic institutions throughout the world today.

Probably because of his promotion of both evolutionary and existentialist thought, Teilhard de Chardin is often praised in the pages of *The Humanist* magazine. One particularly revealing passage that identifies Teilhard with the Humanist movement can be found in an article written for *The Humanist* by Humanist Colin Wilson: "In recent years a new form of humanism has arisen . . . . I mean the evolutionary humanism of Sir Julian Huxley, J. B. S. Haldane, and Teilhard de Chardin."[12] In fact, so admired is Teilhard by the Humanist camp that the commendatory introduction to *The Phenomenon of Man* was written by the militant Humanist, Sir Julian Huxley.

Family Life Division's Guidelines and Programs

Having laid the foundation for a realistic appraisal of Monsignor McHugh and the NCEA, our next step is to examine some of the guidelines and programs being provided to Catholic dioceses throughout the nation by McHugh's Family Life Division in collaboration with NCEA.

Sex Education: A Guide for Parents and Educators

Like many other booklets expressly prepared for parents, *Sex Education: A Guide for Parents and Educators* (published jointly by FLD and NCEA) is fairly innocuous. The approach appears to have been to omit the more controversial and offensive aspects so as to obtain parental support for establishing a program.

Nevertheless, Monsignor McHugh's 35-page booklet has several objectionable features:

1. The introduction recognizes man as a "sexual" rather than a "spiritual" being,[13] — a characterization that can be clearly traced to SIECUS.

2. The use of "open-ended discussion groups"[14] — a sensitivity training technique — is advocated in the *Six-Meeting Parents' Program*

recommended by Monsignor McHugh to help reshape parental attitudes, eliminate personal hang-ups, and enable parents to engage comfortably in sexual dialogue.

3. References are made here and there throughout the booklet to the thoughts of Humanists Erich Fromm and Gordon Allport, casually establishing these authors as "authorities" on human sexuality.

4. The booklet's somewhat limited bibliography includes Gordon Allport's *Pattern and Growth in Personality* and Erich Fromm's *The Art of Loving* and *The Sane Society*.[15] In *The Sane Society*, Fromm falls into his familiar pattern of promoting socialistic Humanism, while at the same time denigrating Judeo-Christian values and attacking the American free enterprise system. His principal contention is that under capitalism, man cannot be mentally healthy; therefore capitalism is the cause of modern man's flight from sanity.

In typical Humanist fashion, Fromm parrots the evolutionist theory that the appearance of man on the evolutionary scene occurred at a point in time when the highest form of animal "emancipated itself from nature by erect posture," its brain having "grown far beyond what it was" in the original state.[16] Further, Fromm views monotheistic religion as "only one of the stations in the evolution of the human race," and predicts that the future will bring about the extinction of theistic concepts in favor of "a new religion."[17] The primary feature of such a religion, according to Fromm, would be "its universalistic character, corresponding to the unification of mankind which is taking place in this epoch," embracing "the humanistic teachings" common to all religions of the East and West.[18]

Another work listed in the FLD teacher's booklet is *Learning to Love* by Marc Oraison, a French Roman Catholic priest whose writings have been censured by Cardinal Ottaviani's curial office at the Vatican, as reported in the August 24, 1966 issue of *Christian Century* magazine. The Vatican has requested that this priest be barred from lecturing on moral theology.

Still another recommended book is Joseph and Lois Bird's *The Freedom of Sexual Love*, reviewed later in this entry.

Sex Education: A Guide for Teachers

Like the parents' guide just discussed, *Sex Education: A Guide for Teachers* (also issued jointly by the Family Life Division and NCEA) was edited by Monsignor McHugh. This 86-page booklet contains a short series of articles on certain aspects of sex education, followed by several pages containing a set of "Guidelines for the Formation of a Program of Sex Education" for teachers, and a bibliography containing recommended reading, films, and recordings. Although certain areas of this teacher's guide focus on traditional modes of raising youth and offer some good advice, enough of it is noxious to cause the overall content to be rated as highly unacceptable. For example:

1. It lays a foundation for acceptance of the humanistic philosophy of SIECUS and associates; establishes SIECUS and the AASEC as legitimate authorities in the field; and encourages public support of SIECUS-generated sex education programs. Consider, for example, the following passage:

SEX RESEARCH INDUCES NEW REALISTIC OUTLOOK

Thus, the burden is shared and parents now have many sources, some of them professional, to guide them. In recent years, for instance, sex educators, professional experts in a new field, have studied sex behavior and customs intensively. Their work is providing practical guidance, *and from it has evolved a realistic and humanistic philosophy with regard to sex and sex education.*

Within the past few years, a number of national organizations have done pioneering work in this field. Among these organizations would be *the Sex Information and Education Council of the United States (SIECUS), the American Association of Sex Educators and Counselors (AASEC)*, and the Interfaith Commission on Marriage and Family. *Under this impetus, several communities have set up programs of education in human sexuality* that extend from the early grades through high school. *These undertakings deserve the support and participation of parents, teachers, and clergymen.*[19] (emphasis added)

2. The teacher's guide subtly promotes the new morality.[20] Teachers are encouraged to direct the student to various "alternatives" available in the selection of a value system,[21] rather than to the traditional Catholic code, and are then asked by Psychologist Michael Carluccio, a contributor to this booklet: "How do you teach children what is right and wrong in the use of sex?" Carluccio's answer to the question is flimsy, and falls far short of orthodox Catholic doctrine:

. . . Do we state that the moral law forbids sexual intercourse outside of marriage and that chastity is a value which cannot be modified or changed? Or do we take the position that all sexual intercourse between individuals is morally justifiable as long as there is mutual consent and no immediate harm done to the social order? Can there be a middle position? I do not think there is an easy answer to these questions. It will take psychologists, philosophers, theologians, sociologists and other professionals years of searching for truths in their respective fields before we can hope to have a synthesis of knowledge and the necessary insight to work out a solution. The present situation seems to be one of confusion and flux.[22]

3. Close to 75 percent of the films in this guide's bibliography are SIECUS-recommended. Among them are *The Game, Human Reproduction*, and *Phoebe*, which were reviewed earlier in PART II.

4. The above bibliography's recommended reading portion offers works by SIECUS directors Evelyn Duvall and Walter Imbiorski; Humanists Erich Fromm and Gordon Allport; and the French priest Marc Oraison, mentioned earlier. Also listed is *The Freedom of Sexual Love*, by Joseph and Lois Bird. Incredibly, celibate nuns and priests as well as Catholic lay teachers are advised to read this book, which explicitly describes oral-genital contacts, erotic stimulation, vaginal and clitoral orgasms, sex play, techniques for prolonging ejaculation, and various positions for intercourse. So far removed from traditional Catholic instruction is the content of the Bird book that, in the foreword, Monsignor J. D. Conway acknowledges that ". . . a book like this would not have received Catholic approval a few years ago."

In view of the above, it is most unlikely that *Sex Education: A Guide for Teachers* will in any way help teachers accomplish the basic purpose of Catholic sex education, which is defined in this booklet itself as being "to help the child achieve a fuller knowledge of himself as a person *and as a Christian.*"[23] (emphasis added)

Becoming a Person Program

The *Becoming a Person* (BAP) program currently being used in Catholic schools is a revised edition of an earlier program by the same title that originated as a Sex Education Pilot Project of the Cana Conference of Chicago. Material for the Chicago project was chiefly taken from experimental work of the American School Health Association,[24] a group whose sex education program was largely structured by SIECUS officials Sally R. Williams and Evalyn Gendel, and Dr. Joseph S. Darden, a Humanist. The Chicago project was tested for three years on approximately 30,000 children.

Curriculum materials for BAP's revised edition were published by Benzinger, Inc., under the chief editorship of SIECUS official Walter J. Imbiorski, the quondam Catholic priest and director of the Cana Conference of Chicago, who later renounced his vows in order to marry. The Cana of Chicago and Benzinger editions have identical teacher and parent bibliographies.

In attempting to enlist the support of Catholic parents for the BAP program, educators have sought frantically to divorce it from SIECUS. During sensitivity-type meetings, parents have been told that Father Imbiorski remained on the SIECUS board for only one year, presumably to discover what the organization was up to. The educators further claim that he does not subscribe to the SIECUS philosophy.

In view of the following indisputable facts, it becomes obvious that, whether intentionally or not, certain Catholic educators are parroting a clear misrepresentation. First, Father Imbiorski served on the SIECUS board of directors for a period of three years (1968–1970), rather than for one year only as his supporters claim.

Second, he continued to defend SIECUS publicly. For example, when speaking at the Divine Word Seminary in Bordentown, New Jersey, in September 1969, while still on the SIECUS board, he reaffirmed his approval of SIECUS as having "the best family life experts and educators in the country."[25] Later, following his term with SIECUS, Father Imbiorski attacked SIECUS critics at the National Catholic Educational Association's annual convention in April 1971, stating that they "are going to have to answer before God" for "slander" against SIECUS.[26]

Finally, the same year saw the publication of Father Imbiorski's book, *Beginning Your Marriage*, written in collaboration with SIECUS director Father John L. Thomas. This could hardly have come about had Father Imbiorski become disenchanted with SIECUS.

Father Imbiorski's close association with Father Thomas was still more questionable in view of the fact that the latter had associated himself with the pro-abortionist Planned Parenthood–World Population, at least to the extent of having been the first priest ever to attend an annual banquet of that organization.[27]

Despite all this, Walter Imbiorski's influence has been widely felt in this country. While still a priest, he established Family Life Divisions and Christian Family Living groups in at least forty Catholic dioceses in the United States. The Benzinger edition of BAP, which is generally considered to be a "cleaned-up" version of the original program, was approved for use in fifty-two of the 135 dioceses in the United States by 1973, according to the publisher. Every diocese in the state of New Jersey has consented to use the BAP program, with the exception of Newark, which uses the Fox program, (to be reviewed later).

Major consultants for the Imbiorski-edited BAP program were Monsignor James McHugh and Mary Perkins Ryan, who, with her husband, John, wrote *Love and Sexuality: A Christian Approach*. According to an evaluation of this SIECUS-recommended book by the New York organization, Holy Innocence Safeguarded:

> . . . the Ryans resort to the argument that contraception is a "brake" on abortion. They do not even condemn abortion unreservedly, for they quibble about the period in which the fetus can be called animated and leave the impression that, at times, abortion could be lawful. Nor is it evident from this book that they consider premarital relationships sinful.[28]

As a further indication of Mrs. Ryan's unorthodox leanings relative to the Catholic Church, her book, *Love and Sexuality*, recommends further reading of such authors as the following:

- Gordon Allport — a Humanist and Communist-fronter.

- *Eric Berne* — a Humanist who before his death was a psychiatrist at Esalen Institute, a mecca for sensitivity training activities that include "nude-ins." Berne's BAP-recommended book, *Games People Play*, published by the notorious Grove Press, appears in a number of bibliographies as a sensitivity training reference.
- *Robert T. Francoeur* — a Humanist and ex-priest, now married, and author of works that promote scientific human breeding and an evolutionary view, including the BAP-recommended book, *Perspectives in Evolution*.
- *Erich Fromm* — "Humanist of the Year" for 1966.
- *Richard Hettlinger* — a SIECUS-recommended author, whose BAP-recommended book, *Living with Sex: The Students' Dilemma*, carries the following endorsement by Humanist Mary Calderone: "Mr. Hettlinger's approach to his subject is immensely refreshing in its openness, candor, realism — *and particularly in its lack of authoritarianism, moralism, and dogmatism.*"[29] (emphasis added)

So far as its content is concerned, the book is propaganda for the acceptance of homosexuality, masturbation, premarital petting to orgasm, and premarital intercourse under certain circumstances. It advances the argument that religious traditions do not permit young people to enjoy sex and that Christian teachings are psychologically damaging. A goodly portion is devoted to a specific attack on the Judeo-Christian moral code, and to ridiculing various religious beliefs, religious groups, and Christian saints. Among those named by Hettlinger as "authorities" in the field of human sexuality are SIECUS; Humanists Mary Calderone, Lester Kirkendall, and Isadore Rubin; Fabian Socialist Havelock Ellis; and the late Alfred Kinsey.

- *Ira L. Reiss* — a Humanist and SIECUS director.
- *Carl Rogers* — "Humanist of the Year" for 1964.

Despite its questionable contents, the Ryan opus, *Love and Sexuality*, is offered as further reading for teachers in the BAP program's bibliography, presumably to guide them in teaching "Christian" morality to their pupils.

Overall, the content of the BAP program takes a naturalistic approach to education in human sexuality, cleverly camouflaged in moral platitudes and sudden bursts of discourse about God's plan. Or, in the lucid words of one critic, James Likoudis, in his scholarly critique of BAP:

> The *Becoming A Person* program is an unsavory potpourri of pronouncedly humanistic psychology and sociology sprinkled with the holy water of Christian "God-language."[30]

At another point in his analysis, Likoudis says:

> . . . it is spiritually barren, betraying the influences of secular human-
> ism, naturalistic personalism, and Freudian pan-sexualism. It embodies a
> distortion of supernatural realities so profound as to result in youth
> becoming spiritually malformed, if molded for eight years according to the
> pattern intended by the authors.[31]

Occasional references to God in the BAP program suggest supernatural design in man's procreative process, but God's sanctions against
sins of the flesh are not mentioned. And noticeably absent from the
eight volumes of children's reading texts are the words *Catholic* and
soul, any mention of the doctrine of *original sin* and the *fall of man,*
and many other spiritual components intrinsic to Catholic doctrine. The
word *sin* is used only twice, and the Ten Commandments and the value
of prayer get one mention each. Yet the BAP program is being sold
to parents as the answer to Vatican II's call for "positive and prudent
sexual education" within a Catholic framework.

Other features also make it unfit for Catholic consumption:

1. *The texts contain an overall denial of any fixed moral absolutes,*
with substitution of a personal value system that may extend beyond
the boundary of Divine Law. Traditional concepts of *divine law* and *sin*
are blurred or minimized in the minds of the teachers and students. An
example is the coverage of homosexuality in the teacher's manual for
grade seven, which is so bland as to neutralize opposition to the
practice. This softening up is evident in such statements as:

> We have seen such developments as the Roman Catholic hierarchy in
> Great Britain agreeing with the government Wolfenden Proposals that
> homosexual activities between consenting adults should not be classified as
> crimes, and sporadic attempts by various church groups to minister to
> homosexuals by trying to help them with their problems . . . .
> The causes of homosexuality are various and not completely known, but
> they have to do with the way an individual personality develops. It is entirely
> possible for a homosexual to be a good and moral person.[32]

The BAP's text's omission of the Bible's unswerving condemnation of
homosexual activity as perverse and sinful* is of significance here. The
treatment given to other areas of morality in the text is similarly divorced from traditional Catholic doctrine, resulting in a further neutral-
ization of the faith. This paves the way for the reorientation of Catholic
children to what appears to be a naturalistic "love-ethic" that is essentially man-centered, empirical, and existential in character.

2. *The BAP texts place gross emphasis on the nature of men,*
women, and children as "sexual persons," rather than as the "embodied

*Leviticus 18:22; Romans 1:23–32; I Corinthians 6:9–10.

spirits" that Christian doctrine teaches they are. They teach that "masculinity" or "femininity" — rather than spirituality — constitutes the human person.

3. *In the lessons on animal life, similarities between animals and human are stressed, after the fashion of the evolutionists.* In Grade Three, when the opportunity arises to focus on man's unique distinction from the animal kingdom, it is emphasized that the difference lies in man's privilege of *choice* relative to his own destiny,[33] while his possession of an immortal soul is totally ignored. Moreover, the Christian doctrine that the soul was created by God at the moment of his conception is never conveyed clearly to the child.

Among numerous secular selections in the bibliography for teachers at the lower grade level are the books in the *Time-Life Nature and Science Library.* A reading of this series reveals such evolutionary allegations as this:

> How does man fit into this picture? We know from a steadily increasing body of fossil evidence that our species has in fairly recent geological times evolved from apelike animal forms. However unique our species seems at first glance, this uniqueness must rest on differences of degree: our apparently "novel" characteristics must have evolved from animal roots.[34]

4. *Much emphasis is placed on role-playing, group discussion, and other sensitivity training techniques, as the teacher is made to assume the role of classroom therapist.* For example, the Grade Two teacher's text suggests as an exercise for the seven-year-old students:

> Dramatize a family quarrel between two sisters over doing dishes, between two brothers over cleaning the yard, etc. Have children take turns being parents showing how they would settle the dispute.[35]

It is incongruous that precious school time should be spent urging children to reenact morally negative situations which arouse feelings of animosity toward other members of their family or each other. The propriety of causing students to record on paper deeply personal or confidential family matters, which is encouraged in portions of the BAP series, is also questionable.

By Grade Seven, the teacher's manual introduces such topics for class discussion as parents' jobs, their preferences, hobbies, fears, likes, and dislikes, what they approve and disapprove, their customs and rules.[36] The next unit in the same booklet advises the teacher to divide the class into small groups of eight or ten, to have each group appoint a "recorder" and then discuss:

> If you had just one wish, what one thing would you (or your group in discussion) want to change about your parents? Count the votes. See what the consensus is.[37]

The above activities are typical of the *antiparental syndrome* which haunts the BAP program, despite its lofty claim that it inspires better communication and understanding between parent and child. Moreover, youth's current sense of anxiety and alienation from parents can only be intensified by experiences that coerce students into analyzing themselves and their parents and participating in *group confession* to disclose family shortcomings and inadequacies.

Commenting on this delving into family life experiences in the classroom, Dr. Rhoda Lorand, a New York physician who has practiced child psychoanalysis and psychotherapy for more than twenty years, has this to say:

> Autobiographies, role-playing and discussion of family life are not only an invasion of privacy but often arouse anxiety and guilt. Furthermore, since the parents will be living in a fishbowl, it will disturb the spontaneity of family life. Even if teachers acquire professional discretion and never mention to their colleagues the interesting revelations made by their pupils, the pupils themselves will certainly report to their families what they have learned about the other children's parents and home life.[38]

5. *Students are subjected to the usual SIECUS-style erotic stimuli and sexual preoccupations, which can only disturb, excite, and embarrass them, as well as interfere with the latency period.* The material presented on sexual reproduction is inappropriate and far too detailed for the age levels to which it is directed. For example, passages like the following are found in the Grade Five student's text (for ten-year-olds):

> The penis is a fleshy, tube-like organ located between a man's legs in front of the scrotum. Most of the time it is small, soft, and flexible because it is composed of soft, spongy tissue.
> At certain times, blood rushes into the cells of this spongy tissue and the penis enlarges. It becomes longer, wider, and much firmer. This enlarging process is called an *erection*. In order for the sperm cells in the semen to leave the body of the father, the penis must be in the erection stage . . . .
> When semen is sent forth from the body of the male, it comes out of the penis in a series of spurts. This process is called *ejaculation*.[39]

As early as Grade Three, eight-year-olds are induced to use such words as *vagina, sperm, uterus, birth canal, conception*, and *internal fertilization*. The same grade level exposes the student to unnecessary descriptions of animal reproduction that are reminiscent of the filmstrip, *How Babies Are Made*.

Further, Grade Five students are forced to dwell on the sexual experiences of their own parents. After being reminded that parents sleep together and told of a "deep special union that exists between mothers and fathers" that expresses itself in a "private form of love," the text reveals to ten-year-olds:

> . . . This love act is called intercourse and during their special closeness and embrace the father places his penis in the mother's vagina and sends millions of sperm cells into her body.[40]

In sworn testimony delivered before the Superior Court of the State of California by Dr. Lorand concerning the practice of exposing grade school children to such information, the physician notes:

> At this age, anxiety and sexual excitement are aroused when the child is forced to think about the sexual nature of his and his parents' bodies.
>
> These emotions, far from promoting mental health, put the children under a heavy burden. They have to try to repress the sexual excitement which the material arouses in them, thereby creating an unhealthy split between sexuality and emotion, and draining off energy much needed for the mastery of academic subjects. Further, our experience has shown us that such forcing of sexual preoccupation on the elementary school child is very likely to result in sexual difficulties in adulthood, and it can lead to disturbed behavior in childhood.[41]

6. *A perusal of the general bibliography prescribed in the BAP teachers' edition confirms that the overall program is rooted in hypocrisy.* Were it truly a Christ-centered curriculum, its selected reading material would be compatible with Christian doctrine in concept and philosophy. Instead, one finds a wide assortment of works by SIECUS personnel, Humanists, Socialists, and other SIECUS allies such as:

- *Helene Arnstein* — a SIECUS-recommended author; former vice president and current board member of the Humanist-founded Child Study Association of America.
- *Isaac Asimov* — a Humanist.
- *Dorothy Baruch* — a SIECUS-recommended author.
- *Jessie Bernard* — a SIECUS board member.
- *Joseph and Lois Bird* — discussed earlier in this entry.
- *Henry Bowman* — a SIECUS-recommended author whose BAP-recommended book, *Marriage for Moderns*, was identified by a California State Legislature Joint Fact-Finding Committee as one of a group of books that "strike at the sanctity of marriage, at the family, and religion."
- *Evelyn Duvall* — a SIECUS director and former advisory board member of the Humanist-founded Child Study Association of America.
- *Erik Erikson* — a Humanist.
- *Erich Fromm* — a Humanist and member of both the Socialist Party and the left-wing, pro-abortion American Civil Liberties Union.
- *Dr. Haim G. Ginott* — a SIECUS-recommended author whose

ties to this organization are so close that he was guest speaker at SIECUS' Third Annual Dinner in New York on October 20, 1969.[42] Dr. Ginott was a member of the 1970 White House Conference on Children, in company with various SIECUS officials and Humanists. One of his books, *Parents: Freedom and Responsibility*, had Humanist Carl Rogers as co-author. Another, *Between Parent and Teenager*, which is in BAP's bibliography of recommended books, has this to say about masturbation — a practice that is severely frowned upon by the Catholic Church: "Masturbation is so self-centered: In splendid isolation, one need not please anyone but oneself. . . . Instantly, a teenager can have the world at the command of his fantasy. This illusion is no catastrophe. . . . Masturbation is helpful as a temporary escape from tension. But it can become an easy substitute for effort and exploration. . . . However, when a teenager's main satisfactions come from personal relationships and social commitments, self-gratification is not a problem, it is merely an additional solution."[43]

- *Henry Grunwald* — a SIECUS-recommended author and managing editor of *Time* magazine. Grunwald edited the BAP-recommended book *Sex in America*, which was listed as suggested reading for Humanists by the late Isadore Rubin in his "Humanist Bookshelf on Sex" in the Spring 1965 edition of *The Humanist* magazine. Some of the contributing authors to *Sex in America* are Humanists Mary Calderone, Lester Kirkendall, Rollo May, and Walter Stokes.

- *Richard Hettlinger* — whose BAP-recommended book, *Living with Sex: The Students' Dilemma,* was briefly covered earlier in this entry.

- Virginia Hilu — editor of the BAP-recommended *Sex Education and the Schools*, which peddles the propaganda of Humanist Dr. Mary Calderone; her former colleague at Planned Parenthood–World Population, Humanist Alan F. Guttmacher; and the Reverend Richard Unsworth, a member of the Planned Parenthood League of Massachusetts' board of directors, and consultant to the U.S. Office of Education. (Portions of this book were quoted in the entry for *National Association of Independent Schools* elsewhere in PART II.)

- *Warren Johnson* — a SIECUS director who also served on the advisory board of the American Association of Sex Educators and Counselors with Monsignor James McHugh. Johnson is author of SIECUS Study Guide No. 3, *Masturbation*, which presents affirmative arguments for the practice. His BAP-recommended 1963 edition of *Human Sex and Sex Education* is nearly unobtainable and is rapidly being replaced by a second edition (1968) titled *Human Sexual Behavior and Sex Education: Perspectives and Problems.* The latter is anti-religious, anti-Catholic, and generously garnished with explicit vivid descriptions of the male and female reproductive structures and their functions. Not surprisingly, the Johnson book's bibiliography contains a lengthy listing of works by Humanists and SIECUS directors.

- *Sidney M. Jourard* — former president of the American Association for Humanistic Psychology, wich was founded by Humanists and is promoted by the American Humanist Association.
- *Clifford Kirkpatrick* — A member of the National Council of the socialistic League for Industrial Democracy, whose membership encompasses a wide spectrum of individuals from the far Left: Communist-fronters, one-worlders, Humanists, American Civil Liberties Union members, pro-abortionists, and population control advocates.
- *Judson Landis* — a SIECUS-recmmended author.
- *Marc Oraison* — covered earlier in this entry.
- *Carl Rogers* — a Humanist who was instrumental in the development of sensitivity training. Interestingly, the BAP program bears nearly the same title as Rogers' book, *On Becoming a Person.*
- *John and Mary Perkins Ryan* — mentioned earlier in this entry.
- *Adrian Van Kaam* — founding sponsor of the American Association for Humanistic Psychology and editor of *Humanitas* magazine, mentioned in Chapter 3.
- *Clark Vincent* — a SIECUS board member.

In addition to the above influences, which make up a large part of the BAP teachers's bibliography, BAP's general bibliography for students at Intermediate and Primary Grade levels includes works by the following individuals:

- *Karl de Schweinitz* — whose book, *Growing Up,* promotes evolutionary concepts (for a review, see the entry for *American Academy of Pediatrics,* elsewhere in PART II).
- *Sidonie Gruenberg* — a Humanist, Communist-fronter, and member of the socialistic Public Affair Committee (Public Affairs Pamphlets). Two of Mrs. Gruenberg's books are recommended reading in the BAP bibliography; one of these is the SIECUS-recommended *Wonderful Story of How You Were Born,* which was briefly described in Chapter 4.

- *Jules Power* a SIECUS-recommended author and director of children's programming for ABC-TV. Powers' book, *How Life Begins*, was inspired by his award-winning program for children, *Discovery*, which was shown on ABC-TV some time ago. *How Life Begins* is written within a purely "clinical" framework and is completely devoid of any reference to God. Moreover, it is another in the long line of books gracing the sex education bibliographies which subtly propagate the message of evolution. For example, in portraying the story of reproduction, the author frequently lumps man together with mice, dogs, horses, and monkeys as just another mammal.

  Like other authors in the pro-evolution clique, Powers dutifully offers comparison drawings of fish, chicken, cow, and human embryos in their various stages of growth, making the expectable comment, "In the earliest stages of development, a human embryo looks very similar to that of a fish, a chicken, or a cow."[44] The drawings accompanying the text are skillfully done, so as to show almost no difference between human babies and animals in the first stage of development.

- *Earl Ubell* — a SIECUS director and Humanist.

The actual curriculum content and bibliography of the BAP program are a far cry from the high-sounding ideals uttered by the initiators and promoters of such courses. In New Jersey, for instance, a portion of the preamble of the *Guidelines for the Formation of a Program of Education in Human Sexuality*, approved by the five Bishops of that state, emphasizes that materials selected for use in Catholic sex education programs "should reflect a Christian view of man and the true values of life, morality and the family."[45]

This noble objective might be praiseworthy, were it not for the fact that the ecclesiastically approved BAP series is simply an expertly camouflaged SIECUS production. Fortunately, some church leaders are beginning to recognize its flaws and to take a stand against it. Two such leaders are John Joseph Cardinal Carberry of St. Louis and Bishop Walter P. Kellenberg of Long Island, who have both banned the BAP series from use in their dioceses. Realistically speaking, the church authorities who continue to sanction BAP's presence in Catholic schools either have not scrutinized its content sufficiently, have ignored its noxious assault on Catholic faith and morals, or have themselves succumbed to an unholy compromise with the deadly forces of humanistic naturalism that have shaped the BAP philosophy.

Life Education Program

Although the BAP series seems to be the current pet project among the USCC Family Life Division's approved programs, and by far the most widely used, other Catholic sex education curricula are scattered through the country. One, authored by Drs. James and Marie Fox, is known as *Life Education*, also commonly referred to as the Fox Program, its complete title being: *Pilot Program for Use in Elementary Schools — Life Education — A New Series of Correlated Lessons.*

While the Family Life Division does not as yet list *Life Education* as an officially approved program, Monsignor McHugh nevertheless stated that when he reviewed it several years ago he considered it a good program. Since then, *Life Education* has received the prestigious sanction of Archbishop Thomas A. Boland of the Newark Diocese.

That diocese initially utilized the series as an experimental program in a small group of schools in Newark. Then, in June 1973, Joseph F. Wagner, Inc., publishers of *Life Education*, disclosed that the Newark Diocese was increasing the number of schools using this curriculum, and that the diocese was purchasing the remainder of Wagner's supply of texts for its use.

The curriculum content of the *Life Education* series is so repugnant and so inappropriate for the age levels to which it is directed that it is only necessary to examine a few lesson plans at random to discover the program's utter worthlessness to any truly religious institution. As examples, consider just the following brief excerpts:

KINDERGARTEN, LESSONS 10 AND 11, "THE CHRISTMAS STORY" — "We all know that the baby Jesus was a boy baby and that He grew up to be a man, but after the little baby Jesus was born, how did the Blessed Mother *know* that He was a boy baby? Because, right after He was born, the Blessed Mother rocked Him in her arms and she looked at His body and she saw that He had the very special parts of His body that *all* little boys have — between his legs he had a scrotum and a penis."[46]

(This passage might more appropriately have been titled "The Humanization of Christ.")

GRADE TWO, LESSON 3, "PLAYING WITH THE PENIS OR VAGINA" — "Boys and girls notice when they touch the penis or vagina that it gives them a special pleasure. They may notice this when they wash themselves. Some children have the idea that something bad will happen to them after they have touched these parts. This is not so. You shouldn't play with your penis in the same way that you shouldn't play with your nose. You shouldn't put anything into your vagina just as you wouldn't put anything into your ear.

"If you find yourself touching your penis or vagina, do not be afraid and do not worry about it."

Life Education dwells on the subject of masturbation as early as Kindergarten and continues through Grade Eight, where such detailed descriptions as the following are given:

"For boys this [masturbation] usually means stimulating the penis with the hand or against a mattress. This creates sexual excitement until climax is reached and seminal fluid is projected from the penis. . . .

"For girls masturbation usually means stimulating the area between their legs by pressure against an object. Fondling of the breasts or nipples is another form of arousing excitement in themselves."

Portions of the remaining test are sympathetic in tone. One later passage points out only that masturbation is *biologically* (rather than *morally*) wrong.

GRADE FOUR, LESSON 3, "THE BABY CHICK" — "Show Creative Scope Slides 11 through 20 . . . . Creative Scope is a set of slides which are excellent, simple visual aids." (The reference is to the slides, *How Babies Are Made,* produced by Creative Scope. The consultant was SIECUS.)

GRADE SIX, LESSON 13, "RELIGION" — "You may be shocked that you were led to believe that Adam and Eve were the first man and woman. It is true that the bible has been around for hundreds of years and the story of Adam and Eve was very clearly told to generation after generation. For the last hundred years or so archeology and anthropology have been digging up evidence of prehistoric humans found in China, Java and Europe making it very difficult to believe that Adam and Eve were actually the first man and woman.

"But if we treat the story as a parable instead of as history, we will find in it rich insights into the relation between early man and God."

GRADE SEVEN, LESSON 17 — The subject for this lesson is the viewing of the film, *Human Reproduction,* which was made in consultation with Humanist Mary Calderone. Instructions to the teacher include the following: "Boys and girls should view the film together. Time should be left for a discussion and a question and answer period."

The *Life Education* program does further damage in that it:

- Encourages rebellious attitudes toward parents.
- Employs sensitivity training techniques to break down traditional attitudes.

- Promotes propaganda about overpopulation, coupled with a thorough coverage of artificial birth control methods.
- Includes a vocabulary of unnecessarily explicit sexual terms.

Among the books listed as suggested reading in the *Life Education* program are those in the following annotated list:

GROWING UP, by Karl de Schweinitz — reviewed later in PART II.

THE NAKED APE, by Desmond Morris — Totally devoid of Christian principles and ideals, this book's central theme is evolution. Moreover, Chapter 2, titled "Sex," is almost entirely hard-core pornography.

SUMMERHILL: A RADICAL APPROACH TO CHILD REARING, by A.S. Neill (now deceased)— This book's title, *Summerhill*, derives its name from a totally permissive school founded in 1921 in Suffolk, England, by atheist A.S. Neill, who became its headmaster. Students at Summerhill are considered to be equal with their teachers. The school is operated by a children's government in which the "bosses" are the children themselves.

Pupils are not required to attend classes and may be absent from lessons "for years if they want to." Conventional concepts such as authority, discipline, obedience, punishment, assignments, homework, and examinations are banned. The children are never reprimanded, and are given complete freedom to do whatever they like. Some educators admit that the current education fad, the "open classroom" approach, is to some extent a modification of the Summerhill prototype.

With regard to sex, Neill's book reflects a decidedly humanistic philosophy. He believes in total sexual freedom for children, adolescents, and adults. Included in the practices he sanctions are masturbation, the reading of smut by any child who is interested in it, and the parading of parents in the nude before their children. The author relates that he and several of his faculty members have been known to go bathing in the nude, in company with some of the older boys and girls, during evening visits to the seaside.[48]

So frankly humanistic is the Summerhill story that the inside cover of the book carries hearty endorsements from Humanists Carl Rogers and Ashley Montagu. There is also a foreword by Humanist Erich Fromm, who significantly observes:

> Summerhill School does not offer religious education. This, however, does not mean that Summerhill is not concerned with what might be loosely called the basic humanistic values. Neill puts it succinctly: "The battle is not between believers in theology and nonbelievers in theology; it is between believers in human freedom and believers in the suppression of human freedom."

Neill's callous contempt for Christian values is evident rather frequently in the book, in such iconoclastic statements as:

- "Religion to a child most always means only fear."[49]
- "The Bible says, 'The fear of the Lord is the beginning of wisdom.' It is much more often the beginning of psychic disorder."[50]
- "All too often, to be religious is to be joyless."[51]
- ". . . a heaven and a hell are infantile fantasies founded on nothing but human hopes and fears."[52]

After defining contemporary religion as "antagonism to natural life" and rejecting an identification with it, the hedonistic headmaster offers an alternative to the Christian way of life and all organized conventional religion, as follows:

> Some day a new generation will not accept the obsolete religion and myths of today. When the new religion comes, it will refute the idea of man's being born in sin. A new religion will praise God by making men happy. . . . Religion will find God on the meadows and not in the skies.[53]

After a reading of *Summerhill*, it staggers the mind to realize that the Catholic authors of *Life Education* have placed this book in the program's bibliography with the apparent intention of exposing teachers to its nihilistic, anti-religious philosophy.

THE WONDERFUL STORY OF HOW YOU WERE BORN, by Sidonie M. Gruenberg — reviewed earlier.

SEX EDUCATION AND THE NEW MORALITY — A SEARCH FOR A MEANINGFUL SOCIAL ETHIC, Proceedings of the 42nd Annual Conference of the Child Study Association of America, March 7, 1966, published by the Humanist-founded CSAA — Besides featuring the views of such speakers as Humanists Mary Calderone, Lester Kirkendall, Helen Southard, and Algernon Black, this conference presented a special award to Humanist and Communist-fronter Sidonie Gruenberg for her book, *The Wonderful Story of How You Were Born.*

In general, *Sex Education and the New Morality* makes a strong plea for the adoption of the new morality, while rejecting the moral absolutes of God's divine law. Its presence in a Catholic sex education program — or any program, for that matter — should be further questioned on the basis of such statements as the following:

> Certainly, we can anticipate that for a minority of young people greater freedom to indulge in sexual intercourse may have negative consequences on the personality. *But for a large majority of young people, development in contraceptive technology can provide an opportunity for healthy sexual freedom*, depending largely on the capacity of the larger society to make realistic adaptations.[47] (emphasis added)

To sum up, *Life Education* is a typical SIECUS-Humanist conglomeration of grossly explicit sex instruction, evolutionary doctrine, anti-parental attitudes, behavior modification, and sensitivity training, with a looming potential for rendering Catholic children more receptive and vulnerable to the favorite arguments of the contraception-abortion mentality.

Education in Love Program

A third sex education syllabus being used in Catholic schools is *Education in Love* (EIL), also known as the Rochester program. This text is an officially approved program of the USSC's Family Life Division, having been published (1971) by the Catholic publishing house, the Paulist Press.

The Paulist Press might well be described as the Beacon Press of the Catholic Church, inasmuch as it promulgates the writings of Humanists, leftists, and others of similar persuasion. Take as one example the Paulist Press's contemporary religious education program for teenagers titled *Discovery*, which is intended for use in Catholic high schools and Confraternity of Christian Doctrine (CCD) classes throughout the nation. Resource materials used in the composition of the "Discovery" program were written by many who have been in the forefront of the anti-Christian movement, such as Communist Pablo Picasso, Socialist Michael Harrington, black revolutionary Eldridge Cleaver, and existentialist Teilhard de Chardin, plus such known Humanists as Isaac Asimov, Albert Camus, John Dewey, Erik Erikson, Betty Friedan, Edgar Z. Friedenberg, Robert M. Hutchins, Aldous Huxley, Archibald MacLeish, Eugene McCarthy, Margaret Mead, Carl Rogers, Bertrand Russell, and others.[54]

The Paulist Press edition of *Education in Love* is an outgrowth of an original text published by the Diocese of Rochester's Committee on Sex Education, under the chairmanship of Dr. Gerard T. Guerinot, a member of the SIECUS-controlled American Association of Sex Educators and Counselors.

Although the *Education in Love* syllabus is seemingly written within a traditional Catholic framework and is laced with scriptural and theological references, its concealed message is essentially identical with that of the *Becoming a Person* and *Life Education* series. Such familiar SIECUS-generated approaches and techniques as sensitivity training, mind probing, delving into private family matters, explicit discussions of sexual intercourse, identification of man as a "sexual being," undermining of the Judeo-Christian sexual morality, stressing of humanistic naturalism, and a bibliography loaded with works by members and comrades of the Humanist-Socialist complex, are all to be found in this program. Despite all this, however, this program's introductory pages declare that the EIL syllabus is chiefly directed to "education in Christian sexual love,"[55] with the objective of inspiring students "to work for a society in which Christian attitudes toward sex and sexuality thrive."[56]

One particularly disturbing feature of this series is the bizarre attempt, in its "Theological Introduction," to fuse Freud with Christian theology, resulting in a nearly blasphemous assault on the divinity of the triune God. For instance, although the author of the introduction* states, "There is no sex act in God," he nevertheless refers to an intimate relationship within the Trinity that is comparable to with the sexual intimacy shared by husband and wife.

In suggesting an appropriate manner of leading children into a discussion of sex, the author tells the teacher:

> . . . this is where to begin, with the striking analogy between God's relational life in the Trinity and human sexuality.[57]

This analogy is extended to identify the act of human sexual intercourse, in which "the two become one flesh," with the "total communication existing continuously in the Trinity."[58] In a later reference to the above passage and its context, under "Notes for Teacher," the text offers the following bizarre analogy:

> To stress the sanctity of the union of sperm and ovum, the teacher may recall the analogy used in the Introduction [to the text], Jesus, the High Priest, and the priest at the altar at Mass unite their efforts to change bread and wine into the body and blood of Christ, extending Christ's redemptive act in time. So, too, the husband and wife collaborate with God the Father to transform ovum and sperm into a new human person, extending in time God's creative act.[59]

Among other passages in the EIL series that render it inconsistent with traditional Catholic doctrine are those concerned with abortion, contraception, homosexuality, and other similarly sensitive topics. In fact, certain areas of EIL's Elementary Teacher's Manual are so defective that they were recently censured in a pastoral letter by Bishop Floyd A. Begin of Oakland, California. Bishop Begin wrote, in part: "The following chapters entitled 'Understandings' in the teacher's manual (Nos. 21, 22, 23, 25, and 26) do not adequately emphasize the authentic moral teaching of the Church."[60] No. 21 deals with birth control; No. 22 with abortion; No. 23 with prostitution and promiscuity; and No. 25 with homosexuality. No. 26 explains necking, petting, "making out," and nudity — to eighth graders.

*The author of the "Theological Introduction" was Father John McLaughlin, S.J., who acted as consultant in the preparation of the Rochester program.

"Understanding 21" (for Grade Eight), gives thorough coverage of contraception at the same time it subtly introduces the child to a study of overpopulation problems. Although the teacher is reminded that the Church approves only the rhythm method as a means of birth control, the entire spectrum of unapproved contraceptive methods is also dealt with — condom, diaphragm, intrauterine loop, "the pill," and chemical creams, jellies, and foams.

"Understanding 22" is chiefly concerned with the matter of abortion. The text declares that both therapeutic and criminal abortions are forbidden by the Fifth Commandment. However, following a discussion of the various medically accepted reasons for performing therapeutic abortions, the text appears to equivocate by advising the teacher: "Care must be taken to respect the conscience of doctors who perform therapeutic abortions for what they consider to be valid reasons." Of course, there is no end to what may be considered "valid" reasons in today's terms, including one mentioned in the EIL text that is a favorite argument of the pro-abortionists — to prevent "severe emotional damage" to the mother.

Although the text acknowledges that the baby is a "distinct personality" from the time it is conceived, it makes no specific mention of the creation of a *soul* by God at the moment of conception. Instead, it equivocates again with such statements as this: "Theologians continue to discuss at what point the human soul exists and what conflict may exist between the rights of the mother and those of the child." Nor is any reference made to the fact that abortion is murder.

Interestingly, even as the EIL program is subjecting both teachers and students to this softening-up process, EIL's handbook for parents is warning:

> Because even an unborn infant is a person with the right to live, therapeutic and criminal abortions are both considered murder by the Church.[61]

Further study of the texts used in the *Education in Love* programs shows that the doctrine taught by the texts is shot through with the teachings of the notorious and heretical Dutch Catechism[62] and strongly influenced by the views of Marc Oraison, the censured French priest mentioned earlier. Another prevailing influence is Elmer Witt, whose pseudo-religious Freudian dissertations in the Lutheran Church's Concordia Sex Education Series have already been examined earlier in PART II. Besides being included in EIL's bibliography, Witt's irreverent literary work, *Life Can Be Sexual*, occupies a key position in the EIL program itself, having served as the sole basis for the "Final Thoughts" at the conclusion of the Grade Twelve syllabus.

Nor does it come as a surprise to discover that Humanist Isadore Rubin's major competing value systems table, though not identified as such, is included in the Grade Twelve text. It will be recalled that this table strategically places the Humanist philosophy at the halfway point between traditional Judeo-Christian morality and sexual anarchy, creating the illusion that Humanism is the safe, "middle-of-the-road" choice.

In addition to many of the same materials offered in the *Becoming a Person* and *Life Education* texts,* EIL's teacher's guide recommends for use of the teacher and/or students a number of additional books and visual aids that do nothing to honor or contribute to a genuine Catholic concept of morality or the family. They include those in the following annotated list:

- *Approaching Adulthood*, by Helen Southard (SIECUS official and Humanist) and Marion Lerrigo; consultant, Dr. Milton J. E. Senn, a Humanist and a SIECUS-recommended author.
- *Becoming a Person* program, by Rev. Walter J. Imbiorski and Frances Marzec.
- *Beyond Birth Control*, by Sidney Cornelia Callahan — a clear-cut defense of mechanical birth control. Known dissenters against the Encyclical *Humanae Vitae* (which denounces all forms of birth control except the rhythm method) who are also represented in EIL's recommended reading list include John Catoir, Rosemary Haughton, and José de Vinck.
- *A Curriculum Guide in Sex Education*, by SIECUS associate Helen Manley. (For a review of this program see entry for the *American Association for Health, Physical Education and Recreation* elsewhere in PART II.)
- *Encyclopedia of Mental Health* (six volumes), editor-in-chief, Communist-fronter Albert Deutsch.
- *The Journal of School Health*, Vol. 37, May 1967, published by the American School Health Association. This issue contains sex education guidelines developed in part by Humanists Joseph S. Darden and Evalyn Gendel of SIECUS. (See entry for *American School Health Association* elsewhere in PART II.)
- *The Jungle*, by veteran Communist-fronter Upton Sinclair.[63] Recommended by EIL for eighth graders, this book is a stinging attack on the American free-enterprise system. (In 1905 Sinclair

*Including such books as *The Freedom of Sexual Love*, by Joseph and Lois Bird, *Growing Up*, by Karl de Schweinitz, and *The Wonderful Story Of You*, by Benjamin and Sidonie M. Gruenberg; also the films *Boy to Man, Girl to Woman*, and *Human Reproduction*.

helped to found the Intercollegiate Socialist Society, whose first treasurer was Ethical Culturist Owen R. Lovejoy.)

- *Out of Wedlock*, by Leontine R. Young of SIECUS.
- *Psychology of Women*, by Helen Deutsch (two volumes). Dr. Deutsch is described in the *New York Times Book Review* as a "revolutionary" and "socialist."[64] The *Times* also made note of her attendance at the 1910 Socialist Congress in Stockholm, Sweden, and the fact that Dr. Deutsch was chiefly influenced in her early years by Sigmund Freud and Karl Marx. So well attuned to leftist philosophy is *Psychology of Women* that it was used extensively by Simone de Beauvoir as source material in the writing of her book, *The Second Sex*. (Miss de Beauvoir, the common-law wife of Marxist-Humanist Jean-Paul Sartre, is a militant atheist. Her Marxist leanings were described in an article in the *New York Times Magazine* of July 11, 1971.)
- *A Woman's Guide to the Methods of Postponing or Preventing Pregnancy*, published by Ortho Pharmaceutical Corporation.
- *The Game.* (See entry for *McGraw Hill, Inc.*, elsewhere in PART II, for review.)
- *Guidance Associates Family Life/Sex Education Program*, made up of four filmstrips: (1) *I Never Looked at It That Way Before*; (2) *Sex: A Moral Dilemma for Teenagers*; (3) *The Tuned-Out Generation*; and (4) *Values for Teenagers*.

    These Guidance Associates filmstrips have one feature in common: they all contribute toward the widening of an artificially created "generation gap." This is accomplished by repetition of the idea that many parental values should be subject to question and that parents have "tuned out" their children, frankly admitting that they are unable to communicate with them. The 1971 Guidance Associates catalog, describing *Values for Teenagers*, says that youth's confusion and bitterness is caused in part by "adult hypocrisy."

- *Human Growth*, by Lester F. Beck. The author acknowledges that the main purpose of this film is to transmit facts on human reproduction without subjecting students to ideas of "right" and "wrong." (See also entry for *E.C. Brown Trust Foundation*.)
- *Love and the Facts of Life*, by SIECUS director Evelyn Millis Duvall.
- *3M Transparencies* — for Grade Eight and upward. Grade Nine bibliography includes Transparency #4362, titled "Comparing and Contrasting the Structure of the Male and Female Reproduction System." On this transparency, one slide shows a drawing of

a nude female figure lying with one leg bent upward. A side view of the uterus, cervix, and vaginal canal is shown, with the note: "Vagina is the passage for penis to deposit sperm." The companion slide shows a drawing of a nude male figure, standing, with penis fully erect. The explanatory note on the transparency says: "Erection of penis makes sperm deposit possible." The two transparencies are to be matched in projection, in order to demonstrate how "sex organs complement each other." The result, of course, is a graphic depiction of penile penetration into the vagina, which might better be labeled "X-rated."

- *Phoebe.* (See entry for *McGraw Hill, Inc.,* elsewhere in PART II.)
- *Parent to Child About Sex*, produced by Wayne State University under the direction of SIECUS board member Frederick Margolis.

As has been shown by this discussion, *Education in Love* is essentially identical in design, approach, and character with other sex education programs, Catholic, Protestant, and secular, in that the material presented shows the pervasive effect of an expertly concealed SIECUS-Humanist influence. Like the others, it disturbs or destroys the serenity of the latency period, weakens the parent-child relationship, and skillfully reorients Catholic youth toward the position regularly advanced by the population control advocates. And it is certain that religiously educated children will suffer significantly more than their peers from the irreverent nature of the thoughts, fantasies, and feelings aroused in them by such instruction.

A diabolical aspect of the *Education in Love* series is that, like the Catholic *Becoming a Person* program, it was designed primarily for mixed classes, and for integrated use in the regular curriculum, from which there is little or no chance for the child to escape. Such usurpation of parental authority undermines the God-given right of parents to act as the sole educators of their children in such sensitive and delicate matters. James Likoudis explodes the hypocrisy of those behind this act of usurpation by saying:

> . . . it is ironical that the people who wish to impose sex education are the very people who in the name of Vatican II demand complete freedom in the realm of theology and dogma.[65]

But perhaps the most significant paradox to consider in the overall Catholic perspective is that the same priests, bishops, and nuns who loudly proclaim their opposition to abortion and population control are in fact reinforcing this sinister, atheistic movement by their consistent support of persons, organizations, and sex education programs that foster the very anti-life mentality that they so vigorously condemn.

Young Men's Christian Association of the U.S.A. and Young Women's Christian Association of the U.S.A. (YMCA, YWCA)

600 Lexington Avenue, New York, New York

Like the Child Study Association of America, the YWCA has been actively pressing for sex education since 1900. Since then, and with the gradual influx of secularism into its ranks and those of the YMCA, the two "Y's" have become just two more cogs in the socialist-Humanist wheel.

For example, veteran Communist-fronter Kirtley F. Mather labored in the highest echelons of the "Y" from 1948 through 1960, holding such positions as president of the YMCA's National Council, executive committee member of the World Alliance of YMCA's, and Alliance representative at the United Nations. (Mather is also affiliated with the American Civil Liberties Union, having been an official of the Civil Liberties Union of Massachusetts.) Another exemplar of secularism in the ranks of the "Y" is Louis Gomberg, who serves on the board of managers of the Golden Gate Branch of the YMCA in San Francisco. Gomberg is also a member of the board of directors and a former president of the American Humanist Association of San Francisco.[1]

Nor are the "Y's" without their own SIECUS influence. Such SIECUS personalities as Humanists Helen Southard* and Deryck Calderwood also play prominent roles in the organizations. Mrs. Southard is associate director of the national YWCA's bureau of research and Dr. Calderwood is a YMCA executive. Dr. Calderwood, it may be remembered, was the primary author of the X-rated Unitarian-Universalist Association sex education series, *About Your Sexuality*, which is currently being used in training programs for some "Y" leaders. The closeness of the link between SIECUS and the YWCA is further evidenced by the fact that the wife of the Rev. William Genné, a SIECUS director, is national vice president of the "Y."

---

*Formerly Helen Southard held the position of family life consultant to the national YWCA (1949–1960). Mrs. Southard writes monographs under her maiden name, Helen Fairbairn.

389

Also worthy of note is the fact that Laurance S. Rockefeller (brother of John D. Rockefeller III, a chief strategist of the world population control movement) is a former president and current member of the YWCA's board of trustees, the financial arm of the "Y."

Not surprisingly, the technique of sensitivity training has become a preoccupation of the "Y." Some 1200 YMCA secretaries had participated in sensitivity training groups by 1971.[2] Christian boys who are "Y" members have also been subjected to sensitivity training in recent years, with the result that many of them now doubt at least some of the tenets of their faith. Humanist William Schutz of Esalen Institute in Big Sur, California, for example, observed in the July 1968 issue of *Redbook* magazine:

> . . . When a Christian organization like the YMCA puts its boys through an encounter group to develop their independence, they may find some of the boys questioning Christian principles. These are not only possibilities; they happen. But they are necessary risks for individual development.[3]

Radical endeavors of the formerly traditionalist YWCA include forming coalitions for the purpose of public demonstrations with such controversial groups as the National Organization for Women (women's lib), the Black Panther Women, the Attica Brigade, World Federalists U.S.A., the Women's International League for Peace and Freedom, the American Civil Liberties Union, and various lesbian organizations.

Local YWCA programs are not without their share of internationalist orientation. Members are escorted on prearranged trips to the United Nations or urged to join and participate in the activities of the "Y's" World Fellowship Committee. The "Y" is further linked to the UN through Mrs. Richard Persinger, a member of both the YWCA National Board and the United Nations Association of the U.S.A. Both the World Young Women's Christian Association and the World Alliance of Young Men's Christian Associations are allied with the United Nations as "Non-Governmental Organizations with Consultative Status."

And finally, as may be recalled, the YWCA has further demonstrated its close alliance with the forces of secularism by its consistent support of such Humanist causes as the movement to legalize abortion. (For additional coverage of the YWCA's pro-abortion stance, see section headed "Familiar Friends of the Court" and elsewhere, in the entry for *National Association for Repeal of Abortion Laws*.)

Conclusion

Conclusion

> *For we wrestle not against flesh and blood, but against principalities, against powers, against the rulers of the darkness of this world, against spiritual wickedness in high places.*
> *Wherefore take unto you the whole armour of God, that ye may be able to withstand in the evil day; and having done all, to stand.*
>
> — Ephesians 6:12-13

The Humanist Revolution

THIS STUDY HAS BEEN AIMED primarily at exposing SIECUS as the nucleus of a larger, interlocking power structure of which sex education is the chief — but not the only — concern. The author earnestly hopes that this endeavor has unmasked the folly behind the thinking of those who contend that SIECUS and sex education are separable; the rationale that says, "We will structure our own program, one that suits the individual needs of our community, without using SIECUS materials." As we have seen, this rationale is incompatible with present-day reality.

But after exploring the wider periphery of the data presented in the total SIECUS story, the reader is by now aware of an ideological undercurrent of much greater magnitude and import than sex education *per se* — an international subversive movement whose aim is no less than world domination by way of the destruction of Christianity, traditional morality, and the whole fabric of society.

Judging by the evidence at hand, it seems reasonably certain that among the major components of this worldwide conspiracy are Humanism, Socialism, Communism, the Council on Foreign Relations, the tax-exempt foundations, and occultism. However, due to the covert nature of the movement, it is difficult to determine which one actually dominates the central core of operation. It is possible that yet another agency sits at the controls to direct them all; or perhaps the top echelons of the several arms of the conspiracy together compose the center of power. The least likely possibility is that each component operates independently of all the others, for it is impossible to witness the perilous events occurring about us without recognizing a related harmony of purpose.

Humanism has been stressed in these pages largely because of its close identification with such issues as sex education, pornography, homosexuality, drugs, ecology, euthanasia, abortion, and population control movements; and also, simply, because it is to date the least explored of the conspiratorial arms. But the possibility that Humanism is itself the eye of the whole conspiratorial movement, or is at least the actual "religion" of the inner circle of initiates, should not be totally disregarded.

In this connection, it cannot be overemphasized that Humanism's central thrust is directed at splitting asunder all hallowed tradition, uprooting the Christian ethic, and imposing what is essentially a minority "religion" on the rest of society. Humanism is therefore not a popular movement, as its supporters claim, but rather a coordinated scheme to establish a system of secular, so-called "ethical" values that are diametrically opposed to the noblest aspirations of the Judeo-Christian culture which undergirds this nation. Humanism is now engaged in a militant religious war, its Godless army having by now reached into almost every phase of our national existence: religion, education, the arts, government, labor, business, finance, and private agencies.

But perhaps its most significant impact has been felt in the communications media — the stage, movies, radio, television, the literary field, the press — which daily spread abroad their message of anti-religious hedonism via a dedicated minority of secularists who remain unidentified as such. Little known to the public is their most cunning tactic: the art of labeling and quoting each other as "experts" and thus conveying the impression that their nihilistic principles have been embraced by a wide majority of the people.

In trying to assess the chaotic condition of our country and find a solution for the problem it presents, Americans must first be willing to take a stand and defend the hallowed principles upon which our nation was founded. The lethal vapors of apathy that have engulfed America should be recognized as being just as deadly as the powers of darkness that would destroy our culture. We can no longer afford to be intimidated and neutralized into standing silently by while every spiritual value our forefathers fought and died for is ridiculed and trampled into the dust.

Every dedicated Christian can begin by renewing his own faith, and then work earnestly to restore an awareness and acknowledgment of the Creator to every aspect of our national and family life. For without God there can be no true order in society, no morality, no conscience. Civilizations survive only so long as they are stronger morally and spiritually than the forces that oppose them. We must live genuinely as "one nation under God" if we are to invoke His protection and divine mercy. As for our young people they are simply suffering from the fatigue, anxiety, and exhaustion that result from attempting to manage their own lives without the guidance of God or religion — a condition carefully nurtured by the Humanist cartel, and unfortunately ignored by many parents. The faith of youth, too, must be rekindled.

Secondly, in concert with the above step, every faithful American must work diligently to enable others to recognize members and allies of the Humanist-Socialist camp wherever they may be found. This can be done through an educated awareness of the atheistic principles they espouse and the programs and tactics by which they carry them out. Once the anti-God forces are identified, each lover of liberty must be prepared to follow through and unmask them publicly. This conspiracy can be destroyed by the spotlight of exposure, for, like all conspiracies, it can function with impunity only in the dim shadows of secrecy. Thread by thread, the Humanist web has been patiently woven around our laws, institutions, and national life. It must be unraveled to reveal the hidden spinner.

And finally, a coordinated effort must be made to rout the conspirators and their sympathizers from their positions of authority and public trust, and to replace them with men of high caliber, men of faith and integrity, who are willing to fight for the restoration of our God-given freedoms. Whether or not we are willing to recognize it as such, our present civilization is in the throes of a Humanist revolution by which Humanism is gaining the role of a state religion, and we are rapidly approaching the point at which we can no longer depend on our present government to protect us. As it was so aptly put by the magazine *Christianity Today* (February 16, 1973), after the sweeping decision of the U.S. Supreme Court that favored the Humanist-spearheaded abortion movement:

> . . . Christians should accustom themselves to the thought that the American state no longer supports, in any meaningful sense, the laws of God, and prepare themselves spiritually for the prospect that it may one day formally repudiate them and turn against those who seek to live by them.

The crisis we face is awesome to contemplate. That our beloved, once-Christian nation is now on a collision course with the Humanist-Socialist juggernaut is no longer a matter for speculation. It is imperative that the battle be fought *now*, while it can still be won. Indeed, as Americans and believers worthy of our forebears, we should stand against this onslaught gladly, and welcome it as the spiritual challenge of the century.

Beware lest any man spoil you through philosophy and vain deceit, after the tradition of men, after the rudiments of the world, and not after Christ.

— Colossians 2:8

Appendixes

SIECUS Board and Staff
— All known members, past and present

BOARD MEMBERS

Robert L. Arnstein, M. D.
Chief Psychiatrist
Department of University Health
Yale University
New Haven, Connecticut

George Auslander
Chairman of the Board
Valley National Bank
Valley Stream, New York

David Ausubel, M.D., Ph.D.
Professor of Psychology and
    Education
Ontario Institute for Studies
    in Education
Toronto, Canada

John C. Ballin, Ph.D.
Secretary, Committee on Maternal
    and Child Care
Assistant to Director, Div. of
    Scientific Activities
American Medical Association
Chicago, Illinois

**Father Robert C. Baumiller,
    S.J., Ph.D.**
Asst. Professor of Obstetrics
    and Gynecology
Georgetown University
Washington, D. C.

Alan P. Bell, Ph.D.
Senior Psychologist
Institute for Sex Research
Bloomington, Indiana

Jessie Bernard, Ph.D.
Research Professor, Honoris Causa
Pennsylvania State University
University Park, Pennsylvania

George Packer Berry, M.D.
Former Dean
Harvard Medical School
Boston, Massachusetts

Clark W. Blackburn
General Director
Family Service Association of
    America
New York, New York

Diane B. Brashear, M.S.W., Ph.D.
Assistant Professor of Social
    Service
Indiana-Purdue University
Indianapolis, Indiana

June Bricker, Ph.D.
Professor and Head of Department
Home Economics Extension
University of Maryland
College Park, Maryland

Carlfred Broderick, Ph.D.
Associate Professor
Department of Family Life
Pennsylvania State University
University Park, Pennsylvania

Marjory Brooks, Ph.D.
Dean, College of Home Economics
University of Maryland
College Park, Maryland

The Reverend Thomas E. Brown
Teaching Fellow, Psychology of
    Religion
Yale Divinity School
New Haven, Connecticut

Mary Bunting, Ph.D.
President, Radcliffe College
Boston, Massachusetts

John Gagnon
Senior Research Sociologist
Institute for Sex Research
Indiana University
Bloomington, Indiana

Evalyn S. Gendel, M. D.
Chief, School Health Section and
   Assistant Director
Division of Maternal and Child
   Health
Kansas State Dept. of Health
Topeka, Kansas

**Reverend William H. Genné,
   B.D., M.A.**
Director, Commission on Marriage
   and Family Life
National Council of Churches of
   Christ in the U.S.A.
New York, New York

Sadja Goldsmith, M.D., M.P.H.
Medical Director, Teenage Services
Planned Parenthood of San
   Francisco
San Francisco, California

Ketayun H. Gould, Ph.D.
Assistant Professor
The Jane Addams Graduate School of
   Social Work
University of Illinois
Urbana, Illinois

Georgia Neese Gray
President, Capitol City State Bank
Topeka, Kansas

Perry E. Gross, M.D.
Dallas, Texas

**Father George Hagmaier,
   C.S.P., Ed.D.**
Associate Director
Paulist Institute for Religious
   Research
New York, New York

Boone E. Hammond
Associate Professor of Individual
   and Family Studies
Pennsylvania State University
University Park, Pennsylvania

Reuben Hill, Ph.D.
Director and Professor of
   Sociology
Minnesota Family Study Center
Minneapolis, Minnesota

Joseph S. Himes, Ph.D.
Professor of Sociology
North Carolina College
Durham, North Carolina

John Holloman, M.D.
Practicing Physician
Former President, National Medical
   Association
New York, New York

Father Walter S. Imbiorski
Cana Conference
Chicago, Illinois

S. Leon Israel, M.D.
Professor of Obstetrics and
   Gynecology
University of Pennsylvania
   Medical School
Philadelphia, Pennsylvania

Marcus H. Jaffe
Editorial Director
Bantam Books, Inc.
New York, New York

Virginia Johnson
Reproductive Biology Research
   Foundation
St. Louis, Missouri

Warren R. Johnson, Ed.D.
Professor of Health Education
University of Maryland
College Park, Maryland

G. William Jones, M.Th., Ph.D.
Associate Professor of Film Art
Southern Methodist University
Dallas, Texas

Richard W. Kay, M.Ed.
Director, Dept. of Community
   Services
Grosse Pointe Public School
   System
Grosse Pointe, Michigan

Luigi Mastroianni, Jr., M.D.
Professor and Chairman, Department
  Obstetrics and Gynecology
Hospital of University of Penna.
Philadelphia, Pennsylvania

Jane R. Mayer
President, Marriage Council and
  Family Guidance, Inc.
New York, New York

**Cyrus Mayshark, H.S.D., M.Ed.,
  M.S.Hyg.**
Associate Dean
College of Education
University of Tennessee
Knoxville, Tennessee

James L. McCary, Ph.D.
Clinical Psychologist and
  Family Counselor
Houston, Texas

The Rev. Robert H. Meneilly, D.D.
Director-Minister
United Presbyterian Church
Prairie Village, Kansas

Roy W. Menninger, M.D.
President, The Menninger
  Foundation
Topeka, Kansas

Catherine Milton
Assistant Director
Police Foundation
Washington, D.C.

John Money, Ph.D.
Associate Professor of Medical
  Psychology and Pediatrics
Johns Hopkins University
Baltimore, Maryland

W. Ray Montgomery
President, Realty Trust Company
Dallas, Texas

Dean Morrison
President, Morrison Homes, Inc.
Piedmont, California

J. Robert Moskin
Editor and Writer
World magazine
New York, New York

Emily Mudd, Ph.D.
Professor of Family Study in
  Psychiatry
University of Pennsylvania Medical
  School
Philadelphia, Pennsylvania

John W. Mudd, M.D.
Columbia University
College of Physicians & Surgeons
New York, New York

Richard A. Myren, LL.B.
Dean, School of Criminal Justice
State University of New York
Albany, New York

Moni Nag, Ph.D.
Associate Professor
Dept. of Anthropology
Columbia University
New York, New York

Ethel Nash, M.A.
Asst. Professor of Preventive
  Medicine
Associate in Obstetrics and
  Gynecology
Bowman Gray School of Medicine
Winston-Salem, North Carolina

Jerome Nathanson
Leader, New York Society for Ethical
  Culture
New York, New York

William L. Peltz, M.D.
Professor of Clinical Psychiatry
University of Pennsylvania
Philadelphia, Pennsylvania

James Peterson, Ph.D.
Chairman, Dept. of Sociology and
  Anthropology
University of Southern California
Los Angeles, California

Harriet F. Pilpel, LL.B.
Senior Partner
Law firm
New York, New York

Wardell Pomeroy, Ph.D.
Private Practice of Psychotherapy
  and Marriage Counseling
New York, New York

Father John L. Thomas, S.J., Ph.D.
Cambridge Center for Social Studies
Cambridge, Massachusetts

Wilhelmina B. Thomas, M.A.
Principal, Walker-Jones Elementary School
Washington, D. C.

Patricia Thompson
Program Director
Monroe County Bar Association
Pre-Trial Release Program, Inc.
Rochester, New York

Harvey J. Tompkins, M.D.
Director, Dept. of Psychiatry
St. Vincent's Hospital and Medical Center of New York
New York, New York

Earl Ubell
Science Editor, WCBS-TV News
New York, New York

Paul Vahanian, Ed.D.
Associate Professor of Education
Teachers College
Columbia University
New York, New York

Robert M. Veatch, Ph.D.
Associate for Medical Ethics

The Institute of Society, Ethics and the Life Sciences
Hastings-on-Hudson, New York

Joseph Van Vleck, Jr., Ph.D.
Visiting Professor of Sociology
Hampton Institute
Hampton, Virginia

Clark Vincent, Ph.D.
Director, Behaviorial Science Center
Bowman School of Medicine
Winston-Salem, North Carolina

Bennetta B. Washington, Ph.D.
Director, Women's Center Job Corps
Washington, D.C.

Sally Robinson Williams, R.N., M.A.
Coordinator, Family Life & Sex Education
Anaheim School District
Anaheim, California

Leontine R. Young, D.S.W.
Executive Director
Child Service Association
Newark, New Jersey

Note: Listed affiliation of each SIECUS director is that shown on SIECUS publication at the time of appointment

STAFF MEMBERS

Mary S. Calderone, M.D., M.P.H., Executive Director

Frederick E. Bidgood, M.A.,
Education and Research Associate

Miss Frances Breed,
Associate Director, Community Services

Jean Bruce
Publications Assistant

Derek L. Burleson, Ed.D.
Director of Educational and Research Services

Mrs. Lorna Flynn
Distributive Officer
Sales and Distribution

Mrs. Muriel Glasser
Publications Officer

Mrs. Esther Gold
Administrative Assistant

Miss Leanore Greenbaum
Administrative Officer

Miss Constance Kelly
Development Consultant

Miss Sally Lydgate
Public Information Officer

Mrs. Frances O'Brien
Director of Development

Agnes Pilgrim
Administrative Assistant

Mary Ratcliffe
Administrative Officer

Sol Reich
Director of Development

Victoria Sanborn, M.A.
Publications Officer

Gerald Sanctuary
Executive Director

Esther D. Schulz, Ph.D.
Associate Director

Mr. Benjamin Sherman
Executive Officer

Mrs. Jennifer Sonsini
Publications Assistant

Mr. Rawn Spearman
Associate Director

APPENDIX B

Humanist Manifesto (1933)

Published in *The New Humanist,* May/June 1933

THE TIME has come for widespread recognition of the radical changes in religious beliefs throughout the modern world. The time is past for mere revision of traditional attitudes. Science and economic change have disrupted the old beliefs. Religions the world over are under the necessity of coming to terms with new conditions created by a vastly increased knowledge and experience. In every field of human activity, the vital movement is now in the direction of a candid and explicit humanism. In order that religious humanism may be better understood we, the undersigned, desire to make certain affirmations which we believe the facts of our contemporary life demonstrate.

There is great danger of a final, and we believe fatal, identification of the word *religion* with doctrines and methods which have lost their significance and which are powerless to solve the problem of human living in the Twentieth Century. Religions have always been means for realizing the highest values of life. Their end has been accomplished through the interpretation of the total environing situation (theology or world view) the sense of values resulting therefrom (goal or ideal), and the technique (cult), established for realizing the satisfactory life. A change in any of these factors results in alteration of the outward forms of religion. This fact explains the changefulness of religions through the centuries. But through all changes religion itself remains constant in its quest for abiding values, an inseparable feature of human life.

Today man's larger understanding of the universe, his scientific achievements, and his deeper appreciation of brotherhood, have created a situation which requires a new statement of the means and purposes of religion. Such a vital, fearless, and frank religion capable of furnishing adequate social goals and personal satisfactions may appear to many people as a complete break with the past. While this age does owe a vast debt to the traditional religions, it is none the less obvious that any religion that can hope to be a synthesizing and dynamic force for today must be shaped for the needs of this age. To establish such a religion is a major necessity of the present. It is a responsibility which rests upon this generation. We therefore affirm the following:

First: Religious humanists regard the universe as self-existing and not created.

Second: Humanism believes that man is a part of nature and that he has emerged as the result of a continuous process.

Third: Holding an organic view of life, humanists find that the traditional dualism of mind and body must be rejected.

Fourth: Humanism recognizes that man's religious culture and civilization, as clearly depicted by anthropology and history, are the product of a gradual development due to his interaction with his natural environment and with his social heritage. The individual born into a particular culture is largely molded to that culture.

Fifth: Humanism asserts that the nature of the universe depicted by modern science makes unacceptable any supernatural or cosmic guarantees of human values. Obviously humanism does not deny the possibility of realities as yet undiscovered, but it does insist that the way to determine the existence and value of any and all realities is by means of intelligent inquiry and by the assessment of their relation to human needs. Religion must formulate its hopes and plans in the light of the scientific spirit and method.

Sixth: We are convinced that the time has passed for theism, deism, modernism, and the several varieties of "new thought."

Seventh: Religion consists of those actions, purposes, and experiences which are humanly significant. Nothing human is alien to the religious. It includes labor, art, science, philosophy, love, friendship, recreation — all that is in its degree expressive of intelligently satisfying human living. The distinction between the sacred and the secular can no longer be maintained.

Eighth: Religious humanism considers the complete realization of human personality to be the end of man's life and seeks its development and fulfillment in the here and now. This is the explanation of the humanist's social passion.

Ninth: In place of the old attitudes involved in worship and prayer the humanist finds his religious emotions expressed in a heightened sense of personal life and in a cooperative effort to promote social well-being.

Tenth: It follows that there will be no uniquely religious emotions and attitudes of the kind hitherto associated with belief in the supernatural.

Eleventh: Man will learn to face the crises of life in terms of his knowledge of their naturalness and probability. Reasonable and manly attitudes will be fostered by education and supported by custom. We assume that humanism will take the path of social and mental hygiene and discourage sentimental and unreal hopes and wishful thinking.

Twelfth: Believing that religion must work increasingly for joy in living, religious humanists aim to foster the creative in man and to encourage achievements that add to the satisfactions of life.

Thirteenth: Religious humanism maintains that all associations and institutions exist for the fulfillment of human life. The intelligent evaluation, transformation, control, and direction of such associations and institutions with a view to the enhancement of human life is the purpose and program of humanism. Certainly religious institutions, their ritualistic forms, ecclesiastical methods, and communal activities must be reconstituted as rapidly as experience allows, in order to function effectively in the modern world.

Fourteenth: The humanists are firmly convinced that existing acquisitive and profit-motivated society has shown itself to be inadequate and that a radical change in methods, controls, and motives must be instituted. A social and cooperative economic order must be established to the end that the equitable distribution of the means of life be possible. The goal of humanism is a free and universal society in which people voluntarily and intelligently cooperate for the common good. Humanists demand a shared life in a shared world.

Fifteenth and last: We assert that humanism will: (a) affirm life rather than deny it; (b) seek to elicit the possibilities of life, not flee from it; and (c) endeavor to establish the conditions of a satisfactory life for all, not merely for the few. By this positive *morale* and intention humanism will be guided, and from this perspective and alignment the techniques and efforts of humanism will flow.

So stand the theses of religious humanism. Though we consider the religious forms and ideas of our fathers no longer adequate, the quest for the good life is still the central task for mankind. Man is at last becoming aware that he alone is responsible for the realization of the world of his dreams, that he has within himself the power for its achievement. He must set intelligence and will to the task.

(Signed)

J. A. C. Fagginer Auer
E. Burdette Backus
Harry Elmer Barnes
L. M. Birkhead
Raymond B. Bragg
Edwin Arthur Burtt
Ernest Caldecott
A. J. Carlson
John Dewey
Albert C. Dieffenbach
John H. Dietrich
Bernard Fantus
William Floyd
F. H. Hankins
A. Eustace Haydon
Llewellyn Jones
Robert Morss Lovett

Harold P. Marley
R. Lester Mondale
Charles Francis Potter
John Herman Randall, Jr.
Curtis W. Reese
Oliver L. Reiser
Roy Wood Sellars
Clinton Lee Scott
Maynard Shipley
W. Frank Swift
V. T. Thayer
Eldred C. Vanderlaan
Joseph Walker
Jacob J. Weinstein
Frank S. C. Wicks
David Rhys Williams
Edwin H. Wilson

Humanist Manifesto II (1973)

Published in *The Humanist*, September–October 1973

Preface

It is forty years since *Humanist Manifesto I* (1933) appeared. Events since then make that earlier statement seem far too optimistic. Nazism has shown the depths of brutality of which humanity is capable. Other totalitarian regimes have suppressed human rights without ending poverty. Science has sometimes brought evil as well as good. Recent decades have shown that inhuman wars can be made in the name of peace. The beginnings of police states, even in democratic societies, widespread government espionage, and other abuses of power by military, political, and industrial elites, and the continuance of unyielding racism, all present a different and difficult social outlook. In various societies, the demands of women and minority groups for equal rights effectively challenge our generation.

As we approach the twenty-first century, however, an affirmative and hopeful vision is needed. Faith, commensurate with advancing knowledge, is also necessary. In the choice between despair and hope, humanists respond in this *Humanist Manifesto II* with a positive declaration for times of uncertainty.

As in 1933, humanists still believe that traditional theism, especially faith in the prayer-hearing God, assumed to love and care for persons, to hear and understand their prayers and to be able to do something about them, is an unproven and outmoded faith. Salvationism, based on mere affirmation, still appears as harmful, diverting people with false hopes of heaven hereafter. Reasonable minds look to other means for survival.

Those who sign *Humanist Manifesto II* disclaim that they are setting forth a binding credo; their individual views would be stated in widely varying ways. This statement is, however reaching for vision in a time that needs direction. It is social analysis in an effort at consensus. New statements should be developed to supersede this, but for today it is our conviction that humanism offers an alternative that can serve present-day needs and guide humankind toward the future.

Paul Kurtz, Editor, *The Humanist*

Edwin H. Wilson, Editor Emeritus, *The Humanist*

*   *   *

The next century can be and should be the humanistic century. Dramatic scientific, technological, and ever-accelerating social and political changes crowd our awareness. We have virtually conquered the planet, explored the moon, overcome the natural limits of travel and communication; we stand at the dawn of a new age, ready to move farther into space and perhaps inhabit other planets. Using technology wisely, we can control our environment, conquer poverty, markedly reduce disease, extend our life-span, significantly modify our behavior, alter the course of human evolution and cultural development, unlock vast new powers, and provide humankind with unparalleled opportunity for achieving an abundant and meaningful life.

The future is, however, filled with dangers. In learning to apply the scientific method to nature and human life, we have opened the door to ecological damage, overpopulation, dehumanizing institutions, totalitarian repression, and nuclear and biochemical disaster. Faced with apocalyptic prophesies and doomsday scenarios, many flee in despair from reason and embrace irrational cults and theologies of withdrawal and retreat.

Traditional moral codes and newer irrational cults both fail to meet the pressing needs of today and tomorrow. False "theologies of hope" and messianic ideologies, substituting new dogmas for old, cannot cope with existing world realities. They separate rather than unite peoples.

Humanity, to survive, requires bold and daring measures. We need to extend the uses of scientific method, not renounce them, to fuse reason with compassion in order to build constructive social and moral values. Confronted by many possible futures, we must decide which to pursue. The ultimate goal should be the fulfillment of the potential for growth in each human personality — not for the favored few, but for all of humankind. Only a shared world and global measures will suffice.

A humanist outlook will tap the creativity of each human being and provide the vision and courage for us to work together. This outlook emphasizes the role human beings can play in their own spheres of action. The decades ahead call for dedicated, clear-minded men and women able to marshal the will, intelligence, and cooperative skills for shaping a desirable future. Humanism can provide the purpose and inspiration that so many seek; it can give personal meaning and significance to human life.

Many kinds of humanism exist in the contemporary world. The varieties and emphases of naturalistic humanism include "scientific," "ethical," "democratic," "religious," and "Marxist" humanism. Free thought, atheism, agnosticism, skepticism, deism, rationalism, ethical culture, and liberal religion all claim to be heir to the humanist tradition. Humanism traces its roots from ancient China, classical Greece and Rome, through the Renaissance and the Enlightenment, to the scientific revolution of the modern world. But views that merely reject theism are not equivalent to humanism. They lack commitment to the positive belief in the possibilities of human progress and to the values central to it. Many within religious groups, believing in the future of humanism, now claim humanist credentials. Humanism is an ethical process through which we all can move, above and beyond the divisive particulars, heroic personalities, dogmatic creeds, and ritual customs of past religions or their mere negation.

We affirm a set of common principles that cam serve as a basis for united action — positive principles relevant to the present human condition. They are a design for a secular society on a planetary scale. [Emphasis added.]

For these reasons, we submit this new *Humanist Manifesto* for the future of humankind; for us, it is a vision of hope, a direction for satisfying survival.

Religion

First: In the best sense, religion may inspire dedication to the highest ethical ideals. The cultivation of moral devotion and creative imagination is an expression of genuine "spiritual" experience and aspiration.

We believe, however, that traditional dogmatic or authoritarian religions that place revelation, God, ritual, or creed above human needs and experience do a disservice to the human species. Any account of nature should pass the tests of scientific evidence; in our judgment, the dogmas and myths of traditional religions do not do so. Even at this late date in human history, certain elementary facts based upon the critical use of scientific reason have to be restated. We find insufficient evidence for belief in the existence of a supernatural; it is either meaningless or irrelevant to the question of the survival and fulfillment of the human race. As non-theists, we begin with humans not God, nature not deity. Nature may indeed be broader and deeper than we now know; any new discoveries, however, will but enlarge our knowledge of the natural.

Some humanists believe we should reinterpret traditional religions and reinvest them with meanings appropriate to the current situation. Such redefinitions, however, often perpetuate old dependencies and escapisms; they easily become obscurantist, impeding the free use of the intellect. We need, instead, radically new human purposes and goals.

We appreciate the need to preserve the best ethical teachings in the religious traditions of humankind, many of which we share in common. But we reject those features of traditional religious morality that deny humans a full appreciation of their own potentialities and responsibilities. Traditional religions often offer solace to humans, but, as often, they inhibit humans from helping themselves or experiencing their full potentialities. Such institutions, creeds, and rituals often impede the will to serve others. Too often traditional faiths encourage dependence rather than independence, obedience rather than affirmation, fear rather than courage. More recently they have generated concerned social action, with many signs of relevance appearing in the wake of the "God Is Dead" theologies. But we can discover no divine purpose or providence for the human species. While there is much that we do not know, humans are responsible for what we are or will become. No deity will save us; we must save ourselves.

Second: Promises of immortal salvation or fear of eternal damnation are both illusory and harmful. They distract humans from present concerns, from self-actualization, and from rectifying social injustices. Modern science discredits such historic concepts as the "ghost in the machine" and the "separable soul." Rather, science affirms that the human species is an emergence from natural evolutionary forces. As far as we know, the total personality is a function of the biological organism transacting in a social and cultural context. There is no credible evidence that life survives the death of the body. We continue to exist in our progeny and in the way that our lives have influenced others in our culture.

Traditional religions are surely not the only obstacles to human progress. Other ideologies also impede human advance. Some forms of political doctrine, for instance, function religiously, reflecting the worst features of orthodoxy and authoritarianism, especially when they sacrifice individuals on the altar of Utopian promises. Purely economic and political viewpoints, whether capitalist or communist, often function as religious and ideological dogma. Although humans undoubtedly need economic and political goals, they aleo need creative values by which to live.

Ethics

Third: We affirm that moral values derive their source from human experience. Ethics is *autonomous* and *situational,* needing no theological or ideological sanction. Ethics stems from human need and interest. To deny this distorts the whole basis of life. Human life has meaning because we create and develop our futures. Happiness and the creative realization of human needs and desires, individually and in shared enjoyment, are continuous themes of humanism. We strive for the good life, here and now. The goal is to pursue life's enrichment despite debasing forces of vulgarization, commercialization, bureaucratization, and dehumanization.

Fourth: Reason and intelligence are the most effective instruments that humankind possesses. There is no substitute; neither faith nor passion suffices in itself. The controlled use of scientific methods, which have transformed the natural and social sciences since the Renaissance, must be extended further in the solution of human problems. But reason must be tempered by humility, since no group has a monopoly of wisdom or virtue. Nor is there any guarantee that all problems can be solved or all questions answered. Yet critical intelligence, infused by a sense of human caring, is the best method that humanity has for resolving problems. Reason should be balanced with compassion and empathy and the whole person fulfilled. Thus, we are not advocating the use of scientific intelligence independent of or in opposition to emotion, for we believe in the cultivation of feeling and love. As science pushes back the boundary of the known, man's sense of wonder is continually renewed, and art, poetry, and music find their places, along with religion and ethics.

The Individual

Fifth: The preciousness and dignity of the individual person is a central humanist value. Individuals should be encouraged to realize their own creative talents and desires. We reject all religious, ideological, or moral codes that denigrate the individual, suppress freedom, dull intellect, dehumanize personality. We believe in maximum individual autonomy consonant with social responsibility. Although science can account for the causes of behavior, the possibilities of individual *freedom* of choice exist in human life and should be increased.

Sixth: In the area of sexuality, we believe that intolerant attitudes, often cultivated by orthodox religions and puritanical cultures, unduly repress sexual conduct. The right to birth control, abortion, and divorce should be recognized. While we do not approve of exploitive, denigrating forms of sexual expression, neither do we wish to prohibit, by law or social sanction, sexual behavior between consenting adults. The many varieties of sexual exploration should not in themselves be considered "evil." Without countenancing mindless permissiveness or unbridled promiscuity, a civilized society should be a *tolerant* one. Short of harming others or compelling them to do likewise, individuals should be permitted to express their sexual proclivities and pursue their life-styles as they desire. We wish to cultivate the development of a responsible attitude toward sexuality, in which humans are not exploited as sexual objects, and in which intimacy, sensitivity, respect, and honesty in interpersonal relations are encouraged. Moral education for children and adults is an important way of developing awareness and sexual maturity.

Democratic Society

Seventh: To enhance freedom and dignity the individual must experience a full range of *civil liberties* in all societies. This includes freedom of speech and the press, political democracy, the legal right of opposition to governmental policies, fair judicial process, religious liberty, freedom of association, and artistic, scientific, and cultural freedom. It also includes a recognition of an individual's right to die with dignity, euthanasia, and the right to suicide. We oppose the increasing invasion of privacy, by whatever means, in both totalitarian and democratic societies. We would safeguard, extend, and implement the principles of human freedom evolved from the *Magna Carta* to the *Bill of Rights,* the *Rights of Man,* and the *Universal Declaration of Human Rights.*

Eighth: We are committed to an open and democratic society. We must extend *participatory democracy* in its true sense to the economy, the school, the family, the workplace, and voluntary associations. Decision-making must be decentralized to include widespread involvement of people at all levels—social, political, and economic. All persons should have a voice in developing the values and goals that determine their lives. Institutions should be responsive to expressed desires and needs. The conditions of work, education, devotion, and play should be humanized. Alienating forces should be modified or eradicated and bureaucratic structures should be held to a minimum. People are more important than decalogues, rules, proscriptions, or regulations.

Ninth: The separation of church and state and the separation of ideology and state are imperatives. The state should encourage maximum freedom for different moral, political, religious, and social values in society. It should not favor any particular religious bodies through the use of public monies, nor espouse a single ideology and function thereby as an instrument of propaganda or oppression, particularly against dissenters.

Tenth: Humane societies should evaluate economic systems not by rhetoric or ideology, but by whether or not they *increase economic well-being* for all individuals and groups, minimize poverty and hardship, increase the sum of human satisfaction, and enhance the quality of life. Hence the door is open to alternative economic systems. We need to democratize the economy and judge it by its responsiveness to human needs, testing results in terms of the common good.

Eleventh: The principle of moral equality must be furthered through elimination of all discrimination based upon race, religion, sex, age, or national origin. This means equality of opportunity and recognition of talent and merit. Individuals should be encouraged to contribute to their own betterment. If unable, then society should provide means to satisfy their basic economic, health, and cultural needs, including, wherever resources make possible, a minimum guaranteed annual income. We are concerned for the welfare of the aged, the infirm, the disadvantaged, and also for the outcasts — the mentally retarded, abandoned or abused children, the handicapped, prisoners, and addicts — for *all* who are neglected or ignored by society. Practicing humanists should make it their vocation to humanize personal relations.

We believe in the *right to universal education.* Everyone has a right to the cultural opportunity to fulfill his or her unique capacities and talents. The schools should foster satisfying and productive living. They should be open at all levels to any and all; the achievement of excellence should be encouraged. Innovative and experimental forms of education are to be welcomed. The energy and idealism of the young deserve to be appreciated and channeled to constructive purposes.

We deplore racial, religious, ethnic, or class antagonisms. Although we believe in cultural diversity and encourage racial and ethnic pride, we reject separations which promote alienation and set people and groups against each other: we envision an *integrated* community where people have a maximum opportunity for free and voluntary association.

We are *critical of sexism or sexual chauvinism* — male or female. We believe in equal rights for both women and men to fulfill their unique careers and potentialities as they see fit, free of invidious discrimination.

World Community

Twelfth: We deplore the division of humankind on nationalistic grounds. We have reached a turning point in human history where the best option is to *transcend the limits of national sovereignty* and to move toward the building of a world community in which all sectors of the human family can participate. Thus we look to the development of a system of world law and a world order based upon transnational federal government. This would appreciate cultural pluralism and diversity. It would not exclude pride in national origins and accomplishments nor the handling of regional problems on a regional basis. Human progress, however, can no longer be achieved by focusing on one section of the world, Western or Eastern, developed or underdeveloped. For the first time in human history, no part of humankind can be isolated from any other. Each person's future is in some way linked to all. We thus reaffirm a commitment to the building of a world community, at the same time recognizing that this commits us to some hard choices.

Thirteenth: This world community must *renounce the resort to violence and force* as a method of solving international disputes. We believe in the peaceful adjudication of differences by international courts and by the development of the arts of negotiation and compromise. War is obsolete. So is the use of nuclear, biological, and chemical weapons. It is a planetary imperative to reduce the level of military expenditures and turn these savings to peaceful and people-oriented uses.

Fourteenth: The world community must engage in *cooperative planning* concerning the use of rapidly depleting resources. The planet earth must be considered a single *ecosystem*. Ecological damage, resource depletion, and excessive population growth must be checked by international concord. The cultivation and conservation of nature is a moral value; we should perceive ourselves as integral to the sources of our being in nature. We must free our world from needless pollution and waste, responsibly guarding and creating wealth, both natural and human. Exploitation of natural resources, uncurbed by social conscience, must end.

Fifteenth: The problems of *economic growth and development* can no longer be resolved by one nation alone; they are worldwide in scope. It is the moral obligation of the developed nations to provide — through and international authority that safeguards human rights — massive technical, agricultural, medical and economic assistance, including birth control techniques, to the developing portions of the globe. World poverty must cease. Hence extreme disproportions in wealth, income, and economic growth should be reduced on a worldwide basis.

Sixteenth: Technology is a vital key to human progress and development. We deplore any neo-romantic efforts to condemn indiscriminately all technology and science or to counsel retreat from its further extension and use for the good of humankind. We would resist any moves to censor basic scientific research on moral, political, or social grounds. Technology must, however, be carefully judged by the consequences of its use; harmful and destructive changes should be avoided. We are particularly disturbed when technology and bureaucracy control, manipulate, or modify human beings without their consent. Technological feasibility does not imply social or cultural desirability.

Seventeenth: We must expand communication and transportation across frontiers. Travel restrictions must cease. The world must be open to diverse political, ideological, and moral viewpoints and evolve a worldwide system of television and radio for information and education. We thus call for full international cooperation in culture, science, the arts, and technology *across ideological borders*. We must learn to live openly together or we shall perish together.

In closing: The world cannot wait for a reconciliation of competing political or economic systems to solve its problems. These are the times for men and women of good will to further the building of a peaceful and prosperous world. We urge that parochial loyalties and inflexible moral and religious ideologies be transcended. We urge recognition of the common humanity of all people. We further urge the use of reason and compassion to produce the kind of world we want — a world in which peace, prosperity, freedom, and happiness are widely shared. Let us not abandon that vision in despair or cowardice. We are responsible for what we are or will be. Let us work together for a humane world by means commensurate with humane ends. Destructive ideological differences among communism, capitalism, socialism, conservatism, liberalism, and radicalism should be overcome. Let us call for an end to terror and hatred. We will survive and prosper only in a world of shared humane values. We can initiate new directions for humankind; ancient rivalries can be superseded by broad-based cooperative efforts. The commitment to tolerance, understanding, and peaceful negotiation does not necessitate acquiescence to the status quo nor the damming up of dynamic and revolutionary forces. The true revolution is occurring and can continue in countless non-violent adjustments. But this entails the willingness to step forward onto new and expanding plateaus. At the present juncture of history, commitment to all humankind is the highest commitment of which we are capable; it transcends the narrow allegiances of church, state, party, class, or race in moving toward a wider vision of human potentiality. What more daring a goal for humankind than for each person to become, in ideal as well as practice, a citizen of a world community. It is a classical vision; we can now give it new vitality. Humanism thus interpreted is a moral force that has time on its side. We believe that humankind has the potential intelligence, good will, and cooperative skill to implement this commitment in the decades ahead.

*   *   *

We, the undersigned, while not necessarily endorsing every detail of the above, pledge our general support to *Humanist Manifesto II* for the future of humankind. These affirmations are not a final credo or dogma but an expression of a living and growing faith. We invite others in all lands to join us in further developing and working for these goals.

Lionel Abel
Professor of English, State University of New York at Buffalo

Khoren Arisian
Board of Leaders, New York Society for Ethical Culture

Isaac Asimov
Author

George Axtelle
Professor Emeritus, Southern Illinois University

Archie J. Bahm
Professor of Philosophy Emeritus, University of New Mexico

Paul H. Beattie
President, Fellowship of Religious Humanists

Keith Beggs
Executive Director, American Humanist Association

Malcolm Bissell
Professor Emeritus, University of Southern California

H. J. Blackham
Chairman, Social Morality Council, Great Britain

Brand Blanshard
Professor Emeritus, Yale University

Paul Blanshard
Author

Joseph L. Blau
Professor of Religion, Columbia University

Sir Hermann Bondi
Professor of Mathematics, King's College, University of London

Howard Box
Leader, Brooklyn Society for Ethical Culture

Raymond B. Bragg
Minister Emeritus, Unitarian Church, Kansas City

Theodore Brameld
Visiting Professor, C.U.N.Y.

Brigid Brophy
Author, Great Britain

Lester R. Brown
Senior Fellow, Overseas Development Council

Bette Chambers
President, American Humanist Association

John Ciardi
Poet

Francis Crick, M.D.,
Great Britain

Arthur Danto
Professor of Philosophy, Columbia University

Lucien de Coninck
Professor, University of Gand, Belgium

Miriam Allen deFord,
Author

Edd Doerr
Americans United for Separation of Church and State

Peter Draper, M.D.,
Guy's Hospital Medical School, London

Paul Edwards
Professor of Philosophy, Brooklyn College

Albert Ellis
Executive Director, Institute for Advanced Study of Rational Psychotherapy

Edward L. Ericson
Board of Leaders, New York Society for Ethical Culture

H. J. Eysenck
Professor Psychology, University of London

Roy P. Fairfield
Coordinator, Union Graduate School

Herbert Feigl
Professor Emeritus, University of Minnesota

Raymond Firth
Professor Emeritus of Anthropology, University of London

Antony Flew
Professor of Philosophy, The University, Reading, England

Kenneth Furness
Executive Secretary, British Humanist Association

Erwin Gaede
Minister, Unitarian Church, Ann Arbor, Michigan

Richard S. Gilbert
Minister, First Unitarian Church, Rochester, New York

Charles Wesley Grady
Minister, Unitarian Universalist Church, Arlington, Massachusetts

Maxine Greene
Professor, Teachers College, Columbia University

Thomas C. Greening
Editor, *Journal of Humanistic Psychology*

Alan F. Guttmacher
President, Planned Parenthood Federation of America

J. Harold Hadley
Minister, Unitarian Universalist Church, Port Washington New York

Hector Hawton
Editor, *Question*, Great Britain

A. Eustace Haydon
Professor Emeritus of History of Religions

James Hemming
Psychologist, Great Britain

Palmer A. Hilty
Administrative Secretary, Fellowship of Religious Humanists

Hudson Hoagland
President Emeritus, Worcester Foundation for Experimental Biology

Robert S. Hoagland
Editor, *Religious Humanism*

Sidney Hook
Professor Emeritus of Philosophy, New York University

James F. Hornback
Leader, Ethical Society of St. Louis

James M. Hutchinson
Minister Emeritus, First Unitarian Church, Cincinnati

Mordecai M. Kaplan
Rabbi, Founder of Jewish Reconstruction Movement

John C. Kidneigh
Professor of Social Work, University of Minnesota

Lester A. Kirkendall
Professor Emeritus, Oregon State University

Margaret Knight
University of Aberdeen, Scotland

Jean Kotkin
Executive Secretary, American Ethical Union

Richard Kostelanetz
Poet

Paul Kurtz
Editor, *The Humanist*

Lawrence Lader
Chairman, National Association for Repeal of Abortion Laws

Edward Lamb
President, Lamb Communications, Inc.

Corliss Lamont
Chairman, National Emergency Civil Liberties Union

Chauncey D. Leake
Professor, University of California, San Francisco

Alfred McC. Lee
Professor Emeritus, Sociology-Anthropology, C.U.N.Y.

Elizabeth Briant Lee
Author

Christopher Macy
Director, Rationalist Press Association, Great Britain

Clorinda Margolis
Jefferson Community Mental Health Center, Philadelphia

Joseph Margolis
Professor of Philosophy, Temple University

Harold P. Marley
Retired Unitarian Minister

Floyd W. Matson
Professor of American Studies, University of Hawaii

Lester Mondale
Former President, Fellowship of Religious Humanists

Lloyd Morain
President, Illinois Gas Company

Mary Morain
Editorial Board, International Society for General Semantics

Charles Morris
Professor Emeritus, University of Florida

Henry Morgentaler, M.D.,
Past President, Humanist Association of Canada

Mary Mothersill
Professor of Philosophy, Barnard College

Jerome Nathanson
Chairman, Board of Leaders, New York Society of Ethical Culture

Billy Joe Nichols
Minister, Richardson Unitarian Church, Texas

Kai Nielsen
Professor Philosophy, University of Calgary, Canada

P. H. Nowell-Smith
Professor of Philosophy, York University, Canada

Chaim Perelman
Professor of Philosophy, University of Brussels, Belgium

James W. Prescott
National Institute of Child Health and Human Development [of HEW]

Harold J. Quigley
Leader, Ethical Humanist Society of Chicago

Howard Radest
Professor of Philosophy, Ramapo College

The following signers were added after the original publication date. This is only a partial listing, since many names were not obtainable.

Joseph Chuman
Leader, Ethical Society of Essex County

Gordon Clanton
Assistant Professor, Trenton State College

Daniel S. Collins
Leader, Unitarian Fellowship of Jonesboro,
  Arkansas

William Creque
President, Fellowship of
  Humanity,Oakland, California

M. Benjamin Dell
Director, American Humanist Association

James Durant IV
Professor, Polk Community College, Winter
  Haven, Florida

Gerald A. Ehrenreich
Associate Professor, University of Kansas
  School of Medicine

Marie Erdmann
Teacher, Campbell Elementary School

Robert L. Erdmann, Ph.D.
IBM

Hans S. Falck
Distinguished Professor, Menninger
  Foundation

James Farmer
Director, Public Policy Training Institute

Ed Farrar

Joe Felmet
Humanist Counselor

Thomas Ferrick
Leader, Ethical Society of Boston

Norman Fleishman
Executive Vice President, Planned
  Parenthood World Population, Los
  Angeles

Joseph Fletcher
Visiting Professor, School of Medicine,
  University of Virginia

Douglas Frazier
Leader, American Ethical Union

Betty Friedan
Founder, N.O.W.

Harry M. Geduld
Professor, Indiana University

Roland Gibson
President, Art Foundation of Potsdam, New
  York

Aron S. Gilmartin
Minister, Mt. Diablo Unitarian Church,
  Walnut Creek, California

Annabelle Glasser
Director, American Ethical Union

Rebecca Goldblum
Director, American Ethical Union

Louis R. Gomberg
Humanist Counselor

Harold N. Gordon
Vice President, American Ethical Union

Sol Gordon
Professor, Syracuse University

Theresa Gould
American Ethical Union

Gregory O. Grant
Captain, U.S.A.F.

Ronald Green
Assistant Professor, New York University

Le Rue Grim
Secretary, American Humanist Association

S. Spencer Grin
Publisher, *Saturday Review/World*

Josephine R. Gurbarg
Secretary, Humanist Society of Greater
  Philadelphia

Samuel J. Gurbarg

Lewis M. Gubrud
Executive Director, Mediator Fellowship,
  Providence, Rhode Island

Frank A. Hall
Minister, Murray Universalist Church,
  Attleboro, Massachusetts

Harold A. Kansen
President,Space Coast Chapter, AHA

Ethelbert Haskins
Director, American Humanist Association

Lester H. Hayes
Public Relations Director, American Income
  Life Insurance Company

Donald E. Henshaw
Humanist Counselor

Alex Hershaft
Principal Scientist, Booz Allen Applied
  Research

Ronald E. Hestand
Author and Columnist

Irving Louis Horowitz
Editor, *Society*

Warren S. Hoskins
Humanist Counselor

Mark W. Huber
Director, American Ethical Union

Harold J. Hutchison
Humanist Counselor

Arthur M. Jackson
Executive Director, Humanist Community,
  San Jose; Treasurer, American Humanist
  Association

Linda R. Jackson
Director, American Humanist Association

Steven Jacobs
Former President, American Ethical Union

Thomas B. Johnson, Jr.
Consulting Psychologist

Robert Edward Jones
Executive Director, Joint Washington Office
  for Social Concern

Marion Kahn
President, Humanist Society of
Metropolitan New York

Alec E. Kelley
Professor, University of Arizona

Marvin Kohl
Professor, SUNY at Fredonia

Frederick C. Kramer
Humanist Counselor

Eugene Kreves
Minister, DuPage Unitarian Church,
Naperville, Illinois

Helen B. Lamb
Economist

Jerome D. Lang
President, Humanist Association of Greater
Miami, Florida

Harvey Lebrun
Chairman, Chapter Assembly, AHA

Helen Leibson
President, Philadelphia Ethical Society

John F. MacEnulty, Jr.
President, Humanist Society of
Jacksonville, Florida

James T. McCollum
Humanist Counselor

Vashti McCollum
Former President of AHA

Russell L. McKnight
President, Humanist Association of Los
Angeles

Ludlow P. Mahan, Jr.
President, Humanist Chapter of Rhode
Island

Clem Martin, M.D.

James R. Martin
Humanist Counselor

Stanley E. Mayabb
Co-Founder, Humanist Group of Vacaville &
Men's Colony, San Luis Obispo

Abelardo Mena, M.D.
Senior Psychiatrist, V.A. Hospital, Miami,
Florida

Herbert J. Muller
Professor, University of Indiana

Robert J. Myler
Title Officer, Title Insurance & Trust
Company

H. Kyle Nagel
Minister, Unitarian Universalist Church of
Kinston, N.C.

Dorothy N. Naiman
Professor Emerita, Lehman College, CUNY

Muriel Neufeld
Executive Committee, American Ethical
Union

Walter B. Neumann
Treasurer, American Ethical Union

William Earl Proctor, Jr.
President, Philadelphia Area, AHA

James A. Rafferty
Lecturer, USIU School of Human Behavior

Anthony F. Rand
President, Humanist Society of Greater
Detroit

A. Philip Randolph
President, A. Philip Randolph Institute

Ruth Dickinson Reams
President, Humanist Association National
Capital Area

Bernard L. Riback
Humanist Counselor

B.T. Rocca, Sr.
President, United Secularists of America

M. L. Rosenthal
Professor, New York University

Jack C. Rubenstein
Executive Committee, AEU

Joseph R. Sanders
Professor, University of West Florida

William Schulz
Ph.D. candidate, Meadville/Lombard,
University of Chicago

Walter G. Schwartz
Director, Humanist Committee of San
Francisco

John W. Sears,
Clinical Psychologist

Naomi Shaw
President, National Women's Conference,
AEU

R. L. Shuford, III
Instructor, Charlotte Country Day School

Sidney Siller
Chairman, Committee for Fair Divorce and
Alimony Laws

Joell Silverman
Chairman, Religious Education Committee,
AEU

Warren A. Smith
President, Variety Sound Corporation

Robert Sone

Robert M. Stein
Co-Chairman, Public Affairs Committee,
AEU

Stuart Stein
Director, American Ethical Union

Arnold E. Sylvester

Emerson Symonds
Director, Sensory Awareness Center

Carolyn Symonds
Marriage Counselor

Ward Tabler
Visiting Professor, Starr King School

Barbara M. Tabler

Erwin Theobold
Instructor, Pasadena City College

Renate Vambery
Ethical Society of St. Louis, President, AHA
St. Louis Chapter

Nick D. Vasileff
St. Louis Ethical Society

Robert J. Wellman
Humanist Chaplain, C. W. Post Center,
Long Island University

May H. Weis
UN Representative for IHEU

Paul D. Weston
Leader, Ethical Culture Society, Bergen
County

Georgia H. Wilson
Retired, Political Science Department,
Brooklyn College

H. Van Rensselaer Wilson
Professor Emeritus, Brooklyn College

James E. Woodrow
Executive Director, Asgard Enterprises, Inc.

BANGLADESH

Abul Hasanat
Secretary, Bangladesh Humanist Society

CANADA

J. Lloyd Brereton
Editor, *Humanist in Canada*

Andrew Malleson, M.D.
Psychiatrist

Eleanor Wright Pelrine
Author

Bernard Porter
President, Toronto Humanist Association

FRANCE

Pierre Lamarque

Jacques Monod
Institut Pasteur

Jean-Francois Revel
Journalist

GREAT BRITAIN

Sir Alfred Ayer
Professor, Oxford

Sir Julian Huxley
Former head, UNESCO

INDIA

G.D. Parikh
Indian Radical Humanist Association

A. Solomon
Coordinator, Indian Secular Society

V.M. Tarkunde
President, All Indian Radical Humanist
Association

NIGERIA

Ernest N. Ukpaby
Dean, University of Nigeria

PHILIPPINES

Gonzalo Quiogue
Vice President, Humanist Association of the
Philippines

SOVIET UNION

Zhores Medvedev
Scientist

SWEDEN

Gunnar Myrdal
Professor, University of Stockholm

WEST GERMANY

Walter Behrendt
Vice President, European Parliament

W. Bonness
President, Bund Freireligioser Gemeinden

D. Bronder
Bund Freireligioser Gemeinden

Still later, these signatures were added in response to an open invitation:

Mihailo Markovic
Professor, University of Belgrade, Yugoslavia

William Adler-Geller
Chicago, Illinois

Terry L. Bowersock
South Bend, Indiana

Hugh Carter
Washington, D.C.

O.E. Catledge, Jr.
Decatur, Georgia

Sue H. Catledge
Decatur, Georgia

Linda Chessick
Evanston, Illinois

Marcia Chessick
Evanston, Illinois

Richard D. Chessick
Professor of Clinical Psychiatry,
Northwestern University Medical School,
Evanston, Illinois

Harold C. Clausen
Pittsburgh, Pennsylvania

Dewey Collett
Erlanger, Kentucky

Marcia DeMarco
Endwell, New York

Stephen J. DeMarco
Endwell, New York

Gloria Goldman
Livingston, New Jersey

Howard T. Gonsalves
President, Humanist Association of
Berkeley, California

Jai-Hai Choi
Professor,Seoul National University, Seoul,
Korea

Otto Krash
Associate Professor, Lehman College, CUNY

Robert Hall
Professor, College of Steubenville, Ohio

Luis R. Marcos, M.D.
American Institute for Psychoanalysis

Henry D. Messer, M.D.
New York, New York

Julius Novick
Associate Professor of Literature, SUNY at
Purchase

Sang-Eun Lee
Emeritus Professor, Korea University,
Seoul, Korea

Edward H. Schiller
Professor of History, Nassau College, SUNY

Hugh J. Stern
Vice President, American Ethical Union,
New York, New York

Ralph E. Wager
Panama City,Florida

Wou-sung Son
Sungkyun Kwan University, Seoul, Korea

Gaylord David Swing
Phoenix, Arizona

G. Alan Robison
Professor, University of Texas

Evelyn M. Weil
President, National Ethical Youth
Organization

Anthony S. Russell
President, Ethical Culture Society of Los
Angeles

Wolfgang Teuber
West Germany

A.J. Lorenze
Bethany, Connecticut

Charles White McGehee
Jacksonville, Florida

John D. McCluhan
Shreveport, Louisiana

James A. Gould
Professor, University of Southern Florida,
Tampa

Adolf Grunbaum
Professor, University of Pittsburgh

Leo P. Mulcahy, Sr.
San Diego, California

Horace L. Bachelder
Minister, First Parish, Plymouth,
Massachusetts

Andrea Y. Blumberg
Tulsa, Oklahoma

Gora
Editor, *The Atheist*, Andhra Pradesh, India

Oliver J. Worthington
San Diego, California

Alfred S. Cole
Unitarian-Universalist Minister,
Wilmington, Vermont

Thomas J. Moore
Birmingham, Michigan

Ruth Weston
Boca Raton, Florida

Robert T. Weston
Unitarian Minister Emeritus, Boca Raton,
Florida

Thelma S. Daniel
Ft. Lauderdale, Florida

H. Nassif
Professor of Anthropology, Washington,
D.C.

John T. Bregger
Clemson, S.C.

Freeman Champney
Finksburg, Maryland

Donald B. King
Unitarian Minister, Geneva, Illinois

Edward A. Frost
Unitarian Minister, Waltham,
Massachusetts

Carl Seaburg
Unitarian Minister, Medford,
Massachusetts

Charles Stephen, Jr.
Unitarian Minister, Lincoln, Nebraska

J. Donald Johnston
Unitarian-Universalist Minister, Niagara
Falls, New York

Lolly Poole
Ormond Beach, Florida

Kenneth W. Phifer
Unitarian-Universalist Minister, Canton,
Massachusetts

Curtis D. MacDougall
Evanston, Illinois

George R. Geiger
Professor, Antioch College, Yellow Springs,
Ohio

Robert S. Brumbaugh
Professor of Philosophy, Yale University,
New Haven, Connecticut

Petra Karin Kelly
EEC, Brussels, Belgium

Richard M. Gale
Professor of Philosophy, University of
Pittsburgh

Hee-Jin Kim
University of Oregon, Eugene

Richard C. Myers
Unitarian Minister, Kansas City, Missouri

Max E. Guernsey
Waterloo, Iowa

William R. King, Jr.
Cincinnati, Ohio

John Burton
Washington, New Jersey

Byron Davidson
Edwardsville, Illinois

Randall J. VanNetten
Grand Rapids, Michigan

Gregory O. Grant
Cocoa Beach, Florida

Allan H. Russcher, M.D.
Kalamazoo, Michigan

Amzie R. Miller
Phoenix, Arizona

Samuel Asinovsky
Piedmont, California

Joseph J. Jelinek, M.D.
Glendale, California

Margaret M. Jelinek
Glendale, California

Ralph Lewis
Santa Barbara, California

Melba Byers
St. Louis, Missouri

Mildred L. Davis
Kansas City, Missouri

Lowell H. Coate
San Diego, California

Ronald William Ball
San Diego, California

Allen R. Korbel
Milwaukee, Wisconsin

Harry H. Lerner
New York, New York

Fred Swenty
Cincinnati, Ohio

John T. Porter
Sierra Vista, Arizona

Ronald Van Orden
Iowa City, Iowa

Ernest G. Baker
Oakland, California

Bernard T. Rocca
San Francisco, California

G. Bradley Millar
San Jose, California

Samual Wolffe
Washington, D.C.

Felix R. Bremy
Paterson, New Jersey

Joseph Ackerman
San Francisco, California

Paul A. Wilson
Wichita, Kansas

Henry Mikes
Cary, Illinois

Kay French
Nashua, Iowa

J. Hammond McNish
Lawrence, Kansas

Thomas J. Dorsey
Miami, Florida

Lilian M. Schiller
Miami, Florida

Jesse I. Fuchs
West Palm Beach, Florida

Genevieve Kerr
Boulder Creek, California

Samuel Berkowitz
Columbia, Maryland

L. Francis Griffin, Sr.
Farmville, Virginia

John H. Humphreys
Knoxville, Tennessee

John E. Montreal
Solvay, New York

Rose Hamill
Tucson, Arizona

G. B. Asselstine
St. Paul, Minnesota

Eugene H. Messal
Kansas City, Missouri

Kathleen M. Bell
Los Angeles, California

Bert Logan Duncan
Clarksville, Indiana

Gerhard Coler
Bridgeport, Connecticut

Sidney M. Weisman
Los Angeles, California

Michael A. Vicario
Lansdale, Pennsylvania

Symbols of Humanism

There are various symbols for Humanism; there will be many more. Here are a few, excerpted from an IHEU pamphlet titled *What Do You Mean, "Religious Humanism"*?

"The Happy Man" is fast becoming the most universal humanist symbol.

Used by The American Humanist Association and The Fellowship of Religious Humanists, these circles were inspired by Edwin Markham's praise of tolerance: *He drew a circle that shut me out/ Heretic, rebel, a thing to flout/ But love and I had the wit to win/ We drew a circle that took him in.*

The overlapping circles symbolize the merger of Unitarians and Universalists; the lamp, knowledge and the appeal to reason. Used originally by the Unitarian Universalist Service Committee, it has been adopted widely by liberal churches.

A conventionalization of the universal man of Leonardo da Vinci; until recently used on the cover of *International Humanism*, this symbol has more recently been used by The American Ethical Union.

I.H.E.U. is the International Humanist and Ethical Union organized in Amsterdam in 1952 with 33 Humanist organizations from 23 countries related to it in 1970.

Among humanists the peace symbol symbolizes the global hope for a shared world at peace where all men may realize security, brotherhood and creativity.

Organizational Members of International Humanist and Ethical Union (IHEU)

Reprinted from *International Humanism*, 1972, No. 3

FULL MEMBERS

American Ethical Union
2 West 64th Street,
New York, N.Y.10023, U.S.A.

American Humanist Association
Humanist House
125 El Camino del Mar
San Francisco, Calif. 94121, U.S.A.

Bund Freireligiöser Gemeinden Deutschlands
Josephstrasse 22
Hannover 3, West Germany

British Humanist Association
13 Prince of Wales Terrace
London W. 8, U.K.

Humanist Association of Canada
P.O. Box 230, Victoria Station
Montreal 6, Quebec, Canada

Humanistisch Verbond, Belgium
Luxemburgstraat 44
Antwerp 2, Belgium

Humanistisch Verbond, Netherlands
P.O. Box 114
Utrecht, Netherlands

Indian Radical Humanist Association
c/o Mr. V.M. Tarkunde
D-426 Defence Colony
New Delhi 3, India

Rationalist Press Association
88 Islington High Street
London N. 1, U.K.

MEMBERS WITH CONSULTATIVE STATUS

Centro Coscienza
Corso di Porta Nuova 16
Milan, Italy

Fellowship of Religious Humanists
105 W. North College St.
Yellow Springs, Ohio 45387, U.S.A.

Human-Etisk Forbund i Norge
Pilestredet 30
Oslo 1, Norway

Humanist and Ethical Section of the Yugoslav Association of Philosophy
Studentski trg br. 1
Beograd, Yugoslavia

Humanitas
J.W. Brouwersstraat 16
Amsterdam-Z., Netherlands

Korean Humanist Association
c/o Seoul National University
Department of Philosophy
Chongro-ku, Seoul, Korea

Ligue Française de l'Enseignement
3 rue Récamier
Paris 7e, France

ASSOCIATE MEMBERS

Asociación Humanista Argentina
Sarmiento 2071
Buenos Aires, Argentine

Freigeistige Aktion
Deutscher Monistenbund
Munzelerstrasse 50
Hannover, West Germany

Gesellschaft für Ethische Kultur
12 Zaunergasse
1 Stiege 4, Vienna III, Austria

Humanist Association of Finland
Box 10793
Helsinki 10, Finland

Humanist Society of Canberra
c/o Griffin Centre,
Canberra City, A.C.T. 2601, Australia

Humanist Society of New Zealand
Box 943,
Auckland I, New Zealand

**Humanist Society of South
   Australia**
Box 270 G.P.O.
Adelaide 5001, South Australia

Humanist Society of Victoria
23 Anderson Street, East Malvern
Melbourne, S.E. 5, Australia

Indian Humanist Union
New Blyth Cottage,
Naini Tal, U.P., India

Indian Secular Society
4 Joothica, 22 Naushir Bharucha Rd.
Bombay 7, India

Institut de l'Homme
5 rue Joseph de Maistre
Paris 18e, France

Irish Humanist Association
Clonard, Torquay Rd.
Foxrock, Co. Dublin, Ireland

New South Wales Humanist Society
72 Tooronga Terrace,
Beverly Hills, N.S.W., Australia

CONTACT GROUPS

**Associazione per la Libertá
   Religiosa in Italia**
Via Bassini 39
Milan, Italy

Bangladesh Humanist Association
31 Topekhana Road,
Dacca-2, Bangladesh

**Humanist Association of the
   Philippines**
2129 Singalong St.
Manila, Philippines

Humanist Institute
1430 Masonic Avenue
San Francisco, Calif. 94117. U.S.A.

Nigerian Humanist Association
P.O. Box 409
Yaba, Nigeria

Sozo-sha
35-3, 3-chome Shimoigusa
Suginami-ku, Tokyo, Japan

Testimony Identifying Isadore Rubin as a Communist: An Excerpt from *Investigation of Communist Activities, New York Area — Part III*

Hearings before the Committee on Un-American Activities, House of Representatives, Eighty-fourth Congress, First Session, May 3 and 4, 1955

(The following portion of the testimony of Mildred Blauvelt is found on pages 853 and 854. Relevant segment is in bold type.)

Mrs. BLAUVELT. . . . Rhoda Price, who also used the party name of Pierce, P-i-e-r-c-e. She attended many of the meetings at the Flatbush Club.

John Rogers, R-o-g-e-r-s; he was one of the members also, who was transferred with me to the Parkside Club. He attended many of the meetings and in the fund drive which started in 1946, he pledged $25.

Alex Rosen, R-o-s-e-n, was editor of the club bulletin which was prepared by the Flatbush Club. He was on the executive committee of the Flatbush Club and recruited Betsy Blom into the party. Alex Rosen was a teacher but subsequently retired.

Mr. TAVENNER. Did that club bulletin have a name?

Mrs. BLAUVELT. I believe it had just the title that appears on there: "Community." Perhaps one of the others would show it a little better. [Reading]:

Harold Rosenberg, R-o-s-e-n-b-e-r-g, 2604 Bedford Avenue. He assisted in the American Labor Party petition campaign in 1945 and also assisted with the December 6, 1945 rally being held in the name of Americans United for World Organization.

Nat Rosenberg, at a meeting of the club held on December 11, 1945, volunteered to help in the press drive by securing subscriptions. He was transferred with me to the Parkside Club.

Elsie Rosenbluth, R-o-s-e-n-b-l-u-t-h, 174 Woodruff Avenue; she was on the executive committee of the Flatbush Club. She was also a member of the Flatbush consumers council.

Nat Rosenbluth, 174 Woodruff Avenue; he was the chairman of the Flatbush Club, and upon its reorganization, or the reorganization of the party, which took place in January of 1946, became the section organizer which included both the 21st and 11th A.D. Clubs and was known as the Flatbush section.

Judith Rosenfeld, R-o-s-e-n-f-e-l-d; on January 9, 1945, at a meeting of the Flatbush Club, was nominated to the executive committee because of her affiliation with the American Youth for Democracy.

Jean Rothman, R-o-t-h-m-a-n; she was elected to the elections committee, and did attend meetings of the Flatbush Club.

Isadore Rubin, R-u-b-i-n. In March of 1945 while he was in the Army in Italy, he sent $10 to the party's fund drive. Upon his return from service, he did attend some of the meetings of the Flatbush Club. Now, there was a club bulletin issued under date of November 28, 1944, which gave his name and listed his address as 1030 Ocean Avenue, with the notation that he was the winner of an essay contest which had been conducted while he was in the Army. Isadore Rubin was a teacher in the New York City school system who was dismissed in 1951, after trial.

I did read some testimony which he had presented to the Senate Committee on Internal Security in September of 1952. At that time he gave his address as 20 Rugby Road, and it was in connection with the teachers union, I believe, that these hearings were being held; and I was particularly interested in reading the testimony because he invoked the privilege of the fifth amendment concerning his Communist affiliations.

Mr. TAVENNER. I have before me the April 23, 1955 issue of New York Teachers News, and apparently published by the Teachers Union of New York.

Mrs. BLAUVELT. That is correct.

Mr. TAVENNER. I notice the name of the editor appears on the editorial board and staff of this issue. Will you examine this issue and state what you see to be the name of the editor?

Mrs. BLAUVELT. The name of the editor is Isadore Rubin.

Mr. TAVENNER. Is that the same person to whom you have referred?

Mrs. BLAUVELT. Yes, sir.

Mr. TAVENNER. As having been known to you as a member of the Communist Party?

Mrs. BLAUVELT. Yes, sir, it is the same person.

Mr. TAVENNER. I desire to offer in evidence that part of page 2 of the issue of April 23, 1955, of the New York Teachers News which indicates the editorial staff; ask that it be marked "Blauvelt Exhibit No. 18," and that it be incorporated in the transcript of the record.

Mr. DOYLE. It is so ordered.

APPENDIX G

The National Committee For Responsible Family Life And Sex Education

(Signers of the SIECUS ad in the *New York Times*, October 16, 1969)

Mr. and Mrs. Morris B. Abram
Raymond Pace Alexander
Shana Alexander
David Aloian
Walter C. Alvarez
Mrs. Max Ascoli
Lester F. Avnet
J. Martin Bailey
Charles R. Baker
Laurence S. Baker, Ph.D.
Margaret Culkin Banning
Stringfellow Barr
Thomas A. Bartlett
Eric Bentley
Milton and Ruth Berle
Dr. George Packer Berry
Theodore Bikel
Clark W. Blackburn
Julian Bond
Dr. Harold A. Bosley
Rabbi Balfour Brickner
Henry J. Browne
Ralph J. Bunche
Mrs. Mary I. Bunting
Raymond Burr
Dr. Allan M. Butler
Red Buttons
Rt. Rev. George L. Cadigan
Godfrey Cambridge
Vincent Canby
Florence Carpenter
John Mack Carter
Bennett Cerf
Bette Chambers
John Chandler, Jr.
Stuart Chase
Leo Cherne
Paul and Julia Child

John Ciardi
Lammot duPont Copeland
Norman Corwin
George S. Counts, Ph.D.
Judith Crist
Reverend Charles E. Curran
Rev. Professor Robert E. Cushman
Mrs. Norris Darrell
Benjamin DeMott
William M. Dietel
Marriner S. Eccles
Irving M. Engel
Mrs. Loy Everett
Mrs. James Farmer
Dana L. Farnsworth, M.D.
W.H. Ferry
John H. Fischer
Dr. Morris Fishbein
Eugene P. Foley
Henry Foner
Mr. and Mrs. Walter B. Ford II
John Forsythe
Sonny Fox
Jerome D. Frank, M.D.
James M. Gavin
The Rev. William H. Genné
Rabbi Roland B. Gittelsohn
Arthur J. Goldberg
Lloyd Goodrich
Reverend Dana McLean Greeley, D.D.
Edward D. Greenwood, M.D.
Chaim Gross and Mrs. Renée Gross
Ernest Gruening
Peggy Guggenheim
Alan F. Guttmacher, M.D.
Reverend Herschel Halbert
Mrs. Oscar Hammerstein
Dexter L. Hanley, S.J.

Rev. Dr. Donald Szantho Harrington
Walter W. Heller
Reverend Theodore M. Hesburgh
Hugh B. Hester
Hudson Hoagland
Prynce Hopkins, Ph.D.
Dorothy Houghton
Frederick L. Hovde
James Howard
Marsha Hunt
Reverend R. Claibourne Johnson
Frank E. Karelsen
Alfred Kazin
Gene Kelly
Rockwell Kent
Walter Kerr
Alan King
Mrs. Donald Klopfer
Philip M. Klutznick
Dr. Mathilde Krim
Ann Landers
Burton Lane
Edith A. Lehman
Mrs. Gerald D. Levy
Bishop John Wesley Lord
Ferdinand Lundberg
Dwight MacDonald
Archibald MacLeish
Gertrude Macy
Gerri Major
Marya Mannes
Mrs. John E. Marqusee
Walter Matthau
Berwyn F. Mattison, M.D.
Jean Mayer
Floyd B. McKissick
Robert S. McNamara
Stewart Meacham
Roy W. Menninger, M.D.
W. Walter Menninger, M.D.
Burgess Meredith
Lee Metcalf
James A. Michener
James W. Miller
Hans J. Morgenthau
Robert W. Morse
Robert Motherwell
Lewis Mumford
Dr. Lonny Myers
Reverend Richard John Neuhaus
Reverend Reinhold Niebuhr, D.D.
Mrs. Ursula M. Niebuhr, D.D.

John H. Northrop
Mildred Scott Olmstead
Joseph O'Meara
Frederick O'Neal
Robert Osborn
Vance Packard
Joseph Papp
Rosemary Park
Augustin H. Parker
The Reverend Robert L. Pierson
Robert S. Pirie, Esq.
Francis T.P. Plimpton
Robert Pressnell, Jr.
Mr. and Mrs. John Raitt
Geraldine E. Rhoads
Charles S. and Linda J. Robb
Mrs. Louis J. Robbins
John Rock, M.D.
Mrs. Kermit Roosevelt
Samuel B. Ross, Jr.
Leo Rosten
Albert B. Sabin, M.D.
Gene Saks
Dr. Jonas Salk
William G. Saltonstall
James H. Scheuer
Mr. and Mrs. Nathan H. Schwerner
Reverend John B. Sheerin
Madeleine Sherwood
General David M. Shoup
Cornelia Otis Skinner
Mrs. Germaine Smith
Stephen E. Smith
Albert J. Solnit, M.D.
Ernest L. Stebbins, M.D.
Rt. Rev. Anson Phelps Stokes, Jr.
Mr. and Mrs. Irving Stone
Richard J. Stonesifer
Miss Anne Lord Strauss
Albert Szent-Gyorgyi, M.D., Ph.D.
Helen B. Taussig, M.D.
Harold Taylor
Bishop Donald Harvey Tippett
Arnold E. True
Ralph W. Tyler
Harold C. Urey
Abigail Van Buren
Mark Van Doren
Gore Vidal
Kurt Vonnegut, Jr.
Harry M. Wachtel
Reverend Matthew M. Warren

Robert C. Weaver   Kenneth L. Wilson
Theodore S. Weiss   Teresa Wright
Elizabeth Weston   John Charles Wynn
Dr. Paul Dudley White   Andrew J. Young
Dr. Jerome B. Wiesner   Whitney M. Young, Jr.
Mr. and Mrs. Herman Will, Jr.

Several of the above signatures were received too late to be included in the *New York Times* ad itself. These names appeared in the March 1970 SIECUS Newsletter and have been fused into the list above.

APPENDIX H

Complete List of SIECUS Sponsors

Walter C. Alvarez, M.D.
Leona Baumgartner, M.D.
Eugene P. Foley
Henry Foner
Rabbi Roland B. Gittelsohn
Chaim Gross
Renée Gross
Ann Landers

Stewart Mott
Albert Solnit, M.D.
Anna Lord Strauss
The Hon. Percy E. Sutton
Helen B. Taussig, M.D.
Harold Taylor, Ph.D.
Mark Van Doren, Ph.D.
Paul Dudley White, M.D.

Officials and Members of Temple of Understanding

Adapted from official flyer

THE TEMPLE OF UNDERSTANDING, INC.

A Non-Profit, Tax-Exempt Educational Corporation organized to be

A CENTER FOR THE STUDY OF THE MAJOR WORLD RELIGIONS

1346 Connecticut Avenue, N.W., Washington, D.C., 20036, U.S.A.

BOARD OF DIRECTORS

Mrs. Dickerman Hollister
Chairman of the Board

Charles J. Mills
President

The Reverend Lowell R. Ditzen
Vice President

Thomas B. Gilchrist, Jr.
Treasurer

Rabbi Samuel M. Silver
Secretary

Mrs. Harold Holmyard
Recording Secretary

John S. Gillooly
Executive Director

Mrs. Charles H. Babcock
Mrs. B.K. Birla
Lathrop Douglass
Finley P. Dunne, Jr.
Miss Elizabeth Gempp
James V. Goure
Mrs. G. Clay Hollister
A. Sanford Kellogg
Stephen Kittenplan
Hon. Arthur Levitt
Robert C. Livingston
Mrs. Bertil Malmstedt
Mrs. Frederick Nicholas
Mrs. Wallace W. O'Neal
Mrs. William H. Rea
Mrs. Ogden R. Reid
Mrs. Josephine Richardson
H.E. Mr. Zenon Rossides
Mrs. William L. Van Alen
Mrs. James Van Dijk
Dr. John Yungblut

INTERNATIONAL COMMITTEE

Chairman
Mrs. B.K. Birla—India

Honorary Member
Dr. Sarvepalli Radhakrishnan—India

Dr. Tetsutaro Ariga—Japan
Mrs. Marjorie C. Artus—U.S.A.
Pasteur Henry Babel—Switzerland
Miss Norma E. Boyd—U.S.A.
The Reverend Marcus Braybrooke—England
Dr. Amiya Chakravarty—U.S.A.
Lady Chapman—Great Britain
Dr. Chang Chi-yun—Republic of China
Munishri Chitrabhanu—India
Mrs. Gordon Clemetson—Great Britain
His Holiness The Dalai Lama—India
H. S. H. Princess Poon Diskul—Thailand
Mrs. Stephen Martin Ecton—Japan
The Most Reverend Emilianos—Switzerland
The Reverend Pierre Fallon, S.J.—India
Pri Shinsho Hanayama—Japan
Dastoor N. B. Minochehr Homji—India
H. E. Sir M. Zafrulla Khan—The Hague
Pir Vilayat Inayat Khan—France
The Reverend Joseph Masson, S.J.—Italy
Mr. Asha Mirchandani—India
Sister Barbara Mitchell—U.S.A.
Dr. Stuart Mudd—U.S.A.
Dr. Seyyed Hoosein Nasr—Iran
Lord Abbot Kosho Ohtani—Japan
Dr. V. Raghavan—India
Bishop A. J. Shaw—India
Dr. Ezra Spicehandler—Israel
Dr. Wei Tat—Hong Kong
Dr. Syed Vahiduddin—India
Rabbi Mordecai Waxman—U.S.A.

The purpose of The Temple of Understanding is to foster education, communication and understanding among the world religions, and to establish The Temple of Understanding as a center and symbol of this undertaking.

American Civil Liberties Union Officials — 1974

BOARD OF DIRECTORS

Chairperson
Edward J. Ennis

General Counsel
Norman Dorsen
Osmond K. Fraenkel
Ruth Bader Ginsburg
Marvin M. Karpatkin

Vice Chairpersons
David B. Isbell
Rolland O'Hare
Harriet F. Pilpel
Barbara Preiskel
George Staff

Treasurer
Winthrop Wadleigh

Corporate Secretary
Frank Askin

Sheldon Ackley (N.Y.)
Michaels S. Battles (D.C.)
Jewel Bellush (N.Y.)
Robert Bierstedt (Va.)
Algernon D. Black (N.Y.)
Ralph S. Brown, Jr. (Conn.)
Ronald Brown (D.C.)
Bob Campbell (Mont.)
David Carliner (D.C.)
Lynn S. Castner (Minn.)
J. Levonne Chambers (N.C.)
Linda K. Champlin (Ohio)
Ramsey Clark (N.Y.)
John W. Cleland (Tenn.)
Carl Cohen (Mich.)
N. Jerold Cohen (Ks.)
Mary Coleman (D.C.)
Gilbert Cranberg (Iowa)
Richard L. Cummins (Okla.)
Patt Derian (Miss.)
Alan Dershowitz (Mass.)
Lolis Elie (La.)
Ronald Elberger (Ind.)
Hazel Erskine (Nev.)
Richard Y. Feder (Fla.)
Irwin Feinberg (Calif.)
Edgar Feingold (Md.)
Ellen Feingold (Mass.)
Monroe H. Freedman (D.C.)
Celeste Frierson (La.)

Donald Hackel (Vt.)
Franklyn S. Haiman (Ill.)
Marjorie Pitts Hames (Ga.)
David G. Hanlon (W. Va.)
Brook Hart (Hawaii)
John Hay (Ariz.)
Samuel Hendel (Conn.)
Lawrence Herman (Ohio)
Philip Hirschkop (Va.)
Jeanette Hopkins (N.Y.)
Howard Jewel (Calif.)
Thomas M. Kerr, Jr. (Pa.)
Edward King (Miss.)
Ralph Knowles (Ala.)
Arthur Kobler (Wash.)
Jim Lawing
Ken McCormick (N.Y.)
Paul R. Meyer (Oregon)
Grace Olivarez (N.M.)
Frances Fox Piven (N.Y.)
Janet Pollak (Ill.)
Suzy Post (Ky.)
Judy R. Potter (Me.)
William F. Reynard (Ohio)
Joseph Rhodes, Jr. (Pa.)
Suzanne Rhodes (S.C.)
William G. Rice (Wisc.)
Catherine Roraback (Conn.)
Ben Roth (E. Mo.)
Marvin Schacter (Calif.)

PPBS: One Result of Court Decisions Outlawing Local Financing of Schools by Property Taxes

Court rulings denying local financing of schools through local property taxes have indirectly provided for the implementation of the Humanistic indoctrination process of the Planning-Programming-Budgeting System (PPBS). PPBS is a systems management tool made possible by computer technology to effect planned change in human thought and behavior. This highly sophisticated computerized program, which has been adopted by a substantial number of state educational systems, often parades under a fictitious characterization. In New Jersey, for example, the law that paved the way for the introduction of PPBS into the schools was termed "thorough and efficient"; however; as a general rule, "accountability" is the key slogan-word used to sell the concept of PPBS to the educators and the public.

Applied to public education, PPBS works something like this:

1. *Planning* certain political, economic, and social goals and objectives to meet predetermined state policies; then measuring behavioral compliance with those policies by means of psychological testing.

2. *Programming* to indoctrinate teachers and students with the Humanist ideology by cycling them through a maze of values-clarification techniques until their knowledge, attitudes, and reactions to certain conditions comply with state policies. Throughout various stages of the PPBS process, personal data on school personnel, students, and parents are fed into a central computer bank for future reference.

3. *Budgeting* to set the program into action and lock in state policies through the power of the purse. This is accomplished by transferring local budget approval to the state and using the revenue sharing plan to force local school districts to comply with Humanistic state guidelines.

PPBS is often described by its promoters as simply an innocuous system of accounting, but in reality it is a carefully planned computerized formula for controlling people, with the finished product a new man with a new consciousness and a new set of values that are completely devoid of loyalty to God, family, and country. Family Life Education is only one component of this process; for the primary thrust of PPBS is the establishment of a one-world political, economic, and social order based on the total Humanist ideology through application of the behavioral sciences and coercive use of the budget.

* * *

The following is a speech originally prepared by Mrs. Mary Thompson of Campbell, California for presentation to the Santa Clara Republican Women Federated. Subsequently Mrs. Thompson presented the speech to a number of other political organizations, parent organizations, and teachers.

PPBS
(Planning, Programming, Budgeting System)
by Mrs. Mary Thompson

When I was first asked to speak to you about PPBS I inquired whether the topic was to be in its broad application, or whether it was to be addressed to PPBS as applied to education. I shall deal with it at the education level today; however you should remember that PPBS is a tool for implementing the very restructuring of government at *all* levels in every area of governmental institutions. What is involved is the use of government agencies to accomplish mass behavioral change in every area. The first agency of government to fully implement PPBS was the Defense Department when Robert McNamara invited the Rand Corporation to help him reorganize planning and budget procedures at the Department of Defense. In August of 1965 the President introduced the PPBS approach throughout the vast federal government. So, as I develop my remarks about PPBS as pertaining to education, keep in mind that the "process" involved is simultaneously being employed to restructure every agency of government.

PPBS is a plan being pushed by Federal and State governments to completely change education.

Now, what is it? The initials stand for PLANNING, PROGRAMMING, BUDGETING SYSTEM. Mr. and Mrs. John Q. Public hear that, and they think in terms of accounting. Budgeting conjures up concepts of orderly, identifiable expenditures for commonly understood expense items within a designated time span. "Accountability" is the key slogan word used to sell the idea of PPBS to the public and to the educators. This isn't accidental, of course, because the idea of public officials being accountable for public money is universally desired. What isn't universally understood, however, is that PPBS is more than an accounting tool using modern computer hardware. The accountability involved in PPBS means accountability to the state's predetermined education goals. To understand PPBS it must be understood at the outset that PPBS is a total system. Its component parts, PLANNING and PROGRAMMING and BUDGETING, cannot be isolated from the SYSTEM. In other words, you do not have PPB, or PBS, or BS, or PS — PLANNING, PROGRAMMING, BUDGETING, constitutes a SYSTEM of management. One leader of educational innovation has called it "A systematic design for education revolution." (Shelly Umans — *Management of Education*)

In a systems management of the education process, the child himself is the product. Note — *the child* — his feelings, his values, his behavior, as well as his intellectual development.

PPBS is the culmination of the "people planners'" dreams. The seeds have been alive for a long time. There have always been the Utopians, those who envisioned a perfectible controlled society. Those who have envisioned the creation of a "new mankind" in the image of whatever the prevailing philosophical elite envisioned at any given time. In contemporary history there have been the Huxleys, the John Deweys, the Bertrand Russells . . . right on down to current behavioral science educationists who control education today. The germination of Federal control of education has been going on for a long time too. For instance in 1933 a government spokesman said, "The individualism of Americanism must go, because it is contrary to the purpose of the New Deal which is remaking America. Russia and Germany are attempting to compel a new social order by means typical of their nationalism — compulsion. The United States will do it by moral suasion. We expect to accomplish by education what dictators in Europe are seeking to do by compulsion and force . . . the general public is not informed on all the parts of the program, and the schools are the places to reach the future builders of the nation." (*Monroe Evening News*, Monroe, Michigan — September 13, 1933)

Until recently the people planners were frustrated by the resistance of the American public to Federal planning and Federal financing for education.

Meanwhile, back at Bethel, Maine — the NATIONAL TRAINING LABO-RATORY was established under the auspices of NEA (National Education Association) about twenty years ago. The establishment of NTL was a "milestone" in the development of the restructuring of the very concept of education. The active training of the agents to effect the change started there and NTL has continued to train "change agents" (their term) to facilitate predetermined changes in education as well as every other walk of life . . . religious institutions, government, industry and service organizations. NTL is most often associated with sensitivity training and the role sensitivity training plays in the process of planned change. Out of NTL we also find "how-to-do-it" manuals such as "Concepts for Social Change," published through a contract with HEW by the way. So, for a quarter century NTL and various similar centers throughout the country have been systematically training leaders to effect the changes we see coming to fruition all around us and especially in our local schools. These change agents know how to facilitate the group process and other techniques to change the attitudes and behavior of school personnel, the community, and in turn to effect the indoctrination of the children. Individuals who refuse to compromise their principles by allowing themselves to be neutralized by entering into the process (I'll explain that further later on) are systematically isolated by the process. It is regrettable that straight-thinking people who operate on the basis of principle become worn out in six months' time battling one phase or another of the restructured education, never realizing that they are dealing with a totally different entity from what they have known traditional education to be.

Until recently the agents of planned change have had fragmented success in introducing innovative programs which the general public regarded with skepticism. Until 1965 there was the situation where responsive channels of representative government at the local level existed in the form of elected local school boards and state heads of education who made direct decisions regarding education programs which were funded at local or state levels. *That* was accountability in the traditional sense — accountability to parents and taxpayers.

Then in 1965 the means for accomplishing the actual *restructuring of education* was provided in the ELEMENTARY AND SECONDARY EDUCATION ACT (ESEA). President Johnson has said that he considered ESEA the most significant single legislation of his administration. Recall that it was also the same year of 1965 when the presidential order was given to introduce PPBS throughout the entire federal government. 1965 was the year which unleashed the actual restructuring of governmental processes and formally included education as a legitimate Federal government function. Since then we have seen the national administration institute a Federal Office of Human Resources, Office of Child Development, Early Learning Program, National Institute of Education, Committee of School Finance, etc. All these are *national offices* leading to total development of the coming generations of children by the state.

PPBS is the systems management tool made possible by technology of computer hardware to effect the planned change. As Assemblyman Robert

Burke expressed it, "If you know what you have to start with and you know what you want to end up with, it's possible to design a system that will make the precise changes required."

With continuous training of change agents through various levels of on-going in-service training, from NTL down to the local teacher in-service training, and with Federal money to finance the continuous on-going process designed to remake a population in the image of a "new mankind," all that's missing is the fool to implement the process, an uninformed and unsuspecting public, and teachers who are too busy teaching to sort out all the pieces.

In order to make an explanation of PPBS intelligible you must also know that education itself has been redefined. Simply put, it has become the objective of education to measure and diagnose the child in order to prescribe a program to develop his feelings and emotions, values, and loyalties toward predetermined behavioral objectives. Contrast that with the traditionally understood function of education of being that of acquiring knowledge and developing skills. How you feel and react becomes more important than what you know. Conditioning people to behave according to predetermined behavior patterns becomes the objective of education institutions. Drawing it right down to basics, we are talking about conditioned responses in human terms. Pavlov experimented on dogs! This is not fantasy of futuristic prophets. The "new education" is in effect RIGHT NOW! A reading of teacher guides, reveals that education no longer means development of the intellect in order to equip the student to make independent decisions which will determine his behavior as a free man. PPBS incorporates the machinery to accomplish the restructuring of a system — specifically, education — and then locks in the process. The term the educationists use for this is "unfreezing and freezing the system." Once the process is locked in, it is to become self-generating.

Taking each element of PPBS will show how the process is accomplished. PLANNING — The planning phase (please note that the process involved with a systems approach is always described in terms of "phases") always includes the establishment of goals committees, citizens committees, needs assessment committees — these are referred to as "community involvement." The committees are always either self-appointed or chosen, never elected. They always include guidance from some trained "change agents" who may be administrators, curriculum personnel or local citizens. Questionnaires and surveys are used to gather data on how the community "feels" and to test community attitudes. The ingeniousness of the process is that everybody thinks he is having a voice in the direction of public schools. Not so — for Federal change agencies, specifically, regional education centers established by ESEA influence, essentially determine terminology used in the questionnaires and surveys. Federal Regional Centers are the instruments for much of the training of local administrators and teachers, and often analyze and compute the data collected in surveys for local school districts. The change agents at the district level then function to "identify" needs and problems for change as they have been programmed to identify them at the training sessions sponsored by Federal offices such as our Center for Planning and Evaluation in Santa Clara County. This is why the goals are essentially the same in school districts across the country. It also explains why three years ago every school district was confronted with the Family Life Education issue at the same time. It was not coincidental. In fact FLE was the first national application of the process made possible by ESEA money and using the techniques of PPBS on a national scale. Anyone who became involved in that issue knew that they were dealing with a different ball game from previous school controversies. So, whether the issue is FLE, district unification, alternate schools, flexible scheduling, multicultural curriculum, or what have you — the process remains the same. Now, unknowing citizens committees are used by the process to generate acceptance of goals already determined. What they don't realize is that professional change agents are operating in the behaviorist's framework of thought and Mr. or Mrs. Citizen Parent is operating in his traditional education framework of thought. So the local change agents are able to facilitate a group to a consensus in support of predetermined goals by using familiar traditional terms which carry the new behaviorist meanings. If you doubt this, a Joint Committee Report on Educational Goals and Evaluation was established in 1969 by our state legislature. Two of that committees conclusions read as follows: "The value of setting goals is as much in the process of participation as the final outcome" — then the report continues further on, "Those with authority for educational policy should take a role of leadership in identifying goals of education." Participants in citizens committees may feel good about participating, but they have had no *real* decision-making powers.

Identification of opposition to a program or goal is a necessary part of the process of PPBS and planned change. Any opposition to a concept that might be brought up in one of the citizens committees, and which cannot be allowed to be brought into the preordained consensus, *must* be identified. Any ideas expressed within citizens committees or answers on surveys are considered systems data. Data gathering is not to find out what *you* want, it is to find out where you are now — what you think, how you feel, so they can more quickly get you where they want you. Reports from these citizens committees are eventually presented to school boards, who, by the way, are the elected officials who rightfully have decision-making power in a true democratic republic. However, these school board members are now asked to assess committee reports and material which all emanates from a central source. These same school boards, with a few exceptions, have been conditioned by constant exposure to school administrators who operated in the behaviorist framework, by School Board Association dinners and conferences where they hear speakers such as William Glasser and Richard Farson telling them all about the needs they then receive from the citizens committee constituents!

A paperback book, *Management of Education* by Shelley Umans, says it very well: "If people are involved, then whole new strategies must be developed to 'engineer' people into accepting change. Projects that do not take into account the need to involve the people affected, are not likely to succeed . . . in discussing strategies for affecting change, we are talking about broad plans, the over-all design for gaining acceptance. How will the person out there be convinced that he wants to adopt the change?" They call it "people technology" further on in that same book. So, involving the potential adopter in the development of innovation is the strategy for overcoming resistance within both the academic community and the general public.

Another name for this process is Participatory Democracy, a term, by the way, which was coined by SDS in their Port Huron Manifesto, to identify the process for citizen participation in destruction of their own political institutions. Participatory Democracy is not to be confused with participation in representative government. A subject for a speech in itself would be the historical development of enabling. A key legislative act which set the process in motion in California schools must be mentioned. That is the much touted SB-1 which required the setting up of goals committees in the name of local control.

PROGRAMMING — Since I am not trained in the technology of computer programming I shall not attempt to get into illustrations and terminology of the application of the operation of computer hardware — the computers themselves. But to continue with an explanation of the political process involved, let's remember that once a district school board, wittingly or unwittingly, has gone through the charade of adopting policy or authorized a pilot project on the basis of citizen committee consensus reports, the PROGRAMMING of PPBS is put into operation. Sometimes the PROGRAMMING has already gone into operation before a "predictable" school board decision is made, and once in a while a school board's predictability is misjudged and there is temporary embarrassment for the facilitators of change when alert citizens point out that implementation is *preceding* legislative mandate. If PPBS is fully implemented, legislative mandates to authorize government action may only be a memory anyway, for programmed phases become impossible to identify except for the top level programmers.

Programming involves curriculum writing (remember the redefined education), text book adoption (textbooks also planned and programmed to conform to the "new education" objectives), teacher training, etc. Constant evaluation is going on as part of this process — as feedback is collected from all segments involved in the process. Data on community acceptance, data on teacher response, data on student response are fed into data banks to provide a continuous picture of how effective the process is, and just how and where to adjust the programming to make the program effective. We are receiving many inquiries from teachers who are in a position to know firsthand the pressures from the constant demands for in-service training and evaluation procedures. Actually, teachers are the only ones in a position at this point to halt the process by protecting their professional integrity, internally.

Now for the BUDGETING of PPBS. PPBS uses "on-going" five to seven year projections of programs which are constantly reassessed and altered along the way. You do not have line item budgets which are based on the concept of estimating the costs of a program until a designated time, then reassessing the program to see if results of that warrant the rebudgeting of the cost of a program. The yearly budget concept won't work with PPBS because it is impossible to project costs for five to seven years' programming because of the nature of continuous evaluation and self-generating change process during the five to seven years. Remember, constant re-evaluation means assessing teaching personnel, students, and community to determine the degree of effectiveness of the planned-change behavioral objective. Translate that: continuous data collecting. Until PPBS is fully implemented, and the system frozen or locked into operation, this can be a wide variable of unknown dimensions. There may still be unexpected straight-thinking resistance in the community, in the classroom, or in the faculty lounge — which will slow the process and make human recycling costs more than the planners anticipate in any five to seven year projection. It is only during the interim between the introduction of PPBS and the full implementation of it, however, that resistance will be much of a variable. The resistance will be isolated and the products of PPBS education will have no "memory" of anything other than this dialectical process called PLANNED CHANGE.

Richard Farson of Western Behavioral Sciences Institute made a report to the Office of Education in Sacramento in 1967. He said it this way: "The application of systems analysis is aided by several phenomena that would be of help in almost any situation of organizational change. First, it is relatively easier to make big changes than to make small ones — and systems changes are almost always big ones. Because they are big, it is difficult for people to mount resistance to them, for they go beyond the ordinary decision-making, policy-making activities of individual members of an organization. It is far easier to muster arguments against a $100 expenditure for partitions than against a complete reorganization of the work flow."

In order to accommodate these difficulties it is necessary to do away with traditional concepts of accounting by which specific plans and costs can be identified and financing for programs *can* be defeated at local level. The process of planned change needs a fluid central source of funding to orches-trate the national thought control. People planners or "engineers of humanity" must have central controlling factors — money being the enabling element. (1) They cannot have local property taxpayers with power to vote "no" on tax increases, which is a limiting factor to the planners. Note recent court decisions declaring local property taxes for education unconstitutional. (2) Note the push for statewide property tax (you don't vote on those rates). (3) Note the increase in Federal Funding for education. Now we have just been introduced to the idea of a Value Added Tax (VAT) to finance education. Once that becomes fact no one will be able to afford property anyway. Think about it. So you see budgeting of PPBS cannot be considered apart from the whole concept of PPBS, the system. You will be told that the state has already legislated the budgeting portions of PPBS but not the rest of it. If pressed on the point, however, proponents at the local level will usually admit that budgeting of PPBS cannot really be implemented as an independent component.

The "S" of PPBS is what makes PPB a System. And when a school district adopts PPBS it locks itself into a *national* system.

Signers of "A New Bill of Sexual Rights and Responsibilities"

In its January/February 1976 issue, *The Humanist* carried a document titled "A New Bill of Sexual Rights and Responsibilities," drafted by Humanist Lester Kirkendall of SIECUS at the request of the American Humanist Association as a supplement to the brief statement on sexuality in *Humanist Manifesto II*.

Kirkendall's new bill is a clear call for the abolition of all the moral standards set up through nineteen centuries of Judeo-Christian civilization. Labelling traditional values as "repressive . . . archaic taboos," Kirkendall set forth a definitive Humanist sexual code intended for all human beings. Following publication by *The Humanist*, the bill was published as a booklet, lavishly illustrated with photographs of nudes in various suggestive poses. Advocated in its pages are free love, adultery, masturbation, homosexuality, bisexuality, abortion, sterilization, pornography, decriminalization of prostitution, and access to sexual relations for persons in mental institutions and prisons.

The signers of Kirkendall's new bill were a group of Humanist authors, editors, and educators, many of whom are in the forefront of humanistic sexology. SIECUS board members are indicated in the following list by asterisks.

SIGNERS

Gina Allen, member of the National Task Force for the National Organization of Women; coauthor of *Intimacy*.

Alan P. Bell, Institute for Sex Research, Indiana University; coeditor of *Homosexuality*.

Maj-Briht Bergstrom-Walan, head of the Swedish Institute for Sexual Research, Stockholm; coauthor of *Sex and Society in Sweden*.

Bonnie Bullough, California State University at Long Beach.

Vern Bullough, professor, California State University, Northridge.

*Deryk Calderwood, New York University.

Elizabeth Canfield, Student Health and Counseling Services, UCLA.

Emanuel Chigier, secretary, International Symposium on Sex Education, Tel-Aviv, Israel.

Helen Colton, director, Family Forum, Los Angeles; author of *Beyond the Sexual Revolution*.

Joan M. Constantine, Acton, Massachusetts; coauthor of *Group Marriage*.

Larry L. Constantine, Tufts University/Boston State Hospital; coauthor of *Group Marriage*.

Albert Ellis, executive director, Institute for Advanced Study in Rational Psychotherapy; author of *The Sensuous Person.*

Anna K. Francoeur, Fairleigh Dickinson University; coauthor of *Hot And Cool Sex.*

Robert Francoeur, professor of human sexuality, Fairleigh Dickinson University; author of *The Future of Sexual Relations, Perspectives in Student Sexuality;* coauthor of *Hot and Cool Sex.*

Tilde Giani Gallino, Turin, Italy.

Evalyn S. Gendel, State Department of Health, Division of Child Health, Topeka, Kansas.

Sol Gordon, professor of child and family studies, Syracuse University; author of *The Sexual Adolescent* and *Sex and the Family.*

Helen M. Hacker, Department of Sociology, Adelphi University.

Marian Hamburg, New York University.

Yoshiro Hatano, assistant professor of physiology and kinesiology, Tokyo Gakugei University.

Preben Hertoft, M.D., Rigshospitalet Psykiatrisk Poliklinik, Copenhagen, Denmark.

*****Lester A. Kirkendall**, professor of family life, Oregon State University; author of *Premarital Intercourse and Interpersonal Relationships* and coeditor of *The New Sexual Revolution.*

Garrit A. Kooy, department of sociology, Wageningen, Netherlands.

Paul Kurtz, professor of philosophy, State University of New York at Buffalo; editor of *The Humanist.*

*****Daniel H. Labby**, professor psychiatry and medicine, University of Oregon Health Sciences Center, Portland.

Birgitta Linner, marriage counselor, Abo, Finland; coauthor of *Sex and Society in Sweden.*

*****Judd Marmor**, USC School of Medicine; former president, American Academy of Psychoanalysts; author of *Psychiatry in Transition.*

*****John Money**, professor of medical psychology and associate professor of pediatrics at the John Hopkins University; editor of *Sex Errors of the Body* and coauthor of *Man and Woman, Boy and Girl.*

James W. Prescott, National Institute of Child Health and Human Development of HEW, Washington, D.C.

*****Ira L. Reiss**, University of Minnesota; author of *Family System in America* and *Social Context of Premarital Social Permissiveness.*

Robert Rimmer, Quincy, Massachusetts; author of *Proposition 31, Adventures in Loving,* and *The Harrad Experiment.*

Della Roy, Pennsylvania State University; coauthor of *Honest Sex.*

Rustum Roy, Pennsylvania State University; coauthor of *Honest Sex.*

Michael Schofield, social psychologist, London, England; author of *The Sexual Behavior of Young People.*

References and Notes

References and Notes

Foreword

1. SIECUS, *SEX . . . is not a four letter word*, 1970.

2. SIECUS form letter (undated), posted January 11, 1971.

3. This paragraph represents a digest of material gathered from the following sources: (a) *Fifth Report, Un-American Activities in California, 1949*, Regular California Legislature, Sacramento, page 265. (b) *Fourth Report, Un-American Activities in California, 1948, Communist Front Organizations*, Regular California Legislature, pages 49, 61. (c) "The New Drive Against The Anti-Communist Program," *Hearing before the Subcommittee to Investigate the Administration of the Internal Security Act and Other Internal Security Laws of the Committee on the Judiciary, U.S. Senate, 87th Congress, First Session, July 11, 1961,* pages 4, 5, 26.

4. *Human Sexuality — A Book List for Professionals* (SIECUS, 1970), pages 25, 29, 35, 40, 43.

Part I

Chapter 1: A Round of Rudiments

1. *The Humanist*, November–December 1964, page 184.

2. *Impact of Science on Society*, Vol. XVIII, No. 4, October–December 1968 (published by UNESCO).

3. *Ibid.*, page 286.

4. Julian Huxley, *Our Crowded Planet, Essays on the Pressures of Population*, edited by Fairfield Osborn (Doubleday & Co., Garden City, N.Y.), page 229.

5. George Brock Chisholm, "The Psychiatry of Enduring Peace and Social Progress — Reestablishment of Peacetime Society," *Psychiatry*, Vol. 9, February 1946, pages 1–35. (William Alanson White Memorial Lectures, Second Series.)

6. UNESCO Conference of the International Union of Family Organizations, held in Rio de Janeiro, July 1963.

7. *Journal of Marriage and the Family*, Vol. XXVI, No. 1, February 1964.

8. Conference Proceedings, 1960 White House Conference on Children and Youth, March 27–April 2, 1960, pages 140–145.

9. *Congressional Record*, March 17, 1969, "Population Policy: A Time for Action," entered by the Honorable George E. Brown Jr., pages E2073–E2081.

10. *Boston Herald Traveler*, October 30, 1969.

11. "Planned Parenthood Head Foresees Use of Coercion," *New York Times*, July 6, 1969, page 47.

12. Alan Guttmacher, "Unwanted Pregnancy: A Challenge to Mental Health," *Mental Hygiene*, October 30, 1967, pages 512, 515.

13. *U.S.A.* magazine, August 12, 1955.

14. *Atlanta Journal*, February 19, 1970.

15. Department of Health, Education and Welfare, *Implementing DHEW Policy on Family Planning and Population* (HEW, Washington, D.C., 1967), page 14 *et seq.* Attachment B.

16. *Denver Register*, May 11, 1967.

17. *Boston Globe*, August 10, 1968.

18. *Los Angeles Times*, September 4, 1969.

19. *New York News*, December 13, 1967, page 4.

20. Paul Ehrlich, "World Population: Is the Battle Lost?" *Stanford Today*, Winter 1968.

21. *Congressional Record*, March 17, 1969, *loc. cit.*

22. *Ibid.*

23. *Health Education, Sex Education and Education for Home and Family Life*, Report on Expert Meeting, February 17–22, 1964, published by UNESCO Institute for Education, Hamburg, West Germany, 1965.

24. *Ibid.*, page 34.

25. Birgitta Linner, *Sex and Society in Sweden* (Pantheon Book, a Division of Random House, New York, 1967), page 104.

26. *Ibid.* pages 104–105. See also *op. cit.* in Footnote 23.

27. *The Humanist*, special issue, Spring 1965, page 78.

28. *Family Life Education — A Community Responsibility*, Proceedings of a Symposium on Sex Education for those involved in any aspect of Education or Counseling, held in Toronto, Ontario, September 23, 1967 (sponsored by Ortho Pharmaceutical Limited of Canada), page 5.

29. *Playboy*, April 1970, an interview with Dr. Mary Calderone.

30. "Educator Sees Sex Changing . . . For the Better," *Washington Star Ledger* Washington Bureau, November 1968.

31. *The American Revelation*, St. Louis, Missouri, Vol. 2, No. 1, First Quarter, 1970, page 11.

32. Address by Dr. Mary S. Calderone, Hoffman-LaRoche Pharmaceutical Corporation, Nutley, N.J., April 2, 1969.

33. "Woman Favors Sex Testing by Adolescents," *Minneapolis Tribune*, October 13, 1965.

34. *Playboy*, April 1970, interview with Mary S. Calderone.

35. *Ibid.*

36. California Legislature, 1953 Regular Session, *Eleventh Report, Senate Investigating Committee on Education*, pages 18, 19, 22, 32, 33, 115.

37. California Legislature, 1951 Regular Session, *Eighth Report, Senate Investigating Committee on Education*, pages 52, 68.

38. California Legislature, 1953 Regular Session, *Eleventh Report, Senate Investigating Committee on Education*, pages 18, 19, 23, 33, 40, 46, 132, 141. See also California Legislature, *Fourth Report, Un-American Activities in California, Communist Front Organizations* 1948, pages 107, 145, 151, 179, 181, 194, 200, 244, 247, 333, 338, 351; and Francis X. Gannon, *Biographical Dictionary of the Left*, Vol. I (Belmont, Mass., Western Islands Publishers, 1969), pages 220–222.

39. See Chapter 4, "A Round of Subversion."

40. California Legislature, 1953 Regular Session, *Eleventh Report, Senate Investigating Committee on Education*, pages 21, 29, 45, 115–119, 141.

41. *Sexology*, April 1969, page 602.

42. John Steinbacher, " 'Girlie' Show Link To Sexologist Told," *Anaheim Bulletin*, Anaheim, Calif., March 6, 1969.

43. SIECUS, *Questions and Answers About Sex Information And Education Council of the U.S. (SIECUS) and Sex Education*, page 1.

44. The Levering Act consisted of a loyalty oath for teachers and was strictly enforced. California Legislature, 1953 Regular Session, *Eleventh Report, Senate Investigating Committee on Education*, pages 9, 13.

45. Information from files of Committee on Internal Security, U.S. House of Representatives, in special correspondence dated February 10, 1970, lists William Genné as affiliated with the following Communist fronts: 1949 — Committee for Peaceful Alternatives to the Atlantic Pact; 1950— World Peace Appeal; 1951 — National Committee to Repeal the McCarran Act; (See also *Congressional Record*, June 26, 1968, "Sex Education Fad," address by the Honorable John R. Rarick, page E5851.)

46. *Journal of the American College Health Association*, Vol. 15, May 1967, "Proceedings of a Symposium on Sex Education of the College Student" (held October 19–21, 1966), page 60.

47. *Sexology*, December 1968, page 353.

48. *Called to Responsible Freedom, The Meaning of Sex in the Christian Life*, National Council of Churches, 1961, pages 6–7.

49. *Newsweek*, June 26, 1967.

50. *Investigation of Communist Activities in New York City Area, Part VI*, House Committee on Un-American Activities, July 7, 1953, pages 2075–2077.

51. "Issues Presented by the Air Reserve Training Manual," *Hearings*, House Committee on Un-American Activities, February 25, 1960, page 1303.

52. "The Negro American — A Reading List," National Council of Churches, 1957. See *Congressional Record*, entry by the Honorable Donald L. Jackson, House of Representatives, April 20, 1960, pages 7843–7844. (Many school systems are currently following suit by incorporating works of these same authors and many others of Communist persuasion into their curricula, under the guise of "American Negro History.")

53. "Network for World Control," Ed Dieckmann Jr., *The American Mercury*, Winter 1969, page 1.

54. *Issues in Training*, edited by Weschler and Schein, National Training Laboratories and National Education Association, page 47.

55. Newcomb, Theodore, *Personality and Social Change* (Dryden, New York, 1943), *passim*.

56. *Journal of American College Health Association*, Vol. 15, May 1967, "Proceedings of a Symposium on Sex Education of the College Student" (held October 19–21, 1966), page 52.

57. *Sexology*, June 1969, page 773.

58. *The Educator*, Vol. 1, No. 2, September 1969, page 1.

59. *Health Education — A Conceptual Approach to Curriculum Design*, School Health Education Study (SHES), 1967, page vii.

60. See Nos. 38 and 50 above.

61. California Legislature, 1948, *Fourth Report, Un-American Activities in California, Communist Front Organizations*, page 107.

62. David E. Gumaer, "The A.C.L.U.," *American Opinion*, Vol. XII, No. 8, September 1969, page 89.

63. *Limited Survey of Honoraria Given Guest Speakers for Engagements at Colleges and Universities*, Report by Committee on Internal Security, U.S. House of Representatives, 91st Congress, Second Session, U.S. Government Printing Office, Washington, D.C. 1970, page 6.

64. Committee on Un-American Activities, House Report 3123 on the National Lawyers Guild, September 21, 1950; originally "related" September 17, 1950. See also *Guide to Subversive Organizations and Publications*, House Document No. 398, page 121.

65. California Legislature, 1951 Regular Session, *Eighth Report, Senate Investigating Committee on Education*, page 54. See also *Investigation of Un-American Propaganda Activities in the United States*, Special Committee on Un-American Activities, Appendix IX, "Communist Front Organizations," 1944, pages 384, 764, 1066, 1274, 1374f., 1614, and 1777.

66. California Legislature, 1951 Regular Session, *Eighth Report, Senate Investigating Committee on Education*, page 54.

67. California Legislature, 1953 Regular Session, *Eleventh Report, Senate Investigating Committee on Education*, pages 130–133. Fritchman is still an active supporter of subversive causes, having recently pledged a donation of $2,000 from his church (The First Unitarian Church, Los Angeles) to the militant Black Panther Party. (See "Extent of Subversion in the 'New Left,' " Testimony of Robert J. Thoms, Sergeant, Los Angeles Police Department, in *Hearings before the Subcommittee to Investigate the Administration of the Internal Security Act and Other Internal Security Laws of the Committee on the Judiciary, U.S. Senate, 91st Congress, Second Session, Part 1*, January 20, 1970, page 10.)

68. California Legislature, 1953 Regular Session, *Eleventh Report, Senate Investigating Committee on Education*, pages 116–117. (Lamont is a former member of the American Association for the United Nations, and is also associated with the ACLU and NAACP.)

69. *Investigation of Un-American Propaganda Activities in the U.S.*, Special Committee on Un-American Activities, House of Representatives, 78th Congress, Second Session on H. Res. 282, *Appendix IX*, "Communist Front Organizations," pages 362, 381, 523, 546, 670, 673, 728, 730, 775, 977, 1096, 1101, 1206, 1375, 1531, 1672, 1774. See also California Legislature, 1953 Regular Session, *Eleventh Report, Senate Investigating Committee on Education*, page 57; and *Biographical Dictionary of the Left*, Vol. I, pages 244–245.

70. Testimony of J. Edgar Hoover, Director, F.B.I., Before House Subcommittee on Appropriations on February 10, 1966, Regarding Demonstrations Protesting U.S. Policy Toward Vietnam, U.S. Department of Justice, Washington, D.C., page 2.

71. "Four Schemes for World Government," U.S. House Report, 81st Congress, First Session, April 19, 1949, pages 155–156. See also California Legislature, 1953 Regular Session, *Eleventh Report, Senate Investigating Committee on Education*, page 115.

72. See No. 38.

73. In former years, according to House Committee on Un-American Activities documents, Arthur J. Goldberg was a sponsor of the Chicago Conference on Race Relations, which had well-known and publicly avowed leaders of the Communist Party among its sponsors. He was also president of the Chicago chapter of the National Lawyers Guild, cited as "the foremost legal bulwark of the Communist Party," as well as a sponsor of the Conference on Constitutional Liberties in America and the National Emergency Conference — both Communist fronts. (See *Investigation of Un-American Propaganda Activities in the U.S.*, pages 610, 653, 1206, 1228; also *Guide to Subversive Organizations and Publications*, House Document No. 398, page 121.)

74. *Paterson* (N.J.) *News*, January 19, 1970.

75. California Legislature, 1953 Regular Session, *Eleventh Report, Senate Investigating Committee on Education*, page 40.

76. *Ibid.*, pages 57–58. See also *Guide to Subversive Organizations and Publications,* House Document No. 398, pages 115–116.

77. *The Humanist*, September–October 1969, page 18.

78. Edith Kermit Roosevelt, "A Temple of Propaganda," *The Wanderer*, July 14, 1966.

79. *Ibid.*

80. Temple of Understanding brochure, List of Sponsors, pages 41, 42, 43, 45, and 48.

Chapter 2: A Round of Philosophy

1. Joseph F. Fletcher, *Moral Responsibility — Situation Ethics At Work* (The Westminister Press, Philadelphia, 1967), page 34.

2. *Journal of the American College Health Association*, Vol. 15, May 1967, "Proceedings of a Symposium on Sex Education of the College Student," page 63.

3. *Ibid.*, pages iii–iv.

4. SIECUS General Information brochure.

5. *Ibid.*

6. Dr. Albert H. Hobbs (Associate Professor of Sociology, University of Pennsylvania), *Seek for Sex Education and You Shall Find* (America's Future, New Rochelle, N.Y.), page 11.

7. René A. Wormser, *Foundations: Their Power and Influence* (Devin-Adair, New York, 1958), pages 100–105.

8. "An Open Letter from SIECUS — Questions and Answers About Sex Information and Education Council of the U.S. (SIECUS) and Sex Education," February 17, 1969, page 1.

9. *Philadelphia Inquirer Magazine*, January 2, 1966.

10. "An Open Letter from SIECUS," *op. cit.*, pages 1,4. See also SIECUS Study Guide #9, *Sex, Science, and Values*, pages 9, 21.

11. Lester A. Kirkendall, SIECUS Study Guide #1, *Sex Education*, fourth printing, January 1969, pages 6, 8, 16.

12. *Journal of the American College Health Association, op. cit.*, page 7.

13. Ira L. Reiss, SIECUS Study Guide #5, *Premarital Sexual Standards*, reissued October 1967, pages 15, 16, 17.

14. Harold T. Christensen, SIECUS Study Guide #9, *Sex, Science and Values*, February 1969, pages 6–9.

15. *Ibid.*, pages 21–22.

16. Isadore Rubin, SIECUS Study Guide #10, *The Sex Educator and Moral Values*, February 1969, pages 8–9.

17. Isadore Rubin, "Transition in Sex Values — Implications for the Education of Adolescents," reprinted in *Journal of Marriage and the Family*, May 1965. (This paper was originally presented at the annual meeting of the National Council on Family Relations, Miami, Florida, October 1964.)

18. *Ibid.*, pages 186–187.

19. *Ibid.*, page 188.

20. *Sexology*, July 1970, page 68.

21. Dr. Arthur H. Cain, *Young People and Sex* (The John Day Co., New York, 1967), page 98.

22. *The Humanist*, March–April 1970, pages 19, 24.

23. *Ibid.*, November–December 1965, page 262.

24. Citizens for Improved Education, *Sex/Family Life Education and Sensitivity Training — Indoctrination or Education*, a report presented to the California State Board of Education (San Mateo, California, C.I.E. Information Center, P.O. Box 241, February 1969), pages 34–35.

25. SIECOP, Special Newsletter, Subject: Documentation of SIECOP's Statement Regarding the Pornography Commission's Report, April 17, 1971.

26. Thomas J. J. Altizer, *The Gospel of Christian Atheism* (The Westminster Press, Philadelphia, 1966), page 127.

Chapter 3: A Round of Religion

1. Sex Information and Education Council of the U.S., Inc. (SIECUS), *SIECUS General Information* (New York, SIECUS, 1968–1969).

2. Lester A. Kirkendall, *Sex Education*, SIECUS Study Guide No. 1, Fourth printing, January 1969 (New York, SIECUS Publications Office), page 15.

3. American College Health Association, "Proceedings of a Symposium on Sex Education of the College Student," *Journal of the American College Health Association*, Vol. 15, Special Issue (Ithaca, N.Y., ACHA, May 1967), page 8.

4. Kirkendall, *op. cit.*, page 12.

5. American Humanist Association, *American Humanist Association — Philosophy, Purposes, and Program* . . . (San Francisco, AHA, undated).

6. *New Humanist*, Vol. 6, No. 3, 1933 (Yellow Springs, Ohio, AHA).

7. Harold R. Rafton, *The Humanist*, Issue No. 3, 1953.

8. Martin Hall, "A Defeat for California's Fundamentalists," *The Humanist*, March–April 1970, page 41.

9. Lisa Kuhmerker, "Curriculum Kits," *Ethical Education*, Vol. 1, Fall 1969, page 7. (Professor Kuhmerker is a member of the Department of Curriculum and Teaching at Hunter College in New York City.)

10. This information, as well as the previous list of SIECUS board members who are Humanists, was gathered from Humanist publication sources too numerous to cite in the space available.

11. *Ethical Culture Fact Book, 1876–1966* (New York, Ethical Culture Publications), page 11.

12. *Ibid.*, page 7; unnumbered pages 12, 14. See also brochure, *For This We Stand, This Is Ethical Culture* (New York, The American Ethical Union.)

13. *Ethical Culture Fact Book, 1876–1966*, page 3.

14. Algernon D. Black, *Ethical Culture — A Living Faith for Modern Man* (New York, The New York Society for Ethical Culture, 1963), page 36.

15. *Ibid.*, page 36.

16. *Ethical Culture Fact Book, 1876–1966*, pages 25–26.

17. *Ibid.*, page 16.

18. *Ibid.*, page 28.

19. "AEU Brief Supports Conscientious Objector," *Ethical Culture Today,* November–December 1964, page 1.

20. Werner, Klugman, "Ethical Forum Joins The Humanist," *The Humanist,* March–April 1969, page 1.

21. Edwin H. Wilson, "Humanism's Many Dimensions," *The Humanist,* November–December 1970, page 35.

22. *The Humanist,* January–February 1974, page 3 (contents page).

23. International Humanist and Ethical Union, "Humanist News," *International Humanism,* Vol. III, One, 1968, page 20.

24. Wilson, "What Do You Mean 'Religious Humanism'?" (Yellow Springs, Ohio, Fellowship of Religious Humanists, undated leaflet).

25. David E. Gumaer, "Peace Symbols — The Truth About Those Strange Designs," *American Opinion,* June 1970, page 56.

26. Rudolf Koch, *The Book of Signs,* (New York, Dover Publications, 1955), page 83; Gumaer, *loc. cit.,* page 50.

27. Gumaer, *loc. cit.,* page 56.

28. William E. Dunham, "Correction, Please!" (*The Review Of The News,* April 28, 1971, page 21.)

29. Staff Report, "Alternatives," *The Humanist,* July–August 1966, page 115.

30. Senate Investigating Committee on Education, California Legislature, 1958 Budget session, *Sixteenth Report,* "Curriculum Changes" (Sacramento, Calif., State Senate, 1958), pages 264–266.

31. See Chapter 4 for documentation.

32. "Is World Government Dead?" (editorial), *The Humanist* (July–August) 1968, page 1.

33. The Editors, "Ethical Forum," *The Humanist,* November–December 1970, page 8.

34. Art Jackson, "News from Humanist House," *The Humanist,* March–April 1967, page 66.

35. Staff Report, "Alternatives," *loc. cit., page 114.*

36. *A Living Will* (New York, Euthanasia Educational Fund, leaflet, 7th Printing, May 1971).

37. "Humanist and Ethical News," *The Humanist,* March–April 1969, unnumbered page 33.

38. "Humanist and Ethical News," *The Humanist,* July–August 1970, page 47.

39. *New York Times,* September 24, 1971, page 48L.

40. The NAACP Legal Defense Fund, incidentally, received an allocation of $15,000 in April 1971 from the United Presbyterian Church's Emergency Legal Aid Fund, for an unstated purpose. This was the same Fund that granted $10,000 to the self-proclaimed Communist, Angela Davis. See *The Presbyterian Layman,* July–August 1971, page 7.

41. *Long Island Press,* October 13, 1971.

42. *Ibid.* Although the Reverend James P. Collins is officially chaplain at Elmira prison, he was on the scene during the insurrection at Attica.

43. John and Evelyn Dewey, *Schools of To-Morrow* (New York, E.P. Dutton & Co., 1915).

44. Committee on Church and State of the American Humanist Association, *In Defense of Separation of Church and State — A Humanist Viewpoint.* AHA Publication No. 53 (Yellow Springs, Ohio, AHA), unnumbered page 13.

45. *Ibid.,* unnumbered pages 14–15.

46. Staff Report, "Alternatives," *loc. cit.,* page 114.

47. *Ibid.,* page 113.

48. *New York Daily News,* September 8, 1971.

49. Donald J. Cantor, "The Homosexual Revolution — A Status Report," *The Humanist,* September–December 1967, page 160. (An article on the subject of divorce, titled "A Matter of Right," with the byline of *David* J. Cantor, appeared in the May–June 1970 issue of *The Humanist.* The author was described in both cases as a practicing attorney in Hartford, Conn., who contributes articles on moral issues and the law to the *Atlantic Monthly.* It is possible that Mr. Cantor's first name is David, and that he writes under both names; it is also possible that the magazine made an error in his name in one article or the other.)

50. *Ibid.,* page 163.

51. American Medical Association Committee on Alcoholism and Drug Dependence and the Council on Mental Health, "Dependence on LSD and Other Hallucinogenic Drugs," *Journal of the American Medical Association (JAMA),* Vol. 202, October 2, 1967, page 47.

52. Maggie Scarf, "Normality Is a Square Circle or a Four-Sided Triangle," *New York Times* Magazine, October 3, 1971, page 45.

53. *Ibid.,* pages 45–48.

54. Tolbert H. McCarroll, "Religions of the Future," *The Humanist,* November–December 1966, page 191.

55. *Ibid.,* page 192.

56. *Ibid.*

57. *The Humanist,* March–April 1967, page 67 (classified advertising).

58. *Ibid.*

59. (See Nos. 21 and 24.)

60. Howard Radest, "A New Opportunity," *The Humanist,* March–April 1969, page 2.

61. Lloyd and Mary Morain, *op. cit.,* page 5.

62. Special Committee on Intergroup Relations, "Intergroup Relations of the American Humanist Association," *The Humanist,* January–February 1963, page 25.

63. *Complete Catalog — Books from Beacon Press* (Boston, Beacon Press, Fall 1969), 4th cover.

64. (See No. 24).

65. *Ibid.*

66. Lester Mondale, *Religious Humanism* (Yellow Springs, Ohio, Fellowship of Religious Humanists, undated leaflet).

67. *Ibid.*

68. (See No. 24.)

69. Fellowship of Religious Humanists, *Religious Humanism,* Winter 1969, editorial page.

70. *Ethical Culture Fact Book 1876–1976,* page 21.

71. International Humanist and Ethical Union, "Declaration of the Congress in Amsterdam Which Inaugurated IHEU on August 26, 1952," *International Humanism,* Vol. III, 1968, 2nd cover.

72. *Ibid.*

73. "Humanist and Ethical News," *The Humanist,* November–December 1969, unnumbered page 37.

74. International Humanist and Ethical Union, *International Humanism,* 3d cover.

75. *Ibid.,* 4th cover.

76. "AEU Brief Supports Conscientious Objector," *loc. cit.,* page 7.

77. Alfred E. Kuenzli, "Friends Among the Friends," *The Humanist,* January–February 1963, page 27.

78. *Ibid.*

79. *Ibid.,* page 28.

80. *An Introduction to the American Friends Service Committee* (Philadelphia, American Friends Service Committee, undated booklet), unnumbered page 7.

81. *Ibid.*, unnumbered page 2.

82. Morain, *op. cit.*, page 40.

83. *Ibid.*

84. *Ibid.*, page 4.

85. (See No. 24.)

86. "AEU Brief Supports Conscientious Objector," *Ethical Culture Today,* page 1.

87. Edward L. Ericson, "Humanist Conscientious Objection," *The Humanist,* May–June 1969, center section.

88. Corliss Lamont, *The Philosophy of Humanism*, Fifth Edition (New York, Frederick Ungar Publishing Co.), page 24.

89. *Webster's New World Dictionary of the American Language*, 2nd College Edition (New York–Cleveland, World Publishing Co., 1970), page 1200.

90. Holy Bible (King James version), Proverbs 14:12.

91. Donald Grey Barnhouse, *Man's Ruin* (Grand Rapids, Michigan, Wm. B. Eerdmans Publishing Co., 1952), Vol. I, page 248.

92. *Ibid.,* page 248.

93. S.S. Chawla, "A Philosophical Journey to the West," *The Humanist,* September–October 1964, page 151. (At the time this article was published, Mr. Chawla was assistant editor of *The Tribune* of Ambala, India.)

94. Hector Hawton, "Humanism's Opportunity," *The Humanist,* March–April 1970, pages 3–4.

95. Robert W. McCoy, (then president of the American Humanist Association, Golden Valley, Minn.) in "Letters to the Editor," *Minneapolis Star,* July 27, 1968.

Chapter 4: A Round of Subversion

1. J. Edgar Hoover, *On Communism* (New York, Random House, Inc., 1969), page 108.

2. Public Hearing before the New Jersey Senate and General Assembly Committee on Education (*re*: Sex Education in Public Schools), Vol. 1, August 14, 1969, page 68.

3. *Paterson Evening News*, January 30, 1969.

4. Committee on Un-American Activities, *Guide to Subversive Organizations and Publications*, House Document #398 (Washington, D.C., U.S. Government Printing Office, Revised, December 1, 1961), page 5.

5. *Ibid.*, page 120.

6. Hoover, *op. cit.*, page 127.

7. *Guide to Subversive Organizations and Publications*, page 1.

8. Hoover, *Masters of Deceit* (New York, Pocket Books, Inc., 22nd Printing, 1966), page vi.

9. "The Communists Are After Our Minds," *American Mercury*, October 1954.

10. Robert Morris, *No Wonder We Are Losing* (New York, The Bookmailer, 9th Printing, 1958), pages 5–17.

11. *Ibid.*, page 17.

12. Most Reverend Cuthbert O'Gara, Bishop of Yuanling, *The Surrender to Secularism* (St. Louis, Missouri, Cardinal Mindszenty Foundation, 1967), pages 11–12.

13. Julian Huxley, *The Coming New Religion of Humanism* (Yellow Spring, Ohio, American Humanist Association, Publication No. 204, undated leaflet), unnumbered page 2.

14. House Committee on Un-American Activities, Report, "The Communist Mind," 85th Congress, May 29, 1957.

15. Hoover, *Masters of Deceit*, pages 321–322.

16. David Mace, "New Morality," *Sexology*, April 1968.

17. Hoover, *Masters of Deceit*, page 322.

18. Karl Marx, *Economie Politique et Philosophie*, Vol. I, pages 38–40.

19. *Socialist Humanism*, proceedings of an international symposium, edited by Erich Fromm, page v.

20. Congressman James B. Utt, Washington Report # 69-4, March 26, 1969.

21. Luther Baker, *The Rising Furor Over Sex Education* (SIECUS Publication Office, June 1969), page 4.

22. *Ibid.*, page 7.

23. Paul Putnam, *Critique of "The Innocents Defiled,"* National Education Association Commission on Professional Rights and Responsibilities, page 2.

24. "Subversive Influence in the Educational Process," testimony of Isadore Rubin before the Senate Internal Security Subcommittee, September 8, 1952, page 146.

25. Interview with J. Edgar Hoover, *Industrial Security,* April 1962.

26. *Guide to Subversive Organizations and Publications*, pages 115–116, 178. See also reference 45, Chapter 1.

27. Senate Fact-Finding Committee on Un-American Activities, *Fifth Report — Un-American Activities in California*, 1949 Regular California Legislature (Sacramento, California, Senate, 1949), page 482.

28. *Guide to Subversive Organizations and Publications,* page 65.

29. Committee on Un-American Activities, U.S. House of Representatives, Part 2, *Communist Political Subversion* (Washington, D.C., U.S. Government Printing Office, 1957), pages 7378–7380.

30. *Guide to Subversive Organizations and Publications,* page 33.

31. *Ibid.*

32. Fifth Report — Un-American Activities in California, page 534.

33. Senate Investigating Committee on Education, *Eleventh Report — Opposition to Loyalty*, California Legislature, 1953 Regular Session (Sacramento, California, Senate, 1953), page 58.

34. *The Population Crisis: Implications and Plans for Action*, Larry K. P. Ng, editor, and Stuart Mudd, co-editor (Bloomington, Indiana, Indiana University Press, 1965.)

35. Miriam Allen de Ford, "Implications and Plans," *The Humanist*, January–February 1966, page 21.

36. Special Committee on Un-American Activities, U.S. House of Representatives, *Investigation of Un-American Propaganda Activities in the United States, Appendix IX, Communist Front Organizations*, First Reprint Edition (Washington, D.C., U.S. Government Printing Office, 1944), Vol. 1, page 1009. (Referred to hereafter as *Appendix — Part IX.*)

37. *Guide to Subversive Organizations and Publications,* page 101.

38. Appendix IX, *op. cit.*, Vol. 1, page 1005.

39. Committee on Un-American Activities, U.S. House of Representatives, *Trial by Treason — The National Committee to Secure Justice for the Rosenbergs and Morton Sobell*, Eighty-Fourth Congress (Washington, D.C., U.S. Government Printing Office, August 25, 1956), page 72.

40. *Guide to Subversive Organizations and Publications*, page 40.

41. *Ibid.*, page 116.

42. Felix Wittmer, *Conquest of the American Mind* (Boston, Meador Press, 1956), page 230–231. See also *Hearings before the Subcommittee to Investigate the Administration of the Internal Security Act and Other Internal Security Laws of the Committee on the Judiciary, United States Senate, 82nd Congress, First Session, on the Institute of Pacific Relations*, Part 2, August 9, 14, 16, 20, 22, and 23, 1951, page 563.

43. Senate Investigating Committee on Education, *Eighth Report*, California Legislature, 1951 Regular Session (Sacramento, California, Senate, 1951), page 66. See also *Appendix IX, op. cit.*, pages 332, 349, 357, 362, 365ff., 372,

377f., 380f., 383, 391, 396, 409, 417, 471, 535, 537, 589, 635, 668, 673, 758, 776, 917, 921f., 949, 1086f., 1089, 1096f., 1163, 1177, 1179, 1202, 1205, 1207, 1209f., 1300, 1355, 1357, 1375, 1379, 1384, 1388, 1447, 1457, 1478, 1483f., 1490ff., 1602, 1617, 1649, 1641.

44. Wittmer, *op. cit.,* page 238. (For more information on the American Student Union, see *Guide to Subversive Organiztions and Publications,* page 31.)

45. *Appendix IX, op. cit.,* pages 313, 667, 671, 962, 966, 1275, 1624, 1642.

46. *Sixteenth Report,* Senate Investigating Committee on Education, California Legislature, 1958 Budget Session, page 176. See also *Fourth Report, Un-American Activities in California, Communist Front Organizations,* 1948 Regular California Legislature, Sacramento, page 248; *Fifth Report, Un-American Activities in California,* 1949 Regular California Legislature, Sacramento, page 540; *Appendix IX, op. cit.,* page 1772.

47. Testimony of Walter F. Steele before the House Committee on Un-American Activities, July 21, 1947, pages 40–41.

48. Wittmer, *op. cit.,* pages 230, 232.

49. Information from files of the Committee on Internal Security, U.S. House of Representatives, special correspondence dated March 9, 1970, pages 1–2. See also *Sixteenth Report,* Senate Investigating Committee on Education, California Legislature, 1958 Budget Session, pages 242–244. (For citations of organizations mentioned, see *Guide to Subversive Organizations and Publications,* pages 118, 62, 65, 138, and 216.

50. *Sixteenth Report,* Senate Investigating Committee on Education, California Legislature, 1958 Budget Session, page 243.

51. Wittmer, *op. cit.,* pages 237–238.

52. *Fourth Report, Un-American Activities in California, 1948, Communist Front Organizations,* page 279; *Third Report,* 1947, page 96. See also *Guide to Subversive Organizations and Publications,* pages 219, 33.

53. Senator James O. Eastland, speech in U.S. Senate, *Congressional Record,* May 26, 1955, pages 7117–7124. See also report, *Sex/Family Life Education and Sensitivity Training — Indoctrination or Education?* presented to California State Board of Education, February 1969, by Citizens for Improved Education, P.O. Box 241, San Mateo, California.

54. *Appendix IX, op. cit.,* page 357. See also pages 328ff., 334ff., 348, 360, 362, 674, 778, 928, 977, 980, 1206, 1338.

55. Information from Files of the Committee on Internal Security, U.S. House of Representatives, special correspondence dated March 9, 1970, pages 1–6. See also *Fourth Report, Un-American Activities in California, 1948, Communist Front Organizations,* Regular California Legislature, Sacramento, pages 192, 202, 208, 228, 229, 230: *Fifth Report, Un-American Activities in California,* 1949, Regular California Legislature, pages 455, 457, 458, 482, 483, 490, 491, 500–503, 505, 506, 512, 515–517, 520, 522, 523, 526, 527, 531, 534, 546, 689; *Sixth Report, Un-American Activities in California* 1951 Regular California Legislature, pages 271, 281, 286.

56. Information from the files of the Committee on Internal Security, U.S. House of Representatives, special correspondence dated March 9, 1970, page 6.

57. *Appendix IX, op. cit.,* pages 362, 381, 523, 546, 670, 673, 728, 730, 775, 977, 1096, 1101, 1206, 1375, 1531, 1672, 1774. See also *Eleventh Report,* Senate Investigating Committee on Education, California Legislature, 1953 Regular Session, page 57; also Francis X. Gannon, *Biographical Dictionary of the Left,* Vol. I, pages 244–245.

58. Joseph Fletcher, *Moral Responsibility — Situation Ethics at Work* (Philadelphia, The Westminster Press, 1967), page 39.

59. *Investigation of Communist Activities in the New York City Area — Part*

5, Hearing before the Committee on Un-American Activities, U.S. House of Representatives, 83rd Congress, First Session, July 6, 1953, page 2017.

60. *Ibid.*

61. Review of the Scientific and Cultural Conference for World Peace, Committee on Un-American Activities, U.S. House of Representatives, April 19, 1949, pages 8, 23, 26, 31, 32, 34, 37, 38, 40, 50, 51. See also the Committee's Report on the Communist "Peace" Offensive, A Campaign to Disarm and Defeat the United States, April 1, 1951, pages 23, 36, 37, 38; and *Biographical Dictionary of the Left,* Vol. I, page 329.

62. Erich Fromm, *The Art of Loving,* 27th Printing, (New York, Bantam Books, Inc., 1969), page 110.

63. *Ibid,* page 111.

64. *Biographical Dictionary of the Left,* Vol. I, page 337.

65. *Ibid.* See also the *Guide to Subversive Organizations and Publications,* page 115.

66. Information from the files of the Committee on Internal Security, U.S. House of Representatives, special correspondence dated March 9, 1970, pages 1–2. See also *Eighth Report,* Senate Investigating Committee on Education, California Legislature, 1951 Regular Session, pages 62, 68; and the Committee's *Eleventh Report,* 1953 Regular Session, pages 15, 19, 22–24, 27, 34, 35, 41, 123, 128, 138, 142, 176.

67. Letter from Harry A. Overstreet to Congressman Harold H. Velde, dated July 21, 1953.

68. *Biographical Dictionary of the Left,* Vol. I, page 476.

69. Edward Janisch, "What We Must Know About Overstreet," *American Opinion,* October 1959, page 44.

70. *Ibid.*, pages 44–45.

71. (a) *Herbert Aptheker* — see Testimony of John Edgar Hoover, Director, Federal Bureau of Investigation, Before the House Subcommittee on Appropriations, on February 23, 1968, Regarding Communist, Racial and Hate Groups, pages 3–4. (b) *W. E. B. DuBois* — see *People's World,* December 2, 1961, page 9. (c) *Langston Hughes* — *Eleventh Report,* Senate Investigating Committee on Education, California Legislature, 1953 Regular Session, page 18. (d) *Maxwell S. Stewart* — see No. 42. (e) *Victor Perlo* — Whittaker Chambers, *Witness,* first paperback edition (Chicago, Henry Regnery Co., 1952), page 543.

72. (a) *E. Franklin Frazier* — Speech of Senator James O. Eastland in U.S. Senate, *Congressional Record,* May 26, 1955, pages 7117–7124. (b) *Carey McWilliams* — U.S. House Report, 81st Congress, First Session, April 19, 1949, *Four Schemes for World Government,* pages 155–156. See also *Eleventh Report,* Senate Investigating Committee on Education, California Legislature, 1953 Regular Session, page 115.

73. Wittmer, *op. cit.,* pages 71–72, 106.

74. G. Bromley Oxnam, Testimony in Hearing before Committee on Un-American Activities, House of Representatives, 83rd Congress, First Session, July 21, 1953, pages 3640, 3661. See also *Appendix IX, op. cit.,* pages 350, 353, 668, 1125, 1206, 1240, 1356, 1650.

75. *Guide to Subversive Organizations and Publications,* page 110.

76. *Appendix IX, op. cit.,* Vol. 1, page 410. See also *Guide to Subversive Organizations and Publications,* page 23.

77. *Guide to Subversive Organizations and Publications,* pages 115–116.

78. *Eleventh Report,* Senate Investigating Committee on Education, California Legislature, 1953 Regular Session, pages 15, 28, 29. See also *Appendix IX, op. cit.,* page 665.

79. *Eleventh Report, op. cit.,* page 27.

80. Senator James O. Eastland, speech, *Congressional Record,* May 26, 1955, pages 7117–7124.

81. *Ibid.*

82. *Appendix — Part IX*, pages 1067, 1076.

83. *Eighth Report, Un-American Activities in California*, 1955 Regular California Legislature, page 392; *Fifth Report*, 1949 Regular California Legislature, pages 480, 502, 506, 510, 512. See also *Appendix IX, op. cit.*, pages 307, 433, 1206.

84. *Fifth Report, Un-American Activities in California*, pages 369, 276.

85. *Fourth Report, Un-American Activities in California, 1948, Communist Front Organizations*, Regular California Legislature, page 247.

86. *Castro's Network in the U.S.*, Hearings, Senate Internal Security Subcommittee, Part 6, February 8, 1963, pages 339–350.

87. Undated advertising brochure issued by Lyle Stuart, Inc., New York, N. Y.

88. *Fourth Report, Un-American Activities in California, 1948, Communist Front Organizations*, Regular California Legislature, pages 141, 151, 198, 199, 234, 357, 358. See also *Biographical Dictionary of the Left*, Vol. I, page 545.

89. Terence Shea, "Learn All About Sex in an Explicit New Sunday-School Course," *National Observer*, August 23, 1971.

90. "Humanist and Ethical News," *The Humanist*, July–August 1972, page 47.

91. *Evergreen Review*, April 1969, page 87.

92. Committee on Un-American Activities, U.S. House of Representatives, Hearings on Communist Training Operations, 86th Congress, First Session, 1959, Part 1, page 999.

93. David E. Gumaer, "Satanism — A Practical Guide to Witch Hunting," *American Opinion*, September 1970, page 71.

94. *Guide to Subversive Organizations and Publications*, page 149.

95. *Annual Report of the Committee on Un-American Activities for the Year 1953*, Washington, D.C., U.S. Government Printing Office, February 6, 1954, page 40.

96. *Guide to Subversive Organizations and Publications*, page 122.

97. *Sixteenth Report*, Senate Investigating Committee on Education, California Legislature, 1958 Budget Session, page 242.

98. *Appendix IX, op. cit.*, pages 1335–1338.

99. *Sixteenth Report, op. cit.*, page 137.

100. J. L. Moreno, *Who Shall Survive?*, page 11.

101. *Eleventh Report*, Senate Investigating Committee on Education, California Legislature, 1953 Regular Session, pages 18, 19, 22, 32, 33, 45, 115, 156, 165, 172–174, 176, 177.

102. *Sixteenth Report, op. cit.*, page 138.

103. *Fifth Report, Un-American Activities in California*, 1949 Regular California Legislature, page 499.

104. *Third Report, Un-American Activities in California*, 1947, Fifty-Seventh California Legislature, page 323.

105. *Ibid.*

106. *Ibid.*, pages 353–354.

107. J. Edgar Hoover, article, *The Lion Magazine*, October 1957.

108. Congressman John R. Rarick, address, *Congressional Record*, June 26, 1968, page E5852.

109. Nesta H. Webster, *Secret Societies and Subversive Movements*, Ninth Edition, (Hawthorne, California, Christian Book Club of America, 1967), page 342.

110. W. Cleon Skousen, *The Naked Capitalist*, (Salt Lake City, W. Cleon Skousen, 1970).

111. *Ibid.*

112. Webster, *op. cit.*, page 337.

Part II

American Academy of Pediatrics

1. Karl de Schweinitz, *Growing Up*, seventh printing (The Macmillan Co., New York, 1964), pages 27–28.

2. Dr. George W. Corner, *Attaining Manhood*, page 57; *Attaining Womanhood*, page 81 (both second edition, Harper and Row, New York, 1952).

3. *Ibid.*, pages 65 and 69 respectively.

American Association of Marriage Counselors, Inc.

1. *The American Association of Marriage Counselors, what it is . . . what it does*, undated promotional brochure, page 1.

2. *Paterson News*, November 18, 1970, page 15.

3. *The American Association of Marriage Counselors, what it is . . . what it does*, unnumbered page 2.

4. *Ibid.*, unnumbered page 3.

American Association of Sex Educators and Counselors

1. *AASEC Application for Membership Enrollment*, leaflet.

2. *AASEC Program of Second Annual Conference,* April 11–13, 1969.

3. *Ibid.*

4. *AASEC Newsletter*, Vol. 6, May 1973, page 7.

5. *Ibid.*, pages 1–2.

American College of Obstetricians and Gynecologists

1. *Family Life (Sex) Education — A Professional Responsibility*, Fourth Edition (American College of Obstetricians and Gynecologists, 1968), page 4.

2. *Ibid.*, inside front cover.

American Medical Association

1. Marion O. Lerrigo and Helen Southard, *Finding Yourself* (American Medical Association, Chicago, 1968), page 17.

2. *SIECUS Newsletter*, April 1969, page 4.

3. *American Medical News*, April 26, 1971, pages 8–9.

American School Health Association

1. "Growth Patterns and Sex Education," *The Journal of School Health*, Vol. 37, No. 5a, May 1967.

2. Public Hearing before the New Jersey Senate and General Assembly Committees on Education (*Re:* Sex Education in Public Schools — Assembly Concurrent Resolution No. 69), State House, Trenton, N.J., December 17, 1969, Testimony of Mrs. Richard Preston, page 23.

3. *The Individual, Sex, and Society*, Third Edition, Carlfred Broderick and Jessie Bernard, co-editors (Johns Hopkins Press, Baltimore, 1970), pages 53–63.

4. Lois Willie, "Teaching guide warns youth of drug dangers," *Newark Star Ledger*, November 8, 1970.

5. Drs. Harold Kolansky and William T. Moore, "The Effects of Marijuana on Adolescents and Young Adults," *Journal of the American Medical Association*, Volume 216, April 19, 1971, page 487.

6. James C. Munch, "The Toxicity of Cannabis Sativa (Marijuana)," *Current Medical Digest*, June 1968, page 692.

7. *Journal of the American Medical Association*, November 4, 1968.

8. Robert Musel, "Says Pot Bad For Hair and Complexion," *Paterson Evening News*, September 2, 1970.

9. *New York Sunday News*, April 14, 1974, page 90.

10. Lawrence K. Altman, "Drug Use Linked to Heart Attack," *New York Times*, October 10, 1971, page 70.

American Social Health Association

1. *The Educator*, September 1969, page 2.

2. Undated leaflet titled *The American Social Health Association*.

3. *The Humanist*, September–October 1970, page 9. (See also *The Humanist*, September–December 1967, page 185, for entry on Fiedler Defense Fund.)

4. *The Humanist*, July–August 1967, page 115.

5. Dr. Charles Winick, "Drug Addicts Getting Younger," reprint from *The PTA Magazine*, September 1970, reprint page 3.

6. Dr. Charles Winick, *The Underground Bird*, A Discussion Guide (American Social Health Association, New York, 1968), page 1.

7. Dr. Charles Winick, *The Narcotic Addiction Problem* (American Social Health Association, New York, revised May 1968), page 21.

8. *Ibid.*, page 14.

9. *The Humanist*, May–June 1966, page 107.

Association Press

1. Francis X. Gannon, *Biographical Dictionary of the Left*, Vol. II (Western Islands Publishers, Boston, 1971), page 564.

2. Association Press brochure entitled, "Frank, Specific Up-to-Date Answers from Evelyn Millis Duvall to Questions About Sex, Love and Marriage for Pre-teens, Teens and Adults," advertising her books, *About Sex and Growing Up, Love and the Facts of Life, Why Wait Till Marriage, The Art of Dating, When You Marry, Being Married, In-Laws: Pro & Con*, and *Today's Teen-Agers.*

3. Evelyn Millis Duvall, *Love and the Facts of Life*, Fourth Printing (Association Press, New York, 1968), pages 164–165.

4. Association Press brochure, *op. cit.*

E. C. Brown Trust Foundation

1. *Guide To Sexology*, compiled by editors of *Sexology*, 1965, pages 238–240.

2. *The Humanist*, 25th Anniversary Issue, Fall 1965, page 246.

3. *Ibid.*

4. Education Information, Inc., *Sex Education and Sensitivity Training: A Report on Secular Humanism and The Behaviorists* (Post Office Box 2037, Fullerton, California), undated, page 12.

5. *Ibid.*, page 13.

6. SIECUS Study Guide No. 7, *Film Resources for Sex Education*, pages 12, 16, 17.

7. "Sex/Family Life Education and Sensitivity Training — Indoctrination or Education?" (presented to California State Board of Education, February 1969, by Citizens for Improved Education, P.O. Box 241, San Mateo, California), page 54.

8. E. C. Brown Trust Foundation, *Early Marriage,* film guide for teachers and discussion leaders, page 23.

9. E. C. Brown Trust Foundation, *Sex Education: K Through 6*, a guide to the use of the films, *Human and Animal Beginnings* and *Fertilization and Birth*, page 8.

10. E. C. Brown Trust Foundation, *Human Heredity*, film guide for teachers and discussion leaders, page 14.

11. Perennial Education, Inc., Family Living, *Human Growth and Human Development Materials* (Northfield, Ill.), undated catalog, page 17A.

12. *Ibid.*

13. *Ibid.*

14. E. C. Brown Trust Foundation, Printed Materials catalog, pages 5–11.

The Child Study Association of America

1. Undated leaflet published by the American Ethical Union, titled *The Ethical Culture Movement — Retrospect and Prospect.*

2. *Sex Education and the New Morality — A Search for a Meaningful Social Ethic* (Child Study Association of America, 1967), table of contents.

3. SIECUS Newsletter, October 1968, page 9.

4. The Child Study Association of America, *You, Your Child and Drugs* (The Child Study Press, New York, 1971), page 34 *et seq.*

Churchill Films

1. Churchill Films Catalogue, 1968–1969, pages 11, 13, 15, 32.

2. Study Guide for *A Quarter Million Teenagers*, unnumbered page 1.

Family Life Publications

1. Family Life Publications, *Information About Counseling and Teaching Aids*, Fall 1969, page 2.

2. *Ibid.*

3. Gelolo McHugh and Jay C. Williams, *Discussion Guide To Accompany A Drug Knowledge Inventory* (Family Life Publications, Durham, N.C., 1969), pages 19–21.

4. Dr. Henry Brill, "Why Not Pot Now? Questions and Answers About Marijuana," *Medical Counterpoint*, Vol. 1, No. 2, April 1969, pages 29–34.

Family Service Association of America

1. *Agency Sources for Material on Sex Education*, B-22F, January 1969; *Bulk Rate for Magazine and Newspaper Articles — Reprints*, 68/11–684; *Reading References on Early Marriage*, B-22C, January 1969; and *Reading References on Marriage, Parenthood and Family Relationships*, B-22A, revised October 1969. (All materials published by FSAA.)

2. Charles Winick, Ph.D., *The Underground Bird, Discussion Guide,* page 1.

3. Rose Leiman Schiller, *The Underground Bird*, page 25.

4. Charles Winick, *op. cit.*, page 7.

Foundations and Grants

1. *Journal of the American Medical Association* (JAMA), Vol. 212, No. 11, page 1864.

2. *Look*, July 28, 1970, page 60.

3. Gary Allen, "Beware Metro," *American Opinion*, Vol. 16, January 1973, pages 22–25.

Group for the Advancement of Psychiatry

1. Group for the Advancement of Psychiatry, Symposium No. 9, *Pavlovian Conditioning and American Psychiatry*, 1964, unnumbered page 156.

2. *Ibid.*

3. *Ibid.*

4. Group for the Advancement of Psychiatry, *The Right to Abortion: A Psychiatric View,* Vol. VII, No. 75, October 1969, pages 198–200.

5. SIECUS, *Human Sexuality, A Book List for Professionals*, 1970, pages 40, 58; Group for the Advancement of Psychiatry, undated form letter.

6. Group for the Advancement of Psychiatry, advertising leaflet, *Announcing a New Publication from GAP — Sex and the College Student*, dated December 1965.

7. Group for the Advancement of Psychiatry, *The Right to Abortion: A Psychiatric View*, Volume VII, No. 75, October 1969, GAP card attached to front cover of booklet.

8. *Ibid.*, page 218.

9. *Ibid.*, pages 205, 218.

10. *Ibid.*, page 219.

11. *Ibid.*, page 223.

12. *Ibid.*, page 219.

13. Group for the Advancement of Psychiatry, Publications List and Order Form, March 1969, pages 2–3.

14. Group for the Advancement of Psychiatry, Symposium No. 9, *Pavlovian Conditioning and American Psychiatry*, 1964, unnumbered page 213.

Guidance Associates of Pleasantville, N.Y.

1. Guidance Associates/Harcourt, Brace & World, "Family Life and Sex Education," catalog, 1969.

2. James Lincoln Collier, "Sex Education: Blunt Answers for Tough Questions," *Reader's Digest*, June 1968, page 80.

3. James Collier, "The Procreation Myth," *Playboy*, May 1971, page 193.

4. David E. Smith, John Luce, and Ernest A. Dernburg, "The Health of Haight-Ashbury," *trans action*, Vol 7, April 1970, page 35.

5. "Expert Asks 'Sensible' Drug Laws for State," Paterson (N.J.) *Evening News*, September 10, 1970.

6. "Pot Commish Calls Alcohol Worst Abuser," *New York Daily News*, September 9, 1971, page 62.

7. R. E. L. Masters and Jean Houston, *The Varieties of Psychedelic Experience*, Eleventh Printing (Dell Publishing Co., New York, 1966), front cover.

8. *Ibid.*, pages 3–4.

9. *Ibid.*, page 314.

10. *Ibid.*, page 4.

11. Guidance Associates, Discussion Guide on *Marijuana: What Can You Believe*, page 47.

12. Masters and Houston, *op. cit.*, pages 37–38.

13. *Ibid.*, page 257.

14. *Ibid.*, pages 148–149.

15. Robert A. Wilson, "420 Psychedelic Travelogs," *The Humanist*, January/February 1967, page 26.

16. Guidance Associates, *Guidance Catalog*, Vol. 10, 1971, pages 2–6.

17. Guidance Associates, Discussion Guide on *Marijuana: What Can You Believe?*, page 10.

18. *Ibid.*

Henk Newenhouse, Inc.

1. *SIECUS Newsletter*, March 1970, Vol. 5, page 10.

The Lutheran Church — Missouri Synod

1. Concordia Publishing House, *I Wonder, I Wonder*, brochure advertising Concordia Sex Education Series, unnumbered page 3.

2. For an excellent analysis of this viewpoint encompassing "the latency period" and other psychological aspects as well, see Dr. Rhoda L. Lorand's "A Psychoanalytic View of the Sex Education Controversy," *Journal of the New York State School Nurse Teachers Association*, Vol. 2, No. 1, Fall 1970. (Reprints are available at $1.50, the cost of printing and mailing, from NYSSNTA's Editorial Office, 23 Point View Dr., East Greenbush, N.Y. 12061.)

3. Eric W. Johnson, *Love and Sex in Plain Language*, (Bantam Pathfinder Edition, New York, 1967), pages 60–61.

4. *Ibid.*, front cover.

5. Elmer N. Witt, *Life Can Be Sexual*, (Concordia Publishing House, St. Louis, 1967), page 13.

6. *Ibid.*, pages 85–86.

7. Concordia Publishing House, *loc. cit.*

8. Martin Wessler, *Christian View of Sex Education*, (Concordia Publishing House, St. Louis, 1967), page 79.

9. *Ibid.*, pages 83–85.

Marriage

1. *Marriage*, May 1971, unnumbered page 1.
2. *Marriage,* March 1970, page 19.
3. Joseph Fletcher, *Moral Responsibility: Situation Ethics at Work*, (Westminster Press, Philadelphia, 1967), page 88.
4. *Marriage,* March 1970, page 67.
5. *Ibid.*, page 71.

McGraw-Hill, Inc.

1. McGraw-Hill Films (a Division of McGraw-Hill Company), *Guidance,* undated catalog.
2. McGraw-Hill Films, *Sociology*, undated catalog.
3. The National Film Board of Canada, *Films 1968–69* catalog (Roger Duhamel, F.R.S.C., Queen's Printer, Ottawa, Canada, 1968), page 64.
4. McGraw-Hill Films, *Sociology*, undated catalog.
5. *Ethical Culture Fact Book, 1876–1966,* page 28.

Medical Aspects of Human Sexuality

1. *Medical Aspects of Human Sexuality*, Vol. II, June 1968, page 5.
2. *Ibid.*, unnumbered page 4. (According to the October 1971 issue of this journal, the same four SIECUS officials were still serving as consulting editors at that date).

Mental Health Materials Center

1. SIECUS Newsletter, Vol. 4, October 1968, page 10.
2. "Humanist and Ethical News," *The Humanist*, November–December 1971, page 47.
3. *Ibid.*
4. *Ethical Culture Fact Book, 1876–1966,* unnumbered page 20.
5. Mental Health Materials Center, undated advertising brochure for *Teach Us What We Want To Know.*
6. *Ibid.*
7. New Jersey State Department of Education, *Guidelines for Developing School Programs in Sex Education* (The Department, Trenton, N.J., undated booklet), page iv.
8. *Ibid.*, page 1 (for Policy Statement on Sex Education, as adopted by the New Jersey State Board of Education on January 4, 1967). See also Lester A. Kirkendall, SIECUS Study Guide No. 1, *Sex Education* (originally published October 1965), reissued October 1967, page 4.

National Association of Independent Schools

1. National Association of Independent Schools, *NAIS Sex Education Program* (leaflet), dated May 1968.
2. *Sex Education and the Schools*, Virginia Hilu, editor (Harper and Row, New York, 1967).
3. *Ibid.*, page 33.
4. *Ibid.*, page 38.
5. National Association of Independent Schools, *NAIS Sex Education Program* (leaflet), dated May 1968.
6. Marjorie F. Iseman, "Sex Education," *McCall's*, January 1968, page 118.

National Association for Repeal of Abortion Laws

1. Herman Schwartz, "The Parent or the Fetus? — A Survey of Abortion Law Reform," *The Humanist*, July–August 1967, page 123.
2. "Readers' Forum," *The Humanist*, January–February 1967, page 31.
3. Judith Yellen, "News from Humanist House," *The Humanist*, January–February 1967, page 34.

4. Advertisement for the Society for Humane Abortion, *The Humanist*, January–February 1966, page 30.

5. "An Appeal to Our Readers," *The Humanist*, July–August 1968, page 19.

6. Advertisement for the Society for Humane Abortion, *The Humanist*, page 30.

7. American Humanist Association, *Free Mind* (Membership Bulletin), March 1971, page 1.

8. Hearings before the Committee on Internal Security, U.S. House of Representatives, *New Mobilization Committee to End the War in Vietnam*, Part 2, Ninety-First Congress, Second Session (U.S. Government Printing Office, Washington, D.C., 1970), page 4288.

9. National Association for Repeal of Abortion Laws (NARAL), *How to Win Repeal*, October 1970.

10. NARAL, Form letter requesting donations, undated, reverse side listing organization members.

11. NARAL, *Speaking Up on Abortion — Statements by Organizations*, undated leaflet.

12. NARAL, *National Organizations Recommending Repeal of Restrictive Abortion Laws* (leaflet), February 1972.

13. *Readings in Humanistic Psychology*, edited by Anthony J. Sutich and Miles A. Vich (The Free Press, New York, 1969), page ix.

14. Harriet F. Pilpel, *Know Your Rights About Voluntary Sterilization*, undated Association for Voluntary Sterilization pamphlet, back cover giving committee listings.

15. Margaret Fisk, Editor, *Encyclopedia of Organizations*, Seventh Edition, Vol. 1, (Gale Research Company, Book Tower, Detroit, 1972), page 424.

16. *The Village Voice*, April 27, 1972, page 39.

17. American Civil Liberties Union, *Appendix from 1970 Biennial Report*, page ii.

18. Advertisement for The Friends of Animals, Inc., *The Humanist*, November–December 1971, page 45.

19. *Ibid.* page 45.

20. Gary Allen, "Life and Death — The Little Murders of Big Brother," *American Opinion*, Vol. XIV, June 1971, page 12.

21. Father Nugent, *Three Ways to Murder a Baby* (The Oratory, P.O. Box 1326, Lexington, Ky.), undated leaflet.

22. Gary Allen, *loc. cit.*

23. "Nurses Fight Loosening of Abortion Code," *The Wanderer*, January 13, 1972, page 1.

24. Herman Schwartz, *op cit.*, page 126.

25. Gary Allen, *op. cit.*, page 3.

26. *Ibid.*

27. *Ibid.*, pages 3–4.

28. David A. Noebel, "One Christian's View," *Christian Crusade Weekly*, November 14, 1971, page 2.

29. John M. Langone, "The Medical Evidence," *Boston Herald Traveler*, November 17, 1971.

30. *Ibid.*

31. Valerie Vance Dillon, *In Defense of Life* (New Jersey Right to Life Committee, Trenton, N.J., 1970), Appendix, page 99.

32. "Claims Pro-Abortionists Are Shifting Their Arguments," *The Wanderer*, August 12, 1971.

33. Mary Kay Williams, "Abortion and Morality — Do Pro-Life Forces 'Impose Morals' on Others?" *The Beacon*, February 10, 1972, page 7.

34. *Ibid.*

35. James H. Townsend, *The Educator*, September–October 1970.

36. NARAL, *National Organizations Recommending Repeal of Restrictive Abortion Laws* (Leaflet), February 1972.

37. "Humanist Views," *The Humanist*, January–February 1969, page 33.

38. NARAL News, Summer 1971, page 6.

39. "Humanist and Ethical News," *The Humanist*, May–June 1969, page 33.

40. *Ibid.*

41. NARAL, *National Organizations Recommending Repeal of Restrictive Abortion Laws* (leaflet), February 1972.

42. John M. Langone, *loc. cit.*

43. *Ibid.*

44. NARAL form letter requesting donations, undated, reverse side listing organization members.

45. American Humanist Association, *Free Mind* (membership bulletin), March 1971. page 2.

46. *Eleventh Report, Un-American Activities in California*, Report of Senate Fact-Finding Subcommittee on Un-American Activities to the 1961 Regular California Legislature, Sacramento, 1961, page 109.

47. National Right to Life Committee, *Special Legal Report: Courts Defend the Unborn*, March 1971, page 7.

National Council of Churches

1. *American Atheist*, August–September 1964, front cover.

2. SIECUS, undated fact sheet on Dr. Mary S. Calderone.

3. John H. Phillips, *Sex Education in Major Protestant Denominations* (Council Press, National Council of the Churches of Christ in the U.S.A., New York, 1968), page 2.

4. *Ibid.*

5. *Ibid.*, page 8.

6. SIECUS Newsletter, Vol. 6, February 1971, page 5.

National Council on Family Relations

1. *Journal of Marriage and the Family*, Vol. 33, August 1971, inside front cover.

2. National Council on Family Relations, *Invitation to Membership*, undated leaflet.

3. *Journal of Marriage and the Family*, Vol. 34, February 1972, inside front cover.

4. *SIECUS Newsletter*, Vol. 7, December–January 1971–72, page 3.

5. *Ibid.*, Vol. 6, October 1970, page 13.

6. Minnesota Council on Family Relations, *Family Life: Literature and Films*, August 1967, page i.

7. "Communist Political Subversion, Part 2," *Appendix to Hearings Before the Committee on Un-American Activities*, Eighty-Fourth Congress, Second Session (U.S. Government Printing Office, Washington, D.C., 1957), pages 7116, 7382, 7384, 7401, 7525, 7526, 7812, 8183.

8. *Journal of Marriage and the Family*, Vol. 34, February 1972, inside front cover.

9. *Ibid.*, Vol. 30, May 1968, page 379.

10. *Ibid.*, Vol. 34, February 1972, inside front cover.

11. *National Council on Family Relations, Invitation to Membership*, undated leaflet.

National Education Association

1. William N. Alexander, "The Community Can Save Its High Schools from Mediocrity," *The Humanist*, May–June 1971, page 13.

2. *NEA Journal*, Vol. 57, April 1968, page 15.

3. *NJEA Review* (New Jersey Education Association), Vol. 45, October 1971, pages 41,44.

4. *NEA News*, press release, May 27, 1969, page 6.

5. *SIECUS Newsletter*, Vol. 5, March 1970, page 4.

6. Alan Stang, "The NEA — Dictatorship of the Educariat," *American Opinion*, Vol. 15, March 1972, page 59.

7. Francis X. Gannon, *Biographical Dictionary of the Left*, Vol. II (Western Islands Publishers, Belmont, Mass., 1971), page 129.

8. *Ibid.*, page 117.

9. *Ibid.*, pages 117–118.

10. *The United ·Nations Association of the United States of America*, Invitation to membership, undated brochure.

11. *The New York Times*, October 20, 1962.

12. *The Woman Constitutionalist*, Vol. 8, April 8, 1972, page 6.

13. Harold G. and June Grant Shane, "Forecast for the '70's," *Today's Education*, Vol. 58, January, 1969, page 30.

14. *Ibid.*, page 31.

15. Ibid., page 29.

16. Alan Stang, *loc. cit.*, page 70.

17. Hearing before a Subcommittee of the Committee on Government Operations, U.S. House of Representatives, Ninety-First Congress, Second Session, *Federal Involvement in the Use of Behavior Modification Drugs on Grammar School Children of the Right to Privacy Inquiry* (U.S. Government Printing Office, Washington, D.C., 1970), September 29, 1970.

18. *Ibid.*, page 101.

19. *Ibid.*, page 156.

20. Harold G. and June Grant Shane, *op. cit.*, page 32.

National Institute of Mental Health

1. *Encyclopedia of Mental Health*, Albert Deutsch, editor, Second Printing (Franklin Watts, Inc., New York, 1963), Vol. 3, page 1098.

2. Senate Investigating Committee on Education, *Eleventh Report — Opposition to Loyalty*, California Legislature, 1953 Regular Session, (Sacramento, Senate, 1953), pages 31–32.

3. *The Encyclopedia of Mental Health*, Albert Deutsch, editor, Vol. 2, page 479.

4. *Ibid.*, Vol. 6, pages 2060–2061.

5. Charles Secrest, "Counter point," *Christian Crusade Weekly*, Vol. 12, April 23, 1972, page 2.

6. George Brock Chisholm, "The Psychiatry of Enduring Peace and Social Progress — Reestablishment of Peacetime Society," *Psychiatry*, Vol. 9, February 1946, pages 1–35.

7. *The Encyclopedia of Mental Health*, Vol. 6, page 2061.

8. Whittaker Chambers, *Witness*, Fifth Printing (Random House, New York, 1952), page 28.

9. *World Health Organization Constitution*, Preamble.

10. *SIECUS Annual Report, 1967–68*, unnumbered page 5.

11. Steve Carter, "Seeks to Change Attitude Toward Homosexuals," *Paterson Evening News*, December 3, 1969.

12. Isadore Rubin, "The Humanist Bookshelf on Sex," *The Humanist*, Special Issue, Spring 1965, page 99.

13. *SIECUS Newsletter*, Vol. 6, December 1970, page 3.

14. *Ibid.*, page 6.

15. Steve Carter, *op. cit.*

16. *Glide In/Out* Newsletter (published by Glide Memorial United Methodist Church), Vol. 2, February 1971, unnumbered page 3.

17. *The Encyclopedia of Mental Health*, Vol. 1, unnumbered page 5.

18. Paul Scott, "Big Brother Develops Thought Control," *The Review Of The News*, Vol. 8. February 9, 1972, page 46.

19. Lee Belser, "Preserving Nation's Psyche," *Baltimore News-American*, January 12, 1972, page 2B.

20. Congressional Record, November 18, 1971, "Agnew Discusses Child Development," an address by the Honorable Samuel Devine, Page H11302.

21. Lee Belser, *loc. cit.*

22. Paul Scott, *loc. cit.*, page 47.

23. *Ibid.*

24. *The Humanist*, March–April 1971, page 2.

25. Congressman John G. Schmitz, "Steps Towards Mind Control," *The Review Of The News*, Vol. 8, March 29, 1972, page 40.

26. National Institute of Mental Health, *Recent Research on Narcotics, LSD, Marihuana and Other Dangerous Drugs*, Public Health Service Publication No. 1961, October 1969, page 3.

27. National Clearinghouse for Mental Health Information, NIMH, *Resource Book for Drug Abuse Education*, Public Health Service Publication No. 1964, reprint January 1971, page 1.

28. Hearing before a Subcommittee of the Committee on Government Operations U.S. House of Representatives, Ninety-first Congress, Second Session, *Federal Involvement in the Use of Behavior Modification Drugs on Grammar School Children of the Right to Privacy Inquiry*, (U.S. Government Printing Office, Washington, D.C., 1970), September 29, 1970, page 148.

29. National Clearinghouse for Drug Abuse Information, NIMH, *Marihuana*, Public Health Service Publication No. 1829, revised August 1970, brochure.

30. "The Playboy Forum," *Playboy*, March 1972, page 45.

31. *The Leaflet*, Newsletter, National Organization for the Reform of Marijuana Laws [NORML], Vol. 1, January– Febrary 1972, page 6.

32. "U.S. Mental Health Chief Opposes Jail for Drugs," *Paterson Evening News*, October 16, 1969.

33. *The Leaflet* Newsletter, *op. cit.*, page 5.

34. *Statement in Suppport of the Need to Reform the Marijuana Laws*, NORML, no date, unnumbered page 3.

35. Dr. Joel Fort, "Pot: A Rational Approach," reprint from *Playboy*, October 1969, distributed by NORML, reprint page 4.

36. *New York Times Book Review*, September 26, 1971, page 38.

37. *The Leaflet* Newsletter, *op. cit.*, page 5.

38. "Top Psychiatrist Urges Easing Marijuana Laws," *Paterson Evening News*, February 12, 1972.

39. "Evils of Marijuana — More Fantasy Than Fact?" *U.S. News & World Report*, April 3, 1972, page 37.

40. National Commission on Marijuana and Drug Abuse, undated press release concerning Endicott House Proceedings for the benefit of the National Commission, page 2.

National Sex and Drug Forum

1. *Glide In/Out* Newsletter, Vol. 2, February 1971, unnumbered page 3.

2. *Ibid.*

3. *Ibid.*, March 1971, unnumbered page 2.

4. *Ibid.*, February 1971, unnumbered page 2.

5. Albert Ellis, *The Case Against Religion,* Institute for Rational Living, Inc., pamphlet.

6. *Screw*, No. 10, April 25, 1969, page 2.

7. *Fund-Raising Reception in Honor of Wardell B. Pomeroy, Ph.D.,* The Mattachine Society of New York, April 1, 1967, printed invitation.

8. Hard-core pornography promotional brochure, untitled, undated, published by Lyle Stuart, Inc., New York, N.Y., page 3.

9. Promotional leaflet for *The Photographic Manual of Sexual Intercourse*, undated, published by Regent House, North Hollywood, Calif.

10. *Glide In/Out* Newsletter, Vol. 2, December 1971, unnumbered page 3.

11. *Ibid.*, Vol. 2, October 1971, unnumbered page 1.

12. *Fourth report, Un-American Activities in California, Communist Front Organizations*, 1948 Regular California Legislature, Sacramento, page 183; *Guide to Subversive Organizations and Publications*, House Document 398, U.S.

House Committee on Un-American Activities, Washington, D.C., December 1, 1961, page 33.

13. *Guide to Subversive Organizations and Publications*, page 33.

14. *Ibid.*, page 107.

15. Special Committee on Un-American Activities, House of Representatives, Seventy-Eighth Congress, Second Session, *Investigation of Un-American Propaganda Activities in the United States, Appendix IX, Communist Front Organizations*, page 1523. See also *Guide to Subversive Organizations and Publications*, page 198.

16. *Fourth Report, Un-American Activities in California*, "Communist Front Organizations," 1948 Regular California Legislature, Sacramento, pages 239–241.

17. *Committee on Internal Security, Annual Report for the Year 1971*, Ninety-Second Congress, First Session, U.S. House of Representatives, Washington, D.C., 1972, page 167.

18. *Glide In/Out* Newsletter, Vol. 2, March 1971, unnumbered page 3.

19. *The Review Of The News*, Vol. 5, November 19, 1969, page 29.

20. Doyle H. Payne, Jr. "An Open Letter to the United Methodist Bishops," *Christian Crusade Weekly*, Vol. 12, June 18, 1972, pages 1–3.

21. *Communist Political Subversion, Part 2*, Appendix to Hearings Before the Committee on Un-American Activities, U.S. House of Representatives, Eighty-Fourth Congress, Second Session, November–December 1956, page 8303. See also *Guide to Subversive Organizations and Publications*, page 18.

22. *Eleventh Report, Senate Investigating Committee on Education*, California Legislature, 1953 Regular Session, Sacramento, pages 56–60.

23. *Communist Political Subversion, Part 2*, pages 7188–7194.

24. *The Review Of The News*, Vol. 7, November 10, 1971, page 59.

25. *Glide In/Out* Newsletter, Vol. 2, July 1971, unnumbered page 3.

New Jersey State Department of Education

1. Special correspondence from Mr. Clyde E. Leib, Special Assistant to State Commissioner of Education for New Jersey, dated June 9, 1969, page 1.

2. Geraldine Lux Flanagan, *The First Nine Months of Life*, Fourth Printing (Simon and Schuster, New York, 1962), page 72.

3. *Ibid.*, page 72.

4. *New Jersey Education Newsletter*, New Jersey Department of Education, Office of the Commissioner, Vol. 5, May 1971, page 6.

5. *Ibid.*

6. Joseph S. Darden Jr., *Sex Education Bibliography*, compiled for Newark State College, June 1967, pages 1–10.

7. William Paterson College, *Course Proposal on Human Sexuality*, undated, page 6.

8. Charity Eva Runden, "The Soul Lags Up the Puddled, Sighing Stairs," *The Humanist*, July–August 1964, page 106.

9. Charity E. Runden, "Sex and the Teacher," *NJEA Review* (New Jersey Education Association, Trenton, N.J.), Vol. 42, October 1968, page 42.

10. Nora Kerr, "Abortion Law Scorned," *Bergen Record*, June 18, 1970.

11. *SIECUS Newsletter*, Vol. 7, February 1972, page 3.

12. "Humanist News," *The Humanist*, March–April 1968, page 33.

13. State of New Jersey, Assembly Bill No. 1056 (Approved June 3, 1970), page 2.

14. Division of Drug Abuse, Department of Public Health and Preventive Medicine (now the Department of Preventive Medicine and Community Health), New Jersey College of Medicine and Dentistry, printed program for the Drug Abuse Institute for Educators, June 22–July 10, 1970, inside front cover.

15. *Ibid.*

16. Earl Ubell, *The Television Report, Drugs: A to Z* (Columbia Broadcasting System, New York, 1970), page 18.

17. Drs. Harold Kolansky and William T. Moore, "Effects of Marihuana on Adolescents and Young Adults," *Journal of the American Medical Asssociation (JAMA)*, Vol. 216, April 19, 1971, page 487.

18. *SIECUS Annual Report 1967–68,* unnumbered page 2.

19. Dr. Joel Fort, "Pot: A Rational Approach," printed from *Playboy,* October 1969, reprint page 2.

20. *Ibid.*, page 4.

21. Mary Ann Hamren, "Drugs, Sex, Narcotics, Pornography and the Philosophy Behind Them," *Congressional Record*, June 25, 1969, page E-5244.

22. *Ibid.*

23. National Organization for the Reform of Marijuana Laws (NORML), *Statement in Support of the Need to Reform the Marijuana Laws,* undated, unnumbered page 4.

24. Edward Hershey, "Pot Has Its First Lobbyist in Albany," reprinted by NORML from Newsday, February 9, 1972.

25. NORML, *The Leaflet* (Newsletter), Vol. 1, January–February 1972, page 2.

26. James L. Goddard, review of book, *Marihuana Reconsidered, The New York Times Book Review*, Section 7, June 27, 1971, page 1.

27. *Ibid.*

28. "Psychologist Who Lived with Manson Family Tells About Commune," *The Los Angeles Free Press*, Vol. 7, January 23, 1970, page 8.

29. *Los Angeles Times*, January 17, 1968.

30. Guidance Associates of Pleasantville, N.Y., *Guidance Catalog*, Vol. 10, 1971, page 2.

31. Dr. Donald B. Louria, *The Drug Scene*, Ninth Edition (Bantam Books, Inc., New York, July 1970), page 89.

32. *Ibid.*, page 107.

33. *Ibid.*

34. *Ibid.*, page 106.

35. "Ex-No. 2 Drug Enforcer Backs Legalizing 'Pot' Use," *Paterson News*, February 10, 1972, page 8.

36. George Gallup, "Marijuana Use Among Adults Rising — The Gallup Poll," *Newark Star-Ledger*, Sunday, March 26, 1972.

Planned Parenthood–World Population

1. *The Individual, Sex, and Society,* Editors, Carlfred B. Broderick and Jessie Bernard, Third Printing (The Johns Hopkins Press, Baltimore, 1970), page 86.

2. Jack Rosenthal, "Area of Suburbs Grew by a Third in Decade But Density Dropped," *New York Times*, April 22, 1972.

3. New Jersey Department for Community Affairs, Division of State and Regional Planning, *1966 Land Use by Municipalities and Counties*, "Summary Table for County and State Totals."

4. Jack Rosenthal, "Nation's Births Show a Decline," *New York Times*, December 5, 1972, pages 1, 41.

5. George F. Carter, "Are Population 'Experts' Running Wild?" *Our Sunday Visitor*, (Our Sunday Visitor, Inc., Huntington, Ind.) Pamphlet #84, May 15, 1965, pages 6,7,10,11.

6. Dr. Colin Clark, *Starvation or Plenty?* (Taplinger Publishing Company, New York, 1970), pages 157,160.

7. Miriam Allen deFord, "The Woman Rebel," *The Humanist*, Special Issue, Spring 1965, page 95.

8. David Tribe, "Our Free-Thought Heritage: The Humanist and Ethical Movement," *The Humanist*, March–April 1969, page 21.

9. Miriam Allen deFord, *loc. cit.*

10. Alan F. Guttmacher, "The Role of Planned Parenthood," reprint from *The Pharos of Alpha Omega Alpha*, Vol. 28, July 1965.

11. Special Committee on Un-American Activities, U.S. House of Representatives, *Investigation of Un-American Propaganda Activities in the United States, Appendix IX, Communist Front Organizations*, First Reprint Edition (Washington, D.C., U.S. Government Printing Office, 1944), Vol. 3, pages 1771–1772.

12. *Ibid.*, page 1771.

13. Alan F. Guttmacher, *op. cit.*

14. *American People's Encyclopedia*, Editor-in-chief, Franklin J. Meine (Spencer Press, Inc., Chicago, 1957) Vol. 17, page 17–222.

15. *Ethical Culture Fact Book, 1876–1966* (New York Ethical Culture Publications), page 13.

16. Edward M. Brecher, *The Sex Researchers* (Little, Brown and Company, Boston, 1969), pages 31–33.

17. Arthur Calder-Marshall, *The Sage of Sex — A Life of Havelock Ellis* (G.P. Putnam's Sons, New York, 1959), pages 198–230. See also Edward M. Brecher, *The Sex Researchers*, page 29.

18. Zygmund Dobbs, *Keynes at Harvard: Economic Deception as a Political Credo*, Revised and Enlarged Edition, First Printing (Probe Research, Inc., West Sayville, N.Y., 1969), page 25.

19. Marjorie F. Iseman, "Sex Education," *McCall's* Magazine, January 1968, page 39.

20. *The Humanist*, September–October 1963, page 158.

21. Alan F. Guttmacher, "The Tragedy of the Unwanted Child," reprint from *Parents' Magazine*, June 1964.

22. Alan F. Guttmacher, "Bringing Birth Control to Millions," reprint from *Medical World News*, October 21, 1966.

23. *Guide to Subversive Organizations and Publications*, pages 69–70.

24. *Fourth Report, Un-American Activities in California, Communist Front Organizations*, 1948 Regular California Legislature, Sacramento, page 247.

25. *For This We Stand: This is Ethical Culture* (American Ethical Union, New York), undated leaflet.

26. *Ethical Culture Fact Book, 1876–1966*, page 24.

27. *Encyclopedia of Associations*, Margaret Fisk, Editor, Seventh Edition (Gale Research Company, Detroit, 1972), Vol. 1, page 684.

28. "Planned Parenthood Head Foresees Use of Coercion," *The New York Times*, July 6, 1969, page 47.

29. Glenn White, "What the Planned Parenthood People Are Up To," reprint from *Cosmopolitan* magazine, March 1965.

30. *Planned Parenthood–World Population Annual Report*, 1970, page 7.

31. "Teen Sex 'Clinics' Explained," *The Oregon Journal*, April 1, 1971.

32. *Ibid.*

33. Bob Lardine, "A Day in an Abortion Facility," *New York Sunday News*, July 23, 1972, page 30.

34. International Planned Parenthood Federation, *Her Future in the Balance* (pamphlet), October 1971.

35. Julia Henderson, "Worldwide Private Efforts" section of *New York Times* supplement on "Population: The U.S. Problem, The World Crisis," April 30, 1972, Section 12, page 24.

36. Francis X. Gannon, *Biographical Dictionary of the Left* (Western Islands Publishers, Belmont, Mass., 1971), Vol. 2, page 264.

37. *Guide to Subversive Organizations and Publications*, page 19.

38. *Encyclopedia of Associations, op. cit.*, page 424.

39. Population Crisis Committee, *Population Crisis* (Newsletter), Vol. 8, July 1972, page 1.

40. *Population Crisis Committee Membership List*, Booklet dated January 31, 1969, pages 6–41.

41. *The Victor-Bostrom Fund Report*, "The United Nations Faces the Population Crisis," page 3.

42. *Ibid.*, page 7.

43. *Ibid.*, page 19.

44. *Ibid.*

45. World Bank, *Population Planning*, a Sector Working Paper, March 1972, page 77.

46. *The Victor-Bostrom Fund Report, op. cit.*, page 5.

47. International Planned Parenthood Federation, *Her Future in the Balance* (pamphlet), October 1971.

48. Kurt Waldheim, "The Role of the United Nations" section of *New York Times* supplement on "Population: The U.S. Problem, the World Crisis," April 30, 1972, Section 12, page 14.

49. Office of Public Information, United Nations, *United Nations Conference on the Human Environment, Stockholm*, Press Release HE/143, June 19, 1972, page 9.

50. *Environment — Stockholm*, a special report published by the Center for Economic and Social Information at United Nations European Headquarters, Geneva, June 5–16, 1972, pages 3–13.

51. *The Humanist*, January–February 1972, page 35.

52. *Environment — Stockholm, op. cit.*, page 17.

53. Bertram G. Murray, Jr. "What the Ecologists Can Teach the Economists," *New York Times Magazine*, December 10, 1972, page 70.

54. Carol Lawson, "Ecology Action Gaining Momentum," *War/Peace Report*, Vol. 11, December 1971, page 17, (published by the Center for War/Peace Studies of The New York Friends Group, Inc., New York, N.Y.)

55. Population Crisis Committee, *The Family Planning Services and Population Research Act of 1970*, page 20.

56. Rose L. Martin, *Fabian Freeway* (Western Islands Publishers, Boston, 1966), page 260. See also *Eleanor's Red Record — 120 Citations, Including Eighty-Eight Communist-Front Affiliations of Eleanor Roosevelt* (a booklet listing specific sources of reference; *i.e.*, Senate Internal Security Subcommittee, House Committee on Un-American Activities, etc.), distributed by News for Action, Box 133, Pleasantville, N.Y., pages 1,11.

57. *Eleanor's Red Record, op. cit.*, pages 1–15.

58. *Ethical Culture Fact Book, 1876–1966*, page 18.

59. Robert W. McCoy, "White House Conference on International Cooperation," *The Humanist*, March–April 1966, page 51.

60. Mary Morain, "Panel on Population," *The Humanist*, March–April 1966, page 51.

61. Population Crisis Committee, *The Family Planning Services and Population Research Act of 1970*, page 22.

62. Population Crisis Committee, *Population Crisis* (Newsletter), Vol. 7, March–April 1971, page 2.

63. *Ibid.*

64. Population Crisis Committee, *The Family Planning Services and Population Research Act of 1970*, page 18.

65. Population Crisis Committee, *Population Crisis*, page 1.

66. *Ibid.*, page 2.

67. President Richard M. Nixon, "Message to Congress on Population," *New York Times* Supplement on "Population: The U.S. problem, The World Crisis," Section 12, April 30, 1972, page 3.

68. *Population and the American Future*, The Report of the Commission on Population Growth and the American Future (U.S. Government Printing Office, Washington, D.C., 1972), page 8.

69. *RF Illustrated*, Vol. 1, October 1972 (Rockefeller Foundation, New York), page 5.

70. Advertisement for " 'The Humanist Alternative' on TV," *The Humanist,* January–February 1974, page 39.

71. World Bank, *Population Planning,* page 80.

72. Francis X. Gannon, *A Biographical Dictionary of the Left*, Vol. II (Western Islands Publishers, Belmont, Massachusetts, 1971), page 224.

73. *Ibid.*, page 298.

74. League for Industrial Democracy letterhead, form letter announcing LID's 62nd Annual Conference on April 21–22nd at the New York Hilton Hotel, dated April 1967.

75. *Eleventh Report, Senate Investigating Committee on Education,* "Opposition to Loyalty," California Legislature, 1953 Regular Session, Sacramento, page 32.

76. *Ethical Culture Fact Book, 1876–1966,* page 9.

77. *Eleventh Report, Un-American Activities in California,* Report of the Senate Fact-Finding Subcommittee on Un-American Activities to the 1961 Regular California Legislature, Sacramento, 1961, page 109.

78. *League for Industrial Democracy* letterhead, April 1967.

79. *Population and Family Planning in the People's Republic of China,* a special report published by the Victor-Bostrom Fund and the Population Crisis Committee, Spring 1971, inside front cover.

80. *R F Illustrated, op. cit.*, page 4.

81. Daniel Callahan, *Abortion: Law, Choice, and Morality* (The Macmillan Company, New York, 1970), page 341.

82. *Institute of Society, Ethics and the Life Sciences,* brochure published by Hastings Center, 1972, unnumbered page 3.

83. *R F Illustrated, op. cit.*, page 4.

84. Institute of Society, Ethics, and the Life Sciences, brochure, unnumbered page 1.

85. *RF Illustrated, op. cit.*, page 7.

86. "Ethical Forum," *The Humanist,* September–October 1972, pages 4–18.

87. Barry Commoner, "Science and the Sense of Humanity," *The Humanist,* November-December 1970, page 10.

88. *Time,* June 19, 1972, page 55.

89. *Newark Sunday News,* May 3, 1970.

90. *Population and the American Future, op. cit.*

91. Citizens' Committee on Population and the American Future, undated membership list, pages 1–3.

United Catholic Conference

1. *American Association of Sex Educators and Counselors Newsletter,* Vol. 3, May 1970, page 1.

2. SIECUS, *Film Resources for Sex Education,* No. SP4, 1971, page A-3.

3. Planned Parenthood-World Population, *Publications About Planned Parenthood* (booklet), 1967, page 9.

4. *AASEC Program of Second Annual Conference,* Sheraton-Park Hotel, Washington, D.C., April 11-13, 1969, unnumbered page 1.

5. *Sex Education Bulletin: Toward a Program of Education in Human Sexuality* (Family Life Bureau, U.S. Catholic Conference), undated, page 1.

6. *1973 Catholic Almanac,* Felician A. Foy, editor (Our Sunday Visitor, Inc. Huntington, Indiana), page 613.

7. "The Norman Thomas Endowment, New School for Social Research" ad, *The New York Times,* October 31, 1971.

8. Preliminary Program, National Catholic Educational Association 67th Annual Convention and Exposition, Atlantic City, March 31-April 2, 1970, page 1.

9. "Agnew and Muskie on the Electoral Process," *The Humanist,* January-February 1969, pages 2-3.

10. Francis X. Gannon, *Biographical Dictionary of the Left* (Western Islands Publishers, Belmont, Mass., 1969), Vol. 1, pages 321-322.

11. Francis X. Gannon, *op. cit.*, pages 321-322.

12. Colin Wilson, "A Humanist Religion?" *The Humanist*, July-August 1965, page 154.

13. *Sex Education: A Guide for Parents and Educators,* Rev. James T. McHugh, Editor (Family Life Division, U.S.C.C., and National Catholic Educational Association, Washington, D.C., 1969), page 8.

14. *Ibid.,* page 23.

15. *Ibid.,* page 21.

16. Erich Fromm, *The Sane Society*, Twelfth Printing (Holt, Rinehart and Winston, New York, 1964), page 23.

17. *Ibid.,* page 352.

18. *Ibid.,*

19. *Sex Education: A Guide for Teachers, op. cit.,* page 16.

20. *Ibid.,* pages 17-19.

21. *Ibid.,* page 56.

22. *Ibid.,* page 59.

23. *Ibid.,* page 71.

24. *Becoming a Person,* Preliminary Curriculum Outline on Health, Growth, Psychosexual Development, Familial and Interpersonal Relationships (Sex Education Pilot Project), published by Cana Conference of Chicago, Ill., October 1967, front cover.

25. *The Beacon,* May 20, 1971, page 6.

26. "New Sex Education Program for Schools," *The Monitor*, April 23, 1971, page 7.

27. Glen White, "What the Planned Parenthood People Are Up To," reprint from *Cosmopolitan Magazine,* March 1965.

28. *Sex Education Program of the New York Archdiocese: An Evaluation,* Holy Innocence Safeguarded (Saint Michael Associates, Box 421-Station A, Flushing, N.Y., undated), page 4.

29. Richard F. Hettlinger, *Living With Sex: The Student's Dilemma* (The Seabury Press, New York, 1966), paperback edition, back cover.

30. James Likoudis, *Fashioning Persons for a New Age?* (Catholics United for the Faith and *The Wanderer,* New Rochelle, N.Y. and St. Paul, Minn., 1971), page 15.

31. *Ibid.,* page 1.

32. "Understanding Yourself," *Becoming a Person Program*, Grade 7 Teacher's Edition (Benzinger, Inc., New York, 1970), pages 44, 45.

33. "Life is All Around Us," *Becoming a Person Program,* Grade 3 Student's Edition (Benzinger, Inc., New York, 1970), page 44.

34. Niko Tinbergen, *Animal Behavior*, Life Nature Library (Time, Inc., New York, 1965), page 178.

35. "No One Like Me," *Becoming a Person Program,* Grade 2 Teacher's Edition (Benzinger, Inc., New York, 1970), page 14.

36. "Understanding Yourself," *Becoming a Person Program,* Grade 7 Teacher's Edition, page 16.

37. *Ibid.,* page 20.

38. Dr. Rhoda Lorand, "A Psychoanalytic View of the Sex Education Controversy," *Journal of the New York State School Nurse Teachers Association,* Vol. 2, Fall 1970, pages 39-40.

39. "The Changing You," *Becoming a Person Program,* Grade 5 Student's Edition (Benzinger, Inc., New York, 1970), page 21.

40. *Ibid.,* page 27.

41. Sworn testimony of Dr. Rhoda L. Lorand before the Superior Court of the State of California for the County of San Luis Obispo, in defense of Cyndy Becker, Plaintiff, vs. Board of Education, Defendant, Affidavit No. 35322, pages 2-3.

42. *SIECUS Newsletter,* Vol. 4, April 1969, page 4.

43. Dr. Haim G. Ginott, *Between Parent and Teenager* (The Macmillan Company, New York 1969), pages 169-170.

44. Jules Power, *How Life Begins* (Simon and Schuster, New York, 1965), page 57.

45. *Guidelines for the Formation of a Program of Education in Human Sexuality,* for Catholic Schools and Confraternity of Christian Doctrine Classes, approved by the five Bishops of New Jersey on February 2, 1971 (New Jersey's Boys Town Press, Kearny, N.J., undated), page 3.

46. Drs. James and Marie Fox, *Life Education: A New Series of Correlated Lessons* (Joseph F. Wagner, Inc., New York, 1970), page 12.

47. *Sex Education and the New Morality: A Search for a Meaningful Social Ethic* — Proceedings of the 42nd Annual Conference of the Child Study Association of America, March 7, 1966 (published by CSAA, New York, 1967), page 26.

48. A. S. Neill, *Summerhilll: A Radical Approach to Child Rearing* (Hart Publishing Company, New York, 1960), page 230.

49. *Ibid.,* page 246.

50. *Ibid.,* page 247.

51. *Ibid.,* page 246.

52. *Ibid.*

53. *Ibid.,* page 242.

54. *Discovery: Introductory Information* (booklet, Paulist Press, Paramus, N.J., undated), pages 6-8, 34, 36.

55. *Education in Love: A Program of Family Life and Christian Sexuality,* Teacher Guide, Grades 1-8, prepared by the Committee on Sex Education of the Diocese of Rochester (Paulist Press, New York, 1970), page 8.

56. *Education in Love: A Program in Family Life and Christian Sexuality,* Teacher's Guide, Grades 9-12, prepared by the Committee on Sex Education of the Diocese of Rochester (Paulist Press, New York, 1970), page 10.

57. *Education in Love,* Teacher's Guide, Grades 1-8, page 12.

58. *Ibid.,* page 16.

59. *Ibid.,* page 40.

60. James Likoudis, "Education in Love?" *Social Justice Review,* Vol. 65, September 1972, page 164.

61. *Education in Love: A Program in Family Life and Christian Sexuality,* Handbook for Parents, Grades 1-8, prepared by the Committee on Sex Education of the Diocese of Rochester (Paulist Press, New York, 1969), page 25.

62. *A New Catechism: Catholic Faith for Adults* (Herder and Herder, New York, 1967).

63. *Eighth Report — Education in Pasadena,* Senate Investigating Committee on Education, California Legislature, 1951, Regular Session (Sacramento, Senate), page 64.

64. Barbara Probst Solomon, Review of Helene Deutsch's *Confrontations With Myself, The New York Times Book Review,* June 17, 1973, page 23.

65. James Likoudis, *op. cit.,* page 167.

Y.M.C.A. and Y.W.C.A.

1. American Humanist Association, *Candidates' Biographical Data and Statements, 1970 Election,* unnumbered page 3.

2. Goodwin Watson, "Touch and Go," *The Humanist,* November–December 1971, page 36.

3. William C. Schutz, "Joy," *Redbook,* July 1968, page 60.

Index

Index

This index is a reference only to names and subjects mentioned in the body of the book and not those that appear in the appendixes. The numbers that appear in boldface indicate an extended discussion of the subject to which they refer.

7840